For Phyllis:
Friend, love, partner, muse,
companion, critic,
and working fellow clinician

ALUMNI NOTES

Alumni Notes

Andrew S. Levitas

Alumni Notes
Copyright © 2011
by Andrew S. Levitas

front cover design: Josh Levitas
copy editing: Matthew Levitas

Published by

~ STAR CLOUD PRESS® ~

6137 East Mescal Street
Scottsdale, Arizona 85254-5418

www.StarCloudPress.com

ISBN: 978-1-932842-44-9 — cloth — $ 49.95
ISBN: 978-1-932842-45-6 — soft cover — $ 34.95
ISBN: 978-1-932842-46-3 — e-book— $ 10.95

Library of Congress Control Number: 2010932754

Printed in the United States of America

Epilogue: March 1979

We shall not cease from exploration
And the end of all our exploring
Will be to arrive where we started
And know the place for the first time.
                    —T. S. Eliot, *The Four Quartets*

*A*nd they lived happily ever after.

I put down the chess problem I was fiddling with as the woman of my dreams sailed into the room on a cloud of perfume, and as usual took my breath away. "What you do to a simple black dress," I said. "Now I don't want to go. Or not right away, anyway."

She did a parody pirouette. "No choice," she said, "Command performance. Whose car are we taking?"

"Only one car to take to Bob's."

In the garage I opened the car door for her, watched her duck her head, hold that long hair, swing those long legs in.

"Did you know," she said, "I had a unit in Phys Ed on getting in and out of sports cars with dignity."

I scrunched myself into the driver's seat. "How did you do?"

"Promise to look at me that way on the way home," she said. Gray clouds, darkening in the dusk light, were just beginning to sail in over the Palisades. We sped out of the Bronx, into darkest Westchester, going someplace neither of us wanted to go, for our patients' sake. *They knew that there was nothing that could save them, And so they played chess as they had any night For years, and waited for the stroke of sword.*

"Quite the establishment," she said. "Befitting being made Training Director."

"Looks more like what you'd live in if you were made dictator of a small Latin American country or, say, owned a large cosmetics firm. Or married the daughter of someone who did," I said.

"Now, now."

"On the up side, he won't have to move when he makes Chairman."

The door opened on the entire Department of Medicine. Cardiology, GI, Nephrology, Endocrine; with the exception of the brain every body system was represented, wine glasses in hand.

"Oh, look who's here; Bob, come see who just arrived."

"Hello, Malka."

Malka did the peck on the cheek thing. "So nice of you to come."

"So nice to be invited," she said back.

We put our coats on the pile. "And we washed the stink of the South Bronx off us and everything," I said *sotto voce*.

"Quiet. You have no social skills, do you know that?"

"I have you instead. Time to kiss the Pope's ring."

Bannerman, the current Department Chair, was surrounded; we took a place at the periphery *I am an attendant lord* but he spotted us, *fit to swell a progress* waved. "Ah, the Doctors Seitz." She winced, but waved back with me. Small talk and Departmental gossip, curbstone consults and lunch meeting promises floated around us.

"Is Marvin going to be here?"

"Trying to decide between headache and can't find a babysitter when last seen."

"It isn't safe to have him around Bob anyway."

"Got that right," I said

We went for wine, scanned the room for a friendly face, found one.

"Hello, Sy."

"Paul. I was hoping to run into you. Wanted to discuss a possible publication. Actually I was hoping to see your ravishing better half."

"Hello, Sy. Good to see you too," she said.

We talked about the paper, a new antihypertensive having unexpected side effects; she went for hors d'ouvres and I saw Bob put a hand on her arm, turn her to say something. It became a conversation.

"She really turns heads," Sy said. "Could account for your rapid rise in the Department."

"And here I thought it was my niche expertise and my penchant for dispensing free care and taking Medicaid in Mott Haven."

"You really are one lucky son of a bitch, you do know that."

"Oh yes."

"I was there the day you met. I met her the same day you did."

"No." I took a sip of wine. "That's a long story."

She detached herself from Bob and made her way back to us. "Hate to interrupt," she said. "The Bodaceous One wishes a tete-a-tete avec nous."

"I so love it when you talk dirty."

"You could get any man you ever wanted," Seidenberg said, "And yet you spend your life with this crass scarecrow."

She put her arm through mine. "I did get every man I ever wanted," she said, and, to me, "Shall we get this over with?"

"Any idea what this could be about, Sy?"

"Not a clue," he said, obviously curious.

We maneuvered through the room, trying to avoid spilling wine, *In the room the women come and go* found Bob and waited politely for him to finish what he was saying to whomever he was saying it to.

"Reporting as ordered," I said.

"You needn't put it like that," he said. "It's just…this is a delicate matter. I thought it best to discuss it, ah, outside the office *In other words not legal to discuss it in the office* so let me take you on a tour of the house." He took her arm as if taking a hostage. We walked behind the staircase into the kitchen, to a smaller, more discreet staircase *servants'*

3

corridors; I tried to catch her eye into a hallway, past bedroom after bedroom to a large, airy study. He shut the door.

"Where's Kornbluth tonight?"

"On call for the Clinic," I said evenly.

"No doubt he volunteered. He detests me."

I smiled. "If he ever thought about you I suppose he would."

"*Casablanca*," she said hurriedly. "Bogart says it about Peter Lorre. Rick, about Ugarte."

"Oh. Funny. Well, give him my regards. Look, it's just small talk, I'm trying to find a lighthearted way to…It's like this. The Department has a problem. And you are in a position to do the Department a favor. Both your Departments. And perhaps yourselves as well."

We exchanged a glance meaning, approximately, *What can he possibly mean?*

"Look, I already know you'll think this is stupid. So do I. But. As you probably know, there have been events. An event. Within the Department's activities. Relationships involving students, trainees and instructors, both attendings and house officers. Over the years. In the current climate this has become unacceptable. The most recent incident…it all raises questions as to the integrity of grading. You must know what I'm talking about."

"We're rather up to our necks running a clinic out of a burned out neighborhood storefront near Fort Apache, Bob," I said. "Not privy to the latest doings up north here."

"Well, no real need to go into detail. The point is, the Department needs to promulgate a policy on trainee-instructor relationships. Against. As Training Director, the task has fallen to me."

"Which has what to do with us?" she asked. "Are you asking us to be involved in this?"

"I should think it's obvious."

4

"I'm afraid you'll have to be explicit, Bob. You can see we're quite at a loss," I said.

"The circumstances of your meeting and subsequent relationship are the stuff of legend around the school. Surely you know that."

The real story is better than their legend

"Hear that, Cyrano?" she said. "We're legendary."

"And your relationship remains most…irregular."

"I don't know, Bob. I'm quite regular."

"So am I," she said. "Every day, as a rule."

"You're the Abelard and Heloise of the Bronx. You met as intern and student and…"

"And?"

"Yes, I'm quite aware of your feelings towards me, quite the figure of fun, so why don't I just point out one other obvious fact: your Clinic's perennial financial precariousness, which even your part-time practices at the University Hospital don't quite ever seem to cover. This is, I repeat, your chance to do the Department, upon whose continued good will you depend, a favor. Afford the Department some moral high ground on this issue. Regularize your relationship."

"Couldn't be more regular," she said.

"I would have thought you'd be on my side in this," he said to her. "Your chance to make him make an honest woman of you."

She crossed her legs. "The way Malka did for you."

He adjusted his yarmulke. "The way Malka did for me. Very funny."

"Well, Bob, we must thank you for this opportunity to repay the Department for all its support," I said.

"Oh yes, and to rescue me from Paul's nefarious embraces."

"When you've finished joking, start thinking," he said.

"If I stop joking," I said, "I'll have to begin taking this seriously, and I'll have to tell you very seriously, that this is a private matter which is none of your or the Department's goddamned business."

"Which is why we're talking in private about a private thing that is a favor you are in a position to do for the Department, both of your Departments, which the Department cannot order you to do. I'm extremely, even exquisitely, aware of that. Think of me as a Dutch Uncle. I'm trying to be, believe it or not, a friend, here."

"Bob, we're never going to be friends, but there's no reason we can't work together, be cordial and respectful. So I tell you with the utmost cordiality and respect: First, I don't accept your premise that our marital status or relationship in any way compromises the Department's ability to create a policy on sexual involvements. As you should remember, I recused myself from any involvement in Heloise's grades. Second, our relationship is none of your business, officially or otherwise."

"Well. Think on it. You may come to a different conclusion. But we have a party to get back to. Thanks for coming up."

"What was that about?" Sy asked when we got back downstairs.

"It's about our sudden need to leave," she said.

"Then I shall never forgive him." And to me, "Call me. About the paper." *And whatever else*

Back in the car I was too angry to drive at first, so we sat and talked. Our breaths steamed the windshield, then the windows. "In retrospect, maybe we should have waited the three months," I said.

She shrugged. "*Autres temps, autres moeurs.* Neither of us was going to wait another minute."

"Or could have."

"You think Sy knew about this?"

"He said not."

"He's head of Cardio and he doesn't know?"

"He'd have told us if he did. He's a friend. And not a friend of Bob's. And he's in love with you."

"Please."

"He is. A lot of people around here are. Nice one about Malka making an honest woman of him."

"Serious up, Pavel."

"OK. You heard the implied threat to the Clinic?"

"Certainly did. He isn't subtle. I figure that's why you didn't jump up and hand him his ass. You handled it well, Paulie. No broken crockery."

I sighed. "We could go out west, start a Clinic in the Sangre de Cristos, near Taos, swim naked every summer day in our own pond. That was my Plan B if you hadn't shown up when you did, Heloise. Or we could start a coffee shop called Che's Lounge."

"God, that's awful, Paulie." But she grinned. "Taos sounds great except for the patients we'd be abandoning. If you'd tried to strangle him I'd have helped. No, same outcome."

"Calm down, Comrade. Never use napalm when bug spray will do. We're not without friends and allies. I can call spirits from the vasty deep." She grinned again. "Monday I'll make a couple calls to some old Movement friends, they'll make a couple calls, by Tuesday Bannerman will have a few calls from offices of the Bronx Borough President, a City Councilman, a State Assemblyman, affirming how very valuable we are to the physical and economic revitalization of the neighborhood, and incidentally to the school's state and city contracts. Which will I think remain in his memory when Bob unwisely brings this up."

"You've become an operator, Pavel."

"Studied under your brother. And Parker. Like them, I shall only use the power for good." The rain had moved in, the cold rain of winter, that froze roads and hearts. "Think this will come up in your Department?"

"Psychiatry? You're kidding, right? They change partners more often than a square dance. You really think Sy didn't know?"

"About us being dragged into it? He would have warned us. I told you, he's a friend, and he's in love with you."

"I like Sy a lot. Well, I'm already taken. Plus, what's your old expression, I could eat soup off his head."

"Tell him tomorrow. I'll be calling to tell him about this. The whole policy thing is bound to come up at a Division Heads' meeting; Bob will want to use it to insinuate himself as much as possible into every Division, make some friends and dependents. That's one reason he wouldn't tell Sy, although he'll know I'm going to tell him, so it will be at the next meeting."

"Maybe he thinks you'll cave and be too embarrassed to tell Sy."

"Who knows what goes on under that yarmulke."

"That is a lovely touch. I sense Malka's hand there."

"Sy's assembling an impressive bibliography," I said. "He's a thoughtful writer, a good medical thinker, has his hand in all branches of medical education, he's bringing younger faculty like ourselves along, allies when the time comes…"

"You think he wants to be Chairman," she said. "So soon?"

"No. Eventually. Gendleman will succeed Bannerman, unless he gets an offer elsewhere. Sy'd be a good Chair. And that is one route to the job."

"So is marrying the daughter of a wealthy Orthodox donor and becoming Orthodox."

"The battle lines are clearly drawn."

"Where does that leave us?"

"Swimming naked in our little lake in New Mexico, since you don't like the coffee shop idea."

"Yah, except I know you Pavel, if there isn't a subway to The Strand nearby you'd just shrivel up."

"Didn't you hear? They're extending the Broadway line to Taos."

"This feels familiar. They're making the opening pawn moves. We're pawns in this. Bob takes out a Seidenberg ally," she said.

"Yup. He's setting up his long game. We're the pawns, right."

"No wonder I'm so mad."

"As if there's a shortage of reasons. Only," I said, "We're only pawns if we let ourselves be. Did then, won't now. This time we get to fight back." I put my hand on her knee. "Together, this time."

She put her hand over mine, gently put it back on the wheel. "Seriously, Paul. What happened to the progressive med school we went to?"

"It's still here as long as we are."

"That's very romantic."

"One idea I had…I wonder if we could start bringing in some of our patients, local kids, maybe their parents too, to work with us, maybe like the Cuban and Chinese block health workers, maybe end up helping them into medical careers. Grow our own successors…"

"Could work. Some of my patients—it would get them out of their own heads. It worked for us. Grow our own replacements, yes…Paul, I was thinking…"

But I was thinking too. "I think it's Malka's ambition, not necessarily Bob's. Why stop at Chairman? How about Dean?"

"The traditional female route to power," she said. "Pathetic. You're right, I can't see Bob, that pompous self-righteous horse's ass, as that cunning."

"But Malka is. Or Malka's father is. He really can't lose. He's counting on us getting into a fight about this, telling him off. If we quit, Sy loses an ally, a pawn off the board. We knuckle under, Sy is exposed as too weak to support his friends. Bob gains either a piece or position. Plus, a bonus, he's been looking for a way to stick it to us for six years. He collects grudges as a hobby. And he kills the Clinic."

"Unless we change the game."

"Exactly, Comrade. We're not pawns, we're the Knight and the Queen, remember? We're legendary. Monday I make a few calls."

"I thought you were going to lose it with that *Casablanca* crack. Couldn't resist it, could you."

"Have to call Marvin too. He'll love it."

"Yes, he's just that juvenile. The pair of you."

"And the one about Malka making an honest woman of him. That was really choice. It was a struggle not to laugh."

She did laugh. "I'm sorry Paulie. It's your Department; I should have kept my..."

"Never. Never. It was priceless." *The gamine face, framed by the glorious hair. Hazy moonlight caught the graceful arch of her collarbones That we should want to touch each other, naked, take parts of our bodies into each other's Such a small miracle of love and trust. She is the cure She always has been*

"I know how to change the game, Paul. Really change it. It's something I've been thinking about for a while... in a month I'll be finished with my Boards. If I pass."

"Of course you'll pass."

"It all feels like one big exam. Like they've all been one big exam."

"You'll pass."

"So I'll be finished. Graduation. Finalement. Fertig."

"Yes. So?"

"Let's have a baby. Get me pregnant."

"..."

"Paul?"

The cold rain pocked on the fabric top. Drops formed on the windshield, rolled down, merged, rolled on. *Silence*

"That...would change the game."

"Scary," she said. "I know you, Paulie."

10

"Yes." *There's a curse*

"You have to trust the Universe to do this."

"Trying to."

"And you'll have to trust me. It's scary for me too. I don't know how…may not know how…you're supposed to learn how to be a mother from your mother, and I didn't always have such a great model."

"You did have one eventually."

"Oh. Well. Yes. Finally. Better late than never. I wish I could call her…We'll need to do this together."

"…"

"It means we wouldn't be children anymore," she said. "It means no more hopping on a plane to Europe or bopping up to the Adirondacks or down to the theater or a museum whenever we feel like. We'd have to grow up. You're an only child. You'd have to share me with someone else."

"Will I get a bill for that?"

"Nope. I told you, free psychoanalysis comes with this relationship. Lifetime benefit."

"Isn't that called Wild Analysis, when you just hit someone with a psychoanalytic interpretation out of the blue?"

"Well, I'm working off the clock, here."

"And I'm arguing with a psychiatrist. Great idea." *But it didn't mean she wasn't right She'd been right on target about the worst thing I ever did*

"What I saw in delivery rooms …When Cheryl went into labor…"

"It's 1979, not 1779. Or 1970. That was nearly ten years ago, Paul, it isn't that way anymore. That's one game we changed. Fathers are welcome now. You could be with me every step of the way."

"You know I can't stand to see you in any kind of pain."

She touched my cheek. "That's one reason I love you so much…"

"I caused you enough for a lifetime."

11

"…but I'm volunteering for this, and I won't hurt because I'll know how to do this and so will you because we'll have the Lamaze training and you'll know how to keep me centered and breathing. We'll do it together. That's one game we changed, Paul. My Lamaze coach, the way they did it at Louvain. You could take care of me if it got rough. I'll want that. Very much." *Silence*

So this was Peace. The War is over, the dead are buried, the wounded are still wounded, the missing are still missing, but a Jewish kid from Brooklyn shares life with a Daughter of the American Revolution in the safe harbor they thought they had made.

"We'll need a bigger place. We'll need a house." I jerked a thumb over my shoulder. "Nothing like this."

She grimaced. "Please. But…we'll need a dog."

"I know what kind, and what to name him." *Pause* I grinned. "Marry me."

She sat back against the door, looked at me searchingly *those thousand watt eyes* but with amusement. "Young white male," she said, "Relating in manipulative manner. Speech clear, coherent, goal-directed, without loosening of associations *the standard mental status exam straight from Friedman & Kaplan's Textbook of Psychiatry* but totally delusional. Meshugge in ganz."

"Listen to me. A comedy is supposed to end with a wedding. And besides, if we don't, by Departmental policy our child will be a bastard…"

"Don't you start being a bastard."

"Hear me out. We go to Colorado. And we get married by the Right Reverend Rinzen Rinpoche. The Third."

Silence. Then She laughed. Hard. "Would that even be legal?"

"I have no idea. *Enough to defy an oracle* Would it matter? We'd be married in the eyes of Buddha and the State of Nirvana. Conveniently located adjacent to Eldorado."

"This has possibilities. More than any other proposals you've ever made."

"It would have to be done with appropriate panache."

"Oh, oui, bien sur."

"And, *rolling my eyes toward the house* for our public, fanfare."

"Naturellement." She laughed again. "OK. Relationship Parliament is now in session. There are two motions before the body. One, we make a baby. Two, we get married. I vote we table Motion Two until later and get to work on Motion One."

I sat back against the driver's side door and looked at her. Really looked. The face that had brought me back to the world. *The forest was dark and empty* So eager, so full of intelligence. *And she wanted to have a child with me*

"So I'll be one of those guys at the Strand with a baby snoozing in a backpack."

"And I'll be breastfeeding at the Reggio." *The thousand watt eyes*

"It'll add another chapter to the legend." *We had to meet the way we did. It all had to happen the way it did. To become the people we are. The people we were then. The people we are now. The world as it was then. As it is now. Do we pass through history or does it pass through us? We are history. Atoms of history. God, we were such children. We were children. And now we want to make another* "Motion carries," I said.

She reached over, turned the ignition key. The engine leaped to life, unreliable as ever. The wipers were still useless. "Take me home, Paul." *How did we get here I can connect nothing with nothing We assemble it It falls apart...* I put it in gear.

"About that legend. Think they'd believe the real story? How did we get here, Pavel?" And she leaned over and kissed me on my right cheek, just above where there was a tiny scar. "I don't know that we ever settled on a final version."

April 7, 1973,
7:30 AM – 10:30 AM

*S*wimming slowly into the light. The woman of my dreams was beside me…But it was only the alarm clock. She wasn't there. No one was. No one had been. There was never enough sleep, so never enough time to dream.

Shit, shave, shampoo. The same ragged-haired, bearded scarecrow in the mirror. *Chase me ladies, I'm in the cavalry* Dress. Eat. Drive. Seven years did Jacob labor for Rachel. *Perseverance furthers*

The way it was then, a resident-intern team was a first year resident and two interns or an intern and two sub-interns, a sub-intern being a fourth year student (one on weekends), and a third year student who followed around whatever was most likely to be educational. It was a Saturday, early April, what would be a beautiful time even in the mostly treeless canyons of the upper Grand Concourse, if I ever got to be out in it…Through a gap between apartment buildings I could see the lighted tops of the skyline that I loved so much, poking above the ruins. And I thought about death. Here is how I think about death. First, that all this would wink out, vanish, be gone, lost. Second, that I would be gone, the thing I call "I" will no longer exist. Like before you're born. Extinction. Not that I would miss life, that there would be no "me" to miss anything. That far from winking out, all this would go on, and the part of it that was me would be a tiny hole, and it would heal over, and leave at most a tiny scar. Both these feelings simultaneously. Marcus

17

Aurelius had covered this territory pretty well. *I did not know death had undone so many* A sickness. Manageable perhaps. Not curable.

Marvin banged on the hood. "Wakey wakey. Fire up the V and the W".

"Ah, the late Dr. Kornbluth." As I merged from the Concourse service road into the main road Marvin gave me the bad news: "We have a new sub-intern and a new clerk," and I groaned at the extra work. "No, no," he said, "This is big news, big; I have it from Sarah in Undergrad that we have two women, and not just any two women…you take the Fourth Year and I get the Third Year *this was unusual* and wait till you see—it's the legendary untouchable Lish the Dish. Aren't you glad you team with me?"

"Lish the Dish."

"Hair like brown silk, legs up to her neck, tits on the small side but fill in name of fresh-fruit-of-choice here. Movie-star gorgeous. Guaranteed, 800, 900 millihelens, man."

"Very nice, but you make the assignments in the team, so why do I get this paragon?"

"The Third Year is a redhead, and cute as a bug, and The Dish is way too tall for me—all yours, Tall Paul."

"Wait—there's like maybe ten women per class, and we get two in the same rotation? Did you cook this up with Sarah?" *Look at this schmuck; it's green, for Christ's sake. 77WABC news at the top of the hour Kissinger says bombing will resume if Hanoi violates the agreement*

"I would have if I could. No, this beats all—I shouldn't be telling you this, and definitely not them. They called in all the rezzies except Franny, maybe September last year and asked who had any reservations about working with female med studs. No shit—can you believe this?"

"I'm past not believing anything, bro. We have Orthos in the ranks—could this have been about their shit with not touching women?"

18

"Maybe, but in point of fact only Bodaceous Bob expressed doubt, and the only orthodox thing he is, is an orthodox dick. I on the other hand expressed eagerness. Yes, my motives were mixed. We are a well matched pair of cynics, Dr. Seitz."

"Reminds me—you going to be Chief next year?"

"Dunno. The Bodaceous One has a lock, Sarah says. Don't park under the overhang—a piece fell off on Bob's wheels last night."

"How do you get this stuff?"

"From Mike—I already know our patients. I called him, he signed out to me over the phone. Why I'm late."

"There's always a reason."

"There is. Always. So. You get Lois Lane and I get Lana Lang."

"Are you ever going to grow up, Marvin?"

"When I have to. In 5—4—3—2…"

We pulled in the gate; the ancient gate operator pointed us toward the overhang, partly collapsed over a Chevy wagon. I pulled in next to an old green MG and rubbed sleep around my eyes. I didn't think about the possibility at that point. Not until we were in the elevator. The elevator operator was older than the gate operator. That was when I woke up. "Does Lish the Dish have a last name, or is it just Thedish?" The elevator stopped just above the 8th Floor; The Ancient backed it down, up, down again, opened the gate.

"Archer? Archibald? Acheson? Maybe that's the redhead."

"Acheson. Alicia Acheson." *BEEEEEEP.*

"Maybe, yeah…" He checked his beeper, pushed open the ICU door. "Hello, Bodaceous Bob—couldn't wait for us?" *77 WABC playing all the hits Here's*

"Dr. Kornbluth, Dr. Seitz, so good of you to join us. *Killing me softly with his song, killing me softly* These are Drs. McCulloch and Acheson…" his lips kept moving. The hair was pulled back for work, pinned into a French twist. The gamine face; she had pierced her ears, graced now with gold hoops. *Slender No, slim That was the word Slim Like a rapier* The glasses were a constant now, there was a blue Oxford shirt and whites, a white Department of Health lab jacket a half size too big, one pocket filled with the Washington Manual bedside encyclopedia, stethoscope around her neck in the approved manner (like a scarf) and the Clark's Wallabies we all wore that year (surgeons wore Adidas). *Strumming my face with his fingers* On a lapel, an Equal Rights Amendment button. She was beautiful, beautiful; the heartbreakingly beautiful girl had become a heartbreakingly beautiful woman. Bob was still talking, talking, the speech I'd heard him give for two straight years, the speech he'd given when I was standing where she was.

"Will you please turn down that radio? Just for a minute? *They never do, Bob* Thanks. This is a crumbling old municipal hospital, it opened in 1929, everything is broken or about to be (Marv whispered, "Wait till he sees his car") but as you know, every municipal hospital in New York is now administered by a medical school or its affiliates, and this one's affiliated with the Mother House, so we can do great medicine here. The thing is—and this is key—this is our place. The attendings run the Mother House, and they run us. But they just round here. We run this place. We can practice medicine the way we want. It's ours."

"And a few administrators'."

"Yes, Marvin, except on weekends when even they aren't here." He turned slightly to deliver this to the students head on. "Meaning we, the House Staff, are. Doctors, I'll leave you to it." And he handed Marvin the pile of sign-out cards and swept out the double doors, opening both, leaving a lengthening silence.

Killing me softly.

"Well," said Marvin, "And that was Chief-Resident-Elect Bodaceous Bob, and—this is key—I am Marvelous Marvin Kornbluth, and this is Tall Paul Seitz, and we have been left to it. You will be happy to know Dr. Bob is about to discover his car is under a crumbled portico."

They laughed. Her laugh had not changed. *Like music*

"Katie McCulloch"

"Alicia Acheson. Ali. Dr. Seitz and I know each other. Or did."

"Then that makes it easy—you work with him and Katie works with me. Let's divvy up the cards and start the bloodletting."

"I'm sorry," she said, "Do we not just call the phlebotomy team?"

"At the Mother House we do; welcome to Morrisania," I said. She had a length of rubber tubing tourniquet pushed through a jacket buttonhole in the approved way, but no pocketful of test tubes, and I needed a fresh supply myself, which worked out perfectly, so before Marv could say anything I said, "So our first stop is the roof."

"The roof?"

"Lab is on the roof." She stopped at the elevators. "Stairs," I said.

"Elevators only go to 8. The ICU is on 8 so we can run up the stairs to the lab with STAT bloods. We'd do it anyway; patients could die waiting for us to catch an elevator. This place is a step back in time." I stopped on the stairs, turned to face her. "Which brings us to the question—is this awkward for you?"

"Me?... No. Can you handle it? Is it a big deal?"

I hesitated *if she can stand it I can too. Or maybe for her it is no big deal*

"Wonderful to see you, Alicia, belated congratulations," she said.

I know how deeply I must have hurt her. Was that why I had made no more effort to find her? And why didn't she come to find me? I don't deserve her. But here she is. Where had she come from? I gave the best smile I could manage. "This wasn't the plan."

She smiled too. "How are your mother, and your grandmother?"

"Mom's OK. Grandmother died when I was halfway through my first year. How about your family?"

"Oh. Paul, I'm so sorry for your loss. I know she meant a lot to you. To me too. My family...not so good."

21

"Dickie?"

She smiled again. "Dharamsala."

It furthers one to see the great man "Damn! So he made it. How?"

"Knocked around London, Paris, Amsterdam until he connected with a group of hippies driving across Europe and Asia. Good thing—I was going broke."

"*You* were going broke?"

And then we were on the roof, through the door just like the roof access to any tenement in the city, onto the duckboards.

"What's with the beach chairs and binoculars?"

"See that very large white circular thingy…?"

"Yankee Stadium."

"Exactly. Perfect view of everything except right field. Set up a radio, watch the game until a beeper goes off. One can always jump off the roof."

"That bad?"

Life in the Valley of the Shadow "I put one foot in front of the other. Hope it will all turn out well in the end, be worth it. Save some lives along the way." *Perseverance furthers*

"Very dramatic."

I shrugged "It's been a long year." *A lot of long years So much to ask.* BEEP "Oh shit—ER already."

But it was only Bob to tell us to put a bed on hold for a possible social admission. Relatively good news. "Kenny, this is Dr. Acheson, Dr. Acheson, Kenny. He runs all this and the beach chair concession. Home game today Kenny?"

"Versus Cleveland. Double header."

"Can a brother get some test tubes?"

"A brother can. You, I'm not so sure. She can. Any time."

"Fill your pockets with an assortment of tubes and off we go. Bring some for Katie." Which was all fake, there were plenty of tubes in the

ICU; I had just needed the minutes with her on the stairs to see how this might work *Did she know this?*

"Bye Kenny; nice almost meeting you." *Your scarf it was apricot* She had the quickness still; why shouldn't she? I went through the sign-out cards, looking for the best mix of easy draws and challenges, and oh shit, there was Moby Dick. But the Unit first. *You're so vain, you probably think this song is about you, you're so vaaaain* We moved from bed to bed, reading the necessary morning labs off the charts, not much bedside chit chat since most of the patients were unconscious or close to it. *77 WABC* A diabetic recovering from an episode of KA; two rule out MIs whose MIs had been ruled out and could go to the Floor, an OD waiting to sign out AMA so as not to miss his next fix. Must not be from the neighborhood; we admitted addicts every day, not a single one ever went into withdrawal. A mystery.

"So you think the staff is selling H?" she asked.

"You figure it out," I said.

"I would start by ruling out the elevator guys"

I had not forgotten how dryly funny she could be. "Let's go to the Floor and catch up with Marvelous Marv, tell him Bob is still here. It'll make his day."

"Yes, I quite get that." Also arch. "What is that about?"

"Maybe later."

We clumped down the stairs, pushing a generation's dust and crumbled plaster around. Four West was a big open space with frosted glass dividers separating beds, lit by huge bay windows built when sunlight was the best disinfectant. Layers of dirt over the glass smeared the wan light. It was a warm spring; there were many empty beds. For now. We grabbed charts.

"Morning Mamie," I said to the elderly woman with edematous ankles the size of a Clydesdale's hoof, "Time to check the oil."

"Oh, Dr Seitz, you won't leave me any blood, not a drop, and not a drop of water either." The catheter bag was in fact full; I called over a nurse to change it. "This is Dr. Acheson" I said to Mamie, and added, for her, "The angel in white is Miss Springer." They shook hands, Callie said, "It's Callie. My wings are back at the desk" *Everybody here is a comedian. Everybody here has recently seen MASH.*

She went to draw bloods on Mr. Gordon. Five patients and she hadn't missed a vein yet, a good thing in a med stud. Mr. Gordon could be a challenge. "Very nice looking young doctor," Mamie said. She had terrible veins, what with all the diuretics; I was concentrating on finding the second best one, leaving the best for an IV when the current one failed. "Mmm" I said. She laughed. Then she asked, as she did every day, why we were putting water in her arm and taking it out every place else, and I explained for the umptieth time that we were just keeping a vein open in case we needed to give her something, or took out too much water and more important what was in it. I loved her; she had a big heart and not just because it was failing. "That girl likes you," she said, predictably; I waited for her to say "I just know", then realized I had to say "Why do you think that", *and also that Mamie hadn't said a word—it was in my own head*, so I just said, "We know each other from before" and moved on. Mrs. Feingold, Mrs. Trent, Mr. Jackson…all old, all poor, all sweet and unknown to me except as patients, whatever they had been in life or would be. I liked them, I wanted to heal them; it was a losing battle against time and poverty and my own fatigue. *You're young, you wake up on a gorgeous spring day, and know you have to spend it with the ill and the dying, in a place that people walked by every day trying not to notice until they had to. You still haven't heard about your Public Health Service application, or for sure about the rumored end of the Doctor Draft, residency loomed as more of the same but with the hope of more sleep. Life is a giant round of repetitive work and the only things that help make it bearable are passing on skills to students, gallows humor, and numbness.* I tied off another arm, sank a needle into another vein.

"Qien es la castana?"

"Ella es una medica. Doctor Acheson"

"Es verdad? Ella es muy buena."

"Si. Muy buena."

Of all the hospitals in all the cities in all the world she walks into mine.

September 1964 – January 1965

$\mathcal{O}$nce upon a time a young scholar set out from the provinces for school. There he met a fairy princess. But he was destined to fall in love three times. The third would be the charm. Unfortunately he had no seven league boots, magic cat, magic hat or machine that turned dirt into gold. I had a Railway Express claim check and an RAF duffle bag older than I was, and the hope that my trunk would be in the storage room at the freshman dorm. It was hot and the duffle was heavy with books I couldn't, at the last minute, do without; by the time I got to the campus I was beat. My room was on the third floor; I hauled the duffle as if it were a reluctant St. Bernard on a leash.

The door to 317 was open. On the bed on the right hand side, obviously already claimed, was a pile of clothing, books and records. On the bed on the left was sitting the most beautiful girl I had ever seen. Years later I saw Renoir's "Portrait of Therese Berard". It was as if someone had taken Joan Baez' hair, reaching all the way to her waist, smooth like Veronica Lake's, then added a young Audrey Hepburn's face and body and Marlene Dietrich's legs. And she was none of those, but herself. She sat with those legs primly crossed, but with her skirt slightly above her knees and the shoe on her right foot hanging by a toe.

"Who are you?" she asked.

"Paul Seitz. That's my bed, I think." She didn't move, except to turn slightly towards me. "I'm going to need to throw this duffle on the bed," I said. She still didn't move. "I need you to move," I said.

29

"Where did you learn manners?" she asked.

"Well, not from Marie Antoinette."

She laughed, and her laugh was music. "B+," she said.

"What?"

A voice behind me said, "She said B+, and she doesn't give those out very often. Very strict grader."

I turned to confront, I thought with sinking heart, her boyfriend.

"Richard Acheson," he said, sticking out his hand.

"The Third," she said.

He stuck his tongue out at her. "Dickie," he said.

"Paul Seitz," I said, shaking his hand.

"That's my sister Alicia," he said, and my heart returned to its accustomed place. "You're supposed to mingle," he said to her.

"I am mingling. I met Paul here."

"We call her AA."

"You call me AA. No one else does. I prefer Ali," she said to me. "Are those books in there?"

"Yeah."

"Can I see?"

"Sure." I opened the duffle.

"AA is a great reader," Dickie said.

She rummaged through the books, suddenly exclaimed "Borges. You have *Labyrinths*. I've been looking all over for this."

"You should have tried The Strand, or in the Village."

"The…you're from New York?"

"Brooklyn."

She pulled out the desk chair, crossed her legs again so the skirt rode up, and pulled a pair of glasses out of her purse. I fell in love, or anyway in lust.

"You're an active reader," she said. "These are your notes in the margins, right?"

"Some. Most. Some are my father's. He was a literature professor."

"So you've read it."

"Yeah."

"I shouldn't…look, could I borrow it?"

"Sure," I said *oh god yes*. "Add your notes to the margins, if you like."

Dickie and I started unloading our stuff into the two dressers and two closets, with many "Excuse me's" and "Sorry's". She read, thoroughly absorbed. I was enchanted. We went for our trunks; she was still reading, in another world, when we got back. The room was suddenly full of Dickie's prep school buddies. Creffield Academy, some sophomore Phi Delts returning early for the fun of Freshman Week. She was polite to them, friendly but cool to their greetings, and kept returning to the book. They were all called Macs, Stors, Fields, Bucks, Parks…

"Who's this?" one of them finally asked.

"Seitz."

"Seitmeyer? Seitgeist?"

"C-," Ali said without looking up. She turned to me. "They all have nicknames based on the first syllable of their last names plus 's' unless the result is too awkward, like Achs. You're already Seitz. You're nickname-proof."

A big man appeared in the door, accepted everyone's greetings, and said, "That's my Alicia, in a room full of virile young men she has her nose in a book." She ignored him. "Alicia. Ali. Did you hear me?"

"I'm listening to Jorge Luis Borges. He has more interesting things to say."

"Who's he?"

"Argentine surrealist," I said.

He turned to me. "Your book, is it?"

"Yes sir."

"That's it, encourage her. Who are you?"

31

"Paul Seitz, sir."

"He's my roommate," Dickie said, "He's from Brooklyn."

"Seitz. That's German."

"Sort of, sir. Czech German."

"Germans I know. Was torpedoed by some once. Any relatives in Germany?"

"No sir. All up a chimney at Auschwitz."

Awkward silence.

Finally he stuck out his hand. "Pleased to meet you, Paul. Take care of Dickie, here. He's becoming a reader too. Alicia, we have to go."

"Only if you've finished visiting your frat house. I'm not going over there with you."

"You'll come if I tell you to." The room went silent. Everyone tried to find someplace else to look. She continued to read, or anyway to concentrate on looking at the book. "We're going. Now. And where I say."

Her face worked a little, but she kept her composure, made as if to finish a page. "Do you have a scrap to use for a bookmark?" she asked me.

"Sure." I rummaged around in the desk, found a pad, tore off a page, handed it to her. She did not let a tear fall. My heart broke for her.

"Leave the boy his book, Alicia."

"It's hers, Mr. Acheson," I said. "I finished it yesterday."

"That's quite all right…"

"It's a gift, sir. I can easily get another copy, and she's been searching for it."

"Thank you, Paul," she said, and pushed out of the room with the book firmly gripped. He didn't know what to do, torn between the interaction with me and following her out. We heard the stairwell door slam *Our troops retreated in good order*

32

"Well," he said. "Good meeting you, Paul. Dickie (he hugged him), keep up your good work." And he was gone. Everyone looked away the way everyone does when someone has behaved really badly. Gradually conversation resumed, turned into "see ya's" and other goodbyes.

Dickie watched as I plugged in my radio and desk lamp and arranged my books on the shelf above the desk. "Silent Spring" and "The Fox in the Attic" were the Orientation reading assignments. Borges was gone. I had picked up Pynchon's "V" after reading his short story "Under the Rose" in the '62 O'Henry's. "The Tin Drum". The one that caught Dickie's attention was the one I'd sped through on the four hour train ride up, Philip K. Dick's "The Man in the High Castle".

"Jesus, what's this?" he asked, turning it around in his hands. The cover showed a map of the United States, east of the Mississippi blood red, with a black swastika in white circle, west of the Mississippi, the Rising Sun of the Imperial Japanese battle ensign.

"What's it look like?"

"Iffy history, science fiction, Axis wins World War II, right?"

"Right, and it's 1958, and history hasn't stopped."

"How do they win?"

"Read it."

"Can't. Have to read 'Silent Spring'."

"You didn't…"

"Nope. We've got tonight and half of tomorrow before Orientation Seminar, so I figured I'd skim it. I bet I can read this and still skim it in time."

"Won't that leave you a little unprepared for the seminar?"

"Listen, if there's one thing you learn in prep school it's how to bullshit your way through a class discussion. As long as I know what it's about I can do it. You watch."

"It's about…it's a complicated ecological argument that industrial exploitation of the earth is poisoning the environment and killing the Golden Goose."

"See? Now I don't even have to skim it. I can bullshit my way through that any time. All I need is one good comment that references something I *have* read and I can take off on that. Or the prof will move on to something else."

I shrugged. To each his own.

We had to dress for dinner; jacket, tie, freshman beanie. In fact, the beanie was what would become better known in a very few years as a Doolie Hat, white, with Nott College '68 in the college's Ruby color. This was supposed to be Old Tradition.

"About five years old," Dickie said, "After a huge food fight. They think we don't want to ruin our only good clothes in a food fight, so…gotta wear jacket and tie. I heard," he said as we walked down the stairs to the freshman cafeteria, "That a year or two ago a guy came in wearing a jacket and tie, and that's all."

I laughed. This might be more interesting than high school. But not that night. That night the aged President of the College, flanked by the Deans of Students, Faculty and Admissions, gave a short speech about the important step we were taking, the solemn 150-year tradition we were joining, the long Ruby line of Nott graduates, and the illustrious name of Our Founder, Elkhana Nott. Then he took out a pitch pipe, sounded an A, and as he had for maybe 100 of those 150 years, Sang Us In with the Alma Mater. Unfortunately he couldn't carry a tune in a bucket. I tried to imagine my father or mother as a part of this at Brooklyn College, and couldn't. Of course, at Heidelberg my father might have had to fight a duel. He never said. No scars, though.

I told Dickie, when he saw my expression through all this, what I thought of it.

34

"You have no respect for tradition, then?" he said.

"None. But then again, these aren't my traditions."

"They're supposed to be mine," he said.

We were supposed to memorize the Alma Mater, some 19th century vapors about dreams of ancient Greece and so on, and sophomores were supposed to be able to demand that freshmen sing it or suffer some physical penalty, but that year the History department, led by Professor Goldenberg, threatened to boycott Orientation if Freshman Hazing were allowed to continue. The tradition of Freshman Hazing was duly allowed to lapse, but upperclassmen would not be arriving on campus for another three days and it was unclear whether they'd gotten the word.

Dickie was deep in "High Castle" when I turned off my light and slid into sleep. We dragged ourselves awake next morning, showered, shaved (as necessary), ate breakfast, dragged our empty trunks down to storage and headed out to Registration. Name, home address, campus address, birth date, scholarship and loan numbers, accounting of semester tuition, room and board, total due...religion, mother's maiden name. I knew perfectly well, warned by my parents, that the latter question detected Jews not picked up by the former. Fuck 'em. I filled in Jewish (by senior year I had filled in Druid, Atheist, Pagan...) and Levinovich. *King George won't have to put on his spectacles.*

Next, lunch. My tie was becoming gravy-spattered. The food was uniformly awful. I realized I was becoming homesick. Luckily Orientation Seminar was next; this went by room, so Dickie and I were in the same group. Our seminar leader was Professor Goldenberg himself, the man who had spared us Freshman Hazing (or not; we'd see). After initial wariness his questions began to elicit less tentative contributions.

"What would you see as the major barrier to the adoption of Miss Carson's agenda? Mr. Seitz, your thoughts."

"Ah, I don't think this will go down very well with America's industrial leaders. Her proposed measures they would see as reducing profits and slowing economic growth, inviting government regulation, and of course we can't have that."

"Why not?"

"Because the minute you say business regulation in this country someone yells 'Communism'." *Thank you, Grandma*

"Is that true, the rest of you? Do you think this agenda will be opposed on economic grounds, or be hostage to Cold War concerns?"

Silence.

"Mr. Acheson. You haven't said much this afternoon."

"Well, I agree with Paul that that kind of counterargument is very likely, but I think it may come from deeper roots. This country was founded by people who knew the Bible by heart, and if there was one passage they knew better than any other it was the one giving mankind dominion over the earth. The basis of the Protestant Ethic, as Max Weber had it, was the Calvinist drive for worldly success as a mark of God's favor, and the Elect are not going to abandon their hope of heaven to save a few swamps."

"Interesting. Moving on…"

The discussion ended at four, and we started to leave.

"Mr. Acheson, may I see you a moment?"

I hung back, waiting for Dickie.

"You did not read *Silent Spring*, did you."

"Ah, no sir, I skimmed it, got the gist of her argument, but I have to say, science just isn't my thing."

"I appreciate your honesty, Mr. Acheson, and the ingenuity of your response, a masterpiece of indirection, but let me warn you, such ingenuity will lose you the trust of your instructors. Take this to heart."

"I will, sir."

"You have a question, Mr. Seitz?"

"No sir, just waiting for my roommate."

"Very well then."

"They don't come sharper than that," Dickie said as we walked back across the campus. "Saw right through me." The sun was strong in our faces, and the freshman hats were becoming an annoyance, not to mention the blazers.

"Should have read the book."

"It bored the living shit out of me, if you must know. I have no head for science or math. 'The Man in the High Castle' is another story. Jesus, I feel like I'm still in that world run by the Axis. It's a great, great book, Paul. Thanks. What it says to me, is that even in a world run by the Nazis and the Japanese Empire, there are still moral choices to be made. Hard moral choices."

That was the first indication I had that there was more to Dickie Acheson than the preppy frat boy I had taken him for.

"And what's this oracle, this I Ching, he talks about? You know?"

"I looked it up. It's an ancient Chinese form of divination, telling you what kind of moment—there are 64 types—in the Tao, the flow of time, you're in. You shift yarrow stalks or coins around, generating a pattern, a hexagram, six lines of prose that supposedly tells you what the Superior Man would do in a Moment like the one being divined..."

"That's what's in the book."

"Right. The translation he refers to isn't made up. It's an English translation of a German translation..."

"I wonder if it's in the library."

"We could look."

What we found was a section well-stocked with Taoist and Buddhist texts of all kinds. Elkhana Nott's children had fanned out across the Far East as missionaries, and brought back a trove, unfortunately much of it in near-impenetrable Victorian translations. One exception: The I Ching, the Bollingen Wilhelm/Baynes translation Dick used. Dickie checked it out on his brand new student card. And used it to avoid reading "The Fox in the Attic." In fact, skipped the seminar to read Jung's introduction under a tree in the botanic garden, next to a pair of Chinese stone lions no doubt stolen from a temple.

"Did you know Jung wrote the intro to Wilhelm's translation?" he asked me. I hadn't known. "He says the Book is an example of his theory of synchronicity."

"Synchronicity."

"Stuff that happens at the same time is linked. When you flip the coins or shuffle the yarrow stalks, what you're doing is part and parcel of the Moment in the flow of time, the Tao, when you're doing it, so it tells you what kind of Moment it is, so you know what to do." He seemed physically struck, without ever moving.

"Like sticking your wetted finger up to see which way the wind is blowing."

"Right."

"Except there's no wind—checking the wind with your finger, the wind cools the wetted finger on the side it's blowing from; there's causality there. There's no wind, no causality linking the oracle results to the Moment."

"Not in the western way of thinking, but there is in the Taoist way of thinking. Causality is only one way of understanding the relations between things and events in the world."

We argued right through dinner, apparently boiled owl with cheese whiz; the debate soon involved several more people at adjoining tables. That's how we met Eli McCone, an engineering student with a philosophical bent. Dickie was absorbed, Eli was curious. I was vehement.

"So," Eli said, "The space-time continuum is a great river, the *Tao*, and it flows like a river…"

"Right…"

"And there are eddies and whirlpools and low water and rapids in Time and when you consult the Oracle, flip the coins, you get a hexagram based on the forces of Time, of the *Tao*…"

"A kind of universal spirit. I mean not a live thing, a sort of…"

"Destiny?" I asked.

"An unfolding…"

"But we could throw the coins and get two different hexagrams."

"Because no two men see the same river."

"Heraclitus."

"Sort of."

"So let's try it."

"What?"

"An experiment. Get the book. You said you have the book."

Dickie went for the Book; Eli and I introduced ourselves. "I don't see this being subject to experimental verification," I said.

"Probably not, "Eli said. "But it's something to do. Beats hearing Prexy sing the Alma Mater." *Ah, a kindred spirit.*

Dickie reappeared with the Oracle and fished out three coins. "We'll need six coins," I said. "Or nine." We came up with six and set about throwing them.

"How does this part work again?" Eli asked.

"Heads is 3, tails is 2. Nine and seven are male, Yang, unbroken lines, Six and eight are Yin, female, broken, lines. Nine and six make moving lines, that transform the hexagram into another, tells you where the *Tao* is going."

Eli recorded the heads and tails, moving and unmoving lines. A small crowd gathered.

I threw a tail and two heads for an 8, a broken, Yin, line, at the beginning, then five straight 7's for five solid Yang lines: Hexgram 44, Kou, Coming to Meet: "Of its own accord the female principle comes to meet the male. It is an unfavorable and dangerous situation, and we must understand and promptly prevent the possible consequences. The hexagram is linked to the fifth month (June—July). THE JUDGMENT: COMING TO MEET. The maiden is powerful. One should not marry such a maiden. The rise of the inferior element is pictured here in the image of a bold girl who lightly surrenders herself and thus seizes power…"

Dickie threw three heads for a 9, a Moving Line, a 7, another 7, an 8, and two more 7's: Hsaio Ch'u, The Taming Power of the Small. The meaning of which is that obstacles block the way to success, but success cannot be forced; "Only through the small means of friendly persuasion can we exert any influence…To carry out our purpose we need firm determination within and gentleness and adaptability in external relations." The Nine at the beginning meant "Return to the Way. How could there be blame in this? Good fortune." Meaning it was in the nature of a strong man to press forward, but when he encounters obstructions he should return to the way suited to his situation and not try to obtain anything by force. The transformation of the Nine to a Six in the first place brought hexagram 57, Sun/The Gentle (The Penetrating, Wind): "Success through what is small. It furthers one to have somewhere to go. It furthers one to see the great man."

Someone said, "Long-winded, gnomic fortune cookies," and walked away.

"Wait," Eli said, "Yeah, at first I was thinking this was like reading the astrology column in the newspaper; you could pick any one and it would be as good as any other, it could all apply to anyone. But look, each hexagram is composed of an upper and lower trigram, right? These two hexagrams are each the inverse of the other. Mirror images." It was true; for me, a Yin line and three Yang lines below for the lower trigram, Sun, three Yang lines above for the upper, Ch'ien; for Dickie, three Yangs below, Ch'ien, a Yin and two Yangs, Sun, above. "Interesting. You got two different hexagrams for the same Moment, though."

"Because," Dickie said, "Obviously the workings of the Universe are producing a Moment with different consequences for me and for Paul. It's the same river, different parts. I'm going to hit some rocks, and he's going to meet a girl he should stay the hell away from. In the same Moment. Which has got to mean my sister."

"You met his sister?"

"She was here to see me off to school."

"This the knockout I ran into on the stairs when I was dragging my trunk up?"

"Was she carrying a book?

"Yeah."

"That was her."

"Paul, tell this Oracle to eat shit and die."

"I don't follow oracles."

"You shouldn't. In this case you should follow your testicles."

I was in fact pretty disturbed by it. I hadn't had a lot of encounters with mysticism before, and the result of our divination experiment was, I had to admit, pretty uncanny. I told myself I could read the two hexagrams on either side of Kou and get the same feeling, but when I tried, it wasn't true. Hexagram 43, Kuai, Breakthrough (Resoluteness) read:

> BREAK-THROUGH.
> One must resolutely make the matter known
> At the court of the king.
> It must be announced truthfully. Danger.
> It is necessary to notify one's own city.
> It does not further to resort to arms.
> It furthers one to undertake something.

This was just confusing.

Hexgram 45, Ts'ui/Gathering Together (Massing), read:

GATHERING TOGETHER. Success.
The king approaches his temple
It furthers one to see the great man.
This brings success. Perseverance furthers.
To bring great offerings creates good fortune.
It furthers one to undertake something.

This made no sense to me at all.

I undertook to read the course catalog. Dickie came back from a shower and we turned in. But couldn't sleep.

"I can't make out who the Great Man is I'm supposed to see," Dickie said. "The rest is crystal clear. I was on the wrestling team at Creffield and I'm sick of it. I needed it to get in here. You know anything about wrestling?"

"Haystacks Calhoun? The atomic skull crusher?"

"That's just fake, on TV. I mean varsity wrestling. You on any teams?"

"Chess."

"Okay, then. Wrestling, real competitive wrestling, is chess with bodies. You force your opponent to make moves that result in a physical checkmate. Only the force involves pain, and I had this epiphany last year when I realized I didn't want to inflict pain on anyone anymore. AA and I were messing around out on the raft and I put her in an armlock and she screamed, and I realized I'd really hurt her, I mean we'd been fooling around since we were kids, and she'd screamed before, but it's like that time I like heard her, you know? And it got me thinking, how many other people had I hurt, just to win a wrestling match."

"Raft?" Coming out of the dark, the rest of this was too much to deal with.

"The house is on a lake, and there's a raft in the lake, out about 75 feet. What, you don't have a lake?"

"I have an ocean."

"No shit?"

"I live in Brighton Beach, a block from the ocean."

"I'd love to see that."

"I'd love to see this lake."

"Deal. We exchange visits. Next summer. *And she'd be there* But you'll have to beware the Powerful Maiden. The Oracle gives good advice. You'd be robbing the cradle."

"How's that?"

"She's just sixteen. Jailbait."

"So am I. We're the same age, then." *My heart sang*

"No shit? You're sixteen? How the hell are you in college? Jesus, you must be a tool. She's still in high school, has a year to go. I'm eighteen. What the fuck?"

"In the New York City schools, you can start class if your birthday falls within the school year. Mine is in February, so I started kindergarten at four and turned five halfway through. Then there's this program, the Special Progress classes, the SPs, where you can do 7th, 8th and 9th grade in two years. And graduate at sixteen."

"That isn't something you want to get around. I'll keep that quiet. So should you."

"Why?" I was already starting to nod off.

"Because everyone here is eighteen at least, or will be shortly. Your student card will get you a beer at the Rathskellar, and probably at any local bar too. Shit, you'll be able to drink at sixteen. This is rich. This

43

is really rich. You're going to need help, man. You're the younger brother I never had."

Next day was Class Registration. This was all about satisfying distribution requirements. Being Pre-med, I didn't have any room for choices: Biology 101, Qualitative Inorganic Chemistry 101, Calculus 101, Western Civilizations, English 101. Dickie was general liberal arts: English 101, Mathematical Concepts ("Mickey Mouse Math"), Geology 101 ("Rocks for Jocks"), Western Civ, and a choice of language (which I had Advance Placement tested out of) or an elective. He should have chosen a language, I thought, to get it out of the way, but by now I knew Dickie needed dessert before he had all his spinach.

"You have to think this through," he said. "The most important considerations, little bro, are: no classes before nine, ten if you can do it, nothing after noon Fridays, and dear God, no Saturday classes. You have two lab courses, which makes this hopeless. Eli here is similarly screwed. You will be at it from eight to four no matter what you do. I, on the other hand, demonstrate the superiority of the Liberal Arts."

He picked Eastern Religions.

That's where it started.

We staggered back to the dorm with our textbooks, lighter by some hundred dollars. Eli and I had slide rules, too. We dumped the books on the bed and went to lunch. This was supposed to be a free afternoon before a weekend of intramural games and a traditional tug-of-war across the muddy streamlet in the botanic garden with the sophomore class. The upperclassmen had begun showing up, cars beginning to arrive in the upperclass dorm and frat house parking lots. Freshmen were not allowed cars. In my mailbox, the wholly unexpected: a letter, in aqua ink, from Ali,

North Greenwich, September 3, 1964

Dear Paul,

Thank you so much for the book. It meant a lot to me. I'll return it when I'm done; see if the notes interest you. It was a real pleasure meeting you. Write me back.

Ali Acheson

I tucked it into the Biology 1 textbook, where I used it as a place marker as I flipped pages. *Section 1 The Cell, Origin of Cells, Cells as Organisms, Cell Structure and Processes, The Cell Nucleus, The Chemistry of the Living Cell, Biological Molecules, Section 2: Organisms, Section 3 Evolution, Section 4 Classical Genetics, Molecular Genetics.*

As if the answer were there.

Schenectady, September 5, 1964

Dear Ali,

It was a pleasure meeting you, too. I'm sure the notes will interest me. Keep it as long as you want. There's supposed to be more Borges coming out soon. Stay in touch.

Paul Seitz

I had no stamps; I walked to the post office in downtown Schenectady. The city was built around Erie Boulevard, which had once been the Erie Canal, with the main street perpendicular; a downtown with a few small department stores and restaurants, a movie theater, a hotel; up a block a civic center. Over all loomed the General Electric Schenectady Works, with its giant flashing neon sign:

45

G

E

GE GE GE

GENERAL ELECTRIC GENERAL ELECTRIC

G

E

GE GE GE

GENERAL ELECTRIC GENERAL ELECTRIC

and the occasional unearthly howl from the Jet Propulsion Division visible on the heights across the Mohawk River.

When I got back Dickie had found the letter, seen her aqua ink on my desk and recognized the handwriting. He whistled. "Nice work, man. I have to tell you, The Pater about shat himself when you gave her the book. He's trying to marry her off to a lot more money than we have, which is a lot more, pardon my candor, than you have."

"Fascinating. How does she feel about it?"

"She has other ideas, but, see, there's a plan. There's always a plan."

"Is there a plan for you?"

"Maybe lawyer. Corporate law, I think, but he will tell me in the fullness of time."

"Do you have a plan?"

"Yeah. Not that. No other details yet."

Dickie reminded me we weren't supposed to leave the campus until the end of Freshman Week. I told him where I'd been. He laughed.

"You're ignoring the Oracle, man." *The Oracle could fuck itself.*

I was drying off after a shower when the goon squad showed up. I wrapped the towel around myself, took up a position against the wall, next to a window. *Castle king's side*

"You're without your beanie, froshie," said a guy in the crowd, but the evident leader. Big guy, standard issue street bully but in a team uniform.

"I usually shower without it."

"That's a mistake that usually costs froshies during Freshman Week."

"No more Freshman Hazing," I said, "Or haven't you heard."

A second one also had the power of speech. "No Yid professor is going to end a two-hundred-year-old college tradition."

So that was what this was about.

"It's quiz time, froshie. What's the school motto?"

"Nous sommes tous freres sous les lois de Minerve." Hell, it was on the sweatshirts.

"Well done. What does it mean?"

"We will all be brothers under the laws of Minerva."

"Oh, so close. It's 'We will all be brothers between the legs of Minerva'. That's going to cost you. Now you'll have to sing the Alma Mater."

Maybe they didn't know it either. Maybe nobody knew it but the mummified President. I edged a little closer to the window and sang (I won't claim well), as loud as I could:

> "Allons enfants de la Patrie-uh
> Le jour de gloire est arrivee.
> Contre nous de la tyrannie-uh…"

"What the fuck is that?"

"It's the 'Marseillaise' you dumb shit," the leader said, "Try again, wiseass. Last chance."

For some reason, no one in this entire dorm needed to take a leak while this was going on. I gave them the Internationale:

> "Arise, you prisoners of starvation
> Arise, you wretched of the earth…"

"You lose, asshole. I know what that is, it's the Communist anthem. From each according to his abilities. You get to polish this floor (he reached into a pocket) with this toothbrush." They moved in.

The picture in my memory of Jews forced to clean the streets of Vienna with toothbrushes in 1937 cleared everything else out of my head, and in a move learned in the Lincoln High locker room I whipped off the towel, flipped it into a rat-tail, snapped it at the nearest face, recovered it, re-rolled it and prepared to snap it again. I backed another one off, and by that time Dickie had rushed in, had the leader in a head lock and down, with a knee in his back. It's an agonizing hold.

"Hello Morgan," Dickie said.

"Acheson," He croaked.

"And a gracious hello to the rest of the Junior Varsity lacrosse squad. How about the rest of you guys back away from my roommate; he needs some room to put his towel back on. You don't want to lose an eye if he snaps it again. And trust me, you would."

They didn't move. Dickie applied a little pressure with his knee.

"Back off," Morgan yelped. This time they moved.

"Where are our manners? Paul, this is Jasper 'JP' Morgan, captain of JV lacrosse, late of Creffield Academy, where he was a complete prick. The rest of you boys introduce yourselves."

They did, mumbling.

48

"Gentlemen, most of you know me; this is my roommate and friend Paul Seitz, from Brooklyn, New York, and I want you to remember his face, because you're going to have to tell all the rest of the sophs that he and I are exempt from hazing. In fact, we all are. Freshman Hazing is officially over. We aren't going to take it. Spread the word."

"Why would we do that?"

"Where did I tell you he was from? Think, shithead."

"You said Brooklyn."

"Right. Very good. See, he has a lot more friends than you do. A lot more. And relatives. And they will come up here by the carload to rip off your faces and shit down your necks. Isn't that right, Paul?"

"And don't you fucking forget it," I said.

"Now. Everybody file out, one at a time, real easy. Your Captain's backbone depends on it. Exit the building. Assemble under that window. You will sing the alma mater. All three verses. When you're finished Morgan can join you. Morgan?"

"Do it."

They did. Some crap about a Grecian dream, golden gates of morning. Dickie let Morgan up, but shifted to an arm lock.

"If you think this is over, Acheson…"

"Just go away," Dickie said wearily. "I don't have time for children anymore. Next time, if there is one, I'll fucking cripple you, just to have done with you. I will, Morgan. You can take it to the bank." He vanished down the stairs, past ranks of jeering freshman faces. Dickie could have been class president by acclamation. There was, in fact, no more freshman hazing at Nott College, ever. "And you," Dickie said to me, "Can say you sang The Internationale to JP Morgan. My sister's going to love this story."

So it wouldn't be for nothing. Getting so scared I would have pissed myself if I hadn't just pissed in the shower wasn't all for nothing. And finding out how much anger overcame that much fear. But getting to sleep was difficult for us both.

"Do you think Morgan will just let this go?"

"Well, Morgan isn't all that tough unless he's had a few, none of them is, really. They know how to play a tough sport with a ball, but I know how to wrassle, right? They can't risk another humiliation, in fact they can't risk jacking up some froshies and just being ignored, or laughed at." He sighed. "This is just prep school with more beer. Do you, by the way, have many friends and relatives with vengeance in their hearts?"

"I could turn out about 60% of the New York Chess Club."

"Fearsome." He laughed. "Doesn't matter. They believe it. They'll leave you alone. And me. We're under the protection of the Mafia and Murder Incorporated."

He was right. We were left alone.

Then classes started and we were neck deep in work. I had always read whenever I had a chance, but most of it was voluntary, only a small amount was school assignments. This was the complete opposite. Recreational reading was out of the question until I figured out how best to assimilate this much material in this little time. This was the background music for the next ten years of my life. It got so I didn't even notice it anymore, except when it stopped. The prep school guys were our guides; they had been doing this for years, and, owning their own books, had discovered the Yellow Highlighter. Highlight the book as you read, make notes, study the highlights and notes and lecture notes for the exams, repeat for Midterms which were impossibly far away, ten weeks until Midterms and Fall Weekend, the first time freshmen were allowed to leave town.

The Cell, Origin of Cells, Cells as Organisms, Cell Structure and Processes, The Cell Nucleus, The Chemistry of the Living Cell, Biological Molecules, The Elements, The Periodic Table, Hydrogen, Anions and Cations, Helium, The Inert Gases, Elementary Stoichiometry, Herodotus, Thucidydes, The Fall of the Roman Republic, Suetonius (some fun here), *The Waning of the Middle Ages, The Great Gatsby, Schiller's Joan of Arc, Differentials and Integrals* Jesus my brain was going to explode. But it didn't.

Every Sunday, by prearrangement, a call home. "How are you doing?" "Everything's fine." "Everything's fine here too. Is everything going well with your roommate?" "Yes." "Making any friends?" "Yes." "We love you." "I love you too. I miss you." "We miss you too. We'll be seeing each other in a few weeks."

The High Holy Days came around. On Yom Kippur I cleaned the gravy stains off my tie and jacket, cut class and walked the two miles to a temple on Upper Nott Street that I'd found in the phone book. My family were not observant, were atheists in ideology and in fact, as am I, but every Yom Kippur my father found out what time the Yizkor service was, and we went to say the Mourner's Kaddish for his vanished family, for my mother's father whom she barely remembered, and my grandmother for the husband who had died when she was a young bride (*Had she had lovers in the Movement? I hoped so*). The temple was practically at the Schenectady border with the suburb the Jews had moved to when the Schenectady Works was supplying the whole world with industrial machinery.

Just as at school I was the poor boy at the party, ogling the rich merchants' comely daughters. I had never been to a Reform temple before, and I was shocked by the stained glass, the organ and the choir. Where were the davening old men, with their rich aroma? To me it

51

looked, sounded and smelled like St. Patrick's Cathedral. I sat through an hour of unfamiliar ceremonies and left, taking the little Yizkor prayer booklet with me. I walked the two miles back to campus and my room. Dickie was reading for Western Civ.

"There's something I have to do," I said, "And I'm sorry if I'm disturbing you."

"No, go ahead. What?"

I put on my father's yarmulke, took his tallis out of its bag and draped it over my shoulders.

"What's that?"

"Tallis. Prayer shawl." I opened the booklet and recited the Kaddish:

> "Yis gadal v'ysikadash sh' may rabo.
> B'olmo dev'ro hirusay, v'yamlech malchusay…"

He sat up.

> "Yisborach v'yishtabach, v'yispo-arv'yisromam,
> V'yisnasay v'yishadar, v'yisaleh,v'yishalal…"

He sat forward

> "…Olaynu v'al kol yisroel v'imru Omayn."

"What was that?"

"The Mourner's Kaddish, that you say on Yom Kippur, the Day of Atonement, which is today, as remembrance for a loved one."

"Your father."

"Yeah."

"That's it?"

52

"If you don't believe in God, or don't want to spend a day fasting and praying, that's it. Here, read the English translation."

He did. "This focuses on the power of God, not your grief."

"Exactly. That's my problem with it."

"But you do it."

"It's tradition. I made a promise."

When we went to dinner he said, "I've been thinking about your prayer. I think that's the problem with all Western religion. The focus is all on God. Supplicating or placating. Buddhism, Taoism…very different approach."

Dinner unfortunately was pork chops.

Time passed. The highlighter ran dry. I bought another one. That one ran dry. I bought a three-pack. The exams themselves proved no worse than high school, if longer. Papers also. Dickie struggled. Not with the difficulty of the work; he was more than a match, as demonstrated by his acing Eastern Religion. He just wasn't interested in anything else, or anyway not as interested as he was in that course. I helped him with math (not that he needed much except prodding) and with some of geology (same story). He needed no help from anyone in English and Western Civ; if anything he sharpened me up in Western Civ when we studied together, but he was capable of abandoning anything for his Eastern religion books, which he supplemented with books referenced and found in the library.

He tried to teach me elementary drinking, but failed when I couldn't stand the taste of beer. "Never mind," he said, "It's lousy beer." There was another letter from her, actually the Borges in a small package.

Dear Paul,

I have to thank you again for "Labyrinths". I had only heard of Borges, and it has stretched my mind like a long swim. "The Library of Babel" I have read and re-read. All his libraries; I think I would live in a library if I could. "Deutches Requiem" disturbs me. He predicted our world 15 years ago and more. Look at my notes. I didn't add many. They're in blue. I only write in blue. It's an affectation. I admit it. I should be enjoying "Gatsby" but Borges is a whole new dimension.

What are you guys reading? What is this I Ching Dickie talks about?

I'm supposedly studying for SATs. Which you're not supposed to be able to study for.   Ali

Dear Ali,

I meant it when I said the book was a gift. It has my father's notes, so tell you what, when I get home Fall Weekend, if that ever happens, I'll pick you up another copy. No kidding about "Deutches Requiem". It had the same effect on me. We live in the world the Nazis made. The regime went under, but its ideas and techniques lived on, adopted by its conquerors. It occurs to me this is how violence works. Maybe how history works. What I was reading on the train up was Philip Dick's "Man in the High Castle". It's about the world as it would have been if the Axis had won. Dickie was fascinated by it and that's where he found the I Ching, the Book of Changes. It's this ancient Taoist Oracle, a kind of

54

divination method that told me I should stay the hell away from you that tells you how to behave as the world changes. Our library had a copy, which Dickie I think has permanently checked out.

We're reading "Gatsby" too. I think of you as my Daisy

Paul

In the mailbox: pledge cards. The way this worked: if you wanted to pledge a fraternity you had to prove you had visited a number of them, enough to make what we would nowadays call an Informed Choice. You did this by attending house parties at each of at least ten frats over several house party weekends, or anyway going in and getting your pledge card punched. Each frat had a particular punch, so you couldn't just punch holes in the thing. You really had to go. Which is why Dickie was trying to drag me.

"You're going to pledge Phi Delt, you're a legacy; all you have to do is go in the other houses and get your ticket punched."

"But I need a wingman, and you need to see a part of life that doesn't have to do with books. I say this as your big brother."

"Well, thank you, but free beer isn't my idea of a good time."

"You need to get your head out of your books. You're going to turn into a power tool, Paul, and you have more going for you than that."

"I don't, actually. Anyway…look, Dickie, I have no intention of pledging a frat. I'm what the British call 'not clubbable'."

"There's the Jewish house. Phi Ep is not Phi Delt."

"Dickie…I can't afford it. I don't have the money. There is nothing I can do to have the money. And, news flash, I don't want to."

"Come along for the ride then."

"What, go to a party with you at Phi Delt? Dickie…do you want to get into Phi Delt, or is showing up with me a way of being blackballed without actually, ah, not pledging?"

"A shrewd question, younger bro. I am in fact ambivalent."

"And you don't want to confront your father, who as I recall expects this of you."

"Not at this time, no."

"And I am supposed to feel how, when Morgan comes over to shake hands?"

"Morgs? He's no problem."

"Maybe not for you."

"It's a chance to hit him again."

That got me thinking, against my better judgment. I could easily win a battle of wits with Morgan, if it came to that, and this time on my own. Nice move, Dickie. So I got out the tie and jacket again, found my freshman beanie, and went with Dickie to Pledge Weekend.

It was a zoo. None of the Houses was supposed to serve beer to freshmen; all of them did. Freshmen weren't supposed to bring dates; many did, and many townie girls cruised the campus, hoping to be picked up. Many were. By 10 PM many were plowed shitfaced. Campus lanes were strewn with puddles of vomit. Groups of the less drunk helped the more drunk through the dark. Groups of girls, mostly underage, asked to be taken in with us. Outside the Sigma Chi house I turned one of them down; she grabbed my beanie and pledge card and ran, staggering, in the door. Dickie split a gut laughing. We chased her in and recovered the goods, she hanging around Dickie's neck.

"Where we going next?" she asked.

"How old are you?" Dickie said.

"Eighteen."

"Yeah, in 1967 you will be. How about we get you a cab home."

"How about you fuck off and leave me alone?"

"Deal."

We went back out into the dark. Leaves crunched underfoot.

"Did you know," Dickie said, "That the elms are dying of elm blight? By the time we come back for our 20th reunion they'll be gone. Maybe sooner. Those little lindens next to them are supposed to replace them. Just like we'll be replaced by that girl, and she'll be replaced by another, and the elms will be sold off as cordwood and the lindens will die of whatever lindens die of."

"Why so philosophical just now?"

"Because we have visited nine frats in two hours. Time to tackle Phi Delt."

We got a frosty greeting at the door. They must have been expecting Dickie; I was a surprise. It was like we were daring them, or anyway he was. A guy named Parker I remembered from the attempted hazing handed me a beer and mumbled an introduction. "Parks," he said, "Rush chairman. Look around all you want."

"Hello, Dickie," Morgan said. "Interested in Phi Delt?"

"You know perfectly well I'm a legacy, Morgan. A very useful one."

"Yeah, your father is a good man to know. You I'm not so sure." He faked a left hook; Dickie had him in an armlock almost before he thought. Morgan laughed. "Fast hands, Dickie. I look forward to Pledge Night. Did I mention? I'm Pledge Master."

"That should make it interesting, Morgs," Dickie said, releasing him. "You remember my roommate Paul."

"I do, yes. Still have all your friends at home?"

"Sure do. Some of them know where you live. They're all very interested in my health."

"Thinking of pledging Phi Delt? I would have thought, Phi Ep. Maybe your Greek isn't as good as your French."

"Thinking of going fishing?" I said. "Or visiting the fishes?"

"You see how terrific it is when we all communicate," Dickie said. Morgan turned away. "I have people to greet. See you Pledge Night, Dickie. Can't wait."

We headed back to the dorm. "Was that really wise? You've set yourself up. You said yourself, he's a complete prick, and he's Pledge Master."

"Don't underestimate a wrestler's capacity for pain and endurance."

"It isn't pain. It's humiliation. Why would you put yourself—all of you, why do you do this—through this ritual humiliation? Your entire culture seems to consist of ritualized humiliations. Your religion is based on a god who seems to me to have walked into being executed like a common criminal."

"And yours seems to consist of an obsession with constantly placating a sadistic god."

"Same god."

"Too true. Look, the ritual humiliations, as you put it, create group cohesion. Once we go through it, Morgan is a brother."

"You mean like Army Basic Training?"

"I guess. I don't know. I know that's supposed to happen."
"If you want so much to join Phi Delt, why didn't you stay, hang out with the brothers?"

"Good question."

Eli was looking for me when we got back.

"Not visiting frats?"

"No chance I'd pledge; not interested. I'm surprised to see you out there."

"My roommate had some crying need to wave a red flag at a bull."

"I don't want to know. Listen, I have a proposition. You know I'm a ham radio geek, right? I hang out at W2NC DXing all night. So I got an offer from WRNC, they need to fill the ten to midnight hours on Saturdays, they need a couple of complete social losers to run and engineer a show. I got an engineer, we have compatible senses of humor, and I can play piano. Interested?"

I thought about it for a half second. Dickie was right, I certainly needed something beyond the books, and counting the days to when I could go home; this was more my style than drinking and frat parties would be. "Sure, I'm game. How many listeners will there be anyway?"

"That depends on how inventive we can be."

Dickie began to spend more time at Phi Delt, and I began my radio career. This started with a quick review of licensing regulations (the famous Seven Words You Can't Say On Radio) and the announcers' test. Repeat the following as rapidly as you can:

"One hen." *"One hen."*

"One hen Two ducks." *"One hen two ducks."*

"One hen Two ducks Three squawking geese." *"One hen two ducks three squawking geese."*

And so on through ten tongue-twisters to:

"…Four limerick oysters Five corpulent porpoises Six pairs of Don Albeirzo's Tweezers Seven thousand Macedonians in full battle array Eight brass monkeys from the ancient sacred crypts of Egypt Nine apathetic sympathetic diabetic old men on rollerskates with a marked propensity toward procrastination and sloth Ten lyrical spherical diabolical denizens of the deep who all stall around the corner of the quay of the quivvy all at the same time."

"You pass."

McCone & Seitz went on the air the next Saturday, with Darren Miller as engineer. We read the news, gave the weather, bantered, broke for Eli's jazz piano. Some of the news and weather was accurate, most we made up ("It's raining dead squirrels on North Terrace, while on South Terrace it's partly groundhogs"). One night Eli finished up Brubeck's "Take Five" with a flourish, and I said, "That was the twelve spastic fingers of Eli McCone with Dave Brubeck's 'Take Five', and now a traffic report from the WRNC helicopter: A major pileup of upperclassmen around a woman with a flat tire on South Memorial Drive…" and the Traffic report was born.

Another night a listener called in. "Ah," Eli said, "We have a call from The Listener. Can we put this on air Darren? Yes? Patch him through."

"You guys are so pathetic."

"Thank you sir, we were of course hoping for witty and erudite, but we will settle for pathetic."

"And I'm even more pathetic for listening to you, but it beats the silence. Not by much, mind you."

"I see, I see, you needed a study break…"

"What I need is that woman with the flat tire, but I also could use an answer to the following physics question…"

"Have you been drinking, sir?"

"Is it Saturday?"

Thus was born Homework Help; listeners could call in stumpers and hope another listener could supply a clue. Or more likely a joke. Next Saturday we needed a substitute engineer for the first hour; Darren sang with the choir, which was giving a concert with the girls from Ithaca College. When he turned up at 11:00 it was with a bottle of beer and Sophie from Ithaca. She was the first girl I had been this close to in weeks, and she was a peach. During a commercial break I asked her if she could read the weather. "Sure," she said.

"We're back, and here's Sophie the WRNC Weather Girl."

"Tonight will be cold. Huh. It's October in upstate New York, there's a surprise…well, it's a lot warmer where I am."

Sophie was a hit; we started writing sarcasm and suggestive patter for her, and she wrote some herself, and for two Saturdays at 11:00 Darren put through a call to Ithaca and patched her into the board. Lonely Nottmen called in asking for her number, her picture. But after a few weeks she started dating a guy from Cornell, and we needed a replacement.

"You could try Ali," Dickie said. "She's going to be grounded for like two or three months. She'll be home Saturdays well into next year."

"What did she do to rate that?"

"I don't know. Fraternizing with the enemy. Conduct detrimental to the honor of the family." And when I looked blank he said, "Riding with townies."

"In North Greenwich?"

"From the wrong side of North Greenwich. Yes, there is a wrong side."

"Can you call her?"

"Here's the number. You call her. She has her own line."

It was the easiest time I ever had getting a girl's phone number. When I decided to call her my heart banged like a steam hammer. I reminded myself we'd talked, written. Then I heard her voice saying, "Hello?"

"Ali? This is Paul Seitz."

"Paul. What?—great to hear from you. This is unexpected."

I explained the gag. "So we need a weather girl. Someone we can count on to be there on Saturday nights for the foreseeable future."

"Well, as no doubt my brother told you, that would be me. This sounds like great fun. I can write my own material?"

"Sure. We can write together, maybe. It won't amount to much."

"Oh, it might."

"I give you the Schenectady weather, you take off on that. There are things you can't say. Seven words, actually. And you have to be able to be loose. Repeat after me: One hen…" She passed.

The next Saturday night while Eli spun records and tickled the ivories I called her, ten minutes before the debut, and gave her the local weather. "Then I ask you the weather in North Greenwich and you're on your own." Eli identified the last number, Darren counted down and gave me the Go sign. "Aaaand, it's WRNC Weather Time, with Alicia, the WRNC Saturday Night Weather Girl. What's in store for Schenectady tomorrow, Alicia?"

"Cold and more cold, Paul, with very cold to follow. Tomorrow 40s and cloudy, Monday a dip into 30s. Bundle up, boys."

"How about the weather where you are, on the Connecticut coast?"

"Partly boring, with ennui moving in tomorrow."

"Excellent; well, there you have it guys, a place more boring than Schenectady; Alicia will be back next week with another meteorological prognostication…"

I called her the next day. "They're listening to us in the Rathskellar," I told her. 'You're a huge hit."

"I'm already planning next week. Call me."

We did. I fed her the local forecast, and waited for commercial to patch her in. "How's it going?"

"I've been better. My father did the worst possible thing. You know about the grounding. About which I couldn't care less, it's a relief, to tell the truth. When he figured that out, he took away my library card."

"He *what*?"

"Took away my library card."

"Holy shit. That's a new one. That's…"

"From the Goebbels playbook."

"He's something from another time. Speaking of time, we're on in 5,4,3,2,… Aaaand, it's WRNC Weather Time, with Alicia, the WRNC Saturday Night Weather Girl. What horrible meteorological phenomenon is going to make Schenectady even worse tomorrow, Alicia?"

"Cold. 30s and more 30s. Remember that brass monkey, boys? Well, they've fallen clean off." There were noises in the background, almost a scuffle; a bang as the phone I thought hit the floor. "And how are things in your part of the world?"

"Cold, but heating up quickly."

Suddenly her father was on the line. "Who is this?" he said. Eli and Darren looked about to shit. I signaled them to sit tight, stay patched in.

"This is Paul Seitz, on WRNC Radio Nott College, sir. You're live on the McCone and Seitz Show, and welcome. We were just asking our WRNC Weather Girl the weather there."

"What the hell are you talking about?"

"Whoa, sir, language, we're on the radio."

"At Nott?"

"Yes, sir, through the technological wonder of wired telephony, you are live on campus. I understand you're an alum."

"Uh…I am, I am. Class of '42. And a Phi Delt."

"And a Navy veteran, I understand."

"Yes…"

"So I wonder if you can give us the marine forecast for the Connecticut coast."

"Uh, it's cold, with a rising wind…look, I…"

"I understand, sir, that the weather is so bad the libraries are closed."

"Libraries closed? No…"

"Our Weather Girl was telling us she has been unable to get to the library. To get the meteorological data we need for our broadcasts, and research her material. Her broadcasts are very popular here, right now there are guys listening all over campus, in the Rathskellar, frat houses, and she needs to hit the books."

Silence.

"Sir? The Rathskellar is just across the alley here, and I'm being handed a note from, I understand there's a crowd gathered outside, asking is it really true our popular and well-liked weather girl has been denied books. Wait—there is another offer here to drive down there and bring her books we've done with…"

"Listen, you, I don't know what kind of prank this is, but I'm hanging up. And I'm not happy."

BREAK-THROUGH. One must resolutely make the matter known
  At the court of the king.
  It must be announced truthfully. Danger.
  It is necessary to notify one's own city.
  It does not further to resort to arms.
  It furthers one to undertake something.

Shit. I pulled off my headphones, signaled Eli to fill time, and headed for the office. I called Dickie at Phi Delt. "Were you listening to that?"

"Yeah. Nice try. He took away her library card? Holy shit..."

"Right, look, is she going to be OK?"

"Should be. At this point he's probably angrier at you than at her. And she can take care of herself."

"You're sure?"

"Seen it before. Relax. Really. She'll be fine."

But she wasn't. When I tried to call the next day her line had been disconnected.

Midterms came. No worse than high school, but longer, and more sophisticated questions. Then Fall House Party Weekend. I could go home.

I made it home late Friday night, late trains crowded with students from every college along the line. All the way home, all the way down the Hudson from Albany, I thought about *He took away my library card,* the ingenious cruelty of that. Brighton Beach Avenue, dark under the elevated, was warmed by the stores' neon signs; there was the friendly, familiar sound of trains being shunted 30 feet above the street. The building lobby held the familiar cooking odors. My mother and grandmother hugged me as if for the last time; as they would say, who could say that it wasn't? I didn't know what to do first. I assured them I was OK, everything was alright, it was a good trip, studies were going well, my teachers were good...I fell asleep in my childhood bed, full of plans, knowing I only had 48 hours, like a soldier on terminal leave.

Saturday morning, the old cliché: everything looked smaller. My mother set out lox and bagels for breakfast, with whitefish; a feast. "How are your really?"

"OK really."

"Are you making friends?"

"I said in the letters; I have a great roommate, and there's Eli and Darren on the radio show."

"Which is on Saturday night, which means you aren't socializing much."

"Socializing at Nott, if you don't have a car or a friend with one, means drinking."

"It can't be that bad."

"It is that bad. It's OK, the radio is fun."

My grandmother as usual said what was really on their minds. "It means you don't get to meet girls."

"I met one. The first day. I told you. I think I told you. My roommate's sister. We're corresponding; she's a reader." I told them about that first day. I told them about the library card.

"Her father sounds like...I don't have words."

"What I don't get," I said, "Is how a man who fought the Nazis could act like one, to his own daughter."

My grandmother said, "Some people fought the Nazis, some only fought the Germans. There's a difference."

I thought this over. "I have this idea, whatever else I do this weekend, to go up to The Strand and find her some Borges, send it to her."

"You do that, Paulie," my mother said. My grandmother just looked stricken.

I did. Later that morning, I took the train up to Union Square and dug around in the shelves. I was able to find a used British edition of Borges' "The Aleph" and an Evergreen "Ficciones." She might need a long book, too; I would send her my copy of "V". I happened on a tiny illustrated copy of Byron's "Prisoner of Chillon". I threw that in; I figured she'd appreciate the joke. This didn't take much time. I hung out with friends, ate as much of my mother's pot roast as I could and still buckle my belt, slept, did it again, but of all the things I did that weekend of freedom from Nott College, none meant as much to me, rushing back through the dark in a day coach on the Cleveland Limited, as that.

Dickie was catching a ride home with a Phi Delt brother, Parker, the weekend after Fall Weekend.

"We're going to smuggle her some books," I said.

"Knowing the old man, you can't just mail or walk in a package of books when he took away her library card."

"I thought of that. What we do is, we buy her a Nott sweatshirt, and shove the books into it. They're paperbacks, small. Unless he feels around inside it, no problem. Just make sure she knows there's something under the Laws of Minerva." I set it up and had the bookstore box it with a simple ribbon. She would know who sent the books, but I couldn't resist slipping in a note:

Vive La Resistance. P.

Her phone was still disconnected.

Eli had come up with a new one while we promised a new Weather Girl when communication was restored: a contest. "Men of Nott: Step forward to solve the biggest mystery on campus. First, call in to tell us what you think is the biggest mystery on campus."

We got a few proposals, some sober:

> The purpose of the Memorial Building.
> The meaning of the Alma Mater (this got three calls).
> The exact contents of the dish in the freshman cafeteria
>   fondly referred to as Trainwreck.
> The exact nature of Mystery Meat.
> The formula for the secret fluid that kept the President alive.

In the second hour, between records and the 11 o'clock news, Eli announced that, "None of you has even come close. The Biggest Mystery on the Nott campus is the exact name of the Dean of Students. What does the O in O. Lewis Osterreicher stand for? Best answer wins the chance to share a weather forecast with the new Weather Girl."

The board lit up. Some left names; the best were simply a single word and a hangup; the first was one of these, and it led the field: "Osshole." In the end we decided to keep it going, spread the word beyond our meager audience. "Spread the word," I said, "Send your answers to McCone & Seitz at WRNC. This is Seitz."

"And this is McCone."

(Together) "Wishing you a happy and fulfilling week. It's a great day to achieve. Hail the Grecian dream."

Answers in fact poured in, but the winning answer was an offhand remark from Dickie. He got in late Sunday night. "Tell me how it went."

"Fine. Flawless handoff. The old man didn't suspect a thing. She gave me this for you."

Paul—

    Thank you more than words can say, for the thought and for the deed. I don't know about the Pynchon, but I guess you figured I'd have plenty of time. Don't worry about me. It isn't Chillon. I'll write when I can. —The Weather Girl

She's in hell, Paul. I'm not there to take some of the heat off her, and it's months until she can get away to college. And I didn't even think to bring her books. You did."

"You did bring her the books. You did the hard part."

"Better find a new Weather Girl."

"Did you hear? We have a new thing going. A contest, what the O in O. Lewis Osterreicher stands for."

"It isn't an O. It's a zero."

"That's it," Eli said when I told him. "Winner. And we build an audience by awarding the prize in the courtyard between the station and the 'Skellar. We can put a mike on a long wire."

It worked. The Phi Delts turned out, mostly sloshed, to see one of their legacies accept a large wooden zero from Eli. Well, it was only across the street. With a second mike I interviewed the growing crowd coming out of the Rathskellar (also half bagged), some of whom knew what was going on, some of whom grabbed the mike to say something mildy obscene (Darren had the feed on five-second delay). Dickie swung the trophy over his head, and received a round of mixed applause and catcalls. "I will treasure this great zero, no doubt the first of many I will achieve this year (laughter, jeers), and thank Dean Osterreicher (jeers; two flung bottles smashed against a 166-year-old wall) for his approbation. He's a great sport, isn't he, the Dean? Great sense of humor. We hope (laughter). Oh, what, he's not here? Douche bag."(Not one of the Seven Words).

Dickie wasn't kidding about the zero. He was on his way to an A in Eastern Religions, and a C and lower in his other courses. "I am really going to have to pull this out," he said. "Less time at Phi Delt." You couldn't pledge a frat if your GPI was below 1.5. I didn't know what I had to achieve to maintain my scholarship, but I figured it wouldn't hurt to shoot for Dean's List. I was on course for it. We became, for our different reasons, a pair of power tools. I read, I wrote papers, I did the radio show. Dickie read and wrote.

It became Thanksgiving; four days at home, the Sunday ride back in coaches so old McKinley might have made speeches off the platforms, and as crowded as the subway at rush hour, college kids mostly, a rolling party if you weren't sad and homesick.

It became Christmas. Two weeks off. Or would be if Finals weren't ten days after we went back. One week off.

It became Finals Week. In the freshman dorms guys walked like ghosts, passed each other in the halls, pulled together study groups, sweated over late papers. A few gave up. Most did not. Dickie did not. "If there is one thing prep school preps you for, it's this kind of pressure," he said.

"If there's one thing prep school preps you for, it's convincing people it prepped you for something. How's your sister?"

"Better. Out of house arrest. Don't know how long she'll stay out. The old man is on the warpath. My grades aren't going to help."

"Well, if there's one thing prep school preps you for it's explaining flunking out to the parents."

"Not funny, bro."

"Sorry."

"She sends greetings, my sister. Says you saved her life. I on the other hand have failed her."

We clipped postcards to our bluebooks so we'd get our grades before the official transcripts were mailed out. Got to bed early or pulled all-nighters. Ice coated the exam room windows. One by one we went home in a sweat, despite outside temperatures in the single digits that made the snow squeak underfoot.

Dickie pulled out an A, a B and three C's. I made Dean's List.

The University of Brighton Beach is what we called my father's library. It took up a whole room of the apartment and parts of the adjacent hallway. Books everywhere, in English, French, German…He loved it when I dug around in his library. He always said it wasn't his, it was ours—my mother's and mine as much as his. And some of the books were hers; Dickens, Hardy, Austen, oh yeah, Austen, the Brontes…He was always teaching. It was like he couldn't stop. He had his degrees from Heidelberg, and Prague, and there weren't many teachers of German Literature in Brooklyn, it wasn't very popular at the time he got hired by Brooklyn College. That's where he met my mother. She was in one of his classes; she was about ten years younger than he was. Eventually he taught Central European Lit too, but until recently that was mostly in German, it was Austro-Hungarian Literature. Many of those writers were Jews. Not just Kafka. My father wanted to translate all the Jewish Central European writers. That happened in the 70s; he never had the time. He was always teaching or discussing. I always got a respectful hearing, even when I was quoting 'Amazing Stories'. He was always teaching. He taught me chess. I was maybe six, maybe seven. Maybe five. I can't remember not knowing how to play. He worked chess problems from the *Times*, and I'd be sitting on his lap. I learned how the pieces moved. My mother would be sitting across the room, doing the Times crossword. The University of Brighton Beach, Undergraduate division. Chess was a big deal to my father. When we started to play, he played without a queen. When I got good enough to beat him he played with a queen. When I got good enough to beat him with a queen he coached me. I was in the chess club in junior high, on the chess team in high school. It was the key to popularity. The chicks just fell all over us.

I was maybe 12 the first time I beat him when he was playing with a queen. He clapped me on the back and said now I was good enough to play the real game. This meant a lot; he had played on a team when he was a kid, and an adult too, and I beat him, full stop. He sat back, tipped over his king. He smiled, told me he was very proud of me, that I would go far with chess, probably a lot of other things, I'd have opportunities he didn't have. Then he reached under the board and threw it over. I was stunned. He'd never done anything like that before. He hugged me. He said, "Don't be scared, Paulie. You beat me, fair and square, you won the game, but some day you'll be winning, and you'll lose. Or someone won't play fair. What do you do then?" I said, "I don't know," and he said, "You change the game. You throw over the board. This isn't a chess lesson, Paulie, this is a life lesson." He got up, helped me pick up the pieces, said he didn't have any more to teach me, now I'd have to teach myself. He seemed, in retrospect, to know he didn't have much time.

My term break didn't coincide with my friends' at BC; I spent the week prowling around my father's desk. That's where I found an unfinished paper on "Der Golem".

I remembered when my friend Sam lent me a Superman comic, and my father caught me with it. He sighed, told me it was junk. Told me not to waste my time with junk. That life was too short. Then he leafed through it and asked me what it was about. I explained Superman and he said, "Der Golem". Rabbi Loew of Prague, in the 16th century, makes and animates a clay man who becomes the champion of the Jews of

Prague. He told me about Meyrink's 1921 version, that he'd seen the movies in the 20's.

He loved Weimar cinema, UFA, and its continuation in Hollywood exile. His favorite movie was *Casablanca*. Except for Bogart, Bergman, Claude Raines and Sydney Greenstreet, he told me, every actor and actress in that film was a refugee from Hitler's Europe. Every one. He could identify them all, talk about their European careers.

He never said he was working on, or had abandoned, this paper. I settled into the chair. He had found out that the creators of Superman were two Jewish kids from Cleveland, and made a connection between Superman and The Golem, despite the Golem's muteness and lack of super powers (although his creator, Rabbi Loew, Mahahral of Prague, could, using Kabbalistic spells and amulets, make The Golem, for instance, invisible).

When my mother came home I showed her the paper.

"He was working on so many things," she said. "I haven't had the heart yet to go through his papers. This summer his department is paying a student to catalog his papers there; maybe you could help, and make a little money. Get a taste of scholarly work." I hadn't realized she was still too grief-stricken to sort through his things. I didn't want to know that. When I looked, his suits and ties were still in the closet. She gave me the number. I went over to BC, talked to the head of the department; there was no way they could refuse me the job, and a small stipend. While I was there I took the opportunity to drop by the admissions office and ask about transferring home. Brooklyn College at that time had a set curriculum and distribution requirements, and not all my credits would transfer; to meet all the BC graduation requirements would take me over four years, plus my freshman year at Nott. That would make me draft bait.

It didn't occur to me at that point to look further into the desk. One more train trip up the Hudson.

April 7, 1973,
10:30 AM – 11:30 AM

"*N*ice of you to give me Mr. Gordon." She held up two red-tops and a purple-top tube, inverting the purple-top to mix in the anticoagulant. "Was he a test?"

"Nope. Practice frames. We now go over to 4E to meet Moby Dick. Callie, sweetheart, pass me the phone."

"Get your own damn phone."

"She loves me" (the women grinned). I paged Marvin.

"She good," Mr. Gordon said, passing on the way to the remains of the sun porch, "Prettiest nurse I ever did see."

"She's a doctor, Mr. Gordon."

"You shittin' me?"

"No sir, straight up."

"I'm a medical student, Mr. Gordon, not completely a doctor yet."

"Well, you goin' ta be a good un, an' excuse me, no shit."

RRRRRIIIIINNNGGG

"Hast seen the White Whale?"

"What ho? On the way. And what do you mean you know her already?"

"We need two beds for the two ROMIs in ICU. Bodaceous Bob called to say hold a bed for a social admission."

"Doesn't he plan to go home?"

"In what? His ride's flat. Plus he has no life, so until the wrecker arrives he will stay here and make ours miserable."

"So," she said, "Who or what is Moby Dick?"

"A very mean, very obnoxious woman with out-of-control diabetes who weighs 600 pounds, no lie, they bring her in from the ambulance with a cargo lift; she's too big for the Hoyer. She has no veins and no place to find any that isn't buried in fat. And she has orders for AM fasting glucose and a 5 hour GTT if we can get one, so she hasn't eaten yet and might eat anything that gets too close."

"Does she ever get to be an actual suffering human being?"

"Not right now. Right now she is an immense technical problem for us to solve, and possibly the surgeons, if we have to do a cut-down or put in a central line. After that she becomes a human being again."

"With a name?"

"Miss Fascelli."

"Now, is there some actual human way to do this?"

"Watch." We pushed into 4 East and approached the White Whale's cubicle. Her eyes were closed, or anyway slitted. "Miss Fascelli," I said.

"Go away"

"Yes, I know, getting blood is a chore, I know you hate it but it keeps you alive."

"Overrated."

"Yes, I know you think that; so do I sometimes truth to tell, but you know, maybe so is death. Today I can offer another alternative that will make this go better. My resident today is..."

"That her?"

"No, that's Dr. Acheson. My resident today is Marvelous Marvin..."

"The ball player?"

76

"No again; Dr. Marvelous Marvin Kornbluth, and do you know how he got that nickname? He can find a vein where no one else can. No one. Famous surgeons call him in to find places to draw blood and put IVs."

"I don't want an IV."

"And you won't need one because Marvelous Marvin will find a vein. Dr. Acheson here will wait with you and I will get Dr. Kornbluth." I walked to the 4E door to fill in the Vein Finder; it almost hit me in the face as he came in, Katie in tow.

He grabbed my arm. "In the biblical sense?" he whispered.

"Not now. Ali is entertaining the White Whale while I bring over Marvelous Marvin the Vein Finder. You're going to find a vein and she is going to let us draw her blood."

He walked and sighed. "That's the best you could come up with?" He turned to Katie. "Good thing I love a challenge. Venipuncture is of course a Third Year procedure, but this exceeds even an intern's skills. Watch and learn. None of this is in a book." She grinned.

The Whale looked skeptical, but allowed Marvin to go over her arms and legs while delivering a mini-course on the art of phlebotomy.

"What we are looking for is places in the body where medium sized veins lie near the surface of the skin. The usual place of course to look first is the antecubital space—that's here in the crook of the elbow, sweetheart (he said to Miss Fascelli)—and when those have been scarred by repeated venipuncture, the radial vein called: Dr. McCulloch..."

"The Intern's Friend."

"Exactly, but in this case one too many interns has been to the well. Miss Fascelli, you haven't been keeping to your diet, have you dear?"

"Do I look like I have? I like this guy."

"This leaves us with unusual places that in fact are often less painful places to draw from. Dr. Acheson, any ideas?"

"The dorsum of the hand."

"Yes and—give me your hands a minute darling—these are good but as Dr. Seitz well knows…"

"We want to save those to use for IVs—just in case, Miss Fascelli."

"Moving on, from the standpoint of phlebotomy, the foot is just another hand."

"You're gonna take blood from my foot? The hell you will."

"Miss Fascelli—may I call you that?"

"Call me what you want—you ain't takin' blood from my foot."

"Shhh, darling, listen to me. I'm going to touch you with this pen point on your elbow crook, OK? Now on the top of your foot. Which one was more sensitive?"

"The elbow. OK, you got it. And anyway that's probably the only place on me there's no fat." And she actually laughed (it wasn't true).

"And it's so easy a student can do it—don't worry, I'll guide her. And here's the thing—we're not going to use a regular needle, we're going to use a tiny butterfly, right?"

"That's an IV."

"It's an IV needle. We hook it to a syringe and we take blood out."

And Katie McCulloch, MS-3, got an SMA-12 and a CBC from a 600-pound woman who hadn't had blood drawn in a week because the outpatient phlebotomy team had kept kicking the job into the next day until she went into incipient ketoacidosis.

"Now, Dr. McC, leave the needle in a minute, Miss Fascelli, here's the thing. The reason you keep running into trouble with your diabetes is we don't know how your body is handling sugar over time. If we know that, we can adjust your insulin and make your life a whole lot better, maybe you wouldn't have to see us so often. If we leave this little needle in for only a few hours…"

"How many hours?"

"Five. We can take blood out every hour without sticking you five times. All we have to do is hook up a tiny syringe full of stuff to keep it from clotting, tape it to your foot, and give you some breakfast and Dr. McCulloch can come around every hour and take a little out, and after five hours we take the whole rig out."

"All you have to do is keep this in me for five hours?"

"Yup."

"Sounds good to me. I wasn't going anywhere."

We ran the bloods up to the roof. Ali pulled me back on the stairs.

"I thought you were completely full of shit. Why didn't you do it?"

"Because Marvin really is better than me at that, and it was good for Katie to do it, and he is not completely exhausted by the White Whale." I looked at my watch. "What I am really good at is keeping Marvin on schedule—MARVIN...Teaching rounds." Back down the stairs to ICU, where...instead of an attending, here was Bodaceous Bob.

"Morning, children, are we ready for school? Gendleman called in sick ("Let me know when he calls in dead," Marvin muttered) and we get to round while the dedicated and skilled maintenance staff figure out how to lift a metal rain shield off my car."

Down on the Floor we went bed by bed, over the twenty patients, Marvin and I alternately presenting them; the students hadn't admitted any patients of their own yet, Bob looking for opportunities in the case presentations to quiz them. This was only a mild form of torture for Ali, agony for Katie.

"Mr. Gordon, 55 year old black male with a four day history of increasing abdominal pain pursuant to alcohol abuse, admitted in acute abdominal distress, back pain, severe nausea and vomiting.."

"Stop. Dr. Acheson, what does the back pain make you think of?"

"Pancreatitis."

"Right; Dr. McCulloch, the workup for acute pancreatitis."

"Abdominal exam, SMA-12, CBC, pancreatic enzymes, stool for occult blood."

"And if it's pancreatitis what would you expect to find?"

79

"Abdominal tenderness, electrolyte disturbances, mostly sodium wasting; elevated amylase."

"Stop; Dr. Acheson, what else might you find?"

"If he's an alcoholic, elevated liver enzymes as well."

"Very good. And what if the lytes were normal?"

This one stumped them; they thought he was fishing for a rare diagnosis, which was a pretty shrewd estimate of Bob's character, but it was a technical trick question which either of them would have gotten if this weren't the Lightning Round.

"Dr. Seitz?"

"Probable dehydration from the vomiting—water loss brings the sodium back to looking like normal concentrations."

"So how would you quickly know, and avoid missing the diagnosis?" The bonus question for the students, a chance to get back in the game. *Please, one of you know this, it's so easy, really.*

"Take a pinch of cheek skin; if it tents he's dehydrated." *Nice going, Katie.*

"Anyplace else you can check this?"

"Dorsum of the hand." *And the round goes to our students.*

"Treatment? Dr. Acheson."

"Replace fluids, put the GI tract at rest until the lytes come back to normal, manage pain."

"Which we do how, Dr. McCulloch?"

"I haven't seen a case—uh *please get this* I think, drop an NG tube to drain the stomach and run IV fluids until the patient can tolerate clear fluids."

"Very good. I assume that was what was done."

"Yes, Bob, very much according to the book; we're just waiting for today's lytes and he goes home."

"YES," said Mr. Gordon.

And so it went, until we came around to Mamie, who could not return a greeting because she was having trouble moving air.

"66-year-old black woman with a history of rheumatic heart disease with mitral insufficiency and a long history of increasing congestive failure…"

Bob cut me off, whipped his stethoscope off his neck and got around behind Mamie. I helped her lean forward. "Deep breaths, young lady, deep as you can," he said. Expertly he ran the bell over all the lung fields, finishing in front with the right middle lobe. He beckoned Katie forward, said, "Dr McCulloch, examine this woman's lungs and tell me what you hear—no, wait until everyone gets to listen." Katie moved her stethoscope over Mamie's back, but paused and re-listened over the lowest lung fields. Ali went next, then me, but I already knew what I would hear.

"Dr. McCulloch, what did you hear?"

"Rales and crackles in both upper lobes, nothing over the lower."

"Dr. Acheson."

"Rales in the upper lobe and right middle lobe, no breath sounds in the left lower lobe and lower half or third of the right lower lobe."

"Meaning?"

"Pleural effusion."

"What do we do? Dr. Acheson."

"Labs are already sent; we ask Kenny for them STAT, and we pump her full of Lasix." I was already writing the orders, slowing the IV to lowest KVO (Keep Vein Open) and ordering IM diuretics. They went off to get the lab results. Mamie looked appropriately scared. I took her hand, listened to her cough when she leaned back. "Too much water, Mamie" I said, "And some of it is around your lungs so it's hard to breathe. You take it easy and let the meds clear out the water."

"She hasn't exhausted you." Ali had lingered.

"No. Her I like. Listen, you know the three myths of medicine? You aren't going to know everything, you aren't going to like them all, and you aren't going to cure them all. You try; with some you try harder. You start out trying to try harder with all of them, but you get tired."

We pulled up at the desk.

"Don't wait too long," Bob said, "She looks like she could use a pleural tap."

I nodded, already calling for oxygen. "Consider her on the way to X-ray." I wrote that order and went to tell Mamie she was going for a ride, with her new friend Dr. McCulloch, then went to find Dr. McCulloch. She was pulling the second sugar out of The White Whale's heparin lock.

"Katie, this is your lucky day. You get to escort Mamie to X-ray. We need to know where those fluid levels are, make sure there are no surprises along with them. You have my beeper number? Do NOT trust the X-ray people. Anything tells you Mamie is getting worse you call me before you can even think of it, yes?" She nodded.

The IV was up on its pole, the tech was already wheeling the bed toward the doors. I tossed the chart on the bed and took Mamie's hand one more time. "Your friend and mine Dr. McCulloch is going with you to X-ray. We'll see where that water is and how best to chase it out. You promise to come back for lunch, OK?" The tech pushed, Katie steered, like a hook-and-ladder rig.

"Why not me?" Ali asked.

"I need you here. Ever do a pleural tap?"

"Saw one."

"See one, do one, teach one—we have to start getting the stuff together; Bob is right; we aren't going to drain that with Lasix." She hesitated just a moment—a pleural tap is a big thing to do your first day as a subintern. "Relax, I'll walk you through it. I'm the Marvelous Marvin of pleural taps." Which was almost true.

"The thing about Bob," she said then, "Is that even when you agree with him he makes you hate him. It's a gift: tone-deaf self-righteousness."

"B+" I said.

"I don't do that anymore."

"You can if you want."

"I'm not that person anymore, Paul."

She said my name. I showed her the supply room; we soon had three pairs of latex gloves, a 50cc syringe, a 25-and a 14-gauge needle, a bunch of tuberculin syringes, six amps of Lidocaine ("Make it ten—everybody always underanesthetizes"; she threw in four more), more red-top tubes and a purple-top, and a bunch of vacuum bottles, all lined up on a tray.

"Now what?"

"We wait."

"For her to come back from X-ray."

"No. She'll be in X-ray for an hour minimum. For Marvin to call and say Bob has left the cafeteria so we can all go to lunch. If we have any luck we won't need this and Mamie can live without an unpleasant experience."

"Any real chance?"

"No. But we give it a chance, and we have some lunch; I hate doing procedures on an empty stomach. And we will buy Katie some lunch, or with a little more luck she will get to come too. Now we write chart notes." Which we did, sitting on a table in the staff lounge with our backs against the wall.

February 1965 – July 1965

Second term freshman year was more of the same, made worse by the numbing cold and the feeling that we had to do it all over again, better by the fact that we were now veterans. The routine of accumulating knowledge basic to the understanding of advanced courses, the steady hum. You only noticed it when it stopped. You tried to live around it.

Except for one course. On the way to registration Dickie enthused about Professor Salter's English 102 section. "Word is he's going to try something new. Experimental. What exactly, word doesn't say, but given it's him, it's bound to be interesting."

"When does it meet?"

"Monday Wednesday Friday 1:30."

"Violates your rule about no classes after noon Friday."

"Worth it."

"What's the reading list?"

"Bookstore has 'The Odyssey', Chaucer, Donne, the War Poets and 'The Wasteland.'"

I had to switch around some Bio and Chem labs, but we both signed up for Salter's section. And that, as it turned out, made all the difference.

You made two worlds, the Study World and the Social World. You only noticed when the two worlds collided. Dickie decided to pledge Phi Delt.

He also continued in Eastern Religions. He was curious about my father's paper on the Golem. He had never heard the story. "So the Golem is just a sort of Frankenstein, but benevolent, and this Rabbi has the power and spells to bring him to life and protect the Jews. He's very stupid, and mute, and he follows orders literally. How does the rabbi bring him to life and shut him off?"

"There are a lot of different versions, but all of them involve the mystical use of Hebrew letters and words, the Names of God. The big one is to write 'emess', which means truth, on his forehead to bring him to life, and erase the aleph to make 'mess', death, to put him back to sleep. Aleph is an abbreviation of the Divine Name, so, see, removing the divine name takes away life."

Eli had come in in the middle of this. "You need god for life, " he said.

"That seems to be the message."

"I do," he said. "I can't see a universe without a designer and a purpose."

"That's because you don't understand how organic molecules work," I said. "You're an engineer, you see the universe as inorganic, machinery, you don't see how machinery can exist without a mechanic."

He shook his head. "Can't see it," he said. "How does all this come from soup?"

"Emergent properties of complex systems. Chemistry arises out of physics. Biology arises out of chemistry. Psychology arises out of biology. Literature and history arise out of psychology."

"You have proof of this."

"You know I don't. I guess it's faith of a sort, in the ability of man to understand. But not in a god."

"The universe can have transcendent purpose without a god," Dickie said. "I need to feel that, but not a god. A Golem that runs things. Literal and mute. It doesn't have to be conscious, or even alive. The Tao. Dharma."

"Neither of you has any respect for religion. Or tradition," Eli said.

"Just the family tradition of skepticism," I said.

"Not for Western tradition," Dickie said.

"So why are you pledging Phi Delt?"

"My family tradition," Dickie said. "Which come to think of it isn't serving me that well either."

"Is that why Eastern Religions?"

"At first. Because it wasn't North Greenwich, Connecticut. It was as distant from North Greenwich as I can get."

"Is that why you're interested in things like The Golem? In Jews? We're another Eastern Religion to you? A bit of exotica?" I didn't know what I was saying, suddenly. "Any Jew would do, right?"

"Of course not. For one thing, it's a Western religion." He looked hurt. "Everyone I know is from North Greenwich or some place that wants to be North Greenwich."

"So any Jew would do."

"No, Paul, not any Jew would do…the first hour I knew you, you made my father—a guy with the Navy Cross, did you know that?—look like the horse's ass that he sometimes is. And you got a reaction from my sister that I haven't seen…ever. At Daddy's orders I've been parading guys through the house every vacation. 'Oh it will be so great for you Alicia your big brother will be bringing boys home for you by the bushel basket.' Half of fucking Creffield Academy has filed past her and you're the only one that ever got a response. That's why I think I can get away with pledging Phi Delt. Morgan isn't all of Phi Delt.

There's my father, useful old alumnus brother, and my sister, who I think you agree isn't bad looking. Shit, Parker's been hot for her since fucking first grade. Why do you think he gave me a ride? I'm safe from Morgan."

"There's me. I'm a liability. Do we stay friends?"

"Yeah, you. Back to you. The first week I know you, you take them on. Naked."

"Achilles fought naked."

"He had invulnerability. What did you have?"

"Rage."

"What would you have done if I hadn't heard you singing out the window?"

"I don't know. I remember thinking I'd go back in the showers, turn them all on, get the towel good and wet, do as much damage as I could before getting the crap beat out of me."

"You might have. Look, you're my friend. You turned me on to the I Ching. You make me laugh. You make me think. You seem to think I know how to think. And you're not from North Greenwich."

"And you'll be living at Phi Delt house."

"Yeah. That's the part I...maybe you need a Golem"

Maybe that's what this was about

What Eli wanted was to talk about the radio show.

"Her phone's hooked up again," Dickie said. "You can have your Weather Girl again. Works for me—it'll help the memories at Phi Delt."

"Paul? Is that you?"

"Sure is. What's the weather forecast?"

"Partly crappy."

"Is this going to be OK?"

90

"It should be. He's calmed down again. I'm off the shit list. Dickie's on it—grades."

"We can use 'Partly Crappy'. It isn't one of the seven words."

"Good. I'll introduce myself as Beatriz Viterbo. Give the weather in Buenos Aires."

"Borges' lost love in 'The Aleph'? I love that story."

"Me too, and thank you thank you thank you for the books. God, I'd love to live in a library. I was thinking about Borges' Aleph. If he had one in his library he would never have to leave it."

"You could be a librarian."

"No. I'm not as interested in the books as I am in what's in them." We didn't realize that never again in our lives would we have the luxury of just sinking into a book for days at a time. "I wish I could stay on the line."

"Me too."

"I'll call just before the broadcast, around 10:50. Gives us ten minutes."

"Goodnight Paul."

"Goodnight Beatriz."

Biology 102 Qualitative Chemistry 102 English 102

English 102 was more adventurous than English 101, maybe because we had this new young prof. Given my workload, "The Odyssey" was a gift; my father had read me "The Children's Homer" and I'd read the Rieu prose translation on my own. I checked T.E. Lawrence's translation out of the library and won several bets with people who didn't think Lawrence of Arabia had done something like translate Homer. Dickie and I were still in the same English section.

"Polyphemous is a kind of Golem," Dickie said.

"Are you still trying to find some tangent to take the discussion on to avoid reading the book?"

"No, asshole, I'm really asking. I'm exploring the concept of the Golem. Polyphemous works by a very simple set of rules, like an automaton."

"He turns himself on and off."

"Doesn't matter. What matters is the control of rage. It's like, I learned this wrestling, everyone's got a Golem inside him, the issue is, turning him on and off. Odysseus has his all under control until he lets loose on the Suitors. Then he doesn't quit until he strings up a bunch of servant girls. Golem, man."

It was an interesting argument, and he developed it in a paper. The problem was referencing my father's work. Which was of course unpublished. We went together to the professor's office when he called Dickie on it. I showed him my father's paper and notes.

"Very interesting, " he said, "But not a citable reference. It hasn't been reviewed. On the other hand…" He stared out the window for a time. "You know, you could have presented this as your own argument. Either of you could have. It hasn't seen the light of day anywhere. But you didn't." He stared around some more. "Mr. Acheson, this is an A idea with D references. You rewrite it with the references Professor Seitz used—I mean, you go back to his sources—and I'll read it again, as if submitted on time. Take a week."

"I'll do it," Dickie said as we walked back to the dorm, "Although I don't really have the time. I need the grade."

"Why this grade especially?

"Any grades. My father is worried my grades so far won't get me into law school."

"That where you want to go?"

"You know I don't. But until I have a better plan…one plan I have is staying out of the Army. And he won't pay for anything that doesn't lead to law school. So here we are. English is a lot more palatable to me than math and geo, so it's this and Eastern Rel for A's. Or nothing." I thought: What was different about Dickie: When I read a book I filed the words away, they were there when I needed them. Dickie *incorporated* them, as if he'd read them with his body, as if they had become part of himself. I helped him. It was a labor of love for me, reading through my father's sources, seeing how his mind worked. In a few days Dickie's paper was adequately referenced. And Midterms were upon us.

Midterms were less fraught than last term. Either we were cockier, or more experienced, it wasn't easy to distinguish. We dragged ourselves through it and headed home for Spring Break. Or to ski resorts, or Fort Lauderdale.

I called her from home. The excuse was the radio show, of which she was by far the most popular part. But what I really wanted to do was hear her voice, and ask if she wanted anything from the Strand.

"Dickie's really worried about his grades."

"I know. It takes the pressure off me. The Pater can only worry about one thing at a time."

"What are you doing?"

"For a while I was Reading Flaubert. I've got my library card back. I've run out of Borges."

"There's more in the pipeline."

"I gave up on the Pynchon, Paul, sorry. Must be a guy thing. I'll send it back."

"Ya win some, ya lose some. I thought you'd need something long, and didn't figure you for 'The Magic Mountain'. Or Tolstoy. I haven't tackled Tolstoy yet. I should have sent you Jane Austen."

"We're reading 'The Scarlet Letter' for school. I think it's supposed to be a warning against premarital pregnancy. I'm not seeing it that way."

"Well, that's interesting news…"

"That's no joking matter, Paul. There's at least two girls in my class that just vanished, which is what happens—you get sent to some relative in a distant city, or a Booth Home. It's no joke for a girl. Boys just…it isn't a joke."

"Sorry." *How did this touch a nerve*

"It's OK. I've just been reading Simone de Beauvoir. 'The Second Sex'?"

"Sartre's woman…Sorry, her own woman."

"Right, Paul, that's what the book is about. I'm reading it in French, with a big Larousse open on my lap; it isn't in English yet and when it is it's going to be bigger than Civil Rights. You'll see. Feminism is the belief that women are human beings."

"That's an idea I was brought up on. My grandmother was a suffragette."

"Was she really? I'd love to meet her."

I couldn't see how this might happen, but it was an interesting picture.

"I'm getting called to dinner."

"You guys eat late." (I'd called after six for the lower rates).

"Very patrician. What time is dinner in Brooklyn?"

"Six. Usually. Go. I'll talk to you before the show."

"Bye Paul."

"Bye Ali."

When we got back it was Pledge Week. Dickie, somewhat grimly, pledged Phi Delt. The brothers showed up to kidnap him in the approved manner. They ignored me, gathered around his bed and asked him in solemn tones if he accepted. When he did they demanded he accompany them to the House for the beginning of Pledge Period. From that point I might as well have had a single room. He had to spend all his time outside of class at the House, at the beck and call of the brothers, as a kind of servant. They could demand any humiliating task that came into their heads.

"They were treated that way," Dickie told me, "So they pass it on."

"Wouldn't it make more sense, if you're being treated that way, to get together and kick their ass?"

"Revolution?"

"Yeah, revolution."

"Not our style since 1776."

"Hello, Paul? They said Dickie isn't there, so I'll tell you. I got into Wellsmith."

"Whoa, Ali. Congratulations. That's great."

"Yeah, well it's…I don't know how much is me and how much it's that I'm a legacy; my mother and aunt are alums. I don't test well, my SATs were nothing to write home about."

"Bullshit. You're brighter and better read than most of our classmates here."

"Well. We'll see."

"We will. Who do you want to be this weekend?"

"I'll sign on and off as Simone de Beauvoir, say I have to go construct my female identity."

"That'll get a response."

"Yeah, the wrong kind."

"Not necessarily. OK, maybe."

"Tell Dickie I got into Wellsmith. A pair of legacies."

"I will. But I won't add that."

"Bye Paul."

95

"Bye. Till Saturday. And Congratulations again."

On the board:

> April is the cruellest month, breeding
> Lilacs out of the dead land, mixing
> Memory and desire, stirring
> Dull roots with spring rain.

"What we have done, gentlemen, is begun the semester with one of the oldest epic poems in the Western canon. An Epic is a poem that tells a story. We proceeded through *The Canterbury Tales* for the music of English and some source material, and Donne for the same reasons: these are Eliot's sources for 'The Wasteland', which I contend is a modern epic poem, perhaps the epic of our time, our civilization. I propose that we study it in depth over the next six weeks, one Book per week, line by line. I promise you, this poem deserves such study."

This was a relief; the reading load over the first half semester had about broken our backs.

"Let us begin with Book One: THE BURIAL OF THE DEAD. I'm sure you all recognize the source, or allusion. Mr. Seitz, start us off."

"Uh, seems self-explanatory..."

"No, it's an explicit reference. Mr. Cameron."

"The Burial of the Dead is one of the Acts of Charity, one of the Offices of Christian Mercy, after Matthew, 'When I was hungry thou didst feed me' etcetera; feed the hungry, give water to the thirsty, clothe the naked, succor the prisoner, bury the dead..."

"Actually not one of the original Acts; added after the Black Plague. *Not real up on my New Testament* How about the first line. Mickelson?"

"The Canterbury Tales, sir (he shuffled pages):

96

"When April with his showers sweet with fruit
The drought of March has pierced unto the root
And bathed each vein with liquor that has power
To generate therein and sire the flower;
When Zephyr also has, with his sweet breath…"

"Certainly. Sounds pretty benign, hopeful, a time of rebirth. Can anybody tell me why, for Eliot, April is the cruelest month?"

Silence.

"Are the next lines a clue?"

Winter kept us warm, covering
Earth in forgetful snow, feeding
A little life with dried tubers.
Summer surprised us, coming over the Starnbergersee
With a shower of rain; we stopped in the colonnade,
And went on in sunlight, into the Hofgarten,

And drank coffee, and talked for an hour.
Bin gar keine Russin, stamm' aus Litauen, echt deutsch.

"Mr. Seitz, help us out with your German."

Back in the game "I'm not Russian; I'm from Lithuania, truly German, or, better, completely German, authentically German. The places are I think in Munich."

"So? Nothing? Any other clues?"

"The Order for the Burial of the Dead is from the *Book of Common Prayer*," Dickie said.

"Just so, Mr. Acheson. Eliot is linking April with death, not life. Winter kept us warm, not April. Why should this be? No? When was this poem written? Zigler."

"Around 1921 and earlier, wasn't it?"

"Exactly. What was happening in England at around that time? In Europe? Anybody?"

"The First World War."

"Exactly, Mr. Hoffer. This is a reference to conditions on the Western Front. Which was somnolent during the frozen winter. Offensive operations, with their huge casualty lists, began in April, when the ground thawed."

"Here's the *Book of Common Prayer* again sir:

I will show you fear in a handful of dust."

"Indeed Mr. Acheson; hold that thought."

"This next part, sir:

In the mountains, there you feel free.
I read, much of the night, and go south in the winter.

Is this a reference to Switzerland, which was neutral?"

"I'm not sure one can take this so literally, Mr. O'Connor. In context it seems more like a refuge in childhood, but the allusion to a neutral territory may reinforce the meaning of a refuge in childhood innocence…"

And so the analysis went, line by line, word by word, as we were, as freshmen, introduced to the concept of deep reading. Word had been right; this was the Real Thing.

Two days later, the odor of bio lab still in my nostrils, we continued the dissection of The Burial of the Dead. We proceeded to Madame Sosostris' comically inept Tarot readings.

"Do any of you know the Tarot?" Professor Salter asked.

Silence.

"Paul and I are acquainted with the Taoist Oracle, the I Ching," Dickie said.

"Not the same thing at all, Mr. Acheson, but again, hold that thought. The point is, gentlemen, you can see where otherwise rational men would turn to mystic divination, in a city where

Under the brown fog of a winter dawn,
A crowd flowed over London Bridge, so many,
I had not thought death had undone so many.

Do they find solace, then?"

"It appears not," Ferguson said.

"Just so. And why not?"

Silence.

"How about these other allusions?"

Again, silence.

"Gentlemen, you have to be prepared to follow Eliot's associations. This is a dream he is having for you. Very well. Here is what I propose. Let's break. We will divide up and track down the allusions in Book One and return for discussion next time, each with a brief essay—maybe a hundred words?—on how you think yours fits in the scheme of the poem. Mr. Acheson, you take 'The ships at Mylae'." Mr. Seitz, you have the German, the Irisch Kind…"

"There has to be a scheme behind this," Dickie said. The actual task was not arduous; in Dickie's case look up Mylae, in mine, translate the

German and hit Bartlett's Quotations. Thirty years later we would have had the answers in minutes on the Internet.

Friday's class saw the explication of Belladonna, hyacinths, 'These are pearls that were his eyes', the sources of those undone by death, Madame Sosostris' cards…

"Mylae was the site of a battle in the Punic Wars, between Rome and Carthage," Dickie said, "Fitting the war motif, but not World War One. He seems to be trying to hail a friend whose shared experiences of the trenches might be a basis for some kind of escape from the deadness all around them."

"Very good, Mr. Acheson. Mr. Seitz?"

"The lines are from Wagner's 'Tristan and Isolde', Eliot's note says; the first is from Act I, the second from Act III, both are about Tristan's longing for Isolde; the first one goes, 'Fresh blows the wind to home, My Irish girl, where do you tarry?' The second one, 'Empty and desolate is the sea', is his acceptance that he is dying and she is not coming." *The maiden is powerful. One should not marry such a maiden.*

"So. Where do all these allusions leave us?"

Silence.

"When you don't know, return to the text. Let it guide you."

When we still didn't get it, he said: "What about this; Lines 19 through 22:

> What are the roots that clutch, what branches grow
> Out of this stony rubbish? Son of man,
> You cannot say, or guess, for you know only
> A heap of broken images, where the sun beats

Why are these people flowing over London Bridge so dead inside?"

"Because they've been through a terrible war?" I said.

"That, and…generations before had been through terrible wars. And plagues. I put it to you that they are in the same position as all of you, right now. They, and you, can make nothing of the experience, for you know only a heap of broken images."

We got it. We all got it. He had taken us through an experiential reading of Book One of "The Wasteland." It was a pedagogical tour de force.

"From here forward, gentlemen, the assignment will be to chase down these allusions, and be prepared in class to discuss their meanings."

"Did I tell you?" Dickie said.

"Paul? Hi. What about this weekend?"

"It's going to be frat initiation night. We won't have much of an audience, but what we have will be dedicated members of GDI. Gamma Delta Iota. God Damned Independents. We'll need you more than ever to comfort the social misfits. Of whom I am one."

"My favorite people." *Please crawl through the phone line right now*

"At this point, Athena on the sweatshirts is beginning to look good."

"I'm running out of femmes fatales to be."

"We're doing 'The Wasteland'. No shortage of characters to be, there. How about this week you be The Hyacinth Girl; next week you can be Madame Sosostris, famous clairvoyant."

"I'll have to read the poem."

"You'll need to be living in that library. It's one allusion after another, and Eliot's footnotes don't help much unless you have his sources. The way he's teaching this is amazing."

"I can call you as I read."

"I like that idea." *I really like that idea* "Dickie is going to miss this one. He'll be getting initiated."

"How is he feeling?"

"Still ambivalent, I think. You should see him in English. I'm worried about him, Ali. There's bad blood between him and the Pledge Master. I seriously don't know why he's doing this."

"Because he didn't have any choice. The pater read him the riot act. 'I left you alone your first term and you came home with a GPA barely passable for law school, now I make the rules, you pledge Phi Delt, you bring the GPA up to at least a 3.0 or you can kiss the car goodbye'."

"What car?"

"The one each of us gets when we graduate high school, only freshmen can't have cars so we get it as sophs."

"Well. Nice. Talk to you tomorrow at 10:50. Oh. The forecast. How about April is the cruelest month?"

"Is that from 'The Wasteland'?"

"First line."

"Bye Paul."

"Bye Ali."

Saturday was unusually warm, for Schenectady. No lilacs.

"How you doing?" I asked Dickie.

"Fatalistic."

"I still don't get how this is supposed to be fun."

"You're not helping. Neither is this crap for breakfast. Phi Delt has a decent cook at least."

He left later that morning for the frat house. I did some reading, got bored; Eli was out somewhere, I did some more reading. Lunch. Dinner. More reading. Time to go to the station.

"Big doings tonight at every frat on campus," Eli said, "Especially for our listeners at GDI. Sit back and let us spin you some platters, coax some tunes out of the old pianer, news at eleven and oh, yes, a visit from the WRNC weather girl." The humor was desultory, is all I remember. I called her at 10:50; Darren began setting up the phone patch as Eli ran through jazz arpeggios. I went to the office, put my feet up on the desk and put the call through to her. "Hey, Ali."

"Hey Paul."

"Anything doing?"

"I got the Eliot."

"What do you think?"

"A heap of broken images."

"See? You're getting it." The corner office faced the street to the east, across it Phi Delt house; to the north was the alley across which was the Rathskellar entrance. An off night there, or a big night for GDI. Suddenly lights came on at Phi Delt. I thought I could hear shouting. "Hold on Ali, something's going on over here at Phi Delt." I put my feet on the floor, reached over to open the window. The shouting was still indistinct. Then the porch lights went on, and Dickie, in a black toga, shot out the front door, carrying something, a bunch of white togas in hot pursuit. "It's Dickie," I said, "I'll call back when I can." I broke the connection and yelled for Eli and Darren. Dickie had turned in the street and was swinging the thing in his hand around to keep them off him. "Can you rig a mike on a really long lead?"

"Sure," Darren said. "We have two, but only enough wire for one."

"Eli. Get on the horn. Call out the troops, at the 'Skellar, at the dorms. We need an army, I think." I ran out with the mike; Darren signaled it was hot. I came up behind Dickie just as Morgan pushed to the front of the mob. His nose was bleeding and his cheek was lacerated.

"Hello, guys," I had time to say, "This is Paul Seitz reporting from just outside Phi Delt and the Rathskellar, where there is breaking news. Popular freshman pledge Dickie Acheson has fled the Phi Delt house and is holding the brothers off with, it looks like, the Phi Delt ceremonial paddle." Then Morgan tried to tackle him.

Dickie whipped him around and to the ground on his back, knee in Morgan's groin and the paddle across his throat. He started to apply pressure. Morgan's eyes bugged slightly. I buried the mike in my armpit and shouted "Dickie." He froze—didn't let up, but didn't push harder either. I could hear Morgan's labored breathing. Parker signaled the group back and came up behind Dickie; I waved him over to where he was visible.

Eli sized up the situation and took the mike from me. "We could use some support out here for our friend Dickie Acheson," he said. Lights began coming on in the freshman dorms; people began streaming out of the 'Skellar.

I knelt down beside Dickie. He was grimfaced; a rage in his eyes I had never seen. Morgan was one step from gurgling, I could see. I asked Dickie if he was OK, and he didn't answer. "Dickie," I said, "GDI is turning out in numbers. Eli is calling them on the radio. The show? You're going to be able to walk away from this, and these jerks aren't going to be able to do a thing about it."

"We don't want trouble, Dickie," Parker said soothingly. "You can go home, and we can discuss this another day."

"There isn't going to be another day for this," Dickie said, or rather whispered, through clenched teeth.

"What do you want to do, Dickie?"

Silence.

"Dickie," I said. "Do you want me to negotiate something?"

"Mmm."

"OK." I looked at the crowd. Our side was growing. They had bottles. "First thing," I said to Parker, "I think you'd better get your people back in the house. At least on the porch."

"I agree," he said. "PHI DELT. Go back in the House. Get on the porch."

They did it. I turned to Morgan.

104

"Morgan," I said, "Dickie has you in what is called a choke hold, plus he's added a little touch of his own. If you so much as move your mouth, he's going to either grind your equipment into the street or choke you. Frankly, I wouldn't shed a tear, but Dickie is my friend and I wouldn't want him in any trouble over a piece of shit like you. I'm going to say things and you're going to answer by blinking your eyes, once for yes, twice for no. Understand?" One blink. "Good. Now. Dickie is going to let you up, but only if you agree to crawl back to your friend Parker. Parker is going to walk off to about twenty feet from here and you're going to crawl that far, and he's going to help you up and back to the house. Believe me, you aren't going to want to walk it. Got it?" One blink. I looked up. There were fifty to a hundred frosh and upperclass Independents watching. Every frat brother on campus was involved in initiations; we had the numbers. "Morgan, before we do this, you need to know something. This happened right in the middle of my radio show. We called out every Independent on campus. Everybody else is doing initiations. Just in case you were thinking about anything, you're hopelessly outnumbered. That right, Parker?"

"He's telling the truth, Morgs," Parker said.

I wondered where the campus police were. "Dickie," I said. "Did you hear me? Is this OK with you?" Silence. Suddenly I knew what to do. I reached up and rubbed Dickie's forehead. Still silence. "I rubbed off the aleph, Dickie."

Very slowly his eyes shifted to me. "Did you hear what I said to him?"

"Yes."

"Is it OK?"

"Yeah. Sure."

"OK. Parker is going to walk about twenty feet toward the porch. He's there. Really slowly, let him up."

Dickie first released the pressure on Morgan's throat, then on his groin. Morgan rolled over and crawled toward Parker, who helped him to his feet. He staggered, as predicted. After two steps, Dickie said, "Rabbi, if you have that magic amulet, this would be a good time to make me invisible."

"I can do the next best thing. We'll melt into the crowd."

"Hey," Parker yelled. "Give the paddle back, Dickie."

Dickie turned, looked at the paddle as if surprised to find it in his hand. "You want your fucking paddle?" he shouted. "Here's your fucking paddle." He whirled like a discus thrower and hurled the paddle onto Phi Delt's roof.

The crowd exploded in laughter. A few bottles flew, but it was over. Eli began interviewing members of the crowd while I hustled Dickie into the station office. My heart was pounding. "What the hell just happened?"

"Morgan did something unspeakable and I came very close to killing him, I think. In my head I killed him, that much I can tell you."

"Well, he walked away, or sort of walked."

"More than I can say for myself."

I wasn't sure what this meant. "Are you OK now?"

"Yeah, probably. I think I won't be completing the pledge process at Phi Delt. I think I just joined GDI."

"Glad to have you. I think the mob that turned out to cover your back agrees."

"I don't think that will impress my father."

"Not even if you explain? You showed an awful lot of courage and skill out there."

"So did you. That was brilliant, rubbing the aleph off my forehead."

"Words weren't working."

"We're even."

"I don't keep a count."

106

He grinned. "Neither do I. Thanks Paul."

"Anyway, as long as old Morgs is around, there's always a chance to run up the score."

"He may not be around. He's on academic probation. That's one reason this whole thing never happened. If he gets disciplined it's expulsion. If he gives us any trouble, it will have happened. Awful lot of witnesses you rustled up."

"It wasn't exactly a plan. There's one more witness we'd better call. I was on the phone with Ali when you made your run for it." Out the window we could see a few Phi Delts trying to make a human ladder to reach the paddle on the roof.

"Ali? Hi sis…yeah, I'm OK. Paul rescued me from killing Morgan…No, that doesn't mean he rescued Morgan. Morgan is wounded…yeah, not much chance, I think…How pissed do you think?…That bad? Hmm. OK. Can you get to Alice's? Yeah, here's Paul."

"Hi Ali."

"Do we owe you more thanks?"

"No. As Dickie put it, we're even. How is this going to go down at home?"

"Not good."

"How will it be for you?"

"I'll survive. He won't find out until Dickie tells him. Take care of Dickie. What the hell happened?"

"Don't know yet. Maybe won't. I have a guess, and so do you."

"Yeah. Ugh. Maybe you should have let him kill him."

"I came pretty close. Think. It wouldn't have been worth it."

"Probably not."

"Shit, I have to get back on the air. I'll call you next week. Here's Dickie."

Eli and Darren were doing fine without me, but Eli asked me to put a cap on our "coverage". "We take you to Paul Seitz, our across-the-street correspondent."

"Well, Eli, as nearly as can be determined, remember these are secret ceremonies, the Phi Delt initiation went further than one pledge was willing to go, and he disrupted the proceedings. He successfully defended himself when they chased him out, and the presence of a sympathetic crowd made everyone think better of taking it further."

Unbelievably, that was the end of it. It had taken place in front of maybe a hundred witnesses, been broadcast on the campus radio (which, being carried along power lines, could be heard between the campus and the next transformers in every direction), and nothing else happened. Drunken prank. Boys will be boys. I prowled back and forth in my own skull like a caged zoo tiger. So did Dickie, but he was thinking along different lines. He had to tell his father. In the end, his father called him to congratulate him on becoming a Brother, and Dickie told him he had something to tell him about that, and invited him to dinner at the South dining room. "It will take him out of the house and put him in a public place," Dickie said, "Spare the women and children. Also, no alcohol."

That was my first clue about what they were dealing with; it would be years before I understood. "What are you going to tell him?"

"What Morgan tried to do. Which will leave him with no argument. And that I will under no circumstances have anything further to do with Phi Delt or the fraternity system."

It worked. What happened, or rather almost happened, was more than Mr. Acheson was prepared to countenance—or to publicize by taking it up with the frat, which would embarrass the Achesons and put them at odds with the organization and culture. Dickie presented him no alternative.

Dear Paul—

Is Dickie OK? Father is being very weird and I don't like the sound I get from Dickie himself.

—A.

Dear A

He isn't OK or not OK. Very thoughtful, unusually silent for long periods. I'll call soon.

–P.

Light from the hallway woke me. It was Dickie coming in.

"What time is it?"

"About 3 AM, Mom. I took a walk."

"Problem?"

"Yeah, could be. I keep thinking about me and Morgan in the street. When I sleep I dream I'm back on the street, I have the thing in my hands and I'm pressing down on his throat. Sometimes even during the day it feels like…I'm here and I'm not here. I'm back on the street choking Morgan. Comes back to me like a dream. Mostly just at night. Tonight I dreamed I killed him."

"You didn't."

"Tonight in the dream I did."

"You didn't."

"Because you stopped me."

"You stopped you."

"You erased the aleph. That was cute. In the dream I didn't stop me."

"In real life you did. You want to see a shrink?"

"I want to learn how to meditate. I asked Richards to teach me."

Richards was the Eastern Religions professor. "Will he?"

He climbed into bed. "He said yes."

In the Study World, "The Wasteland" quickly became the high point. Professor Salter, a prematurely bald, goggle-eyed, gangly young man, drew us in, brought us into contact with the world as nothing else that semester. And there was the added factor for me of writing and phoning Ali about it. In the next section, "A Game of Chess", there was more to it than thrill.

> You ought to be ashamed, I said, to look so antique.
> (And her only thirty-one.)
> I can't help it, she said, pulling a long face,
> It's them pills I took, to bring it off, she said.
> (She's had five already, and nearly died of young George.)
>
> The chemist said it would be alright, but I've never been the
>   same.
> You are a proper fool, I said.

"'It's them pills I took, to bring it off.' What, gentlemen, could that mean?"

Silence.

"Is it a quotation?"

"No."

"It doesn't look like something we could look up," Christopher said.

"No, Christopher, it isn't. It's something you have to know. Eliot is counting on your experience of the world here. Look further along."

> HURRY UP PLEASE ITS TIME
> HURRY UP PLEASE ITS TIME

"Anyone? Any of you ever been to England? No? This is the traditional call for last round before closing at the pubs. In the previous segment, seemingly unrelated, a couple go quietly mad. Why? What does he say?"

"'I think we are in rats' alley/Where the dead men lost their bones'," Dickie quoted.

"Suggesting what to you? No? No one? I shall rush out as I am, and walk the street With my hair down, so."

We laughed.

"What if I told you Rats' Alley was a famous section of the Western Front?"

"He has combat fatigue," Finley said, "He can't talk about it. He can't talk to her."

"Right. They called it shell shock; they thought it was a physical effect, all the exposure to bombardments. Although the early Freudians thought it was an effect of anxiety."

"They can't speak because he can't face the memories," Dickie said.

"Yes, Acheson. And it's driving *both of them* mad. The woman, and look at how Eliot sets her up, this upper class drawing room by firelight, can't stand the secrets and silences. This section of the poem is about the effects of the war at home. The constant threat of destruction and loss. Not unlike our situation currently. Did you know the Germans bombed London from zeppelins? So then Eliot cuts to this lower class pub, and this woman is talking to her friend about the relationship with her husband, and she says

It's them pills I took, to bring it off

What is she talking about?"

Silence.

"If this were a girls' school, or coed, we would have the answer in seconds. What can this mean? Go and think."

I called Ali. "Abortion, of course," she said. "How can you not know that?"

I was ready for that next class.

"Exactly Seitz. Did you all know that and not want to mention? One of our society's big secrets. There are drugs, abortifacents, that 'bring it off'. The things you miss, living in a monastery."

On the way back to the dorm Dickie said, "It isn't the memories he can't face, or anyway not the sights and sounds and smells, those are only reminders. What he can't face is how it felt to hate another man so much he wanted to kill him, and to have another man hate him so much that he wanted to kill him. What the war set loose."

"We're not only talking about the poem now."

"No. We're not."

Dickie started meditating. At first he did it alone, when I was at 3-hour chem and bio labs. When he had learned to truly clear his mind, to focus, he did it when I was there, and it quickly lost its eeriness. He looked at peace for the first time in weeks. I called Ali.

"Before anything else, your brother is sleeping again, and seems at peace. The thing with Morgan really messed with his head. I should let him tell it. He's taken up meditation."

"Really? Meditation? Dickie? This I have to see. Are we doing the Weather Girl this week?"

"Absolutely. We never did the Hyacinth Girl, or April is..."

"Got it. If he's meditating he's going to love the next part. Of 'The Wasteland'."

Sweet Thames, run softly, till I end my song.
The river bears no empty bottles, sandwich papers,

112

Silk handkerchiefs, cardboard boxes, cigarette ends
Or other testimony of summer nights.
　　The nymphs are departed.
And their friends, the loitering heirs of city directors;
Departed, have left no addresses.

"What is Eliot talking about here? Seitz."

"Well, he could be talking about the place where Coney Island Creek ends at a bulkhead next to a gas tank. The trash that piles up there."

"Coney Island Creek. Another storied body of water, not unlike the Thames?"

Laughter. "'Or other testimony of summer nights.' What testimony?"

Silence.

"'The nymphs are departed. And their friends, the loitering heirs of city directors.' What have they left behind, with no addresses?"

"French Letters," I said. "Used condoms. We used to call them Coney Island Whitefish."

Shocked silence. "Exactly, Mr. Seitz, exactly. Look at where the poem goes from there; it's unmistakable, isn't it?

The sound of horns and motors, which shall bring
Sweeney to Mrs. Porter in the spring.
O the moon shone bright on Mrs. Porter
And on her daughter
They wash their feet in soda water.

Anyone? No? It's a soldier's song from the First World War. It isn't their feet they wash; Eliot cleaned this up for 1920s publication. And he goes on a few lines later:

113

Mr. Eugenides, the Smyrna merchant
Unshaven, with a pocket full of currants
C.i.f. London: documents at sight,
Asked me in demotic French
To luncheon at the Cannon Street Hotel
Followed by a weekend at the Metropole.

Suggesting what…Acheson?"
    "A homosexual come-on," Dickie said evenly. "And he goes on:

I Tiresias, though blind, throbbing between two lives,
Old man with wrinkled female breasts, can see
At the violet hour, the evening hour that strives
Homeward, and brings the sailor home from sea,
The typist home at teatime, blah blah blah…

I Tiresias, old man with wrinkled dugs
Perceived the scene, and foretold the rest -
I too awaited the expected guest.
He, the young man carbuncular, arrives,
A small house agent's clerk, blah blah blah

The time is now propitious, as he guesses,
The meal is ended, she is bored and tired,
Endeavours to engage her in caresses
Which still are unreproved, if undesired.
Flushed and decided, he assaults at once;
Exploring hands encounter no defence;
His vanity requires no response,
And makes a welcome of indifference.
(And I Tiresias have foresuffered all

114

Enacted on this same divan or bed;
I who have sat by Thebes below the wall
And walked among the lowest of the dead.)
Bestows one final patronising kiss,

It's about the most despairing seduction scene I've ever read."

"What makes it so? Anyone."

From Terrence: "They aren't in love."

"No, exactly, they aren't," Salter said, "But it's more than that, Eliot says. What does he think is leading to all this degraded, loveless sex?"

Christopher quoted:

"By the waters of Leman I sat down and wept . . .
Sweet Thames, run softly till I end my song,
Sweet Thames, run softly, for I speak not loud or long.

The first part is from the Book of Psalms, only it's Babylon…"

"Eliot was in Lausanne, on Lake Leman, when he wrote this…" *site of the Castle of Chillon*

"'Et O ces voix d'enfants, chantant dans la coupole!' I looked up the Verlaine poem; it refers to the Pure Blood of Parsifal, and the pure children's voices singing in the cathedral dome."

"Good, Christopher, excellent, exactly."

"And the rest of the section is repeated references to the history the Thames has seen."

"Exactly, Zigler. What is Eliot getting at? What did he make you see and feel?"

"The despair after the War."

"Of course, but why that despair? What is the source of the despair? He hints at it…What about this:

While I was fishing in the dull canal
On a winter evening round behind the gashouse
Musing upon the king my brother's wreck
And on the king my father's death before him."

Silence. "Did any of you follow up Eliot's footnote about the Grail Legend?"

Amazingly, we hadn't. We'd looked up the quotations in the poem itself, but not in Eliot's notes.

"This is a reference to the legend of the Fisher King, whose wound must be healed for the despair to end."

"Like Philoctetes, sir, who had to be at Troy for the Greeks to win?"

"An interesting comparison, Purcell, but Eliot isn't interested in winning; he has other ends in mind. He's musing on the wreckage, not on the victory. Do you all see the constant counterpoint of the glorious historical Thames of London's past with its sordid present?"

We did, of course. "Then what of this. Line 300:

On Margate Sands
I can connect
Nothing with nothing.

What do you make of that?"

"The people of 1920 London have become disconnected from their past," I said. "I think...it's like the entire population suffers from the same inability as the man in Rat's Alley in the previous section."

"Exactly, Seitz. London, and by extension, European civilization has suffered a self-inflicted trauma that has cut it off from its own past, and that disconnection has robbed their present actions of all meaning. The sexual goings-on have no resonance. No depth. No connection to past generations, to literature, to myth...to anything. You see?"

We did.

"Professor, " Dickie said, "What about the very end of the section. And the title. We haven't connected them."

"Do you have a suggestion, Acheson?"

"Well, yes. I do.

To Carthage then I came

Burning burning burning burning
O Lord Thou pluckest me out
O Lord Thou pluckest

burning

'To Carthage', etc, and 'O Lord Thou pluckest me out', Eliot tells us, are from Augustine, 'to Carthage then I came, where a cauldron of unholy loves sang all about mine ears.' and 'Burning' is from the Buddha's 'Fire Sermon'." And he stood up and declaimed:

"Thus I heard. On one occasion the Buddha was living at Gaya, at Gayasisa, together with a thousand monks. There he addressed the monks: 'Monks, all is burning. And what is the all that is burning? The eye is burning, forms are burning, eye-consciousness is burning, all that is visible, that too is burning. Burning with what? Burning with the fire of lust, with the fire of hate, with the fire of delusion. I say it is burning with birth, aging and death, with sorrows, with lamentations, with pains, with griefs, with despairs. All the senses are burning. The mind is burning, ideas are burning, also whatever is felt as pleasure or pain, that too is burning. Monks, when a noble follower sees thus, he finds the eye, finds distance from forms, finds distance from eye-consciousness, finds distance from eye-contact, and the visible, from that too he finds distance. He finds distance from the ear... in sounds...He finds distance from the nose... in odors...He finds distance from the tongue... in flavors...He finds distance from the body... in tangibles. He finds distance from the mind, finds distance from ideas, and whatever is felt as pleasure or pain. When he finds that distance, passion fades out. With the fading of passion, he is liberated, and knows that he is liberated. He understands: 'Birth is exhausted, the holy life has been lived out, what can be done is done, of this there is no more beyond'."

He sat down. It is fair to say we were astounded, Salter included. "I take it, Acheson, that what we just heard was the Fire Sermon."

"It was, Professor. An abridged version of my own."

"I know Augustine, of course, but I admit I never sought out the Fire Sermon. I assumed I knew its gist...So Eliot brought together the seminal works of East and West on asceticism. Do you all follow?"

We did. Each in our own way.

"Thank you, Acheson. I'd appreciate a copy of the full text, if you would."

"Certainly."

He had more than memorized it. He had incorporated it.

Ali was equally astounded. "He had memorized the entire thing?"

"The thing entire, but his own abridgement. And not just memorized. You had to have been there."

"Yes, well, no girls in the tree house. Cooties."

"Salter thinks that too. He remarked that a girl in the class would have gotten the meaning of 'to bring it off' in a second.

"And you might want a hand with, wait a sec, here it is

> She turns and looks a moment in the glass,
> Hardly aware of her departed lover;
> Her brain allows one half-formed thought to pass:

'Well now that's done: and I'm glad it's over.'"

"God, is that a horror?"

"One that Tiresias alone can fully appreciate, having lived as both man and woman. Lacking a Tiresias, coeducation might be a good idea."

"You can say that again." *I want to reach through the phone*

From that moment Dickie dominated the class. He was a man inspired, not to inspire us but himself. He had seen something, perhaps for the first time clearly, something he had not known, or had only dimly known, he needed. The class, and surely Dickie, made short work of the Death By Water section and its obvious adumbration of the theme of mortality; as Salter put it, the need for death to focus our attention on what is important. We began the finale, "What the Thunder Said", worked our way through its beginning, so reminiscent in tone to Lamentations and Ecclesiastes, then

> Ganga was sunken, and the limp leaves
> Waited for rain, while the black clouds
> Gathered far distant, over Himavant.

"Acheson?"

"The sacred river Ganges; Himavant is a Himalyan peak."

> DA
> Datta: what have we given?
> My friend, blood shaking my heart
> The awful daring of a moment's surrender
> Which an age of prudence can never retract

"Da. Datta, dayadhvam, damyatta. Acheson?"

"Give, sympathize, control. It's from the Upanishads."

"What about the English? 'The awful daring of a moment's surrender/ Which an age of prudence can never retract'?"

"I think," I said, "Eliot means, if you forget those commands, humans risk irreparable violence."

"Individuals and nations," Dickie said.

"Well put, Acheson. Eliot hints at this, who can...?"

> "Cracks and reforms and bursts in the violet air
> Falling towers
> Jerusalem Athens Alexandria
> Vienna London
> Unreal,"

Christopher quoted.

"Yes. And what is the remedy, for Western man?"

I said,

> "I sat upon the shore
> Fishing, with the arid plain behind me
> Shall I at least set my lands in order?
> London Bridge is falling down falling down falling down...
>
> 'These fragments I have shored against my ruin'"

"So we must shore fragments against our ruin?"

"What we can remember of culture before the War. Maybe only fragments, but maybe enough. And maybe not..."

"Indeed, exactly Seitz, all of you, maybe not." He sat up on the desk. Put the book down. "Gentlemen," he said, "It is the tragedy of the man and woman in 'A Game of Chess' that he cannot connect the tragedy of the trenches with the suffering of earlier wars, of the man and woman in 'The Fire Sermon' that sex devoid of the deep link to romance, and romantic love, is a tragic, empty exercise. If all you know is the present, your life lacks resonance. When you know your actions to be linked to those of the past, to the great themes of the human condition, they acquire depth and meaning. This is Eliot's great warning to a century whose experience had been sundered from the past by the horror of the first industrial, technological war. That war was an unspeakable horror; men as young as yourselves and younger dying anonymously and uncomforted in mud. So they cut themselves off from any memory. The War is a chasm. And if they forget?" He picked up the book again.

"Why then Ile fit you. Hieronymo's mad againe.

They did it again less than twenty years later. And we're still doing it."

"It's hard to escape the conclusion that Eliot saw Buddhism and Christian asceticism and self-control as the only preventative for the violence inherent in human society," Dickie said.

"Not a path everyone is prepared to follow, Acheson."

"I know it, Professor."

"Eliot's 'Wasteland' is a dream you have to have, a maze you have to navigate, in order to learn how to read 'The Wasteland'. Now go home and read the poem. Read more Eliot. Read more modern poetry." There was a brief burst of applause. We knew we had done something.

Dickie meditated for long periods, and except for the periods of intensity in class, maybe including them, he seemed at peace.

I had a great idea. "A dramatic reading of 'The Wasteland'." Eli said. "Well, it's certainly in the grand tradition of our twisted approach to radio. Sure. Why not. Who'll do the reading? You?"

"I was thinking, me, you, Darren, Dickie, and the Weather Girl can do the womens' parts." *Under the firelight, under the brush, her hair Spread out in fiery points*

"I didn't know there were womens' parts."

"We've been here so long we've forgotten about womens' parts."

"Speak for yourself. Can this be done in under two hours?"

"Definitely."

I told Dr. Salter about it. "That would be wonderful. I'd be glad to take a part." I hadn't counted on that. "Sure." We got together and split up the sections, and rehearsed. Ali would have to be cued; we weren't sure she'd be able to hear clearly through the phone speaker.

"Did you know there is a recording of Eliot reading the poem?" Salter told me.

"Really? Could we get hold of a copy?"

"I don't know if you could play it without paying royalties. I can find that out for you."

I thanked him and called Ali. "You in?"

"Oh, I'm in. How big an audience do you think we'll have?"

"Well, after you became the Weather Girl, and your brother launched his on-air assault on the fraternity system, we have a solid listenership in GDI. We'll publicize it, but who knows, that might lose us listeners…maybe we should spring it as a surprise."

Eli thought so, and the next Saturday night, the weekend before Spring House Party Weekend, guys listening to WRNC at about 10:15 were surprised to hear Eli announce, "Tonight we're going to try something unusual. A few of you have had the recent experience of reading T.S. Eliot's famous poem 'The Wasteland'. Tonight the WRNC Radio Players are pleased to bring you a dramatic reading of the poem in its entirety."

And we did. Dr. Salter began: "April is the cruelest month…" Eli read "A Game of Chess", and I had Ali on the line. I read the first half of "The Fire Sermon", and I will never forget Ali picking up from there:

> "At the violet hour, when the eyes and back
> Turn upward from the desk, when the human engine waits
> Like a taxi throbbing waiting,
> I Tiresias, though blind, throbbing between two lives,
> Old man with wrinkled female breasts, can see
> At the violet hour, the evening hour that strives
> Homeward, and brings the sailor home from sea,
> The typist home at teatime, clears her breakfast, lights
> Her stove, and lays out food in tins.
> Out of the window perilously spread
> Her drying combinations touched by the sun's last rays,
> On the divan are piled (at night her bed)
> Stockings, slippers, camisoles, and stays…"

The Young Man Carbuncular arrived:

> "A small house agent's clerk, with one bold stare,
> One of the low on whom assurance sits
> As a silk hat on a Bradford millionaire…"

…engaged her in the caresses unreproved if undesired, but this time we had the part not read out in class, from her, the woman's part:

> "Bestows one final patronising kiss,
> And gropes his way, finding the stairs unlit . . .
>
> She turns and looks a moment in the glass,

> Hardly aware of her departed lover;
> Her brain allows one half-formed thought to pass:
> "Well now that's done: and I'm glad it's over."
> When lovely woman stoops to folly and
> Paces about her room again, alone,
> She smoothes her hair with automatic hand,
> And puts a record on the gramophone."

Her voice speaking those lines moved me strangely, but all I could say when I called her back at eleven for the weather segment was "Great job."

"When lovely woman stoops to folly."

Or unlovely man

Dickie had brought it home with "What the Thunder Said".

> Datta. Dayadhvam. Damyata.
> Shantih   shantih   shantih

I told him too, "Nice job."

"I don't know, Paul. I think I've taken a different meaning from this than you have."

"Your Buddhist studies."

"It's becoming more than just studies. Everything else I do feels like a waste of time. A prison."

"Really?"

"Really really. Everything else I'm doing. And everything else I'm doing dampens it.

> Dayadhvam: I have heard the key

Turn in the door once and turn once only
We think of the key, each in his prison
Thinking of the key, each confirms a prison

Eliot has that exactly right."

Spring Weekend passed. Finals week approached. We settled into typing final papers. Dickie put his major effort into Eastern Religions, and a paper nailing down all the Hindu and Buddhist allusions in 'The Wasteland'. Those were going to be his two A's. Everything else could go to hell.

I puzzled out integrals, solved stoichiometry equations and electron subshells, memorized the evolutionary tree. We did the last radio show. Took drunken calls from the dorms. "You guys gonna do any more poetry?"

"Actually we hope to have a recording of Eliot himself reading 'The Wasteland'."

"Oh, crap." Hmmmmmmmmmmmmmm.

Eli gave me a "thumbs up".

I called Ali for the last time. "Who do you want to be tonight?"

"I think I'll just sign off as 'The WRNC Weather Woman of Mystery."

"I like that. Not 'Weather Girl'. This has been fun, Ali."

"For me too, Paul."

"Think we can do it again next year?"

"Can't see why not. Through the wonder of wired telephony."

"Does Wellsmith have a radio station?"

"Not as far as I know."

"I was hoping they needed a weatherman."

"I was hoping we'd see each other, Paul."

"Were you? Me too. Maybe we could meet in the City."

"Maybe. I'm traveling with my aunt part of this summer, but we'll find some way."

"Stay in touch." *Out of my league* I hung up. *Coward*

A few days later, Professor Salter called me at the dorm. "I have that record of Eliot reading," he said. "I live up Van Orden Avenue, not far. You're welcome to come to dinner, you and Acheson. Listen to it, see if it's radio-worthy."

We knocked on the door of a neat little house among trees just off Van Orden. Everything was blooming, after the long winter. *Winter kept us warm.* The door was opened by...if Ali Acheson was the most beautiful girl I had ever seen, this was the most beautiful woman. She was curved and trim and then curved again, then long-legged, and she smiled a welcome. "You must be Acheson and Seitz. Or Seitz and Acheson."

"Seitz is the taller one," Professor Salter called from the kitchen. He came out with a bottle of wine, put an arm around her, introduced us properly. We were awkward, a little; neither Dickie nor I had ever socialized with any of our teachers, and it took me a while to realize I had socialized with plenty of teachers all my life, just not mine. I would have thought of this sooner, but my mind that night was on just one thing. *Salter is a brilliant and fascinating troll. And this glorious woman married him. If he could do it so could I*

Over hors d'ouvres she said, "I understand you two are responsible for some remarkable moments in Robert's class. The radio performance is the tall one's, right? And you (she indicated Dickie, with an outstretched hand) delivered the Buddha's Fire Sermon."

"Correct, my pet," Professor Salter said.

"I'm not your pet," she snapped.

"He's probably the most inspiring professor on this campus," I said quickly.

"Assistant Professor," she said. "That's like Magician's Assistant. You get to be sawn in half and clean the rabbit crap out of the hat." She slammed down her plate and walked quickly into the kitchen.

"I'll just…" Salter followed.

"Baby, it'll be OK," we heard him say. "I'm up for a raise, after this I can write my own ticket."

"To where? Another rinkydink college in East Shithole? I'm not your baby. This is your baby, in here. Who's going to pay for it?"

Salter came out of the kitchen. "Men, this is awkward. My wife…my wife and I have had some news, she's upset, and…"

"That's alright sir," Dickie said. "We can make this another time."

The walk back to campus was nearly wordless. What to say? We never did get the record.

If he could do it so could I A few days later the opportunity presented itself. Dickie got a letter, opened it, smiled. "I got a job as a counselor at a camp for mentally handicapped kids. Damn, I wanted this."

"Really? That sounds great."

"I would have told you about it but you have to be at least nineteen."

"It's fine. I have a job at Brooklyn College, helping organize my father's papers. There's stuff I know…"

"Yeah, that does sound good. When do you get done? I mean, are you taking any time completely off?"

"End of the summer I could. Why?"

"I told you, I want to show you our lake, and see your ocean." *She'd be back by then*

"Sure. You bet. Will this be OK with the 'rents?"

"Not a problem."

We did the postcard-in-the-bluebook thing again. I made Dean's List again. Dickie was in the shithouse.

The grad student working on my father's papers, Nancy Goodman ("Call me Nan") was a lesbian, the first I'd met, to my knowledge. She was completely dedicated to German literary scholarship, and to the light it shed on homosexuality in pre-War Germany and German-speaking cultures, a topic in which I had no interest at all at that time. It made our work and relationship easier, in a way.

"I know German culture and literature, and how to organize scholarship," she said the first day. "You know your father, and where we might turn up the missing pieces of his work." It turned out there were many such, papers and translations that came to abrupt ends, only to find pages later on; references or notes pointing to other work, unsent letters and early drafts alluding to ideas and works perhaps pursued, perhaps not.

"I assume my mother has been some help with this."

"Not as much as…some help, yes, but…Paul, she's still so grief stricken she won't really go near his things. But she told us you already turned up his translation of 'Der Golem', and we're all very eager to see that. We thought he had discarded it, that it was totally lost."

"I never knew him to discard anything," I said. "You tell me what you're looking for, and I bet we turn up half of it at least. For instance, I know he was always sending things to friends for review and criticism. I used to take the packages to the post office."

"See? That's what we need. We all know the literature. You know your father."

I wanted to tell her I knew quite a bit about the literature too, but I just didn't care to impress her (I was seventeen!) and I was struck by the thought that maybe, just maybe, my knowledge was neither as great nor as sophisticated as hers. It was possible, I had to concede (I repeat, I was seventeen). We ate lunch in the cafeteria and watched girls together. She asked me if her being a lesbian made me uncomfortable.

"A little," I said, "But it's something I'd rather get over."

She laughed softly. "Your father would have approved of that answer. He was comfortable with it, having spent the time he did in Weimar Berlin. Homosexual culture was wide open then, or did you know that."

"Not something we talked about." She pointed to the ambiguous sexuality of Weill, of Lotte Lenya and Marlene Dietrich, Ufa personnel in general. Read Isherwood, she said; the Berlin stories. Was my father more sexually experienced and sophisticated than I had ever thought about? Would we ever have had that conversation?

As it turned out, she was trying to make a friend. Most of the papers we were dealing with were miscellany; the good stuff had been picked over by his friend Dr. Spielvogel at Yale, editor of the festschrift. Shopping lists, lecture notes, letters; it was a treat to hear his voice again, but it was like listening to him on the phone with his dentist. There was one exception: a few pages of what looked like miscellany, which Nan had recognized as the first of Kafka's "Zurau Aphorisms". Of which I had never heard. Nan explained, sounding like the introduction she eventually would write.

"In late 1917, Kafka developed unmistakable signs of the tuberculosis that was going to kill him. He retreated to his sister's house in the country, in Zurau, until April 1918. Depending on how you count, he wrote about 109 or 110 aphorisms. Brod put them together with some other short work and published them in 1953. There is no English translation yet. Unless there is."

"You think my father was working on this? There's only the first one." But she showed me what could be fragments of others. "Do you think he was working on this at home, or do you think he finished and sent it out for review by a friend?"

129

"You tell me. I think he was trying to increase his understanding. Look here." She pointed to faint pencil marks; it looked like it said Increase Dig.

"Increase Dig? He almost never used slang, especially hipster slang." But a few days later I dropped the deodorant I was putting on as I put it back in the medicine chest, and it rained medicine bottles and cosmetics. One bottle said Digitalis. His name was on the label, and a date in early 1964. I asked my mother if he had been taking Digitalis. She told me he kept that kind of thing to himself; she didn't intrude. I called his doctor and explained the situation, that if he had instructions to increase Digitalis the date could give us a clue to the whereabouts of a lost manuscript. Or anyway the whenabouts. He went for the chart, found the note.

"He called me in February 1964, a few days before he died, to say he was having more trouble breathing. We made an appointment and I told him to increase the Dig." He pronounced it "Didge". "Terrible loss."

I thanked him and hung up. He had been increasingly secretive, almost paranoid as his breathing got worse, and I'd already found the Golem MS secreted in the desk. It wouldn't be a huge MS; he couldn't have gotten far if he was translating them consecutively. The desk seemed like a good place to look. It would have even without the clues.

When I was about nine my father taught me how to shake a tail. How to lose someone who's following you. Spy tradecraft he'd learned during the war. We were at the Strand Bookstore. He was in an antic mood, rare for him. I think he'd just picked up a James Bond book out of a Used bin, and it made him laugh so hard he had to take his glasses off and wipe his eyes. I asked him what was so funny, and he showed me all the heroics and nonsense, told me how ridiculous it was, that real spies try to be invisible. And he said, 'Want to learn how to shake a tail?' I said sure, and he showed me.

"You're on a city street, you check your back, and your expected path too, by watching, stopping at store windows and looking for reflections. If someone stops when you do, or you see the same face over and over, you suspect a tail." An experienced agent, he said, knows where all the places are with two entrances. One can duck into one and go out the other before the tail can catch up. One can duck into an alcove, or an alley, and make the tail pass you, then head back another way. That catches him. You can go into a store, hide in a dressing room, buy another coat and hat and discard the one you're wearing. You can go into a store and browse—bookstores are good for this, so are coffee shops, and catch the tail outside. And duck out a back entrance. He demonstrated all this, using the stores all around Union Square.

"Want to play spy?" he asked me. It was like playing tag, only better. First I was the tail, and had to keep him from shaking me. He shook me every time, and caught me from behind. He was showing me how to go from fox to hound. Then I was the fox. I couldn't shake him. Until I ducked down into the subway, hid behind a pillar, and came up another way. He met me five minutes later at the Strand entrance. He congratulated me, the way he always did when I mastered a new skill. Then on the way home, we were standing on the train, he suddenly ran out the door as it was opening. I watched where he went—back one car. I used the doors at the end of the car to change cars, but he wasn't there. I went to the seat behind the motorman's cab at the end of the car. At the next stop, I sat tight, figuring he'd done the same thing and would double back. He did, and I caught him. He laughed, he hugged me, said, "Can't fool you. You know your old Papa too well."

I think, now, that he was increasingly skeptical of politics, of the strident nationalism that he saw replacing the internationalism of the war years, the transnational unified resistance that he'd participated in, against an evil, in the war. There were things he wasn't allowed to talk about, but from remarks he made over the years, plus what we know now, I think he was involved in, or anyway knew about, how at the end of it we made some exceptions for useful Nazis. He used to walk out of the room when Werner Von Braun was on the news. In 1956, during the Hungarian Uprising, he got some phone calls that sent him to his study in silence. The last one he hung up on. He couldn't talk about a lot of things, but no one ever said he couldn't teach his son some low level tradecraft. It turned the city into a giant playground. And his desk into a hiding place.

There was nothing more in the drawers. I stepped back, looked the desk over. I pulled it away from the wall. I tapped the sides, listening for differences in sound. Behind the second drawer was a hollow sound. I got a ruler, measured the inside depth of the drawer and the outside dimensions of the desk. The drawer was short; there was a space behind it. I called Nan and told her I would be working from home that day. Taking out the drawer on its hardware was an afternoon's work. How he got things in and out I couldn't figure.

In the compartment were several sheets with what I now recognized as translations of the "Zurau Aphorisms". There was also a simple copybook. The first pages were in fountain pen, his flowing script; some later pages, later drafts, were in ballpoint, picking up in the middle of the line as if he'd run out of ink and didn't want to pause to refill his pen. The title page said Fur Laura, my mother's name. The first line read "Ihre Kuss im Nacht." Your kiss in the night. It went on in that vein, more personal than poems meant for publication. These were love poems to my mother, started in 1946, reworked over eighteen years. It was as if he was trying to resurrect German as a language for love lyrics. I presented her with the notebook when she came home. She sat and cried, absorbed for an hour. She'd had no idea he was working on this.

"He talked a lot about what he worked on, with me," she said, "But not until he was far enough along for me to have something critical to say. He must have regarded these as first drafts. Or zero-th drafts, just notes toward a draft."

"Why do you think he hid these things? This, the Golem?"

"I don't know," she said. "He had lived in this clandestine world, he called it, for eight years, and in Nazi-occupied territory, or places that were about to become Nazi-occupied territory, for years before that. Then in McCarthyite America. Friends of his lost their jobs, were blacklisted. I know he had a paranoid cast of mind about…nations in general. He must have altered his desks, in ways he'd been trained to do. As he got sicker he got more withdrawn, even dreamy…I loved him insanely, you know."

"As he did you."

She ran a hand back through her hair, and for just one moment I caught a fleeting glimpse of the beautiful girl he must have seen in 1946. It was the first time I thought of my parents as anything but *my parents*. "That's probably the only way to love anyone." She gave me a motherly kiss. "Maybe we should take the desk apart." I assured her I had been all over it; there was nothing else removable.

I brought a tape measure and ruler to work and went over his office furniture. There was a concealed space behind a drawer, but it was empty. I confronted Nan. She admitted she had found several of the Aphorisms there. And the copy of the German original he was working from. Next day we called a few of his colleagues; they were excited about an English translation of the Aphorisms, but he hadn't shared anything about such a project. More evidence these were rough notes.

"I won't lie to you," she said, although in a sense she already had. "This is a career-maker. I could edit these, and work on the rest, following his notes and his leads. It would be shared credit."

It would be a career-maker for anyone in German Lit. I didn't know what to do.

"What do you want to do?" my grandmother asked.

"I don't know. I mean, I did know, now I'm not sure. I wanted…want…to be a doctor, but this…This is his legacy, and I could have a thesis out of it, maybe a book, by Seitz and Seitz, I'd be collaborating with him…I could do this."

"But do you want to."

"I don't know."

"Paulie," my mother said, "No matter what you do you continue your father's work. You have his mind, and mine. You have his weltanschauung, his outlook on life. He thought art could heal. If you become a doctor, you'll be the kind of doctor he would have been."

I needed to kick this around with a friend. On Saturday I went down to Washington Square to find Sammy, hustling Speed Chess. I sat with him during a lull, told him the story.

"So the dyke thinks there's a book in this."

"More than one, but one commercial book."

"And you could share in the take, even if you didn't do another lick of work on it."

"Maybe. Yeah. A little. It isn't about that."

"Sure, sure. That's why she didn't tell you she already had some of it. Nice for it not to be about that. It's always about that, Paulie. Let's have a game. Off the clock. Straight chess."

We set up the pieces, played a fierce game that I won. By that time we had gathered a crowd.

Sam tipped over his king. "Break time, folks," he said to the crowd, "Back in a minute." He headed for the noisome men's room, me following. "Paulie, you have to do what you want. This dyke chick will get your father's work into print. As long as you can play a game of chess like that you're continuing his line."

"I hope I didn't mess you up, winning that game."

"You're kidding, right? A bunch of people just saw you beat me. They think I'm beatable. Then I turn the clock on. I'm gonna do land office business all day."

"Did you let me win?"

"Never, Paulie. But don't play me on the clock."

I was out of my depth. Mom came with me to lunch with Nan. We came to an agreement. She would produce an edit of the existing translations, which we would go over together. My mother would get acknowledgment, I would get a mention; we would have a photocopy of the originals. Copyright, if any, would be jointly held.

"The first step." Nan said, "Is to get a grant." Much of the remaining month was spent creating a list of potential granting agencies and contacting them. Repeatedly.

That is how I discovered I didn't want to do this for a living.

April 7, 1973,
11:30 AM – 12:30 PM

.

"Is it always so quiet around here in the morning?" she said.

Meaning, where are the admissions.

"You so eager for an admission?"

"I want to see what it feels like to have my own patients."

"That sounds like the Alicia Acheson I knew."

Longish silence. "I'm tying to make out if that's a compliment."

"About 80 per cent."

"So where are the admissions?"

"This is Saturday morning at Morrisania Hospital, AKA Morris's Anus, AKA The Anus. Nobody is desperate enough yet. A block south of here is the 167th Street crosstown bus that runs across to upper Manhattan and stops at Presbyterian. Anyone sick in Morrisania or Mott Haven or surrounding neighborhoods and well enough to get as far west as Jerome Avenue and 167th will keep going to Pres. That would be those wise enough to get an early start to an ER. Because there are no neighborhood clinics, which is what's really needed down here so people can get regular care instead of waiting until they're at death's door. As the day wears on, sicker people will begin to board that bus, and some will be unable to get past Walton Avenue and will wash up, reluctantly, at the Anus. So when you do get an admission, it will be someone requiring a great deal of doctoring, and we will hope that not too many arrive at once."

139

BEEEEP.

"Shit, X-ray, it's Katie." But it wasn't; it was Marvin.

"GI rounds."

"What are you doing in X-ray?"

"Keeping Mamie and Katie company and writing a discharge note on the AMA . Checked the ER. Coast is clear. Mamie is in with the shadow-gazers."

"What's in the ER?"

"You know it's bad luck to ask. Throw salt." *Click.*

"Come," I said to Ali, "GI rounds."

"On a Saturday?"

"Lunch."

The cafeteria was on the ground floor, and had once been something else. Ali and Katie were probably anticipating the legendary Mother House feast, free to students, supposedly only to those actually doing rotations at the Mother House, but who would know, so students from all over the school would take lengthy study breaks and pool gas money to eat there. This was, however, the Anus, so on the distribution list for all municipal agencies. We said they served the same food in the hospitals, the schools, the prisons and the zoos. We filled our trays with sandwiches and coffee, found a table. Easier than on a weekday.

Ali asked Marvin, "So where did you learn to find veins beyond the usual locations?"

"Lewisburg Federal Prison."

"Interesting."

"Public Health Service posting. The place was overrun with addicts who had calcified, infected and otherwise rendered useless the routine phlebotomy and IV sites. These guys were shooting between their toes. The staff were all COs, they knew their stuff. They taught me a lot."

140

"Sounds dangerous," Katie said, "More dangerous than I would want to try."

"That's not the most dangerous thing Marvin ever did in his life," I said.

"What is?"

"Tell them."

He wiped some mustard off his chin and sat back. I had heard this story before. "My brother and I were tail gunners on our father's seltzer truck." They laughed. "Oh, sure, it's hard to keep a straight face when anyone mentions seltzer, but in Brooklyn and parts of the Bronx it was the sovereign remedy for every GI disorder known to man, a medicinal beverage worthy of respect. That's how I got into medicine."

They were still smiling, not sure how to take this. "Explain 'tail gunner'," Katie said."

"Ah. First I must explain—look, when I say seltzer, other than Claribel the Clown, what do you think of?"

"The stuff you mix with Cola syrup at a soda fountain; carbonated water."

"Nah, that is to seltzer as a firecracker is to an H-bomb. Seltzer delivered to the homes of elderly Jews is so highly carbonated it cannot be shipped in single-hulled ships; it will blow the bottoms out. Seltzer explosions have leveled towns in Eastern Europe. It is under such pressure that it must be bottled in thick glass bottles…"

"Traditionally clear, blue, or green," I added.

"Correct, but the important part is, thick, with the levered dispenser so beloved on Howdy Doody…" They were trying not to laugh. "And the tail gunner's job is to ride the back of the truck and when it stops, run the bottles up the stairs of these five-story walkups, exactly what you can see out these windows, while the driver keeps the motor running and curses at your slowness."

"So where is the dangerous part?"

141

"Well. I recall mentioning the high pressure contents of these glass bottles. On day one of every summer my father would remind us of what he called The Most Dangerous Sound in the World."

"Which is?"

"*PING*. On the back of a truckload of seltzer bottles the most dangerous sound in the world is '*Ping*'. Because this is the sound of a bottle rupturing, which will send shards of glass all over, probably rupturing other bottles in a chain reaction…"

We were all openly laughing now.

"Oh, you laugh, but my father told us: You ever hear '*Ping*'and you jump off the truck, no matter what. Or you will die in a horrible seltzer-related catastrophe."

When the laugh subsided, Katie asked, "Is your brother a doc too?"

"Nope. Lawyer. Largish firm downtown."

"Which one?" Ali asked.

"Oldwasp, Irish, Jew, Jew and Jew."

Ali rose. "Pit stop," she said. Katie joined her.

"Not cool, ace."

"Why?"

"Her father is Oldwasp."

"You think I offended her?"

"You'll know, if you did. You brought Irish into it too."

"So how do you know her?"

"My college roommate's sister. I spent a few weeks at their place one summer."

"No shit. You bang her?"

"No, Marvin, I did not."

"Did you want to bang her?"

"*PING*."

"You never thanked me for reuniting you, Paulie."

"Yes, thanks heaps. How are you getting on with Katie?"

"Our first child will be a cardioliogist, the second will be a lawyer."

"So *you* should be thanking *me*." Minutes passed.

"Ladies," Marvin said, "Our colleague Dr. Seitz indicated to me that I may have offended. If so, I apologize from the bottom of my heart."

"Your comic ethnic resentments are only a small portion of the shit we have had to take around here," Ali said.

"Such as?"

"If you can't play football you can't practice medicine."

"What kind of crap is that?"

"It's a paraphrase, Marvin," I said, "From a famous feminist essay by Virginia Woolf."

"Really?"

"A boy I once knew gave me a copy," she said.

Marvin looked from one of us to the other. "Well, I can assure you that Dr. Seitz and I harbor no such sentiments."

"Dr. Seitz I know doesn't. He was the boy."

August 1965

$\mathcal{D}$ickie's phone call rescued me from a late summer of utter boredom. "Time to show you that lake," he said. "I'll be home Saturday. Pack for ten days minimum. Swim gear definitely included. Be at Greenwich station at noon Monday. Any questions?"

Will your sister be there? "None," I said. I needed a new bathing suit. It took hours to find the right one; usually I bought clothes by the pound. *Don't blow this*

My mother and grandmother were glad for me to be with a friend. "But you have to get a hostess gift, for his mother."

Oh do not ask what is it Let us go and make our visit "A what?"

"A gift, a token something, she's going to be cooking for you and so on for a week or two."

"You mean like a bobka from Moskowitzes? I think they have a cook."

It was a puzzle. I knew to bring Ali something from the Strand. I knew Dickie would like to see a copy of the "Zurau Aphorisms". Jewish pastries would not survive August in a subway and train. I had no idea.

My grandmother did. "Schrafft's," she said. "Candy from Schrafft's. They go to Saks and Bergdorf's, they eat at Schrafft's." Saturday I made the trip to the Strand and walked up to Schrafft's. I stopped to see Sammy in Washington Square Park, to give him the windup of the story, tell him about going to North Greenwich.

147

"Slumming?" he said. I got the chocolates home in time to refrigerate them.

The challenge had been to find something for her at the Strand. There was no new Borges. What could I get her? Nothing jumped off the shelf. Then I thought: If she were here, what would she want? The answer jumped out of the W's: Virginia Woolf's 'A Room of One's Own'.

The famous essay by Virginia Woolf, in which she claims a woman can achieve anything if only she has £ 500 and a room of her own

My mother noticed it in the bag; you couldn't get a book into our house without everyone passing it around. She approved heartily. "You think she'll read this?"

"She's already reading de Beauvoir's 'Second Sex'. In French."

"I already like this girl."

Monday morning I kissed them goodbye and caught a train for Grand Central. I might as well have been going to Mars.

The familiar tunnel under Park Avenue and bridge over the Harlem River gave way to unfamiliar neighborhoods in the Bronx that would, ten years later, be as familiar to me as my own. The train ran express past the Botanic Gardens and the Zoo, up the stagnant Bronx River, then began making stops in Westchester. It was maybe 45 minutes to the Connecticut border and Greenwich. Dickie met me at the station in a cliché of a station wagon. He grabbed my bag and threw it on the rear deck. "Great to see you, man. I've been waiting for this all summer."

It was hot and humid, but cooled by a breeze off the Sound. We drove into the leafy northern regions of the township, the houses becoming bigger and further apart. A few turns took us onto Lake

Drive. A turn onto an anonymous dirt track between two stone walls took us to the house. "Home sweet home," Dickie said. Home sweet home was a Carpenter's Gothic pile of extraordinary proportions, with two chimneys, two porches (one fronting the drive, one the lake), a clerestory cupola, bay windows and gables galore. William Dean Howells slept here. I whistled.

"Yeah," Dickie said, "It's a real monster. We live in about half of it or a little more. You get the guest wing. Instead of twenty guests for a weekend we have one for two weeks."

"Two weeks?"

"If you want."

It looked like paradise, and I hadn't even seen her yet. I hauled my bag into the foyer; Dickie threw the car keys onto an end table that looked like John Adams had maybe once put his hat on it. The rest of the furniture was pretty much like that. "Come on to the kitchen, have some lunch." There was a cook, a middle–aged Negro woman who would live to be called black, live to be called African-American, to see an African-American President. If the past is another country, this part of it was, I thought, paster than most. "Pat, are there any leftovers?"

At that moment Ali came in from the lake. She was in a two-piece bathing suit, still dripping, her hair just shaken loose from a bathing cap. I hadn't seen her in almost a year; now I was seeing as much of her as I legally could, and I was stunned, literally stunned. She just had time to say, "Hi Paul," when a dog the size and color of a small oak dresser ambled over to sniff me. I patted his head as he squirmed around, checking me out. "That's Riley," she said, "As in 'Life of'. He's a golden retriever, getting old and a little arthritic now, aren't you boy, yes you are." Riley had quickly lost interest in me and sat down in front of her expectantly; she knelt down and took the dog's head in her hands as he kissed her, slopping his tongue over her face, his tail thumping the floorboards. I wished I was Riley. *Remember to breathe*

Dickie came back in with a salad bowl, some tuna and white bread and a jar of mayonnaise. "Hey, Ali's here, and you met Riley. C'mere Riley." But Riley wasn't going to move as long as she was petting him, and I could see Riley's point. He settled to the floor, turned up his belly.

"You're here just in time," Ali said, wrinkling her nose. "Riley needs a bath." We finished lunch, and took my bag to the guest wing, which was indeed separated from the family bedrooms by a huge central hall. "Best accommodations in summer are shaded by the magnolia," Dickie said. He opened the shade on a view of the back lawn and the branches of a magnificent magnolia, one bough of which reached to the window. There was a tennis court, weedy, a pool, empty, and the lake with a raft about 75 feet out from a dock. Ali was walking down to the dock, Riley trailing.

"I thought we were going to bathe Riley."

"She is. Why? Want to help? Dig out a bathing suit."

I figured this involved hoses, raincoats, I don't know. Here's how we bathed Riley:

1. Dickie and I yelled to Ali to wait up.
2. Dickie and I each changed into bathing suits.
3. Dickie and I arrived separately at the dock.
4. Ali dropped a huge old towel on the dock, took a plastic bag with a string, inside which was a huge spray bottle of dog shampoo, rigged it to the bra strap of her suit top, called Riley, and knifed off the dock toward the raft.
5. We followed.
6. Riley woofed and, giving no evidence of arthritis, ran off the end of the dock into the water, in which he proved to be an aquatic mammal, as graceful as he was awkward on land.
7. At the raft, Ali clambered aboard and Dickie and I hoisted, pushed and otherwise manhandled Riley aboard.
8. We all stood back as Riley shook himself of half the lake.
9. We chased Riley around the raft, or tried to hold him, as Ali attempted, with varying success, to squirt reluctant, struggling Riley; as if he knew what a sad sight he was all soaped up, his coat dragging and bubbling.

150

10. Ali cajoled and hauled Riley to the side of the raft and tipped him into the lake, following him gracefully over the side. Riley paddled around, Ali playing with him, splashing water over his back until he was completely rinsed, trails of spent shampoo trailing in his wake, herding him toward the dock.

11. We swam to the dock and took up position to receive Riley and towel him dry.

This is where things went off the rails. Riley reached the dock, but by catastrophic mistiming I failed to throw my end of the towel in time, and Riley began the process of shaking himself dry. "Swim for your lives," Dickie shouted, "Abandon ship." He dived off the dock, but my way was blocked by Riley. Ali climbed onto the dock and threw the towel over a quiescent Riley; I threw myself in the lake, smelling like wet dog. Did I mention that the Achesons, possibly including Riley, were laughing uproariously?

"Oh sure, laugh at the city boy," I said. "You want to shampoo me now?" *Her laugh was music* Riley ambled off; we went back in the lake. We made casual chit-chat, getting re-acquainted; I tried to look around, keep it from being obvious that I couldn't take my eyes off Ali. Lake Vere was big enough for many of the houses on it, some as grand as the Achesons', some more modest, to have small boats. There was a rowboat pulled up on the shore a few tens of feet from the dock, oars shipped.

"Hope you like lake swimming," Ali said. "The pool is having problems again."

"Again or still?" Dickie said. "Is Chaskis working on it?"

"Oh yeah," Ali said. "Apparently it is, as usual, a complicated diagnostic process."

At some point we heard a car in the drive. The afternoon whiled away.

Their mother had come in; that was the car we'd heard. I was formally introduced. This was the time to proffer the Hostess Gift; I dug it out of the bag and came back down. "Schrafft's," she said, with a pleased tone. "A taste of the City. We so seldom get there anymore. We'll put these out after dinner."

"Ah," I heard Dickie murmur, "He grafts a gift." *From "High Castle"*

"I brought something for each of you guys," I said. I showed Dickie a copy of the 'Zurau Aphorisms' and explained what they were.

"That's amazing," Ali said. "You found these in your father's desk?"

"And for you," I said, and handed her "A Room of One's Own".

"Oh," she cried, "How do you do it? How do you always know? Oh, thank you so much Paul." And she suddenly kissed me on the cheek, just where, many years later, there would be a tiny scar.

Silver clinked on fine china. "I understand your father was a Professor of German language and literature, Paul."

"Yes, at Brooklyn College."

"How interesting for you. How did he come to pursue that subject?"

"He was born in Austrian Prague, and studied in Weimar Germany. He sort of knew Kafka's friend Max Brod, and that circle."

"Fascinating. And your grandparents? His parents?"

"I don't know much about my father's family, other than that they went up a chimney at Auschwitz."

I knew the word "blanched" from literature; I had never before seen anyone actually do it. There was a slight pause before conversation resumed.

After dinner I cornered Dickie as soon as I could. "I don't know that I like being used as a battering ram in your battle with your family."

"What do you mean?"

"It's perfectly obvious your mother didn't know I'm Jewish."

"So? Why should that make any difference to anyone?"

"Should and does are two different things. You embarrassed us both, her and me."

"Momentarily. Look, Paulie, Johnson just signed the Civil Rights Act. You helped integrate Nott College, help me integrate the Acheson house."

"Glad to, Dickie, just tell me first."

We sat out on the porch, watching the sunlight fade over the lake. Crickets and fireflies chrred and flashed. Bats swooped. It started to cool. Ali stood. "Gotta go," she said, "Have to have 'The Scarlet Letter' re-read by Orientation."

"What a waste," Dickie said, "It's just Orientation, you already read it, you have this knocked."

She kissed him on the head. "You have your ways and I have mine," she said. "Besides, I need to spend some time in a room of my own. Goodnight Paul." And she was gone.

Breakfast provided the next occasion for social awkwardness when bacon and eggs were served.

"Oh my, Paul, I'm so sorry," she said, "I wasn't thinking."

"It's quite alright, Mrs. Acheson. My family never observed the rituals or dietary laws. We're Socialists." And I dove into the eggs, to prove it.

Ali's eyes showed delight; she barely suppressed a laugh.

I swam out to the raft. "Dickie still meditating?"

"As far as I know. Oh, there may be bacon at lunch."

"See, we have a saying. Don't ever worry you'll forget you're a Jew, some Goy will remind you."

"Goy?"

"Gentile. Non-Jew."

153

"So that's what I am. A Goy."

"Nope. You're much more dangerous than that. You're that most dangerous of creatures, the Shicksa."

"Shicksa?"

"Female Goy. Capable of making nice Jewish boys forget they're Jewish. Or wish they weren't. Or forget it makes a difference. If you were blonde you would be a Golden Shicksa, the most dangerous variety."

"Yes, I was a great disappointment to my father. I was supposed to be tall, blonde and athletic. Instead I'm tall, brunette and bookish."

"For me, much more dangerous."

She turned on her side. "Really?'

I gazed down the length of her. "Extremely really."

"Tell an intelligent girl she's beautiful and a beautiful girl she's intelligent."

"What do I do with one who's both?"

"Teach her something. Make her laugh."

"Teaching you Yiddish will fill the bill, believe me."

"Is there a word for a male Goy?"

"Shaygetz."

"So Dickie is a Shaygetz."

"Yes. And I'm a Yid. And you know what the church bells say? 'Goyim, goyim, goyim'."

"Paul. I'm going to say this once. One time. And I never want to have to say it again, ever."

"What?"

"To me it makes no difference, you being Jewish. None. Nada."

"Really. By what miracle?"

"First, I'm not a jerk. Second, I know all about being…disliked for something I am. I just told you."

"Gour nicht."

"What?"

"Gour nicht. It means 'nada' in Yiddish."

She reached over into the lake to get her finger wet, and dripped cold lake water on my chest. It was electrifying. "Gour nicht," she said. And touched where the damp was, down my chest. Which was even more electrifying. I took her hand; we interlaced our fingers. *Stay on the raft, Huck*

"So you really don't go for the blondes?"

"What? Marilyn Monroe? Jayne Mansfield? Brigitte Bardot? Is this a trick question?"

"Yes. So who are your favorite actresses?"

"Oh, I don't know…Myrna Loy. Lauren Bacall."

"Jewish."

"I know that. There isn't a kid in Brooklyn who doesn't know that."

"So you really don't go for the blondes."

I shrugged. "Blonde, brunette, redhead, it would make no difference. I'm only going to tell you that once."

She laughed. "Well, my bad luck I won't date older men. I took an oath."

"Older than what?"

"Me."

"I'm not older than you. You're seventeen, right? We're the same age."

"So how are you a year ahead of me in school?"

"Skipped a grade." I explained the convoluted mathematics of the New York City public schools.

"So I wouldn't have to violate an oath." Her fingers were still twined in mine. *How was this happening*

"You could always go to Kol Nidre, if you had to."

"What's that?"

"Evening service, the night before the ultra-solemn Yom Kippur, the Day of Atonement. You say this prayer, and it absolves you of any foolish or ill-considered or coerced oaths."

"Handy."

"In a culture often facing forced conversion, it was."

"Oh. Yes. I see. Do you go?"

"No. I say the Mourners' Kaddish for my father on Yom Kippur. I promised. But I'm not a believer."

"In anything?"

"Not in anything traditional, or organized. In skepticism. That's the family religion. I had a bar mitzvah. Got a nice copy of the Five Books of Moses."

"Did you read it?"

"Is it a book? Sure. Quit after God hardened Pharaoh's heart. Not a God I could warm up to. You a believer?"

"Not in much."

"In Christmas. All goyim go gooey over Christmas."

"Not me. Not here. It's the family closeness they go gooey over. None here. Or anyway none that's real." Her grip tightened, just perceptibly.

Suddenly Dickie's head broke the surface. We hadn't heard him at all. We unlocked our hands as surreptitiously as we could. "You guys dissected any literature this morning?" He hoisted himself onto the raft.

"You find inner peace this morning?" she said.

"Close enough. Jesus, it's summer. We're supposed to be having conversations about, like, when Superman changes in a phone booth, where does he put his clothes?"

"Was this something you were meditating on?"

"Not until now."

"He has a pocket in his cape."

"They would get all wrinkled."

"What about the hat?"

156

"It's a collapsible hat."

"What, like a top hat? That's only top hats. He wears a fedora."

And so on, for the rest of the day.

After dinner their mother suggested they take me on a tour of the house.

"Oh, you haven't been to North Greenwich, Connecticut until you've had the Acheson House Tour," Ali said. "Follow me." We were a bit mystified.

"What exactly are the purposes of this tour?" Dickie asked.

"Anthropological," she said. "Paul has never seen a large Yankee Gilded Age home."

"It's not the Vanderbilt Mansion."

"But it's not a Brooklyn apartment either. Come on. You never know what you'll learn. Follow me. Yes, no visit to North Greenwich, Connecticut is complete without a tour of historic Acheson House, a Gilded Age lake cottage beautifully set at the southern tip of Lake Vere, just north of the Dark Satanic Mills. Come this way." We did. Riley followed, tail thumping. "We first cross the magnificent entryway and central hall, pausing to admire what would be the magnificent sweep of the staircase, if it weren't a miniature of a Vanderbilt Mansion original which loses something in the shrinkage. We come now to the front parlor, where only last week we had Dolly Madison."

"Really?"

"Yes, a pint of strawberry and a pint of butter brickle. We proceed to the drawing room, which in summer draws flies, and in winter, unwanted attention."

"There's a chessboard."

"There is," she said. "I play. Not at your level."

"She knows you're a rated player."

"I'm a competent amateur player. I'm not Bobby Fischer…"

"We now mount the almost-magnificent staircase, pausing to note the stain in the carpet where the cat threw up last week. Several similar stains will be noted in the second floor hallway. This is the main bedroom..." Thirty years later it would be the most expensive room in a four star B & B; the tour would be much the same.

"And here is my room," Ali said, "Where we might find the cat, if she hasn't hidden under the bed. Nope, no cat." Riley wound around and around us, sniffed, gave a deep "Woof." The room was as big as my parent's master bedroom; bigger even. The desk and shelves overflowed with books and stuffed animals, almost covering a pink Princess Phone.

"I assume this is where the Weather Girl broadcasts from."

"Indeed it is. Moving on...we now come to the Young Master's room, also known as the Trophy Room." Dickie's room was less populated with books but the walls were covered with Creffield banners and horizontal surfaces with wrestling trophies. "The guest hall you know."

"What's this door?"

"Ah, the alert tourist has detected a subtle feature of Gilded Age Cottage architecture. Behold." The door opened on a narrow, completely unadorned corridor and staircase, a surprise after the ornate moldings, wallpaper and other decoration of the rest of the house. "Servants' corridor," Ali said. "Come on in. It's a shortcut." The corridor led to a maze, with hidden doors to each room and hallway. Steep, narrow stairs led down to the kitchen and up to the third, servants' floor under the eaves. The cook's room was in use; the others were sealed off (thirty years later: the Historic Servants' Suite). "The servants could at all times reach the bedrooms and their own rooms without being seen. Ingenious, yes? A feature copied from English Great Houses, mentioned in 'Northanger Abbey'."

"Where?"

"Jane Austen. Come. I'll demonstrate." A second later we were in her room, by way of a door I'd assumed was a closet. We went down the stairs toward the kitchen.

"Where does this door lead?"

"Outside. Servants could come and go invisibly. There's a key above the transom. Very discreet."

"But there's only the cook."

"Alas. The service corridors have long been good only for games of hide and seek. And other conspiratorial activities."

"I attacked her with water balloons when we were ten and twelve," Dickie said. "For example."

"You didn't have the nerve to take me on by frontal assault."

"Riley sleeps in front of your door. Had to evade the sentry."

"Woof," Riley said.

Ali hit the books again and Dickie suggested a row around the lake. We pushed the boat out and threw ourselves in. Dickie rowed us out to the middle of the lake and we watched the day fade.

"This year's gonna be different," he said.

"How so?"

"In a few days I pick up my MG, and we can get the hell out of Schenectady. Like up to Slidell, man, find us some nookie."

"How does this square with Buddhism? Meditation?"

"I've been reading 'Siddhartha'. Read it?"

"No. My father warned me away from Hesse. Called him a cheap obscurantist, *Actually he told me he was full of shit up to his eyebrows, Dickie* a romantic masquerading as an Eastern mystic."

"Well, he suits me for the moment, maybe longer. You know what he says the road to ultimate enlightenment is?"

"Nookie?"

"Yes, actually. Experience. Worldly experience. Only through worldly experience do you find what is true about the world, and what should be kept and what rejected."

"You mean, what Augustine said. 'Make me pure, Lord, only not yet'."

"Yeah, exactly. You know what I did all summer, Paul? I took care of mentally retarded kids and showed them how to have a good time. They don't get much of a good time, everybody's always trying to teach them enough to not be retarded, life is all work, they never get shown how to play, and they never find out. I showed them, or rather took them, me and my co-counselor, who was this Swedish girl who didn't know a lot of English. But did she ever know how to have fun. In sex she was eloquent. I busted my cherry clean off. One day I started to think, I didn't know how to have fun either. I had the Hesse book, and I was meditating on all this, and it came together for me: How do I know what is Ahimsa, what is Maia, unless I experience it and meditate on it?"

"So you fucked the Swedish girl's brains out and then meditated on it."

"I did."

"And did you come to any conclusions?"

"I came to the conclusion that I would drive the wheels off the MG, and fuck as many Slidees as would let me, and I would keep meditating until I was sure what the next step is. Which is what Siddhartha did, pretty much. He achieved enlightenment. And he had a faithful friend who came along for the ride: Govinda. The position of Govinda is open."

"I'll make out an application. So your plan is to ride to Nirvana in an MG?"

"Yes. That is exactly my plan."

Many a truth said in jest. We sat out on the lake late enough to see a few stray Perseids.

Next morning I heard what turned out to be the smack of tennis balls. She was practicing serving. In a short skirt and T she flung the ball up, went up, up on her toes, arced the racket around in a way that lifted her small breasts, and slammed the ball…mostly into the net.

"Paul. Thank God you're here. Pick up a racket, hit them back to me so I don't have to chase them. Assuming I ever hit one over."

"I've never played. I've played Paddle Ball, which is like handball with this very short racket."

"Squash."

"If you say so."

"Well, it doesn't matter. We're evenly matched. I'm a total spaz."

"Well, I'm hopeless at sports. We only have street games. Stickball, boxball, stoopball, and I'm a klutz."

"A what?"

"Klutz. Clumsy oaf. Yiddish for spaz."

"More Yiddish. It's like a secret language you have."

"No secret. It's just medieval German written with Hebrew letters, with a lot of Hebrew loan words. An international language. A Jew from Brooklyn could talk to a Jew in Poland, or Czechoslovakia. If there were any Jews left in Poland or Czechoslovakia."

"Unbelievably horrible, what happened. I sometimes think, how many Germans were diverted from the war fronts to carry that out. It's like the Jews were a human sacrifice, pinning down Germans, war casualties."

"Some actually fought back. There were revolts in every ghetto, even in some concentration camps. The Allies did nothing to help. Except Stalin. He armed Jewish partisans."

"Did nothing? We won the war. My father...it damn near killed him. He was..."

"I know. Torpedoed."

"He'll tell you all about it. I came this close to not existing."

"I hear he has the Navy Cross."

"It's the cross we all have to bear. What did your father do in the war?"

"I don't know all of it. He was with the forces of the Czech government in exile. My real name is Pavel. He was seconded to British Intelligence, then the U.S. Army. Very murky. I know some of it...whatever it was, it made him sick of war."

"Tell you what I think. People aren't that good. We fall into violence and it kills our thinking and we get pulled further in and it kills more of our thinking and we spiral down and we can't stop until one side is exhausted. And even then some can't stop. They live as if the war were still on. In their heads."

"Not my father. I don't think. Maybe."

"No, I promise you, your father was a healer. He became a teacher of German literature. Amazing. We're a fine pair of klutzes."

"Klutzim. The plural is klutzim. As in Hebrew. A lot of Yiddish words follow Hebrew grammar."

"Hebrew I know about. From Midnight Mass."

"From..."

"Midnight Mass at The Cathedral of St. John the Divine."

"The one on 110th Street? The one we call the Cathedral of St John the Unfinished?"

"That's the one. Midnight Mass, we sing, oh, wait, Sh'ma Yisroel. I don't remember all of it..."

"Sh'ma, Yisroel, Adonai Elohenu, Adonai ehud. Hear O Israel, the Lord Thy God, the Lord is One."

"That's it."

162

"You sing the Sh'ma?"

"I bet that's something every kid in Brooklyn doesn't know."

"We're not getting in a lot of tennis."

"Screw tennis. I'm just doing this to try to test out of a Phys Ed requirement. I hate it. That's why I'm not in prep school. One reason, anyway."

"I wondered about that."

"Can you see me at a prep school? Field hockey. Tennis. Ugh. They tried to put me there three years ago, and I wouldn't. Demanded to be taken home, to go to public school with my friends. The few friends. Threatened to flunk out. They tried to put me in therapy, but the therapist told them there was nothing wrong with me—my reasons were perfectly rational. I think my father was just as happy to have me in public school, save the money for college."

"Few friends?"

"There once was an ugly duckling," she sang.

"Ugly duckling? You must be kidding."

"Gawky, brainy and braces isn't a formula for popularity."

"I'm trying to picture that. Not succeeding."

"Well, some people think I'm a swan. How about you?"

"My best friend, Sam Rabinowitz, was almost as uninterested in sports as me. Except the Dodgers of course. The local religion. We read *Mad Magazine*, which my parents wouldn't let in the house, we watched the Three Stooges on TV. And Dodger games. And the Civil Rights demonstrations and marches. We went to the Ingersoll Library on Grand Army Plaza, that's the central Brooklyn Public Library, when we'd run through all the books we wanted at the local library branches. We rode all over for free or nearly free on school bus passes. We went to the museums, took the trains to the end of the line, just to see what was there. We'd just hang out on Brighton Beach Avenue, digging the odors: knishes, pickles, smoked meats. Some of the stores still had NRA

163

eagles in the windows. The woman in the bakery who gave me cookies, one day her sleeve pulled up and she had a concentration camp tattoo, the 7's all had swastikas in circles at the tails. On the boardwalk were guys in berets, they were veterans of the Lincoln Brigades…We had snowball fights on the beach. Ever seen the beach after a snowstorm? Quiet, smooth, nothing there but gull tracks. In a snowball fight we were always on the same side, me and Sam. When we played handball we were always a team, me and Sam…"

"Was he on the chess team too?"

"No, he wasn't that kind of player. He was very unorthodox, a speed player, not a book player, never memorized the openings. He was my sparring partner when my father thought he had taught me all he could."

"I never had a friend like that."

I looked down, touched her hand with a finger. "You do now. Was North Greenwich High any better?"

"Not much. But at least I didn't have to play field hockey, and I could read as much as I wanted without a hassle. And I could keep Riley company. Some good teachers."

"Same at Nott. About Phys Ed. I couldn't pass any sport, so I have to take classes. I took archery."

She laughed. "I'm a klutz too. We're a pair of klutzim. I'm all legs, I trip over myself. Grandma was a ballerina."

"Really?"

"No. More likely a Follies girl, my aunt says, and they cleaned up the story. From the Mayflower to North Greenwich, the Achesons have taken a lot of cleaning up. My mother is a Daughter of the American Revolution. My father, as you know, is a Son of a Bitch." When I finished laughing, she said, "I got the legs, not the athleticism or dance skill."

"Looks good from here," I muttered.

"What? No secrets."

"I said looks good to me. All legs. I'm sorry, I've embarrassed you."

"Embarrass me some more. Any time." Suddenly she froze. Her mother was walking toward the pool with a man in coveralls. "Mr. Chaskis," she said, "The pool service. Must be another attempt to fix the pool."

Dickie showed up about then. "Jesus, if you two were dropped down into the Running of the Bulls at Pamplona you'd sit down and talk. This is a tennis court. One plays tennis."

"One does not play tennis. One has never played tennis," I said.

"And she can't play for shit. Tell you what, the only way to learn this is to do it. I'll take you both on. We won't even keep score, how's that?"

We did, and I got to watch her serve some more. They tried to teach me how to serve, and balls went flying all over. Her serves continued to go into the net. Eventually some volleys occurred, but laughter overcame us all after awhile, and the heat, and we quit. She showed me how to put a racket in a press while Dickie retrieved the overs.

"I like the way you look at me when I serve," she murmured to me.

"I've embarrassed you again."

"I said I liked it."

The afternoon was too hot for anything but the raft.

After dinner she disappeared again, to read for school. Dickie and I swatted mosquitoes on the porch, and eventually lighted a citronella candle.

"I meditated on your father's comments on Hesse."

"What's your conclusion?"

"Twofold. Imprimus, Hesse is good enough for a second-rate mind like mine. Secundus, enlightenment through worldliness. The only way

I will win this argument with you, so you'll concede the point, is to get you laid."

"So I'd win either way." We watched the dark.

That night I sat up thinking about her. I had never met a girl who talked like this, so forthrightly. I had never met a girl I could talk to like this. I had never met a girl who took pleasure in my regard. And said so. Fireflies winked on the lawn, echoing the stars. The lake was a blacker pool in the darkness. A door opened; someone let Riley out for a few minutes, called him back in. Too good to be true? What was wrong with this picture? She was so affectionate with me. But so was she with Riley.

She was waiting for me on the raft. "The Woolf is great. How did you know it was what I would want?"

"I just thought, if you were here, what would you get? I read the back cover, thought of de Beauvoir…"

"Have you read Virginia Woolf?"

"No," I said, "In fact I only knew the name from the play."

"What female authors have you read?"

I thought, with surprise, "None." Not even my mother's beloved Jane Austen. "I have to admit."

"Who are your favorite female characters?"

"Is this like 'Who are my favorite actresses'?"

"Sort of. Come on. Humor me."

"Catherine in 'Farewell to Arms'. Maria in 'For Whom the Bell Tolls'. Oh, Linda Snopes, in the Faulkner trilogy…"

"All created by men. I'm re-reading 'The Scarlet Letter', right? And Hawthorne I think had no conscious idea what was in Hester Prynne's head. I thought, what if this book had been written by a woman?"

166

"By that argument, she wouldn't have known what was in Dimmesdale's head, or Roger's."

"Except women make a study of men. We have to, don't we. And we have so much more literature to work from."

"Very comforting. So how do *you* think I managed to get just the right book for you?"

"How do you think you did? How did you know what I would have wanted if I'd been there? You got it right; this is an extra-credit question."

I thought about it, and it suddenly came to me. "Why would a man not be able to empathize? I'm in the same position as you, I'm supposed to be tall, strong, athletic, and I'd rather read, play chess, look at art, and travel. It isn't a sex thing. It's a brain thing."

She lay back and thought this over. "Girls still have it worse. I think you're right, but it's worse of the same thing." She was suddenly up on her knees, leaning over me, her hair sweeping across her face, staring into my eyes. "Do you think you know what's in my head? Really?"

This was, I remember knowing, an Important Question. I remember feeling that. "That's how," I finally said. "By analogy. Connection. I use some fraction of my experience to understand yours. Approximate it. Like you know what it feels like to be Jewish in America."

"Empathy."

"That's the word."

"It gets you part way. It makes you think you know. But you still don't really know." She was still looking intently into my eyes.

"I want to know."

"Then you'll have to listen."

"I am listening."

She leaned back. "You are. I know it. But you should read more female authors."

"I should."

"It isn't enough to make an analogy to what you're feeling. You have to listen to what they're saying. Walk in their shoes."

I thought back over what she had told me. "Like to know that WASPs were hurt by World War II too."

"That surprised you?"

"I'm ashamed to say it did. I never thought about it."

"So I taught you something."

"You teach me something almost every time you open your mouth."

"We're even, then." She lay back, relaxed.

"Oh yes." I turned to her, moved close to her ear, and whispered, "I like the way you talk to me." *Such a fierce intelligence, this girl*

We swam in to the dock when Dickie came out, heralded by Riley's barking. We toweled off. Ali shook her hair out. "Did you say you wanted to travel?" she said, head cocked to dry out an ear.

"I did."

"Where have you been so far?"

"All over New York City. Schenectady. North Greenwich, Connecticut. Where I'd really like to go is, like Mt. St. Michel, other places in Richard Halliburton's 'Book of Marvels'. It was in the back of the classroom in elementary school. I must have read it five times."

"If you'd like to add Cos Cob to your list, come with to pick up the MG," Dickie said. "It's here."

"What's with this car?" I asked.

"I told you," Dickie said.

"Daddy promised us both a car when we graduated high school, and when we could have it on campus," Ali said, "But I forfeit mine until I comply with some parental wishes."

"Which ones?"

"They want her to come out," Dickie said.

"Sorry. What?"

"Come out. Debut," she said.

"As in 'debutante'?"

"You got it."

I didn't know what to say. "What does that involve?"

"A kind of cross between a fancy dress ball and a slave market. You come out in a fancy gown and everyone makes a fuss over you. Not my thing. Extremely not my thing. The threat is, no debut, no car. Who cares?"

"But I now have a car," Dickie said. "We can go out tonight. Make trouble."

After lunch Mrs. Acheson drove us all in the wagon to help Dickie take delivery of the car. It was sleek, British Racing Green with a rallye stripe. Dickie and the sales manager took it out for a shakedown, ran through the gears, lecture on breaking it in, no highway driving or speeding for the first thousand miles, blah blah blah. With the top down, me scrunched in the back bench, we drove home. Ali's hair streamed in the wind, sometimes blowing in my face. *More please*

We were left a dinner. Mrs. Acheson came down the stairs, looking, as my mother would say, like she just stepped out of a bandbox. Ali asked her where she was going. "A Board meeting," she answered vaguely, and left. The wagon crunched down the gravel drive.

"Board meeting?" I asked.

"Library, hospital, charity, Junior League," Ali said. "One or another."

"Well, they say, if you want to know what a girl is going to look like in twenty years, look at her mother. I'd say you have nothing to worry about."

"That's a great compliment to my mother. Tell me, do they say how to know what a girl will sound like in twenty years?"

"Ahhh…" She twisted her hair into a ponytail, clipped it. *A new look to admire.*

Dickie twirled the car keys, waiting for dusk. "PC?" he asked. Ali shrugged. In those days, the drinking age in New York was eighteen, in Connecticut twenty-one. If you wanted to drink, the first town you hit over the border was Port Chester. The roadhouse parking lot was full, high school and college kids knocking back beers.

"Nice wheels, Acheson."

"Whooo Hooo, Dickie's MG. About time."

We went in. "At least one of you better be eighteen," the waitress said.

"That would be me," Dickie said, pulling out his license.

"She's not legal," the waitress said.

"I just want a coke," Ali said.

"Me too," I said.

"Beer for me, " Dickie said. "Celebration."

The din was overwhelming. You could barely hear the jukebox. When Dickie went for another beer a bit of local talent slid into the booth. "AA. Who's this?"

"This is Paul. Paul, this is Doug. Doug is just leaving."

"Just like that? Not cool, AA."

"You're drunk."

"Not yet."

"Then go get drunk."

"What a welcome. You used to be so much more friendly…"

"And now I'm not. Get lost, Dougie."

"I don't think so."

Dickie was just coming up behind the booth.

"The lady wants you to leave," I said.

"Who's gonna make me. You, Sticks?"

"Me? No. He might. I'll help, though."

170

Dougie turned.

"Douglas," Dickie said. "You're in my seat."

"I just wanted to talk to your sister, and she gives me the cold shoulder. Then I have to take shit from this guy."

"Yes, Douglas, life is full of odd reversals. Why don't you go someplace and think about them."

Doug weighed up the odds and decided on the better part of valor.

"Do I have to take on all your old boyfriends, AA?"

"He should be the last."

This was rapidly becoming very unpleasant.

"Ali has spent her senior year slumming," Dickie said. She sipped her coke. "The parents were most upset. Not the way a prospective debutante behaves at all."

"That was the idea, Dickie."

"Conduct unbecoming a debutante."

"Yes. In ten days I leave for Northampton," she said. "Chapter closed."

"Plenty of townies in Northampton," Dickie said.

"No more rude mechanicals, Dickie, OK?"

"Don't throw yourself away, Ali."

"I don't think I will Dickie. I don't think I did. Not as much as you think."

She went up to her room when we got back, with only a muffled goodnight to us. I sat out with Dickie.

"She was wild all winter. That's how she got grounded, running around with townies. Nothing serious. Part of her revolt at the deb thing, I think. I don't blame her. But I'm really tired of being the big brother, intimidating or humiliating everyone that...shit; Dougie, Morgan. I feel like shit afterward."

"Morgan had it coming. Both times."

"True, but I feel like shit afterward, no matter how good it feels at the time. Or is supposed to feel."

"I know what you mean," I said. "The one time I ever did something like that I ended up feeling like shit too."

"I can't imagine you…"

"When the Aquarium opened in Coney Island we went there almost the first week. That was a memorable trip. Because we got to see the electric eel. And I became aware on that trip of a dawning interest in Naomi Ackerman."

"Who was she?"

"Nobody. A girl I thought was the best looking in the class. Also, I saw Olaf the Walrus for the first time."

"What was the big deal about Olaf the Walrus?"

"Well, he was a walrus. Huge. Swimming around in this not so huge tank. Just around and around. In Brooklyn. You could watch him under water, and this huge clumsy creature became a thing of grace and beauty. Or you could go up on the roof and stand at the plexiglass fence and lean over and watch him. But if you did that, Olaf would surface to breathe, and in the process blow huge quantities of disgusting, fishy-smelling spray all over you. Or on that day, all over Kenny Warhaftig."

"That's great," Dickie laughed.

"Yeah, I about laughed my ass off, along with everyone else in the class except Kenny Warhaftig."

"What did he do?"

"Tolerated, or pretended to tolerate, the nickname 'Fishface' for the next seven years. But the real story is…My cousin Cynthia. Total bitch. My father had…has?…a paternal half-brother. My paternal grandmother was my grandfather's second wife. What happened to the first one, my uncle's mother, is murky. I don't really know. Whatever it was, it left bitterness between my uncle and his father and my father. He went to America in maybe 1909, maybe 1908, around the time my father was born, so there must have been bitter feelings for some time before that, whatever it was, my father's birth capped it. Huh. I never thought about that before. That connection. He would have been fourteen, fifteen, sixteen. Jesus. Imagine him all alone, landing at Ellis Island. Actually, he was, from what my father told me, more than up to the job."

"How so?"

"He was what is called in Yiddish a *galut*. A *shtarker*. A *vilda chaya*. A real bruiser. A Wild Animal. Looked a lot older than he was. I think he got into the rackets. It's more than a little dim. The Lower East Side at that time was full of Jewish gangsters. It isn't talked about much. Murder Incorporated was a Jewish operation, remember? Arnold Rothstein fixed the 1919 World Series. I think Dutch Schultz. The older people in Brighton still talked about some of these guys."

"Meyer Wolfsheim in 'Gatsby'."

"Right. My uncle was in there somewhere. However he got the money together, in the 20s he owned a good sized fish restaurant, and that's where the family fortune was made."

"At a fish restaurant?"

"Prohibition. The freighters full of wine and liquor sit off the coast just outside the three mile limit. Fishing boats bringing in their catch, maybe not so full a hold, maybe want to put a little icing on the cake, baby needs a new pair of shoes, they stop, load up, stow the bottles and cases under the catch, offload at the Fulton Fish Market, and the seafood restaurants get their fresh fish and a bonus of fresh booze. Most of the seafood restaurants in New York at that time were speakeasies."

"I notice a theme here. A great deal of this has to do with fish."

"I'm a very fishy person."

"How does this link up with humiliating people?"

"When I was about eleven, my mother succeeded in a long campaign to get my father to try to reconcile with his brother. She had no family, he had no family, I don't know…anyway, my father ended up inviting his brother and his family to our place for dinner. My parents didn't drive, so there was no way to easily get to Long Island. Not West or East Egg, but pretty close. This dinner was a pretty big accomplishment, because my uncle had ignored my grandfather's pleas for money and help in getting out of Europe, or at least getting my father out of Europe, in the 30s, when the Golden Door had been shut.

"So the big day arrives, my mother gets all fapootzed, which is comic Yiddish for gussied up, she makes her best pot roast because, espionage experts that we are, we have found out that Uncle Sol favors pot roast. Hates fish. Uncle Sol shows up, looking like a Thomas-Nast-cartoon Robber Baron, in a Caddy, of course; he pays one of the older kids on the street to watch it for him, his wife is a good thirty years younger, also fapootzed, and there are my cousins Cynthia and Linda. Cynthia is maybe 14, her nose is so high in the air I can see up her sinuses, she's also dressed like for a state dinner, which this is. Linda is a squirt.

"The apartment is so small there's really no room for us all to sit. They have to move books. My mother tells me to show the girls around, show them my room. More books, the chess set, a window overlooking the El. Cynthia says, 'Is that it?' I say, pretty much. She doesn't play chess. I offer to take them on a tour of the neighborhood high points, which are the boardwalk, the beach, Coney Island and the Aquarium. 'How far is it?' she asks. 'I can't walk far in heels.' I tell her not far.

"Outside the guys are playing stickball. Cynthia says to Markie Hymowitz, who I think was already shaving in the third grade, 'Hey, you're supposed to be watching my father's car.' All the guys go 'OOOOOOOHHHHH.' Hymowitz comes over, says 'Hi gorgeous. Look, we're playing stickball *right here* so we can keep a good watch on the Caddy. So, what's your name, you wanna watch?' She tells him to drop dead, but Uncle Sol had already slipped him a five, so there wasn't much she could do. Hymo says, 'She your girlfriend, Paulie?' I say no, my cousin. I put my finger up to the tip of my nose and pushed it up, meaning nose in the air, stuck up. She's a head taller than me, and in heels. Hymo says, 'When you want a real man, come see me.' I'm trying to remember if this was about when 'Lady Chatterley' came out and the hot parts got passed around. Like 'Candy' last year in the dorm. She just made a face.

"The quick way to the Aquarium is on the boardwalk. She almost breaks a leg three times trying to walk on it, and she blames me for this. 'It's so dirty,' she says, 'Our beaches are clean, and private. No one can get in except residents'. I had never heard of a private beach. The concept was beyond my experience. Beyond my ability to conceive."

"You're sort of on one now."

"Well, my education has been furthered. 'Why does your house's hallway smell like fish?' she says. I explain that many people lived there, and cooked there, and you got used to it, some of the cooking odors were pleasant, like home. 'It just stinks,' she says, and 'How far is it? I'm getting tired'. I tell her, maybe a block and a half, it's right over there, you can see it from here. 'It better be,' she says.

"Now we're there, and don't you know I have to pay her admission, as if we were on a date. She sees the footbridge from the West 8th Street Station, and she says, 'Why didn't you say we could have taken the train,' and I say, 'Because it's only one stop, and we'd have had to walk almost as far, and it's another 30 cents each.' And she says, 'Thirty cents? You made me walk all this way for 30 cents?' I was having my first real experience of class consciousness. But I knew it was important to my parents to put up with this monster. And it was fun looking at her legs. To be completely honest."

"Better than Naomi Ackerman's?"

"About the same. Her sister just kept running around us. Her I could have killed, too, just for being annoying."

"So we go to see the electric eel, which she pronounces 'boring', and we look at all the fish, which I realize she has probably seen enough of in her life, and she makes the face about ten more times, and finally tells me this whole day was turning out as boring and aggravating as she thought it would be. So I ask her if she's ever seen a walrus, which is not a fish. No, she hasn't. Little Linda is fascinated, so she sighs, shifts her gum, and we go to see Olaf in his tank. And he's doing flips and Immelmans and just about turning himself inside out, and she says, 'Borrrringgg', and I say let's go up and watch from the deck. That's the best view. And exactly as I hoped, she leaned over and Olaf gave her a face full. I mean, he'd just been fed, so his whiskers had a full load of fish fragments. And he splashed her as he went under.

"At first, it was the most satisfying feeling of revenge, of relief of frustration, that I'd ever felt. At first. Then she cried. 'My dress, it's my favorite and it's ruined. Oh god, I'm going to smell like fish for the rest of the day. I can't go home like this...' and on and on. I felt awful. I didn't know how devastated she could be; I mean I figured she'd just get meaner and meaner, and I guess I anticipated feeling more and more justified. But she didn't. At least not at first.

"Then Linda started laughing, and she smacked her. And turned on me, said this was my fault, I knew this would happen."

"Which was true."

"Which was true. I didn't do it, but I had no idea at that time, I was eleven, that you could feel just as bad about not preventing a cruelty as about perpetrating one."

"What happened?"

"We went back to the apartment. I offered her my hand on the boardwalk; we couldn't even think of the subway. I remembered Kenny Warhaftig and what he smelled like on the train, and this was worse. My uncle was, the only word is, enraged. He blamed me too. And my father. For exposing her to this hazard. My mother went into her closet, found her some clothes that sort of fit. Threw the dress into a plastic bag, everyone's arguing about whether it's dry-cleanable, everyone has an opinion. I snuck off to my room. Except, Linda followed me. She played with something. Finally she comes over and whispers to me, in my ear, I was lying on my bed, 'She had it coming. She deserved it.' I said, 'Nobody has that coming.' Dinner was pretty frosty. We walked them down to their car, and that was that."

"How did your parents react?"

"They were...my mother couldn't stand my aunt, and my father had no more desire to see his half-brother than he ever had. My mother hadn't believed they could be as obnoxious as my father said; she said she was wrong. They regarded the whole Olaf thing as an accident. Which it sort of was. But not. I just felt miserable. I wish they had just punished me some way. My father asked me what I was feeling. I told him I didn't know it was possible to feel so bad about even passively embarrassing someone, especially someone as awful as Cynthia. He told me everyone has his or her humanity, and you never know when you're going to see it, or what it's going to be like, and to never forget that, and that he learned in Germany in the 30s that it's almost as painful to witness someone's victimization as it is to be the victim. You feel guilty in some way. You feel somehow *complicit* if you just pass by. Then he sighed, and said it wouldn't matter. The next time I'd ever see Cynthia or any of them was at a funeral."

"Was that true?"

"Yeah. The next time I saw them was at a funeral. His."

"How old were you when he died?"

"I was sixteen. He lived to see me get the scholarship to Nott, and not much longer.

"What's the saying?" he said. "Revenge is a dish best eaten cold? Yeah. I see that. The passion cools and you wonder, 'why did I ever do that?' It just adds to the sum total of misery in the world. I feel like going back and buying Dougie a beer. Should have done it then—just said, 'C'mon, Dougie, I'll buy you a beer', and taken him away. He'd have gone, and I wouldn't feel like this. Shit."

"After years," I said, "I still feel bad about Cynthia. I wonder where she is now?"

"Probably taking it out on some other guy."

A night of troubled sleep. *Was she slumming with me now?*

You realize, I'm leaving a lot out. Laundry, grocery runs, pizza runs, throwing a ball around with Riley, finding an old croquet set in a shed and making up our own rules, finding an old Monopoly set and making up our own rules (you could declare Socialism), skipping stones at the lake, rowing over to a little store for ice cream. Watching clouds, fireflies and stars. Kid stuff. Ali and I still had one foot in childhood, for all the deep reading; Dickie was, I think now, still clinging to his. He had burned all his bridges with his friends from Creffield and Phi Delt. And we read. Ali read "The Scarlet Letter" and "A Room of One's Own"; I read a copy of "Jacob's Room" that she gave me (it knocked me out); Dickie read "The Tibetan Book of the Dead" and the MG Repair Manual. The return to school loomed over all three of us. Far away, cities burned, a war was growing. I'm leaving a lot out.

I swam up to the raft. She was lying on her back; I rested my elbows on the edge next to her, all but my head and shoulders in the water. "What are you doing?'

"Getting a nice athletic tan."

"I should too. My mother hopes I'll come home not looking like a Yeshiva bocher."

"A what?"

"Yeshiva bocher. A pasty-faced orthodox Jew who spends his days in the Yeshiva, the school, studying Torah, which is the first five books of the Old Testament, to you. As if there was only one book."

"There is. It consists of all the books ever written."

"Is that in Borges?"

"Maybe. I don't remember. What are you doing?"

"Admiring the view."

"Of what?"

"Of you."

"Like what you see?"

"Very much." *Very much*

"Enough to want to touch?"

"What?" *What?*

"Enough to want to rub some suntan oil on my back?"

"Part of the view is of your mother sunning herself on the porch and incidentally watching our every move."

"Even better."

"Yeah, right, see, I understand about the debutante thing, I know the game you're playing…"

"It isn't chess."

"No, it isn't. Not worthy of you."

"So, will you?"

Oh, you know how much you want to, she seems to know too, she's counting on it. Bitch. Tease.

"Convince me you'd want me to even if your mother wasn't watching."

She turned on her side, looked me straight in the eye *sincerity; if you could fake that* and said, "That she's watching is a bonus, Paul, I won't deny it, but with you…yes I would. You're not part of the game. She doesn't know about our letters and phone calls. And she won't find out. Not from me, anyway. I would ask you, whether she was there or not. I don't think I knew she *was* there."

A life turns on such tiny, insignificant things. Chance things. The phone rang; we could hear it. Hear the screen door slam as she went in to take the call. Ali didn't take her eyes off me. "Now, Paul," she said softly.

I hauled myself up on the raft. Her skin felt like…no simile came to mind. Touching her was like nothing else. She moved under my hands, flexing her back and slipping the straps down so I could cover her shoulders as I worked in the oil. *If this is what her back feels like, what would I feel touching her breasts? Her thighs?*

"Thank you, Paul. Turn over; I'll do you."

And that was another sensation for which there was no comparison. I was stunned at what the simple touch of hands on skin could excite. We lay together on the raft, prone under the sun, faces turned toward each other. *We could just float away*

"Now you can go home with a tan." The raft bobbed gently. "Turn over. No more than five minutes on a side. Don't you know how to do this?"

"I grew up at the beach. You get a tan just walking around. Five minutes on a side and you'd char. Or I would, anyway."

"I'd like to see it."

"What? Me char?"

"No, the beach. Brighton Beach. Brooklyn. Where people in New York actually live. Smell the pickles and smoked meats."

"Mmmmmmm."

Did she know? At dinner her mother said to us, "Why don't you kids go to the City tomorrow? The pool people will be here, and they're going to have to dig and patch—there's a crack in the casing, there's going to be heavy equipment all over the place."

"We could just go to Greenwich Beach," Ali said.

"The MG won't fit three, not on the Merritt, the cops will pull us over in seconds," Dickie said.

"You are not taking that little car into the City," Mrs. Acheson said, "You'll drive it to Greenwich and take the train."

"It'll be hot as a crotch in the train," Ali said.

"Alicia! How is that a way to talk. Let Paul show you his city. I have to supervise major work here tomorrow, and I don't want to have to worry about you, too."

When we sat out on the porch that night she murmured, "She's afraid I'd be hanging out with townies on Greenwich Beach." *I thought that's what you wanted her to think*

With Ali in this mood we were as happy to have her as she was to be there. But in the train she brightened up, as if freed of a spell. "I love the City, " she said, "Where should we go? I vote Museum of Modern Art."

"Metropolitan" Dickie said, "I want to see the Asian collections. You're outvoted."

I thought she'd go sulky again, but she didn't. "You don't know how to get there except by car."

"But we have a native guide."

"Fast way?" I said, "Lexington from Grand Central to 86th, walk to Fifth; slow way, Madison Avenue bus to 82nd."

"The subway? I've never been on the subway." Her eyes glowed at the prospect.

"Subway it is, then." *Now you're on my turf* "We can catch the Lex without even going outside, but take a minute to walk," I said. I took them out onto 42nd Street; we walked from Park to Fifth, took in views of the Empire State and the Chrysler Building at each end of the walk, "And that's the central New York Library," I said. She couldn't resist a quick look in. "There's a legend," I said, "If a virgin passes, the lions will

181

roar." She laughed. In the middle of the 42nd Street Fifth to Sixth block is a striking modern building; she asked what it was. "World Headquarters of McCann-Hertz," I said.

We walked back to Grand Central and I showed them how to buy a token and use the turnstiles, how to make the train come by looking intently up the track, how far back to stand—subway skills. "Oh," she said. "McCann-Hertz. I just got that." She punched me lightly on the arm.

At the Met Dickie pulled us into the Hindu/Buddhist collections, but we were quickly bored and agreed to meet him in two hours at the restaurant. She became sparkling and animated as we walked through Greek and Roman, on the way to 19th Century European, where Renoir's "Luncheon of the Boating Party" was on loan from the Phillips Collection. She suddenly took my arm, pulled me closer, put her other hand on my arm; she was rapt.

"If we could just walk into the painting, into that afternoon."

"Why that one, particularly?"

"They look happy together."

"They all had their problems too. It's easy to look so free and happy out drinking on the river."

"But they all got out of themselves—they were artists and artists' models, struggling with how to get a vision on canvas. Not with…neurotic shit."

"That too."

"OK, probably, but they got a vacation from it. In their work. In their art. It took them out of themselves. And their families."

"That makes sense. I never thought of it that way. Reminds me of the Brighton Beach Pavilion. It's part of the boardwalk. Just working class people, gathering on the boardwalk, musicians, chess players. Even some Spanish Civil War vets, Lincoln Brigade people, old Socialists…"

"Can we go there? I'd love to see it."

"Slumming?"

"What? No, idiot. Instead of jumping into the painting. Something real. Could we?"

"Too late today. Maybe another time."

"Damn."

Silence.

"If we could just walk into the painting."

"They're artists and their models. The power dynamic…" I said.

"Yeah, I know. The one on the left, with the little dog, look around the gallery, Renoir painted her like a thousand times."

"And married her. Not until like 1890, but he did. Her name's Aline *Did he ever call her Ali* That's Jean Renoir's mother."

She was silent for a moment; longer actually. "Then that's, and I should have known from the red hair, the Madame Renoir from the 1910 portrait."

"What 1910 portrait?"

"The one in the Wadsworth Atheneum."

"Where's that?"

"Hartford. Connecticut? There are museums outside New York, Paul."

"You have proof of this?"

But she was in her own head. "I think maybe he felt the same about her even when she was stout and middle-aged. Same fond brush strokes. And," she pointed to another picture of young Aline with a little dog, "Same little dog." *Silence.* "What if Monet had married Berthe Morrisot. Or Mary Cassatt?"

Silence. "OK," I said, "What if? You mean can men and women ever be equal?"

"No, I mean, can they ever be equal *and* happy together. At the same time. Virginia Woolf married Leonard Woolf; they even wrote a book with a novella by each of them. But a lot of the time they were miserable. Hah. You know what she called him? 'My penniless Jew'."

"Very nice. Manet had a thing with Berthe Morrisot, didn't he? *How about my parents? Weren't they equals? Were they? I didn't know. Sure looked like it.* Considering how they met, I think my parents were. Why not?"

"I don't know. How did they meet?"

"He was the kind of teacher who on a final exam in his Trends in German Thought class would ask a question like 'Who was the most persuasive social diagnostician: Kafka, Marx, Weber or Freud?'"

"How can you answer that?"

"That's what he wanted to know. One student answered that the question was unanswerable, and proceeded to defend her answer. He married her. The discussion was the substance of dinner conversation on and off for seventeen years."

"Why do so few couples manage it?"

"I don't know," I said. *Silence* "I joined in the conversation when I could."

"That's the childhood I wanted."

"It was terrific, up to the father dying part."

She kept my arm as we walked through the centuries of Greek ceramics on the way to the restaurant. In red and black, nymphs cavorted with satyrs, goddesses with men, gods with women, men with women, men with men. Laughter from the odd Silenus.

After lunch we made a desultory tour of the European collections, but enough was as good as a feast, and despite the heat we walked back to Grand Central along the Park, caught a late rush hour train back to Greenwich. It was Friday; most of the suit-and-tie crowd had left earlier. She had been right about the heat in the trains; what air conditioning there was didn't work well. As we came up the drive I asked if their father was going to be home for the weekend.

"Ask him yourself," Dickie said. There was an E-type Jag in the driveway.

"Oh, goodie," Ali said. "Daddy's home."

Dickie was late getting to an already late dinner. Her mother sent her to fetch him; she came back alone, sat next to me.

"So where's your brother?" Mr. Acheson said, shaking out a napkin. There was a cocktail glass in front of him.

"He's turned into a bug."

I laughed.

"Obviously that remark was for your benefit, Paul."

"It's from Kafka, sir. 'The Metamorphosis'. The son turns into a beetle."

"She's well read, isn't she? If she could only play tennis as well."

She kept silent, attended to the meal; Dickie had appeared. There was food, I'm sure of it, but I don't remember what. Riley circulated, hoping for a handout. Dickie asked about the boat; Mr. Acheson grunted, said he'd called and the repairs were done, the marine forecast was good, they could pick it up tomorrow and have a sail. "Everyone turn in early, we'll give her a good run."

"I have reading for school," Ali said.

"Bring it with you."

"I can't read on the boat."

"You do nothing but read on the boat. You're coming. It's an order, Missy."

"It's for school."

"What is?"

"'The Scarlet Letter'. We have to read it and be prepared to discuss it at orientation."

"It's about adultery. End of discussion." He was smiling. He was being funny.

185

"It isn't," she said. "Everybody thinks it is, but it isn't."

"How not? She has a baby by the reverend, she's married to another guy, she has to wear the red A, the reverend grows a big burning A on his chest, end of story."

"That's how it is for everybody else. For Hester—her name is Hester—she has to work as the deathbed nurse. She gets to be present for the death agonies of everyone who engineered her punishment. It's about female rage at mistreatment. Hypocritical mistreatment. No one ever really tries to find out who the father is."

"Female rage. I get enough of that all day. It's about adultery, and that's the end of it."

I couldn't let this go. It was happening right in front of me. Maybe even because of me. "Mr. Acheson, with respect, I think Ali has a very valid interpretation. It's novel, I agree, but I've read the book and I have to say, what she says makes sense. The sex part is obvious, but the anger part is more subtle…"

"So subtle it isn't there."

Her mother didn't miss a forkful.

I followed her out after dinner. "Ali."

"What?" Sullenly.

"My mother teaches English. We could call her and run your idea past her. I bet she'd back you up."

"You think so?"

"Sure. I owe her a call anyway." But the phone rang and rang. "Must be walking on the boardwalk. We'll try later." We played fetch with Riley until dark, then went up to her room to call. Her parents were bustling around for an early night. She was there at the second call, and thought Ali's interpretation was ingenious and quite valid. She said she might try it out next time she taught the book, and thanked Ali for a stimulating idea.

I intercepted her father in the hall. "Mr. Acheson, my mother has a Masters in American Literature, and she teaches Honors and Advanced Placement English at Erasmus Hall High School in Brooklyn. We just got off the phone with her and she says Ali's reading is valid and quite ingenious. She wants to use it the next time she teaches the book."

"Well, she would say that."

"Only if she meant it, Mr. Acheson."

"I didn't mean to suggest she didn't. I meant because she's a woman. But I'm much more interested in the fact that you are in my daughter's room with the door closed."

"I'm here too, Dad," Dickie called.

"Oh. I'm sorry, Paul. It's just…Alicia can be headstrong, and can be careless about the social proprieties. I'll count on you to remember that."

I went back into her room.

"Jerk," Ali said.

How is this asshole allowed to live when my father is in a hole in the ground

I couldn't sleep; it was too early. The early start would have to be a tiring one. I had no idea what to expect of "a sail". I stared out into the dark. Something occulted the green light at the end of the dock. Someone was out there who couldn't sleep any more than I could. It had to be her or Dickie; I was willing to bet the farm it was her. I slipped downstairs as quietly as I could; when Riley woofed I knew it was her. I stopped to pat him and he escorted me to where she sat at the end of the dock, swinging her legs over the water.

She was crying. I started to put an arm around her but stopped. "He hasn't missed a single chance to humiliate or belittle or demean you," I said. "What is it with him?"

187

"He's a jerk." In the bouts of tears I caught a glimpse, just for a minute, of the little girl she had been, bringing her father little witty gifts. Jokes, remarks, the fruits of her intelligence, all of them rejected, redirected with a frown instead of met with a loving smile. Little girls didn't do that. Little girls didn't behave that way. What could that have been like?

"Your mother isn't…"

"Much use. No, she isn't."

"Why?"

She ignored that. "What was your father like?" she asked.

"The opposite. He supported my mother, my grandmother, me, his students, his culture. What we call in Yiddish a Mensch."

"That just means 'man'."

"The connotation is 'man among men'. Upstanding man. A good man."

"Never did anything jerky?"

"Well, he died before he should have. One thing weird…he taught me chess. He played competitively in Europe. The first time I ever beat him, he turned over the board. To show me how to turn the tables on someone who was beating me, he said."

"I wonder," she said, "If it works like that for women. Can you tell the kind of man a boy will be from his father?"

"I don't know. I think, like you say, men have more choices."

"You're a mensch, Paul."

"That's a great compliment. I don't know that I deserve it."

"As far as I'm concerned you do. You've been my champion."

"You mean like Ivanhoe? I'd prefer Cyrano. Closer physical resemblance. I hated Ivanhoe."

"I mean like Ivanhoe."

"That makes you Rebecca. I really will have to teach you Yiddish."

"I guess."

"Ali. You need to be your own champion. I'm not always around."

"That's a lot harder. He isn't *your* father."

"Yeah. I can dig that."

We stared out over the lake. Clouds moved to reveal a quarter moon, perfectly reflected in the water. A Chinese poem.

Ten years later I could have figured this out in a minute. But I was seventeen.

The next morning Mr. Acheson was surprised to find I had no driver's license; I had to explain the math again of how I was seventeen and about to start my sophomore year at Nott. "You must be some kind of genius," he said. "Unfortunately what we need right now is two drivers. Dickie has to come with me to the boatyard to take the boat out. We'll be docking at the yacht club. We need to move the car there too. That's it; Alicia is coming. Dickie, wake your sister." I knew we would be getting the evil twin.

"You really don't have a license?" Dickie said. "The driving age here is sixteen, I thought it was the same in New York."

"Upstate. In the City, eighteen. Anyway, we don't have a car."

"Wow. I never thought."

So she drove us to the yacht club. "I'm sorry," I said. "You almost got away clean." She was wearing the two-piece again, with a shirt tied over it, a hair band and sunglasses.

"It's OK. I brought my book. And he would have dragged me anyway. I have an important role to fulfill. Come on, parking at the Club is a bitch. You're going to need sunglasses." She reached in to the glove compartment, grinned at the pair she found. "You really don't drive?"

"Nope. No reason to. Or not until now."

The boat was not the modest day sailer I expected from the anchorage at Sheepshead Bay. It was a formidable craft, obviously seagoing, with a big cabin and a roomy foredeck. Dickie and his father brought her in under power. In that tiny harbor she was like a bear pacing a small cage. They picked up a mooring. "Come on," Ali said again, and led me to a dory. "I'll row."

"I can row."

"Let's both row. Each take an oar."

We pushed off from the dock, bobbed in the gentle swells, and tried to row in a coordinated way, which we finally accomplished by counting "stroke, stroke", when we weren't giggling like fools. Dickie pulled us in with a boathook; we climbed aboard awkwardly and let Dickie pull the dory forward and tie it to the mooring buoy. Mr. Acheson gave us a mild glower for not taking sailing seriously enough, or something, maybe told himself we were only kids, and invited me into the cockpit. *Here is the man with three staves, and here the Wheel…Fear death by water*

She went below, and I followed, for a tour. There was a small galley, with table, and bunks for four. Two could be pushed together. Everything was polished, neat, orderly…shipshape, I guessed. My only knowledge of sailing was Forester's "Hornblower" novels, and Errol Flynn in "Captain Blood" and "The Seahawk" on TV.

We motored out of the yacht club anchorage, leaving no wake (per the signs) and out into the channel. "Red Right Returning. Going out you keep the black or green channel marker buoys to starboard—that's the right, Paul." We proceeded down crowded Greenwich Bay under bare poles.

The barges wash/Drifting logs/Down Greenwich reach

"I know that sir. Starboard right, Port left."

"Know how too read a chart? Look here." He showed me a map of Long Island Sound; it looked to me like the negative of a map of Long Island. There were unfamiliar markings, some obviously depth, some, I saw, lighthouses with their codes.

"There isn't much nautical tradition among my people, Mr. Acheson."

"Untrue, Paul. There was Solomon's Fleet. Your people sailed with the Phoenicians."

Phlebas the Phoenician, a fortnight dead...
Gentile or Jew
O you who turn the wheel and look to windward,
Consider Phlebas, who was once handsome and tall as you.

"And the German Navy, at least the surface fleet, in the twentieth century was a liberal institution in need of your people's mathematical skills. Did you know that the captain of the Bismarck when the British sunk her was by Hitler's racial laws a Jew?"

"I was certainly not aware of that, Mr. Acheson." Of all the strange things he ever addressed to me, this strangest turned out to be true, although it took me decades to verify it. A stopped clock is right twice a day.

"I was captain of an LST in the war, Paul, did Dickie tell you that?"

"Yes sir, he did."

We had cleared the point and were out in the Sound. "OK, men, time to hang out the laundry. Dickie, show Paul how to raise sail."

Dickie showed me how to hoist the mainsail, which caught the wind instantly and bellied out *To leeward, swing on the heavy spar*

"We're out in the Sound now," he said, "The old man wants to take her upwind first, and treat us to a downwind run. Could go as far as the Bronx." We hoisted the jib, climbing over Ali, who sat against the mast,

191

tying back her hair, ignoring us. *Here, said she, Is your card, the drowned Phoenician Sailor,(Those are pearls that were his eyes. Look!)* She went forward to the prow once the jib was hoisted and took up position there.

Here is Belladonna, the Lady of the Rocks, The lady of situations. "Are you OK?" I asked her. "Have I taken your jobs?"

"Oh no. Most assuredly not. I am now doing my job. I'm the figurehead."

"What?"

"Look around at all the other boats coming up and down the reach. What do they all have in common? Or almost all."

This was obviously a trick question, but I got it suddenly, by seeing it through her eyes. "A pretty girl at the prow. Wait—there's one with none, and one with two. So an average of one."

"He makes me feel worthless," she murmured, just loud enough for me to hear.

"I find plenty worthwhile about you."

She turned on her side, swept a hand in the air down her body. "You mean this?"

"You know I don't mean just that. I mean sure, it got my attention, but by itself it wouldn't be enough…"

"Right. Sure."

"All of our conversations before this week were on the phone or in letters. They held my attention without the visuals."

Silence. Then, "That's true."

"See?"

"That's the part of me that *I* like."

"It's the part that keeps me interested."

"So if I was a one-eyed hunchback…"

"Were. Extremely contrary to fact takes the conditional." She laughed. "So," I said, "What if *I* were the one-eyed hunchback?"

"Oh, what a…"

"No, it's a fair comeback. What if?"

She settled back. "OK, we're all superficial, sexual creatures. Point taken."

I became aware that my name was being called. "Come aft, Mr. Seitz, Paul. We're going to teach you how to sail a boat."

"Come on," I said to her.

She shook her head. "No girls in the tree house," she said. "You go."

"Take the wheel, Paul," Mr. Acheson said. "Keep her pointed at that headland. That's Kings Point, our port tacking landmark. Moving upwind, Paul, when the sail starts luffing, flapping like that, it means you've fallen off the wind; center the rudder. That's it." I saw Ali lie back and cover her eyes. "Sail's luffing again, Paul. That's it. Yeah, I was at Sicily, Salerno, Anzio, and the big one, Omaha Beach. Had one sunk from under me by a U-boat in the Med. Always best to sink in warmer waters."

"That must have been…"

"It was, but not as scary as Omaha Beach. Bodies floating everywhere." He looked away, took a drink. "We weren't to go in until the beach was secured, but without our tanks and artillery the beach wasn't going to be secured. We had a 105 battery aboard, and they broke out shells and added our little fire to what was going over our heads from the big guns. It probably didn't help much but it felt good to be shooting back, what with all the shit they were throwing at us, pardon my French." I thought of the warship firing into the empty coast of Africa in "Heart of Darkness". I thought of the whiteness of the whale. "Sails are luffing again, Paul."

"Sorry sir."

"Watch your telltales, the strings along the sail. Almost time to go about anyway. Dickie, wake up, we're going to show your friend how to tack. OK. On my command 'Ready About', you, Paul are going to

193

spin the wheel to leeward and yell 'Helm's Alee' and Dickie is going to throw the boom over our heads. You're going to find the new heading and steady up towards it while Dickie pulls in the mainsheet to catch the wind. Ali will do the same with the jib. Understand?"

I nodded. I understood "Spin the wheel to leeward." The new course should be at the same angle to the wind, but to starboard instead of port. Everything else was gibberish.

"Ready About."

"Helm's Alee." We moved sloppily onto the starboard tack, the Bronx bridges still ahead.

"All small boat sailors were Naval Reserve, Paul, did you know that? They called us all up, believe me. Nott had a training course for naval officers. It's how I got there. What did your father do in the war?"

"He was in intelligence."

"Field or analysis?"

"I think both, at different times. He didn't discuss it much."

He took the helm again in the more crowded waters off the Bronx, between the Throggs Neck and Whitestone bridges. We could see planes coming in low to LaGuardia; far enough upwind. He brought the boat about, Dickie and Ali handling sails. Now we were headed downwind, and he turned the helm over to Dickie briefly. When we cleared Little Neck Point Mr. Acheson called out, "What say, Dickie, we show Paul a spinnaker run?" He took the helm, sent me forward to help Dickie unpack the spinnaker.

Ali, sullen, moved out of our way. "Don't mind me. I'm just cargo."

"I'm sorry," I said," I think I've usurped your place at the helm."

She smiled wanly. "I don't have a place at the helm. I'm doing my part, I told you."

Dickie hooked the spinnaker to the yard; on command we hauled it up, tightened the sheets and dropped the jib to let it catch the wind. The big sail filled, bellied out in rainbow colors, and pulled us east

194

before the wind. We seemed to skate across the water. "She's a good downwinder," Dickie said. He went aft to the helm.

I plopped down next to Ali. "Your mother doesn't like sailing?"

"No more than I do, but she gets to say no and mean it. Better excuses. I have none."

"What's wrong with sailing? The only other boat I've ever been on is the Staten Island Ferry. It's beautiful out here."

"Maybe. Where would you like to go?"

"Uh…"

"Exactly. Trust me—the shores of Long Island Sound look exactly like this, right to the end. One part looks like every other part."

"Synechdoche."

"Isn't that where you and Dickie go to school?"

"Very old joke. Look, isn't there anyplace to go on shore?"

"Must be. I wouldn't know. We just sail. For the sake of sailing. It's some sort of pointless display of athletic skill, or mastery. A very male thing. I don't pretend to understand. I'd much rather be on the Staten Island Ferry. Going someplace."

"Put it like that…"

Silence, except for water lapping past the prow. Then I saw she wasn't just sullen. Two tears left trails down her cheeks.

"Paul," Dickie yelled over the slapping of sails and rigging, "Take the helm. I'm going below."

I looked back toward the cockpit. Only Dickie. I stood. "Come on," I said, and put out my hand. She looked at it, suddenly took it, pulled herself up. We made our way aft, stepping over and around rigging, cleats, stays. Dickie went below.

"Take the helm," I said to her.

"You don't know what you're…"

"Take it, come on. It's your turn. You want me to take one side?" Again the hesitation, but she took it, stepped up and held the wheel. The boat surged eastward, the spinnaker taut and full.

Five minutes later Mr. Acheson poked his head out of the hatch and lost his mind. "What are you doing? What the hell do you think you're doing?"

"She's taking her turn at the helm, Mr. Acheson."

"Dickie pushed up behind him. "He didn't know, Dad."

"But she does."

"What?" I said.

"Letting a woman touch the helm is bad luck. Very bad luck. She knows that."

With as much dignity as she could muster, glowering at her father, she made her way forward to the prow and sat, hugging her knees. Her hair streamed in the wind. She was the loveliest thing in view. Dickie took the helm.

"Shit," I said.

"Don't worry about it. He cools off as fast as he explodes. He'll be around to apologize to both of you."

"I'll just…" I made my way to the prow, balanced myself against the stays. "I'm sorry," I said.

"I knew what I was doing." She wiped her eyes.

"But I didn't, and I'm sorry. Look, I'm pretty certain that stuff about a woman touching the helm is bad luck is pure bullshit."

"Quite a lot of what comes out of his mouth is bullshit. Could be bad luck for you, though."

"Nah. I'll be fine."

She laughed. "Sit by me. Keep me company. That was really very good of you."

"I didn't know I was taking a risk."

"All the more impressively gallant. I thought he would be too embarrassed to humiliate me and throw a show in front of a guest, so I went along. You know what the best part is? Dickie went below to heave. He gets seasick. Motion sick. I don't."

We sat on the afterdeck, Richard Acheson, Esq, sipping port.

"This really takes me back to my Navy days."

This seemed the time to say, "I hear you have the Navy Cross, sir. There must be a story." *Why are you sucking up to this asshole So he's her father so what*

"There is, but it's more a story of survival than heroism. Playing a bad hand well. Sunk in the Med, on a run from North Africa to the Salerno beachhead. Torpedoed by a U-Boat. If they'd surfaced to machine-gun us we wouldn't be having this conversation, but he was afraid of being caught on the surface by our aircraft. I'd radioed for rescue and air cover as we went down and he probably heard it. Maybe that's what I got the medal for—thinking to radio while she was burning and going down. Loads of flammable stuff on board. Didn't lose a man; just the boat."

"Boat?"

"An LST. This was no John Kennedy grandstanding, rescuing his men after almost killing them, going up against a cruiser with a PT boat. Silly bastard almost got us all killed taking us up against the Russkies, and ended up giving away the Turkish missiles anyway. Dick Nixon would never have done that."

Silence.

"You realize," he went on, "That after Tonkin Gulf we're in a real shooting war. Firing on a naval vessel is an act of war."

"If it happened," Dickie said.

"It happened, alright, and if it didn't we should act like it did. This will be your generation's war. Make men of you."

197

"Of me too?"

"No, Alicia, not of you." He took another sip of port.

"How do you like sailing, Paul?"

"Very interesting, Mr. Acheson, a great skill."

"Very few of your people are any good at it, I believe" He seemed to have forgotten his remarks of the morning. "Great navigators, though. Good with numbers. Ron Goldberg, navigator on the flotilla's lead boat. Ended up commanding her, at Normandy. Good with numbers. Navigators, supply officers, weathermen, technical people. Rickover, I believe, yes, one of your people. Same in the Air Force; navigators, bombardiers, quartermasters; Italians, now, they fit in tail turrets, ball turrets, antiaircraft gun seats in the Navy."

"I know some pretty tall Italians, sir."

"Bet you're good with numbers, Paul." *A stopped clock...*

"I hope so, sir, Organic Chemistry and Physics are coming up. Some of my Protestant professors are awfully good with numbers."

"My point is, winds and tides, sailing takes instinct, local knowledge, not book knowledge. Half these watermen can't even read a newspaper." We slapped mosquitoes. "Think I'll go back to the City tonight. Piles of work." Ali and Dickie exchanged a glance. "Paul, I could drive you if you like."

Oh no "No thank you, sir, I'd just as soon have another few days on the lake, if it's OK with you."

"Of course, son, you stay with your friend. I was just being polite." He lurched slightly getting to his feet. "Good night," he said, and swung himself over the side into the dinghy. We took the dory.

"You realize he thought he was being complimentary," Dickie said.

"It's OK. I know that." *The hell I did*

"He's a jerk," Ali said.

"Ali."

"He is, Dickie. And you know it."

198

"Do I assume the offer of a ride was genuine, or just politeness?"

"I wouldn't know. All part of a plan, I'm sure. There's always a plan. You know the plan for me," Ali said.

"Is there still a plan for you?" I asked Dickie.

"Still Corporate law. I'm supposed to become a lawyer, but a real one, on Wall Street. He can use his connections. And who knows —politics. As it gets less palatable it gets more elaborate."

"Jesus."

"Yeah."

But he changed his mind; when we got back to the house he was there on the phone. He slammed it down, cursed under his breath. "Guess I'll be here overnight after all," he said.

I was awakened by a rumble of thunder. I couldn't tell whether it was inside or outside the house, because there was also door-slamming and Riley barking. She wasn't at breakfast; Dickie and I noodled around with the car, tuning the carburetor. This would turn out to be a weekly necessity. We cleaned the tools, cleaned the grease off our hands with DAP and went in to lunch.

She wasn't at lunch either. The squalls were coming in thick now; thunder and lightning all over. No movies worth seeing nearby. In the drawing room Dickie settled down to read some Buddhist tract; I picked up the Sunday *Times*. No Ali. Mr. Acheson prowled the house like a burglar casing it, making repeated phone calls with no answer, slamming down the receiver and pouring the occasional drink. The cat finally made an appearance, deciding to curl up in my lap.

"You're in her chair," Dickie explained. When Riley came in I thought she'd be next, but she wasn't; Riley settled down next to me. Mr. Acheson came in, drink in hand, said, "Ah, the Peaceable Kingdom," and left again for the phone. Mrs. Acheson was God knows where. I hid behind the Times.

Late in the afternoon she came into the drawing room. She had made her hair up more elaborately, most falling straight down her back, some gathered toward the center by a clip and falling away. She looked more beautiful than ever. She stood by the chess board, Riley curling around her legs, which should have been the cat's job. "Give me a game?" she said.

"You're making a mistake," Dickie said. "He's the intramural champ, campus-wide. He's a rated player, remember?"

"I could spot you a Queen," I said.

"Not a chance," she said.

"Now you're making a bigger mistake."

"I didn't think you'd go for it but I had to make the offer," I said to her, and to Dickie, "Maybe she doesn't mind losing."

"Now *you're* making a mistake," Dickie said.

"I don't mind losing to a stronger player," she said, and to me, "Not to you. And maybe I won't lose. How many female chess players do you know?"

"Yeah. Huh. Damn few. One, in high school."

"And you dated her, I bet."

"Ah, no."

"But not because she could beat you."

"Nope."

"Because she was ugly as a bag of doorknobs," Dickie said. She hit him on the shoulder.

"Unfortunately, pretty close."

She held out a pawn in each fist; I got black and was treated to a Queen's Pawn opening. She was an unorthodox player, no patzer. I expected to have her on the ropes in ten moves, but it took more than thirty; she was a strong tactician, had a good middle game. When she looked disappointed I said, "You're good, and I mean that; you stood thirty moves against someone with Master's Points, and…"

"Let's see what happens when I play you again."

"Sure." It passed the time, and there was the added bonus of being able to watch her across the chessboard. I quickly grew to love her look of quiet concentration; just before she decided a move the tip of her tongue would just peak out between her lips. Chess is intensely interesting to those who are playing it, boring to those who watch, and to describe to anyone else. Suffice to say: I opened King's side, Pawn to King Four (in the chess notation of the time, P-K4), the King's pawn to the fourth square in front of the White King. A very standard opening move. She followed at first with the orthodox replies, as we developed our pieces, moving them out to control the center. She quickly saw I was playing by the book and started making unorthodox moves, developing her Queen's side pieces and castling Queen's side. Trust me, this was slightly unorthodox. Zwischen-zug: Game-changing. For me it was suddenly like playing harpsichord in a jazz combo. It drew my game offside to counter; the massacre of the pawns began, and the exchange of Queens, the exchange of knights for bishops, bishops for rooks. And all the time, her look of quiet concentration; the tip of her tongue just peaking out between her lips. When the smoke cleared, she was only slightly behind in the traditional scoring, with her pair of knights, a pawn and of course her king, to my king, bishop and rook, but I had better position and to win she had to queen a pawn. The endgame would be trench warfare.

The way to checkmate with a King, bishop and rook is to use the two pieces to attack alternately, using the King for defense. An attacking knight disrupts the ability to do this; it's the game's trickster, able to move in an L-shape and jump over other pieces. A pair of them are murder. I put her in check and snapped up the pawn; checkmating with a pair of knights and a king is quite a feat but she could always force a stalemate. We hopped all over the board, until her father suddenly came in and over to observe.

201

After a few minutes' study he said, "Give it up, Ali, it's mate in three."

I couldn't see it. I could not see myself checkmating her in three moves. In fact, I thought I was in trouble; she used the knights well. Was he being polite to a visitor? Breaking up a budding friendship/romance? Just his usual treatment? What?

Ali studied the board, that look of quiet concentration; suddenly she looked up at me—and threw it over. Pieces flew.

"Very nice," her father said, "Hardly sportsmanlike."

She stood and walked quickly, wordlessly, out of the room as Dickie walked in. "What's that all about?" he asked.

"Your sister has staged one of her famous walkouts. She insisted on playing against a rated player. That's a mistake I wouldn't make."

"It's how you learn, Mr. Acheson. It wasn't our first game and she was holding up very well. I dare say she could take you on. You play her, you'd lose. She has an unorthodox but very effective game."

"Of that, I'm certain," he said, and sipped his drink. "Tell me something, son. Did you really have me on the radio that time?"

"Yes."

"He did, Dad."

"Really? I thought you were bluffing."

"I'm a chess player, sir, not a poker player. I don't bluff."

The phone rang, and he walked away. *How is he alive* This time he didn't slam it down. He wasn't at dinner, and neither was she. She took dinner in her room. Dickie went up to meditate. I set up the pieces and studied the position. It was still raining, with the occasional growl of thunder. *What the thunder said* When I saw Riley head for the porch I knew she was out there. It was so dark I couldn't see her at first, but I could hear the glider squeak.

"Are you talking to me?"

"Of course I am. Whyever not?"

"I thought you might be mad that I beat you…"

"You didn't."

"I know. That's what I came to tell you. I've been studying the position since dinner, and I don't see mate in three, or ten for that matter. Or at all. I think your father's wrong…"

"My father is never wrong. Just ask him."

"…or bullshitting. So it's him you're mad at."

"Not about just the game."

"It's a real roller coaster with you, Ali."

"It is for me too. I'm sorry, Paul. I apologize in advance for all my craziness. Oh God, I've never talked to any boy the way I talk to you. I've never talked to anybody the way I talk to you."

"I said, I like the way you talk to me."

"I apologize for how I am…"

"Yeah, when you're around them it's like you're a completely different person."

"Not one I like."

It made me wonder for a moment how much of her evident feelings for me were based on that. But she showed those when we were away from the Enchanted Castle too, so…?

Abruptly she said, "My father treats me like a brain is some sort of hideous growth on a girl."

"It's the most exciting thing about you."

"To you."

"Yes. To me. I'm only going to tell you once." My eyes were dark-adapted now, and the clouds had parted enough for us to be illumined by a hazy moon.

"So it isn't just this." She pointed to her body.

"I thought we had settled that."

"Well, you've been looking in my eyes this whole time, so maybe it's true."

"All I know is, since I met him, he hasn't missed a single opportunity to be cruel, dismissive or demeaning…"

She started to cry, but it was brief. "What did I *do*?"

"Nothing. I mean that I've seen. Except try to frustrate his plans for you. Maybe if you could lighten up on this debutante thing."

"I can't, Paul. I can't. It isn't anything I do that frustrates his plans; it's what I am. I told you, it's a cross between a ball and a slave market. You come out. You debut. Don't you see? I thought you understood this."

"Am I missing something here? I mean, I understand the symbolism and how offensive that is to you, but isn't it all just a big Sweet Sixteen party?"

"It means you're eligible. For marriage. You're on the market."

"Surely not before you finish your education."

"Wrong. From that day." *I had to endure mortal marriage, much against my will*

"He's trying to marry you off?"

"He's trying to get rid of me to the highest bidder. The sooner the better. Look at this house, Paul. It's half closed off. There are termites, mold, horizontal cracks in the basement. It's a contractor's dream. He's being practical. And he never loved me. Never. I was always a disappointment." And this time she cried for real. I went in and got some tissues. She gestured thanks, said again, "I'm intelligent and he treats me like that's some kind of defect."

"Doesn't he treat everyone that way?"

"Women."

"Not just you."

"But especially me." She cried again. "I should have had your father. I should have been your sister."

"That would make some of my feelings very awkward."

"Huh." I was starting to understand that "Huh" was a laugh through tears.

"So he has a plan for you. Always had. And who you are and what you want for yourself…your plan frustrates his plan."

"Who I am frustrates his plan."

"Well, yes. So maybe he doesn't know how to love anybody. Only his plans for them, only…" I was just seventeen, I didn't know how to say it. "There's a plan for Dickie too, and he isn't too happy with it."

"That's a reckoning he can postpone. Mine is here. Now."

"You're starting at Wellsmith in a week."

"He can pull me out any time. You didn't hear what went on this morning."

"I heard doors slamming…"

"I thought my mother supported me. This morning I found out I can't count on her, either."

We sat in silence, listening to the eaves and shrubbery dripping.

"Dickie told me what you said to him. After I staged my protest. Thank you again, Ivanhoe."

I walked in on breakfast Monday and this was happening:

<u>Mrs. Acheson</u>: "Mr. Chaskis and his crew will be here again today. When they dug up the case last week he thinks they cracked a pipe. Why don't you all go to the City again?"

<u>Ali (sulkily)</u>: "I don't want to. I have reading to do."

<u>Mrs. Acheson</u>: It will be too noisy to read. There's going to be heavy equipment and men tramping in and out all day."

<u>Ali</u>: "I don't want to go." (Stamps out of room, with tray of toast).

Mrs. Acheson chased her into the dining room. "Alicia, be reasonable. It will be sheer hell here all day, and I'm sure the boys will be glad of your company, won't you, Paul?"

"We certainly would…" She shot me a look.

"They'll be fine without me."

"Alicia, I want you out of here, out of the way. You walk around here heedlessly, chasing Riley, running out to the lake. Wearing next to nothing, as if we lived in the desert, and there's going to be an army of workmen…"

"Is that what this is about?"

"It is, Alicia, and this discussion is over. You will go to the City with the boys. Paul at least seems eager for your company."

We walked out. "Sorry," I said, balancing a glass of OJ, "I thought I was helping."

"You weren't."

But she did her hair up again, tied a kerchief over it to keep it from blowing around in the MG, and marched silently to the train. This time she was sullen, angry really, all the way in. It was hot and humid in Grand Central when we emerged into the roar of ventilators, motors, compressors. The odor of electrified metal and machine oil was stifling.

"Museums are closed Mondays," I said. "I have a cool idea— literally. How about we ride the Staten Island Ferry? Great ride, great views, nature's air conditioning."

She perked up a little at that. "How do we get there?"

"Easiest thing in the world. Lexington Express to Bowling Green, shank's mare to South Ferry." We went up to the concourse and down to the subway. The old cars groaned over the oldest tracks in the city. There was a sea breeze at the tip of Manhattan, and the Ferry never fails, a 40-minute ride past the Statue of Liberty, through the most dramatic shipping lane in the world, away from, then back toward, the towers of Lower Manhattan and the Brooklyn Bridge and the other East River bridges on one side… "And on the other side?" she asked.

"Brooklyn," I shouted over the roar of wind and engine. Gulls cried, riding the draft created by the big boat, hoping for a handout. All for a nickel. She had kept the kerchief, and sported a pair of sunglasses much in fashion at the time. She looked to have stepped out of a movie. The Statue of Liberty as usual charmed, but the approach to the Battery ferry slip is the highlight of the trip, and we were perched at the prow, the best seats in the house. The big boat tooted, the crew took stations, the captain overshot slightly to compensate for the tide and current, then swung the boat into the palisade, bouncing off and grinding along it, stirring the water in the slip. Chains and pulleys rattled and clanged; under us the propeller suddenly came on to kill forward way, churning the stew of tidal water, machine oil, diesel, fish entrails and God knows what into a boil. The gulls wheeled and squawked. She loved it. Dickie looked a little green.

She found a mirror on a gum machine and restored her hair, clipping it so the side fall was gathered in a central braid and the rest cascaded down her back under it. Her mood was obviously restored as well. Dickie asked what it had been all about the day before. She took the clip out of her mouth, her hand behind her head lifting her breasts slightly, and said, "Mother wants me to cut my hair short."

"Don't," I said sharply.

Dickie gave me a look; I looked away.

"No chance," she said. "Where to now?"

"The Village," Dickie said. "I want to see where the Beats hang out. There's Buddhism happening there."

East Side, West Side/All around the town We hopped a Broadway Local at South Ferry and got off at Christopher Street. The West Village at this point was still the hippest place in the known universe, the center of the Post-War arts scene. I showed them the White Horse Tavern (they wouldn't let us in), the Blue Note, the Village Vanguard; Dylan and Baez and Phil Ochs and Ginsberg and Coltrane and Bruce—for Dickie their spirits were all there, even in the glare of a humid August day. Posters for peace groups, anti-war graffiti abounded. We blew the dust off books and records at stores along Bleeker, thought

207

maybe we'd see a movie at the Waverly… "How about some lunch?" Ali said. "I didn't get a lot of breakfast."

We popped into the Reggio, where the tables were chessboards. She had her first espresso. "I had my first one here too," I said.

"Give me a game?"

"Sure."

"I know better," Dickie said.

"I'm not trying to win; I mean I am trying to win, but whatever happens I'm trying to learn," she said. *If I knew love the way I know chess*

"You kibbitz," I told Dickie.

"Do what?"

"Kibbitz. Watch actively, moving from side to side, commenting on the action, stopping just short of annoying. Every game needs a good kibbitzer."

"See?" she said, "Already we're learning something." *She had said it the New York way, instead of "we're learning something already"*

She picked white and opened Queens Pawn again, but this time I was ready for her; it lasted twenty-five, maybe thirty moves. "Do you always open Queen's side?" I asked.

"It's a matter of principle."

"Idea. Someone you might enjoy meeting, if he's here." I explained speed chess on the few blocks over to Washington Square Park. He was there, hustling.

"Paulie, how's the man."

I introduced the Achesons, watched as Sammy appraised her. "She plays, Sammy," I said.

"Yeah?"

"She just stood me around thirty moves, and yesterday she damn near beat me."

"No shit, pardon me kid, how fast can you think?"

"I don't know," she said.

"Want to see how fast Paulie can think?"

This time I knew I was a loss leader. "Sam, I'm not shilling for you, I just wanted them to meet an old and impressive friend."

"On the house," he said.

"It could cost you trade."

"It's a slow day."

At twenty moves we were locked in pointless maneuvering, and I quit, not wanting to cost him a paying customer.

"I'd like to try this," she said. "And it doesn't have to be on the house. It's education."

"Cost you five, little lady."

I realized she was attracting a crowd for him; she was oblivious or didn't mind. She lasted ten moves, banging the clock like she'd been doing it all her life. And lost, laughing.

"How about you, Mr. A? Care to give it a try?"

"I'm just the kibbitzer," Dickie said.

Sam smiled. "Been learning Yiddish from this one?"

"Among other things."

We watched Sam take ten dollars from two duffers, signaled goodbye and nice meeting you, and walked across the park, at a loose end for what to do next. It was fun watching heads turn as she went by. She stayed oblivious until she drew whistles at a construction site over toward Broadway; then she grimaced, suddenly turned and began shouting. "You want it?" she yelled at them, "Come get it. Open house, boys." This brought jeers, catcalls, a couple of obscene offers. "Sounds good to me," she shouted back.

Dickie and I dragged her off around a corner. "Are you crazy?" he said.

"Yes. Absolutely. Everybody seems to have some plan for me, or anyway for my body, starting with Father, on through Mother, and working all the way down to total strangers on a scaffold. In the past hour, here's a running total. First, you two decide whether I should play chess or not, and how to open. You never *asked me*. I've been called kid, and little lady, and I'm the same age as Paul here. I've been ogled by every guy we passed, and I've been publicly humiliated in the street by a gang of complete strangers."

"And you did a pretty good job of egging them on."

"Didn't I just. Make sure it gets back to Father."

"Is that what this is about?"

"Yes. That's what this is about. It's about me not having a say in anything. Not a goddamned thing in this world. Nothing."

I thought I knew what to say. "Ali, where would you like to go? What would you like to do? It's your day now."

"I don't think…"

"Dickie, shut up. Her choice."

"Damn right," she said.

"Or she'll make us miserable for the rest of the day?"

"Damn right again."

"Ali, what do you want to do?"

"I want to see the ocean. I want to go to Brooklyn."

"Slumming?" Dickie said.

"Thanks," I said.

"No. I want to see what Paul calls the Real City. Where people live. And I want to see the ocean."

"If that's what you want. "

"That's what I want."

I got us a Brighton Express at Union Square (I showed her The Strand, but she said, "Another time"). "Show you something," I said, and took them to the first car, to watch out the front window. "You're the motorman," I said.

"Don't patronize me."

Oh I'm so sorry your fucking highness "Sorry. Jeez." *That's a shit thing to say Ali I wanted to share that*

The air was fresher at Brighton but still smelled, as usual, of the sea and bunker oil. It was a Monday but the beach was still mobbed. And it was hot. Very hot, with little breeze.

"What smells?"

"Everything."

We walked the boardwalk toward Coney Island, past the Pavilion, past the handball courts, past the Aquarium. She was still sullen. Nothing satisfied.

"It is *really* hot."

"We don't have climate control. Only climate."

"Cute."

When we got to the Cyclone, Dickie wanted to ride.

"Come on," he said, "This is a great-looking, classic roller coaster. It's famous. Legendary even. You can't be here and not ride this."

"Are you telling me again what I can and can't do?"

"Jesus, Ali, that wasn't what I meant and you know it."

"How do I know it?"

"Suit yourself. We're riding. Paul?"

"No thanks. I had my fill of rides as a kid. The Wonder Wheel, maybe. No Cyclone." Did I say this because I wanted to be alone with her, without Dickie? Was I afraid for her in this mood? I honestly don't know, to this day. I wanted to help. I remembered her father treating her like a four-year-old. Did I think what I was doing helped? Did I think I *could* help?

"Well I'm going. Meet you here."

Ali walked to the weather-side rail and looked out to sea.

"You wanted to see the ocean."

"I thought I did."

"Well, you're looking out over New York Bay. That land in the distance is Jersey. We used to say, 'That's America'. Here. Turn part way to your left." Two freighters were headed out. "That's the open Atlantic." *Thalassa. Thalassa*

"I wish I could just swim away in it."

"It's that bad?"

"Yeah, it's that bad. And you've seen it, so you should know. If you don't, I don't have much use for you."

"You mean the first time we met, and your father made that crack about all the virile young men and you with your nose in a book? And your mother and her crack about the pool crew?"

She faced me. "You do get it."

"I think so. You can't win either way."

"Right. And they want to marry me off."

"So what are you going to do about it?"

"What I am doing. Acting like a complete jerk until they back off. Or until I ruin my reputation so thoroughly it's too embarrassing to have me at a party. Isn't this stupid?"

"Yeah. Why not just tell them? Straight out: No way."

"You met them. What do you think? They don't give a damn for my wishes. Or for me. I got switched at birth with the one they wanted. Now they want to make me into the one they wanted."

I put my hand on top of hers, where it rested on the railing. "You're pretty angry."

"Angry? Paul, I'm not angry, I'm desperate. And I'm taking it out on everybody. I'm not good with angry and I'm not doing well with desperate." She put her other hand on top of mine. "Look, no matter what I say or do, don't think I've forgotten what you did the day we met, or with the books, or on the boat, or today. Crap, I thought Dickie understood, but now, I don't know...silly bastard, insisting on going on the roller coaster, when he's seasick on a calm day."

Sure enough, Dickie wobbled across the boardwalk, looking like five pounds of shit in a three pound bag.

"Nice ride?" she said.

"Great," he said. "I've been to Coney and ridden the Cyclone."

"For Christ's sake, Dickie, you look like you're going to blow lunch. You think I've never seen you heave over the side of the boat?"

"You're so wrong, AA. I have already blown lunch. And thank you so much for you'll pardon the expression bringing it up."

"You OK?"

"I will be. Give me a minute. I thought, you know, it's on land. And I don't get carsick."

"You used to, when we were small."

"Again, thank you, Alicia."

"It isn't anything to be ashamed of. It isn't like wetting the bed."

"You little…"

"I never said you did, I meant it isn't the same. I'm sorry, Dickie. Paul, I'm very sorry if I gave the impression that my brother was ever a bedwetter. He wasn't."

"Thanks, Ali. That will convince everyone."

"I believe it. Or don't care. Did someone say something? All I heard was the ocean. Want to walk on the beach?"

We took off our shoes and scrunched sand between our toes, and when it was too hot we made our way through the crowd to the shingle and walked in the cool mud. That left the dilemma of sand stuck to our feet, and walking barefoot on the boardwalk, which was splinter city, which left us using the concrete steps up to the Aquarium. "Hey, want to see the electric eel?" Dickie was enthusiastic about the eel, and Ali was mildly interested in the exotic creatures. The eel did his thing, the rainbow fish rainbowed, the clownfish clowned, the sharks glided by with their idiot grins, nothing coming back from their ancient eyes. Which left Olaf the Walrus, the neighborhood character.

"You gotta see this," Dickie told her, and he winked at me. Well, where were my loyalties here? It was never even a question. I mounted the steps to Olaf's outdoor gallery, with a mounting sense of déjà vu. How many times, Olaf?

"If you lean over," Dickie told her, "You can watch him surface; he's as graceful as a porpoise, Paul told me." And she started to lean over the tank. And Olaf started to surface. I pulled her back just in time; Olaf's lungful of spume dispersed harmlessly into the space I had just pulled her out of.

"You miserable bastard, Dickie. You knew that was going to happen. Thank you, Paul. Thank you very much." And she walked off down the stairs.

"Why the hell did you do that? She needs to come down a peg or two."

"That's more than a peg or two, Dickie. You know that, I told you that."

"You're stuck on her. That's what's happening here."

"Stuck on her? I like her, yeah. I don't like what she tells me about your father's plans for her. I don't like how he treats her. I don't like how you sometimes treat her. There you have it. Straight up."

"You like her. Face it."

"I just told you I did."

"Did you tell her?"

"Should I?"

"Are you asking me? Is she wanting you to ask me?"

"Ya got me. I'm a schmuck."

"Damn. You like my sister. This is a development."

"Am I going to have to listen to this for the next three years?"

"Possibly."

She was waiting at the exit. Where could she go?

"Where to now?"

"Well, my mother should be home from work in an hour. My grandmother should be there now. What the hell. Come to my place. Dry off." I led them away from the boardwalk into the shade of the trees where Surf Avenue becomes Ocean Parkway, hoping for some relief from the heat. She moped along. Well, we all did. The El thundered overhead, providing a little more shade. The building was cool after the heat of the beach and the streets. As usual the lobby smelled of last night's cooking. Or last week's. They were polite and didn't comment. Up the stairs, the stucco walls echoing our footfalls. The lobby was suddenly dark and small to me, the doors with their judases like a cellblock in the Lubyanka. But my grandmother came to the door when I turned my key, her eyes wide with surprise and delight. She hugged me and made Ali and Dickie welcome.

"A pleasure to make your acquaintance, Mrs. Levinovich," Dickie said. "Paul has told me so much about you."

"Hi, I'm Dickie's sister, Alicia."

"Aren't you lovely. Paulie she's lovely. And so tall. Come in, I was just making tea. Can I get you some?"

"No, please, don't trouble."

"It's no trouble, dear. Paulie, show them around. Go, go. Shoo."

"That won't take long."

"Stall them. I'm old and I'm slow." She started pulling out mugs, and a glass for herself. If you are imagining a scene out of "The Gertrude Berg Show" you aren't far off.

I showed them my room, with the view of the El. A train was just making its way into the terminal, banging over the points. The sea view from the living room was much more impressive. "Great in a storm," I said. That left the library. "Welcome," I said, "To the University of Brighton Beach."

"Oh," she said. She was enchanted. She ran her hands over the spines of books, pulling out and examining treasure after treasure. She

215

pulled out the Prague Kafka. "This is a First Edition of *Der Prozess*; 'The Trial'."

"It is."

"Do you know what this is probably worth?"

"To my father? To us? I don't know. Priceless. There's a story, of how he got it out of Europe…"

"And here's all the Borges. And Grass, in German and English. Oh, Paul." And suddenly that tall, lovely, brilliant girl burst into tears. She collapsed into my father's reading chair like a marionette with its strings cut. She cried with her whole body, shaking and gasping, trying to stop, to catch her breath, then not even trying. She just wept.

"Ali," Dickie said. He knelt down beside her. "Are you OK?" She shook her head, waved him away.

"Ali, what is it?" I said. "What can we do?" She shook her head, still in tears of utter despair. "Ali, I want to help but I don't know how." It wrung my heart. "What can we get you? Anything?" *Anything*

She shook her head again, quiet now, but tears still falling. My grandmother was suddenly there, a box of tissues in her hand. "Come here, dear, come with me. What is it? You boys get lost for a while."

"This is where I want to be," she said, "This is what I want. This room. What's in this room." She said this in tones of utter despair.

"Come," my grandmother said. "We'll have tea, we'll send the boys out for something for dinner. We'll have what to eat, and see what we can maybe make better." She hugged her, and Ali's head fell on her shoulder, where mine had fallen whenever I was hurt. "You'll stay for dinner," she continued, "Pavele, here's a ten, you and your friend, go get some cold cuts by S&G, get knishes by Mrs. Stahl's."

"Let me pitch in, Mrs. Levinovich," Dickie said.

"Don't be ridiculous, you're a guest. Paulie, go. Let the women talk."

216

We hit the bricks. Down the stairs to Brighton Beach Avenue, past the eternal stickball game. *The tots play Ring-around-Rosie*

"This is stickball," Dickie said.

"Yes. The park ranger will be by any minute to explain it to you."

"Quit it, Paulie. I don't deserve that."

"No, you don't. I'm sorry. I'm just…I'm worried about her."

"You and me both. She's been…I've never seen her come apart like that before. I didn't know it was this bad. I really didn't know. She's right. You're right. My father's a son of a bitch. Not so much to other men. To women. All right, to me too, pressuring me to join Phi Delt, and the lawyer thing. With me out of the house for a year I don't know what he's been doing to her head. I used to at least distract him. I think."

"Let my grandmother do her thing. She never took crap from any man, that I know of. I'd say Ali picked the right place to come unglued. Our job is to take as long as we reasonably can to pick up some delicatessen."

"Lovely word. Says it all."

We started with a selection of corned beef, pastrami and tongue from the steam table at S&G, known throughout the neighborhood and beyond as Essen Gay. "Gay essen," I explained to Dickie, "Means 'go eat' in Yiddish. See the blue NRA eagle still in the window?"

"In my neighborhood they think Roosevelt was a traitor. What's tongue?"

"In this neighborhood we think he's God. Tongue is a cow's tongue, pickled and steamed."

"As much as I enjoy another tongue in my mouth…"

"Stick to the corned beef. I'll have the tongue." On to Mrs. Stahl's for knishes, "A pastry filled with potato and onion. Here," I took one out of the bag. "Try a bite."

"Mmmm. This is good. Now I know what the street smells of."

"Mrs. Stahl's is a local institution. On weekends you can't get near the place. Surrounded by cars from Jersey and The Island." We sat awhile on the boardwalk, near the Baths, let some time pass. "You mind that we did this trip?"

"No. Nah. Siddhartha, man. All experience is good, the more random, the better. But you have to face something."

"What?"

"You like my sister, man."

"Dickie…"

"Stop. I'm glad for you. For her too."

"She's a touch volatile. Mercurial."

"Not her fault. She'll be leaving it behind when she goes to school."

"Doesn't she have any girlfriends she can work some of this stuff out with?"

"That's part of her problem. The ones who aren't from our little world don't understand this and think it's ridiculous. The ones from our world think she's poison now."

I looked at my watch. "Think it's cool?"

"Most likely."

It was. They were still drinking tea, Ali out of a cup, my grandmother the Eastern European way, out of a glass, with a sugar cube between her teeth to sweeten it.

"You OK Ali?"

"Yes. For the first time today. Look, I'm sorry. I started to tell Paul while you were on the Cyclone. I'm…I was…desperate. Despairing. You know Father's been pressuring me to come out, and you know what that means, and how it goes against everything I've ever wanted for myself. I can't do it. I won't do it. I can't go down that road, not for anything."

"OK."

"Yesterday he roped Mother into it. He got her to work on me. She told me she wouldn't support me if I refused. I don't know what he'll do. Threaten to do. I know he regards education for women as optional."

"I told her she has to change the game," my grandmother said. "She's been trying to sabotage it, but that just costs her, not him. She has to tell him straight out, No, and No is No. But she needs an ally, she's only seventeen. Just going to start college, that she's desperate to do. Believe me, this I understand. That room in there has been my college."

"Mine too, Grandma."

"So you know why she broke down; yes Alicia?"

"Yes."

"I'm sorry, Ali," Dickie said, "I had no idea it was so bad. When I left Mother was still on your side."

"She was. Not anymore. Things have changed."

"I see."

"Is there any other family to turn to?" my grandmother asked. "This is what we're up to."

"How about Aunt Alice?"

"He won't listen to her."

"Better than nothing. Maybe much better. Maybe Mother will listen to her."

"It isn't her they have to listen to," I said to her. "It's you."

"You have to make it clear to him that No is No. That you won't play his game. You play your game. Tell her, Paulie."

"He has been, Mrs. Levinovich."

"Has he. Well, we taught him well."

That was when my mother showed up. She was surprised and delighted in turn. We made introductions and Grandma filled her in on the story. "You must be the girl with that brilliant interpretation of 'The

Scarlet Letter'," she said. "I agree. You must be absolutely straight with him. Tell me something. Paul says you've read Simone de Beauvoir. 'The Second Sex'. And Betty Friedan?"

"Feminists. Yes, I've read de Beauvoir. And Betty Friedan I've heard of."

"You know what we say at Womens' Strike for Peace? Feminism is the radical idea that women are human beings."

"She told me that one, Ma."

"His father and I tried to raise our son to understand this. I hope he does. I hope both these young men do."

"I think Paul does, Mrs. Seitz. He brought me 'A Room of One's Own'. My brother I think is almost there."

"Well Jeez, thanks, Ali."

The laugh broke the tension. We had dinner, a festival of banter, cold cuts and hot knishes.

"Professor Seitz must have been some teacher," Dickie said. "I read his paper on 'Der Golem'."

"A good teacher and a good man," my grandmother said.

"And a great husband," my mother said.

"Paul has told us some things about him, Mrs. Seitz," Ali said. "It must have been a tremendous loss. I so wish I could have met him."

"He would have been intrigued by your reading of 'The Scarlet Letter'."

"That's what Paul said—no, wait, that you would be, Mrs. Seitz."

"He would have, too. I suspect so was Paul."

"Books are the way to our hearts," I said.

"They were his great love," my mother said.

"Apart from you."

She laughed. "Sometimes I wondered." She turned away for a moment, to shed a few tears, I knew. "But he'd never read Jane Austen."

I touched her shoulder. "I doubt lack of Jane Austen killed him," I said.

She turned back, grinned. "It wouldn't kill you to read Jane Austen."

"I have him reading Virginia Woolf, Mrs. Seitz," Ali said, "'Jacob's Room'."

"Really. Well now. Paul never read anything but what he wanted."

"Are you starting to feel outnumbered?" Dickie said to me.

"Surrounded," I said. "Possibly outgunned."

Then it was time to go. They shook hands with Dickie, hugged and kissed Ali, wished her luck, hugged and kissed me. "I'll be back in a few days," I said.

"Help her out, Paul," my mother whispered, "She's so bright, and she's in pain."

"I'll try, Ma. I like her."

"Good." Then, louder, "Do you need more clothes?"

"No. I'm fine. I'll see you day after tomorrow."

The eternal stickball game was still on. The older guys were home from jobs. Mark Hymowitz couldn't resist; he called Time Out and stopped us less than ten feet from the lobby door.

"Another cousin, Paulie?"

She took my arm, tightly. "I'm not a cousin," she said.

I introduced them. "I've never seen this game," Dickie said.

"Stickball? Like baseball but with a broomstick. You hit for distance. Distance determines a single, a double, a triple, a home run. Caught ball is an out, three whiffs is an out."

"How far do you have to hit for a run?"

"Two sewers."

"Two sewers?"

"The distance between three manhole covers," I said. "Home plate is a manhole cover. Mark here is a two-sewer hitter."

"Want to try?"

"Sure, why not."

"This is harder than baseball—thinner bat. Really takes an eye." Dickie whiffed one after another until Mark served him up a creampuff and he bounced it off the hood of the Steinguts' Buick. "Ground rule double," Hymo said. "You're catching on. How about you, Sis? Want to try?"

She pulled me closer. "I'll stick to chess."

"Chess? You got lucky, Paulie."

"What are your chances for the Olympics?" I turned to the Achesons. "Mark is determined to be the captain of the first American Olympic Stickball Team."

"I wish you all the luck in the world with that," Dickie said. We made some goodbyes and headed for the train. I wished it were October; it would be just cool enough and the beach would be empty and we could sit in private and watch the sunset and listen to the waves coming in off the Atlantic. As it was, I took them to the first car, up to the front window. The train emerged from the half light onto the Manhattan Bridge just as the sun was setting and the lights were coming on. The skyline, the river and the other bridges unfolded on either side of us as the train labored up the grade. She took my arm again. "Thank you, Paul," she said, "Thank you for this day."

"Yes," Dickie said, "Thank you, Paul."

"The hardest part was arranging the sunset."

"Wiseass." She squeezed my arm.

Boys and girls together
Me and Mamie O'Rourke

We arrived back, exhausted, to a dark and empty house, the only light the green light at the end of the dock. Ali and Dickie exchanged a look. "Home sweet home." Riley gave us his usual enthusiastic greeting. We opened windows for a breeze, brought some cold drinks out to the porch. The moon was down behind some trees; the Pleiades were clearly visible, a reminder.

"Gotta start school soon."

"Days away," Ali said. "I'll have to do some shopping with Mother."

"Don't cut your hair." I said.

"I'd sooner cut my throat."

"Scared?" Dickie asked her.

"A little. Not really. More relieved than scared."

"We'll get you through."

"I'll get me through."

"I meant orientation. I don't have any worries about your abilities. I'm the one with the grades problems."

"You're the one with the motivation problems. I'm not the only one that has to confront Father, am I."

"No. You aren't. But I have to plan it very carefully. And not step on your lines. Keep me informed, will you?"

"I will, Dickie." She finished her soda and sat forward on the chair.

"Bedtime," she said. Last fun day tomorrow. I apologize from the bottom of my heart for today."

"It ended well. Stop apologizing; we understand."

"Paul, I want to hear all about your father some time."

"Some time," I said. *The heart is half a prophet*

Dickie and I sipped some more soda and watched nothing on the lake.

"Now that we've fixed her, we can work on me," he said. "She's right, I have to explain to my father that I'm not going to be a lawyer."

"The doctor is in."

"You're lucky. You don't have any expectations to meet."

"Yeah. Nothing makes that easier than a dead father."

"Yeah, that was a stupid way to put it. I mean, you were always free to pursue what you wanted, right?"

"Not entirely. I could as long as the Brooklyn Public Library and the subway system held up, and the odd ancient college with a public relations problem came up with a scholarship and we could get by on my mother's salary…"

"OK, I mean you didn't have to fight with your parents over what to do with your life."

"That's true."

"I think if I were my sister you'd be more sympathetic."
I laughed. "That's probably true too. Sorry. I'm listening. Sympathetically."

"Here's the thing. She can't do anything right in his eyes. I can do no wrong, as long as I meet expectations. And I can't. I've done it up until now and every bone in my head says it's over. I could be a good lawyer, I bet; I enjoy analyzing texts as much as you and Ali, but the texts I'm interested in are Buddhist. That's what turns me on. That's what I want to study."

"And you have to tell him."

"Eventually I do. I have to stay in school or leave the country—if I drop out I get drafted, or have to enlist. That's not how I want to get to Asia. And I will not be part of organized killing. I will not. I have to pick my time very carefully with this. He'll stop tuition if I make a wrong move."

"He's that…"

"Yeah. Look, I know this sounds bad, but Ali has to make her move now, or he'll put her on the marriage market."

"That's what she says. At seventeen? Really?"

"Not married, engaged. Plenty of upper-crust types do that; it's falling out of fashion but it still goes on. You get engaged and go through college with a ring. Or you marry some guy in law school or the Navy and go to school and get your bachelor's. And your MRS."

"MRS?"

"Misses, dolt."

"This is a whole other world for me, Dickie."

"So's stickball, for me. It's how my parents did it. She came out, they got engaged while he was in school, she started school, he got pulled into the Navy, they got married and pregnant when he came back stateside to pick up a new boat after he got sunk. She lost that one and I got started when he didn't get shipped to the Pacific. Thank you, A-bomb. I owe my existence to the worst single act of violence in human history. Anyway, I have more time, and I get to see how Ali's move works out. Which, I know, stinks."

"So the problem for you is how to stay in school without going nuts, but it's the same problem as hers, which is to get the education she dearly wants."

"That's it."

"How about if you major in Poli Sci? He'd love that."

"Forget it."

"Dickie, you could run for any office and win. You charmed Mark Hymowitz, who was trying his best to embarrass you. That's a real skill in my eyes. You charmed my people; you had to rescue me from yours. That's a real skill."

"A skill I'd rather not cultivate. I'm working hard to not be so good at it."

"History?"

"My father's given it a bad name. It's just one war after another, one case of desire gone crazy after another. That's why Buddhist philosophy appeals to me. Peace. After listening to them fighting for the past eight years or so, a system of life that offers peace is mighty attractive."

"Philosophy. Why not major in philosophy? It can lead to law school. And I bet the reading includes Eastern."

"Jesus, Paul, you fucking *are* a genius. That's great. I've been so sunk in how to approach him—see, that's the political skills part—I never thought what to approach him *with*. No reason you can't major in Philo and apply to law school. That can keep him happy for another three years. Until…"

Silence. The chrrrr of crickets.

"Until what?"

"Until whatever the next step is. That's all I know now. I have to go meditate on my actions at the Aquarium. I'm still a chip off the old block, and I don't like the block."

I went up too. I was just as tired.

Too early, there was tapping on my window frame. It was Ali, in the magnolia. Dickie was out there too.

"Come on out. You're missing the best part of the day. Come watch the sun come over the trees."

"Give me a second." Pee, pull on pants, climb out window onto magnolia limb.

It was going to be a hot one. As the sun cleared the trees the lake began to sparkle invitingly. Last day. Her hair was in a ponytail. Her legs dangled from an upper branch. "Come view our kingdom on the day before we abandon it. It's a ceremony. Every year we invite one commoner to share our panorama." In the early light, from this vantage, the expanse of lawn down to the lake was magnificent, perfect. Another word from books came to me: "Idyllic," I said.

"The reign of the current sovereigns has not been an idyll," she said.

"Not in the least Tennysonic," Dickie said.

"An embattled kingdom," she said.

"Dickie was saying. For the past eight years?"

"About. That lawn used to be full of people. Friends, cousins, cousins of friends, friends of cousins. Barbecues, swim parties. That weedy tennis court was in constant use. Riley (N.B: at that moment jumping at the base of the magnolia) was in dog heaven. There were even other dogs."

"What happened?"

"The King started to have trouble sleeping and got a little too deep into the wine cellar."

"Oh."

"Not deep enough to require a Regent, but deep enough for things to start going to hell."

"And you're leaving the kingdom next week."

"I am," she said.

"How's it feel?"

"Not as good as I thought. But good enough."

"I propose," Dickie said, "That we spend the day in the most ridiculous ways possible."

"I believe we can," she said. "Mother left me a note about a beauty parlor appointment. I left a note telling her to cancel it."

We climbed down and began with a big breakfast, substituting food for sleep and laying the groundwork for future cardiac problems. Toast with every kind of butter, jam, jelly, marmalade, coffee, more toast, more coffee. It was a no-limit buffet. Riley got his portion and then some, especially when the bacon was broken out. Next came free-form croquet, with numerous non-sanctioned rules. In the midst of this, Dickie went to find a broomstick and electrical tape; I demonstrated my skill in wrapping the handle, and he began practice for his triumphant return to Brighton Third Street. Ali even played outfield, which involved a lot of running around; I'd never seen stickball played without boundaries of parked cars and other impedimenta. Riley chased whatever got past any of us, which was plenty; of course it was his ball we were using. From his point of view it was the most elaborate game of fetch ever staged. I loved watching her run. I loved watching Dickie laugh and swear trying to hit my lobs. It may have been the first time in my life I ever enjoyed anything athletic.

We were draped over various articles of porch furniture, deciding between lunch and a pre-prandial swim, when their mother came to the door. "Alicia, it's time for your beauty parlor appointment."

"I told you, Mother, to cancel that appointment. I'm not doing anything to my hair."

"Alicia, we are not having a discussion about this."

I waited for the explosion, but it didn't come. She kept an even tone. "Mother. We visited every one of the Seven Sisters, or, if you like, just focus on Wellsmith. My hairstyle is very much in fashion. Most girls today would kill for long straight hair. I think it's my most attractive feature."

"Alicia, I said clearly that this is not a discussion. Say goodbye to the boys and come with me."

Then Ali did something extraordinary, something that would blossom in time to come, something I never expected, something I would not, and even Dickie with all his social skill, could not, have done, and would not be able to do for many years. She changed the game. Changed it utterly.

She was as tall as her mother. She put her hands over her mother's shoulders and looked her straight in the eyes. "Mother," she said, "Do you remember being my age? Starting off for college? It's *my* hair, Mother."

And her mother relaxed. Ali dropped her hands back and her mother took one. "Very well," she said, with some warmth, "Since you feel so strongly about it."

And that was that.

After lunch it got hotter and hotter, so oppressive we couldn't even get out of the water onto the raft except to dive off it again. She had a graceful dive, gathering her whole body and uncoiling straight out, a gorgeous spring. We splashed and surface dived, juggled a beach ball between us. Riley, still excited from the morning, joined us in the water. We played to forget; she that she was about to leave home for good, Dickie that he was returning to the guerilla battle with his father, me that I was going to start the legendarily difficult Organic Chem, make or break for pre-meds. And that I would not be seeing her until...when? The afternoon passed slowly, but it passed, last afternoon in Paradise. At dinner Mrs. Acheson was unusually affable, not the remote matron of the estate she had been playing. As if Ali had melted something in her. And in herself.

"You're all facing school again, Ali, you for the first time. Are you all ready?"

"As ready as we're going to be," Dickie said.

"It passes so quickly," she said, "Youth. It feels like an afternoon lasts an age, but when you look back it's an eyeblink. Ein augenblick, yes, Paul?"

"Yes, Mrs. Acheson; I didn't know you spoke German."

"I did languages at Wellsmith."

"Mother, what was it like, starting college then?"

"Oh, very different in some ways, not so in others...we knew a war was coming."

"We have one now," Dickie said.

"Not on the same scale. We didn't know how we would be involved, and the boys we went with, whether we'd ever see them again. I was engaged to your father, you know that story, and I was terrified he would be killed, or come home maimed. Or...changed in some way. He seemed the same..."

Silence.

"Your aunt; that's my sister, Paul, wanted to fly airplanes. I mean, she knew how to fly, she wanted to fly for the military..."

"Didn't Dad want to fly?" Dickie asked.

"He did, but he washed out of pilot training. I was so relieved—I thought he'd be safer at sea. In this war the Navy seems to be the safe service..."

"Not for the Vietnamese," Dickie said.

It was still hot after dinner; we lolled around on the porch, played a desultory game of Scrabble, books forgotten, plenty of reading to do soon enough. The heat kept constant even after dark; the sky intermittently lit with heat lightning. Dickie went up to meditate. *Om mani padme hum*

"I thought I'd be sleepy by now," Ali said, "But I'm not, and it's too hot to sleep anyway. I have an idea, Paul: Night swim."

We tripped the light fantastic It was warm enough, that was for sure. We changed back into bathing suits and swam to the raft. It was lit dimly by the moon, now obscured by heat haze, and by the occasional heat lightning.

"That was amazing," I said, "What you did with your mother."

"I changed the game. I changed my own game. It's just...I loved her when I was little, and she loved me. Liked me. For just a moment I reconnected with that. I think...I think I touched the girl she once was, I mean, she was once me, if you see what I'm saying."

"I don't know how you did that."

"Neither do I. I might be able to do it again. But I don't think so."

"You mean with him."

"I mean with him."

"You could maybe touch the boy who loved her."

"You *are* a romantic. I don't know if he ever did. This house was her family's." She gave a single sob...then stopped. "I don't think I'm

230

desperate anymore, Paul. I think I can talk about this without the tears or drama." But some tears came anyway. Not desperation, just sadness. "It's like this. If you're a girl, and your father doesn't love you, you think, whoever will?" And then she did cry. "Don't you see? If I confront him, and I know I have to, I lose any chance, any hope there ever was, that he'll ever love me or care about me. Then I'm scared, who ever will?"

What to say? "Well, your brother thinks you're pretty terrific. He'd about kill for you. And he says there's a Phi Delt who's been hot for you since like elementary school. And, who knows, sometimes a complete stranger shows up out of nowhere that…"

She turned to me, fire in her eyes. "He treats my intelligence as if it were a defect."

I put my arm around her, pulled her to me. "I told you, I think it's the most exciting thing about you."

She put her head on my shoulder. "I'm not crazy Paul."

Aren't you? "Not very."

"Not very. Thank you, Paul."

"Stop thanking me. You're always thanking me. You thank me for things no one should have to be thankful for."

"You keep doing things that deserve thanks."

"I do them because…"

"Because what?"

I hugged her tighter. "I can't stand seeing you bullied. I know what it feels like. Also *in for a penny in for a pound* because you're the most beautiful thing I have ever seen. Because everything I like to do is ten times more fun if I do it with you. Because you surprise me all the time. Because when you're away from this place you light up like a Roman candle. Because you won't settle. Because you fight back."

Because I love you. I don't know. Do I? Maybe. Maybe this is love. Is that the right thing to say? You can't say that to someone in this condition.

It's—what would she expect if I said that? (It was 1965). Engagement? Marriage? That was what she was fighting against. I was excited. And frightened. At the same time. By the intensity of my feelings for this girl. And about her feelings, period. Waves of desire and fear washed over me like tides. I was as crazy as she was.

But it turned out that I had said enough. At that moment she needed to feel she was lovable, capable of inspiring love, not that she was loved. We were seventeen, and had a lot to do. It was enough. She kissed me again, where one day there would be a tiny scar.

"You always know what to say to me."

"Huh. I've never known how to talk to girls."

"You know how to talk to this one. I need at least one male in my life who knows what I need."

"There's Riley."

She laughed. "Yes, there's Riley." *And sometimes the odd penniless Jew turns up* "But I can't talk to Riley, or anyway he can't say much back. You say I'm beautiful and intelligent and sometimes I even believe it, but until today I feel like I wasn't allowed to enjoy either one. So I must be worthless, unlovable, is what I thought. Felt."

"You aren't either one."

"The other day when those construction guys were yelling at me I felt trapped in my body. When you look at me I don't. I like it. Why is that? I only ever met one boy I could enjoy my whole self with, and I've probably done what I do, which is go too far with him, and scared him."

"Who?"

"You, you idiot. You've seen me at my absolute worst."

"It all makes sense."

"Well. And I won my mother over. I didn't cut my hair. The hair remains intact."

"So it does."

"I have to get some sleep."

"Yeah."

"Really."

"I know."

"I don't want to go."

"I don't want you to go."

"I don't want you to go, Paul. It's been such a …it's been a privilege getting to know you, I mean, getting to spend all this time. It's been…oh, hell" And suddenly she rolled over on top of me, planted her mouth on mine, and kissed me. I could feel the entire length of her on me, our legs sandwiched, her breasts through the thin bathing suit top, her soft belly against mine; I could feel the tip of her tongue gently part my lips, and I opened my mouth slightly, touched the tip of her tongue with the tip of mine, started to put my arms around her, but as quickly as that she rolled off me, over the side of the raft, and was gone.

I was in no condition to swim after her. I was hard as a rock, my body in a state of aroused disbelief. I realize now that she took me so by surprise because I was so focused on my own feelings, on what to say and do, that—and I won't blame this entirely on the dark and on being seventeen—I completely missed the cues to what *she* was feeling. I couldn't believe (I mean, I saw myself in the mirror every morning) that I had inspired a moment of passion like that in a girl as spectacular as I thought she was. I still can't. What I really could not believe (I mean, her brother had said, "Face it, you like her", not "Face it, she likes you") was that the passion I felt for her was returned. That she felt it too. I couldn't believe the luck.

I couldn't believe. *I couldn't believe.* I couldn't trust.

I heard the splashes of her swim to the dock, rolled on my side to see her climb out and run up the lawn in the moonlight. Riley met her at the porch. I heard the screen door bang. There was nothing left but the green light at the end of the dock. I lay for a few minutes; what

233

could I do? Chase her to her room? Savor the moment. Try to slow my heart. Get a moontan. When I could, I slipped into the water and swam back to the dock, sat and dried off, and went into the silent house to sleep.

Only I couldn't sleep, couldn't hope to sleep. I lay in the dark completely unable to sleep. I had never been more awake. I mean, I had been attracted to girls since sixth grade, learned enough social skills to do some noncommittal dating in high school; the feelings were like a storm, sated by simple contact and clumsy runs to first base (as we said then), a pleasant fire in the blood. This was a hurricane, an earthquake. I wanted this girl. I wanted to be with this girl. I had never felt anything like this before, and the power of it awed me. I had to talk to her. No. I had to finish the kiss. She had kissed me with her whole body, and I hadn't had time—hadn't been able, to react. I was stunned to find myself capable of this response. Such a commonplace thing, for adults, the experience of sexual excitement, but for a boy, and one who had lived almost exclusively in his head for seventeen years, it was a revelation. It was a drug, this feeling. *And I knew she felt it too*

I could not afford to make a wrong move, but what would be a wrong move? Going to her room? Trying and risking being caught? What kind of scene would that create? But not going, not trying, could be a different kind of wrong move. Could I trust my own judgment? I could not. I knew that. Could I live with a decision to not try? I could not. I knew that too. I lay there as images of us together washed over me, the storm surge. When I got to her room, what would happen? What could we do? Sit and talk in the dark? I could slip into bed beside her. What then? How to negotiate taking our clothes off? Do I get into her bed naked? Did she sleep naked, in the heat? Then what? Roll against each other, caress…I had no condom, couldn't get one (it was still illegal to sell them to anyone under 21 in Connecticut; oral contraceptives were still experimental, years away). *Couldn't ask Dickie for one, now, could I?* What could two bright, but, as was commonly the case back then, sexually naïve teenagers, do? Stumble around substitutes for intercourse? Such sex education as we had did not cover oral sex (which in fact was still illegal according to the sodomy laws of several states). Interracial sex (which according to many peoples' definitions, this would be) was similarly illegal, and would be for several more years. The phrase "dry humping" was at best vague. I didn't hear the words "coitus interruptus" until medical school, and then as reference to an antique practice. How to do this? A King's Pawn opening probably wouldn't help here. I didn't know much, but it was an article of faith at that time, as it had been for over a century if not a lot longer, that The Man would know what to do to get sex going.

What was going to happen? I could get her pregnant. She would be gone for a year, gone to Switzerland, or Puerto Rico, baby in trash can, dead in a back alley. We could run away, elope to Las Vegas. It could end in bitterness, poverty, disgrace. Her father could prosecute; the spectacular trial of the two lovers, splashed over the tabloids, you remember the case. But this isn't any of those stories. Boy meets girl, boy loses girl, boy gets girl. This isn't that kind of story either, or not the usual version. *Do I dare to eat a peach*

Apparently I did The floorboards in the hall creaked like a haunted house, and her familiar slept at her door; one woof from him and all was over. At the window the easily-climbed magnolia. Full moonlight. The service corridors. It was like a chess problem. I was as good as there. What would I do if she was asleep? Or surprised? She wouldn't be. She couldn't be.

Crickets chrred, fireflies sparkled in the cooling night. The moon, partly silvered by an obscuring cloud, was reflected in the lake, *image from a Chinese poem*. The green light at the end of the dock. *Do I dare disturb the universe* I kept to the shadows, doing a broken field run from tree to tree. And ducked behind one when I saw the pool man striding across the lawn as if he owned it. I saw him take the key from over the transom, unlock and enter the service door. A few seconds later a light went on in her room, then off. *A bold girl who lightly surrenders herself* I slumped against the tree, staring out across the dark lake, sick, disgusted. The dock light mocked. I would say this was like a punch in the gut, but I'd been sucker-punched by a playground bully when I was nine, and this was much worse. What was all this crap she'd been feeding me for two weeks? She was beautiful, she was rich, she was intellectual, a "brain" like me, and she was attracted to me. She was a dream. She was an answer to prayer. And like most answers to prayer, like the Delphic Oracle, it came with a catch. Like most dreams, it was a fantasy. *Maybe you're the Queen's Pawn, Ace.* But the hurricane would not abate. The fire would not go out. I climbed back up the magnolia, but could not sleep. Her involvements with townies, her "rude mechanicals". Her joke vow about not dating older men. Her campaign to shock her parents out of pushing her down the debutante road? Her need to know her father loved her, or anyway a father. Obviously her mother tried to get her out of town every time the pool guy showed up. No wonder she was so mercurial. She had two lives, a secret like that.

No wonder she could kiss like that

This went around and around in my mind, in something like rage, until there was faint light in the sky. Then I thought, maybe this was what she was trying to escape from, which in about a week she would. Maybe that was it; she was getting away from this mess, and really did want me; I mean, I could rescue her, that's obviously what she wanted and needed. Only this: I would need to catch up with her—not disappoint her. That was it. Toward dawn I fell asleep. And dreamt of her. Of her body against mine. That, anyway, was no lie.

I woke around noon, judging by the light. Right. Maybe the pool guy, this whole mess, was what she was escaping from, and I was part of the escape. I was the normal relationship she could escape to. Him

236

showing up last night was just bad luck. A last time. That's when I saw the note on the floor, obviously shoved under the door while I slept.

Paul—
I couldn't let you leave without a goodbye, but my mother is dragging me out for last-minute college equipage and I haven't been alone long enough to sneak away to wake you and say the goodbye I want to say. Please keep in touch with
— The Weather Girl

After such knowledge, what forgiveness? Maybe she had thrown him out. Told him it was over; get lost. And waited to say a real goodbye to me. She had been involved in this unhealthy thing, and then I showed up, and she had broken it off. One thing was for sure. I'd need some experience to keep up with her in the sack. Pee, open door, check hall. No one. Her door was closed. I snuck into the service corridor and through it to her room. On the desk "A Room of One's Own" was open to this passage:

"…if through their incapacity to play football women are not going to be allowed to practice medicine…"

I sat in her chair for no few minutes. Feeling again the indignation on her behalf. No matter what else, this, too, was true. What to say? Everything that had brought us together was summed up in that passage.

Dear Ali
Just to say: I can't play football worth a damn, and I don't intend to let that keep me out of med school. If that's

what you want, don't let it keep you out either. I can't and won't believe this is goodbye. I'll be calling, and we'll be on the radio. And maybe again on the raft.

I thought about that last sentence, took it out, rewrote the note, put it back in again, and signed it:

Au revoir — Paul

I closed the book on it, so she'd be sure to see it. *The awful daring of a moment's surrender Which an age of prudence can never retract* I snuck back out to my room, shaved, showered, came down to find Dickie in padmasana position on the dining room floor. We made plans for stuff to bring to school, for the trip back. "I should stay long enough to thank your mother for the hospitality," I said.

"I'll tell her you said so," he said. "Ali wanted to see you again, but I have no idea what time they'll be back; she's won mother over again, so it could be tonight."

I really had to go. "I don't think I'll ever forget this visit, Dickie," I said.

He grinned. "You aren't the only one," he said.

I thought it the better part of valor to leave it at that.

...On the sidewalks of New York When I got back to the neighborhood the perpetual stickball game was of course still on. Markie Hymowitz couldn't let me pass without a ragging about her. "Where's the movie star, Paulie? Or is she a model?"

A very fine swan indeed

"Both," I said. *Schmuck.*

A quarter century later, a day after his New Rochelle high school gym class carried him to an ambulance, and minutes before I threaded a cardiac catheter into his femoral artery and up into his coronaries, Coach Mark Hymowitz asked me, "Hey, Paulie, that girl you showed up with that day, the real looker, the one her brother hit the ball off Steingut's Buick. Whatever happened to her?"

She was that memorable. The anesthetic was starting to take effect, so I just said to him, "Long story, Hymo. Complicated. I'll tell you when you wake up."

April 7, 1973,
12:30 PM – 2:00 PM

"Page from the Floor—Mamie's back, it's show time." We stopped in X-ray and looked at the films. "What do you see, Dr. McCulloch?"

"Opaque bilaterally from the diaphragmatic gutters to the fifth intercostal space."

"Very good." She had counted ribs down from the collarbone, for a landmark.

Marvin headed off to scope out the ER. The elevator creaked its way up. There was the usual three-step landing. The cage banged. I thought Ali's heart rattled; mine would have. A pleural tap is a tough procedure for a rookie. There was nothing I could say to her that wouldn't be condescending.

Mamie's breathing was an effort just to watch, even with the oxygen. I took her hand. "Mamie my love, Dr. Acheson and Dr. McCulloch and I are going to get you breathing again. Here's what we're going to do. We're going to numb up two spots on your back and we're going to put a very small needle into the big puddle of water around your lungs that's squeezing them in there and take it out so there isn't pressure on your lungs *Only from the fluid still actually inside the lungs* and it will only hurt at one part, and then only a little. OK dear?" She nodded, knowing this was a lie, eyes closed, like "What choice do I have?"

We went for the equipment tray. "You ready for this?" I asked her. "If not now, when?"

"I guess it is a revolution, kind of." We gloved up.

We sat Mamie up and all percussed Mamie's chest, then auscultated, making sure of our landmarks, using a pen to mark where we stopped hearing resonance and breath sounds.

"Katie, wipe some betadine around the spot; be generous. OK, good. First step, Mamie, we put in a load of Novocaine." I put my hand in hers. "You're going to feel a little stick and some itch when she puts in the first Novocaine . If you feel any pain after that you squeeze my hand." She nodded again. "OK, here we go. Katie, pop open an amp of Lidocaine." She did, and Ali drew it up. "Where are you going in?" I asked Ali. She pointed to a spot on Mamie's left back, just above where we estimated the diaphragm's downward curve to meet the chest wall. "Perfect," I said, and she inserted the little needle under Mamie's thin skin, rotating it and raising a bleb through which the rest of the anesthetic could painlessly go. Mamie jumped a tiny bit. "OK dear, that was the little stick. Now we wait a minute for the Novocaine to work. Another amp." Katie popped another ampoule of Lidocaine; Ali drew it up; going through the bleb, she squirted Lidocaine in all directions. "Another." In all, 4 amps of Lidocaine, squirted while going in, and while pulling out. "OK, this last one is for the money—you're going to try to push gently until you feel it give; then you're going to pull back a micro and try to numb the pleura." This was the hard part, and the part I had warned Mamie about. "Mamie, hold my hand tight and try not to move; Dr. Acheson is going to put in one more thing of Novocaine in a sensitive spot." She drew up the Lidocaine, breathed deeper than Mamie could, and did it. Mamie jumped slightly and squeezed my hand hard, and settled as the Lidocaine took effect.

"Now, hook up the…" From behind her, out of Mamie's sight, Ali twisted the big 14 gauge needle onto a 50cc syringe the size of a turkey baster. "Katie, line up some red- top tubes and a purple-top. Label them 'Pleural Fluid'. Same for the sterile bottles, and swab the tops of the bottles with betadine."

I checked everything; it looked as good as this could.

"OK, step two: Mamie, take my hand again. Dr. A., gently go in until you feel the membrane again, but this time go through with a little back pressure and stop pushing when you feel the resistance stop and pull back for fluid." No amount of Lidocaine will completely cancel out the feeling of a 14 gauge needle going through skin and muscle, and Mamie bucked a little and squeezed my hand half off. "Good, dear, you're doing well." They both were; there was a tiny pool of straw-colored, maybe slightly bloody fluid in the syringe. "Good," I said again. "Now pull back on the plunger. Katie, break out another syringe and be ready to take this one from Ali. You're going to very carefully and sterilely put a small gauge needle on the syringe and put samples in the culture bottles first, then two red-tops, and the purple-top." Marvin was back. He handed Ali the second syringe and she took off another 50cc. In all we got about 175cc from the left pleural space before the fluid stopped coming easily, and Mamie was straining less.

"Whoa," I said. "Enough; you don't want to suck lung up against the sharp end. Almost done this side, Mamie dear; let me go help Dr. Acheson now." To Ali: "You're going to slowly pull back out and Katie is going to whip a 4X4 full of betadine over the hole and you're going to apply pressure. Then you're going to tape up." She nodded, and smoothly backed the big needle out. Katie handed her the betadine-soaked gauze and she pushed it as hard as she could against the puncture site. There was sweat on her forehead. "That was beautifully done—so good you get to do it again immediately. See one, do two."

With Callie's help we turned Mamie around so Ali could use her right hand to get to Mamie's right back, percussed and auscultated again. This time Katie put in the Lidocaine (she'd done it before, on

Surgery), and I guided her through the tricky part numbing the pleura. More fluid, more bottles and tubes for the lab. I held Mamie's hand and let Ali order the equipment up from Katie.

"Let Katie do some pulling now," I said. She got nowhere at first, not having before felt the tension in a 50cc syringe pulling at a 14 gauge needle, but got the hang of it. Ali labeled tubes and bottles for her, betadined the culture bottles, spread out some 4X4s, sprinkled betadine liberally. We had Katie remove the needle and slapped on another pressure bandage.

Mamie was breathing well for the first time today, and was hopping mad. "I thought you were my friend," she said as we pulled the sterile gloves off.

"Me too," I said, "What, did that hurt more than I said?"

"Of course it did, but what I want to know is why you let a couple of nurses stick needles in my back." She had been sufficiently hypoxic to not recall the earlier introductions.

"Mamie, this is Dr. Acheson and Dr. McCulloch. Dr. Acheson is a senior medical student, she'll be a full-fledged intern in three months, and Dr. McCulloch is a junior medical student."

"No lie?"

"No lie, Mrs. Tolliver, my name is Alicia Acheson and Dr. Seitz should have introduced me or I should have introduced myself. And this is Dr. Katie McCulloch."

"Well now, is that ever special. I thought about being a doctor when I was your age. I thought I'd never see it, women doctors. I lived to see that, Praise God. There any black women doctors?"

"Two, in my class," Katie said.

I looked at my watch. "She has to go and get a last blood sample. Leave in the butterfly."

We had to get the specimens to the lab; Mamie had no fever but there was always the possibility of infection and we'd want to know soonest. I went; Ali wrote the chart note. When I got back down Ali had the note for me to countersign:

4/7/73 Pleural tap yielded 175cc of straw-colored fluid, slightly blood-tinged, left, 150cc right. Fluids sent for electrolytes, cells, cultures X3. Patient tolerated procedure well — Alicia Acheson, MS4

I countersigned it. "Very well done, " I said.

"You're a good teacher," she said.

"I try to be," I said. "It's one of the few good things about this job. Mostly it's blindingly routine, and lonely. I mean, if it was just me and Marvin and another intern, I would have done that all by myself, and neither Mamie nor Callie is much of a conversationalist. We always say students double the work, but actually they double the companionship."

"Pretty scary, sticking a big pipe like that into someone's chest." She pushed some hair back; her forehead was still wet.

"Yeah, and you did it twice, perfectly..........Look, a year ago I was where you are. Now I've stuck so many sharp things into so many places I can't count them all. They're all stories, though."

"Like the time you taught your college roommate's kid sister how to do a pleural tap."

"No. That one's not going to be a story."

"Do you realize," she checked her watch, "This is the first conversation we've had in over six hours without any banter, jargon or wising off?"

September 1965 – March 5, 1967

Dickie called a few days later. He was still breaking in the MG and was short of the thousand miles. He couldn't use expressways to get to Schenectady, so he proposed meeting me at one of the railroad stations along the Hudson and driving up the Post Road. Since our trunks were going Railway Express (and wouldn't have fit in the MG) this sounded like fun. He picked me up in Peekskill and we headed north through the Highlands, the panorama the Hudson River School artists had painted a century before, dotted with Robber Baron mansions.

"How's Ali?" I asked.

"Off to orientation at Wellsmith, with apparently a last blessing from you. She showed me the note. You really think she can make it into med school?"

"Why the hell not?"

"I don't know what to think. I'm just making sure you're not blowing sunshine up her ass."

"I can always catch a train in the next town, Dickie."

"Whoa, Jesus but you're touchy."

"You're suggesting I'd lie to her to, like, what...?"

"I'm her brother. This is my job."

"I'm not Dougie."

"OK, chess players don't bluff, got it. But it's a big challenge, Paul. I know the kind of shit she's had to put up with from the old man, it

251

didn't just start when you showed up, and you're not the only one she talks to. I don't want to see her fail, especially not because of prejudice against women. She can't afford it."

"You're right, Dickie, I'm sorry I…"

"No, I put it badly. Not seriously enough. I touched a nerve." And he grinned slightly.

"What?"

"Nothing."

"I think she has the stuff, anyway as much as I have. She certainly has the brains. That much I know. The crucial thing, they say, is Organic Chem. If she can get through that, she can do it. Period. I wonder if I can." It was a glorious day, with glorious views. I had never sat in the front of a sports car before. "It feels like my ass is right down on the road."

"It's not sprung like an American car; the suspension's so tight you feel every curve, every bump. You'll see."

"I already see." *Every curve, every bump*

"I mean when you drive it."

"You know I don't drive."

"You can, up here. Get a permit and I'll teach you, Govinda. I wonder if we'll be in Schenectady in time for dinner."

I pulled out the map, added up the miles, knowing he could do at most 50, and did the math. "We'll make it by half an hour, maybe fifteen minutes with traffic in Albany."

"You did that in your head?"

"Distance equals rate times time, solve for time."

"But you did it in your head. Faster than I could with a slide rule."

"So? I'm a Brain."

"It took you seconds, you know that?"

"I have a feel for numbers. There are tricks. To multiply by 5, add a zero and divide by 2. To multiply by 7, multiply by 5, multiply by 2, add the results. Break it down into easy steps."

"Easy for you."

"Just a parlor trick."

"A useful one I bet." Another prophetic statement.

In Albany we had a surprise. Damned if a downtown theater wasn't playing *A Man and a Woman*.

"We have to see this," Dickie said. "All the European counselors said I have to see this. We can come back later, put some more miles on the car."

The oldest upperclass dorms at Nott dated, picturesquely, to 1804; those rooms were prized despite their age because the dorm sophomores usually ended up in faced the bell tower of St. Jude's (by no coincidence, patron saint of lost causes) RC Church. Forget sleeping in Sundays and Saints' Days. Dickie's wasn't the only MG in the lot. We hauled the small stuff upstairs and went after the trunks. We were now entitled to eat at the upperclass dining room, where we found Eli, traded news of summer. He was unusually quiet about it, and appalled at Dickie's report of his spirituosexual quest.

"That's disgusting," he said.

"To the Western religious mind, maybe," Dickie said.

"It does remind me, though. Paul, I assume you want to continue the show."

I had been turning this over in my mind. The Weather Girl segment was a way to keep in contact with her, but at a distance. See how things went. "I do."

"Then we have to talk about the Weather Girl. Ever since I showed up here I've been getting questions, how's the Weather Girl, are you still going to have the Weather Girl, when can we meet the Weather Girl…"

"I don't think there's a problem; she just started at Wellsmith. We just have to find a phone there…"

"That isn't the problem. The problem is I'm more and more uncomfortable with it."

"With what?"

"How sexualized it's becoming."

"There has never been anything in the segment…"

"I know; it isn't her, it isn't you, it's the audience."

"We don't control that, Eli."

"We don't have to encourage it."

"Encourage what? Listening to the voice of a very intelligent woman making literary references and showing that girls have the same concerns and intelligence that men have? I'm sure she's fully clothed when we're talking, Eli. And I can guarantee feminist content; I know what she's been reading over the summer."

"Who is she, exactly?"

"My sister, "Dickie said.

"Oh. I'm sorry if I…never mind."

"De nada, Eli. Uh, Eli, we were thinking of going over to Albany to see *A Man and a Woman*. You in?"

"I don't…"

"It isn't pornographic, Eli."

"……I guess."

"Friday."

I was in three courses plus Organic, but Orgainc consumed everything. It was a six-credit course at Nott, with two labs and four lectures a week. Grueling is the kindest thing one could say about the Organic schedule, and it left little time for anything else. Much of it was brute memorization, but for sheer brute memorization it couldn't beat Comparative Anatomy, dissecting representative animals from the most primitive (shark) to the most advanced (mammal) phyla, learning the body plans and variations underlying evolutionary thinking. Imagine having to memorize the New York subway system, learning by digging up each tunnel, assuming you also had a time machine and did it in the 1910's, 20's, 30's 40's and 50's. Oh: also two labs per week, plus whatever extra time you needed to complete the dissections. Most of the week I smelled like either a mortuary or a duPont plant. A's in these courses got you into med school. B's might. C and below, don't bother applying. It was that simple.

Professor Uppenough (pronounced "Upenow", the jokes were legion, make up your own)—Uppie—was an enthusiast. "It's called Organic Chemistry, gentlemen, because it is the chemistry of life. All known life is based on the carbon atom's ability to form four bonds. This simple property enables carbon to form a tremendous variety of compounds with very interesting properties according to a few simple rules. In the weeks to come you will learn these rules." He turned to the board. "Let us set to work."

Things hadn't cranked up to full blast by Friday, so we headed for Albany to see what all the fuss over *A Man and a Woman* was about. More miles on the MG, Eli scrunched in the back. While we stood in line for tickets I told them about the first day in Organic.

"You really believe that?" Eli said. "That organic chemistry explains life?"

"It explains the mechanics of living things. The chemistry underneath it."

People in nearby seats shushed us; the famous samba theme was coming on. Anouk Aimee and Jean-Louis Trintignant performed the timeless dance of attraction against a background of international road racing and rallye driving; all I could think of was how much Anouk Aimee reminded me of Alicia Acheson without looking anything like her. Luckily there was little plot to follow, *Boy meets Girl, Boy loses Girl because Girl can't forget Other Boy, Boy gets Girl by making all the right moves— UN HOMME ET UNE FEMME as seen by a seventeen year old* but I thought if Eli had trouble with the Weather Girl this was going to be a long night. I was right, but the problem came from an unexpected direction.

"You just saw that movie. You think chemistry explains that? The look on her face when he shows up at the train, you think chemistry explains that?"

"At one level, sure. It doesn't explain the experience of it, of life. I know that." *Don't I know* With the MG's top down the wind blew away any attempt at conversation until we got back to the dorm.

"You think chemistry explains anything about life?"

"Yeah, Eli, the mechanisms. Illness, disease. I know how the MG's engine works but I know that doesn't explain how I'll feel when I drive it. Like Duroc says, 'You feel the engine through your whole body'. "

"So you're going to learn to drive, Govinda?"

"Maybe, Dickie."

"Knowing how an engine works means knowing that somebody made it, right?"

"Right."

"So, knowing the intricacies of organic chem, biochem, you know there must be a Creator."

"No. I know that is one hypothesis. An engine is made of inorganic material. Iron, aluminum, they don't have the chemical properties of carbon and organic molecules. Organic chem is different from inorganic. Organic molecules can make more of themselves, all by themselves. I don't see a need for a Creator."

"Where do you stand on this?" he asked Dickie.

"I stand where I see that this is the kind of argument that has led to bloodshed. That the universe is whatever it is, and man is whatever he is, and he should seek peace with himself and whatever is."

"Seek peace. Not truth."

"Peace and truth are one."

"What if they aren't?"

Which is when Parker and a bunch of Phi Delts walked into the lounge. "Evening gentlemen," Dickie said as Eli and I went to Red Alert, "To what do we owe the honor?"

"Came to deliver a piece of news, Dickie. Morgan isn't back. We just heard he joined the Marines a month ago."

Silence.

"We thought you'd want to know."

That night I had a dream. I was on the Brighton line and the doors opened and Ali was there. "Do you think you know what you're doing?" she said.

"You think chemistry explains anything about life?" On some level I *think I did.*

We started up McCone and Seitz again, but the lightness was gone. Eli was struggling with something, tormented by something. "We can't do the Weather Girl, Paul. I can't. I'm sorry."

"It's OK, Eli. You do the show. I'm up to my ass in work." *On the minus side it got me out of contact with Ali On the plus side it got me out of contact with Ali But I had to call her*

Dickie meditated. And meditated. And meditated. He also drank, but still in moderation.

"It's not your fault, Dickie. He was well on his way to flunking out already."

Silence.

"Paul! It's been weeks. I thought you'd joined the football team."

"Organic chem, Ali. Comparative Anatomy. Ten hours of lab a week. It's killing me. Eating me alive. You'll see. Ali, there's another reason. McCone's gone nuts over something; he's had a religious, I don't know…it's his show, and he says no more Weather Girl."

"What…the…hell."

"I know. I can't shift him. He doesn't even know who you are, Ali. He maybe saw you once, the first day of school last year, it isn't you, it's any whiff of…sex. It's more of the same shit you…"

"Yeah. Where do you stand on this, Paul?"

"You have to ask?"

"No, I'm just mad. Tell me something. Did you…?"

"What? Did I what?" *Did you try to come to my room that night*

"Nothing."

Dickie's drinking went from moderate to heavy.

I had an idea. "Dickie. I took the test. I got a learner's permit. You're going to teach me to drive. You're going to need a wingman." He looked up. And grinned. "Good going, Govinda. And you're going to need a license too, because by bus it's four hours to Northampton and four back and no place you can stay so if you're ever going to visit my sister you'll have to go by car because if not by the time you get there it'll be time to leave."

We started out in a parking lot in an empty mall that Sunday, and graduated to streets. He just needed something to do to set the karmic balance right. "Did you know," he said, "It was me taught Ali to drive." But he wasn't just teaching me to drive, he was, intentionally or not, teaching me to *incorporate* what I learned, the chemistry of thought into action. *The alchemy*

His drinking slowed but did not stop. Not entirely. On his desk I found a note: "There are questions we could never evade if it weren't for our Selves." One of the "Zurau Aphorisms".

A letter from Ali:

Dear Paul,

Don't share this letter; I think I'd prefer it to be between us. Orientation was great; I love it here, the chance to wake up every day and have my mind stretched. I might even put up with the field hockey. I didn't pass out of tennis, no thanks to you! I met my advisor, and when I told her about thinking about being pre-med she warned me about the odds. When I didn't scare, she made me tea. I should introduce her to your grandmother, who I want you to send my special regards. And, yes, thanks.

Here's the first burr under the saddle, and I want you to know about this. This evening we had a compulsory (!!) frosh mixer with Amherst. We had to get cards punched just like you did for fraternity rush. I don't know what the thinking is behind this, or maybe I don't want to know. Anyway, had to go. I didn't want to. I don't want to meet anyone else. So here's what I did: (1) I wore heels, which as I expected made me a head taller than 90% of the boys in the room and (2) I carried a book, and why do things by halves (do I ever?) I brought "Labyrinths". Maybe should have brought the Woolf, but any boy who got past that would be pretty special. I figured the risk was pretty low. There's only one Paul Seitz. I reread Borges all night and thought of you.

Write me — Ali

And just like that, the fire was relit. Only I wondered:

Dear Ali

Not much time; I'm plowed under with lab work; this may smell of formaldehyde. I was thinking, after I finished laughing, if I were an Amherst Froshie, would I have had the nerve to approach you? I don't know.

— Paul

And this continued to bother me.

It was illegal for a student driver to drive over the road test course, but not to be a passenger in a car driving over it. "Be careful," Dickie said, "They try to trick you, tell you to take the 'next available left' and the next *possible* left is one way the wrong way; you go to the next one after. Shit like that."

The examiner was impressed that I was going to take the test in a stick shift car. "It's my roommate's," I said.

"You at Nott?"

"Yeah."

"Where do you live?"

"Brooklyn."

"You won't be able to drive there for another six months. If you pass."

I told him I knew. I passed.

Naomi Ackerman was going to Hunter, commuting from home. I got her phone number from Information. She was pretty surprised when I called, and I was about equally surprised when she said she'd go out with me. Hell, I was surprised I'd had the nerve to call her. Well, I went to an out-of-town college, a Big Deal in the neighborhood.

"Starting at the top of your wish list," Sam said. It was a warm mid-October night. I'd startled a New York Central conductor when he came to collect my ticket; I was dissecting a dogfish shark head at the time, in a shoebox on my lap. My mother and grandmother weren't too crazy about having it in the refrigerator either.

"It's the only way I have time to get home," I said.

"How's your roommate?"

"Fine," I lied.

"And his sister?"

"I don't really know. Off to Wellsmith."

"Were you able to help her out?"

"I think you really helped her, Grandma. She asked me to send her special regards."

"When?"

"…In a letter."

"So you do know."

"Only sort of."

"And you're going out with a girl here, tomorrow night."

"That's the idea."

It was the idea, and I tried to imagine explaining my reasoning. *You see Grandma I'm infatuated with the other girl, nuts about her in fact, but she's been sleeping with a grown man, so if I'm ever going to have a shot with her I have to get some sexual experience, so I'm going out with my grammar school crush so I can maybe try some moves out on her.* The wonder is, it made perfect sense at the time. There is a saying in Yiddish: "Wenn der Putz steht, ligt der Sechel in Drerd," which means, "When the penis stands up, wisdom goes to hell". It might as well mean, "A hopelessly naïve and aroused adolescent boy can rationalize anything". *There are questions we could never evade were it not for our Selves.*

Here's what happened, in brief. I met Naomi at her parents', passed the usual fatherly scrutiny as she delayed her entrance by the standard ten minutes, and took her to see *A Man and A Woman* in Manhattan. Naomi was no dummy, not by any means; I found myself having a better time than I had planned to have, and was feeling more and more queasy about my project. It is so simple, but I could not have put this together at the time. I was seventeen. A young seventeen. She was in fact a few months older than me; maybe just eighteen to my seventeen-and-a-half. Anyway, with Ali, we'd met as people, not as dates. I'd known Naomi at school only at ogling and moping distance. It was only in the course of the evening that she was becoming a human being to me. I am not proud of this. Or of what followed. We walked, we talked on the subway. She told me, to my immense shock, that she had been aware of my regard, and had always hoped I'd ask her out and wondered why I never had. The night continued warm; we walked along the boardwalk, looking out to sea, listening to the gulls' cries, and I maneuvered her into a ride on the Wonder Wheel. I settled us into the seats, pulled in the safety bar. And slipped my arm around her. The ride began, with its dizzying panorama of New York, rising to view the entire city, falling back to the purlieus of the Coney Island Bowery. I pulled her closer. On the third circuit, the great wheel stopped. The tiny annunciator in the cab buzzed; a voice said, "Sorry folks, we're having a problem down here. Just sit tight, it'll be a few minutes and we'll have it running again." Jackpot! I pulled her to me, the face I'd adored for seven years, brought my other hand over the nylon-clad knee I'd longed to touch for five of those seven years, and she stiffened ever so slightly and said, "Paul, I want you to know, I've always trusted you." Images of deflating balloons, stalled locomotives, collapsing towers. I relaxed my arm, retreated; at length the wheel resumed its revolutions, took us back to earth, to her home, where we kissed each other on the cheek and she told me to call again, she'd had a wonderful time.

Dickie about split a gut laughing. "She meant she trusted you to make a good job of it. Idiot." *Which is what your sister calls me* We were doing advanced driving lessons, high speed highway driving on lonely stretches of the partially completed Northway, the Albany-to-Montreal section of I-87. The mountains were spectacular, but clouds were lowering and the trees were bare; it would be snowing hard soon. "Govinda, we really have to get serious about Sour Hour." *Which is how I knew he wouldn't tell her*

The Necturus. In CAT lab we had moved up to amphibians. In Organic, Alkanes, Cycloalkanes, Atomic Orbital Models, Alkenes.

Sour Hour was the Ladies Drink Free time in Saratoga, seat of Slidell College (Women). It seemed to me at that time that drinking was an athletic contest to these people, this society. A route to respect. And for the first time in my life, I was in a place where being smart and funny were not. And, outsider by age, class, and ethnicity, those were my only assets. I didn't want to throw them away; they were all I had. The first expeditions were disasters. Girls came to the bars in groups of two, minimum, for the same reason we did. Too drunk to walk, two could prop each other up. Dickie had no trouble charming any one of them; my appeal proved more elusive. Several times, over two weeks. Whether I spoke or kept silent, the results were the same. I was able to analyze the situation quite easily. "I think, Dickie, that there are two components to our problem. First, you go for girls with the same background as you. Suburban. Second, they aren't enchanted by my exotic urban background the way you are."

"That and the fact that you don't drink." He was slumped against the passenger door as he said this. "Means you're not sociable. Also suggests to them that you're trying to get them drunk while you stay sober. Suggests possible attempts to take advantage of their putative virtue."

I thought about this for some little time. "I was not aware of that. I learn something new every day. But I don't like drinking, don't like beer, can't afford it either. And one of us has to be sober enough to drive. Maybe you should do this alone for a while. I have work anyway. I have a turtle to dissect." But he was asleep.

Love was what they needed. Sex was what they would settle for. Drunk was what they got.

In the morning there was a message on the door for Dickie: "Riley's dead. Call me immediately." Dickie was ferociously hung over; I called her.

"I loved that dog, Paul. He was the best gift I ever got. I took care of him…I wanted to be a vet, until I got the idea I could be a doctor. God, I loved that dog."

"He loved you, Ali. He guarded you."

"He was my friend. And my father killed him."

"What?"

"I said, Father killed him."

"Like, ran over him accidentally in the drive…?"

"No, took him to the vet and had him put down."

"Why?"

"They said his arthritis was getting worse; I think he was just more than they wanted to take care of. I said, I was the one that took care of him. I can't talk anymore. Tell Dickie. He loved Riley too."

That was the first time I ever heard her say she didn't want to talk further; it scared me. I woke Dickie, and through the fog he said, "She's really pretty cool, but…OK, we have to go see her. You're going to have to do the driving, Govinda. I need aspirin, coffee and fluids."

264

The lessons had been just in time.

Through hangover fog, thick-voiced, Dickie said, "She started out wanting to be a vet. She practiced on Riley when she was little, and he let her wrap him in gauze. The cat wouldn't let her."

I imagined the little girl wrapping gauze around the big, patient dog. The little car flew; I looked down at the speedometer and found it up to 80, 85, 90, without knowing how it got there. Where the cops were I'll ever know. We were in Northampton in under two hours. Dickie was starting to recover; we took her out to a lunch, found a booth. She told him what had happened.

"They just called and told you?"

"Yes. I am—we are—supposed to go home for Thanksgiving and they didn't want me to just come home and find no Riley."

"That's nice of them."

I kept quiet, trying to melt into the leatherette.

"Will you still come home?" Dickie asked her.

"Oh, yeah. I'd been thinking about when to tell them straight out to forget about me ever making a debut, and this looked to be the time."

"Don't just do it out of anger. Don't just be angry."

"That's why I decided against. I'll be angry, Dickie, but cool. I have a week to rehearse. But I can't rehearse his lines, so this can't be the time to drop the big one. I'll save that for another time, or they'll just think it's me being angry about Riley, and they can discount it. I'll have to postpone that. Damn. I'd like to have that over with. Damn him."

"Coffee," Dickie said, "And keep it coming."

"Burger, fries, coffee," I said.

"BLT down," she said, "And coffee."

It was a grim lunch. She thanked us for coming.

"Worried for nothing," I said. "You were right, she's gotten pretty cool here."

"It's my father I'm worried for. She's going to fucking kill him. You maybe don't understand about the dog."

"I think I maybe do understand. You in shape to drive?"

"You drive, Govinda. Get good at it."

I think the plan started to form in his mind that day.

They called me Thanksgiving Day to tell me what happened; put another way, two Organic and three CAT labs later.

"Mother picked me up at the bus in Stamford," Ali said, "And she was already nervous, said stuff like 'It had to be done, Alicia, the poor animal was suffering'. 'Not this past summer,' I said. 'Alicia, he was pining for you. (Here she started imitating their voices) He hung around me like he hung around you, but I have no time for that'. 'So this is my fault somehow?' I said, and she just made some noncommittal noise to that. So we come down to dinner and he says Hello Alicia I'm sorry about the dog but he was suffering and I think pining for you and I realized they had settled on a story, you know?"

The words were just piling out of her, as if she was racing against her emotions.

"So I said I had come home for just one reason, and that was to tell him that he was a miserable excuse for a father and a miserable excuse for a human being and he turned purple and said he didn't regret killing Riley, he'd killed a lot more than that and I said if there was no difference for him between a German soldier and a defenseless dog (she paused for a brief sob) he should be ashamed of that Navy Cross not proud of it, I sure was, and he said Is this where you stage one of your walkouts and I said no, not anymore, if he couldn't stand it he could leave, and he said you know you're grounded for the rest of this holiday and Christmas too and I told him I didn't give a damn I had enough

266

work to do because I wrote that paper about The Scarlet Letter and got an A and they asked me if I was interested in majoring in English but I was going to be pre-med and he really exploded then, slammed his glass down and said no daughter of his was going to spend four years in some hospital in Harlem or somewhere doing God knows what and I told him I wasn't asking anyone's permission, that my advisor and an actual pre-med think I have the stuff and he said who and I told him you, Paul, and oh by the way you had told me I hadn't lost that chess game, not in three moves or any other number, and speaking of numbers I had his."

"Where was your mother during all this?"

"Right there. Quiet mostly. He had the carving knife in his hand and I think she was worried what he'd do with it. I wasn't. Let him kill himself, for all I care."

"Ali…"

"Anyway my mother says, when I brought up med school, 'Richard, if she goes to medical school she stands a good chance of marrying a doctor.' I was going to unload on her, too, but I realized she was trying to calm him down. Well, she has to live with him. You know what? It worked. He got himself under control, harrumphed a few times, said I don't know who you think will pay for that young lady and I said loans if I had to, and pay it back when my trust comes due, because I never wanted another thing from him, the only thing he'd ever given me that I liked was Riley and he'd found a way to take that back. Med school is covered, Paul. No worries there. I…"

What did she mean, med school was covered? Chaskis? Blackmail? Was she still seeing him?

"…he was so angry. *What had she been saying? Never mind*

"Then what?"

"He turned red, purple, took a drink. Asked me if that was all I had to say and I told him that about covered it and I started eating dinner."

"Jesus, Ali."

"Finished it, too. Pretty quiet. I think Mother cried a little. Didn't she, Dickie?" I had forgotten he was on the line too.

"A little."

"You know, if I'd told him about the coming out thing and then he'd killed Riley I would have figured it was punishment, revenge, but it was for no more reason than they didn't want to be bothered feeding him. That's how much they care, Dickie."

"So are you OK?"

"OK? What does OK mean?"

I'll never see that house again, I thought. I was wrong. But any ideas of meeting her in the City, or of being invited for Christmas, were gone.

I was elated for her, disgusted...and sympathetic. In turn. She needed me; my original plan of getting her away from the pool guy was the right course. When she graduated med school, I'd be a year ahead, we could get married, I'd be getting a salary a year ahead of her, begin paying the loans off. Or we could erase the loans by going to some underserved remote town, which would get her away from...disgust alternated with restless planning. Crazy? I was not yet eighteen. I could have maybe discussed this with a father. Discussing it with my mother or grandmother seemed out of the question. That left Sam.

"Could work," he said. "You really think she's sleeping with this guy? Or was?"

"I don't know for sure," I lied. "But I want to act like it's true, to be sure. It'll get me the necessary experience." These were the years of the rumors of the Kennedy Brothers sleeping with Marilyn Monroe before her suicide, if it was suicide; I figured I was rescuing her from upper class behavior. Working Class Hero.

268

"Well, a girl looks like that, plays chess like that, it's worth a try. Worst thing can happen, you get laid. How can you lose?" Years later, this would be called, by Sam, Analysis of Downside Risk. "You want experience, try Maxine Cohen."

Maxine! Second runner-up in the high school longing list. Something of a reputation, for the time and place. "You know where she lives?"

"Somewhere in Gravesend, one of the numbered streets. I don't know exactly."

I got out the Brooklyn phone book. There were 37 pages of Cohens. I got a ruler and went down the pages one line at a time, copying down every Cohen with an address on a Gravesend numbered street. There were over a hundred, that I could whittle down to 75. I went to work.

"Operator, I'd like to place a Person-to-Person call to Maxine Cohen at…" and I'd give the number. After four or five "No one by that name here"'s, the operator said, "Look, kid, I know what you're doing, I bet you think you're the first one to think of it, and I can't stop you, but how many numbers do you have?"

"About seventy left."

"Seventy. Look, hang up, wait two minutes, call again, distribute the work, OK? And good luck, I hope you find her."

Her number was 46th on the list; I hung up and called back while they called her to the phone. Total cost: Zero. My, but I was clever. I apologized for the short notice, considered really rude at that time, but I was only in town for a limited time. And damn if she didn't agree to come out with me Saturday afternoon. Not the prime Saturday night slot, but great for short notice.

It was cold but she wanted to walk, so we took a stroll in Central Park, then down to Rockefeller Center to see the skaters and on down

Fifth Avenue to see the store windows, then across 34th to Macys. Talked about the old days, where so-and-so was now. *God I wish this was Ali* I took her hand, she didn't object; I put my arm around her, she didn't pull away. The kiss goodbye was a real kiss, on the lips. No tongues.

Alkynes, Alkadienes, Nucleophilic Displacement and Elimination Reactions, Alkyl, Cycloalkyl, Alkenyl, and Alkenyl Halides, Organometallic Compounds.

Alcohols and Ethers.

Just like in the war movies, my last mission as wingman was the hairiest. We walked into the Lead Balloon and behind the door the place was a wall of noise. We pushed through a mob of Dartmouth, Williams and Nott jackets to the bar to give the market the once-over. Reconnaissance was brief; Dickie locked onto a target in a far corner virtually instantaneously and for instantly comprehensible reasons. Her long black hair in a plait, wearing a sari, in Saratoga in 1965 she was both totally out of place and a homing beacon for Richard Acheson III, apprentice Buddhist. The sullen girl with her was tall and blonde and looked like she should be carrying a tennis press. She was already half bagged. There was a drink in front of her, not a beer.

"May we sit and get better acquainted?" Dickie asked the girl in the sari. "I'm Richard Acheson. Dickie."

"I'm Bitsy Reade," the blonde girl said. Dickie didn't take his eyes off the girl in the sari. "This is Paul Seitz," he said. "And you are?"

"Bina."

"Just Bina?"

"Visarasantha." Her accent was British yet not British exactly.

"Oh good," Bitsy said. "I get the sidekick."

270

"Can I get you a drink?" I asked her.

"I already have one."

"So you have."

"I've already had three."

"Too many for me to catch up with. I'm driving."

She shrugged. "Aren't you the good boy." Dickie and Bina were deep in conversation; he'd quoted the Upanishads to her and this and his offhand manner *the part of Connecticut I come from, we all know the Upanishads by heart* had put her completely at ease. It was a marvel. Bitsy was another matter.

"You're at Slidell."

"No, I'm at UCLA. Of course I'm at Slidell." She took a swig.

"Look, I'm just trying to be pleasant."

She leaned closer to me. "And I'm trying to swallow the fact that I just lost a preppie like Dickie Acheson to my social loser roommate." She swallowed some more of her drink, too.

"She's your roommate?"

"My, but you're quick. Yes, she's my roommate. The only one who'll room with me. I keep late hours and I'm not always sober. Or discreet."

"No, well, I can keep a secret."

"Want to know another one?"

"Sure."

"I'm pretty polluted."

"I'd never have guessed."

"Jesus. Sarcasm. If you want some action you're going to have to try harder." She stood up. And sat down again, unsteadily.

"Are you going to need a ride home?"

"I don't know. Maybe. Are you going to give me a ride home, Nottman?"

"If you want." *That's an old old joke*

271

"When I want."

"When you want."

"You're a good sidekick."

I tapped Dickie's shoulder. "Keys."

He unlocked his eyes from Bina and flipped me the MG keys. "Nice going," he said.

"I'm going to have one more," she said, "And then you can take me home. This place is starting to depress me. Get me a vodka tonic." When I hesitated she handed me a five. "Take it out of this"

I got carded but brought her the drink. It smelled like the lab. She chugged it. She got up. "I'm going to take your arm, Nottman," she said, and I guided us through the wall of sound. The sudden quiet when the door shut behind us was startling; there had been a muffling fall of snow. I maneuvered us to the car; she told me which House. I asked her, "Are you going to heave?"

"No, Sir Galahad, I'm not. I'm going to pass out. Probably." I helped her into the car as best I could, exposing a great deal of leg in the process. She was past caring. She was also as good as her word; by the time we'd gone a block she was out cold. So, now what? *Nah. You have to be kidding* Once at her House I was stumped. How to get her inside? And what then? Leave her passed out in a lounge? Men weren't allowed above the first floor of a Slidell House any more than women were at a Nott dorm. I went in to reconnoiter, making the choice to turn off the ignition and with it the heater rather than risk her waking up and deciding to take a drive. Inside a mousy-looking girl was sitting behind a desk.

"Can I help you? Who are you here for?"

"Bitsy Reade."

She made a face. "She's out drinking somewhere. You missed her."

"No, you don't understand. She's done drinking; she's passed out in my car. I need help getting her in out of the cold."

"You son of a bitch."

"How am I a son of a bitch?"

"You have some nerve taking her out drinking and bringing her back in that condition…"

"No, you have this wrong. My roommate is back at the Balloon talking to her roommate…"

"To Bina?"

"Yeah, Bina…"

"Bina is talking to a guy?"

"Last I saw. Must still be. It's his car."

"Is your roommate Indian?"

"No, an aspiring Asian Studies major."

By this time we were at the car, Bitsy slumped against the passenger side door. "She's majoring in alcoholism," Minnie Mouse said. "OK, how do you want to do this?"

"Open the door, catch her head, grab her bag; I'll get her under her arms. When I have her out we each take her under one arm and see if she revives enough to walk, walk her in if she doesn't."

"You've done this before."

"No, I've had a mile of icy driving to think about it."

It worked, but Bitsy was completely out; her head lolled. We got her to the lounge at the foot of the staircase, which bore a curious resemblance to the one chez Acheson; this was a summer mansion redone as a dormitory. I started to lower my side of Bitsy into a chair, but my helper said, "Oh no, we can't leave her here, we have to get her to her room."

"We? Can't you call someone from upstairs?"

"They're all out. I would be too, but it's my night on the duty desk. You'll have to help me get her up to her room."

"I seem to recall a rule about that. I'd be in as much trouble if we're caught as she'd be. And you."

"There's no one to catch you but me. And I doubt it's the most serious rule you'll have broken tonight."

"Meaning what?"

"Just help me get her upstairs, please."

"Sure. What the hell." We resumed the wounded march, pausing to try, and fail, to pick up her shoes when they dropped off. It was easier without. She stirred slightly, her eyes fluttered when we dumped her on her bed; I remembered something and tipped her on her side, "So she won't aspirate if she barfs," I said.

"Well," Minnie Mouse said, "That was fun."

"Yeah. She's been a whole lot more fun since she passed out."

"I just bet. Bastard."

"Look, what are you insinuating?"

"I think it's clear enough. I'll give you this, you did a much better job of getting her clothes back on her than they usually do, every button in place, and you were decent enough not to just dump her on the porch, which is what they usually do in warmer weather, or just dump her and honk, which is what they do when it's cold."

"Jesus, woman, you have this completely wrong." I was so angry I walked out and down the stairs, but I found her shoes and stopped to bring them back up. "Here. More points for me."

"You didn't…"

"Call me a romantic, I prefer women to be conscious. What I meant when I said she was more fun passed out is that she was unbelievably obnoxious before."

"She's a nasty drunk."

"I'll say."

"I owe you an apology."

"You sure as hell do. Christ. What kind of stuff have you seen…"

"I told you."

"Yeah. I guess you did." We walked down to the desk.

"She's been destroying herself since her coming out party *Oh hell* …Look, I'm really sorry," she said.

"It's OK."

"No, I mean you aren't finished yet. You have to check her back in." She took out a box of index cards, exactly like a library card catalog drawer, and shuffled until she found:

Reade, Barbara (Bitsy)

Out: Date: <u>12/4/65</u>   Time: <u>6:00 PM</u>

With: <u>Albert Myles</u>

Address: <u>Box 217, Williams College, Williamstn, Mass.</u>

Destination: <u>Downtown Saratoga Springs</u>

Signature <u>Albert Myles</u>

Estimated Return: <u>12 AM</u>

Actual Return _____

Signature: _____

"You have to be joking. *I want to live in the library* You each have a card, and guys check you in and out like library books?"

She shrugged.

"And you go along with this?"

"It's for our safety."

"To protect you from the likes of me."

"Yes. Or anyway to protect Bitsy."

"Yeah, that's working well. You don't find this demeaning? I do."

"Just sign the card, Albert." She filled in the time, 10 PM.

"Only one problem. I'm not Albert Myles."

"Yeah, I kind of figured that."

"I mean I'm not the guy who signed her out. I wouldn't have."

"I doubt there is an Albert Myles. If there is, he dumped her. Just sign it, or she'll have to. Or I will."

"You go right ahead. I won't be a party to this." I walked out, started up the car, looked over at the passenger seat for anything that might have fallen out of her coat or pocketbook. Nothing. There was the gentle snowfall, patiently beginning to fill the streets. *Was this what Ali was fighting to escape, what she would be if she lost the fight? Jesus, anything to escape this waste. She had to be freed from the depredations of wealth.* And this: *If this is how our society treats its wealthy, what must it be doing to the poorest?*

I went back to the Lead Balloon to find Dickie nursing the dregs of a single beer, deep in conversation with Bina. I told them what happened. Dickie tried hard not to laugh, just barely succeeded. Bina thanked me gravely. There was an Albert, she said, or anyway a guy, he had indeed dumped her, and she had returned to the House determined to get smashed. Bina had come out with her, faut de mieux, to try to keep her from as much harm as possible. I rode the rear bench for a return trip to the House. The mousy girl was surprised to see me again, more surprised when Bina backed my story.

Now Dickie had her address and phone number without embarrassing her by asking. "I owe you," he said, as the wipers tried and failed to cope with the snow. "It was the best thing that happened tonight, hell, all semester, me meeting Bina."

"The best thing that happened tonight," I said, "Was that Tipsy Bitsy didn't yark in the car." *The best thing that's happened tonight is that you're driving back to Schenectady, stone sober*

Aldehydes and Ketones. Reactions at the Carbonyl Group. Unsaturated and Polycarbonyl Compounds; Reactions Involving the Substituent Groups.

Dickie's relationship with Bina was one of mutual fascination. Bina was the daughter of an Indian diplomat, at the time posted to the United Nations in New York; she had lived in England, Czechoslovakia (which gave us a connection), Japan and Egypt. "I'm collecting continents," she said. Dickie had told her about his interest in Tibetan Buddhism within the first fifteen minutes at the Lead Balloon, and she was able to give him some details about the growing Tibetan center at Dharamsala, seat of the exiled Dalai Lama after the 1959 revolt, of which he'd had only the sketchiest notion. And began informing him about life in India, and what a westerner faced there. He, in turn, could inform her about what she faced if she pursued her dream of living in Europe or North America. She had been wearing Indian dress that night because she had been at an International Night get-together, featuring exchange students from nearby colleges (and, to help fill the room, high schools); she had been at the Lead Balloon only to try to protect her roommate, whose binges often ended in post-midnight suicide threats, raging denunciations or tearful terror of pregnancy. We, in turn, had only been at the Lead Balloon, rather than, say, the Saratoga Inn or the Winners' Circle, because it was less favored by the Phi Delt crowd.

All of this, in turn, fascinated Eli. "You see, Seitz, how the Lord works to bring things together. He has a plan for those two."

"Or two plans. One each."

"Exactly. You see how many things had to happen, to bring them together."

"It could have been any other combination."

"But it wasn't. And it stopped Dickie's drinking cold."

"That much I'll say. And he's meditating well again."

"You see?"

"So what was the Lord's plan for me and Bitsy Reade? Seems like the Lord regards her as an expendable part of the plan."

"I don't claim to know. Maybe that was just one of the things that had to happen—give them time to say something crucial to each other."

"Like how an enzyme brings two chemicals together for a reaction that otherwise wouldn't take place."

"Exactly."

"Except, Eli, the enzyme is without consciousness. It doesn't plan, it just works. Organic chemicals can do that…" Besides, I thought, whatever happens can be made to seem inevitable. But I didn't want to have that conversation with Eli just then; I was off to a lab. I was always off to a lab.

The first time I saw Bina in Western dress I almost didn't recognize her. The long black plait was a long fall of black hair; she was trim and attractive in sweater and jeans. An altogether appealing package, except, as my grandmother said, I could eat soup off her head. Too petite for Tall Paul. She was moving toward, for lack of a better word, Americanism, while Dickie was moving toward Buddhism. "We met in the exact middle of our journeys," Bina said, "Like at a rest stop on the Queensway, each of us going in opposite directions, fun while we're at that place." She was already anticipating her father's next posting, in Ottawa she thought.

"The best way to learn about America," Dickie proclaimed, "Is movies." The Janus Film Festival was bringing American classics, European and Asian art films, to American campuses. How it would help Bina to see *Battleship Potemkin*, *La Strada*, *Breathless*, *The 400 Blows*, and the like was difficult to see, but *Casablanca* and *The Maltese Falcon* were, arguably, relevant. Twenty years later one could rent the videotapes; forty years later the DVDs arrived at the mailbox or you texted the title into your cable service; none of these beat being young and sitting in a cold classroom watching a scratchy 16mm print with a wobbly sound track. Especially when Satyajit Ray's *Distant Thunder*, about the Bengali Rice Famine of 1944, caused by the British stockpiling of rice in advance of the Burma offensive of 1945, prompted this from Bina, so quietly you could miss it if you hadn't seen her lips move: "My father was in prison with Gandhi-ji at the time." It was almost lost in the din of the Rathskellar. Dickie was in the john.

"We need to find a girl for you," she said to me, sipping coffee in place of the tea the Rathskellar didn't serve.

"I'm working on that," I said. "At the moment I'm dating Florence Flask."

She leaned forward conspiratorially. "Richard says you are sweet on his sister. Is that the correct term?"

"It is, and Richard is right, but there are complications."

"She seems from his description a most remarkable young girl."

"That's one word for it. I'd have to agree."

"For me and for Richard there are also complications."

I thought she meant that she would be transferring to the University of Toronto, following her family to Canada, but she didn't.

"I have a fiancé in India. Not really a fiancé; someone my parents, or rather my mother, has selected for me."

"…?"

"An arrangement. An arranged marriage." She sipped more coffee. "We were affianced by our respective families in childhood. I haven't seen him since I was eight years old."

"She must be talking about her fiancé," Dickie said, returning from the john.

"I was telling Paul we must find a girl for him."

"Not your roommate."

"No. I think she will not be in school much longer in any case. Tracey Berenstein was much impressed with you."

"Who?"

"The girl on the desk the night we all met." *Minnie Mouse?* "She made that most clear. Your refusal to sign the date card struck her as highly principled."

"She seemed to think me unprincipled in every other way possible."

"That was merely confusion."

"There is the matter of our respective heights."

"My sister is as tall as he is," Dickie said.

"Ah."

"I'll take a rain check, Bina, if you don't mind. I'm overwhelmed with work anyway." I left it to Dickie to explain what a Rain Check was.

"The issue of principles puts me in mind of something Richard and I must discuss. There are many gurus, Richard. One must choose carefully."

I chose that moment to have work to do.

There was never really any question about other gurus. Dickie's abiding interest in the Tibetan version of Buddhism, and the unquestioned authenticity of the Dalai Lama, made his goal absolutely clear.

Carboxylic Acids and Derivatives

Life wound down to Christmas Break. Dickie drove me as far as Tarrytown on the Thruway. I directed him into the maze of streets off Route 9 just beyond the Tappan Zee bridge.

"You know this town?"

"Never been here before. I know it from the map."

"When did you last look at the map?"

"When we left Schenectady."

"And you remember it, in that detail."

280

I shrugged.

"Another parlor trick?"

"My father taught me to read when I was maybe four, or even younger. He taught me to read a map. All kinds of maps. Road, subway, topographic. They stick in my mind. He knew from the War. He was in Intelligence. British Intelligence, actually."

"No shit."

I shrugged and wished him a Merry Christmas.

"How do you say that in Yiddish?" he asked.

I laughed. "Donno. Not sure it's possible. Just, have a good Christmas and New Year. Tell Ali and your parents same to them."

He sighed. "Should be another cheery family dinner. He's still going to be mad at her."

"What are you going to do?"

"In the struggle between yourself and Reality, hold Reality's coat." Another of the "Zurau Aphorisms".

"Think you can?"

"No. But I think I can hold Reality's coat and do some stuff behind it. I was thinking, she's grounded, but maybe I can teach her to drive stick."

"If it gets rough, meet me in the City. Come to Brooklyn. Have some tea. Her too."

"I'll keep that option in mind. But she's still grounded, remember? I'm going to have to be very careful around him, Paul. I'm going to have to be direct with him some time soon. I'm not going to get much further pretending I'm preparing for law school. He isn't stupid. Have a good holiday, Paul."

For the millionth time, I boarded a train. It was good to see them, but my mind was on her, both on what was happening with her, what were the chances of seeing her, and on my plans about Maxine Cohen.

I took Maxine to a movie in the City; I can't remember which one now. I can't remember what we talked about, or if we talked at all. My brain was a war zone. The day after Christmas I called her in North Greenwich. "This number is disconnected or out of service." I called Dickie.

"I sprung her," he said. "The old man is on one of his work binges; he won't find out until I'm out of here. She came home, found her phone disconnected, we worked out a plan. I took her out to teach her to drive stick on day one; on day two we snuck her luggage into the trunk—it's an English car; Bina says we should call it the boot—and she drove us up to our aunt's in Danbury. That's where she's spending Christmas vacation. Want the number?"

I called her, congratulated her on making a break for it.

"I'm not going to put up with being grounded anymore."

"Any chance we can meet in the City?"

"Oh, Paul, I don't know. My aunt's taking me to Boston for New Year's. I have no way of getting to a train until she gets back, and then we leave for the Boston cousins."

"Too cold for a swim in Lake Vere."

"I don't think we'll be doing that again."

What did she mean? Just the estrangement from her parents, or something else?

"Is everything OK between us?"

"Of course. Except we can't ever get to see each other. I don't know why this keeps happening, that everything in our lives keeps pulling us apart. We'll have to keep the Post Office and Ma Bell in business a while longer. How about we plan to meet semester break?"

"You're on. I'm just glad for you, that you have a place to be free of…"

"Thanks Paul. For understanding. As usual."

She was going to be with her aunt, alone for much of the time. I had no time to lose with Maxine.

Maxine was financing her few school fees and book expenses babysitting. The holiday season was one of her most lucrative times. This meant on the one hand we couldn't go out much; on the other hand I could join her wherever she was sitting. We could watch movies on television and let things take their course on the couch, depending on how old the kid was and how good a sleeper. There was a mutual moment when we knew the kid was asleep, and I would put my arm around her. We kissed, and kissed some more, and one night when she started to put some tongue into it *The time is now propitious, as he guesses* I chanced opening a button on her blouse. When she moved so I could do it more easily (Wanting me? Wanting me to not tear off a button?) I opened another. And another. She closed her eyes when I drew back and spread the blouse open like wings. *Exploring hands encounter no defence* There were her breasts, partly visible behind a thick brassiere. We went back to kissing *rounding first base, heading for second* I couldn't figure out how to unhook the thing. Maybe she would do it. She was leaning back against my arm and the sofa back, and I couldn't figure out how to ask her to move without, I thought, breaking the spell. Then I had an idea. Between kisses, I pushed the blouse off her shoulders. Between kisses, I slid one shoulder strap down her arm. Between kisses, the other. As gently as I could, I ran my hand over her breasts, folding the bra cups down, freeing her breasts of them *slid into second* I kissed her gently, ran my hands over her breasts again, circled the nipples. They hardened. I wasn't expecting that; I didn't know they did that. Her eyes were closed, her breathing coming quick. *Koufax takes a long lead off second* I kissed a nipple, ran my tongue around it as it hardened again, heard her moan softly, felt her hips heave toward me *and headed for third on an unexpected base hit* her eyes flew open and she pushed me away, trying to catch her breath. *Game called on account of rain*

"Whoa. Down boy." She started to pull clothing together.

"Sorry. Did I do something wrong?"

"No. You were doing everything right. That's the problem. We were going somewhere I shouldn't and I bet you didn't even bring protection."

"Protection?" *Oh, right*

"That's what I thought."

"I guess I didn't expect things to go that far."

"They weren't. I mean, I don't think so. I mean, you have to be prepared if they do. Look where you are." It was that obvious. "You think you could just stop?"

"I don't...well, you just did."

"Girls can, better than boys."

Listen to the voice of experience "I would never hurt you, Maxine."

"You already have." She was buttoning up.

"What? How?"

"Your move when I pushed you away was to tell me how much you like me. You didn't. You don't."

Silence.

"See? You're supposed to say something like 'Sure I do' or 'How do you know that' or 'Come here and I'll show you'. But you just sit there because I hit you with the truth, didn't I. I bet you haven't even been listening to me. What am I studying in school Paul? What do I want to be?"

"An elementary school teacher. Of course I've been listening."
"OK, maybe I'm wrong on that one, I'm no big brain like you, maybe this is how guys on the chess team make out, but...it feels like all technique with you. No real feeling. That was a very smooth move with the bra, did you learn that in that fancy college?"

284

"I just thought of it."

"So I'm right. You were thinking. This isn't about thinking. If you're thinking you aren't feeling."

"I can feel and think at the same time."

"Not about this you can't."

"I said, I didn't plan for things to go that far…"

"See? Plan. There was a plan. You don't plan making out. Not with me, anyway. Planning is for when it's just sex."

"I didn't mean…"

"Yes you did. Yes you do. Your hands were in the right places, your heart wasn't, and your head is up your ass. Just go, Paul."

I put on my sweater and toggled up my coat in that hallway like the Lubyanka. *And gropes his way, finding the stairs unlit* The tile floor was a chessboard. On the stairs an ancient, battle-scarred cat was coming up; I stooped to pet it and it ran away as if it knew something *I Tiresias, old man with wrinkled dugs.* Outside it was warmer, or I was still warmed by sexual excitement and the knowledge that I had some skills in that fraught arena *One of the low on whom assurance sits As a silk hat on a Bradford millionaire.* A block away an El train screeched around the curve, showering sparks off the third rail *Sexual initiation was a staple of Fin de Siecle German literature Would my father have ever* It was cold; I pulled up my hood, but Schenectady had hardened me to cold and I chose the boardwalk *Were the stories told by all those Sour Hour studs just a way to cope with* At the Pavilion I sat and looked out over the Bay. Overhanging clouds returned city lights; the Ambrose lightship beacon swept across the cloud bottoms. It was much too cold for the lovers who cuddled here in the warmer months, and those who sought more privacy under the boardwalk. Barely visible by reflected light were their initials carved into the wooden railings.

It really had warmed slightly; it was going to snow. *The water in the clouds gives up the Heat of Fusion to turn from liquid to solid phase, the phase change warming the air* I knew the mechanism. I was losing the warmth, the feeling of triumph. I watched the lights of a freighter headed out to sea and thought of her *the coast of the Sound is the same wherever you land I'd rather be going somewhere…sailing is just a skill* Sex without love was exactly the same, prowess without a point. *Well now it's done, and I'm glad it's over* On the other hand, Beatrice to Benedick: "For which of my good parts did you first love me?"

Would my father have How did these things go together, sex and friendship, liking and loving, loving and fucking? Where was the course on that? My independent study program was not going so well. As the first flakes came down I turned for home *This was something she already knew This was what she had been telling me Well, we were even Could my father have helped me with this?* I shied away from that thought.

I knew, or rather I felt, that I owed Maxine an apology I would never be able to give her. For what, I wondered? For using her. As if she were only a collection of body parts. *For which of my good parts…If the answer isn't or doesn't include her mind, give it up, Benedick* It was becoming too cold to be sitting out here; I went home to sleep, to a dream. I was in a railroad terminal, there were parts of a lot of familiar stations. A train was leaving and it was somehow pulling a rusty old boxcar from its siding. I jumped aboard the boxcar and a girl was there, looking out the open door. The train picked up speed, faster and faster through abandoned, weed-choked train yards, under long viaducts, under elevated lines. The boxcar came loose from the train; I asked the girl, How do we stop? She made no answer but the train pulled away and the boxcar went up another track, up a hill. Look out, I shouted, jump before it stops, it's going to tip over. We both jumped but by the laws of dream gravity the boxcar stayed upright and the girl turned to me and of course it was Ali and she said Paul do you know what you're doing and I woke in a sweat and promised myself I'd remember the dream.

286

On the train back to school I wrote to her, first thing.

Dear Maxine,
   I thought about what you said and it made a lot of sense. It doesn't have anything to do with fancy colleges. This place isn't so fancy. It has to do with me. Maybe some day you can give me another chance, but I wouldn't blame you if you didn't.

I started to write, "Thank you for the first chance" but had enough sense to see how much worse that made it. She was completely right. The whole thing had been as calculated as an organic chemistry equation, and everyone deserves to be treated as more than that, even if that's what we are. *Get it, Paul? We're organic chemistry equations that can be hurt* Instead I wrote:

You deserve better. Sorry I wasn't it.
                                    — Paul

The letter came back marked, in her handwriting, Return To Sender. Well, screw her. Maybe she didn't deserve better.
But she did. Everybody does.

Back to school, back to school.
"Did you talk to her?" Dickie asked. "Did she tell you what happened?"
"Just that she wasn't going to tolerate being grounded anymore, being treated like that."

"It didn't end there. Father called her, told her if she wasn't prepared to live by his rules in his house she wasn't welcome at home. Then he tried to ground *me*. Demanded the car keys."

"What did you do?"

"Told him I was twenty years old and he could shove it. I've had it with him too."

"Jesus."

Study Week. Eli stalked the halls, looking for a fight. "You have no respect for religion," he said.

"Well, damn little."

"Then you have no respect for me."

"I don't see where that's the case. You and I disagree about a lot of ideas."

"This isn't about just an idea. You don't just disagree, you think I'm a fool for being a believer."

"I think…" I said slowly, and then I stopped because I realized it was true.

"You see?" he said.

"I do see, Eli, and I'm sorry. I think…I think the idea of religion is…"

"Foolish."

"Not…OK, look, here's how I think about this. I respect your critical thinking in every other way, but not in this one. Thinking about it this minute, I guess that means you have an experience of, I don't know, God, that I don't, and that's the basis of the difference."

"A fool's experience."

"No. I did not say that. I most definitely did not say that and I don't feel that."

"But you imply that if I exercised my critical faculties in this one area the way I do in others it would go away."

288

"It's not something within my experience. My family are atheists. Yeah, OK, I guess I feel that but I could be wrong."

"So there might be a God."

"I didn't say that. I said I could be wrong about the ability of critical intelligence to deal with religious experience and belief. So I don't think you're a fool."

"That still means you think I have some defect in my critical intelligence if I abandon science and engineering and go to divinity school."

"I said what I mean. That you've made me see that this is not something intelligence will resolve."

"That's very good of you."

"You're determined to pick a fight about this. With me."

"With this whole place."

"I get to represent Nott College? That's rich."

"You represent this attitude better than anyone I know. It's why I have to leave."

"Is that what this is about?"

"Yeah. I think I want to transfer to a school with a religious orientation, maybe even become a clergyman. No matter what you think."

"What I, personally, think?"

"What everyone here thinks. But you especially."

"Why me?"

"Because if you can't talk me out of it, nobody can."

"That's crazy. Have you talked to anyone else about this?"

"My parents. My advisor. God."

"What do they say? No, wrong question. What do *you* say, Eli?"

"You don't want to know what God said?"

"I assumed that would be part of what *you* say."

"You reject the idea that I could have a call from God?"

"Eli, I have no experience of these things. I don't know how to answer you without offending you."

"I'm going to tell you that I prayed over this and the voice of God told me that I am called."

"That must have been a powerful experience."

"It was. It filled me with joy. For the first time in my life, Paul, real joy."

So, I thought, you follow what brings you joy, even if that's just the twitch of a neuron, a flow of neurotransmitter, it was powerful enough to overrule everything else in your head. Like love. It was then I realized she brought me joy. Whatever else she brought.

"That I understand, Eli."

"Your roommate's been awfully quiet in this conversation. I would think you'd have something to say here, Dickie."

"I don't have a dog in this race. Buddhism isn't a religion, in the western sense. It's more a philosophy. And its goal isn't ecstasy. It's peace. Peacefulness. Not the fulfillment of desire. The end of desire."

"Well at least that's an anchor for your life. Paul here has none. He's doomed to a life of anxious skepticism."

"The skepticism *is* the anchor, Eli. At least you don't have me doomed to hell."

"Sounds like hell to me, Paul."

Joy. Did everything I thought and felt lead back to her? Perhaps not everything.

The Student Aid Office called me in. "Mr. Seitz. Good to see you. As you know, your scholarship decreases every year, the funds to be made up by grants in aid. It isn't too early, it never is, to begin planning for your grant in aid jobs for next year. The early bird gets the worm, right?"

I had gone up to Schenectady with my father for my admission interview maybe a few weeks before the Kennedy assassination. We took the train, straight up the east shore of the Hudson, the American Rhine, the scenes painted by the Hudson River School artists right out the window; he loved it, but he was taking the occasional Nitroglycerine. I carried the bags, or rather bag—only overnight, only the two of us. He told me not to worry—I had a sure spot at Brooklyn College, all paid for, which was not much; like all of City University at that time it was nearly free. This was a lark. Word was out that in the wake of the Civil Rights movement a lot of these Little Ivy schools that had been avoiding admissions from New York were in trouble over it, and were looking to clean up a potential public relations mess. We shared a bed. He slept peacefully, I thought. I didn't. Out the window was the sign on the General Electric plant. It cycled every few minutes, lighting up

G

E

GE GE GE

GENERAL ELECTRIC GENERAL ELECTRIC

G

E

GE GE GE

GENERAL ELECTRIC GENERAL ELECTRIC

We had some toast and coffee, went over to the college. The admissions director introduced himself, shook my father's hand. "Professor Seitz," he said, "We're very interested in your son."

"What about him interests you?" he said.

"His gift for literature and languages, but also sciences and math, his accomplishments on the chess team."

"The fact he comes from Brooklyn," my father said. The admissions director humphed a little, but he took it. He invited me in, asked me the usual questions, why was I interested in Nott, what did I want to study, blah blah blah...he didn't even seem to be interested in my answers. When I stopped talking he said he was prepared to offer me Early Admission with a substantial scholarship if I dropped my applications to all other schools. I said I hadn't applied Early Admission, and he said they'd convert my application to Early Admission. He told me to think it over, and to call my father in, to discuss it. When my father came in he listened to the offer, and he sat back to look like he was thinking; he did that to gain time. Rubbed the side of his nose with his finger, like he did when he was thinking out a chess gambit.

"It's a very handsome offer," he said, "But there is no point in being admitted to the candy store if you haven't the money to spend there."

The admissions director upped the figure for the first two years, said I'd have to apply for loans and a grant-in-aid position my junior and senior years. They worked the numbers on the loans, and my father nodded to me, asked me did I want to do this. I don't know, the place looked like College to me. Like in books. And I wanted to get away from Brooklyn. I don't know why. Or maybe I do know why...I wanted to escape seeing him dying.

I limped into Finals, once again doing what I did best, substituting thought for feeling. I would not disappoint, I told myself. Semester break. Everything I did was wrong except on exams. And it was all for nothing. I came back from my Organic final to find a letter: she would be spending Semester Break with the Boston cousins, she was sorry, she couldn't go home. I understood, I wrote back. *I deserved it*

Suddenly in the middle of semester break there was a phone call from Dickie: "Can you meet me at the Reggio Saturday? And bring Sam. I have a proposition that should interest both of you."

"Sam will be right down the block hustling speed chess if it's warm enough. I'll get him there. Can we know what it is?"

"Saturday."

Sam was intrigued. What could this be about? "One thing is for shit sure, Paulie. It'll involve money." Even I had gotten that far. "Mine, not yours. You haven't got any." Too true.

The windows of the Reggio were opaque with condensation from the espresso machine. Was this part of the plan? I told Sam to circle the block with me.

"Why?"

"Humor me." No surveillance that I could detect.

"Gentlemen, welcome to my conference room. A round of coffees," he said to the waitress.

I said, "How about we skip the crap."

"Right. Guys, I need money. I'm about to be a big disappointment to my old man, and he's going to do his best to cut me off. I've been on short rations since Christmas; Paul knows why. I thought of a scheme. I have an MG. I just invested in some suspension and fuel line parts to make it rallye ready. I think there's money to be made on the rallye circuit when school starts up."

"What's the rallye circuit?" Sam asked.

"Point to point racing over a set road course. You have to meet precise timing at each stage. It's usually done by teams, a driver and a navigator. I'm a pretty good driver, but that's where Paul comes in. The navigator carries maps, clock and a slide rule. Paul *is* a map/clock/slide rule. He has eidetic memory for maps, and he can do distance/time calculations in his head faster than I've seen them done with a slide rule.

293

He's also becoming a pretty fair backup driver and second wrench. There's a professional circuit in Europe…"

"We all saw *A Man and a Woman*," Sam said.

"I don't mean the professional rallye circuit. Here college kids do it for fun."

"Tell me about the money part," Sam said.

"There's often a small purse, but that's negligible; mostly it's like sailing. Done pour le sport. The money is in side bets."

"With the rich college kids."

"Precisely."

"And you need backing."

"We'd need a loan, to start the betting off. Believe me, you'll be repaid. Paul, all the time I was teaching you to drive in the mountains we were driving over the rallye courses. Both of us know every inch." Sam shook his head. "I don't do loans. I do investments. We put up shares and split the take."

Dickie didn't blink; he'd probably expected this. "Makes it more complicated," he said. "We'll need to set up an account. We couldn't risk that much cash under a dorm bed."

"I don't have the money to buy in," I said.

"No problem, Govinda; I'll stake you, you pay me back out of the winnings."

"Can I make a few suggestions?" Sam said. "I've been at this a few years now."

"I was hoping you would."

"My clients over in the park have included Yalies, Harvard men, Columbia men, plenty of my own from NYU, Brooklyn, City; I strongly suggest the cash gets put up first and held by a neutral party, or in a neutral place. My biggest welchers are from the Ivy League."

"Are you suggesting that the people who stole and looted this continent are not trustworthy?" Dickie said. We laughed.

294

"Deal," Sam said. "How much to start?"

"A thou apiece." Serious money in 1966. "The operating expenses for the car are going to have to come out of this."

We sipped espresso. "Here's another idea. Sam taught me this. We lose the first one, and occasionally another one. Makes us look beatable."

"Cute. Yeah. OK. I'm going back up tomorrow. There's snow, ice and all kinds of shit all over the mountains. I'm going to do some practice, get the feel of the new suspension. See you in a few days."

On the way home Sam said, "So you have been listening, Paulie."

"Sure."

"Tell me something. How is he going to disappoint his father?"

"Not sure exactly, but I have a pretty good idea. It involves travel. I think this is a short term thing, get in, get out." I told him about Bina.

"Yeah. Make it a joint account, Govinda."

"You know...?"

"I haven't stopped reading, Paulie."

It sometimes feels to me—it feels to me now even more strongly—that everything I said and did the first half of my sophomore year was wrong. My only excuse is, it was based on so much wrong information. And worse, wrong interpretation.

Another train ride up the American Rhine, another semester, another registration. I was carrying Sam's check for the thousand. This time the CAT lab was in fact an actual cat. I like cats. I did not like dissecting one.

Eli did not return. We had a postcard from him from a church-related school in Ohio.

Carbohydrates. Conformation of carbohydrates. Glycosides. Disaccharides. Polysaccharides.

Thank God for English 324: The American Short Story.

We opened a checking account at Schenectady Savings under the name MG Enterprises. It was that simple. A sudden brainstorm led me to the Schenectady Public Library's map collection. As I'd hoped, topographic maps of the Adirondacks, Catskills, Green and White Mountains. We could anticipate inclines, precalculate performance. Just before our first practice run, an old engineer's trick, I greased my slide rule with Vaseline, to Dickie's disbelief. "Insurance," I said. I did the math and off we went. Slick as the proverbial whistle. Meanwhile Dickie made the rounds of bars and collected phone numbers, hustling bets. The first real race, it was all we could do to intentionally lose.

It was in fact a lot of work; in addition to the mountains of time consumed in the labs, there were now the maps and calculations, and the mountains of time consumed in the mountains. Driving and navigating required intense concentration. It only occurred to me that there was real danger involved when Dickie misjudged an ice slick and we skidded off a road outside Ausable Forks, snapping a tie rod. From a wagering standpoint it was advantageous; the next bets against us doubled. The MG Enterprises account kept even.

I did a lot of my reading as Dickie drove us to and from the rallye sites. I stayed up until all hours in the chilly lab doing the dissections and memorizing the insides of an animal I would have preferred to be playing with and memorizing chemical formulae. What I did not do a lot of was sleeping and writing to Ali.

Exhausted after a three hour session one night in the freezing CAT lab I returned to a message on the door: "Call me as soon as you get in. I have a Biological Emergency."

Laughter on the floor. *Was she pregnant? Nowhere else to turn? What the hell?*

"Ali?"

"Paul, hi, thanks for calling back. Been awhile, man."

"Yeah, you'll take Organic and CAT and you'll understand." *What a miserable excuse*

"Plus road racing."

"That doesn't help."

"I called with a question about the Hardy-Weinberg Equilibrium. It's a take-home open book quiz question, extra credit, the answer isn't in the book, so I thought I'd call a guy who's read other books. I think it's a trick question."

"What's the question?"

"It's in two parts. First part, there are three traits that assort separately and it gives the population frequencies…"

"And the question is, what are the gene frequencies, right?"

"Right, and what are the frequencies of people with the combinations of traits."

"OK. How do you approach this?"

"I'm hung up on it being three traits. I've been thinking all night and I'm not getting it. Or I think I'm not; maybe I am."

"If they assort separately what does that mean about the genes?"

"They're independent of each other."

"Right, so each one…"

"Oh, I see. It's three separate calculations. We're supposed to make up traits."

"How about tall vs. short, blonde vs. brunette and athletic vs. bookish?"

She laughed. "Love it. Then just multiply the frequencies together to get the frequencies of tall, blond and athletic, short blonde and athletic, on down the line. Just set up a 3X3 square."

"You got it. What's the second part?"

"A trait with three alleles. Make one up, use the assigned population frequencies to calculate the gene frequencies. This one I'm completely stumped by. I admit it."

"OK. First the traits. How about hair color: blonde, brunette, redhead. The frequencies are…"

"…p, q…"

"And r. Three alleles; p + q + r = 1."

"Oh, of course. A quadratic with three factors."

"There you go. Only thing, it won't give the frequency of brunette with red highlights." *Under the firelight, under the brush, her hair/Spread out in fiery points*

"Thanks so much. I knew you would know this."

"Of course. I'm a sophomore, froshie."

"Yah. Rub it in." *Like suntan lotion*

"It's good to hear from you, Ali."

"It's you that stopped writing."

"I can fix that."

"You do that."

"They might be short letters. And illegible if Dickie takes a curve too fast."

"I don't care. We'll talk at length Spring Break."

"Will we?"

"It's all arranged. I can get down from Danbury. You'll see. Write to me."

"I will."

Organic Nitrogen Compounds, Amines,
Amides, Nitriles and related compounds

I wrote, swaying and skidding over an unguarded cliffside road: *"Tall, brunette and bookish is the rarest combination. There is only one Ali Acheson." She could have gotten the answer to that Bio question anywhere, if she really didn't know it*

Slowly the MG Enterprises account began to grow, fed by skipped meals (we were too tired to wake for breakfast anyway), and then to throw off a trickle of cash. What Dickie, with his usual political skills, was counting on was the competitive tradition of the leisure class (what, really, is a sailboat race about? Or a tennis match?). An upstart team of drivers had come out of nowhere, out of a second-tier college, didn't use slide rules or timers, one of them was reputed to be a scholarship student *from Brooklyn*, the other a class traitor who had broken open a Phi Delt initiation; well, we can beat that. We have to beat that; the upstarts must be put down. In that atmosphere it was child's play to push bets and get odds. It was a matter of honor to them, Dickie explained, and that's how it seemed to play out; to us it was a matter of money. And suddenly we were making it. Sam's investment began to pay off, and my initial share was just about paid back.

Now into the swing, we would get to the town near the course site the night before, and it would begin at a host's welcome party or at a nearby bar. We were reputed not to drink (proof of our upstart status, as Dickie had taught me, to these people who distrusted anyone who didn't). Dickie held a wine glass, conspicuously barely sipping; I was known to be underage (another challenge to the system). Boasting, bragging, and good-natured competitive psyching, just like at a team chess match, gave way to something darker as the blood alcohol level of the room rose. The moment came where Dickie would ask someone, in this instance a pair of newcomers come up from Yale just to challenge us, if they were prepared to back their words with something more substantial. Others would line up to back the challenge—and fatten the kitty.

This particular time it went like this:

Yalie Driver: "So what are you driving, that beat-up MG with the phony rallye stripe?"

Dickie: "That would be the magnificent product of British automotive engineering that has taken the last three weekends' prizes, son. (He could more accurately have said: "That would be the MG with the concealed beefed-up suspension giving us better ground clearance and 100 lbs of sandbags hidden under a blanket in the boot for better traction.") And what piece of tin are you pushing, if you don't mind my asking?"

Yalie Driver: "The Alfa."

Dickie: "Ah. A terrific choice for the mountains; great mountain car. (Again, he could more accurately have said: "A piece of Italian fluff with a big mill and not enough height to clear a New York pothole.") I believe we face some stiff competition here, Paul."

Me: (with a shrug and my best Brooklyn accent): "Not much. These are flatlanders. We're in the mountains."

Yalie Driver: "We're gonna wipe the floor with you."

Dickie: "Think so? Feel strongly enough about it to back that with a little friendly wager?"

Dickie was in fact a smoother, more polite version of Sam. Why had I never noticed this before?

That particular race required topographic maps and forethought. Teams could choose one of three routes; the challenge was to match the capabilities of the car to the route. The shortest involved a winding mountain road with several steep climbs and wicked switchbacks, ending in a hairpin turn into a one-lane bridge. Perfect for European sports cars. On the map. Larger American cars—Mustangs and the like—could take the longer but straighter route. What we knew from having driven every road in the Adirondacks was: the winding mountain road had suffered unrepaired damage from a late fall ice storm, likely to rip the exhaust system out of the low-slung Alfa, and probably any unmodified Triumphs, MGs and Sunbeams that ventured up it.

The referees drove out to the checkpoints and we picked one, a Holyoke girl, to hold the money. The Alfa started two cars ahead of us. Just for fun, and to stir future cash-backed enmity, we lumbered off the starting line, just to make the inevitable finish more striking; we made up the time on a straightaway two miles ahead. The first casualties were a couple of guys from Williams who had a road map but hadn't consulted the topographics; they ended up in a ditch with a front wheel at an unnatural angle. I waved, to continue to look as cocky as possible. Dickie double-clutched down to take the curve, then upshifted, and soon shifted back down for the next upgrade. He played tunes on the gearbox for the steep up- and downhills. I warned him to slow for the checkpoint and stay left; I gave him the "Next left" sign and reminded him it was a 180-degree turn into the rough road. He hit it perfectly, downshifting to use engine-braking on the curve, and catching the upgrade with some oomph. Just the other side of the curve a Triumph sat steaming; overheated or punctured radiator. Another wave to a couple from Hobart. The road got rougher as it rose, pounding the suspension and our kidneys. Dickie had to let go of the wheel periodically when he couldn't take the vibration; I passed him the padded gloves, held the wheel while he pulled them on. Two more switchbacks and we topped the summit; the downhill side was the roughest part, with blind curves, we knew, hiding the badly holed pavement. We had time to exchange a grin; it couldn't be long now, and surely there was a shard of tailpipe, and there was the Alfa, its muffler hanging. We saluted them, made the next two checkpoints, and drove back to pick up our winnings, which between alcohol and upper-class machismo had swelled to over two thousand dollars. More than enough to wash the mud off the car. I would take the check for his third home to Sam at Spring Break; for the first time I had some serious walking-around money.

Amino Acids, Peptides, Proteins and Enzymes

Outside this little world, a war worsened. We were insulated from all of it.

I was becoming an accomplished driver and navigator. Also an accomplished liar, con-artist and conspirator. Just like everyone I knew. *How did my father get along in Heidelberg? In Berlin? In Warsaw? In the War?*

I met them at the Reggio as planned. Ali looked radiant, triumphant, and I told her so.

"It's because I did it. Absolutely in no uncertain terms did it. Told them no debutante ball, no party, not ever. Finalement."

"Fertig."

"Fertig?"

"Yiddish. Final beyond finalement. That's wonderful, Ali.

"What is?" Bina had materialized behind me. "You must be Alicia." She sat. "I've heard so much about you."

"And I've heard so much about you. What's wonderful is I told my parents they were not going to force me to have a Coming Out Party." And she explained to Bina what this meant.

"You intend to defy your parents' attempts to arrange a marriage for you."

"In essence, yes. I intend to be a doctor."

She sipped her espresso. "Allow me to say, Alicia…"

"Call me Ali."

"Ali…in my country you could be killed for this. Slowly starved into submission. At the very least exiled from home."

"I am exiled from home."

"In fact?"

"True," Dickie said, "Our father told her not to return unless she was prepared to be married well by the time she finishes college."

"At least he didn't threaten to pull me out. He can't." *There was that again*

"He could make it most difficult, I assume," Bina said.

"Probably. But not impossible. I think he figures if I'm in college, and not just any college, I stand the best chance of…"

"Making an advantageous match," Bina finished. "I am in approximately the same situation, vis-a-vis my father. I am already in violation of my mother's expectations that I marry a man I last saw when we were both eight years old."

"You can't be serious."

"This is the custom among upper-caste Hindu families. It is one I intend not to follow."

"She's gone as far as abandoning the sari, at least outside the house," Dickie said.

"You've been pretty quiet, Paul."

303

What to say? "I think…" I said slowly, trying to frame the thought as well as I could, "That in every culture on earth, wealth oppresses the holders of it as much as it does the poor. Only they don't realize it."

"Gandhi-ji believed the same thing," Bina said.

"Well, I wouldn't put myself in that company."

"It oppresses women most. What privileges there are go to men," Ali said.

"In this I must agree," Bina said softly, "But that boy in India must feel much as I do." She always spoke softly in those days, especially in disagreement.

We had pastries. I congratulated Ali on her confronting her parents, and Bina on her determination to follow the same path. "To liberation," Dickie said, and we clinked demitasse cups.

"Where to now? Ali asked.

"Only one place possible," I said. "Today I show you the Holy of Holies."

Bina asked, "What could that possibly be?"

"The Strand Bookstore."

Dickie and Bina walked slowly; Bina paused to look in every shop window. Ali and I walked on ahead. It was early April; the forsythia had blossomed, foretelling Spring, but there was still a chill. Ali walked with her hands in her pea coat pockets, a scarf, and her hair, that hair, streaming in the breezes funneled down the narrow crosstown blocks.

"So you did it."

"I did it. I made an appointment. Told them we had something very important to discuss. Dickie picked me up at my aunt's place and drove me down, I told them, and here we are."

"It's wonderful, Ali."

"Not completely wonderful. I'm still living out of my aunt's house, she's always running around for work." She took my hand, we walked along, swinging our linked arms. My heart sang. I was at the Strand, browsing the shelves with money in my pockets, with a beautiful, fiercely intelligent girl who played chess and loved books. And thought I was special. And I was prepared for her now. The getting of experience was behind me, her aunt was forever out, leaving Ali alone in a house for days at a time. Truly, I had reached the sunny uplands of life.

Ali picked through books. "Paul, there's a catch, but maybe one we can use."

??? "What catch?"

"He's really angry, Paul. More angry than I've ever seen him. Scary angry. He told me to my face to get out, he never wanted to see me again. I don't care about that; he'll cool down, but I know him, he'll only redouble the pressure if I'm around, so I have to not be around. I have an idea, so listen to my logic here. I need advice. Pre-med advice."

"You have a faculty advisor…"

"Who can tell me the party line. You can tell me the emess."

"Where are you learning Yiddish?"

"News flash: Wellsmith College now admitting Jews."

"West Coast stations please copy."

"Yeah. So. I have to meet two simultaneous goals: Fulfill my pre-med requirements, and stay away from home. So here it is. Wellsmith offers a sophomore semester abroad. In Paris."

"…"

"Paul?"

"Yeah. Wow. Paris."

"Right, Paris. Look, Paul, you know I have fluent French and here's the thing, if I can't get into an American med school I have more than a shot at Paris or Louvain."

"You're going to get into an American med school."

"A male with my grades, assuming I do well in Organic, would have no problem. My advisor said this. Maybe things will be different in three years but I can't depend on that. So, anyway, the courses I could take there include Physics, which is mostly math, Comparative Anatomy which is mostly pictures and dissection, and I can get a bunch of language and social science distribution requirements out of the way. Then I do the second semester of Physics and Comparative Anatomy here, and I can pull them out if I bomb out in Paris. You've done CAT lab; am I being crazy here?"

"No. Actually you're making a lot of sense. The worse for me. I won't be able to see you for like six months or more."

"Well, where have you been for the last six?"

"Working my ass off in Organic and CAT. I didn't want you to see me without it."

She gave the laughter snort, then laughed outright. "A soft answer turneth away wrath. A funny answer turneth away questions."

"When do you leave?"

"I'll go with my aunt to Europe in June and not come back until winter break next year. That way I won't have to spend any time with my father until he has something else to worry about."

"Meaning Dickie."

"Maybe." She turned away, picked through a few more books.

"There's only one flaw in the plan. There's something I want to do more of here, and I can't, with this plan."

"What's that?"

"Hang out with you, idiot. What do I have to do, wear a sign? So I was thinking, with the money you've been making rallying with Dickie, you could come to Paris for a week, Christmas. Paris, Paul. We could spend days like this, only in Paris."

April is the cruelest month

"Ali, I'm glad for you, and it all makes sense, and I don't care if it's Paris, it could be Jersey City, but the money…the way my scholarship works, every year the direct grant decreases and the loan and payments increase. My father's life insurance took care of the first two years, but now I have to work and bring in money and save every penny…"

"Oh, Paul. I never thought. I had no idea how it worked." She slumped against the shelves. "I thought I was freeing us. I thought…"

"It's OK, it's OK." I thought I saw a tear, and I didn't want her to cry. "We'll always have Brooklyn."

"…Maybe I have the money…"

"No. I couldn't."

"Yes you could."

"No I couldn't. He won't support you in med school. You need every penny too."

"I have a small trust fund. It doesn't kick in until I'm 21. I could borrow from my aunt…"

"Ali, no. I won't be the reason…I'm not that good a person."

"Neither am I. Paul, I may never make it to med school."

"You will."

"If I don't, the separation, it's all for nothing."

"You will. You can do this. I can do this. *Can I?* I have to do the thinking for both of us. You have to get on that plane, Ilsa."

"What?"

"*Casablanca.*"

"Oh. Right…We'll have to keep the post office in business. Those onion-skin airmail pads. I'll be leaving straight from school. We won't see each other or talk for *another* six months, and it's been six months since…"

"So we can do this. That's how we know we can do this. Go. Get away from there. Let him know you're determined." *I can do this. In that six months I had dated, if that's the right word, two other girls. All to be sure I could satisfy her. Or that's what I had told myself. I can do this. I owe her this.*

"Come," I said. "This requires a sendoff. A memento." I knew what I wanted; it was easy to find, a battered bilingual edition of *Cyrano deBergerac*. I ran to the cash register and paid for it before she could object. "I need a pen," I said. She had followed me slowly to the front of the store. I paid, and bumped into her as I turned to write in the inside cover:

To my Roxanne, from her Gascon cadet

This time she did cry, one or two soft tears. We kissed quickly. I don't remember the rest of that afternoon well; I know we must have kissed again when Bina and I put her and Dickie on the train at Grand Central. Were we too embarrassed by the depth of our feelings, to kiss in public *with Dickie there* or maybe—too frightened by it ourselves? The kiss I remember is the one at The Strand.

Arenes. Electrophilic Aromatic Substitution

"By my calculations, Govinda, you're eighteen years old. Can I buy you a drink?"

"You can let me drive the MG down Brighton Third Street."

There were birthday cards and a call from my mother and grandmother. And a call and a card from Ali.

"How does it feel?" she asked.

"Honestly? Nothing. No different. *I'm too down in the dumps about not seeing you for six months I don't feel anything much*

"I just want to know if I'll wake up any different."

"I'd love to be there to see it."

"Mmmm. Maybe my nineteenth. Our nineteenth. "

"I'm thinking of getting a calendar, like a jailed revolutionist, to cross off the days. Oh. I did get one other card. Besides yours I mean."

"Who from?"

"Selective Service System Local Board No. 39, Brooklyn 24, New York. Says Paul Seitz, Selective Service Number 52-38-48-270, Date of Birth February 21, 1948, Place of Birth Brooklyn, NY, Color Eyes Blue, Color Hair Brown, Height 5ft 11 in Weight 140, Other Obvious Physical Characteristics None. I have no other obvious physical characteristics."

She laughed. "Anything else?"

"The law requires you to have this certificate in your possession at all times…"

Silence

"Paul? You still there?"

"Yes."

"Learn Organic. You're going to get me through it."

"Yes, ma'am."

As it warmed and the roads dried, the rallye speeds got higher; we had to change from winter to summer oil and adjust the timing and carburetion. None of the rallye sites was anywhere near Northampton. The sandbags came out of the boot. Summer tires went on—Michelins; the MG Enterprises account was fat and getting fatter.

Aromatic Compounds

Everything blossomed. Dogwood bloomed. Dickie still meditated faithfully, did enough work to maintain Gentleman's C's. He spent more and more time with Bina, driving up to Saratoga and picnicking at the Yaddo art colony's formal gardens, a notorious trysting place in a time when college students could not visit each other's dormitories or check into a motel and a sports car had no room for more advanced amorous activity. They still came to movies at Nott. One night at the

309

'Skellar Bina said again, "We really must get a girl for you. We can't properly go out together until we do. Do agree, Paul; I'm running out of information on India for Richard. I haven't been there since I was ten."

"Very well. Only as a favor to you. Just something casual."

"To fill out a luncheon party. Well, one never knows, but we can make this most clear." *We?*

She was pretty in the conventional way of that time, styled hair, long-limbed, filled out a sweater. A knockout, really, I suppose. I supposed. The open car precluded conversation. We took the picnic blankets and basket out of the boot. Statues of The Four Seasons; a sundial inscribed: "Hours fly, Flowers die, New days, New ways, Pass by, Love stays." Vines hung down from a pergola; behind was a thick wood where we spread the blankets. Fruit, cheese, small sandwiches, thank you, Bina.

"We're going to take a stroll in the woods," Dickie said, throwing one of the blankets over his shoulder. Bina smiled, and they were gone. Birds sang. Insects buzzed.

"That leaves me with the wingman," she said.

"You know that term?"

"My father is a General? In the Air Force?"

"My father was in the RAF." She looked blank. "Royal Air Force."

"What's that?"

"British. Battle of Britain? Churchill? Nazis?"

"Oh."

Silence.

"Well," she said.

Silence.

"Can I ask you a question?"

"You just did."

"What?"

"I said, you just did."

"What?"

"I said, you just did. You just asked me if you could ask me a question. That's a question." She looked blank again. "Go ahead," I said.

"How old are you?"

"Eighteen last birthday."

"Eight…Jesus, I'm twenty. Nearly twenty-one."

"Really?"

"Yes, really. Jesus, this is really robbing the cradle."

"I'm sorry if…"

This time it wasn't a question. "You're a virgin."

"No. Yes, OK?"

She laughed. "So I'm a part of the Dickie Acheson Phys Ed course?"

"What?"

"Look, I'm obviously no genius, but I didn't just fall off the turnip truck. I'm supposed to be your first time, right?"

I didn't answer. She lay back on the blanket, took another pull on the wine bottle. "So, you want to?"

"I thought…"

"I'm starting to warm up to the idea. You're not bad looking."

"Thanks. Neither are you."

"Oh, gee, thanks for the enthusiasm."

"Sorry…Look, I don't even have…"

"I do. I have a thingy." *Diaphragm* She sat up, put her hand on my shoulder in an almost motherly way. "Look, kid. Paul. I'm twenty…My first time, times really, it was, like, you either wanted the guy enough, or you wanted the sex enough. The very first time, I wanted the guy enough, then later…anyway, I guess it's the same for guys. But it's a

311

bigger deal...you aren't my first virgin and for guys it's a...it can be...you have to want the girl or the sex more than you're scared." That sounded true. And I didn't. This wasn't the right girl at all.

"I'm not her, am I."

"Who?" *Dappled sunlight played over her face, her body*

"Whoever it is you thought would be your first."

"Oh. Right. You're right."

"Like I said, I'm no genius, but some things I know. You're a nice kid. I think. You haven't tried to get me drunk. Or yourself. Points for you."

"Thank you."

"What are you going to tell Dickie?"

"I don't know. What would it be best for you for me to tell him?"

"Jesus, you *are* a nice guy. Are you sure you don't want to do this?"

The bar for Nice Guy didn't seem to be set that high.

"Looks like you don't. Look, don't worry about me; you tell him anything you want."

I want your sister so it's awkward to have you get me laid

The Chemistry of Natural Products

"Well," Dickie said, "You've pretty much screwed up your chances with every girl in Saratoga until a new frosh class shows up. One would think you didn't want to get laid. Hey math head, ever seen this equation?" And he threw over an index card that read:

$$\int e^x = f(u)^n$$

"You don't know calculus. That equation requires limits." I realized he didn't get the joke about limits. *But she would* "At a minimum, Dickie, I'd like to be able to hold a conversation before and after."

"The only girl I've ever seen you hold a conversation with of any length is my sister."

And Jacob went in also unto Rachel, and he loved Rachel more than Leah.

Silence.

"Wait a minute. Wait a minute here Seitz. About the only guy I ever saw her hold a conversation with, of any length, and without insults, is you. Holy shit. I must be fucking blind."

"Dickie, you know we're friends…"

"Don't try to deny this, Paul. It isn't that she's hard to look at, either, and the two of you are walking libraries. Jesus, how have I been missing this?"

"Missing what? You know I like her…"

"Like her, yeah. She sure didn't get whomped with the ugly stick…"

"No, she didn't, sure, but she's just a tad bit…unstable, don't you think?"

"Crazy? Yeah, was, but not nearly as crazy as you thought, is she, or as people thought, and not at all since she left home for school. As you know. She put it all out there with the parents, didn't she, and got some support from Mom, and she's finally where she fits. How did I miss this? You don't just like her."

"Dickie…"

"You're serious about her."

"Dickie, we've been down this road…"

"OK, Paul."

How do I say, Dickie I know something about your sister that you don't, and it's a really big thing. Or did he know and he was shopping her to the poor kid? Or what? Or did he know, and not think of her as damaged goods, which obviously I did, and what right did I have to think that? That has to stop.

313

Jacob loved Rachel more than Leah but he had eleven sons and a daughter with Leah, Bilhah and Ziporah.

What do I feel for her?

That night I had a dream. We were on the raft, and she was naked and so was I. She smiled and asked if I wanted some suntan wine. I asked her what suntan wine was, and she kissed me and rolled over on me, reached down and stroked me; she mounted me and we rolled over and over, and I exploded inside her and I woke up stuck to the sheets and knew I was hopelessly in love with her. Completely and totally. I wanted her desperately. I wanted to get back into the dream. I wanted to jump in the MG and drive straight to her. Nothing else mattered. I fell back to sleep, woke up in a more sober frame of mind but still ecstatic from the dream. I had to talk to her, if only to be sure she was real. *If I drove over to Wellsmith, where would we go?*

She was out. Dickie found me at the phone, trying for a third time. He saw the pile of quarters, knew it couldn't be home I was calling; home I called collect, he knew.

"You're in love with my sister."

"Possibly. Probably."

"You turned down a roll in the hay with a famed courtesan, Govinda. You've got a bad case. You're serious about her."

And Jacob loved Rachel...

"Maybe. Eventually."

"Now. Not eventually. Does she feel the same way?"

"I don't know. I know she likes me."

"Do you want me to find out?"

"No. Thank you, Dickie, but stay out of it. If there's something there I want it to grow by itself, without any fertilizer from you. There's

314

been enough of family pressure, you could screw it up if she read it that way…"

"She wouldn't."

"Just let it be."

"She's leaving for Paris in days."

"Let it be."

"This must be the way chess players play love."

"As opposed to wrestlers."

"Ex-wrestlers."

"Ex-wrestlers, then."

"I will never lay angry hands on another human being, Paul. Never."

I wrote to her.

Cherie
Think of me in Paris. Bon voyage.
— Votre Gascon Cadet

A postcard came back. It said only:

Chaque jour.
—A.

Finals came again. The Nott and Wellsmith academic calendar did not overlap exactly. When she was halfway across the Atlantic I was in the middle of my Organic Chemistry Final. I got an A, and an A for the course. Nothing stops that. Nothing, nothing, nothing. The B+ in Comparative Anatomy was good enough. I had walked out of lab for two days when in the final stage of the cat dissection I'd opened the lower abdomen and found a uterus filled by four almost completely developed kittens. It was a warm day; I went into the Gardens and just sat. *Under a boddhi tree, Dickie would have said.* How many things had to die for me to get to medical school?

The last phone call with her hadn't gone well either.

"I have half a mind to quit this and just come back here for the fall semester," she said.

"Don't," I said. *Tell her you love her*

"I don't know what I'd…my aunt is staying in Europe for a few months; I could only come back to school. Paul, I was always ambivalent about this."

"You have to go." *If I tell her I love her she won't get on the plane* "Ilsa, you have to get on that plane."

"What? Oh, *Casablanca*."

"Yeah. Where I'm going you can't follow; what I have to do you can't be any part of."

Silence.

"*Casablanca* again," I said.

"Oh. But I thought we were headed in the same direction."

"We are. But there may be a detour." *Tell her you love her*

"What detour?"

"Dickie's going to tell your father…"

"Oh no. That's not going to go well."

Tell her you love her Tell her you love her Tell her you love her If I tell her I love her she won't go That isn't fair She has to go

"It isn't, and you can't be here when it doesn't."

"You're right, and I hate that you're right."

"So do I." *It's tearing me apart Tell her you love her*

"Ali, I…"

"What?"

316

"Nothing. When exactly—*exactly*—do you get back? And where exactly will you be?"

"I sent a letter this morning with the address in Paris. I don't know where we'll be before that; my aunt isn't a planner and she has lots of friends. We'll be in Venice for at least a week or two, that's all I know. I'll be at the Paris address September 2nd. I can write to you, but you won't probably be able to write back before we've moved on. It's crazy, I know. I know I'll be back for second semester. It's an open ticket." *Tell her you love her tell her* "You'll find a letter waiting. We won't lose each other, Ali."

"No we won't…Paul? Saratoga's a lot closer than Paris."

"Not to me it isn't." I didn't tell her about the kittens. I didn't tell anyone. Not then, anyway.

If I tell her I love her and she stays, where could she go? She'd go to Europe with her aunt for the summer. Then where? Back to school. Then what? What could I offer her? Refuge in Brooklyn? Would her aunt just give her the house keys for Thanksgiving and Christmas, for us to shack up? You know why you won't say it Coward You don't deserve her

"I just got off the phone with my sister."

"So did I."

"Yeah. She said. She says you told her she had to go. Thank you, Paul. That must have been very hard."

I shrugged. "It was the right thing to do."

"Not from the look on your face."

"This better be worth it, Dickie. It had really better be worth it."

"It will. I owe you. I'm going to talk to him. I'll tell you how it comes out. I'll make it good, Paul. I'll figure a way. I'll be meditating on it."

Yeah. That's how we got here I invented a reason to go to the CAT lab.

The semester dragged itself to a close. Dickie and I took shifts driving as far as Tarrytown. Railway Express hauled the rest. All except my heart. That was in Europe.

It was time to tell my mother and grandmother about the rallyes. "It isn't racing for speed," I explained. "It's precision driving *over dangerous mountain roads covered in ice and snow and worse* and Dickie is very very good at it. So am I, now."

They looked very doubtful. "It's real money. I can afford breakfasts, and this year I might even have time to eat them."

"You've been skipping breakfast?"

"Only on lab days. I took Organic and Comparative at the same time. I ate snacks in the lab."

"You work too hard, Paulie. No breakfast means too hard."

"It'll be better this year. The hard part is done." I didn't tell them about the betting, only the purses. I brought Sam his share. "Nice," he said. "How long until someone catches on to this racket?"

"Don't know. I'm surprised we've gone this far." Money was too tight for argument. It was too tight to be choosy about a summer job, too. The "Zurau Aphorisms" weren't going to see print any time soon. A friend of my mother's knew of a job, a summer project, in an insurance office downtown. The money was good. The office was at Wall and William, a block from the Stock Exchange. I got off the train every day with brokers, runners, floor traders; taxis disgorged the millionaires on the street above. The job involved auditing applicants' responses and medical exam results. The trains were hot and humid. Time passed. I got a lot of reading done. The War heated up; there was

318

a big offensive in Quang Tri Province, U.S. Marines and South Vietnamese Army, something called Operation Hastings.

There were letters, mostly brief, often just postcards. *Dear Paul Moving on from Florence to Pisa Tuscany is gorgeous beyond gorgeous but ungodly hot More later Ali Dear Paul Too hot to go to Pompeii I don't care I'd love to see it heat or no heat but maybe this is better because I'd rather see it with you Ali Ciao Paulo The Vatican museums are cool and spectacular God touches Adam's finger with his and gives life If only we could just touch fingertips for a moment Some day we must come back to the Forum Romanum and Ostia Ostia is the silted up port of Imperial Rome intact ruins like Pompeii but cool and shaded Te Amo Ali.*

Pretty office girls flocked to coffee shops and to the nearby piers to eat lunch. When they moved me up to the midtown office (same job, different day) there were more, behind the Library in Bryant Park. The older ones treated me as a mascot, the younger ones as maybe something more, or maybe I was feeling, since I was attractive to one girl I was attractive to all the others. A guy could dream. And one day she called from JFK, breathless, she had just got in, she couldn't stand being without me another day, she said, and I told her to get a cab to Brighton Beach and I walked out of the office, told them I wouldn't be coming back, when I got home I helped her out of the cab she was wearing a light summer dress and the stickball game paused and sighed, and I paid the cabbie and he winked at me and we went upstairs Where are your mother and grandmother? Visiting friends they won't be back for days and she smiled and unzipped the dress and threw herself into my arms and I whirled her around down the hall into my bed and she pulled my clothes off and I kissed her from top to bottom and back to the top and she laughed and then I slowed and stroked her breasts and kissed them and she moaned and reached for me and gasped when I came inside her and when the ecstasy faded we did it again and this never happened but it happened over and over again, over and over.

Succubus [med.L., masc. Form (with fem. meaning) corresp. to Succuba, after Incubus]. A demon in female form supposed to have carnal intercourse with men in their sleep. (Oxford English Dictionary).

August 29, 1966

Mlle. Alicia Acheson
Hotel de la Harpe
19 Rue de la Harpe
Paris V
France

Hold For Delivery

Dearest Ali — Dear Ali —

I can't stand another day without you. Bienvenue a Paris. *I have to come to Europe, and I have to see it with you.* I loved your descriptions of Italy and southern France. They helped pass a dull and lifeless summer. *Your tender expressions of longing triggered sexual fantasies of such power and depth I thought everyone around me could hear them.* I fear another fall and winter of relentless work and ceaseless longing for your company. *If I don't feel your dear flesh soon I will crawl straight out of mine.* Luckily I have provisioned myself with distractions from the Strand. I'm reading Joyce, who, like *me, longed for Paris and the angel of mortal youth and beauty a woman. I love you desperately and completely.*

Tout mon amour, ma cherie, mon coeur, Votre Paul

Love, Paul

Dickie called to set up the rendezvous in Tarrytown. "Negotiations have opened," he said.

"How they going?"

"Not going. Not going anywhere. Just, the topic is opened."

He explained on the drive up to Schenectady. Richard Acheson Jr. was horrified at the idea of a son of his studying Buddhism, not just as a scholar but as an adherent. Not unexpectedly, the doctrine of Ahimsa, nonviolence, respect for life, left him unpersuaded. Left him choking, actually, in Dickie's account. The notion of Dharma, duty of right living, also failed to strike a familiar chord. He failed utterly to be able to take the ideas and doctrines seriously, his son's heartfelt interest also. I suddenly realized what Eli McCone had seen in me. I filed that away. On Dickie's recommendation I took "Metaphysics and Epistemology" ("Give us something to talk about in the car, and clarify for you all the arguments you were having with Eli," he said). That left Physics and Advanced Organic and Biochem. The reading list for The 20th Century English Novel included Joyce's *Portrait of the Artist* and Woolf's *Jacob's Room* and *Mrs. Dalloway*, so I was already ahead on the reading. Good thing. By September 9 there was a package: a beret and a clutch of books: Camus, and a British translation of Sartre's *Roads to Freedom* trilogy.

September 9, 1966

Dear Ali

I can't begin to thank you for the books. I know about the Sartre from my father; they deal with the run-up to the War, including Munich, and the Fall of France; there is no American translation that I know of. This is a treasure. And Camus! I'll be discussing Woolf soon; I can read the Sartre because I've already, thanks to you, read the Woolf.

How's Paree?

— Paul

I tried on the beret. It didn't look right, but I knew what I needed to do. I stopped shaving and started to let my hair grow. But I didn't get to read the Sartre. Not yet.

The news spread by the end of the first week of school. Morgan was dead, killed in that Operation Hastings in Quang Tri. I feared for where Dickie would take this, but he merely continued to meditate serenely, after a grimace. "I considered him dead after he enlisted," he said, but his meditation became more intense, and he was preoccupied. That night he took no meat course, and by Monday he had quietly, without announcement, become a total vegetarian. On his desk I found "Zurau Aphorism" # 96:

"The rewards of life are not life's, but fears of living a higher life; the pains not its pains, but self-torture due to this fear."

Being a vegetarian was not easy at the Nott dining rooms. On the way to the first rallye of the season I expressed concern.

"It's my next step," he said.

"Dickie, I know why you're doing this."

"That a fact."

"I know about Morgan's death too, and I can't say I'm all that broken up about it." *I'm ashamed of that Father*

"It wasn't you who had his neck under your hands," he said shortly.

There was a long, long silence as we drove north of Saratoga, north of Lake George. "In the mountains, there you feel free," he quoted. Apparently no answer was expected.

14 Septembre 1966

Cher Paul,

OK, I've been here long enough to get settled, and have enough to write about to keep you interested from an ocean away. Glad you liked the books. They were a pleasure to seek out, and as for thanks, they are only a small down payment on the thanks I owe you. It isn't a matter of thanks anyway.

So. This is an old hotel in a narrow street (off the Boulevard St Michel, the Boul Mich, just at its intersection with the Boulevard St Germain, at the foot of the Pont Neuf; it's the crossroads of the Quartier Latin) done over as a student hostel. My view is of just below the rooftops, but the south tower of Notre dame is visible over the roofs. I've already been to the bell towers; the gargoyles remind me of you. Hah! Most of the classes are at the University of Paris, the Sorbonne to you. Paris reminds me of New York, but mostly of Brooklyn (anyway, this part). It hasn't recovered from the War. There are cars, tiny Renaults, Citroen Deux

Chevaux, and bigger Citroens, buses Hemingway rode, and everywhere motorcycles, motor scooters (Vespas) and motorized bicycles. The odor of cheap gasoline and pissoirs is ubiquitous and oddly delightful. I would say Romantic, but the romance lacks a crucial ingredient (my first Parisian flirtatious remark). Catnip for a Socialist: The Rive Gauche is full of bullet holes and little brass memorial plaques wherever a Resistant fell in the Liberation, Mort Pour La France.

Speaking of, we were on a weekend excursion to Normandy, take les jeunes filles Americains to see Omaha Beach, and Paul, a propos a long-ago conversation, these were not empty beaches, they were the beaches Monet and Boudin painted and Proust wrote about. They told us that as many French civilians were killed on D-Day as allied troops. Those little plaques are all over Caen and the smaller villages which were completely wrecked in the fighting. I wonder how many innocents were killed by my father's artillerymen (I'd love to ask him if we were still on speaking terms) like little boys playing with firecrackers. Of course the Nazi regime had to be rooted out, but at what cost? And to whom? Your father's response, his disgust with war, makes sense to me. Paul, do not go to a war. There is no such thing as a Good War. Ginny Woolf thought so, and said in "3 Guineas" (it's bitingly sarcastic and hilarious) if women had more of a role in politics war would be impossible, that Feminism could help end war. Anyway, your father's response I understand. My father's, I don't. I am trying.

We saw Mt St Michel; what a wonder of medieval

architecture, and pictures in Halliburton do it no justice. It must be seen in color, by sunset light.

The countryside still shows signs of war damage, wrecked war machines and burnt out fortifications still on the beaches and in the hedgerows. Normandy and Calvados were shattered, Paul. It's all new construction. I found a book, at one of the Quai bookstalls, about the Liberation (Le Tragique Ete Normande, by Helene Dufour, a woman of course), and it was a slaughter. There were 29,000 civilians killed from June to July 1944, and their livestock, and their towns. I wonder how many my father's artillerymen killed. And how many dogs?

I wrote a paper, but I left out the dogs.

— Amour et baisers, Ali

P.S: Ginny Woolf: 3 Guineas: n20: "For just as I was told that desire for learning in woman was against the will of God, so were many innocent freedoms, innocent delights, denied in the same name". It's from a book by a Mary Butts (don't laugh). Sound familiar? Woolf calls the male subjugation of women "The Infantile Fixation". It isn't something wrong with me, Paul. It's him. This deserves study.

P.P.S: There is a harmless crazy man, he's called The Rat Man, who stands at the corner of the Boul Mich and St Germain. When a girl he thinks is pretty goes by he flashes a toy rat in her face. She jumps and everybody laughs and tells her what a compliment this is. I was complimented yesterday. My life is complete.

325

September 19, 1966

Ali —

I've read and reread your letter. I am ashamed to admit I didn't know, and never thought about, the civilian casualties of the Liberation. I guess I never thought past the destruction of Hitler and the films of the waving civilians and the girls climbing on tanks. Stupid, especially considering our own casualty. A few hours after I posted my letter to you we heard that Morgan had been killed in Nam.

I was worried Dickie would take it very badly, but he has not, at least not in the way he did when Morgan dropped out and enlisted. He is meditating more deeply, and has become vegetarian. His immersion in Buddhist practice deepens by the day. When I try to tell him this is neither his fault nor his responsibility he only says I was not the one with my hands on Morgan's throat. I have no answer to that, and more and more I think he's right. I think he was on this road already, and Morgan's death only accelerated it.

I don't know if he is writing you, but he approached your father with a proposal to study Buddhism full time. As painful as it is for me to say this, be glad you aren't here. He regards it as the opening round. There is more to come.

— Kisses back to you, Paul

P.S. Of course it's him. I thought we'd settled that.

P.P.S: I applaud the Rat Man's aesthetic judgment but not his critical methods.

P.P.P.S: My mother and grandmother are both members of SANE and Women's Strike for Peace.

Dickie made his trip downtown to deposit the last weeks' rallye winnings and came back with two backpacks and two sleeping bags and air mattresses. "No rallye this weekend, Govinda. We're taking a hike."

"Any special place?"

"Top of Mt. Marcy. Has to be this weekend; it might not be warm enough much longer."

"Any special reason?"

"Something I have to do at the top. You'll love it."

On Dickie's desk: Zurau Aphorism # 103: "You can withdraw from Reality's travails, if you will, but that is the only travail you can avoid."

These were free translations my father was experimenting with; for instance in this context he had rendered "Die Welt" as "Reality", not "The World". Under it I wrote: " 'In the struggle between yourself and Reality, hold Reality's coat', and by the way, write to your sister."

We spent Friday evening provisioning. It was raining slightly when we set out Saturday; we took shifts since Dickie thought I needed more practice on wet mountain roads. Mt. Marcy is the highest mountain in the Adirondacks, the highest in New York at 5344 feet. It is nested in a cluster of peaks of nearly the same elevation; to reach it some trails take you over the slightly smaller peaks. It is a day's climb, or rather uphill hike. We reached the trailhead at around noon; fortunately the rain had stopped and it was summer-like, just past the equinox. The trail led ever upward, through deep woods, over streams swollen with recent rains. I fell into a fantasy, looking around for sites for guerilla camps, arms caches, Castro and Che in the Sierra Madre. I had never done such hiking with a backpack; I wasn't winded but I wasn't in good enough shape to reply to Dickie's conversational sallies without becoming winded. He was of course in terrific physical shape; the conversation became a lecture; maybe it would have been anyway. It was as if he were musing aloud, thinking but wanting me to be in on his thoughts.

"The Buddha was a prince pursuing sensual pleasure full time. He wandered six years. Then he had a revelation. He sat under a pipal tree seeking Moksha; enlightenment, liberation. True liberation was peace, the absence of desire. Desire caused only suffering. Liberation from desire was enlightenment."

"I was there for the Fire Sermon, Dickie."

We struggled up a steep slope, over a field of scree. "Seek no other refuge but yourself, and let truth be your light. The truth is Dharma. Dharma is The Way of Life. The Eightfold Way. Respect for life, compassion, nonviolence."

"That's threefold."

"I'm not being exhaustive," he said patiently, passing between two boulders before a narrow canyon. We rested, had some raisins and chocolate, and watched some clouds come over and darken the trail ahead. The light was strange; the sun was under the cloud layer. We were poorly equipped for this; lightweight trail equipment was years away from invention, we were wearing tennis shoes and heavy lumber jackets. We pushed on, ever upward. The symbolism was almost as heavy as the backpacks.

The canyon was a narrow pass between a huge smooth boulder and a granite cliff. The trail hugged the cliff, parallel to a stream. In the pass the stream was a rocky torrent, but at the other end it widened out into a tiny, deep lake surrounded by low trees and high grass. There were two lean-to shelters. We threw our packs down in the nearest lean-to and just sat, looking back into the mouth of the canyon. High above, a single tree grew out and then upwards from the boulder. We both stared at it. And I don't remember if it was Dickie or me who said, "It's a model of the Universe. Out of inorganic matter, life."

"How did that ever happen?" Dickie said.

"Organic chemicals have amazing properties."

"It was a rhetorical question, Paul, but tell me about that."

"Even simple chains of carbon atoms can spontaneously form polymers. Amino acids spontaneously form protein chains. Before organisms evolved, the chemistry evolved. We don't know every step, probably never will, but we can grasp the general idea."

"I get it. And I get that every creature now alive came from one before it, and so on and so on back to the primordial creature, and so on back to the primordial chemicals. Which means...Paul, say the Universe is eternal, or anyway very, very long-lived. How long since the beginning?"

"Of life? On Earth? Best guess is 4 billion years."

"So if that 4 billion years is like a moment in the life of the Universe, it's all happened in a blink, ein Augenblick, right?"

"I guess so."

"So all life is one—from the point of view of the Universe, everything alive is alive in that instant. All life is one. You see?"

I did, in fact.

"Meaning your organic chemistry and my Buddhism arrive at the same conclusion. All life is one."

"It's all related, certainly. OK, it's One. We cannot kill a blade of grass."

"Not without straying from Dharma. One must be still."

We were, as the sun sank below the level of the surrounding mountains.

"What I don't get," Dickie said, "Is how it all emerges from nothing. Creation ex nihilo."

"Maybe it's our concept of Nothing that's wrong. 'Nothing' is just a human concept, a word. Maybe in the Universe there is never such a thing as what humans call Nothing. There's always a Something, out of which a Universe can emerge."

"You realize Eli would have said the something was a conscious, active God."

"He found it necessary."

"I don't. I don't need a Western-concept God. If what we call Nothing can generate all of this Something, there must be rules about how that works."

"Equations, Dickie. Physics, chemistry, biology."

"Oh, math, no, my Something has to be a Something without math. Or anyway, I don't have to understand the math part."

"You don't. It works without you understanding it. Like a refrigerator. Or the MG."

"But I can still use it."

"Sure. It's just that if you understand the math you can see how it all can work without conscious direction."

"But still by some rules, some kind of predictability."

"Right."

"But not necessarily by the Rules you learn by science. Or, your science is only part of the Rules."

"OK. Sure." *This was interesting.* "This is getting interesting."

We gathered wood for a fire by the waning light, set up a few rods on some rocks and heated some soup. I had a ham sandwich; Dickie had nuts and beans. We listened to the fire crackle, felt ourselves becoming drowsy. As the fire died the stars thickened above us. Something coming out of Nothing. We peed into the lake, fed the large backlog into the fire, pulled the sleeping bags close to it at the edge of the lean-to, and slept the sleep of exhaustion.

When I woke, Dickie was already up and dressed. He had the topo map out. "Know what this place is?"

"The middle of nowhere."

"It's Lake Tear-of–the-Clouds. You're looking at the headwaters of the Hudson River. Pee into that and it'll be in Brooklyn in a few days."

It was all the inspiration I needed.

Juice, bread, instant coffee, roll up sleeping bags, repack packs, and off again, upward. I was well rested, stretched out, more able; plus, for a time the going was less steep. The trees began to get shorter, the gaps between them wider. Mt. Algonquin and the other surrounding peaks began to appear. In late September there was no one else this high on the mountain. Altitude began to affect me; though it was less steep, there was less oxygen. And Dickie began to pick up rocks. I called a halt.

When I had enough breath I said, "It seems to me the last thing anyone would want right now is to pick up more weight."

"That would depend on one's plans for the journey."

"I thought the point was to reach the top."

"I have something to do there."

We reached the tree line and crossed to bare rock. Not far to go to the summit, and I was practically crawling. At the summit I threw off the backpack and lay panting. Dickie dropped his load of rocks and went to gather more, larger rocks. I watched this for a while, wondering when he was going to tell me what he was doing, maybe ask for help. He seemed not to need to, and to need not to. When he began to pile the rocks in a particular pattern, I asked him what the hell he was doing.

"Building a stupa."

"A what?"

"A stupa," he said patiently. "The Buddha's landing zone. One of them." He took out a small piece of what looked like leather and placed it under the stupa. I suddenly knew without asking that it had Morgan's name on it. Then he sat down next to me and contemplated the view. Which was spectacular. In full sunlight, the 360–degree panorama of the highest peaks in the Adirondacks. We just sat for a time, conscious that we had accomplished something important, and assimilating the feeling that very few things are more satisfying than the accomplishment of a self-assigned mission.

"This is a wonderful place," he finally said. "The Adirondacks are a wonderful place."

"You say that like you won't ever see it again."

"I will, but not for much longer. I have to leave here, Paul. I mean leave the country. It's the only way to go where I want to go."

"To study Buddhism full time."

"Exactly. The Dalai Lama has started a Tibetan Buddhist study center in a place called Dharamsala, in India. I have to figure out how to get there. Maybe how we could get there, Govinda."

"Not my thing, Dickie."

He sighed. "I know. Committed Socialist Physician. Doctor to the People."

"Something like that. Somebody has to treat the casualties. And I don't think I can pursue enlightenment until everyone is free to."

"Everyone is free to."

"Not really. They have to feed their families. They have to survive with all kinds of health problems. I don't think I can fully embrace nonviolence, either; it seems to me those are things worth fighting for."

"Socialism," Dickie said patiently. "Communism. Democracy. We're like the bull in the bullfight, always falling for the cape when we should be watching the sword."

"You lost me."

"The cape is the rhetoric of any scheme that brings its proponents to power. A psychopath like Hitler can outline a utopia and all the opposing effort goes into refuting the rhetoric. Which the Communists and capitalist democrats did most ably, and constructed other tyrannies. The sword is human desire, the desire for power and wealth. The rest is just justification, rationalization. It all leads to the same place. Capitalism, Fascism, Communism, they're all based on exploiting the Universe and ultimately man himself."

"And the answer is?"

"Get out."

"Of town?"

"Of Desire."

"Buddhism isn't another rhetoric, another bullfighter's cape?"

"Nope. Because: No sword. The goal is not power over others, or the Universe, it is the individual's loss of that desire."

"You could be a hell of a politician, Dickie. Quite a progressive."

"You know when I said about Morgan, that you weren't the one with your hands on his neck? You know what I was feeling when that was happening?"

"Rage."

"No. Fear. Of myself. Of what I might be capable of. In India's history there was a king, Ashoka. He ruled a huge bloody empire, from Persia to modern India except the south, Kalinga. He was cruel, ruthless. So he launched the Kalinga War. And something happened. He saw the slaughter from the front lines, and he became so appalled that he renounced war entirely. He built schools, hospitals; he tolerated all religions, allowed women to be educated. He built stupas everywhere, propounded Buddhism all over his realm. He embraced the Dharma. You don't want to feel what I felt that night. You do not."

Going down a mountain is almost as difficult as going up. You use muscles you usually don't. They start to hurt, along the shins, around the hips. When we reached the trailhead we found that someone had parked us in. We sat in the car, Dickie still seemingly infinitely patient.

"I feel I never thanked you enough for what you did that night in front of Phi Delt," he said.

"No thanks necessary."

He stood, found his backpack, found what he was looking for, and handed me a picture, a diagram of The Eightfold Way. It looked exactly like a ship's wheel. "Here," he said. "You are no longer Govinda. I declare you an avatar of the Snow Lion. Protector of The Buddha." He laughed. I was beginning to wonder about his sanity, and he sensed it.

"Relax, Paul. I'm not going nuts. I'm trying to work out how to get where I have to go. First thing is to try my sister's route. Think they'll give me a year abroad?"

"In India?"

"No. But once I'm out, I don't have to come back. Here's where better grades would have helped."

"Dickie, your Desire didn't kill Morgan. His did."

"You're correct, Snow Lion. Only it wasn't that simple. It was his Desire in collision with mine. I can only do something about mine. He'll have to work his out in another life." It was almost two hours until the other hikers showed up, apologized, moved their car. Dickie showed preternatural patience. If he had done so a year ago I would have regarded it as a pose. Now I regarded it as genuine. And it continued.

27 Septembre 1966
Cher Paul—

'Ca va? I write to you so as not to forget mon Anglais. I make it a point to conduct my life entirely en Francais. Some of the girls wonder why the French go all frosty when addressed in English (accent Americain) and pay for things in dollars. Je parle Francais seulement and I change my dollars for Francs, 5 to the dollar counting the exchange fee (cheaper at American Express).

They bussed us to Chartres on another weekend excursion. We were inside the cathedral and it was dark from an approaching storm, and I was staring up at the great rose window when it was completely illuminated by a lightning bolt that just fired every pane of stained glass in the church. Amazing. It was as if you were there.

Tout mon Amour, Ali

But I wasn't

October 3, 1966
Cher Ali

Physics now calls. I could calculate the energy in your lightning bolt, give you the frequencies of the light absorbed and transmitted by a Chartres Bleu window, calculate the refraction I took Dickie's advice and signed up for Metaphysics and Epistemology, so I could also talk with you about the ideas behind the church's construction. None of this would bring me to stand with you when the lightning lit it up. Thank you for sharing the moment. Also the insights about the War.

— Votre Paul

8 Octobre 1966
Mon Cher—

Honetement, I believe some of les jeunes filles Americains just came to Paris to shop. No shortage of chic shops, or jeunes filles Americains to haunt them. Myself I am learning the SNCF the way you know the New York Central. I took myself to Versailles today and became a Socialist. You would not believe the opulence. You can't until you come from a dump on the Rive Gauche and stroll through the Hall of

Mirrors and into the gardens Marie Antoinette had remodeled whenever the whim took her.

The shop I do haunt is Sylvia Beach's Shakespeare & Co. and it isn't The Strand but I did find a copy of Harrington's "The Other America". Is what I felt at Versailles what you felt stepping into Chez Acheson? If you don't mind my asking.

— Yours in Revolutionary Solidarity, Ali

October 13, 1966
Comrade Acheson

I don't at all mind you asking. Yes, I did feel that, at least a little bit; it came out in a sarcastic remark I had no right to make to Dickie in Brooklyn while you were upstairs with my grandmother. But I never felt it toward you, or Dickie either, I think because I knew you as people, and because it became clear to me that your wealth was bringing you no happiness, that as I said to Bina that time it oppressed you almost as much as it oppressed the masses.

Actually that wasn't it. It was that I was so entranced by you the class thing stopped mattering. Vive La Revolution. Vive l'amour.

— Votre Paul

But what did she think of my home?

336

18 Octobre 1966

Cher Paul—

CAT lab is no better en Francais. I get the vertebrate body plan and variations, I really do. Dissection is not my thing. I cannot imagine being a surgeon. Lucky I don't want to be; that's the last tree house with a No Girls Allowed sign. The art is the relief. Everywhere I look, exquisite cathedrals, exquisite architecture, museums stuffed with royal loot. Stopped in Ste Chapelle yesterday; the windows are huge and the stonework so fine, filigree really; it's as if it's made of light itself. I wanted to take a picture, but that wasn't enough; I wanted to copy the experience from my brain into yours. To share this with you. What if you make a huge bet on the MG and win—could you come over then? There are youth hostels you could stay in for practically nothing.

Letter from Bina. She refused to go back to India with her mother to meet the fiancé. Big flap. Huge. In the end her father supported her and her mother backed down. See what we started? Tell Dickie and give him my love.

— Tout mon Amour, Ali

P.S. I now dream in French. Paul, vous etes mon reve. Non. Tu es mon reve. If it's true the wealth/class thing doesn't bother you let me buy you a ticket to Paris. Please Paul.

Was she crazy about me, or just crazy?

I had just left Schenectady Savings with a cashier's check for Sam when a woman with a baby carriage asked me for a light. "I'm sorry," I said, "I don't smoke."

"Good for you," she said, "It's a nasty habit, but it keeps the weight down. It's Paul, isn't it?"

It was Mrs. Salter. The baby was wrapped all in pink against the weather; the little face, so kitten-like, peeped out of the roll of blankets, asleep, at peace. "She's beautiful, Mrs. Salter. What's her name?"

"That she is. It's Roberta. And I must apologize to you. I behaved very badly the night you were over. I had just found out I was pregnant, and I was very anxious, and I don't handle anxiety well. Not without cigarettes or a drink, and I couldn't do either, I think, being pregnant, so…"

"That's alright, Mrs. Salter, we understood."

"Did you? I only learned later that night that your own father had been a professor. I hope I didn't offend you."

"Certainly not."

"Well, please convey my apology to your friend Acheson. I know his family slightly. His father did some legal work for mine. Where did your father teach?"

"He was a professor of German literature at Brooklyn College."

"Really? Walk with me," she said.

There was no civil way of leaving her short of my next stop at the Post Office.

"How exciting to be able to teach in a place like New York, not…" She shifted the box she was carrying from Geissner's, the women's specialty store next to the bank. "White gloves," she said, "For tea with the President's wife. You must know what that's like, from your mother."

"Not…No, not really. My mother taught English at the high school level. Still does. I don't think they have teas at Brooklyn College."

338

She put the box of gloves into the carriage.

"Your husband's a brilliant teacher," I said.

"Yes," she said, "He is." We were at the Post Office. "Amazing to think that this little one's prospects in life depend as much on what Prexy's wife thinks of my gloves as it does on her father's brilliance."

There's a war. Cities are burning. A people are waking up. What planet is this I've landed on?

A surprise at the next rallye: An older (25+) couple with a classic MGA. "It's a beauty," Dickie said. "Gotta be at least fifteen years old, maybe older. I love it."

"And it could be a ringer. Same as us. If Sam were here he'd wait for dark and be under it looking for modifications."

"Feels like Sam *is* here. Flashlight batteries warm?"

"Should be."

"I'll just go have a friendly chat."

In the night we made a long arc around the motel parking lot to approach it from the far side, we hoped out of sight of the rooms. I carried a bedspread to block light from under it. Dickie crawled under, moved the light around, snapped it off and we were done.

"As you thought. Look, these models were built rugged, for 1940s roads, practically jeeps, and the suspension he has in there would be enough to run the Baja. And he has Michelins. Our rallye days are over, Govinda."

"If they follow the same strategy, we have one more winning ticket. Tomorrow. We could score big."

"Can't risk it. They may not be as devious as us—just get in and win. We can risk what we planned, no more." He was right. We won, but they were right on our tail. No more next times.

October 24, 1966

Ma Cherie

The longing could not be greater and the timing could not be worse. Last weekend brought a new couple to the rallye circuit, with a car built like a tank. This thing is going to blow everything else off the road. I don't know how I feel about having you pay my way to Paris. Did Virginia pay for Leonard? It isn't just the air fare; it's meals, Metro fares, I don't know what else. It isn't the wealth/class thing, it's a male/female thing, and I'm ashamed I can't get past it, the thought of you paying my expenses. What picture does that conjure up? This is idiocy on the grand scale, I tell myself, look at what you're turning down, Paris with I almost wrote The Girl Of My Dreams you, what is this? I confuse myself. Here it is: You could bring me to Paris and I couldn't even buy you dinner.

— Votre pauvre Paul

Silence from Paris for three weeks. Then a huge, fat envelope. *Uh oh. A Dear John*

1 Novembre 1966

Mon Pauvre—

I'm sorry for not writing sooner, but this one took a long time to write, because I had An Adventure, and I had to wait for the conclusion. Actually I still don't know it.

340

I don't remember if I told you my cousin Eleanor is here too, with the Vassar Junior Year Abroad Program. She was always my favorite cousin on my father's side. I was with her and a friend of hers from her program at the Jeu de Paume, which is the Impressionist Wing of the Louvre. It's funny, whenever I go to a museum here, which is every week or more often, I feel like you're with me. I've seen a lot of paintings I'd like to step into. Maybe some day. Anyway, here we were and it's obvious this guy is ogling us, following us. Which isn't that strange; Eleanor makes me look like—what did you and Dickie say? A bag of doorknobs?—but he's young, very dashing-looking, well-dressed, not some poor Sorbonne student with his tongue hanging out. He looks Parisian, though. Finally in front of Monet's Rouen Cathedrals he approaches us and says, Pardonnez moi, mes jeunes filles; vous etes Americains, non? Which is pretty obvious, but next he says, Well so am I, I'm Phillipe de Contigny, from the Embassy, and I'd like to take the three of you to dinner to discuss something. Maxim's.

So here it was, what the faculty chaperones had told us about, some guy in CIA wanting to use us, or one of us, as a courier on our next visit home. I wonder why they don't want something in the Diplomatic Pouch, who might be reading what, what private stuff. Eleanor is really cool, she tells him to take himself off somewhere so we can discuss it. Her friend thinks maybe this guy is a creep who wants to get us all in bed, Eleanor says that would have to be some big bed and anyway he'd have to buy us that dinner at Maxim's first. Ha

341

Ha. No, she says, this guy is CIA, and I agree, and we've been warned about this, and Eleanor says But Maxim's, and we just have the best meal Uncle Sam ever bought anybody and tell him a polite No or We'll Think About It. It sounded like a great joke, and she said she'd call home and check out his bona fides.

So we take his card and agree to meet him at Maxim's Thursday night, (this was Sunday); if Eleanor gets a red flag we just don't show up. But Eleanor calls to say the de Contignys are genuine American peerage, well how nice for them, and even though I have a queasy feeling about this Eleanor was always the daring one that set up all the games and on and on.

Thursday night I get to Maxim's, little black dress; the heels trick won't work with him, he's as tall as you are. Shit Shit Shit Anyway, no Eleanor, no Eleanor's friend, I figure they must be inside, but they aren't, only Phillipe, and he's at a window seat hidden between two potted plants, at a table for four. I should have turned around right then, but I wasn't that suspicious yet. Only just enough, because he gets up, pulls out my chair, tres gallant, takes my coat to the checkroom and pockets the check. I ask him for the check and he smiles this charming smile and says he'll keep it and I say give me the damned check it's my damned coat. Which he does. I say the others must be late and he says no and shows me a note; last minute cancellation, surprise exam tomorrow. Right. There's wine, he opens it, sniffs it, tastes it, approves, pours me a glass, pours himself a glass, I take a sip, he takes

342

a swig, he looks around for the waiter, I pour ¾ of my wine into one of the plants. Which is what I used to do with Riley when they served something disgusting. He makes small talk, where are you from, where he's from, what are you studying, blah blah blah and I wait for him to ask me when I'm going home but he doesn't, he goes on as if this were a blind date. The food comes, by this time I've poured half the bottle of wine into the plant and he's poured the other half into his gut.

The meal is over and he's asking about dessert, and still no courier pitch, so I ask him straight out when he's planning to ask me to carry something back to the States, I wasn't born yesterday you know, and he grins and says this isn't one of those things, he's not on official duty, it was the only way he could think of to get me to come out with him, my father had told him if he just called me and introduced himself I probably wouldn't. In vino veritas. The son of a bitch just doesn't ever give up. Did Eleanor really cancel, I ask him, or did you cancel on her, and he says, I did, and grins wider. Quel romance. So, he says, now you know how much I wanted to meet you, do you want to go back to your little apartment or someplace more interesting. This was now officially scary, Paul. I don't want to come off sounding like I was so cool and high handed and in control. This was scaring me. You know my vow, and it isn't for nothing; I'm not that socially adept. So I grinned back and said someplace interesting sounded, well, interesting, and I would just go powder my nose while he ordered us dessert. I actually said Powder My Nose. I did use the powder room (there was actual powder) and then I picked up my coat and asked the checkroom woman (I almost wrote girl) for one of those note things and this is what I wrote:

Phillipe:
   Tell my father he can go to hell.
   While you're at it, why don't you join him there?

I thought about a taxi, but I anticipated, correctly as it turns out, that I wouldn't be getting this month's check from home. I'm starting to know the Metro as well as you know the New York subway. One meal at Maxim's (sans dessert) and since then I've been stretching my funds eating at little cafes in the Quartier Latin and the Marais (that's the Jewish neighborhood, what's left of it; can't get a knish though). I was pretty proud of myself for handling this, at first, but now I feel ashamed I let myself get dragged into it just to get a fancy meal. And that poor plant. I don't know how far I can stretch my allowance. Good thing Shakespeare & Co had Frommer's Paris On $5 A Day. I might have to tap my other money.

   Paul. Je suis pauvre aussi, maintenant. Paris is a beautiful city, but I find I prefer New York. And maybe Brooklyn. I spotted de Beauvoir at a student café. She was with Sartre and he was surrounded by women students <u>and she puts up with it!</u> He treats her like crap. I'd heard that and now I've seen it for myself.

344

Tell Dickie this story, he'll love it. I still haven't worked out whether Eleanor was a party to this; I called her and she said de Contigny cancelled on them, didn't he cancel on me? Do I believe her? I haven't called her again. On second thought, tell Dickie so he'll know just how far Father is prepared to go, and who he's connected with.

Courage, mon pauvre, mon brave, Votre,

— Ali Not de Contigny

I did show the letter to Dickie.

"Eleanor is a little snot," he said. "Always was. Ali was always trying to play up to her. For a friend. Which brings me to this: Maybe bad news here, Govinda. She talks to you like a friend. Not good, little bro. Pass me the screwdriver (we were tuning the MG). Start it and rev it." I did; he adjusted the idle. "Like a litter of kittens. No, seriously, Paul, if she likes you as a friend that's not a good thing. Not if you like her like I think you maybe do."

"How about we discuss the fact that your father is pimping her to any…"

"It isn't pimping when the Upper Clahsses do it, dear boy. It's matchmaking. He, or more likely deSheveled or whoever, probably saw Ali's picture on my father's desk, or a relative of his did, and asked about her and that lit a circuit in my father's brain. Or."

"Or what?"

"She told you to share this story with me. What did the letter say? Tell me how far the old man is willing to go, and what? Who he's connected with?"

345

"Yeah."

"Is she trying to tell me…Paul, she knows something I was going to tell you shortly. Now is as good a time as any. I'm planning to confront him over Christmas with my non-negotiable plan to study Buddhism. She's telling me to watch my step. And watch my back."

"For what, the CIA?"

"Yes, Paul. My plan is to study with the Dalai Lama. In India. I wasn't kidding." *It furthers to meet the great man*

"He's going to shit himself."

"More likely shit on me. And yes, CIA, apparently he has connections, some of his Navy friends stayed in the military and other places. Welcome to the WASP establishment, Paulie."

"You're not serious. You are serious."

"I am. I wonder about another possibility—that deBonair was already watching all the Betty Coeds abroad and called the old man for an all clear. She told us about the courier thing…"

"Why not Eleanor?"

"Maybe she was next on the list. Maybe he just likes brunettes. I don't know. I'd dearly love to meet him. Or my old self would."

"She did a pretty good job taking care of herself."

"And told you all about it, Friend. If you know anything about women, you know they don't get romantic with friends. She's telling you all the tricks of the feminine trade. Meaning she isn't planning to use them on you."

Naturally I gave this some thought. First it worried me. Then I thought, he doesn't know about what happened on the raft, or at the Strand, or anyplace else. It didn't seem to have occurred to Dickie, as enlightened as he thought he was, that a man and woman might base a relationship on emotional honesty, or on mutual contempt for these masculine/feminine games. All this expertise about women. These guys—this entire damned school—talked about women as if they were another species. Which given the isolation of the Monastery on the Mohawk they might as well have been. If these guys knew so damned much about women, why were they so desperate all the time? Why did they have to get them drunk? It also occurred to me that he might be right. Or that hers was a more elaborate game. Or that I was just as trapped, not taking the offered trip to Paris. Or that relations between men and women had become so distorted and poisoned it was impossible to tell. There was, of course, Chaskis. Here was another thing: the experience with Chaskis might be to my advantage, and hers; it had turned her away from worse. And there was, of course, that kiss. Reason should see you through anything, shouldn't it? Only reason didn't. Reason was steadily making this worse. What if this guy had been just some guy? Not connected with her father? What if there were other guys? Why had she stayed until dessert? Why, when she saw the empty table, did she stay at all? Why did she agree to go in the first place? *Why did she go to Paris in the first place?* And what was this other money? What did she mean by that? *Where was that ticket to Paris now? If she sent it I'd go in a heartbeat*

You love her but you don't trust her.

I had an odd dream. A female announcer was giving the weather. 'This is WQXN" she said. I woke, felt anxious. The weather girl, that was easy. WQXR was New York's classical music station, the one always on in the apartment as I was growing up. Why WQXN, then?

I didn't write back for almost as long as she hadn't.

December 9, 1966
Dear Ali —
    My turn to be sorry for not writing sooner. Big papers

347

due, all the rallyeing catching up with me. I got to know the Adirondacks and Green Mountains much too well. Dickie and I had a good laugh at the account of your intrepidity. I hope the money thing worked out; I'd hate to think you couldn't afford postage.

I can't stop thinking, though: How did you ever agree to go out with this guy? I mean, if I were a poor student with my tongue hanging out and tried to pick you up at the Met, all I'd really need was a sharp suit and a little French?
— Paul

14 Decembre 1966
(Carte Postale: Ste Chappelle, Interieur)
Dear Paul—
I can't believe it. I've made you jealous! Hah!

December 19, 1966
Dear Ali
It isn't funny. You're in Paris. I'm in Schenectady. I don't have two nickels to rub together. I am jealous. Or something. I can't compete with nobility, American or French, I figure, so I worry. I'm sorry, I do. I'm crazy.
— Paul

Nothing. Silence. No letter. No postcard. Nothing. Why? What had I done? Was Dickie right, that whatever passion had been there a year ago had cooled, I had misread everything, I was just a friend, and now she saw I wanted to be something more? More than she wanted? More than she could give? What? It was a long, sad, frightened, angry Christmas.

3 Janvier 1967

Paul—

I found your letter when I got back from Christmas. One of the instructors took pity and invited me to her Noel. Otherwise I'd have had to spend it alone in the hostel. No young men there. Look, buddy, you have a lot of nerve. There are weekly mixers here for us; Wellsmith isn't the only Semester In Paris program, there are plenty of guys. We get invitations to Embassy parties, gallery events, other stuff. And I go. It's lonely, and these are social events, and I go. Boys at the Sorbonne want to have coffee with Les Belles Americains, and sometimes even one Belle Americain, and sometimes I want to feel like Une Belle Americain. I can't believe I have to be telling you this. I'm not a nun, Paul, and I don't expect you're a monk Did he tell her? He told her No he didn't Shit Shit Shit I'll be home soon, or anyway back Stateside, I'm flying to Boston and on to Northampton from there. We'll talk then. Idiot.

— Ali

Darling. We're having our first quarrel.

Dickie was agitated and meditating when I got in after Christmas. "You look like five pounds of shit in a three pound bag. You told him, didn't you."

"I told him. He about busted a gut. I mean, he was quiet at first, took a drink, thought for a few minutes. Then he said it was fine with him if I dropped out of school, I could always go back, but only if I enlisted in the military. I told him I was becoming a Buddhist, that this meant I was an absolute pacifist, I could not and would not take life and he said fine, be a medic, and I told him I couldn't be a part of any military organization. Then he exploded, went on and on about what I was throwing away, and he would never allow that, and I'd better go back and do well on my exams and think very carefully. I told him I had been thinking very carefully, and this was the conclusion I'd come to and I wasn't going to change my mind. He dropped the anger and said Please Dickie, go back and do well on your exams, and think this over a second time, and we could talk again at semester break. Paul, I think from here forward we should conduct ourselves as if we were being watched."

"Huh?"

"My father's firm sometimes uses investigators. I've met some, when they've come to the house to deliver something, he may start surveillance on me. I think he knows I have my passport. I have a plan. Or part of one. I don't think he knows I have enough money, shit, I don't really…"

"I know how to spot a tail."

"What?"

"I said I know how to spot surveillance. My father taught me."

"No shit? Then we'll watch…"

"No, we can do it more actively…if we really think it's happening."

It had become "we".

Dear Ali, I'm having An Adventure

No word from Paris. No obvious surveillance. Study Week, Finals Week, Semester break for Nott. Not for Wellsmith. But when I got back for second semester there was a letter in my box. On the outside rear of the envelope:

*I never got to send this. It was my last night in Paris
and no one had a stamp.*

19 Janvier 1967

Cher Paul,
    Or should I say Jean-Louis. Finalement, I got around to seeing Un Homme et une Femme at a third run house in a banlieu. There was an empty seat beside me. You were in it.
        Tout mon Amour, Ali

I choked up. There were hot tears in the corners of my eyes.

25 Janvier 1967

Cher Ali, Mon Reve, Mon Coeur
    Je suis tres stupide. Je suis fou. My damned French isn't good enough for this. We'll see each other Spring Break, or sooner. We'll talk as soon as I have your new number. Call me.
    Je t'aime Jean Louis (Paul)

There. That's done. Said it.

But events overtook us. Dickie had met with his father again at the break, and had made it clear he was not going to continue to study anything but Buddhism, and would not join any military organization of any kind, would not join the Peace Corps either (which wasn't draft-exempt anyway) and would not fake a 4-F classification. He was adamant. We walked around frigid downtown Schenectady, trying to spot a tail. And pulled one. I spotted him, Dickie recognized him, guy named Mike, he said; we split up, Mike followed Dickie back to the campus and I followed Mike to a maroon Olds 98 two-door that could probably do 140 on the straight and level. *The game's afoot* We started to limit our off-campus trips, doing a few to keep Mike from thinking we'd spotted him. And started to plan in earnest to get Dickie out of the country.

"This'll make you a draft-dodger, Dickie. A felon. It's a one-way trip."

"You think I don't know that?"

"I'm just saying it's the basis for any plan. So. Plane, train, car?"

"I have to hoard every penny. Can't be plane, then. Train, Mike can take me off it anywhere along the line. Has to be the car. And it has to be both of us, so you can bring the car back. To Ali. That should perk your interest."

It did. "It does."

"While I was home last spring I got the safe deposit box keys from my mother. Told her I was getting my passport to apply for a Semester Abroad. I picked up the MG's title documents. I can make over title to Ali; she's eighteen, she can hold title. It's the car Daddy refused to give her when she told him to shove his coming out party. I can get an India visa in Canada."

"Bina."

"Bina's father, yeah."

"So we drive to Toronto?"

"Too far, all flat terrain, we'd never be able to shake that Olds. It'll have to be a dash, to Montreal. The Northway is finished all the way to the border now, for the World's Fair. And the best part: No state police troop yet. It's wide open. If he follows us there we can lose him in the city. But I bet we can decoy him and leave him wondering."

"How?"

"One more rallye. We sign up and drive part of it, slip down a back road and make a run for the Northway. And we throw him off by doing a rallye south, in the Catskills, not the Adirondacks. Find us a route, Govinda."

"You find the rallye, I'll find the route. Depends on the date, the weather to the north."

There was one. Saturday, March 4, starting in Schoharie and running south into the Catskill Preserve. There were roads north in a wide arc around Schenectady, and sunset would be early enough to hide us on the Northway if by some miracle Mike figured out our play. I had Ali's number by now; but Dickie thought she might be under surveillance too.

"How likely is that? And why?"

"Why take a chance? I'll use a contact at Wellsmith, she can call from a pay phone in the library or somewhere." Well, he knew his father better than I did. "Not yet. Closer to D-Day. We have to keep his eyes off her."

Dickie's meditations left me alone *with him still in the damned room* for hours. I tried to meditate, too, but my mind wouldn't empty. The closest I got was one long Sunday afternoon toward the end, too wet and cold to even work; I was across a chessboard from my father. It was not peace. *"Pavel," he said, "Do you know what you're doing?"* No, I said, *what? The chess pieces were like a city, how they moved seemed to shift with every turn. "Why did you go to Nott?" You wanted me to. "Not without me to..." How was I supposed to know that? He ignored me. "I was as alone as you. Heidelberg, Berlin, Warsaw, London, occupied Prague, I know Pavele, I found out, rage won't keep you company."*

We made a timetable. At D minus 14 we let it be known around, by easing it into conversation, that we'd be at this Schoharie rallye. At D minus 7 we bring Ali into it, and tune the car. At D minus 5 we gas up the car. At D minus 2 we close the MG Enterprises account, distributing it in three cashier's checks (I would use mine immediately to open a savings account). At D minus 1, after dark, Dickie pulls Mike, and I pack the car. That left the planning for D plus 1 and after.

"Just drive back to Schenectady, maybe they'll think I came back too, get a night's sleep, and drive on over to Northampton. End of plan," Dickie said. "My father will go nuts, call you, call Ali, ask where I am, you won't know so don't worry. I think I can disappear pretty quick in Europe. If I go to Europe. Could go the other way. Depends on the financial situation, other factors. Sorry, the less you know the less you can tell him. I'll mostly be improvising anyway."

"You have to let us know you're OK."

"I will."

"I'm still on Dean's List. I have unlimited cuts."

"Relax. You'll be home by Sunday afternoon, call her, grab some money, take a day to go to Northampton, home by Monday night. Whatever you want. Paul?"

"What."

"Until then, radio silence."

I saluted. It was only three weeks away now.

That left only the job of looking completely like everything was routine. And the job of saying goodbye. I'd be without Dickie for the first time since I came to Nott. I hadn't realized until this minute how much I had depended on him. Friendship, support, advice (however inaccurate), transportation...excitement. Without Dickie I'd be a complete and utter tool, a book-bound drone. He had brought to my life almost everything about it that was alive, in Schenectady. Even in New York.

Ali would have the car. She could visit, I could visit her. We could hike in the mountains. We could go to New York. We could...Emotional handoff; one Acheson to another. But Dickie had always had my back. And I had always had his. Then I thought—it was a long time since either of us needed our backs covered. We had moved on to something a lot more sophisticated. Something distance might bear. Something adult. It was time for me to have my own back.

It all went according to plan. We let it be known we'd entered the Schoharie Rallye, we tuned the car as usual, gloved hands still cold, breath steaming, in the parking lot. Dickie talked to Ali, gave her my love, he said, and grinned. We did our school work; Dickie even handed in a last paper. We walked downtown to the bank, ignoring Mike the tail, as if we were just withdrawing the Schoharie entry fee. The night before, D minus 1, Dickie took a walk to Diamante's, nursed a brew for an hour while Mike stood around outside and I packed the two loaded backpacks into the MG's boot, already crowded by the sandbags. I stuffed a small duffle into the rear floor, where it wouldn't be visible in the dark. At the last minute I threw in my sleeping bag. *You never knew.* That was it.

When I think of it, and I do, often, it is as The Big Road Trip. It began routinely enough; a cold dawn, clouds visible over the Helderbergs, rolling through downtown Schenectady *G E   GE GE*

GE   GENERAL ELECTRIC GENERAL ELECTRIC and out under the Thruway, southwest through the rolling country bordering the Catskill Preserve. Behind us, far enough to be innocuous, close enough to keep us in sight, the maroon Olds. Found the meeting point, paid in our entry fee, oh look, the MGA was here, we waved. Here was a Mustang *Bonjour Jean-Louis* the timekeepers deployed, we took our place in the starting lineup, checked gauges a last time (the maroon Olds around a corner, ready to pick us up again at the finish line), engines revved, and one after another we were off. It was midmorning. The clouds were still holding off.

We kept to the course through two checkpoints; at the widest gap, between checkpoints two and three, after opening a lead that left us invisible to the car behind us, Dickie threw the MG into a turn onto a one-lane county road that ran north into a hamlet called Gallupville, dumped us onto New York 7 west to our goal, New York 30. We had made a wide arc around Schoharie; Mike would be knocking back another cup of joe, killing time until we showed up for our prize.

New York highway 30 runs up from the Pennsylvania border in the first, the easternmost, valley in the great spine of ridges, a spur of the Appalachians that had pinned the original colonists to the coast. We picked it up just south of the Helderberg Gap, one of the first passes leading west to the Niagara Frontier. The wagon road that became U.S. 20 out of Albany ran along the Mohawk River; then had come the Erie Canal, the railroad and the Thruway. We crossed them all, speeding northward, past Johnstown and Gloversville, hollowed out by the export of apparel jobs. By the Millennium all of industrial New England would look like this.

"I know Gloversville," I said to Dickie. "It was organized by the ILGWU. My grandmother was an organizer for them, after my grandfather died. It used to be the center of glovemaking. That honor now goes to Italy, with the dollars and the jobs."

"When we pass the IBEW hall in Schenectady they call you Hippie, Govinda; your Workers are nationalist to the core."

"Nationalism is false consciousness, says Marx."

"It's all false consciousness."

"I'm starting to agree with you. Except love, and friendship."

"Even those. But those are the hardest to let go of. They'll be the last to go. If they ever do."

The road skirted the west shore of Great Sacandaga Lake and entered the Adirondack Preserve. The lake was frozen; the cottages, so alive in summer, were closed and shuttered, the tiny towns and their stores mostly dark and empty.

"We were a happy family once, Paul. Mom, Dad, me, and my brainy sister. It went bad, I don't know why. Or I do know why. She discovered the library in town when she was about six. Never looked back. She could hide out from the arguments in her books. Anyway, that's how it started. I saw the same thing you did; he bullied her, he persecuted her. Before that we did the usual brother-sister fooling around, the mock-bullying. But I stopped. I knew to stop. I couldn't stop him, I was just a kid; you know, when you're a kid you just accept anything your parents, hell, all adults, do, as right. But this wasn't right. So I started trying to protect her, you know, and they sent me off to Creffield."

We broke out a snack; the MG hummed along. *In the mountains, there you feel free.* Sacandaga, Hope Valley, Wells. In the middle of nothing but darkening mountain peaks north of Wells was the junction with Highway 8 eastbound. Griffin, Bakers Mills, Sodom (!), Johnsburg, Wevertown, little Loon Lake; signs to the Northway pointed down both forks at the center of town.

"Stay on 8," I said, "The other fork is a side road through town, we can make better time getting on from 8." A few minutes later we were there. Time to gas up, water the flowers. The Northway connects to

357

Autoroute 15 at the Rouses Point border crossing, all, as Dickie had said, new for the upcoming Terre des Hommes Exhibition. It was getting dark now. As Dickie said, the road was as yet unpatrolled. I offered to drive.

"No thanks, Govinda, this may be the last time I'll ever do this." And Dickie made his valedictory drive. It was a beauty; the little car wound out to 100, 110, 120. It was almost too loud for conversation, except at high volume.

"Paul, I have to ask you. Take care of Ali."

"How am I supposed to do that? Does she even want to be taken care of?"

"That's how. You just did it. I told you, I ran interference for her with the old man for years until they shipped me off to Creffield. I made a lousy job of it. I had my own problems with him, and the strategy didn't include confronting him every time he treated her like shit. I'm ashamed to say. But you. You took on the job the minute you met her. Or met him. It makes no difference. *It does to me.* She needs a friend. It wouldn't hurt for you to be more than that. Look, she's every bit as bright as you are, way brighter than me. You're the same age. She isn't hard to look at…"

"We've been down this road, Dickie."

"…and she digs you. She digs you, Paul; she gets you. And you have to admit, not that many people do. Not that many people get her, either. I think all the people who do are in this car. You really appreciate her."

"So what am I supposed to do, that I'm not already doing?"

"More of it. Stop letting a year go by between seeing each other. Bring her the car, and she'll be able to get out of the cage they have her in. She'll be able to visit you. Maybe she can rallye. The two of you."

"That's a picture." *Wait, that really* was *a picture.* "Deal," I said.

"Deal," he said.

"I have a favor to ask too."

"What?"

"Stop saying I, or we—Ali and I—are brighter than you. You see as deeply into things as we do. Into books. Maybe deeper. You're going to take this a lot further. I think you maybe have more guts than either of us."

"I don't know, man. I don't know if I'm doing a courageous thing, or just running away. I guess that depends on where I go, or how far I get."

"How close to the Buddha."

"How close to the Buddha."

Bienvenue a la Belle Province. Quebec, me souviennes. Autoroute 15 Nord. In those days you didn't need a passport to cross the Canada border. It was empty flat country, completely dark, from the border station until the lights appeared across the St. Lawrence. We crossed into the city on Pont Victoria after refueling in La Prairie. The prices were higher; Dickie told me these were Imperial Gallons. I pulled the Montreal map and steered us up Rue Bridge and Rue Peel toward the big cross on Mount Royal and the McGill campus, where I hoped we'd find a room or at least a couch. I needn't have worried; Bina had given Dickie a contact, the first inkling I had that he hadn't told me everything. But I was too beat to think straight.

Morning broke cold in the dorm. It was good to wash and shave. We found a combination bakery/coffee shop near campus off Sherbrooke; croissants and brioche for breakfast, and wonderful coffee. An impulse: I bought a brioche and two birthday candles. American money was welcome, fortunately; we had arrived so late the cambios were closed, and now it was Sunday.

"Back to work," Dickie said. He parked two blocks from the railroad station downtown. He got out, swung his backpack out of the boot, adjusted the straps and grabbed the duffle, and started walking while I scanned his back trail. Nothing. I waited until he'd gone a block, locked up with the second set of keys, and followed. I couldn't see a tail on either of us. I watched him exchange money at the cambio and buy a ticket to Toronto. We met in the station bar.

"One of the reasons you never liked beer," he said, "Is that the 'Skellar and Dio's serve crap. Try a Molson's ale."

"I believe I will."

"This is a banner day. Well. I guess it is."

"I'm going to miss you, man," I said.

"Tell me something. If you weren't so crazy about my sister, would you be doing this?"

I about choked. "Of course I would. You're my friend. You're a damned good friend." *OK I just gave it away*

"I always wondered why. Not because of my sister? I mean, you met her first."

"Dickie…"

"Jesus, your sense of humor goes completely to hell whenever I try to talk to you about her, you ever notice that? It's how I know you're serious, even if you don't."

I refused to take the bait. "I like the way you think. We're from completely different backgrounds…"

"Ah. You like the exotics."

"…but we see things the same way. Value the same things. Think almost the same way, not exactly, enough different to make it interesting…I like the way you take things seriously. Jesus, Dickie, who knows? I like you. And I'm going to miss you." *I'm going to miss you.*

"You do know, and I say this in all friendship, man…that you are a walking mass of class and ethnic resentment."

"I was."

"Still. Some."

"Less, thanks to you."

"More to my sister, I think." He grinned.

"Both of you."

"Look, we taught each other the same things, Paul. How to navigate in each other's worlds. Which…now, they intersect. More and more, they will. Now I have to learn to navigate in another. Learning yours was a first step. Thank you."

"Navigation. I do this for friends." *What was he trying to say*

"Or do you just like fighting with my old man?"

"It isn't like we've spent our entire time doing that. Just the past few weeks. Months."

"The reason I ask…look, I was only building up to this question. I've waited until the last possible minute to ask."

"What already?"

"Do you really like my sister like I think you do, because she could be serious about you."

"Dickie…"

"Or do you just enjoy rescuing her from her cruel, anti-Semitic, anti-intellectual, antifeminist father? Is she just a damsel in distress? Someone who…you could feel just as bad about not preventing a cruelty as about perpetrating one?"

I was stunned by this very obvious question, obvious to anyone but me. Did Ali wonder this too? Had they discussed this? Would they? *Is this why he thought I was back and forth about her Is this why you tested me you son of a Wait it's a very good question* I took a few sips of the very good beer. "That's a good big-brotherly question," I said. "There's no question I feel good when I do that, but I enjoy being with her even more when we aren't fighting with him. *Why don't I just tell him You know why Not just from the father* At the Met that day. On the phone, the Weather Girl thing. At the lake. All those times." *There weren't all that many.*

361

"Don't answer. Think about it. You'll bring her the car."

"You know I will. It'll be a pleasure to see her again. *Oh God* Touch base in Schenectady to throw them off, maybe they'll think we both came back, get some sleep, over to Northampton. That's the plan."

"I think you really *appreciate* her, Paul. Take care of her."

"You keep saying that. She doesn't need to be taken care of. She does a pretty damn good job of taking care of herself."

"Support, I mean. Take care of her that way. Help her get to med school. That's what she wants more than anything. I formally give the job to you, Govinda. Snow Lion. OK?"

"I'll think about it. I took your question seriously, Dickie. It's a good one. I care about her. *You must know that* I'll think about it for her sake, not just yours. My own too. *You do and do not know what you're asking* I'll think about it."

"You do that. I'm going to miss you, too, man." We clinked bottles, paid up.

We went to the platform. "The MG's papers are all in the glove box." He gave me his keys. "Well. I want to thank you again, Paul."

"For what?"

"For your friendship and your help. You taught me a lot."

"Not nearly as much as you taught me," I said. "We're even. Believe me."

We shook hands. Men didn't hug back then.

"See you, man."

"See you."

It was 2 PM. I whispered "*Gay gesunt*". The train hooted, and, slowly, was gone.

April 7, 1973,
2:00 PM – 4:30 PM

*B*EEEEEP

"Oh shit, that's the ER. Phone, phone." She passed me the phone.

"You all done? We got live ones—alky with sweats and arrythmias. Dr. A is first up, yes? You get the little old lady with shortness of breath and swollen ankles."

"What a novelty. On the way."

"An admission?"

"Two. See? Be careful what you wish for."

Down to ER, through the doors separating relative sanity from utter chaos. Rows of wheezers in the asthma room, breathing into pressure gauges; beds with dripping IVs, blood on the suture room floor, people in white uniforms yelling into phones, cops, techs, people holding themselves, folded over themselves, holding small children, listless, eyes closed tight or staring, a dull moaning roar over all of it, or maybe just in my head.

Marvin and Katie held two charts next to two gurneys, IVs already running. This was where Ali started functioning as half an intern; she looked over the large man like a pilot kicking the tires and went up in the elevator with him. I got the LOL; Katie came with me, the traditional Intern/Third Year team. She followed Ali out to the elevator but Marvin pulled me back. "Ali actually will be getting another when it rolls in: Bob's social admission."

"Is he still here?"

"I am *Bob's voice over my shoulder* and I'm staying until he's admitted. Then I'm signed out to you. Interesting guy—they found him stuck on the floor of his apartment when they went to get the OD last night, couldn't get up, hadn't for days. The place was a pigsty, not fit for habitation, we can board him until Welfare can find him a place. No English. I want you to treat him well, he isn't just a bed plug. Give him the most attractive of care. How do you like your students? Very nice stuff."

"Well, Bob, Dr. Acheson, who I assume you mean is the very nice stuff, just did two pleural taps as slick as you could have. She is bright, has persistence and very good hands."

"You let a subintern do a pleural tap?"

"This is Key, Bob—we get to practice medicine the way we want. We were right there supervising, not that she needed much supervision."

"Yeah, good hands, is what interests me most. She's very hard not to like; last year they called her The Intern's Friend. She's a knockout, but she needs to lose the ERA button."

"That is very interesting Bob, but I should tell you that Paul here has known Dr. Acheson for like many years and rather than listen to you on this subject he would be most happy to hand you your ass."

"I didn't realize she was a friend of yours, Paul. My apologies."

"Not me you have to apologize to, Bob; I think she'd be happy to hand you your ass without any help from me. By the way, know what you really call a woman doctor?"

"What?"

"Doctor. And I'd advise you to lay off the ERA button." *Schmuck.*

366

We rode up to 4. "Thanks for dragging me into your feud with Bob, "I said."

"Don't mention it."

I found Katie as the nurses were rolling our new patient into bed and taking the thermometer out of her mouth. Callie was already writing her nurse's admit note. "What have we here?"

"An LOL in NAD named Mrs.Goldstein. BP's a little up."

"In No Acute Distress as long as the oxygen is running… Hello, Mrs. Goldstein, I'm Dr. Seitz and this is Dr. McCulloch, and we're going to get a history and examine you and see if we can figure out how to get you home. Where is home?"

"The Concourse, near Mt. Eden Avenue."

"Big hill there—have you been having trouble getting up the hill?"

"Lately."

"OK, Dr. McCulloch, hit it."

"Mrs. Goldstein, Hi, why did you come to the hospital today?"

"I couldn't breathe. For two days I can't breathe like normal. And I can't get my stockings up my ankles. I know from this."

"It's happened to you before?"

"Oh, yes, I take a water pill and a pressure pill and a heart pill."

"What's their names?"

"Lasix, and the other one I think maybe Inderal, Inder something. And Digitalis."

"Are you on a diet?"

"Sure, no salt. You're a young lady yet, you don't know. Look at you, look at the shape on you, what do you know about diets?"

"I know a little."

"A little, sure."

"So, have you been having any pain in your chest?"

"No, thanks God."

"Heartburn?" I asked.

No."

"Pain in you arms? Get numb around your lips? Fainting? Pain when you breathe…" She ran down the sequence of questions for the differential diagnosis of chest pain, getting a "No" for each, and she only had missed the one. She started the Review of Systems.

"OK, now I'm going to ask about your whole life history, any medical problems you ever had. Have you ever been in the hospital before?"

"Me? No—oh, oh, once a few years ago like now. That's when they put me on the water pill. And the heart pill."

"And the no-salt diet."

"And the diet, yes."

"Any surgeries?"

"No."

"Any diseases that run in the family?"

"Two aunts I had with breast cancer."

"I'm sorry to hear it. Any headaches? Dizziness?"

"No."

"Eye problems?"

"No."

"Problems hearing, earaches?"

"No."

"Sore throats? Trouble swallowing?"

"No."

"Belly pain? Nausea, vomiting? Constipation? Black stools? Diarrhea?"

"No. Wait—maybe a bissel diarrhea last week."

"Still?"

"A little, yes. Usually I have the other problem, I take prunes."

She went through urinary, genital, extremities; all "No." She missed one or two trivial questions; I asked them as she wrote it up.

368

"We're going to examine you now, Mrs. Goldstein."

I drew the curtain around the cubicle and we helped Mrs. G. maneuver the gown around as we looked in her eyes and ears, down her throat, at her chest, percussed her chest, auscultated her chest... "Ooh. Cold." (I showed Katie how to hold the stethoscope bell in her hand to warm it before putting it on the patient's chest)...listened to her heart, palpated her abdomen, optioned the pelvic, finally pushed our fingers into the fluid-swollen ankles.

I showed Katie how to place EKG leads, how to run off a rhythm strip and get a 12 lead. Which in fact they had done in the ER, but education is education. They had sent admission bloods too.

"So, doctors, what do I have?"

"Too much water, Mrs. G. Have you been sticking to your diet?"

"Sure. What am I, a fool?"

Back to the lounge to discuss and write notes.

"What did you see?" I asked.

"An LOL in NAD, even without oxygen, awake, alert, oriented, with a history of mild congestive failure, on low salt, Didge, diuretic and antihypertensive, 2 days of shortness of breath without chest pain..."

"Know why I asked her about heartburn?"

"Uh, no."

"Women especially, but men sometimes, will experience cardiac pain as heartburn. Go on."

"Fluid bilaterally, with dullness and rales in both lower lung fields..."

"Did you check her Right Middle Lobe?" Which unlike the other four lobes of the lungs is auscultated from the front of the chest.

"I did. Full breath sounds."

"Good. A lot of people forget, and fluid likes to lurk there, along with junk that heads straight down the right bronchus. One of God's design flaws. Go on."

"Heart sounds full, no murmurs."

"Is that good news or bad?"

She tried to reason it out. "Good that she has no valvular disease, but bad because if that isn't the reason for the congestive failure it has to be from the hypertension, cardiomyopathy, and that is not good in the long run."

"Very good. Go on."

"She has 2+ ankle edema."

"What did you miss?"

"Can't think what."

"The diarrhea."

"I thought that was a red herring."

"It probably is. But, why is this lady in failure?"

"Her hypertension is a little out of control."

"True, but only a little. Two other possibilities. First one: what is her Heart Pill?"

"Digitalis. Oh, she could be Didge toxic."

"Yes she could. Digitalis, commonly referred to as Dig *pronounced Didge*, the all-purpose cardiac drug, it strengthens the pump and calms the arrythmias, and sometimes it kills you. Nobody ever thinks of it, but about 25% of patients who come in here on Dig are toxic. A patient on Dig, always get a Dig level. Also: Dig can increase blood pressure. She was started on the Inderal after. Second: What month is it?"

This puzzled her. "April."

"Which means?"

"...Sorry."

"No, I'm sorry, that was a 'guess what's in my mind' question. It's April, so Passover, so every LOL on the Concourse goes off her low-salt diet for a bissel gefulte fish, a bissel chicken soup. And rolls into every ER in the Bronx swearing she has kept her diet."

"So what about the diarrhea?"

"May be nothing. May be Dig toxicity. But when we get her to cop to going off her diet, we might also find out she makes homemade gefulte fish, which sets her up for fish tapeworm."

Mrs. Goldstein became:

<u>CC</u>: 67 yo wf in NAD, c/o SOB and ankle edema X2 days.

<u>HPI</u>: No c/o chest pain, perioral numbness, arm pain, heartburn. H/O hosp X1 for SOB "a few years ago"; started on furosemide and propranolol. ?Diarrhea last week.

<u>FHx</u>: Noncontributory.

<u>Past Hx</u>: ROS negative and noncontributory.

<u>PE</u>:

    <u>VS</u>: P=76, BP=140/95, Resp: 6/min, T=98.6F

    <u>HEENT</u>: WNL

    <u>Chest</u>: Dull to P&A over LLL; rales RLL, LLL

    <u>Cor</u>: RSR@76, S_1S_2 no M

    <u>Abd</u>: LSKK, No masses or tenderness

        <u>Ext</u>: 2+ pitting edema bilaterally

        <u>Psych</u>: Awake, alert, oriented X3

    <u>Labs</u>: Pending

    <u>EKG</u>: WNL except sl depressed ST in V1 & V2.

"So what shall we order?"

"Labs…"

I grinned. Time to teach the Third Year how to write orders. "Yes, but not yet. Take dictation. 1.Admit to 4E. 2. Low-salt diet. 3. You want to follow her vital signs: pressure, respiration and pulse, at least every eight hours, so: VS qShift. What about treatment?"

"We're holding Dig pending labs. We want to get her out of failure, so a shot of Lasix…"

"Not a shot. Lasix chases out potassium, which…

"Would increase risk of Dig toxicity."

"So: 4. Lasix 40 mg PO stat. What about her Inderal?"

"Hold off on that too, until we know about the Dig? It could slow her further."

"You win the cigar. Could be some shlepper on the Concourse raised her BP with Dig, then started Inderal…"

"And put her into congestive failure."

"Exactly. So no med orders yet. But, you don't want to get woken up or called for every little contingency: headache, arthritis pain, little fevers, constipation so: 5. Acetaminophen 325 mg q4h prn H/A, other pain, fever>101F, and 6. MOM in PM if no BM in the AM. Now…"

But she exploded with laughter at this.

"What? Every elderly Jew counts bowel movements like gold; they miss one and they will hound the nurses and you until they get some Milk of Magnesia. Remember: The Irish drink and the Jews shit."

"Very nice."

"Passes for cultural awareness in the Bronx."

"Now, labs."

"Yes. We're going to want daily electrolytes, CBC with differential. Trough Dig level in the AM. For now. EKG."

"So she'll need an order to hold her AM Digitalis until bloods are drawn."

"Right. Very good. What about the fish tapeworm?"

Marvin had appeared at the door.

"Stool for ova and parasites?"

"Bingo, stool for O & P."

"I should have got that."

"Something a Katie McCulloch might not know."

"But might if her mother's maiden name was Levitsky."

"Your mother's maiden name is Levitsky?" from Marvin.

"Aye, begorra."

"Go ask Mrs. G. if she maybe had a bissel gefulte and a bissel chicken soup last week." *(NB: She did. But she didn't make homemade gefulte. Sometimes diarrhea is only too much prunes. Or too much Dig.)*

Suddenly there was screaming.

"We could use some help, I'm afraid," Marvin said.

"There is screaming. Why is there screaming?"

"Our newest guest is in DT's, is my guess."

Shaking like the proverbial leaf, Mr. Jefferson was standing up on the bed, pulling at his gown and putting severe stress on his IV, which popped out as we ran over, running blood down his arm and D5W all over the floor. Alicia and Callie were trying, and failing, to pull him down as he screamed, "I have to testify. I have to toostify. I have to tootsify." And he did, he tootsified all over the bed, catching Ali in the backwash.

He calmed slightly with his bladder emptied and allowed us to settle him back horizontal. "Tincture of urine," Marvin said. "This performance was preceded by complaints of ants crawling on him, temperature of 100F. Dr. McCulloch, your diagnosis."

"When was his last drink?"

"He says about 12 to 24 hours since," Ali said, shrugging out of her urine-soaked lab jacket.

"DTs."

"Correct. Now, what do we do for Delirium Tremens?"

"We get an LP, and we start paraldehyde per rectum," said Bob, appearing from nowhere.

"We do not," Marvin said. "We remember our recent New England Journal of Medicine and some cases reported to us by our friends at Kings County and we start Librium 20 mg and taper by 5 mg per day for 4 days."

"That's experimental."

"It most certainly is not. It's been reported in NEJM and is standard now in a lot of places. And what the hell—you're signed out to me."

"As resident. I'm here now covering for Gendleman. Dr. Acheson, this is your patient; where do you stand on this?"

"With Dr. Kornbluth. The mortality rate for DTs is from 20 to 50% with paraldehyde, less than a quarter of that with Librium, which suggests to me that paraldehyde may be part of the problem because the inevitable vomiting dehydrates them further."

"The NEJM study wasn't double blind."

"How can you do a double blind study of paraldehyde? You start paraldehyde and people on the next street can smell it. This is the best data we're ever likely to get, and it means no more shoving tubes up the ass of disoriented, confused people and making them stinking and nauseous."

"So this is about not wanting to get your hands dirty."

"If that was what it was about I wouldn't have shaken hands with you this morning."

Longish silence, contained laughter.

Bob was stone faced. "I'm sorry, I was out of line. Dr. Seitz, I expect I know the answer to this, but where do you stand?"

"I find my colleagues' arguments and the NEJM article persuasive. And if Librium is ineffective we can always run paraldehyde later."

"Reducing the dose by God knows how much because of the Librium."

"Yes, but I bet that won't be necessary."

He walked over to a window, as if the answer were somewhere out on 168th Street. We could almost see the wheels turning: asserting possibly faulty authority vs. mutiny by underlings; if this worked he could take the credit, if not we could take the blame from Gendleman, with who knows what consequences to our careers. Nasty things in our folders. I started transferring books, tubes, reflex hammer, miscellaneous tourniquets from my lab jacket to my tunic pockets. Bob made up his mind.

"OK," he said, "But I'll be calling to find out if he's calming, and if he doesn't within three hours you're going to hang that paraldehyde enema. And you're going to do the LP."

"Why add a huge spinal headache to this poor guy's problems?" Marvin said. "Diosrientation, confusion, formication, alcohol history, including withdrawal. We know he's in DTs. No way. We can do that if his fever persists beyond today."

"I'll leave that to you." Bob said. "You can explain your reasoning to Gendleman on Monday." And, once again, he left.

"Have they got that crap off his car yet?" Marvin asked the air.

"Here," I said to Ali. "Take my jacket."

"Thanks." It fit her better than her own.

"That was great," Marvin said, "Terrific. Backed Bodacious Bob down with data. Not to mention the handshake thing. I'm in awe."

"My temper is going to get me killed in this business."

"Not as long as you have data. Keep up with the literature and you can get away with anything in academic medicine. Need proof? Check out Gendleman. Blows his top on an hourly basis, gets rezzies to cover for him on weekends, never on time for a goddamned thing…"

"You lack the moral high ground on that one, boss."

"…Listen. Last Christmas Eve we couldn't start M&M Rounds until he showed up. Mortality and Morbidity is Murray the G's show. We're waiting like fifteen minutes, twenty minutes—nothing. Suddenly he pops in, and like spontaneously, better than if we'd planned it, someone starts and we all join in: "God rest ye Murray Gendleman, Let nothing you dismay…right Paul?" They grinned, probably having seen the joke coming.

"Truly a Great Moment in Medicine," I said.

"But, and this is the most important part, in his back pocket is rolled up that week's New England Journal, on a Tuesday." *The day before you get it in the mail.*

"Let's get Librium rolling on this guy. Katie, did you get the White Whale's last blood?"

"Hours ago. What's formication?"

"Tactile hallucinations; feeling of ants crawling on you."

Suddenly Bob was back. "Dr. Acheson, you have another admission. The social."

"Paul, go with her and show her how to cut the ER red tape," Marvin said. "Katie, come present me your LOL." He went off with her to write his resident's admit notes and add to Katie's store of knowledge.

Ali sat down for a minute to catch her breath, absently picked up Mrs. Goldstein's EKG. "Slow but GMG," she said. "Gour nicht mit gour nicht." And grinned, and stuck her tongue out at me.

"Wait," I said, and took the ERA button off her discarded jacket and pinned it to mine. "Now we're ready."

Bob started to say something, thought better of it, changed gears. "Dr. Acheson, I believe that's your MG parked near the remains of my car. I always wanted one. BRG, rallye stripe…I was wondering if you'd consider selling it."

She looked like she was considering it. "I wouldn't take a penny under ten thou."

"What? It isn't worth half that even in mint condition."

"It is to me."

"Really? The right rear's all banged up. What's with that?"

"Ask Dr. Seitz. He knows more about that than I do. It involves part of a New England stone wall in the boot, but he never got around to telling me the details."

March 5 – March 7, 1967

$\mathcal{I}$ walked back to the car on autopilot. I had just said a very serious goodbye to one of the two best friends I'd ever had, and I might never see him again. I couldn't imagine at that moment how I ever would, or anyway not for many, many years. But I had to put that out of mind; there was work to be done. *There always was damn it, the lump in my throat.* I watched the street from a block away, trying to look casual. If there was surveillance I couldn't spot it. I double-checked the map and made for the river. Over the bridge Autoroute 15 Sud was as barren of anything to look at in daylight as it had been in the dark. I turned on the radio; French '50's pop, pre-acid Beatles. The road was empty. Nothing to distract from thought. Dickie's question rang in my ears, rattled around in my brain. He was right to ask; in spite of what I'd said, almost every interaction, the ones he knew about, involved me rising to her defense; encouragement, advice, books, subversion of and challenges to her father, a home to cry in. What had they all told me: *Take care of my sister, Paul. Help her, Paul, she's lovely, and she's in pain.* No one ever said, "Love her."

There was that kiss. That kiss. If I so loved damsels in distress, why was I not with Bitsy Reade? But what struck me was the ups and downs in my feelings for her since she had freed herself. That kiss. But the kiss pointed two ways. Either she was passionately in love with me, even then *as I was with her* or she just really knew how to kiss. I was even prepared, a year ago, to have sex with other girls to be able to kiss back, rescue her from the clutches of an adult lover. Or lovers. How could I ever have rationalized that? How could that ever have made sense? *Because I was not prepared to ignore or forget Chaskis entering the service corridor* There was, not only but there was, the undeniable physical attraction, *Oh God, was there*, and it wasn't just to any girl, at least I knew that. It was to her. *Did she think and dream about my body the way I thought and dreamt about hers Did girls do that* But that wasn't enough for it to be Love, capital L, either. Was it? *Mon amour, mon coeur, mon reve* It seemed like a start. I hadn't seen her in close to a year. Maybe she had cut her hair. So what? I had grown mine. For a year I had only known her over the phone or in letters. I had told her the attraction wasn't based on looks, but that was in part, or whole, I didn't know, a lie; for a year her voice, on the phone or on paper, had conjured up the visual memory. But it seemed to me I really did love her mind; I wanted to hear her voice as much as I wanted to see her. *Almost as much as to touch her*

Besides, Dickie's question cut both ways. The thought frightened me—was her attraction to me based on my defying her father? Both her parents, really. But so much of her response to me seemed independent of that...

Does the knight slay the dragon because he loves the princess, or because he loves fighting dragons? Both? Was it OK to feel the one, if one felt the other? Beowulf did it for the glory. Ivanhoe didn't marry Rebecca (where would they have gone?). Perseus loved and married Andromeda; in fact, he fell in love first, asked her father for her hand, then went back and slew the sea monster, who conveniently waited for Cepheus' consent. Bogart never got the girl; in *Casablanca* he gave Ingrid Bergman to Victor Laszlo. For The Cause. Wait; in *To Have and Have Not*, he did get the girl. Got her in real life, too. And how did the princess feel about it all?

It didn't matter. There were no Jewish knights. *Seven years did Jacob labor for the hand of Rachel* The Jewish tradition was to labor for years for the hand of the beloved and then have your father–in–law slip the wrong girl in on you. *Or your brother-in-law* Or was I just scared? None of this should make any difference, should it? It was easy to love a voice, a face; a person was, apparently, another story. But I had loved The Lady of the Lake. Hadn't I? *Do I have to take on all your old boyfriends, AA   He should be the last* Did Dickie know about the pool guy? He couldn't know I knew. Was that his concern? *Why did this matter*

I was not yet nineteen; the birthday candles were in my backpack. It did not occur to me—could not have occurred to me—that, in time, *she* could rescue *me*.

At the border a customs officer pulled me out for inspection, had me open the boot, *why me College kid financing his little trip to Canada with a trunkful of Molson's and Canadian Club*, looked under seats and in wheel wells *not for booze* while I watched. But I watched the booths, too, and saw his partner, looking in the MG's direction, make a call. The maroon Olds swung in behind me at the first exit on the American side, took up position a quarter to a half mile behind. We'd been overconfident, figured he'd just go back to Schenectady; I should have come back across another way, or maybe he'd paid off custom's guys at all the crossings below Montreal when he lost us. But he was overconfident too; we had lost him once, I could do it again. It laid itself out like a high school geometry problem.

> Given: Dickie needed at least 24 more hours to disappear.
> Prove: You can give him that, and more.
> Proof:
> 1. The customs people had told Michael the MG was here, with only one driver, and a description told him it wasn't Dickie.
> 2. It was Sunday; he couldn't call anyone unless he stopped somewhere (cell phones were 25 years away).

3. Michael would follow me to Schenectady or to my first attempt to refuel, giving Dickie less than 24 hours.

4. Therefore: (a) I must evade Michael (b) I must go to ground somewhere other than Schenectady, within range of the gas I could afford.

5. Therefore: I must shake Michael and go to Northampton. QED.

I might have come up with a better plan if my brain were the only organ involved in my thinking, but it wasn't. I should have been scared *Train, Mike can take me off it anywhere along the line* but at that age, when I got scared, I got angry. Which is what made me so dangerous to myself.

I had work to do.

I couldn't outrun the Olds on this road. To evade Michael I needed a place to run off the Interstate out of his sight, a place where I could quickly vanish behind trees or under an overpass, a place where I could easily double back without his seeing me in his mirror. Darkness would help, so it would have to be—I checked the time—at least two hours away. Using one hand and my teeth, I opened the map and added up the mileage. If I kept to 60 mph, a mile a minute, I could conserve fuel and reach exactly what I needed in almost exactly two hours: the entrance we'd used yesterday. There was a long curve; when he was out of sight in my mirror I could floor it, run down the exit to route 8 behind the trees, cut back north through Loon Lake and be back headed northbound before he realized I wasn't in front of him anymore. Then it would really get interesting.

When it really got interesting…suddenly the Olds loomed beside me, the heavy car slamming against the little MG. He ran me off the road; while I was still stunned he handcuffed me and threw me into the back of the Olds. Dickie had been caught. Nice try kid he said we took him off the train in

384

Kingston ran him back through the Thousand Islands in a speedboat old bootlegger's route They'll be waiting for us at the Dean's office Osterricher!! I should have known Code Name Zero He marched me in Dickie face bruised was handcuffed to a chair His father was talking to Osterreicher Good of you to join us Mr. Seitz We were just discussing my son's new plans to apply for early admission to law school weren't we Dickie His German accent was suddenly more prominent and his monocle was flashing reflected sunlight Hah you thought you vere zo cleffer MG Enterprises how juvenile ze banks are all in our hands und ze radio tracking devices pinpointed your effry move exzept fur zome back country in ze Adirondacks which is uff no importance Which was when the lock got shot off the door and she and Sam and the guys from Third Street poured into the room They all had Sten guns The ammo bandoleers crisscrossed her chest and lifted her breasts Her hair poured out of her beret No importance huh Father say hello to The Resistance back away Sam get the keys anyone moves gets ventilated You'll neffer get avay vit zis he shouted as we ran out the door and she threw me a Beretta We hightailed it for the hideout on Mt Marcy Sing the Marseillaise I put a shot right through the monocle That was for Riley Who's Riley Sam asked as

Between the lateness of the hour, the heights of the mountains, and an approaching cloudbank, the sky was beginning to darken. A lucky break. I varied speed, averaging 60, watching him back off when he got too close, speed up when I did. Come on, asshole, think I'm predictable, just a kid. Should have learned better yesterday. Meanwhile I calculated the route to Northampton, weighing up the choices. Purred along.

New York 8
Loon Lake
Hague
1 Mile

Here was the curve. I watched the mirror for the moment we'd be out of sight of each other. There. I killed the lights, hit the gas and the MG took off like the proverbial rocket. I aimed for the exit ramp, skidded but (barely) held the curve, and there was no one coming; I gunned it up the road behind the trees, just caught sight of him speeding over the bridge, headed south at speed; I downshifted and gunned it again, roaring much too fast through Loon Lake and back to the northbound Northway. The gas gauge stood at below a quarter tank, no time to worry about that now, it was five miles past frozen Loon Lake back to the Northway on this road, I made that, careened on to the Northway northbound, killed the lights again, and pushed it to the top end for the twenty or so miles to

New York 74
Schroon Lake
Ticonderoga
1 Mile

Nothing in the mirror. The road was empty. Even if he figured it out, it was fifteen miles to his next turnaround; he'd get off at Loon Lake, check the gas stations. It didn't matter. He'd have no idea where I was going; maybe he'd think I was taking local roads to Schenectady, maybe running back to Canada; this he'd never guess, and he wouldn't follow me into icy mountains, I didn't think. I took the exit at speed again; this road dead-ended on the Interstate, headed east over the mountains. Now was the time to worry about gas; the gauge was at one eighth, maybe lower, but I knew something. Schroon Lake was frozen solid, dimly reflecting in the waning light; the road from there was all downhill. I took the road as fast as I could; when I saw Lake George, also frozen, I threw it into Mexican Overdrive and coasted into Ticonderoga on fumes, into the gas station I knew was there. It was

386

open; I pumped a few dollars worth of gas as fast as I could, anxiously watching for headlights from the west, but there was nothing, and on the roads ahead I would have the advantage. Ticonderoga, Carrillon; the old fortress brooded over the strategic isthmus between the Lakes, looming in the gathering darkness, ice-festooned cannon restored to its gunports as a tourist attraction almost two hundred years after Washington's men sledged them over the mountains to the Siege of Boston. Route 22 led down that narrow, almost uninhabited isthmus, and here was where the snow, after holding off all day, began to come in gusts, mixed with sleet. The wipers began beating their tattoo, moving snow and ice around but not off the windshield. I turned on the heater and defroster; sheets of snow flew across the road in the deepening darkness. I tried not to become fascinated with the vortex of flakes caught in my headlights. There had been an ice storm here; ice encased every branch. It was as if the world had grown feathers.

The MG had only an AM radio, giving quirky reception in the mountains. *Hsssss...Squeal...Hssss...Squeal. No; the unmistakable falsetto opening...In the jungle, the mighty jungle, the Lion sleeps tonight...* Sedaka and the Tokens, a voice from the old neighborhood. I dialed around, looking for news and weather *Squeal... Temperatures continuing to fall through the night with intermittent snow and freezing rain in the northern and midsections of the state west of the mountains; east will see slightly warmer temperatures with rain and freezing rain This is North Country Radio W...hissssssss urlington Vermont You don't need a weatherman to know which way the wind blows How about a Weather Girl*

If Michael had correctly figured out where I was headed he could have come south, could be waiting for me ahead at the marshy southern tip of Lake Champlain in Whitehall, but he wasn't. *How am I doing so far, Papa* I was out of the Adirondacks; ahead were the Green Mountains. It was still snowing furiously, a brief mountain storm I hoped, beating against the upslope, but I couldn't count on that. The area seemed underpopulated and overgrown. This was the original frontier, fought over by English, French, Huron, the land of Fenimore Cooper's Long Carabine and Chingachcook; behind me in the dark as I turned east slept the dead of Saratoga, who had turned the tide and sent Gentleman Johnny Burgoyne and his unbeatable regulars back to Canada. *My dead were in Europe but these too were my dead* It might as well have been Troy. History had left this place to lynx and bear, to sleep and dream; History was elsewhere, this history was forgotten, as ours would be, as our war would be. It would not matter.

It mattered to me. It mattered very much to me. If I didn't kill myself in these mountains I would see the girl I'd been dreaming about for a year *Faithful Penelope.* Route 4 became a main highway into Rutland. The snow squall had stopped, but it had snowed here earlier, and partly melted in the sunlit parts and refrozen; black ice was a real possibility. A new snow layer topped a season's compacted accumulation. I needed to pee, I needed food, I needed coffee, I needed some local knowledge. And it wouldn't hurt to top off the tank. At a diner at the intersection of 4 and 7 lights beckoned. I took the Vermont map in with me. A long-haired young woman with bright eyes welcomed me from behind the counter; except for us the place was dead empty. *What was she doing there on a frozen Sunday night? What was I?* She asked what she could get me *anything, anything* and I felt myself starting to wake from anxious dream. "Coffee," I said; I wanted a burger but there wasn't time, or might not be; I settled for a tuna on white toast and home fries. "You in that big a hurry?" she asked. "It's a bad night to be in a hurry. Gonna get a lot colder and freeze the sleet solid."

"That so? Is it bad in the mountains?"

"Where you comin' from?"

"Saratoga," I said. "I need to get to Hanover the shortest way possible not Route 4."

She looked out the window, saw the MG. "That must be a story. Dartmouth boy?" She leaned forward, raised a leg behind her, leaned further over the counter than she needed to. "I get it. Girl at Slidell, right?"

"You got it. Truth is, I have a big exam tomorrow, and here's the thing, I know I should keep going east on 4, but my friend was killed there last year, rear-ended by a truck, and I thought I'd try 103. Any idea what it's like up that way?"

"Way, way less traffic, sure, but it's prolly iced over, at least in spots. Wicked curves, wicked hills." *But no possibility of a maroon Oldsmobile making it*

"You're right. I'll stick to 4."

"If you go to Dartmouth, how come you're wearing a Nott jacket?"
I need to get better at this "It was my friend's."

"I don't know if that's touching or creepy."

I shrugged. "Look, do you have any seltzer? Soda water? Club soda?"

"Only at the fountain."

"Can you draw some off, into a bottle? I'll pay you for it. I need to clean the crud off the windshield and headlights."

"Sure." She found a near-empty detergent bottle and drew off some soda water.

"What can I give you?"

She sighed. "You guys kill yourselves in these mountains trying to get to Slidell when there are perfectly good girls right here. We're your waitstaff and ski patrol at Killington." She tapped the bottle on the counter. "Don't...you...have ...eyes?"

I wouldn't know. I don't ski. That's not my car. This is not my life.

"I'd say my eyes are being opened."

She poured me another slug of coffee, and chuckled. "Flirting is at no extra charge."

I woke fully from dream. I wanted suddenly to get over these mountains. Now. I went to the bathroom, pulled out a handful of paper towels. "I'll stick to 4," I said, but she probably saw me head south to the junction with 103. Stopped for gas, collar pulled up against the wind, I squeegeed the windshield clear of ice and salt and grit. "Icy in the mountains?" I asked.

"Do bears shit in the woods?"

Vermont 103 East. It was time to run my easting down. The wind pushed the world eastward under bare poles. The empty trees, asleep in winter's grip, whispered again of the futility of History, but I was driven by Desire.

Route 4 runs due east; 103 runs southeast toward Boston, saving many miles and much time, and I could easily outrun the Olds on its twists and blind curves, now that I had left a trail for him to follow if he had figured out where I was headed and run around the south end of Lake George to Rutland. *Shit I really do need to get better at this* The wind was harbinger of more snow, fitful flurries, without the fury of the squall but adding to the slick layer already on the road. Metal surfaces—bridge guardrails, signs—were rimed with ice.

The road began to climb; soon the towns were gone behind, and I was in the forest. We were in the forest; the car was like a living thing in my hands.

> *Midway in life's journey, I went astray*
> *From the straight road and woke to find myself*
> *alone in a dark wood. How shall I say*
> *what wood that was! I never saw so drear,*
> *so rank , so arduous a wilderness!*
> *Its very memory gives shape to fear.*

The woods, so friendly and inviting on a summer day, were Dante's and Frost's and Hawthorne's forest primeval, the trees closing around whatever tiny man should choose to put there. Carillon was a castle in a hopeless wilderness, livened only by Fenimore Cooper's remorseless Huron. The little car whined along; I felt the trees closing behind me as the road curved away before my headlights. Falls of ice grained the rocks, ice gleamed in every bend of the road, threatening to throw me skidding into the frozen creek just beyond the shoulder. The road curved, dropped away, climbed, curved, dropped away again, curved and dropped, curved and climbed; I downshifted, upshifted, trying to make the best possible time and keep the gearbox warm. The wipers smeared ice and grit; the same mix dimmed the headlights. From the radio only static and atmospherics, punctuated by occasional snatches of music when a beam penetrated those silent mountains. At Ludlow an intersecting road even less promising than this, a stone church dim in intermittent moonlight; I stopped to clean the windshield and headlights *Thank you Nausicaa*. There was a brief clearing of the clouds, but this only meant more rapid cooling of the air and a harder freeze. The intersecting roads became smaller, un-numbered, finally vanished entirely.

I came up over a hilltop and the warning sign must have been knocked down; the headlights just caught a double S-curve with another hill in the middle. I killed as much speed as I safely could, braking and downshifting, somehow made the first curve, *This is how Camus died* but wasn't so lucky on the second. The skid took me into a full 180-degree fishtail, which slowed it just enough, and off the road, slamming us into a snow bank. The impact was enough to stall the engine; I killed the lights, radio and wipers and took a few deep breaths to slow my racing heart. In the sudden silence I could hear the sounds of the cooling engine and the burbling of the stream under the ice. Cloud had again obscured the moon; there was only faint starlight.

I got out, inspected the rear end for damage. *I pranged my kite Squadron Leader* There was none I could see beyond surface scratches and dings; the snow drifted up against an ancient stone fence had acted as an impact absorber. I had been damned lucky. The next question was whether the car would re-start; Lucas electrical systems were notoriously unreliable (in England, I later learned, the company was referred to as "Lucas, Lords of Darkness"). But spark was not the problem; it was clear as I tried to turn it over that the engine was flooded. During the moments of sheer terror I had probably braced myself, tensing every muscle including the one pushing on the accelerator pedal, pumping fuel into a stalled engine. Loss of precious time; I couldn't just sit there. It was cold and getting colder. Forest closed in on all sides. Coffee was having its diuretic effect; there was nothing for it but to go write my name in the snow while waiting for the excess fuel in the cylinders to vaporize or drain.

Frozen snow crunched underfoot. Now the only other sound was the water running beneath the layer of ice in the creek, only stars overhead, a few gleams in the forest that might have been ice and might have been the eyes of deer, or catamount, or bear. Whatever it was left me alone. And suddenly I was alone; Frost was gone, and Dante, and Hawthorne, and Fenimore Cooper, all the books that stood between me and the forest, and there was only the forest and just the forest and I said to myself without words *Remember this moment, no matter what happens remember this moment.* I breathed and watched my breath join the atmosphere of the forest, and I wished I could stay there and just breathe, and suddenly she was there with me and I knew I had had a moment like this once before on a raft in a lake on a summer night and I knew what I wanted and there would still be books but there would always be this moment, and the other one.

It was too soon to try to start the car; I couldn't risk draining the battery in useless attempts. I was suddenly taken by the amount I didn't know. So much. My little store of knowledge against that overwhelming bulk. The route to Northampton, Massachusetts, over against what was in a girl's heart. *Father. Papa. I could sure use some help here I don't have a disintegrating Wehrmacht to contend with just one guy who I think I lost hours ago using what you taught me and who would be crazy to take his car up this road but mine is no jeep either and I need to get it started and out of the snow* The dead don't speak but the parts of them that have become a part of you can come to you as a voice or a thought, or an idea. *Use your brain You changed the game the way I taught you Now break this down step by step move by move You only have to know one thing at a time*

The car was lodged in snow, but could not slip further back against the frozen stone wall. First get the engine started; then you have light and heat. I turned the ignition key, *lay off the gas to avoid another flooding, if this doesn't work you can take off the air cleaner and shoot some starter fluid into the carburetor* but it didn't catch and I suddenly remembered how to do this: *the choke all the way in, the gas pedal to the floor and turn the key* and it caught, running rough. I eased the choke out a little; the richer mixture caught and the reassuring roar was back. I found the right mix to keep it running, letting it warm, gradually pushing the choke back in, pulled out slightly more against the possibility of a stall; I would be outside working to get out of the snow bank. *So reassuring, this small display of skill* When I judged it was warm enough I eased it into gear; as I thought, the wheels spun, and I quickly put it back in neutral.

Let us inventory our assets. In the boot was my backpack, the sleeping bag *I could use as a blanket if I had to*, a small snow shovel (*de rigeur* for these climes), cans of gas-line antifreeze and starter fluid, and two fifty-pound sand bags. I didn't need the sand for weight, I suddenly realized; I had an ancient New England stone wall to furnish all the ballast I'd ever need. I could use the sand to spread over the snow. But the stone

393

wall was frozen solid; I couldn't pull any loose *out of this stony rubbish.* *Think* I pulled out the tire iron and the shovel, opened the hood and found room for both atop the warming engine. After five minutes they were warm enough, I figured; I pried under a top layer of ice with the iron, opening a wedge. I went back for the shovel, pushed it into the wedge before it could re-freeze, and pushed. Ice flew off in all directions, freeing a layer of stone; brute force with the tire iron did the rest. *Something there is that doesn't love a wall*

I set about pulling huge chunks of New England shale and granite out of the wall and piling them in the boot; two flat pieces of slate I wedged under each drive wheel. Using the little shovel I made sand patches across our probable path. I opened the hood and heated the shovel again on the engine block to break up some ice in the probable path. *Ready.* I got back in, pushed the choke all the way in, put it in gear, revved it *What are the roots that clutch* and popped the clutch. A few hundredweight of primordial planetary material in the boot made this time the charm. The car shot forward as if from a cannon, slewing around but catching the piled sand; the right wheel spun for a second on the scattered ice but the left caught a patch of dry asphalt and pushed us back onto the road. *Everything tickety-boo Squadron Leader* Spilling slate ballast, I headed back up hill to make the U-turn where I could see any oncoming traffic. None. I kept some of the slate for traction and tossed the rest back toward the wall. No time to repair it. *Sorry* Cursing myself for the lost time I stopped and built a crude stupa. It seemed the right thing to do.

This time I took the curves in second gear, lost time a risk preferable to being killed. It was a different world on the downslope. Still icy, but soon there was a gleam low in the distance; it was the Connecticut River. Sleet continued on down US 5, but the road had been salted and there were no more mountains, not even hills. I upshifted, tried the radio again *...RKN Keene New Hampshire keeping warm on this wet freezing night here's Frank and Nancy Sinatra to tell you about Somethin' Stupid Hsssssssss And then you go and spoil it all by saying something stupid like I Love You* I didn't care what it was, I let them sing to me, I didn't want to think anymore for a while.

The sleet gave way to a frozen fog, then mostly rain. I pulled over long enough to run the paper towels over the crud on the windshield and let the rain do the rest. *When we say "It's raining," to what does the "it" refer?* Salt and slush continued to splash the car; passing trucks threw up mud and oil from the sites where I-91 was under construction; the blurred flashing lights on the detour barriers kept me awake. Finally south of the Massachusetts border parts of the new Interstate were completed; I could throw it into high gear and make my run to daylight.

I pulled into the UMass campus and found a parking space behind one of the dorms. It was very late, empty and silent in cold moonlight. It felt like I was still moving, my hands still vibrating from the thrum of the wheel, my middle ear still sensing motion. The only sound was the crackles and pops of the cooling engine.

A few students were still in the lounge long after midnight. Nobody (this was in the days before college dormitories were "secured") objected to me sacking out on a couch using the sleeping bag for a blanket, or showering and shaving the next morning after a fitful sleep. *The name is Bond, James Bond If I were Michael when I didn't show up in Schenectady I'd have figured out where I'd gone and called reinforcements* I called her from a dorm phone, and she, surprised, gave me directions to the diner in town—a male visitor on a Monday morning would attract attention. I told her to use back doors, try to stay out of sight of anyone watching her dorm. "I'll explain later," I said. I rolled the mud and salt-spattered MG through Northampton. The samba theme from *A Man and a Woman* sounded in my head. *Nice work Jean-Louis*

Who would I be meeting? Who was she now? I hadn't seen her in a year, and…it never occurred to me to wonder if it was the same for her, to wonder the same about me. Who was I now?

She was bundled into a yellow ski jacket, hair spilling out of the fur-lined hood. I watched her come up the street, that colt's stride bringing a sudden smile to my heart.

"What are you doing here so early?" Tense. "This wasn't the plan."

"Hi Paul, glad to see you. Hope you had a good night's sleep on a dorm lounge couch."

She smiled slightly, beginning to relax.

"Let me save us a lot of trouble," I said, and put my hands on her shoulders, looked into her eyes. "I'm an idiot. I admit it. When you left I slowly went crazy." I reached into my pocket and pulled out the beret, adjusting it. "Look. Just like Che."

Now she smiled for real. "You are an idiot. But. And. This wasn't the plan."

We went into the diner. "It wasn't the plan that I be followed back from the border. Dickie and I figured the tail would turn around and go back to Schenectady and be waiting there, and it might take a few days for them to figure out that he hadn't come back from Montreal. But he picked me up at the border. I think he bribed some customs guys to watch for us. I thought, if he followed me in, he'd confront me, maybe even at a gas station, but if I shook him and went someplace unexpected we'd buy that day or two for Dickie to disappear. I have limited money, Ali, so there was only one place to go. Plus: had to bring you your car. If I got caught in Schenectady you'd never get it. It's the least I could do for the Weather Girl."

"No call. No letter."

"Radio silence. For your own protection. Dickie told you."

"And you listened. How is Dickie? I'm worried about him, Paul."
Oh yeah, Dickie. Right.

"Away as planned, and in fine form. The car's intact except for scratches in the right rear quarter panel where I slid into a snow bank on Vermont 103."

Her expression changed. "Are you OK?"

"Sure. Fine. *You'd better believe it* Had hell's own time getting it started again, and out of the snow and back on the road."

"You crossed the mountains? On back roads? In an ice storm?"

"Only way to get here from there without the tail."

"Paul, that's how Camus…"

"I know. That's what went through my head when I fishtailed."

"You could have been killed."

"I wanted to…No. No. I *had* to…"

"What?"

"To see you. It's been almost a year. It wasn't going to be one day longer…"

"Oh, Paul…"

I pulled out the two birthday candles and the brioche, pushed the candles into it and lit them. "Make a wish," I said.

"I got my wish," she said "It's good to see you Paul. Really good."

"You too, Ali. *God, it's been almost a year You left me for Paris* Here's the keys, the registration, and the title transfer. He very much wanted you to have the car. Said it was yours by right. So did I."

"I thought you should have it."

"Me? Couldn't afford to keep it. Besides, he said you'd earned it." She sipped her coffee. "Did he tell you how, or why?"

The waitress was tapping her pencil. "Short stack," I said, "OJ."

"For you, miss?"

"I ate already. Just the coffee, thanks."

"Something to do with confronting your parents, finally. I know there was no coming-out party, so…"

"Exactly. You know. I did what you all advised, finally, when the time was right. You, Dickie, your mother and grandmother, my aunt Alice. You know what I was doing, trying to give them the message that I was too wild and unpredictable to trust at a social event of that significance that I didn't want. But it was costing me, everybody thinking I was crazy. Including you."

"It crossed my mind."

"That's what I realized at your home that day when I broke down crying—that I was acting so crazy, maybe I *was* crazy."

"Stupid, maybe. Not crazy."

"Thanks. You know the story. I never told you the details. I waited for a weekend when they were both going to be home and I told them I had something important to tell them. I called them into the drawing room and I told them that under no circumstances would I participate in a coming out party. My father said he could make me. I told him he could maybe make me be there, but I could promise him I'd make such a scene the family name would be mud for a generation. He went all frosty, said that would be too much to my disadvantage, and I told him it wasn't because I had no interest in or ambition to enter that society, I intended to be some use in the world, and reminded him I intend to go to med school. It really blew him away. You know the rest; told me to get out and not come back until I was ready to be well married. Then red and speechless."

"I would think a lawyer could mount a better argument than that."

"He isn't a lawyer, he's a fixer. A society fixer. He keeps money in families and makes scandals go away. That's why he's tolerated in what he calls the Upper Crust, even without their kind of money. Which was lost years ago. He knows where the bodies are buried and is willing to bury some more. Why do you think he has an investigator who can follow Dickie around?"

"I don't know a lot about the attorney racket."

"That's why it impresses you."

"About the car?"

"Right, the car. He told me he'd pull me out of college. My mother said she wouldn't stand for that, and college was where I'd be meeting guys. I realized she was trying to help again." She shrugged. "She still has to live with him."

"So in the end she stood up for you."

"I have to say she did. The best she could…God, I'm going to have to handle my mother. And I don't know what I'm going to have to do to help…I feel responsible, Paul. For Dickie. He told me he started out with this thing protecting me from my father's…whatever my father thinks he's doing…"

"He told me that too."

"…and it went on from there. Wanting to never hurt anyone, or do any harm. Do you know where he's going?"

"You know where he's…"

"I mean from Montreal."

"Toronto. At least that's what he told me, to get a visa through Bina's father."

"Except her father's in the Vancouver consulate."

He hadn't told me everything "He didn't tell me that."

"He probably didn't tell either of us the whole story. So we couldn't tell Daddy, and Daddy couldn't tell his CIA friends."

"You're serious about that?"

"Remember de Contigny?"

I winced. "Too well."

"You are such an idiot."

"We've established that."

"Have we ever. And what I'm going to have to do now…"

"Ali, I'm much too glad to see you to be having this conversation. We can sort it all out later. Happy 19th birthday, cherie."

"Happy 19th birthday, Cyrano."

"And you never cut your hair."

"Never. You told me not to."

"That's why?"

"Partly. Mostly because I told me not to. But partly."

"I always think of it as the chestnut waterfall," I blurted.

"Chestnut waterfall. Huh. I like that. Anyway, Daddy told me I'd never see a penny. I told him I didn't want any of his money; I was planning to support myself. He told me the car he promised me on high school graduation, I could kiss goodbye. I told him I could live without a car."

"You can use it to visit me."

She smiled, and took my hand. "I can if I can pay for the gas. I have to get to classes…I have to get you back to Schenectady."

"Nobody should ever have to go back to Schenectady. Plus, I go to Schenectady, we get caught today. Thought of a way to buy Dickie a little more time. *And spend a little more time with you* You have to transfer title to the car. That means you have to go to a DMV office in Connecticut. I can get a train to New York from New Haven and stay missing for long enough for Dickie to get his head start. Pick up some money from home, visit the family, go back from there. It'll take them three days to figure out where I am, and where Dickie might be, and that's all the time we ever figured he'd have, and then some."

"I can't do this today, I have a massive psych exam tomorrow."

"Pigeons in Skinner boxes?"

"No, child development."

"No one else can do this. If your father interferes before you get the title change processed, you don't get the car, and I've transported a stolen vehicle across state lines. Across an international border." *I am prepared to undertake dangerous missions for The Weather Girl*

She pondered that one for a second. "OK. You drive, while I read."

I shook my head. "I'm half asleep. I'll get us killed. You drive, I'll read to you."

"That could work."

It sort of did. I flipped her the keys, we paid for breakfast and headed south after she picked up her psych books at her dorm. "Look at me, Nancy Drew."

We stopped to gas up. I looked for a tail, but I couldn't see one, at least on the parts of the route on the Interstate.

"I don't know where there's a DMV office, but there's bound to be one in Hartford, and you can get a bus there to New Haven. Start reading, please. Just the highlighted sections."

It was about the developmental tasks of adolescence, heavy emphasis on Erickson and Blos. "In the opinion of these psychoanalytic thinkers, the major task of early adolescence is to consolidate the gains of Oedipal development in the new atmosphere of real sexual capability. The child of five, in the Oedipal phase, is incapable of real sex; all is symbolic. These conflicts may return to be reworked, in light of real physiologic sexual development..."I paused.

"What?"

"I was just thinking. What if something happens to disturb that process."

"Read on."

"The child requires a period of relative peace, undisturbed by environmental distortions, in which to successfully accomplish the integration of real sexual capability with unresolved Oedipal longings...Who exactly ever gets a period of relative peace?"

"Nobody. That's the point, I think. Read on."

"Failure to do so introduces distortions into the tasks of late adolescence...well, yeah. What kinds of disturbances? A parent dies?"

"That would be one. Major marital instability and parental craziness would be another."

A fine cold rain had begun to spatter the windshield. The wipers pushed the water around ineffectively, smearing the oncoming view. For a while the thumping of the wipers was the only sound.

"The real task of adolescence, undertaken after sufficiently successful resolution of the task of early adolescence, is the development of the capacity for intimacy, or as Erickson put it, 'Intimacy vs. Isolation'. The adolescent's sexual longings change focus from the parental generation to that of peers. The earliest relationships are bound to be ambivalent, as the parties act out and further resolve the conflicts of the Oedipal period..."

"Or the inherent power differences between male and female," she said.

"Or the inevitable social awkwardnesses. Sounds to me like the best textbook for this phase of development would be 'Pride and Prejudice'."

"We're studying it now in English Lit. Don't tell me how it ends."

"Jesus, how do you think it ends?"

"Oh, I know they're going to get married, but I don't know how or why. Or maybe it'll be a forced marriage."

"Elizabeth Bennett? Forced?"

"Forced by circumstances. Or maybe she and Darcy agree to be friends, and he finds her a suitable beau. Rich enough, but, you know, not the real upper crust."

"Ingenious. I won't ruin it for you...The endpoint of psychosocial development comes with the capacity to, first, form an intimate adult relationship, that is, one incorporating both friendship and sexual intimacy, and one capable of nurturing a new generation, as Erickson put it, 'Generativity vs. Stagnation'."

"Or one can always get pregnant in the back seat of a car."

"This car has no back seat."

"Then we are safe from the demands of late adolescence." She sang, "…How to make two lovers, of friends."

"How do these people support themselves?"

"Capable of nurturing…Someone is supposed to have once asked Freud what a normal adult needed to be happy, and he said, 'To love and to work'."

He also asked "What do women want?" I hope it's a bearded chess-playing scarecrow pre-med

Exit signs were starting to read "Hartford". The rain stopped and restarted. The thump of the wipers punctuated my thoughts…she was coming out of a phone booth next to a diner.

"You fell asleep."

"Told you I was beat."

"I hated to wake you. You looked so relaxed. Your face settled into peace."

"You were watching me sleep."

"When I wasn't watching the road. I have the address for the DMV. Not far from here. Want to get lunch first? They're probably closed noon to one anyway."

The jukebox selections were all Sinatra, Bennett, Como, Williams. The Beatles hadn't yet reached this corner of East Hartford. Oh, wait. "She Loves You."

"What'll it be, hon?"

"Tuna on white toast. There fries with that?"

"Home fries."

"And coffee."

"For you, honey?"

"BLT down, light mayo, coffee." When the waitress left she said, "Still won't eat bacon, Paul?"

"Sure I will."

"My mother…she thought she was doing the right thing."

I shrugged. "What's the right thing? What upset her more, that I'm a Jew, or a Socialist?"

"I'll ask her. She'll want to know if there are things Socialists won't eat."

"I don't think your family is going to be too happy with me."

"With me either. I don't think I care anymore what they think."

I looked at her, sat back and had a really good look. The serious expression; she'd grown into it. Cocooned in the puffy ski jacket, the long legs in jeans. She shrugged out of the jacket, the magnificent hair spilling over. I imagined that hair caressing my face. My chest.

"What?"

"I was thinking, you aren't Dickie's kid sister anymore."

"And you aren't Dickie's underage roommate anymore. You're an international conspirator and automobile thief."

"And you're a psychiatrist."

"I hope. The unexamined life is not worth leading."

"You still have to take Organic Chem, Socrates."

"I put it off until Junior year. One more advantage to going to Paris. A lot of us did; the really good prof will be back from sabbatical. It's just…look, all this stuff about the mind. But then Blos and Erickson suddenly acknowledge that biology plays a part. Sexual maturation affects mental maturation."

"Rhymes with…"

"Stop. Be serious. I mean, the mind, the brain. How do they relate? How are they connected?"

"OK, first, the mind has to be in the brain. Stop the brain, the mind stops."

"Obviously. But…*in* the brain?"

"Right. Did this in Metaphysics and Epistemology. Gilbert Ryle? I think Gilbert Ryle. Anti-Cartesian Dualism. Said if there's an Ego, in the brain, you have a reductio. The Ego is a little man, running the brain. What runs the little man? Another brain, and so on...unless Mind and Matter are connected, not separated as Descartes had it."

"So the mind isn't something contained in the brain. The mind is something..."

"...that the brain *does*." We stared at each other. It didn't matter that others had discovered this before. It mattered that we had independently reasoned our way to the same conclusion. It didn't even matter if it was correct.

"Look," I said. "It's like the heart. What is a heartbeat? It isn't something *in* the heart. It's something the heart *does*."

"Exactly. Just as what we call the mind, consciousness, is something the brain *does*. We can't see it, like the heartbeat, but we can feel it. See it in others. Maybe even measure it."

"But in cardiac muscle, you can see how the ion shifts alter protein, causing the contraction."

"So? The coordinated heartbeat is an emergent property of a complex system of many muscles working in tandem..."

"...So the mind, consciousness, would be an emergent property of many neurons in a complex network."

"Exactly."

"How can a thought move a molecule?"

"Wrong question. The moving molecule *is* the thought."

We both sat back contentedly, sipping our coffees. *Solved that one.*

The waitress appeared, to freshen up our coffees and drop off the check.

"Could you tell us how to get to the DMV office?" Ali asked her.

"Sure honey. It's downtown. Take a right out of the lot..." I wrote it on a napkin. We finished our coffee.

405

"The way I see it," she said, "We're maybe going to have medicines for the mind the way we have for the heartbeat. Change the chemistry, change the mind."

"You know, that's not so farfetched. At Nott we have this computer…terminal. It's hooked up to network of computers on other campuses all over the east, colleges, labs…anyway, the thing is programmed, it's the operating instructions they give it, protocols…point is, when the hardware goes blooey the protocols (what we were talking about would one day be commonly called "software") won't run right."

"No different from what happens to a brain after a stroke. Or maybe mental illness. What happens if the protocols go blooey?"

"It can crash the machine, because it feeds back to how the machine works."

"So the mind is protocols, programs, in this scheme. Only in the brain, the hardware gives rise to the protocols, if I follow this. How are you doing for money?"

I checked my wallet. "Can you bust the pennies out of your penny loafers?"

"Penniless no more. How about I get this. You really don't know what you'll need. I don't know what the fare is from Hartford to New Haven or New Haven to New York."

We got back in the car; she drove, I navigated the unfamiliar streets with the help of the napkin.

"What about the soul?" she suddenly asked.

"Ryle pretty much kills that too. If it's Ryle."

"Anyway, the mind is what the brain does. You are what you do. Huh. I hope that isn't all there is to it. I've done some pretty crazy things."

Me too "We're not talking about brain and mind anymore."

"No."

"There it is." Big as life, Connecticut Department of Motor Vehicles. Complete with giant line. We inched forward.

"Title transfer, fill out the form, go to line 4 and present your documents." We took turns on line as the coffee had its inevitable effect on renal function. Inched forward. The clerk gave the paperwork barely a glance. Dickie's signature was in the right place. "Check or cash?" She rooted in her purse for her checkbook. "Have a seat, we'll call you." We slouched in the plastic seats. She shook out her hair, found a rubber band and did a ponytail.

"Almost done."

"Yeah," she said.

"Want to study?"

"No. I want to talk more. About the mind-brain relationship. Listen, here's one that's a puzzle if the mind and the brain aren't connected. Why are you the same person in the morning that you were when you went to sleep last night?"

"Who says you are?"

"You are. This isn't a Borges story. Same temperament, same memories, same routines. So, how?"

"Well, like the heart keeps beating even when you're asleep. It's a continuous chemical process...regulated by the brain, but not consciously. I see what you're getting at, that there must be processes below the level of consciousness that...that must be continuous, ongoing chemical processes going on from yesterday to today..."

"And all our yesterdays," she said, grinning. Her hair had come loose again. That waterfall of hair. Her eyes peeking out from under it. She pulled it back with one hand, again twisted it into a ponytail with the other, raising her breasts.

I grinned back. "Exactly. A continuous train of interlocked biochemical processes leading back and back, to the developing brain, to the moment of conception, to sperm and egg, to our parents that supplied them, to our grandparents..."

The waterfall of chestnut hair.

"And back and back through the evolutionary tree, ancestral simians, mammals, reptiles, amphibians, fish, protozoans, the chemicals that came together in the Urey experiment..."

"Life being an emergent property of complex chemical activity..."

"What we call life."

"Yes, right."

"Right back to the Big Bang."

The hair brushed thoughtfully back, just before speaking.

"Right."

"Dickie would love this."

"Dickie did love this. We had a version of this conversation when he and I climbed Mt. Marcy last year. He said it was the scientific proof of the Buddhist doctrine of the oneness of all Being."

"I wish I'd been there."

"I wish you'd been there too. With all my heart."

She looked at me then. And I thought, what would it be like to wake up every morning with this girl, and have conversations like this. To have days of just driving around, seeing the world and having conversations like this.

"You look pretty good, Paul."

"What?"

"You do. You've grown, you grew your hair. I like the beard and 'stache."

"So have you, Ali."

"I'm too tall. Except for you."

"You're just the right height for me."

"Exactly. With you, I can wear heels."

I filed that picture away for future delectation.

408

"Acheson? Acheson." We went to pick up the title papers and registration. The clerk was humming, and broke into the refrain: "All the way from Cali forn eye aaay on the Atchison Topeka and the Santa Fe. You must get that a lot."

"First time today." (Curtly) *Careful, your highness*

"Sorry. Jeez."

"No, I'm sorry. Big exam tomorrow. Nerves."

The information desk had a map; the bus station was close by. The next bus to New Haven was in a half hour. I wished it were a half day.

"So," she said.

"So," I said.

"I wish I could stay. Show you the Atheneum. Or drive you to New Haven. It would be another two hours…"

"You don't have time, I know. Go. You have to go."

"Not this time. Not until the bus leaves."

"I'm a big boy. I can…"

"I'm enjoying the day. I don't want to go yet. I don't want to go at all, Paul. I don't want you to go."

"The only reason I can go is, you have the car. You'll drive to the train to New York. You'll drive to Peekskill or Poughkeepsie or White Plains to pick me up. I'll find a place in Schenectady for you to stay. I will, I promise." *God, do I promise*

We walked around outside, ignoring the drizzle. There was a blue Chevy that had been parked at the diner. It had Massachusetts plates. I pulled her back inside. "I think we should act from this moment as if we're being watched. There's a blue Chevy about three cars up the street, across from us. See it?"

"Yes."

"It has Mass plates. I'm pretty sure it was at the diner. Watch your mirror going back. You leave first. I'll see if he leaves when you do. We'll see who he's following. If he stays, I'll be watching him from the bus."

"What should we do?"

"I have one idea. He'll report back that I'm getting on a bus. He might not know for sure northbound or southbound unless he follows it, if it's me he's following. Or he'll figure, if I were going back to Schenectady I'd leave from Northampton. So he'll figure I'm going to New York. If he doesn't see me get off in New Haven he'll figure I'm going all the way by bus. I could shake him there, get on a train. If he follows you, well, you're just going back to school." *With the MG*

"He could just ask the guy at the ticket window where you bought a ticket to."

"Yeah. I should have bought a ticket to New York and gotten off in New Haven. Too late now. Well, that was before we spotted him, and anyway we couldn't afford it. Maybe I could crash a night at Yale…I mean, your father is going to catch up with me eventually, we're only trying to buy Dickie some time, I can buy him another day. That should be enough. It's one more than we planned."

"You're enjoying this."

"A little. It's payback, too. I owe your brother a lot." *He introduced me to you*

"So do I. Today was more fun than I've had in a long time, Paul. A year. Talking to you is…"

"For me too, Ali." We heard a bus engine, and it was there.

"…call me."

"…I'll call…" We said simultaneously, and laughed.

"Good luck on your exam. And watch your mirror."

"Take care, Paul, and watch your back." And suddenly she hugged me, and kissed my cheek, just below where one day there would be a tiny scar. I held her, turned her face, kissed her. Really kissed her. She kissed back. We turned into each other's embrace, took a breath and kissed again, deeply, longingly, both of us stunned by the flood of

410

feeling. I couldn't let go of her. And the enormity of what we'd done suddenly hit me. *Where could we go Where could we go*

"Listen," I said when I had breath, "When they finally catch up with us, your parents are going to go ape-shit."

"I can handle them. I've been doing."

We kissed again, even longer, even more deeply. *Where could we go*

"That was maybe only practice. I have some idea from Dickie how your father is going to react. Just…no matter what happens, no matter what Ali, promise me you'll remember this moment."

"Very dramatic."

"Just remember. No matter what happens."

She hugged me tightly; we kissed one last time. Deeply enough for the souls neither of us believed in to mingle. "I'll remember."

They were calling All Aboard, closing the luggage holds. We stepped back, looked at each other, just for a moment.

"Go."

"Ali I can't….Ali. Je pense que je t'aime."

"Go," she said. And, it was almost a whisper "Je pense que je t'aime aussi. Tout meme."

I got aboard, threw my backpack into the luggage rack, threw myself into a seat and looked for her. She was searching the windows. I banged on mine; she found it. And put her hand up to the window. I put mine over hers from my side, mouthed "See you." She smiled, nodded. The bus shifted into gear, and she stepped back, headed for the car. The bus paused at the curb and I watched the street. Please follow me. Please. Please leave her alone.

The MG pulled out, turned the corner, was gone. The Chevy stayed put. Which only meant there was no challenge in finding her. I was maybe a different story.

It was only an hour's ride to New Haven, enough time to think. This was a chess problem. I was a knight being harried by pawns, I thought. *Too cute.* But: Richard Acheson Esquire was a fixer, an attorney. He had an investigator, a heavy, perhaps. Sydney Greenstreet and Wilmer the gunsel in *The Maltese Falcon*. Michael. Michael that Dickie and Ali knew, he'd maybe been to the house. Michael had followed us to the Canadian border but had not crossed it. Why?

Because he was carrying a gun, and couldn't risk it. *Please* Because he wasn't licensed in Canada. *Possibly* Because he didn't have to. He waited for the MG at the border, confident that he wouldn't be spotted. Maybe: he had a contact in Montreal that we didn't spot. More likely: My original thought, he had had a word with the customs people, be on the lookout for a beat up MG. No need to go to Montreal. Dickie might have been caught already. Unlikely; if he was already found, why chase me? He was still OK. Michael had a local guy in Northampton. Or for all I knew, Richard Acheson Esquire had long made a practice of keeping his children under surveillance. Unlikely; I'd have noticed that. So would they, I thought, so most likely a recent development. Since Dickie had argued with him at the beginning of last semester? Maybe. Definitely since Christmas. Anyway, when he needs surveillance outside New York he can call on local talent. With Massachusetts plates. Ali was right; the Chevy hadn't followed her, and his move would be to ask where I'd bought a ticket to. He could have another local guy in New Haven watching the bus station with a phone call.

Or not. A trip to the rear window showed a blue Chevy with Massachusetts plates not far behind. Good. I had pulled one of his pawns.

But he sent Michael to Schenectady. That was special. The big mystery was what Richard Acheson Esquire hoped to learn from all this. They couldn't think I was Dickie—not since I showed up in Northampton. Or maybe not. Maybe the local guy didn't know me from Dickie, thought I was Dickie. *Not if he'd seen that kiss* The only goal that made any sense of all this was to bring me and Richard Acheson Esquire together, under circumstances unfavorable to me. To ask where Dickie had gone—confirming that they'd lost him in Montreal. All I could supply, of course, was the starting point for his journey; presumably they already knew that. And it made no difference: a coffee shop near McGill, off Sherbrooke. So what? So they thought I knew more, is what. I was going to be a great disappointment to them. To him. And the longer I could draw this out, the better for Dickie. Every hour his trail grew colder.

Now. How to lose the tail in New Haven. I already knew where to crash. My father had friends and colleagues all over the country; all over the world, really. At Yale there was Professor Hermann Spielvogel, editor of my father's festschrift, one of his oldest friends, someone he'd known since his Heidelberg days, someone with whom he'd exchanged visiting lectures, written papers, exchanged translations. I could lose my tail at the bus station, maybe, or I could go to the Yale campus and use open quads to spot him or his local contact, a campus full of buildings with multiple entrances and exits. Maybe he'd pick me up again at the railroad station, or maybe Dr. Speilvogel could drop me at another nearby station tomorrow. Maybe he lived in a nearby town with a station.

I closed my eyes and caught a nap. I woke up in city streets, for a moment felt like Ali was there beside me, felt the sadness as the dream faded. I didn't bother to look for the blue Chevy; I was planning to shake him on foot. *Thank you, Papa. How am I doing so far? How had he known No, I was in this* because *of what he taught me*

At Information I asked the way to the college. "Which one? There's more than one."

"Yale."

She showed me on a map. I shouldered my backpack and set off. It didn't take long to spot the tail. He had no idea I knew how to do this. I made sure there wasn't a pair and headed for the campus. My tail was right with me, right across the quad, stay with me Ace, here comes the Big Play. Here was a campus map, here was the Languages building, as usual behind the more favored departments. I went into the library, browsed the card catalog for a while. A long while. I watched him read through the announcements on the bulletin boards at the main entrance. And when he began to really read them, I headed for the stacks.

To him, it must have seemed I'd vanished. He would figure—well, I would, if it were me—that I'd found my book and gone to the stacks. I took up a position at the highest level, saw him come up one flight of stairs, another—same idea I had, search from the high ground. I headed into the maze of shelves. As I hoped, there was another stairway in the older section, a spiral, every library is alike. I took off my shoes, and walked as softly as I could down the spiral. Put my shoes back on and walked as fast as would be inconspicuous out the side door I'd counted on being there, got my bearings and ran around the corner of the nearest building. From there I worked my way around to the Foreign Languages building, staying out of sight of the Library. The directory gave me his office number; I hoped he had office hours after afternoon lectures. If not, it would be another night in a dorm lounge.

Luck held. Through the ground glass windows of his office door I could see light and silhouettes. I shrugged off my backpack, sat back, and realized how hard my heart was beating. He wasn't expecting another student, especially one he didn't recognize. He said his goodbyes to the guy he'd been talking to and turned to me. "Yes? I'm very sorry, I do not recognize you. Are you in one of my classes?"

"No, Professor Spielvogel, I'm Paul Seitz, Martin Seitz's son, I was here checking out the medical school, and I couldn't be here and not stop to say hello…"

His eyes lit up. "Pavel. Look at you. So tall now. Starting to look like your father at that age. I can see Martin's face in you. Terrible loss."

"Yes sir. I miss him every day."

"As do I. You're here about applying to the medical school?"

"Yes."

"A great loss to the field of German Literature."

"Thank you, sir, that's a great compliment, but I'll never have my father's talent for languages. My brain works more along the lines of numbers, math and the sciences."

"But you still read literature."

"Couldn't live without it. Half the backpack is books."

"Can you stay for dinner?"

"I was planning to stay overnight in the dorm."

"No such thing, no such thing. You will stay with us. There is plenty of room. Why didn't you call me in the first place?"

"To tell the truth, I didn't expect to be here today. I was planning to make this trip next week, and would have called you, but I caught a ride that saved me a bundle."

"So you'll have dinner and good conversation and a good nights' sleep, and save another bundle."

"I'd be most grateful, sir."

"Nonsense, it's nothing. How is your charming mother?"

"As always."

"Your grandmother?"

"In good health."

"Knock wood."

"Let me just call Martha." He drove me to a suburb, soon to be in leaf. "Why do you keep looking around?"

"Beautiful town, sir." *No blue Chevy. Lost him.*

Mrs. Spielvogel, like her husband, was little and round. The welcome was warm. Books covered every free space. I started to relax.

415

This was home. There were pictures all over of Spielvogel's children and grandchildren; I vaguely remembered the children, all much older than me.

"I got to this country a good ten years before Martin," he said. "A dessert wine? Yes?" A Liebfraumilch. We were in his library. "I missed the war, or rather, my war was here, teaching German language and culture to the O.S.S. Your father, I know, was in the middle of it. We all honored him for this."

"He was more ambivalent about his experiences."

"I know. It enriched his translations. How are the "Zurau Aphorisms" coming?"

"You'd have to ask Nan Goldman."

"He really had it in secret compartments in his desks?"

I nodded.

"His life was perhaps more traumatic than we ever considered." He shook his head. "He missed the increasing interest in foreign languages beginning just now. He was very well known among us, a big fish in a small pond. I love this expression. A big fish in a small pond. I still use his Rilke translations in my classes."

"I didn't know he'd translated Rilke."

He stood, searched the shelves for a few minutes, tossed me a paperback, a cheap student edition of the "Duino Elegies." "It's practically anonymous. On the back cover his name is mentioned."

It was there, in perhaps six point type: Intro. and tr. By Martin Seitz, Ph.D., Department of Languages, Brooklyn College.

"Keep that, Paul. It's for you."

"We must have a copy at home."

"I have dozens. Keep it. From me. For him."

"Thank you sir. I've not read Rilke."

"He must have been saving him for when you were older. That's

416

why I'm giving it to you. For him. A good thing for a young medical student to have. Did you know your father wrote poetry, in his student years?"

"Really? Seriously?"

"Very seriously." He laughed.

"I never knew that. We also found some later poems to my mother, in his desk. I sometimes think he was trying to revive German as a language for love poetry."

"That will take longer than he had. Than any of us will have."

"Does my mother know?"

"I don't know. He was always a much more astute critic than a poet. I think he concluded he would never be as good a poet as a translator."

"It probably made him a better translator."

"It did. He used to say, you can teach a poet German but it was much harder to teach poetry to a linguist."

"Sounds like him."

Before turning in I took a few minutes to read his introduction. The usual boilerplate, a brief biography, but also this:

Rilke placed himself at the center of the romantic revival then underway in the international culture that immediately preceded the First World War, a culture that would be a casualty of that war. Did he sense that that very romanticism, translated into the political realm, would bring about that war, and all that has followed? Can any man predict all the consequences of his acts, or of his words? The ripples spread from every lived moment, these poems tell us, to places beautiful and terrible.

—Martin Seitz, Ph.D.
June 7, 1959

I fell asleep in the arms of German *Kultur*, the first good nights' sleep I'd had in days, dreamless as far as I can remember.

I showed Spielvogel the Translator's Introduction over breakfast.

417

"I don't know if he was here explicating Rilke or reading into Rilke his own preoccupations."

"A good thing to be preoccupied with, given the turn events have taken."

"That we are wealthy and powerful enough, as a culture, to have aestheticized politics, to have made of government a medium for the realization of romantic, artistic ends?"

"I wouldn't have put it that well."

"He and I discussed this many times. Hitler was a failed artist, at least in watercolors. In government he was wildly successful, he created, in his terms, a masterpiece. And he bequeathed the world his methods. This will always be the central question in German cultural studies."

"And any other cultural studies. I intend to avoid the battle and treat the casualties."

"No one can avoid this battle."

I was tempted to tell him what I was really doing here. I finished my coffee instead. Who would believe the story? Besides, the romantic element was embarrassingly clear.

Before I could say anything he asked, "Where do you need to go? Back to the Medical School?"

"No, I'm finished there. I have to catch a train to New York. I can leave from anywhere; if there's a station close by I can just leave from there. I don't want to take you out of your way; I've done that enough already."

I promised to stay in touch, and meant it. I imagined taking Ali to meet Spielvogel, talk until the small hours, sleep over… He took me to Milford, close by, where I caught a local to New York. What would be their move? If I were Richard Acheson Esquire, or more likely Michael, I would set watchers at the three entry points to New York from Connecticut. Port Authority Bus Terminal, definitely. Pennsylvania Station where the long distance trains pulled in on their way to DC, and Grand Central, where the New Haven commuter trains terminated. If I had enough resources I might put a man at the 125th Street Station, but there were a dozen places in the Bronx to watch too. No, it was much easier than that. If I were going straight back to Schenectady I'd have to go to Grand Central; if not I'd be going home. Best to put a man at Grand Central and a man in Brooklyn. That chilled me. No doubt someone was already watching the Nott dorms. I didn't want to be picked up at home. Invited to meet with Richard Acheson Esquire. What could they do to me in a Manhattan law office? All that would happen was talk. That would be the end of the fun part. Might as well get it over with.

I took out the little book and sank into my father's Rilke.

> We assemble it
> It falls apart. We reassemble
> It
> And we fall apart.

Was that true? Did we organize things, our selves, every day, fall apart in sleep, and have to reassemble ourselves from the same parts every morning? But the parts change over time. I could no longer remember how my ten-year-old self saw the world, much less my five-year-old self. I still collected things, ideas instead of seashells and coins. Did we reassemble ourselves, our selves, every morning, from a subtly changing array of parts? Blos and Erickson. They said we reassemble the parts of our selves at each developmental stage, always the same, always different. The ship Argo, that in the course of its journey had every slat, every spar, every sail replaced; at journey's end, was she the same ship, or not?

The train jerked and lurched, buffeted by passing expresses, the old coaches groaning. I wished Ali were here to discuss this. I closed my

419

eyes, and imagined hers, so animated, so alive. Waiting like a racehorse at the gate for the next opening to launch an idea. Walked like a colt, too; those long legs, a gawky, awkward grace. Her lips on my cheek. Her lips on my lips. I was besotted, I know; I was enchanted. But this was—or was it?—the same girl as two years ago. She was nothing like her, but was her. Inside this girl was that one. Or was she all new, reworked like the Argo? If the MG had a new engine, transmission, drive train, quarter panels, was it still "The MG"? Or was it just "An MG"? What about me? My sudden casual skill at lying and deception? And to a man whose respect meant a lot to me. This was new…

The train rattled through Bridgeport, Stamford. It was after rush hour; trains were crammed in the yards. The factories along the line were humming, machinery rumbling and working, men swarming the outdoor spaces. (Thirty years later, the same journey; these factories would be ruins, dark, boarded up, crumbling, empty, the yards strewn with broken brick, surrounded by razor wire, the jobs gone, the men with them). I dozed briefly, woke up in time to cross Greenwich harbor awake; I wondered if the boat was in the water yet. Too soon, probably.

> *Down Greenwich reach*
> *To the Isle of Dogs*

Then we were over the border into New York, running express; the Westchester suburbs flashed past, Port Chester, Mamaroneck, New Rochelle, Mount Vernon, then the Bronx. Home. Went to the bathroom, combed my hair. The bridge over the Harlem River, past 125th Street, into the tunnel. We roared under Park Avenue, dim lights flashing past, and slowed, began banging over the points. Lights appeared, ends of platforms. One platform began to slide past. Show Time.

It was my intention to be picked up here. I could maybe sneak into the subway, make it home, but I didn't want a scene, didn't want to bring my mother and grandmother into it. *Don't worry your mother.* There was no hurry; give them time to spot me. How hard could it be to spot Jesus Christ in a Nott College jacket and a backpack? I took my time, got a good look at the famous constellations in the Grand Central ceiling, sadly faded (forty years later they would shine, fully restored). It was Michael himself who came up behind me.

"Mr. Seitz. You've led us a merry chase That's very embarrassing for me."

"I'm a chess player, Mike. Knight's gambit."

"So I have to assume you're letting me find you here."

"It's a shorter walk to his office."

"I'll get a cab."

"We'll walk, thanks. I'm not getting in a cab with you."

"Relax Mr. Seitz. Nobody wants to do anything but talk."

"We'll walk. I can use the stretch. Or I could just start yelling my head off right here."

He sighed. "We'll walk if you insist."

It seemed prudent—I was feeling pretty cocky after buying Dickie two more days than we'd thought he'd have—to take note of the entrances and exits from the building, a pre-War between Madison and Fifth in the high 30s. The interior was pretty well appointed, marble or faux-marble floors, walls, two elevators only, past a reception desk with a uniformed doorman/guard. A thick door suggested an interior set of fire stairs. The layout was repeated in the floors above: one corridor with offices opening off it, emergency stairs at the east end. Bradford, Fordyce & Acheson had the whole top floor, the elevator opened onto carpeted space, blond wood paneling, comfortable chairs and couches in muted colors, American Impressionist prints on the walls. On second look, not prints, originals. There was the stairway access at the east end.

There was a central reception and switchboard desk; each office had a secretary/receptionist as well; attractive women bent over the desks. The clatter of typewriters was muted by the carpeting.

"Have a seat," Mike said. He approached a desk; the secretary looked up, checked a schedule, said something. There were magazines on a coffee table, most prominently the National Review. Mike came back. "We can go in in a few minutes."

"We?"

"That's the way Mr. Acheson wants it." Better than having him covering the exit, or maybe there was someone down there too.

"Suits me. Does Mr. Acheson always get what he wants?"

"Kid. Mr. Seitz. I realize you have no experience of these things. Can I give you one piece of advice? Really. From the heart."

"Sure."

"Stop talking like a bad Sam Spade movie."

"I suppose that's more polite than 'Keep riding me, you'll be picking iron out of your liver'."

"*The Big Sleep?*"

"*Maltese Falcon.*"

"So tell me. Did you turn off the Northway by plan, or did you spot me?"

"Maroon Olds, only car on the road, maintaining constant distance, never passed me? Spotted you weeks ago. He wanted her to have the car, I thought of a way to get her the car and maybe buy him another day while you figured out where I went."

"Yeah, get her the car. Pretty girl, that Alicia."

Shit. I shrugged. "If you like the type."

"Mr. Acheson will see you now."

He actually rose to greet me, shake my hand. "Mr. Seitz. What a pleasure to see you again, although we would have wished it a few days sooner, wouldn't we, Michael."

Michael chuckled. "I told him he led us a merry chase, Mr. A."

"Well, I told you Michael, he's a very bright boy. That's why he and my son have been such good friends. Two very bright boys." *Now who was talking like a bad B movie* He indicated a chair right in front of the desk. Mike sat back against the wall behind me and to my right, next to the door, legs crossed, arms stretched out across the couch back.

This was another chess problem. Mike could move easily enough to block the door, but could only come at me diagonally. Like a bishop. Mr. Acheson was behind the desk, like a castled king. The walls were a forest green. To my left was a set of open display shelves full of ceramics, the centerpiece being a magnificent Dresden vase, easily two feet high and almost as wide. It was maybe one step away, out of the corner of my left eye.

"A very bright boy, Michael, so I am certain he will see sense, see where his advantage lies." Mike kept quiet, no doubt a veteran of many similar situations. It was their game, designed to keep me anxious, keep me off balance, keep me from putting them off balance. Not a chess problem, that.

"I assume you know why you were invited here. Cigarette?"

"No thanks."

"Mind if I smoke?"

"It's your office."

"So."

"So, what?"

"You know why you were invited here."

"Invited?"

"Don't play dumb with me, Mr. Seitz. It demeans us both."

"Demean me just a little, Mr. Acheson. Explain to me why this guy pulls me out of Grand Central Station and escorts me to your office."

"Escorts?"

"Now you're playing dumb with me, Mr. Acheson."

"I see you don't know how this game is played. Let me tell you the rules. Each of us has something the other wants. One of us wants it badly enough to use a kind of parallel set of rules to achieve it."

"Parallel rules."

"I don't think I need clarify that further."

"I think you are going to have to."

"Don't fence with me, boy."

"Mr. Acheson, you said I have something you want. You may be mistaken there. You say you have something I want. I'm certain you're mistaken there."

"I want to know where my son has gone. I know he went to Canada and that you aided him in the deception that made that possible."

"Well, Mr. Acheson, if you know that, I suspect you know I wouldn't want to tell you. If I knew."

"That, Mr. Seitz, brings us to what you want. What you want is for your life to continue as it is. But in fact it could go quite a bit better. What would you like, Mr. Seitz, that I could arrange for you?"

"I honestly can't imagine, Mr. Acheson. Nor can I imagine wanting to contemplate such an offer."

"Come on, Mr. Seitz. You can do better than that. You want to go to medical school. That's going to cost money. Your mother and grandmother live in a tiny apartment in Brooklyn. Your mother could use a promotion, for one thing."

"I suggest you leave my mother out of this, Mr. Acheson. I very strongly suggest that."

"Your father left a substantial body of unpublished work, my sources tell me. Work of some cultural significance. Editors and publishers can be found, Mr. Seitz."

"I appreciate your devotion to culture."

"What of that menu appeals to you, Mr. Seitz?"

"You mean, what is my friend worth?"

"That friend is my son, Mr. Seitz. I want very much to speak with him. That is all I want. I want to understand what is in his mind. I think he is pursuing a foolhardy course, from which his and your actions have deprived me of a chance to turn him. I want only to have that chance. To which end, I require from you his current location."

"My understanding is that you have already had that conversation."

"Perhaps your understanding is faulty, or in error."

It was possible. I only had Dickie's word for his interactions with his father. But I had Ali's word too, and I had my own observations. The chess game, for one example. The boat. The library card. Riley. *Who ya gonna trust, me or your own eyes?*

"Possibly. But Dickie helped me fight off a bunch of bullying upperclassmen. You sent out a small army of—with all due respect to Mike here—goons to track me down and drag me up here. I think I'm going to go with Dickie on this one, Mr. Acheson."

"Boy, you do not know what you're playing with."

"Boy? I think we'd better stick to Mr. Seitz and Mr. Acheson, man."

"You're right. But you are beginning to try my nerves, and, forgive me in advance, right Michael? I sometimes become angry when my nerves are tried. You see, I also think you have become involved with my daughter. And my second demand is that any such involvement cease."

"Involved? I delivered her a car. I gave her some books. That's my involvement. Didn't you ever hear that no girl was ever ruined by a book? Cars, I don't know."

"This is no joking matter, son."

"I'm sorry, sir, I just can't take this seriously."

"Do you think I'm blind and deaf, son? Can't see what's going on in my own house, under my nose? Wooing her with books, feeding her dreams. You think I don't know who you are, or what you are? You think you're the first man in the world who wanted my daughter's money? She has the looks and brains to marry very well, and I will let nothing stand in the way of that. *Was this a cartoon?* She needs someone with more blood in his veins." *Don't get psyched, this is like a chess game and this is the psyching part*

"Then you have nothing to worry about."

"I told you not to fence with me. You seem to know how to spot surveillance, but she doesn't. And there is surveillance."

Time to psych back "It is a truth universally acknowledged, that a single man in possession of no fortune, must be in want of a rich wife." They both looked baffled. "Parody of the first line of 'Pride and Prejudice'."

"You're very well-read, young man. Very bright, very clever. That isn't the same thing as power, Mr. Seitz. Chess is just a game. You were seen having breakfast with her yesterday morning."

"And I bet she was seen walking alone to that breakfast. I spent the night on a couch in a UMass dorm and I brought her the car."

"You moved a stolen car."

"Its legally titled owner conveyed it to its new owner. Who gave me a lift to Hartford so she could retitle the car and I could catch a bus. That's my involvement. That's hers. Until I called her yesterday she didn't know a damned thing about it."

"Well, that's very good news for her, Mr. Seitz, because if I thought for one moment that you and she had any further involvement I would cut off her tuition that fast. And those checks are monthly. I sit at the center of a very large web, Mr. Seitz. Half of your school, half of hers, are children of my neighbors, or someone else I know. *I know his family slightly. His father did some legal work for mine* Any attempt at communicating with her, letter, telegram, phone, ham radio—I haven't forgotten the radio thing—or her with you, will disturb the web. You are a biology student, Mr. Seitz, so I assume you know what that means. I repeat, I will pull her out of the school she loves so much. Which I

426

will be telling her before close of business today. And you wouldn't want to be responsible for that, would you. Which brings us to your tuition, Mr. Seitz, which is dependent upon a scholarship and a school job. Either of which I could have stopped in about two seconds. So you have two clear choices here, Mr. Seitz. You can tell me where Dickie is, or how to get in touch with him, or you can join him through your organization. Or get better acquainted with your draft board. I really don't care, you'd be no asset to our army."

"Let me get this straight. You think I arranged some contact for your son with some organization in Canada?"

"The name Acheson means something to the Russians, Mr. Seitz. I know about your mother's and grandmother's hobbies, I know about his friend and yours, the Indian diplomat's daughter. India is a Soviet ally, no matter what they say. I think you could be part of a Soviet front organization, or a dupe."

"That's pretty funny, Mr. Acheson."

"Funny? Why would I think this funny thing, Michael?"

"He shook me off on the Northway, meaning he spotted a professional tail. Then he did the same thing in New Haven. Acts like a pro, sir."

"Of course I did. How smart do you have to be to spot the only other car on the Northway, considering Dickie knew for days or weeks he was being followed? And your guy in New Haven followed me onto a college campus wearing a gray suit and a fedora. He couldn't have stood out more if he'd been wearing clown shoes. I figured he was your man; I guarantee everyone else on that campus thought he was a narc."

"It's alright Mr. Seitz; we know you have no professional espionage training. We have a complete dossier on you. Here." He tossed me a manila folder labeled "Seitz". It accounted for my movements since about age 14, my father's background, my mother's and grandmother's political affiliations—lightly sketched.

I said, "Are my eyes really brown?"

"What?"

"It's from a movie, Mr. Acheson," Michael said. "*Casablanca*? Bogart?"

"Don't wise off to me, Mr. Seitz. You're in no position."

"So you think I subverted Dickie's politics and took the first opportunity to sleep with your daughter."

"If you must be offensive, but yes, that is exactly what I think. Both my children were on quite a straight path until they met up with you, and since then I haven't had a minute's peace. Don't think both of them haven't sprinkled your name liberally in conversation at table."

I saw it then, assuming I could believe him, what they'd done, what they'd had to do: encourage this madman's belief that I had turned them against him. I knew Ali had told him I thought she had the stuff to be a doctor, or anyway a pre-med. It was an easy thing to do; he believed it already and could never be brought to see his own part in that process, never believe any other version. Both his children wanted out; Dickie maybe had done it, but he could still ruin Ali's chances. And she, indirectly but heedlessly, could ruin mine. Maybe already had.

"Know what, Mr. Acheson? I'm quite prepared to meet your demand that I never have anything to do with your family ever again. I think the whole pack of you are crazy."

"Fine, think what you want. That leaves my first demand: Where is Dickie?"

"Mr. Acheson, here's what I know from Dickie. He has lost faith in American values, Western values in general, and over the time I have known him he has more and more embraced Buddhist values and practices, including a radical pacifism. He wanted to drop out of Nott to pursue studies in this area, and he approached you with this proposal. Am I correct so far?"

"Substantially."

"Your response to him was that it was fine with you if he dropped out, but only if he enlisted in the military, for future career considerations. Also correct?"

"Again, substantially."

"Are you aware that his beliefs make such a course of action impossible for him?"

"I'm aware that he fell among political radicals. Drugs, too, I wouldn't be surprised."

"He fell among Buddhist texts, Mr. Acheson, and courses in Eastern religion and philosophy. I'm probably what you would call a political radical, at least on the subject of the Vietnam War, or maybe war in general. For Dickie it goes beyond that, but into spiritual realms, not political."

"And I think you are full of shit, Mr. Seitz. I think you helped him leave this country to hook up with a bunch of international left wingers, Communists probably, and that you yourself are part of such a group. Or a fellow traveler. I don't care which. Now Mr. Seitz, where is he?"

There might be another solution to this. All it required was no conscience.

"I stopped knowing the answer to that question three days ago, Mr. Acheson."

"I think that is a lie, Mr. Seitz, and I think things could go well beyond what I indicated earlier. Far from a promotion, I think your mother could lose her job due to her political activities. She wouldn't be the first at her school. Your father's work might never see daylight. You could be on your way to Southeast Asia in a matter of weeks."

> *BREAK-THROUGH. One must resolutely make the*
> *matter known*
> *At the court of the king.*
> *It must be announced truthfully. Danger.*

429

It is necessary to notify one's own city.
It does not further to resort to arms.
It furthers one to undertake something.

An idea, or rather an action, had been forming in my head. Again, a chess problem, and I thought I had the moves figured out. At least it would change the game, and I had had enough of this one. Well, it had worked once. "I think those are empty threats, Mr. Acheson." I caught the sign I was looking for; his eyes flashed briefly to Michael by the door. I jumped up, throwing the chair to my right and back, blocking Michael, and had the big Dresden vase in my hands and over my head. Fine china, light as a feather. Michael reached over the fallen chair, but Mr. Acheson called him back: "Mike. Stop."

Addressing me, Mr. Acheson said, "Do you have any idea what that is worth?"

"I have some idea how much it's worth to you."

"Put it down, Mr. Seitz. I've been hasty. I have a temper, I'm sorry, it sometimes gets me into trouble."

"Yeah, well, how about Mike moves behind the desk. We're close enough an accident might happen, and he can help you with your temper problem."

"I think you're bluffing. What would your father think, you threatening to destroy a rare surviving work of German art?"

"He'd say no work of art is worth a human life. And I told you once, chess players don't bluff. Tell Mike to get behind the desk with you. Now."

He sighed. "Do as the young man says, Michael." Michael did, his eyes dead.

I backed off toward the door. "Now. Here's how this goes."

"You're in no position to dictate terms, young man."

"As long as I have this I am. My terms are, you shut the hell up and listen carefully. You want to throw around threats, here's a few to think about. Or this valuable art object is going to vanish in a terrible janitorial accident."

"You would be arrested for vandalism."

"I don't think so. Then we'd have to explain what I'm doing here. Dickie, Alicia, all of it."

"All right, Mr. Seitz, I'm listening."

"If you make any attempt to hurt me or mine, if I even think you have, I'm from Brooklyn. Not your part of the New York Metropolitan Area. I have relatives, friends, and they have relatives and friends. And some of them are cops, and some are court clerks and messengers, and building inspectors, and fire inspectors, and elevator inspectors, and title searchers. Is your building up to code? Paperwork in order? How about the elevators? Doors wide enough? Fire stairs clear? Do you like being able to double park outside? Clients like being able to get cabs? Are you getting the picture here, Mr. Acheson? And Mike: Some of my friends of friends are people you would not want to mess with."

"I can make your scholarship go away."

"So I'll go to City U."

"You'll never get into a medical school."

"Now you're beyond your reach, Mr. Acheson. But you can try. If any of that happens this office and all your partners will be so tied up in red tape and violations you'll be lucky to be able to fix a parking ticket. This is still a Democratic town, Mr. Acheson. It ain't Connecticut."

"I take you into my house, show you hospitality, and this is how you repay me?"

You crazy bastard "You call this hospitality? Tell you what, Mr. Acheson, I'll be taking my leave. I'll just take this with me and give it to your secretary in the lobby, in exchange for my jacket and backpack which you are going to tell her to bring down. Assuming nobody follows me. That's a really hard marble floor down there, it could still drop. Call her, Mr. Acheson. Tell her."

He made the call. "Just stay the hell away from my son. Stay the hell away from my family. That's all I want from you. We'll find him without your help. Just stay the hell away."

"Fine by me. I never wanted anything from any of you. Come for a visit and end up in a soap opera."

"Just one thing, Mr. Seitz. One last thing. Did you ever consider the possibility that my son might be mentally ill? Suicidal?"

"If I thought that I would have called you, Mr. Acheson. I assure you he was in excellent humor and had definite plans."

"Thank you for that at least."

"Pacifism isn't a mental illness Mr. Acheson." I opened the door a crack. The secretary was just getting my backpack and jacket. As I watched she stepped to the elevators. "I'll be taking the stairs. You'd better hope I don't hear any footsteps but my own in there, or this thing is going to get to the lobby before I do. Are we clear?"

"What do you think, Michael?"

"Mr. Acheson, I think this kid won't bribe, and he won't threaten. He doesn't have the sense. I can find your son for you. Without any information from him."

"You see, Mr. Seitz? No one will hinder your departure. You can leave the vase…"

"In the lobby, Mr. Acheson, as we agreed."

"Just be careful with it."

There were no footfalls on the stairs other than my own. The vase was a beautiful thing, and I was glad not to have had to destroy it. Would I have? I don't know. Ali was right. Fear turns to anger. Anger gains momentum, and you do things you regret. Why no one stops wars. These people were crazy, and made me that angry, scared and

432

angry, one more healthy reason to give them a wide berth. The secretary was expressionless as we exchanged burdens. I shrugged into my jacket and swung my backpack onto my shoulder. She clicked across the lobby with the vase. What she and the security guard/doorman thought I will never know. Maybe shit like this happened all the time.

I walked over to Fifth, sat on the library steps, bringing my pulse back to cruising speed and looking for a tail. If there was one I couldn't spot him. Too cold to sit here.

> *Chock full o'Nuts is that heavenly coffee*
> *Heavenly coffee*
> *Heavenly coffee.*
> *Chock full o'Nuts is that heavenly coffee*
> *Better coffee a millionaire's*
> *Money can't buy   He never offered me money*

I crossed the park to the Chock Full O'Nuts on 40th and Sixth. Paid for a cup and took a corner table, where I could scan the park and down Sixth. *At the court of the king. It must be announced truthfully. Danger. It is necessary to notify one's own city. It does not further to resort to arms.* Two years ago I would have broken it. Or wanted to. Possibly over his head. *Had I learned something or forgotten something?*

We could get married, move in with my family, go to Brooklyn College. *What about med school*

I am prepared to undertake dangerous missions for The Weather Girl I would have to give her up for now. I would have to, I saw that. I had a plan for her, he had a plan for her, and the one important thing was, she had a plan for herself. That was the one that counted, and the risk, not least to her, was too great. He was that crazy. Paranoid. If I tried to contact her he would know, eventually. There was only the kiss, and a

433

whispered *Je t'aime aussi, tout meme.* Did I have any right to risk her future, all our futures, on that alone? Not without discussing it with her. I took out my wallet. Tapped. Down to three dimes. FDR's face looked away from me, times three. A life turns on such small things.

There was a pay phone on the wall in back. I inserted a dime, leaving two for the new subway fare.

"Operator."

"I'd like to make a collect call to…" I gave the number of her dorm phone. Circuitry clicked. "I'm sorry, sir. That is a pay phone. You cannot make a collect call to a pay phone." *Shit.* The dime came back as it was supposed to, but often didn't, when I hung up. Which meant one more try at Ma Bell's slot machine.

"Operator."

"I'd like to make a Person-to-Person call to Miss Alicia Acheson at…" again I gave the dorm number. It rang and rang, was finally picked up by whom I will never know. "I have a Person-to-Person call for a Miss Alicia Acheson."

"Um…not here."

"Tell her Paul called," I shouted as loudly and quickly as I could, and hung up. This time no dime in the coin return. But a coffee shop full of staring customers. I held out my hands, palm outward, the universal New York gesture for "I'm not crazy."

Enough left for one trip to Brooklyn. One last look at the back trail. I went into the subway at 39th, ran back up at 37th. No one following. I caught a Brighton Express at 34th.

If love meant putting someone else's happiness before one's own, it meant loving her meant having no contact for two years. We couldn't disturb the web. Too much at stake for too many people, riding on one crazy man with enough power to bring grief to us all. Until she graduated. June 1969. Plus a month or two for the summer trip to

Europe. *Two years…How do I give that up?* I tried telling myself that girl, the one I was with yesterday, was also the crazy girl from two summers ago, the one who was sleeping around. That I couldn't trust her. That it was crazy to fall for the first girl that kissed you *Only she wasn't that girl* That a day of wonderful bull sessions and one dream and one kiss didn't override what I also knew. That I wasn't losing anything. *What happened to the intense love I'd been feeling? She scared me. She'd want to defy him. Maybe another time. After she graduated. One shouldn't marry such a maiden* The train rocked across the bridge. *The Moral Compass: Cowardice and Love pointed in the same direction*

At the Beach I ducked down Brighton 4th and took the boardwalk to Brighton 3rd. No one sitting in a car. The stickball game was going on; the kids hadn't seen any strangers on the block. That's when I relaxed. There probably never had been, outside my anxious imagination. Cutting contact with the Achesons, from the vantage point of home, was looking healthier every minute. No more evasive action. *Everything I had done for the past 36 hours had been evasive action Except the time with Ali*

Up the stairs, knock on the door, back up against the wall. My grandmother saw no one through the judas; she stepped out into the hall and her face lit up. I put my finger to my lips *shhh*; she smiled, old conspirator.

"Who's there, Ma?" my mother called.

"No one," my grandmother said. "Total stranger."

My mother turned from the stove, let out a small cry and hugged me as hard as she could. "Paulie, Paulie, where did you come from?"

"From Yale. I got a ride with Dickie (*well, I did*) and went to check out the med school, took the train back. Couldn't pass through the City without stopping to see my best girls."

"Medical school? Paulie, you do want to go to medical school? You're sure?"

435

"I do, Ma, and don't worry about money. City is opening a new med school at Mt. Sinai, or I can get a Regents Medical Scholarship."

"Those are only good in state; why go to Yale?"

"To ask about scholarships."

"You could do that by phone. Or wait, Papa had a friend there…"

"Dr. Spielvogel. I looked him up. He asked after you. He gave me this." I showed her the "Duino Elegies."

"I remember this. Part of his series of Modern German Poets."

"I read it on the train from New Haven."

"You really want to be a doctor, Paulie?"

"I do, Grandma. Pretty sure."

"Promise me one thing. Swear this."

"What?"

"That you'll never join the American Medical Association. Those momzers fought Medicare tooth and nail. Everyone should have Medicare. Promise."

"I don't want to be that kind of doctor, Grandma. I promise." *More like Che Guevara* We ate in silence for a while.

"How long can you stay?"

"Can't. Got to get back tonight."

"Tonight. Overnight at least you can't stay?"

"It's not a vacation. Missed two days of classes already. Most of the backpack is books I should be reading. And I don't have enough clothes. Or money. In fact, I need train fare back to Schenectady."

"Put on a robe, we'll wash what you have."

I kissed her. "I have to go. Spring Break is in a few weeks, and I'll spend every minute with you."

"You work too hard, Paulie."

"No I don't, not really. I work just hard enough."

"You need friends. You need a girlfriend. How is Dickie?"

"Fine ma. He sends regards."

"And his sister?"

"Also fine, as far as I know."

"She liked you, Paulie."

"Not exactly a woman of the people."

"There's more to her, Paulie. A proletarian of course she isn't, but rich people have their troubles too. It's as easy to love a rich girl as a poor one." *No it isn't*

"I'm rich enough, Ma." I held up the Rilke.

"That won't put you through medical school. Your father always worried about what would come after college."

"I'll get a Regents, Ma, and that will come from books."

She kissed me again. "From your mouth to God's ear, Paulie."

"Tell me how you are."

"Fine. The kids, they get wilder every year, and the politics isn't helping. You know I believe in education, but my kids are starting to come home from Vietnam in boxes."

"Something we maybe are going to do something about, Ma."

"Paulie, stay out of any craziness." *This from a '30s Trotskyist*

"I know violence can't be stopped with violence. *Only I'm not so sure about that* Ma, this is a crazy question. Have you noticed anyone around the block, like, watching the house, you…"

"You are mixed up in something."

"No, Ma, nothing, look, I said it was a crazy question, just a prank by some of the guys at school."

"You're a lousy liar, Paulie."

You should only know

"Forget it, Ma, it's just something stupid a friend of mine at school started, it's over, so forget about it, it's nothing."

She chose to be reassured. For the third time in as many days I said a goodbye I desperately did not want to say. The latest, I realized, in a long string. I shouldered the backpack again, headed out. There was one more stop to make.

At the court of the king.
It must be announced truthfully. Danger.
It is necessary to notify one's own city.

I rang the bell in the lobby of Sam's building; his mother came on the annunciator and I asked her to send him down, as so many times when we were kids. Younger kids. "So how are you Paulie," she asked, the annunciator making her sound like a bosun calling Battle Stations. I pressed the button, "OK, Mrs. R." Sam came to the door; we walked to the boardwalk and under it. The sea breeze cut through us; we took shelter behind a buttress. I promised him the last check, told him the story. Most of it.

"So you smuggled Dickie out, ducked the tail, delivered the MG and got the girl. I'm looking for the big red S on your chest, Pav-El."

"Except the old man is fucked in the head. I was wondering if you had any way of finding out if he's as big a threat as he says."

He thought a minute. "Maybe. I can ask people who can ask people. It could take a while."

"How long is 'a while'?"

"A while."

"Thanks, Sam. For whatever you can find out. I have a little money now, if that helps…"

"I could maybe invest it for you. With mine. Horse race futures."

"No, Sam. It's med school money. Application fees, travel for interviews, I can't count on a scholarship, I'll have to buy a microscope, fuck knows what."

"Play it safe, Paulie. I can tell you that without finding out anything."

"You met her, Sam."

438

"Yeah, I met her." He looked away. "Paulie, did it occur to you to call him, tell him you'll tell him where Dickie is if he'll leave the two of you alone?"

"The thought occurred to me. To do it, no. Why would she want anything to do with the guy that did that? Why would I?"

He sighed. "Me too."

Twenty years later, when I was dropping off my taxes for him to do, he asked me how I'd managed it. I told him I knew what I did but I didn't know how I'd done it. That it hadn't been pretty. What I didn't know at the time was, that girl I'd spent the day with, I'd never see again. *That mind. That heart. In that skin.*

As it was, I shouldered the backpack a last time, headed to Grand Central. I caught the Wolverine.

> *And I did not think the girl could be so cruel*
> *And I'm never going back*
> *To my old school*

April 7, 1973
4:30 PM – 6:30 PM

The ER clock said 4:30 but it didn't say it was right. *...today in Saigon the Air Force announced another day of raids backing the ARVN...* We found the head nurse, got her to get a clerk to pull together the chart paperwork and went to look behind Curtain A. Sitting up in the bed was an elderly man, not at all frail looking, but wasted, as if a sturdy old building had been emptied and was waiting for the wrecking ball. It was quickly apparent he spoke very little English, but copious amounts of something else. The clerk had two other charts to put together for surgical and OB admits, so the first thing I taught Ali was to do an admission exam in the ER if one had to; time was never recoverable.

"What is he speaking?" Ali said. "It sounds like Polish or Russian."

"But isn't," said nurse Wanda Elenowska. "It could be a dialect; I can make out some of it but not enough. We know the ambulance crew was out picking up somebody else in his building, which was mostly abandoned, and heard him calling out. They found him on the floor; he could have been there for days."

"And that's all we know."

"That's all we know. The apartment was stripped. He's all yours. Social Services can see him Monday."

"So that's it?" Ali asked.

"No. What do you want to do—he's your patient."

"I want to find a translator."

443

"For what language?"

"And I want to help him get somewhere he'll be cared for."

"First we get a diagnosis."

"Is that all this means to you? To all of you? It's a game, right? Like chess. One up ourselves and each other with the right diagnosis? He doesn't need a diagnosis, he needs a decent place to live."... *another brigade is reporting back home...*

I pulled her into the corridor, found a quiet corner. "Look, you know how this works. It starts with sleep deprivation, or anyway that's the background, the zero-th step in the process. We don't get to sleep. The next is to take the unbearable experience of terribly pitiable people in horrible trouble, hanging on to life by a thread, and turning that into an intellectual game called Get the Diagnosis, and the payoff is, or one day will be, that this ruthless game will, in about one out of three cases, save a patient's life, or anyway postpone death. The unexamined patient is not worth having." She grinned a little at that. "He does need a diagnosis. Why couldn't he get up?"

"It's a very male way of approaching it."

"True. Learn the game. Join the faculty. Change the game. You can change it. It'll take years. But right now...this guy is scary, isn't he?"

"...Yes."

"Why?"

"Because we can't get a history."

"Right. We'll have to go by our exam and labs, and skills at interpreting them that the Game has taught us. He's scary, Ali." A strand of hair had come loose from all the pins. I brushed it back from her face. She had never looked so beautiful to me. She took my hand for as long as it took to move it from her face, and a moment longer, and pulled me toward the ER.

"Do we at least have a name?"

444

"No." I took my stethoscope off my neck and pointed to it. "Sir, we're going to examine you now." He nodded, sat forward. Ali smiled at him *she could make me live just with that smile* and started with a pulse, then his head and neck, looking in his eyes and ears, nose and throat, feeling his neck for nodes, percussing his chest, auscultating (I mimed deep breaths, but he knew what to do) first his chest, then his heart, where she heard something of interest, abdomen, genitalia, then his hands…

"Paul, look at this." He was missing distal parts of three fingers from his left hand, two from his right; she quickly looked at his ears and found a missing right lobe. "Frostbite" she said, "I saw this on the ski slopes."

She was right, it was frostbite. He looked the right age. I pointed to his hands and said "Vlassov?" This set off a storm of speech. He took my hand and would not let go. "Ja, ja, Vlassov," he said, "Vlassov."

"What's Vlassov?"

"Not what, who. General Vlassov, a Ukrainian Red Army general, captured by the Wehrmacht, defected and formed the Russian Liberation Army from Russian POWs. The Germans equipped them pretty well, sent them to fight with Army Group Center in1945, but they didn't trust them entirely and sent them into a frozen swamp. That's probably where he lost the fingers." I turned to him "Ukraine?" I said.

He pointed to himself. "Ja, Ukraine, me."

"So he's speaking Ukrainian, which sounds like Russian and Polish, but isn't either one. How about…Herr soldat, wie heissen Sie? Was ist ihre name?" No dice. "Papieren? Wo ist ihre papieren?"

"Keinen papieren."

"Yeah, that we already know—on the street somewhere. One more possibility, if I can do this…" and I tried to put together the sentences from dimly remembered childhood memory.

"What was that?"

"Czech. I thought he might respond to Czech. Prague? Praha?"

He brightened up again. "Ja, Praha, Praha."

"Not enough Czech, and he won't respond to German. And he definitely will not respond to Russian…Wanda…where's Wanda?"

"Here, Doctor—what?"

"Know anyone who speaks Ukrainian?"

"I do, as a matter of fact, she's on the ICU graveyard shift—tonight, I think."

"There's our first lucky break. Do you think you can tell him in Polish that we'll have a Ukrainian here later?" Ali asked.

"I can try." He seemed to calm. I went over him quickly; nothing significant. Neuro might have to figure out why he wasn't walking.

"What did you find?" I asked Ali.

"Nothing much. I thought I caught a skipped beat, on pulse and when I was listening, but I couldn't pick it up again."

"Me either." I said. "What do you want to do?"

"Get an EKG with a long rhythm strip and keep an eye on his vitals. And hope the Ukrainian nurse doesn't call in sick."

"And put in for Neuro Monday."

There was an EKG from the ER; nothing significant. We got him to the floor and let nursing do its thing, told Marvin the story. "So if he has an arrythmia…"

"It could account for falling, being unable to get up," Ali said. "And maybe confusion from intermittent anoxia."

"Could….Katie."

"*Sir.*"

"As soon as Mr. Ukraine is set up, run a rhythm strip. You know how to do that?"

"EKG, switch to limb leads and let it run a few minutes."

"Run a few of them, five to ten minutes apart. I'm going to grab us some on-call rooms before the surgeons get them all."

Ali and I settled down to write admit notes. "Why did you try Czech? And why would he definitely not respond to Russian?"

"Because when Vlassov's Army, a division actually, got sent to that swamp, they realized the Germans were just using them as cannon fodder to cover their retreat, and that everyone was in a mad rush to escape from the Red Army. They realized their only hope was to surrender to the Americans. So they headed south, toward Prague. Where the partisans had begun an uprising against the German occupiers. The Germans sent in the Waffen SS, and they were making mincemeat of the Czechs until Vlassov's gang showed up. They turned it around, pretty much liberated Prague. And as many as could tried to get to American lines—Patton's Third Army was only a hundred miles or so away. They knew they were marked men for Stalin. A few of them made it; they didn't know the US had agreed to turn all Russian POWs over to the Red Army no matter whether they wanted to be repatriated or not—Stalin regarded POWs as traitors, and Vlassov, well…he was eventually hanged in Moscow. Our man must have made it. Somehow. He was in a German uniform, maybe could fake enough German or just keep mum, like today, to blend in with a bunch of deserters, fool some GIs, end up in a POW camp for Germans. How he got to the States we'll have to ask him—if he'll tell us"

"And you know this how?"

"I know this because one guy they were trying to reach to surrender to was my father."

"Your—wait, how does your father come into this?"

"Because in September 1938 Germany demanded the cession of the Sudetenland by Czechoslovakia…"

"The Munich Pact, I know…"

447

"...and by March all of Czechoslovakia was a German protectorate—two actually. The Prague Jews were part of an ancient German-acculturated community—Kafka? Right? My grandfather probably bought insurance from Kafka—so my father had tried to attend university in Germany. During his graduate years he saw the book burnings..."

"Which explains his library."

"Which explains his library, yes. He came back to Prague to complete his studies, and became a member of a city chess team. In February 1938 he went to Warsaw to play in a tournament. When the Germans rolled into Prague his parents contacted him and told him to stay in Poland. They wired money. They also contacted his older half-brother in New York to start trying to get him to the States. My uncle was less than eager; it was a bitter thing between them for the rest of their lives. Anyway, when the Germans marched in, a whole bunch of Czech Air Force pilots flew their planes to Poland, even though Poland took a piece of Czechoslovakia too. The reasoning was, Poland was next. One of the pilots was a chess player from a Prague club. They took my father on as a batman."

"A what?"

"A servant. European military tradition. It saved his life. When the Germans invaded Poland in '39 they bombed the Polish air force on the ground. The Czechs never got to fly. They fled to England through Lithuania and Sweden, and there they got to fly for the RAF, there were three squadrons of them. My father's talents at chess and languages got him noticed by the Czech Provisional Government. He watched his friends die in the Battle of Britain, one after another. SOE, the British OSS, got interested in the Czechs; the Czechs had their own training facility. Assassinated Reinhard Heydrich? Yes? He had a hand in that. Comes D-Day, Patton's dash across France, the Rhine bridgeheads, Patton's Third Army is miles from the Czech border, the Provisional

Government has signed an alliance with the Soviets; my father joins it with the Social Democrats but by then his half-brother had worked a few connections, and when the U.S. came in, he was seconded to them as liaison to Czech partisans working with Britain, unofficially to keep an eye on Czech partisans working with the Red Army. When Prague rose against the Germans, and Vlassov's gang moved in, he was right there. And I have good reason to think he let anyone through who was running."

"Why?"

"By then he knew his parents and family were all dead. He made a very unauthorized trip to Prague. Stole a jeep, and took another Czech with him, a partisan. Shooting all over the place; Vlassov's people were duking it out with that SS battalion. He went home, found the ruins, found the neighbors. Theresienstadt, Auschwitz, smoke. He found one thing."

"I'll guess. The German edition of Kafka."

"Right. Buried in the yard. He couldn't save them, but he could save what they had saved, what meant that much to all of them. He forced his way into the house; it had been given to some collaborators. I think that may have been the only time he ever pointed a weapon at anybody. He was sick of war, sick of that war. He was sick of death and killing and politics. He was a Social Democrat, a Menshevik, he thought the Soviets were going to keep Czechoslovakia and replace one tyranny with another, that a Social Democratic Czechoslovakia didn't have a prayer. He was a little crazy by then. And his own status was far from clear. He wasn't a British citizen, he didn't want to be one—he told me: once MI6, always MI6 and he didn't want to be a spy, even if they got him a cover job at Oxbridge. The Americans needed his language skills; they had started liberating the camps, they needed his Yiddish and his German. And after that, for the de-Nazification interrogations and the War Crimes trials. And the rocket scientists. He wasn't British, he was Czech; one way to American citizenship was to enlist in the American army. Europe was destroyed, Germany was a charnel house, he had no more ties to Europe, he may have come to America out of disgust. Between his half-brother and his professor friends and his language skills, his desire for American citizenship was looked on favorably, so they let him. But not until 1946."

"So there is a Seitz family tradition of helping refugees."

"I hadn't thought about it that way, Ali, but I guess there is. *Well…Dickie* Also of rescuing books."

"Well, you told me you'd tell me his story some time. I guess this is some time."

"It isn't the whole story."

"I know, Paul."

"There's never been anyone I could tell the whole story."

She touched my hand. "There is now."

I looked at her. *How much could I…* "OK. He had the first heart attack when I was fourteen. By that time I was playing at the New York Chess Club, I was on the school chess team. The more I think about it, about how he stopped playing with me, when he threw the chessboard over, you remember? I think maybe he was starting to have the chest pain. I think he knew. Why he had to give me a 'life lesson'."

"I remember. Did he tell anybody?"

"No. I don't think so. It wasn't his way."

"Your mother must have suspected."

"I don't think she did. Maybe. Anyway, he had been having chest pain, I know that now, but he finally went to see his doctor. Got admitted straight to Downstate. I came home from school, and my grandmother told me my mother was with him, and he was OK, and I could go visit tomorrow."

"How did you feel?"

"Plenty scared. People died of heart attacks, I knew that. I knew anxiety was a part of it, and I knew he was anxious about the world situation. The Bay of Pigs invasion scared him. He was always kind of taking the world's temperature, seeing if it had the fever he had experienced in 1938. Did I mention I had a passport by the time I was two? So I would never be stateless, which is something he knew about. I don't know what else he might have been worried about. Except the chest pain itself. I mean, he would know what it meant. *And about me*

"My mother came home from the hospital, and she was very matter-of-fact, he was OK, resting comfortably, all the things we say, right? And we could visit together tomorrow. But my grandmother stayed over. I went to see him in the CCU the next day, and he really did look OK. He was on nasal O_2, had an IV running. He had asked for books; we brought him Bruno Schulz."

"Bruno Schulz?"

"Jewish surrealist writer. Imagine Kafka crossed with Borges."

"Sounds interesting."

"I still have the book, but it's in German. So. He came home. Took a leave for a few weeks; somebody covered his classes. Except for chess team I came home straight from school. He'd be reading, or working a chess problem. He was reading Gunther Grass, I remember. The Danzig Trilogy. He was planning to assign 'Dog Years' when it came out in English. I'd find him in the chair, asleep over the book."

"How long did that go on?"

"For a few weeks, maybe months. He got his energy back, enough to go back to teaching, go to museums, but we had to use the elevators. It took him forever to climb the subway stairs. But he did it."

"How were you feeling about all this?"

"Scared. Sad. Angry."

"Angry at what?"

I looked away. *At him. For not taking care of himself. For being older. For being sick. For scaring my mother. For scaring me. At myself, for feeling those things. At the world, for scaring him.* "At him. For dying on me, scaring me into thinking he would. At myself…Just before the summer I came to your house I found evidence his Dig dose was increased just before he died."

"You think he was Dig toxic."

"Maybe. I didn't understand the significance until the lecture on Dig in Pharm."

"So you get Dig levels on everyone on Dig."

"That's just good medicine."

"It's that too."

"So one day I came home and found him dead."

"I remember. I'm sorry, Paul. You never told anybody?"

Silence.

"Paulie? What are the odds of a member of Vlassov's Army showing up at this hospital? Today?"

"What are the odds of you showing up at this hospital today? Why did you come to this medical school?" *To find me?*

"Why did you come here?"

"Because so much of the faculty was on McCarthy's blacklist…"

"Exactly, so it's in the forefront of admitting women, and blacks, and whatever."

"How about Women's Medical in Philly?"

"Rejected me. With a 3.6 GPA from Wellsmith. I was rejected from four other schools too. One interviewer asked me did I want to be a doctor or just marry one, and then have babies and retire."

"Jesus. What did you say?"

"I told him if I became one maybe I'd find one worth marrying but it was beginning to look unlikely."

I laughed.

"I already knew that place was a lost cause."

"Daddy couldn't pull a string?"

"Daddy probably was pulling strings. He would much rather I marry a doctor than be one, you know that. But he has no strings at the Little Red Medical School."

"That's what I figured too."

"What?"

"I said that's what I figured too, when I applied."

"Why did you have to figure that…?"

But I interrupted. "Wait. You've been here for almost four years?"

"Nope. Transferred in last year from Louvain."

"You were at Louvain?"

"Oui, bien sur."

"Damn it, I thought of that possibility. That must be a story."

"Low tuition, dollar goes a long way, but yes, there is more to it…"

Which is when Katie ran in. "Look at this," she said, and handed Ali what looked like a mile long rhythm strip. "He kept skipping beats, so I kept running it."

"Ali, page Marvin." When he came on the phone she told him our man was having trigeminal beats. "For this you interrupt my nap? A mere human life? OK, I'm coming. And…"

"So?"

"He says tell you to show me how to transfer him to ICU."

I called the Unit for a bed, warned them to have a bedside monitor ready. "Here's what you do: Get the chart, write up the trigeminal rhythm, write orders: Admit to ICU, Cardiac monitor, and repeat the rest of the floor orders. And Katie…"

"Yes?"

"You just probably saved a life. If this guy is going to have a fatal arrythmia he's going to have it in an intensive care unit. Great work." She ran out.

453

"So, Ali—how did you find out this place is so progressive?"

"From Parker. Who had it from you. So you see, you are responsible for me finally being here."

BEEEEEP

It was Marvin. "We have on-calls 4,7,8 and 10. You on your way to ICU?"

"Yes."

"I'm there already."

"Why did you have to think about my father's inability to influence anything at this school, Paul?"

"Later, Ali, later." *How could she not know*

The nurses were just rolling him into the ICU bed *Layla, you got me on my knees, Layla*; one was unspooling the monitor leads. "Is the nurse who speaks Ukrainian on tonight?" Ali asked. One of the nurses nodded, mouth full of pins and stays.

We filled Marvin in on our patient's history as he ran the EKG strip through his hands. "Well, he isn't just a social admission now. Katie, come here." He hugged her. "You maybe saved a life. Not bad for first day on a Medicine clerkship. We buy you dinner."

We let Ali check his IV, pat his hand and smile at him reassuringly. He was her patient, but he was our project now. We went back to the floor to make sure everybody was stable before risking going to dinner. Mamie was breathing easier, much easier. We'd have to do post-tap chest films; I wrote the order. Mrs Goldstein was sitting up reading a magazine. Mr. Jackson was doing a crossword puzzle and trying to pretend he wasn't watching Ali's every move around the floor. I tried to pretend the same thing. *Louvain* Mr. Gonzalez was sleeping like the proverbial baby, under the influence of enough Librium to stop a locomotive. Infiltrated IV's needed replacing, a Third Year's job.

Ordinarily the intern would supervise, but Marvin's interest in Katie was growing beyond obvious. Now was down time before the evening rush. Back to the lounge to write case notes.

"There's only one case history," I said. "It consists of every case history ever written."

"That sounds familiar."

"You said it about books, eight years ago."

"You remember everything I ever said?"

"Probably."

"I'm more interested in what you have to say now."

Silence

"Time to talk" I said to her.

"You first."

"Why me?"

"It was your turn when the conversation stopped."

"Upstairs?"

"No, six years ago."

"Ali, I…"

"OK, Rock Paper Scissors." We shot.

"Paper covers rock. You go first."

"…What's Dickie doing? Why the hell didn't you tell me you were in Louvain?"

"One: Becoming a Buddhist monk and studying Tibetan Buddhism with the Dalai Lama in Dharamsala. Two: I sent a letter to you here in December '69. It came back addressee unknown."

"Shit. I had moved out of the dorm, to a house."

"Yeah, shit. My turn. Why, Paul?"

Another long silence. "Ali, Ali, I don't know how to start, to talk about…Look, here, for now…I don't have to tell you how wonderful I thought you were back then, how I felt…"

"Tell a smart girl she's beautiful and a beautiful girl she's smart."

"What do I do with a woman who's both?"

"Make her laugh. Tell her something important. Something she doesn't know. Surprise her."

What do I say?

"You taught me how to do a pleural tap. Showed me how to ride the subway in rush hour. You don't have to try to impress."

"Thank you. Neither do you.

Silence.

She said, "So why did you..."

BEEEEEP

"Paulie, the Whale wants to talk to you."

"Join me in a conversation with Miss Fascelli?" She came along, for lack of better.

"Miss Fascelli wishes to know her Glucose Tolerance Test results, and I thought she should hear them from her doctor. I dispatched Dr. McCulloch to the roof to see if they are complete, that we may confer." The Whale was eating this up.

BEEEEEEP

Katie calling to tell us it would be another fifteen minutes minimum. "Miss Fascelli, my colleagues and I must repair to the rooftop laboratory suite to attempt to rush these results. We shall return when we have them."

"Jesus, can this guy talk."

We took the stairs; life was too short for the elevators, and there was the prospect of a half hour on the roof, Yanks vs. Cleveland. We arrived slightly out of breath. Kenny and Katie were already occupying two of the four beach chairs, passing the binoculars back and forth. "What inning?" Marvin asked.

"Bottom of the eighth, Yanks up three-two, one out, Lyle's pitching to Mingori," from Kenny.

Munson gives a sign; Lyle shakes him off, sees something he likes, here's the windup, here's the pitch we could hear the roar of the crowd, or thought we could *and it's a full count, one out, men in the corners, Lyle comes off the mound to talk to Munson...*

"He's pitching to a pitcher, and takes him to a full count."(This was before the D.H.)

"He bats left handed."

"Next one's going to be high and hard; he's warning Munson," Marvin said.

"Bunt," said Katie.

"Sac fly," Marvin said.

"Sac bunt," Katie said. "Pitcher batting, top of the order coming up, chance for a run, advance a runner, take out the force at second."

"Paul, your opinion."

"Not my game," I said. *That great beginning Has seen it's final inning*

"Chess is his game," Ali said.

"I'm with her." Kenny said.

"About chess being Dr. Seitz's game?"

"About the bunt."

"I'll bet you dinner; no, we're already buying you dinner, I'll bet you breakfast tomorrow it's a sac fly."

"You're on."

The windup and the pitch...Mingori gets the bat down, lines a bunt up toward first, Chambliss advances to second, and Houk is coming out to the mound

"Very nice, very nice." Marvin said.

Katie grinned. "Four brothers," she said, "And two years of softball at Kenyon."

"And," I murmured to Ali, "He gets to buy her breakfast tomorrow. Ain't young love grand?" But she walked away.

BEEEEEEEEP

"Miss Fascelli wants to speak to someone about her lab results."

"Tell her they're still cooking." They cooked until the end of the inning (Cleveland moved a run in on a walk to load the bases and a blooper) when Kenny deigned to pull the numbers off the autoanalyzer. I showed them to Ali. "What do you think?"

"I think mate in three."

"It never was mate in three. He was messing with your head. I told you that. What do you think about this GTT?"

"When did you tell me that?" She looked at the five glucose levels. "Needs more long-acting insulin in the AM."

"Dr. Kornbluth?"

"I concur. What is 'mate in three'?"

"You'll bag Katie in three meals." We trooped down the stairs, Katie, fortunately, trailing far enough behind to have missed this witticism. The Whale was, as usual in the afternoon, on the phone.

"I gotta go, Ava, the doctors are here. No, I'll call right back…So, what's the verdict?"

"You could use more long-acting insulin in the morning, my dear," I said, "And we should try that out tomorrow, which should be easy if we leave that rig on your foot." This turned into an argument, which we all knew she would win just by having it. In the end, fifteen minutes of sullenness, mild raging, and tears ended in her agreement to remain long enough to be certain the added insulin would do its job "without making me fall down stairs. You people have done enough to me, I'm like some experiment to you."

"Is that what you think, Miss Fascelli? Really? Would we take such time with an experiment?"

"I don't know, would you? Go, leave me alone. One more day I'll stay, and that's it, you hear?"

"Stay until we get this right, so you don't have to come back so soon." But coming back was what she really wanted.

"What is so wrong, if you're lonely, with wanting to be taken care of?" Ali asked.

"All the lonely people, where do they all come from; all the lonely people, where do they all belong. At Morris's Anus, apparently." I wrote the new insulin orders.

Marvin checked his watch. "GI rounds, children. A hot meal courtesy of the City of New York. And I would like to make a prediction. In fact, a prophecy. I prophesy that Bodaceous Bob will appear as if by malign magic at our table."

"He has to be gone by now."

"Alas, no. Catching Zs in on-call 5 when last seen."

"Not going to happen," Katie said, "You saw yourself, he wants you to screw up and be nowhere nearby when it happens."

"I take note of your regard, and of your perspicacious reading of Bob's character and intentions, and am prepared to wager with you again. If Bob shows up, I take you to dinner *tomorrow* too."

She smiled. "You're on."

The dinner line was long even on weekends; trays banged, silverware banged, a hiss of steam came from somewhere where a dishwasher clanged. Under the glass, unidentifiable meat and wan-looking vegetables floated in water topped with bubbles of oil, evil-looking in the dim light of distant bulbs.

"Those diced carrots are awfully pale."

459

"Not carrots. Turnips."

"Swell."

At the table, Katie was worried by all she had to learn. What she had done that day seemed like fragments to her, of a giant puzzle whose picture she could not yet make out.

"But you don't have to learn all of medicine this year," said Marvin, "That's the beauty of the system."

"So now the Great Vein Finder puts on another hat, that of theorist of medical education."

"I do. Listen, Katie, what did you learn today?"

"You mean aside from that you are a huge windbag, and that you don't know beans about baseball."

"Yes, aside from that, serious up for a minute."

"I learned how to find difficult veins, how to put in a heparin lock, how to do a pleural tap, partly, how to run a rhythm strip and how to spot something dangerous on it, how and why and when to do all those things, how to work up a patient and write it up…"

"Exactly, all things that Ali knows because she's a Fourth Year. And she learned things she'll know so she can be a successful intern. And Paul is almost finished learning what he needs to be a resident. All you have to learn at any one time now is what you need to know to be the next step up the ladder. Then you will teach those behind you, world without end."

"So I'll become Ali, and Ali will become Paul, and Paul will become you, and you will become…Bob?"

"Watch your mouth, young lady."

"Time to tell us what it is between you and Bob," Ali said, and as if by malign magic, he appeared.

"Ah, yes," Marvin said, "I asked them to send over the wine waiter."

Bob ignored this. "I checked on our DTer," he said, "Seems to be doing OK. Sleeping soundly. I thought he was dead, but just snoring peacefully."

"So why are you still here? For God's sake, *go home*."

"I can't. Car is still under the portico."

"Bob, let me let you in on a little secret. The city of New York maintains a miraculous service. Mere blocks from here are two different transit lines, one elevated, one underground. For a mere 35 cents, they will whisk you to whatever rock you sleep under. Really, I've seen this."

"Exactly, Marv, but I need a favor. It's not a free service. My wallet is in the glove compartment."

"You waited until now—all fucking day—to borrow carfare? I would gladly have given you ten times that to get you out of here. Here. Oh shit, who has money in their whites?"

"I do," I said, and reached over to where my jacket lay over Ali's chair back.

"She's wearing your jacket," Bob said.

"Hers is now Mr. Gonzalez' urine specimen," I said.

"Then that must be your ERA button on the jacket. I meant to speak to you about that, you too, Dr. Acheson."

"It's her button, Bob," I said. "But I put it on there when I gave her my jacket."

"I could order you to remove it."

"You could try," she said. Quietly.

Attention all hands Attention all hands Battle Stations Battle Stations This is not a drill Repeat This is not

"Bob," I said, "Do you really want to make an issue of it with us? With all these witnesses? You wanting to be Chief and all."

Silence.

I fished in Ali's—my—jacket, found a subway token. "Go home Bob," I said.

And, finally, reluctantly, he did. Or at least he left the cafeteria. We ate silently, watching to see if he'd come back, but he didn't. Hadn't tried to join us for dinner; just left.

"Thanks," Ali said, "Now, what is it with you two and Bob?"

"You know how it works at the Mother House, with ICU admissions?" Marvin asked. "Very neat system, really, for the patient. Since they'll be going to a Floor, if they make it, they get an ICU team, which does the formal admission, and a floor team they'll eventually be assigned to comes down and examines them and writes admit notes too. The ICU team has responsibility, but the Floor team can write notes, write orders sometimes, and takes over when the patient gets transferred to the Floor. Not an issue here; we just admit everyone and follow them from Unit to Floor, so continuity of care blah blah blah."

"Sounds like a good idea to me," Ali said.

"It is a very good idea, only I'm too exhausted to appreciate it just now. Anyway, this was in October, right Paul? October. Paul and I are on ICU, we have an 83-year-old lady, had an MI in the ER; they get her heart restarted but not in time to rescue her brain. She's been there three months already. We're the third ICU team taking care of her. Heart is pumping, lungs are filling on a vent, fluid is going in one arm and coming out the other end, but nobody's home. The Big Nightmare, right? She's a heart-lung prep. We even have a portable EEG that reads flatline. The family is desperate for her to die, to end this. So Bob shows up with a 'tern and two Third Years; he's her new Floor resident. He reads the chart, and suddenly we find orders for sed rate, antinuclear antibodies, ASLO titers, rheumatoid factor, signed by Bob."

"Why?" Katie asked.

"You tell me," Marvin said.

"That's the workup for lupus, other connective tissue diseases."

"Right on, Dr. McCulloch," Marvin said, "Only…"

"Only why do this to a corpse?" said Ali.

"Exactly," I said. "So Marvin, after I peel him off the ceiling of the Unit, pages Bob, and he comes back down with his retinue, and Marvin asks him…"

"I ask him what the fuck he thinks he's doing, and he picks up the chart and says, 'She's got a reversed A/G ratio; this is what you do to work up reversed albumin/globulin'."

"And Marvin says, 'Yeah, in a live patient'."

"So what happened?"

"We had responsibility for the patient; we cancelled the lab orders. Bob thought about making a stink, but probably realized some people would find this appalling. A lot of people think patients in a vegetative state can still feel pain, can still suffer. On some level. There's talk of declaring flatline EEG a definition of death. Jury's out on this one. But putting this woman, what remained of her, her family, through a workup for lupus was just…"

Silence.

"We did," I finally said, "After some discussion, come to a theory about there being two kinds of doctors."

"Is this going to be another occasion to wise off?"

"No," I said, "Very serious. Two kinds. One kind of doctor gets into medicine to ease suffering. Another kind gets into it to fight disease. No matter how much suffering he or she inflicts in the process. The kind of doctor that has to eliminate every last lab abnormality, every last tic and tremor, no matter the side effects of treatment. The kind that never asks the patient when he or she would like to stop, or can't imagine when that could be."

"Bob is a very good doctor," Marvin said. "Just the wrong kind, for me."

"The kind who would do a spinal tap on a guy in obvious DTs."

"Exactly. Total ego trip."

463

Silence

"So now you're philosophers," Ali said. "Ethicists."

"Front line ethicists," Marvin said, spearing a forkful of, maybe, meat.

"What do you call this? The Kornbluth School of Sardonic Compassion?"

"We do now. Tell me your speculations about Mr. Ukraine."

Ali filled him in on the possible history.

"So you think this guy could have known your dad?"

"I plan to ask him," I said. "It's a long shot."

"Katie tells me you think your LOL may be Dig toxic."

"Maybe. Part of the differential of sudden failure, especially with the Inderal."

"You think everybody is Dig toxic."

"And one out of four times I'm right. You all know what Barnhill says."

"Our drugs are poisons with favorable side effects," they chorused, after our favorite Pharm teacher. *These are fragments I have shored against my ruin.*

"How does it feel to have your own patients?" Marvin asked Ali.

"I don't yet. Neither one of them can speak to me. Right now I have two large technical problems who haven't become people yet."

Three counting me, I thought. What could I say to her? *That I was a coward. That I wouldn't take on her father. That I couldn't trust the person she was then. Which was another type of cowardice.* Postprandial sadness. Nothing now stood between us and the onslaught of Saturday night admissions.

"Tell me something," Ali suddenly said to Marvin, "At Lewisburg, did you run into a conchie named Bill Parker?"

"Sorry, not that I recall. This was two years ago."

464

In the men's room Marvin said, "She's a cool one, and you have a rival named Bill Parker."

"Yes, and no."

BEEEEP.

The Floor. Wash hands and run.

April 1967 – May 1972

$\mathcal{I}$ threw myself into my courses.

Giese: Cell Physiology I learned elementary neurotansmission. I learned we did not yet have the tools to resolve the brain-mind relationship. I learned botanical classification. I learned protozoan physiology. *Life is something chemistry* does

It was Ryle.

The curve of her neck where it meets her shoulder

The Berkeley Physics Course I learned the Michelson–Morley experiment. I learned about Minkowski 4-space. I learned the Lorentz Transformations, mass-energy equivalency and Relativistic Physics; we repeated the Millikan Oil Drop Experiment and calculated the charge on the electron *it came out to −1 on three separate runs, within the margins of error, Eli.* I learned The Bohr atom.

There was a letter from her. Jesus, she had nerve. Didn't she know what she was risking? Did she think she could handle the old man, just like the deb thing?

469

Dear Paul,

I haven't heard from you but I expect you're pretty busy. So am I. Just a note. I passed that psych exam. Actually, I aced it. Must have been the 200-mile study session. Seriously—all that Blos and Erickson? Talked about BOYS' maturation. Nothing about girls, and it's different for us. It has to be, the biology is different, not inferior, or aberrational, as de Beauvoir says in the Second Sex (I know you know that!). And we grow up in different worlds. She says we construct our identities as women. Honestly, I don't know how men and women manage to get together at all. It must be some kind of miracle. There are female psychologists and psychiatrists, Anna Freud hews too much to Daddy's line, but there's Karen Horney, and Margaret Mahler, and Hilda Bruch. I'd love to work with them some day.

Love, Ali

Was she trying to tell me something? About her thing with Chaskis? I didn't answer.

The waterfall of chestnut hair

I learned Quantum Mechanics, the Heisenberg Uncertainty Principle. The Schrodinger Wave Equations. Schrodinger's Cat.

Not a word from Dickie.

"Are you here to tell me where my son is?"

"No, Mr. Acheson, I'm here to tell you your daughter and I are deeply in love, and we will see each other where and when we choose, and if you try to interfere my dark minions will take your little law firm apart. Capiche?"

One day I came in from Advanced Organic Lab and she was there, in my room, with an Assistant Dean of Students barely older than I was, packing Dickie's things. She turned, and it wasn't her, it was her mother.

"Mrs. Acheson," I said.

"Paul." She nodded to me. "I'm here to box up my son's possessions."

"Perhaps I could help."

"Thank you, I think you've done quite enough already."

"I'm sorry if…"

"It is my son who owes me an apology. I understand that you thought you were helping a friend. Have you heard from him?"

I understood, or thought I understood, that her absolution was meant to pave the way to asking that question. "No."

"Would you tell me if you had?"

"I would, Mrs. Acheson, I understand you are concerned for his safety and…"

"A pity you didn't think of that two months ago."

I thought *A pity you didn't* but said only, "I wouldn't want to cause you any unnecessary pain. He assured me he would contact all of us when he reached his destination." Which, I suddenly realized, could be spiritual, and could be decades away.

"Is this his?" She had picked up the I Ching.

"It was. He gave it to me, but…"

"I see, he wrote a dedication to you here. I don't want it; it's part of what led him away from himself."

Or toward himself "Not really Mrs. Acheson; it's Taoism; Dickie is pursuing Buddhism…"

"Neither is the religion or culture he was born into, is it."

"No; he's seeking something different."

"You all seem to be. The world we made just isn't good enough for you."

"No, Mrs. Acheson, I'm afraid it isn't."

"Do you talk to your own mother this way?"

"I don't have to. She agrees. She's a member of Women's Strike for Peace, among other things…"

"Some day, Paul, you will have a child. And I hope you get to feel even a small fraction of what I am going through right now."

And I thought, but did not say, that no matter how many other things I might screw up as a parent, and that could be plenty, I would never, ever demand that my child go to a war.

With the room emptied of his things, Dickie seemed truly to be gone. I guess I had half expected him to turn up, *or just wished it* the path he had chosen not quite good enough. I thought about his mother's curse and the thought came into my head *you could be talking about your own grandchild* and very uncharitably, but I was only nineteen, I wondered if that would matter to her. With the distance of years and the experience of parenthood some of the space occupied by indignation that day has come to be occupied by regret.

A phone call from Sam. "Paulie, from what I can gather, her father is pretty well connected. Play it safe."

"Can I hurt him?"

"Hok mir nicht kein chinek, Paulie. There's a problem someone should bring to your attention."

"What's that?"

"Your foreskin. Has it grown back yet?"

"Not a problem, Sam."

"Sure, Pavel."

"So. Can I hurt him?"

"Enough for a little revenge. Not enough to threaten him."

"You're killing me, Sam."

"Saving you, man."

It does not further to resort to arms.
It furthers one to undertake something.

A cell phone rather than an open dormitory pay phone; e-mail, a social–networking site; these were all a generation in the future. When I called her in Danbury that time I hadn't written her aunt's number down. I only knew a first name and a town. Who was Aunt Alice? Father's sister or mother's? A quick call to Information: No Alice Acheson in Danbury. So: If not a married name (no one ever mentioned an uncle), Mother's sister. Who might take as dim a view of my helping Dickie run, or of a penniless Jew suitor, as the rest of the family.

All the numbers that crowded my head. I knew from repeated use the first twenty primes, all the one- and two-digit Pythagorean triplets, pi to six decimal places, Boyle's Constant, logarithms to base 10 of 2, and 3, (and therefore of 4, 8, 6 and 9), e (Euler's Number), to nine decimal places (well, it's a repeating decimal that far), conversion factors for Fahrenheit to Centigrade and Kelvin and back, English to Metric measures, atomic weights of the first fifteen elements, mileages of dozens of mountain road segments, the exact time from Brighton Beach to Union, Herald and Times Square stations, the Friday and Sunday New York Central Schenectady-to-New York schedule, Avogadro's Number...the one number not in memory was the most important number I'd ever learned, and it was because, with my memory for numbers, I hadn't written it down and I'd used it only once. *Try dialing Avogadro's Number. Idiot*

Mrs. Acheson I'm calling from WOR in New York you're being called at random for our Most Beautiful Maiden Name contest For a pair of tickets to the New York City Ballet What was your maiden name

Hello Mrs. Acheson I thought about what you said I don't know where Dickie is right now but I know where he's headed and I'll tell you if you allow me to date Alicia...
No. Not ever.

Another letter from her.

Dear Paul,
Nothing from you. Lost in the mail? I could come see you; I'm getting tired of watching the mailbox anyway. All it brings is bad news. Bad things are happening in my family. They're grilling me about Dickie, and about you. I'll tell you about it when I see you. When would be a good time? — Ali

I didn't answer. I rocked back and forth in my chair. I drummed my fingers on the desk, the wall. I thought about punching it. I paced. I longed to reach through the paper to her. I put the letter in the desk drawer. With the other one. It was all of her I could safely have. If I got her pulled out of school, even if I somehow swept her out of that crazy man's reach, how long could she love me if it destroyed her dreams for herself? That's what I told myself. Why was she risking all that for a worthless coward like me?

Bad things are happening in my family.

Don't disturb the web.

The eyes gray, or green, wide with surprise or joy

I learned the proof from perfection, Occam's Razor, The Argument of Evil, Pascal's Wager, the meaning of meaning.

The arch of her cheekbones

Roberts & Caserio: Basic Principles of Organic Chemistry, Advanced; Castellan: Physical Chemistry I learned the synthesis of aryl amines. I learned the Laws of Thermodynamics, (and how to remember them: 1. You can't get something for nothing; 2. Things will get worse before they get better; 3. Who says they're going to get better?) I learned the Huang-Minlon Modification of the Wolf-Kischner Reduction.

The arch of her foot

I learned classical history, the triumph over Persia leading to the disaster of the Peloponnesian War, Professor Walker nodding over Thucydides and suddenly fixing the class with a glare: "If our leaders cannot see the relevance of the Athenian catastrophe in Syracuse to our current imbroglio in Southeast Asia they are to be pitied, and ourselves moreso."

The curve of her calf, the taper of her thigh

I learned Nuclear Magnetic Resonance. I learned Information Theory.

The sweet hollows behind her knees

I read Faulkner.

The arch of her back when she sat hugging her knees

I read Woolf.

The direct glance

I read Joyce.

The absent, inward glance

I catalogued books in the library for my grant-in-aid job.

The lips, mobile or still, the times she kissed me

I set up freshman bio labs for my other grant-in-aid job.

The ear or the eye suddenly revealed by a shift of hair

I consulted the I Ching. I got Hexagram 4, Youthful Folly, with no moving lines.

YOUTHFUL FOLLY has success.

It is not I who seek the young fool;
The young fool seeks me.
At the first oracle I inform him.
If he asks two or three times, it is importunity.
If he importunes, I give him no information.
Perseverance furthers.

Perseverance furthers.

The hair brushed thoughtfully back, just before speaking
The thoughtful speech
The concentration over a chessboard

I wrote away for med school applications.

The somehow graceful coltish stride

Baldwin: Dynamic Aspects of Biochemistry; White, Handler & Smith:
Principles of Biochemistry I learned enzyme kinetics.

The sweet swell of exactly right-sized breasts

I learned the Krebs Cycle, the Urea Cycle (quantitative).

The long stretch of her legs

I learned the cytochrome system, the ATP cycle (likewise).

The dimples just above the iliac crests

I learned the structure of proteins and complex sugars and lipids.

The sweet swell of her buttocks, exactly palm-sized

I learned the mathematics of the structure of DNA, the mechanism of DNA replication, translation.

The way her mind worked, so quick

I had the dream again. The woman on WQXN.

Perseverance furthers

> *If you're going*
> *to San Fran cisco*

Summer came again. The Summer of Love. It was also the summer Newark and Detroit burned. I waited table in a third-rate Catskills hotel/bungalow colony. There were armies of us, sleeping in bunks in basement barracks, pulling in good money and fending off underage girls and sometimes their barracuda mothers.

> *I love a waiter, I always will*
> *Because a waiter gave*
> *me such a thrill*

I read Camus. I read the Sartre. *Even though the world was absurd, both joined the Resistance. So, although protected and absolved by his Irish passport, did Beckett.*

The food is terrible, and such small portions. For the waiter $5, for the busboy $3.

I read Marx. I read "Three Guineas".

The way she knifed into the water when she dove

Summer went. This was the Bardo World.

The lips, mobile or still, the times she kissed me

You have the moment in the forest and the moment on the raft What do these tell you

I had a week before classes started. I worked on an old chess problem; the one Mr. Acheson created one insane night. Only this time it occurred to me he was bullshitting. I had outgrown the belief that adults, parents, always told the truth. Instead of trying to see mate in three for white, I played black. And there it was. I had in fact blundered. Black could make a single knight move and create a fork, checking my king, forcing me to move it, leaving me to either move away or protect the rook. If she took the rook, I take her knight and it's a stalemate. Tie game. Or she could choose not to take the rook, keep maneuvering. It wasn't fair to her to not know, to think she had lost that game. I thought about how to tell her. I didn't have her current address at school, couldn't write to her home, even without a return address, even mailing it from somewhere in, say, Jersey. I could try writing to her last address at Wellsmith, mail it from somewhere...

Dear Miss Acheson,

I very much enjoyed meeting you last spring. Look at this chess position again. You'll remember it, I'm sure. It is not mate in three for white. It's black's—your—move. Play it out.

Yours Sincerely,
Albert Myles

I got on a Harlem Line train at Grand Central, got off at Bedford Hills, the WASPiest sounding postmark I could find on a map, and mailed it, made up a return address. She'd know who sent it. That I was still out there. Still in the Resistance.

Senior year meant graduate-like seminars. I was accepted into Professor Goldenberg's "Democracy and Totalitarianism". Most of the others were history or Poli Sci majors; they saw me as taking the course just for fun, as if intellectual curiosity was not a legitimate reason, as if Goldenberg had given a treasured spot to me instead of to one of the apprentice Leaders of the Nation. Parker was there, one of the bathroom assailants. He had shattered a leg skiing the slopes of Killington last winter, had been out all last semester, missed the chance to graduate with his class. He walked with a limp. He was taller, leaner, wore glasses now.

"Mr. Parker, entertain us with your analysis of the similarities between the rise of Hitler and the rise of Mussolini."

"Both rose to power on a wave of resentful nationalism."

"Expand, please."

"Italy had been on the winning side in the Great War, but because of her high casualty rate and meager territorial gains, felt like a loser. Germany of course was a loser, with lost territory, saddled with reparations, burdened with occupation armies. Both populations were ripe for a response to an appeal to nationalism, even ultranationalism."

"Why 'ultra' nationalism?"

"Because…there was a new movement, or rather a newly powerful internationalist movement, Communism, now with a national home. Old elites trembled."

"I doubt they literally trembled. Or if they did, their hands steadied when they found their checkbooks. Good."

Well, I'd been doing the reading. "Another similarity," I said, "Was that both movements started out as Socialist, but found the appeal to nationalism a more successful route to power."

"Yes, but how did that combination prove so potent? Democratic politicians in both countries were hardly internationalist."

"They were statist," Parker said. "When they took power, they expanded the state beyond its previous role. The state became a quasi–religion."

"Some would argue not so quasi. What about those elites?"

"That's where things diverge," one of the Future Leaders said. "In Italy they exercised power behind the scenes, kept their power and property. In Germany they found themselves co-opted by the party they funded. They had their property, but only kept the dividends if they went along."

"What of the Soviet Union? Enlighten us Mr. Seitz."

"The Soviets remained true to their Socialist roots, at least at first. At least until the breach with the Trotskyists they remained internationalists, drove out the old elites and confiscated and collectivized their property. Under Stalin, nationalism returned. New elites grew up, but not until after the second war."

"Are you arguing that nationalism did not appear in the Soviet Union until after the Nazi invasion?"

"Uh, no, but the official party line was internationalism; the regime had come to power as anti-nationalist, nationalism was associated with Czarism…I think it was Stalin's political genius to re-ignite nationalism by claiming to build International Socialism by concentrating on strengthening it in one country. The Socialism of the USSR was International Socialism. Nationalism *was* Internationalism."

"Very amusing Mr. Seitz."

"I don't recall that in the reading, " said another of the Future Leaders.

"Mr. Seitz is fortunate to have grown up among Socialists," Goldenberg said. "He is a supplement to the reading."

The class laughed.

Dear Ali,

You would have loved Goldenberg's seminar today. Democracy and Totalitarianism. Comparing Nazi Germany, Fascist Italy and the Soviet Union. I wish you could have been there when he said—when I said...

"So," Goldenberg said, "Here is the question for next time: what does this teach us about the relations between a nation's economic system and its political system?"

"What do you mean exactly, Professor?"

"Use your imagination, Mr. Cameron. I assume you have one."

The soft hollow below her throat

There was a long letter. Did she get my note? Had I stirred her up again? My fault. I had to end this, send her a signal that we could not *could not* be in contact until she graduated. She couldn't lose her life for a gutless shit like me. I thought about ways to contact her. Through the library? I couldn't think of a way. A letter through a friend? All my friends were from Nott or from Brooklyn; a Brooklyn or Schenectady postmark would be like sending up a flare. Any strange postmark would be a risk. And I also thought, My God, didn't she understand the danger? If not to herself, then to me, to my family? Could she not look beyond her own needs, her own wants? I couldn't sleep.

I knew what to do. I didn't need the damned Oracle. I knew this was irrevocable, or anyway irretrievable until I could talk to her again, when it was safe. But she would understand. Had to. After weeks of being unable to do it, I put her letter, unopened, in an envelope, typed her address. No return address. Mailed it from Albany. It tore me in half. A piece of my heart went with it. *Don't disturb the web*

"There is no necessary connection between a nation's economic system and its political system," I said.

"Wait," Cameron said, "That's impossible. Capitalism only works in a democracy." *So nice to have a target*

"Bullshit. Capitalism worked perfectly well in Mussolini's Italy. I'm not arguing that there is no connection between the economic and political systems, just that there is no *necessary* connection.

"Intriguing, Mr. Seitz. Intrigue us further."

"Well, capitalism as we know it certainly works in democracies, but it also worked more or less well in Imperial Japan, and is working perfectly well in Franco's Spain and Salazar's Portugal. And the Gilded Age United States..."

"What about Socialism?"

"Socialism can work in democracies; take the Scandinavian countries, Britain under Labour. Or it can work under dictatorships, as in the Communist Bloc. By the same token, Democracy can function perfectly well in a Socialist economy as in Scandinavia, or in a Capitalist economy."

"Elaborate, Mr. Seitz."

"I don't know that I can elaborate further, Professor Goldenberg. It seems…"

"Superficial, Mr. Seitz. Your point is taken, on a superficial level, but a comparative study might reveal quite startling differences between the workings of capitalism under those different regimes. What about Nazi Germany?"

"I was thinking, that's a kind of intermediate case…the circumstances of the Versailles reparations…Old Campaigners had to be satisfied, and the ordinary German populace, with welfare benefits, and they had to be weaned from the old Socialist and Communist unions, and industry had to be infused with new capital…so the owner class had to kick in more."

"Where else could the money have come from?"

Silence.

"No one? What about the expropriation of Jewish businesses and the confiscation of Jewish wealth? And that of the conquered nations?"

"You two would bring that up," Cameron said.

Chilly silence, the silence that grows as someone realizes he has behaved really badly.

"As is the case with every statement made in this class, you will have to explain and justify that statement, Mr. Cameron."

"I only meant, sir…" He looked around the room. No one would meet his eye. *You feel complicit.*

"Come, Mr. Cameron. You meant what? That there is some sort of conspiracy between myself and Mr. Seitz?"

"No, sir."

"Mr. Cameron, this seminar is a place for, among other things, future leaders of our democratic society to practice critical thinking and hone debating skills. You are I believe a Political Science major, suggesting to me a future in politics and government, or at least an interest in it, yes?

"Yes sir. Sir, I apologize."

"So you do, Mr. Cameron, but let us for the sake of argument reverse our roles. If I had made such a statement to you, and subsequently made an apology, would you assume I did so sincerely, or would you wonder if the apology were perhaps…tactical? Do you see the problem here, for a political leader? It is impossible to apologize or undo the impact of such a statement."

"I do see sir, and I can only assure you that my apology is most sincere."

"Exactly what you would be expected to say, Mr. Cameron. Do you see?"

"I do sir. I see no way forward. Everything I say now is suspect."

"Exactly, Mr. Cameron. What you risk losing is a reputation for sincerity. That is the point I wish to reinforce. Take the lesson to heart."

"I will sir."

"Now, what about Mr. Seitz' contention that there is no *necessary* connection between a country's governmental—I think that is what you really mean, not political; politics is irretrievably mixed with economics —and its economic systems…"

Dear Ali,

Goldenberg's seminar continues to be a peak educational experience. Tonight I argued that there was no necessary connection between a nation's governmental (I said political, but Goldenberg made that crucial distinction) and economic systems and we chased that one around the room awhile—I think he likes good questions better than good answers. But one of the guys made this anti-Semitic remark, and Goldenberg handled it amazingly, turned it back on the guy for all our educations…

"Did you hear the one about Dickie Acheson's kid sister? Passed out over a piano at a frat party at Yale and made a G-major chord when her head hit the keys." *Damn her No, damn me. I had failed her*

485

Her spending. And Paris. Jesus. Come to Paris, Paul. Sure, when they dig the tunnel

Perseverance furthers

This time the dream woke me. "This is WQXN" It became—had become—a recurring dream.

"Gentlemen, the question we have before us tonight is: Is Democracy inherently unstable? Start us off, Mr. Seitz, from your Classical background."

"Herodotus I think I remember said he had encountered three types of government in his research and travels: Democracy, Oligarchy, and Kingship. He argued that the only stable one was Kingship, because Democracy inevitably devolved into Oligarchy, and the Oligarchs intrigued among themselves until one emerged as King. The history of Athenian democracy and of the Roman Republic would seem to bear this out."

"Elaborate."

"Under stress, Athenians would elect an oligarchy, or even a dictator. As in the war with Sparta. From the start Athens was only a democracy within the city walls. The colonies were subjects. Why they defected to Sparta at the first opportunity. And supported any dictatorship that would help against Sparta, always crying that it should become democratic..."

"You're off your point, Mr. Seitz. I think you were headed for Southeast Asia."

Laughter.

I grinned myself. "Sorry. The Roman Republic followed Herodotus' cycle almost perfectly, devolving into demagoguery, oligarchy and finally Imperial rule."

486

"Hitler similarly used mass media to turn a democracy into a dictatorship," Parker said.

"Go on, Mr. Parker."

"Goebbels was a master at using mass media; newspapers, movies, radio, mass rallies, to raise emotion and muster votes to elect a party that promised to destroy the electoral system that it was using to come to power."

"Are you arguing that there is inherent danger in mass media?" Cameron asked.

"I suppose television could be used to educate, but if it follows the path of radio, and so far it has, we can expect nothing but a further cheapening of national debate."

"Mr. Parker, do you refer to the Kennedy-Nixon debate?"

"I do. I've heard it said that people who watched it on TV thought Kennedy won, and people who listened on radio thought Nixon won."

"Yes, because of his poor grooming, supposedly. It does raise the point that, as happened with Hitler, our politicians could become media stars, or vice versa. Or to put it better, we can perhaps look forward to a time when there will be no border between entertainment and politics. How would that destabilize democracy?"

"I think it would pave Herodotus' path from democracy to tyranny," Parker said.

"And that would be the end? A worldwide totalitarianism, cemented by mass media, as Orwell described? You have all read Orwell?"

Everyone nodded. *Silence.*

"There can be no way out?"

I said, "Totalitarianism has to have some excuse to sustain itself, a promised utopia, an external threat, to prevent revolt. Berlin has written that utopian totalitarianism, like Fascism, Nazism, and Communism are inherently unstable because they are the product of the dissatisfactions of one generation that brings it to power. The succeeding generation, or generations, that grow up in this utopia will have new dissatisfactions, if only those of growing up with a bunch of smug utopians, and seek to change it. Berlin thinks only liberal democracy is capable of absorbing and fulfilling or compromising inevitable conflicts and changes in desires of people generation after generation. Totalitarian states will inevitably over time return to liberal democracy, as did Italy, Germany and Japan."

"So there is a cycle of political history, then?"

Silence.

"That seems to be the conclusion we are heading toward," Parker said.

"Then the trick, gentlemen, seems to be to be born at the beginning of a liberal democratic cycle."

"Professor, who is Berlin? He isn't on the reading list."

"Isaiah Berlin. British political philosopher and historian. No, he is not on the list. Mr. Seitz, have you been doing some unauthorized reading?"

Laughter. The class ended.

"Seitz, can I speak to you? Buy you a beer?" It was Parker.

"Coffee."

"'Skellar or Diamante's?"

"Rathskellar coffee is swill. Dio's." We walked to the Terrace, headed north to Diamante's Pizza, which had recently added an espresso machine. Schenectady's first, probably.

"What would you want to talk to me about?"

"Politics."

"In what context? The context of freshman hazing?"

"I hoped we could be past that. That was three years ago. We were different people."

"Speak for yourself."

"OK, I'm not that guy anymore."

Was that possible? Erickson and Blos thought so...

We took a booth in the rear dark. "What's it to be, gentlemen?"

"Genny"

"Double espresso. So. I'm listening."

"I could apologize, but first of all we have the shining example of Cameron before us, and second, I am not that guy anymore. He was an asshole...I was an asshole, OK? I know that. Look, you know why I didn't graduate with my class? I racked up my leg skiing last January. I spent almost six months at a hospital in Killington, couldn't be moved. Did a hell of a lot of reading and thinking. Hospitals are good for that, you know? Good for almost nothing else. I missed a whole semester, but I got my head out of my ass. So if I apologize, it isn't from the guy you want it from. I mean, I can apologize for him, but it's not the same as him apologizing. You see?"

"See it from my point of view."

"You want an apology."

"Hell, yeah, I want an apology. I'd like a lot more than that, but I'll settle. OK, yeah, I see what you're saying, but..."

"You want me to take responsibility for having been an asshole."

I laughed. "I guess so."

He held out a hand to shake. I took it. "So a pair of assholes can share a drink."

"I have belated greetings for you from Alicia Acheson."

"What?"

"She visited me a few times when I was in the hospital and she was skiing at Killington. She mostly talked about you, Seitz. Damn, she grew up well."

"Is that what you wanted to tell me?"

489

"No, just happened to think of it—should have told you weeks ago. What I wanted to tell you…look, have you read the Port Huron Statement?"

"You mean the SDS manifesto? Students of the world unite, you have nothing to lose but your 2-S and a world to win?"

"Yeah. But it says a lot more, about a world radically reimagined. A way out of the cycles we were talking about tonight."

"Hey Parks, you gone queer?"

"Hello, Dombrowski. You know Seitz."

"Is why I asked."

"Why don't you," I said, "Go find a bottle and crawl into it, and let the grownups talk?"

"No friends with you tonight, Seitz."

I stood up. I was bigger than he was, now.

"He has, Dombs," Parker said.

"I don't waste my time with gimps and queers," Dombrwoski said, and abandoned the field.

"I've been in a number of fights on this campus," I said, "And I've never thrown a punch yet."

"That's because it's all talk. Three years ago if you'd just sung a few words of the Alma Mater it probably would have been enough."

"Dickie didn't seem to think so."

"Oh. Morgan." He looked away. "That was something different, that goes back to Creffield…" He laughed suddenly. "You sang the Internationale. I don't fucking believe you. Look, ignore these shitheads."

" 'Turning queer'?"

"He means you. And Dickie. One rumor that went around when Dickie took a powder was it was because he was queer for you…"

"Dickie isn't…"

"I know that. I was in prep school with him. Believe me, you know who's a homo at prep. Did you know that Goldenberger is?"

490

"Never thought about it."

"There's no need to. Tell me something. Did you really drive Dickie to Montreal, then ditch one of his father's people and drive his MG through a fucking ice storm to bring it to Ali for her birthday? No shit?"

"Yeah." I sipped my coffee. He shook his head. "You still living at Phi Delt?"

"What, with the Dombrowskis? I told you, I'm not that guy anymore."

"So where do you live?"

"Off campus. Huron Street."

This was news. An off-campus apartment was an unheard-of treasure. The college had put up new dorms, and needed the rents. No off-campus housing. But Parker was a super-senior. Off-campus apartment. No restrictions on women visitors. Of course, the bars on Huron Street were good for a few murders a year. A good place for headquarters for a campus political organization. *Among other things*

Agent provocateur?

"You want to start a chapter of SDS?"

"I thought, start small. An Ad Hoc Committee, to organize demonstrations, peace actions, protests. I graduate in January. I thought, get it started, leave it to others to keep it going."

"What are you going to do when you graduate?"

"I don't know. Stick around, be an off-campus agitator."

"Who have you approached?"

"You. Kantrowitz. Shapiro. Paulsen. Stanley, Stratham, Boyd, Carlyle, Miller, Hostings. McCarthy..."

"McCarthy?"

"You'd be surprised."

"What's your draft status?"

"I'm 4-F, Seitz. Gamy leg."

"You got a Blighty. Lucky you."

"Four-F is still part of the System, Seitz. I was thinking of applying for a CO."

We walked back across the darkened campus, he on to Huron Street.

She mostly talked about you, Seitz. Yeah I masturbated. Who the hell doesn't? Liar.

> *Neither fear nor courage save us. Unnatural vices*
> *Are fathered by our heroism. Virtues*
> *Are forced upon us by our impudent crimes*

"Violence is never justified," Parker said.

"The Warsaw Ghetto uprising." "

"The French Resistance."

"The Hungarian Uprising of 1956."

"The Prague Uprising of 1945," I said. Goldenberg shot me a look.

"The Bay of Pigs," Cameron said.

"That merely aimed to replace one tyranny with another, and proves my point," Parker said.

"The proposed exceptions test that rule. In 1942 five Czech partisans assassinated Reinhard Heydrich, ruler of the Nazi protectorates of Bohemia and Moravia, in which he had perpetrated massacres. In July 1944 a conspiracy of senior Wehrmacht officers attempted unsuccessfully to assassinate Hitler and take over the German state with a goal of ending the war and the Nazi regime both. They very nearly succeeded, although it would have been far more impressive if they'd done it when Germany was winning. Would you not have participated in those actions, Mr. Parker?"

"I would serve in a non-combat capacity, I suppose. I see the point."

"Do you? What do these examples have in common? Other than desperate romanticism."

"There were no other available legitimate ways to resist."

"Violence is, then, legitimate if there are no other legitimate means to resist tyranny?"

"I suppose so," Parker said, "But the degree of participation is a personal decision."

"Indeed, Mr. Parker, it is. But even non-combat activities eventuate in casualties. The decision not to take life at first hand is possibly an aesthetic—no, that's unfair—a moral distinction without a difference."

At lunch "…I heard from a girl, Dickie Acheson's kid sister, she like vanishes for days at a time, nobody knows where she goes for vacations, story is some French guy showed up last year and gave her a car…" *Well that one's garbled but what Frenchman? De Contigny? Nah. Bullshit*

I joined the Campus Action Committee. We planted crosses on the ROTC parade ground. We disrupted the Army recruiter, going in, in twos and threes, hands up, chanting "Nicht schiessen, Kameraden". We planted cards in the Chapel bibles: "If You Call Yourself a Christian, Help End the War in Vietnam".

Dear Ali,

I've joined the Campus Action Committee, and we've been doing some small demonstrations, things to register protest and disrupt the System. It was started by your and Dickie's old friend Parker, who sent me your greetings, and thank you.

We disrupted the Dow Chemical recruitment interviews, spraying Lysol and deodorant around the room, in the windows. Not a word from Dickie.

I filled out my medical school applications. *I want to be a doctor because human folly is endless and somebody has to treat the casualties.* I sat for the Regents Medical Scholarship exam and came in 110th; the top 100 got a scholarship to be used in a New York State medical school and I knew I was in the money because the top ten would go to Harvard. I took the MCATs.

The way her skirt slid up over her knees when she sat at my desk

I read Yeats, more Joyce, I read the classical poets. I read Kafka and Rilke and Heine, some in my father's translations, I read Hugo and Stendhal. I read Melville. I read until my eyes bled and whenever I closed my eyes she was there, and I couldn't stop it. *I imagined us together, I imagined us in Paris, I imagined us in bed, I imagined us naked, I imagined her hair brushing my face, my chest. The single kiss became a thousand thousand, I saw her eyes close, I heard her moan softly…*

> *Dear Dickie,*
> *I don't think I can take your path. I don't think your solution would work for me. I cannot rid myself of desire. I don't want to.*

Perseverance furthers

"In my opinion, what makes Democracy unstable, or anyway part of what makes it unstable, part of what makes it easy for demagogues to start the cycle toward tyranny, is people would rather be rich than be free."

"A remarkable statement Mr. Seitz. Can you support it from History, or merely from psychology?"

"The Spartacist Revolt, sir."

494

"You mean Germany, 1919?"

"No sir, I mean as in Spartacus, the slave revolt in ancient Rome."

"As in the movie, Spartacus?" Cameron asked.

"As in what the movie made bullshit out of, Spartacus. He led a revolt of slaves and gladiators, made mincement of every army Rome sent against them, and they escaped over the mountains into Dacia. They won. They were free. And instead of heading for home, or out and away from Rome, they persuaded Spartacus to lead them back into Italy for plunder. They had won their freedom and threw it away for the chance at riches. Just the chance."

"Some people would argue that the only basis for true freedom for the individual is riches," Cameron said.

"Who, other than Ayn Rand and William F. Buckley?"

"He has a point, Mr. Seitz, which you must answer without recourse to sarcasm about second-rate minds."

"You call William Buckley a second-rate mind?"

"Ayn Rand? Don't push it, Mr. Cameron. I suffer fools lightly, but not their fool ideas."

"Some would argue...I would argue that the push for riches undermines freedom in total; maximizing individual freedom comes at the expense of the total freedom," Parker said.

"So the general freedom of the many is enhanced by restrictions..."

"I would say, regulation..."

"...of the freedoms, the *economic* freedoms, of the few."

"So, had the slaves and gladiators pooled their plunder, or used it to finance their escape..."

"Which they did in the movie, to buy passage from the Cilician pirates..."

"It makes no difference," I said, "Plunder is plunder. This is about to turn into an argument about Capitalism vs. Socialism, and you know what, it makes no damn difference. Capitalism, Communism,

Socialism, all have one thing in common: they are all based on exploitation of the planet's resources, and exploitation is exploitation. It all leads the same place. The exploitation of man by man."

"But a very different journey. Intriguing idea, Mr. Seitz. Intrigue me further."

"Well, first, sir, it isn't my intriguing idea. It was the starting place for my friend Dickie Acheson."

Silence. A silence you could slice.

"It led him to his decision to explore Buddhism, as a path to an end of Desire. Of Greed."

"Quietism. An interesting stance. A way of being a Conscientious Objector to the Hobbesian struggle."

Class broke up

"Walk with me, Mr.Seitz."

We walked out into the parking lots behind the Carnegie building. Out front the lights just coming on under the pollarded elms, all dying of blight. The row of tiny lindens that would some day replace them stood further out in the field.

"About your friend Acheson. Inquiries have been made."

"I'm aware, sir."

"Perhaps not fully. Faculty have been questioned about the state of his mental health."

"Yes. He's not insane."

"Also his sexual proclivities."

"I've heard that one too, sir. He is not homosexual."

"Perhaps you are aware, Mr. Seitz, that I am."

"It's been bruited. It's of no consequence to…"

"It is of consequence." We walked quietly into the softening twilight. "Do you know that you are the first Jew from Brooklyn to attend this college?"

"I didn't think, the first."

"And I am the first faculty member with that same background."

"Really? I can't say I'm surprised. You know, you saved my life with your and the department's stand against freshman hazing."

"I did not save your life. I spared you some unnecessary humiliation, that's all. You will experience sufficient necessary humiliation in your life. There is some more unnecessary humiliation we can be spared. Our names have been linked."

"What?"

"Yours, mine, Acheson's. In an investigative theory."

"I can guess the origin of that theory, sir."

"You cannot. You and I are the first Brooklyn Jews in our respective positions at this college, Mr. Seitz. Do you think that is a coincidence?"

I was silent, stunned.

"Your father was in intelligence, in the war, yes?"

"How do you…"

"I was also. In fact, I knew his work."

"What did he do? He never said, not in any detail."

"SOE. He trained and ran agents in Czechoslovakia. The Heydrich assassination, yes? He had a hand in that."

"No wonder he never mentioned. He would have been ashamed to have been involved in the death of another human being. Not to mention the reprisals after."

"Later, perhaps. Not at that time. Some would dispute the application of the term 'human being' to Reinhard Heydrich. He also knew Berlin."

"Like the back of his hand, sir. He studied there…"

"Isaiah Berlin. Who was also in British Intelligence. And whom I also knew slightly. We were all analysts, although earlier your father had those dealings with SOE in the Heydrich assassination. Coordinating arms drops to the partisans, passing orders. I assume you found Berlin's books in your father's library."

"I did."

"So when your father called me…"

"When what now?"

"Your presence here is not a coincidence, Mr. Seitz, in the eyes of those who see the world as a huge conspiracy, rather than what it is, a series of opportunistic capitalizations on coincidence and connection. When you expressed interest in coming to Nott he called me, to explore what the climate would be like for you. I assured him Nott continues to offer what it has for over a hundred years: a good 19th Century education."

I laughed, although it was an old joke.

"It's what he wanted for you. What he had. An experience that encourages critical thinking, yes? Rather than mere credentialing. But to some minds this indicated collusion, conspiracy. The Elders of Zion."

"Before I forget sir, I wanted to say, I've wanted to say for some time, how much I admire your handling of Cameron's anti-semitic comment. Unlike my own experiences it did not involve any violence or threat of it."

"I'm glad you take that lesson from it, and that the lesson in pedagogy came across. It is my job to teach them, Mr. Seitz; I don't have to like them all. But you've missed a point. The remark was not necessarily anti-semitic."

"No?"

"I thought it referred to the possibility of homosexual connection."

There seemed nothing to say to this. "Cameron is an idiot, and he'll be dead in Vietnam in a matter of months."

"Mr. Cameron will never go anywhere near Vietnam. He will get a deferment, or join the National Guard, and some day he will order

498

others to go to some other Vietnam. And he is not an idiot. Or not enough of an idiot to not be aware of a level of knowledge around here to which you have only just been admitted."

"It does seem, sir, as if...I have the sense of a giant web, of conspiracy, or of opportunistic coincidence that might as well be a conspiracy, supported by silence, lies, half-truths..."

"Welcome to the world, Mr. Seitz, yes?"

"There must be a way out."

"There is no more territory to light out for, Mr. Seitz."

"Dickie found some."

"Mr. Acheson did not find a way out, from what you say; he found a way *in*. It is said you are applying to medical school. Is this true?"

"It is."

"Have you included the medical school of Yeshiva University in your applications?"

"I have."

"I assume you know its history. No? Very progressive." He chuckled, a bass note.

"I was hazily aware of that, sir."

"You will ask me for a reference, yes? It would be my pleasure to supply it. Your father would be proud of you."

"Thank you sir. I was thinking of asking."

"Another unnecessary humiliation I've spared you. I might spare you another. You are involved, with Mr. Parker, in the protest actions on campus, yes?"

"I am."

"Take care, Mr. Seitz."

"We're essentially engaged in pranks, Professor. No more than that."

"Take care. All of you. Your cause is right, but The Establishment, as you call it, does not have a sense of humor. Or of irony or sarcasm.

Except perhaps in France."

It had become full dark, a wind sweeping the lamplit shadows of the dying elms over us.

"I'll take care, sir. We all will. Professor, one question? An odd one?"

"Surely."

"Do you know a professor of German literature at Yale, Dr. Spielvogel?"

"Never heard of him, sorry."

Was he lying? I couldn't tell, and I knew why. For months I had been lying to people I knew and loved or cared for: My mother, my grandmother, Spielvogel. It had been so easy. There was a way out, or rather a way *in*. I could stop lying. I could stop right now. There was a late train, an express I could just catch. I could call from the station, tell them I was on my way. It was Thursday night; I only had two Friday classes. It made more sense to take a morning train, but this wasn't about sense. I threw clothes in the backpack, just made the train. After we left Albany and ran along the icy river it was pitch dark; the windows only reflected, dirty and scratched, the interior of the coach, and my own face. I read; I dozed.

Dear Ali,

I just had the most remarkable conversation with Goldenberg. Apparently your father put Michael to investigating Dickie's whereabouts, and he developed a theory that either Dickie is insane or homosexual and managed to spread this idea while supposedly engaged in clandestine inquiry. You'd have thought the Morgan incident would've convinced him otherwise, or maybe this was just revenge. I briefly thought of initiating my sabotage of his office in retaliation, but so far there are no obvious consequences. I am tired

*of lying, Ali, and tired of secrets. The world seems to run on them,
and like Dickie, and like the signers of the Port Huron Statement,
I am looking for a way out of that world. I am on a train right now
to New York, to tell my mother and grandmother about our
adventure last year, and I will write to Dr. Spielvogel, or go out to
Yale to tell him that...*

Lights blazed in the yards at Croton-Harmon where electric
locomotives replaced diesel for the run into New York, familiar
mechanics of a world that was vanishing even as I mastered it. Lights
appeared outside the windows. Commuter town stations flashed past,
the hulk of Sing-Sing, the diadem of the Tappan Zee Bridge, the
Phelps-Dodge and Otis Elevator factories in Yonkers, and we were in
the Bronx, the familiar skyline beginning to appear over Harlem.

I called home from Grand Central; as usual they were delighted to
see me, not questioning why I should suddenly arrive late on a
Thursday until I walked in the door and after hugs. We sat down to tea,
my grandmother still drinking it the Eastern European way, through a
lump of sugar held between her teeth. Which meant I could speak
uninterrupted, at least by her.

"I came home tonight because I have something to tell you I should
have told you months ago." They exchanged glances; *how had they
waited this long?* "You remember the last time I showed up
unexpectedly, last year?"

"When you were at Yale," my mother said.

"That's the time."

"If you have a secret, Paul, you're old enough..." *She thought it was
a girl*

"It isn't something I should keep secret. I don't know why I did. I
didn't want to worry you. I still don't, and I don't think there is
anything to worry about..."

"So tell us, already."

I told them how we'd helped Ali confront her father, about MG Enterprises, how I'd helped Dickie leave the country, being followed, delivering the car to Ali, helping her register it, being tailed, hiding out at Spielvogel's, and the meeting with Acheson. "The money's in a savings account in Schenectady Savings," I said. "It will pay the expenses of med school applications and interviews and so on."

"Oy, Paulie, what are you mixed up in?" my grandmother said.

"Nothing," I said, "I mean, that was it. Finished. Fertig."

"You broke up a family, Pavele."

"It was already broken up, and Dickie was 21. He was of age, and he would have done it anyway. He just needed company, and for me to bring her the car."

"The two of them could have done it without dragging you into it. You could have told him that," my mother said.

"But then she would have been at her father's mercy. *So I hadn't failed her completely* This way we kept her out of it, she's free to go her way…"

"So you do care about her."

Shit "Yes. No. I don't know. It's complicated. Yes, she lights things up. She lights me up, yes, but there are things about her I don't like. Things that come from being rich and careless. She kept writing, even though she knew the risk, not just to her but to me, to all of us. Not just her, you. Us."

"So she likes you enough to…"

"And she's all over the frat party circuit, skiing in Vermont, there are stories about her…she's…"

"She wants to be a doctor, Paulie. She's beautiful, she's intelligent, so she's not a saint. Who is? What do you expect from people, Paulie?"

"I don't see her headed that way anymore."

"So she'll be what she'll be. She writes because she's lonely and she likes you…"

"She needs to like me enough to wait."

"He really scared you, the father, didn't he."

"Sam said he has the connections."

"Sammy said. Nobody's that powerful, Paulie." *Maybe nobody you know*

"This professor told me to be careful. If Papa were here maybe we could have taken him on."

"If Papa were here we'd have sat down with you and had a good long think. He might have gone to speak with him. I don't know if it would have come out different, but we would have thought about it all together."

"Sometimes, Pavele," my grandmother said, "You do the right thing because it's the right thing. *Which was what?* It doesn't always come out right."

"And that's it?" my mother asked. "Where's Dickie now?"

"No idea. Or word from him. I said I'd keep away from them and I meant it."

"Nobody is following you anymore?"

"No, and I'd know. I've been involved in protesting the War…"

"I thought you said fertig."

"That isn't part of it. It's separate."

"This is what you get," my mother said to my grandmother.

"What?"

"He was maybe three years old, you're taking him to rallies for the Rosenbergs."

"You were there too," my grandmother said. "Don't worry Paulie, we're proud of you. As long as you keep away from any craziness."

"I told you, I don't think you can fight violence with violence."

"That still leaves the girl. Alison. Alicia. She had problems, Pavele."

"Yeah, too much money."

"You think rich people don't have problems?" my grandmother said. "You think rich people, rich girls, are free of oppression? I was a Suffragette, Paulie, which was against Socialist doctrine, Socialism was supposed to free us, but I wanted to vote before the country woke up to the advantages of public ownership. Some of those girls were the richest in town. They went to jail just like us. Some of our leaders were upper class. Some of the best. Not all like that, but that girl...that girl's problems were not of her making. It's as easy to love a rich girl as a poor one, Pavel."

"She's out of my league, Grandma. And I have no doubt her father will pull her out of school if I go near her. And told her, too."

She came around the table, kissed me on the head. "Working class hero," she said, "You had to run home to tell us this? You haven't been lying, Pavele, just keeping a secret." *Old conspirator*

"Not exactly 'The Scarlet Letter'. It isn't a crime Paulie," my mother said. "Stupid, yes. Really stupid. You should have talked to us, Paulie."

"It felt like lying. The secrets—no more secrets. The only way I could get together with her is, more secrets. More mishigas. The lies, the secrets. It's how these people live."

"It's how everybody lives. There's never no more secrets, Paul. That isn't what I'm angry about. It's that you never consulted us. Discussed any of this." She sighed. "We wanted for you to be independent. You're nineteen now, but..." She looked away, thought for a few moments. "You could have gone to Paris."

I hugged her. "Schenectady is far enough. Too far, Mom. I'm sorry I ever left. It always felt wrong, going up to Nott..."

"Nonsense, Paulie. Your father always said, New York isn't the first stop in America, it's the last stop in Europe. It's what he wanted most for you. What we wanted. We've missed you terribly, but..."

"I should have transferred back to BC."

"Then it would all have been for nothing. No more of this, Paulie."

"Do we—did Dad know a history professor at Nott, Dr. Goldenberg?"

"I don't think so."

"He taught my freshman history section, and I had him for Modern European. He took me into his Democracy and Totalitarianism seminar, even though I'm pre-med. More like a mentor. It's like he's always trying to tell me something, and this afternoon he did. He told me he was the first Brooklyn Jewish professor at Nott and I was the first student, and I should be careful. And he told me Papa had called him about conditions there."

"Is that what sent you flying down here? I knew he called someone."

"So that wasn't a secret."

"Not from me. We wanted you to feel you were handling things on your own. We knew there would be plenty to handle; Goldenberg said it wouldn't be so bad. But your father died with secrets he never had time to tell, Paul. Again, no Scarlet Letter."

"Does Spielvogel know Goldenberg? Is that who told Papa about him?"

"No idea. You could ask him."

"I owe it to him to tell him I was lying to him about how I came to be at Yale that day."

"You find a way to tell him. I suspect he'll understand student craziness. It sounds so crazy, Paul."

"Seems so now."

At Union Square you change for the Lex to Grand Central, but you can also change for the Canarsie Line out to Cypress Hills; on impulse I took that train instead, rode out to the cemetery. The riots had touched close to here; I walked warily from Broadway Junction up to Bushwick Avenue. Visiting the grave of a parent is an obligation under

Jewish tradition; the gates were open and would be until the Sabbath began at sundown. I walked the quiet paths, the familiar, spectacular skyline shining behind the rows of angled headstones and more elaborate tombs. It had been more than three years.

We wouldn't need a big room, we thought, but members of his department came, his grad students, some of his undergraduates. Told us what a great teacher he was; well, we knew that. Mom wanted to sort his papers but couldn't bring herself to do it. You know that story. I did it. Uncompleted journal articles, starts of translations was all we had then. They talked about a festschrift. A rabbi said some generic stuff. None of us could speak; we were still too stunned. At the graveside an old man who did this for a living led us in a prayer we had no belief in, in a language we didn't understand.

I wasn't there to pray. It was his voice I sought, not God's. *You have to ask yourself why you didn't consult your mother before getting involved in this narishkeit Is this the time for the Socratic Method Papa It is Pavel You're talking to yourself Foolishness you call it I was getting my friend out of a war, like your brother should have done for you Dickie knew that story Yes he did I told him Why didn't you ask your mother I was afraid she'd say no Next you have to ask yourself what you thought you were doing, lying, swindling, sneaking across borders What you did in the War, what you taught me Papa I was fighting a genocidal maniac with a nation in arms You're fighting a rich man who annoys you It's her battle not yours But I can help He's the only available face of what you fought You can't fight my war You have your own war to fight You've been playing their game They could have done it without you just the two of them We I wanted to keep her out of it Pavel You need to get clear in your mind what you want with this girl Everything I want to be with her and talk with her and discuss with her and play chess with her and swim with her and travel with her and go to museums and movies with her and read books with her and I want to make love with her and wake up with her in the morning She makes me so angry but I can't stay angry… With the girl I think she will be Then not with the one that is You have to want the whole person Pavel not just some parts You don't get to pick out the parts you want This is Love, Pavel So you have to ask yourself Are you in love with her or just with some idea of her That's just a version of what Dickie asked me in Montreal Nobody's perfect not even your mother I could never get interested in Jane Austen This isn't just about Pavel it doesn't matter Why does it feel like it matters then You have to change the game You have to change your game Knights Gambit you mean be the first Jewish knight I don't know what to do I don't know the right moves This isn't chess Pavel I don't know who she is now That isn't why You know why Perseverance furthers Pavel* Knowing I was only talking to myself.

I put a stone on his marker, as tradition demanded, shook off the old man who offered to pray for those who no longer knew the prayers, called him back, gave him a dollar. Looked once more at the skyline behind this city of the dead; I looked at it again from the elevated platform, then from the train, until we went underground.

It's as easy to love a rich girl as a poor one. Spoiled party girl. What's the old Arabic proverb? What you can't have, shit on? Now I wasn't lying to anyone anymore.

Just to myself.

Winter closed in. That winter, of 1967/68, is still talked about by anyone who was there. Upstate New York and New England were in the grip of an Arctic air mass that would not shift. For weeks temperatures hovered at zero and below, as much as 40 below. Ice rimed every window, thickened into layers. Food refrigerated on window sills froze solid. Motorcycles were moved indoors. Car batteries were pried out, brought indoors, kept warm in beds. Radiators froze and cracked.

Engines seized when summer weight oil would not flow. Eyes and noses ran, freezing facial hair, freezing eyelids closed. We wrapped our heads in scarves under hoods, wore two pairs of gloves. Winds whipped tiny ice crystals across the tops of snow drifts, excoriating any exposed skin. Pipes froze. People froze. Thought froze. Emotion froze.

I started going to med school interviews. They were all the same. After enough repetitions of my feelings about my father's death I began to get the nagging feeling I was exploiting it. I could hear Dickie's whisper *It's all exploitation, everything is built on corpses*. I already had the scholarship, a big advantage. Plus the good grades from a good school. Plus Goldenberg's reference. Which meant a lot in the Bronx. Christmas came, Christmas went, Finals came, Finals went. I had a med school acceptance. Nothing could hurt me now. I was invincible. All I had to do was finish up my Senior Thesis, a few papers for The Modern American Novel, ace Advanced Organic and not outright fail Phys Chem. I could graduate Summa. *Big deal*

Problems not of her making. That waterfall of hair. Her eyes peeking out from under it. The hand running back from her forehead to push her hair back, raising her breasts

Ask Parker to ask her about the aunt. Then Parker tells a friend and he tells his sister and she tells a parent who mentions it at The Club and the web starts to vibrate

Still no word from Dickie.

The War was widening and deepening; hundreds of thousands of draftees were landing in Nam, the bodies began to come back in numbers. The Tet Offensive proved we were right about the War, the War could not be won, should not be fought, it was frightening being right. Parker graduated. Nott had an authentic off-campus agitator, and Parker had more time to devote to planning demos. He had a terrific idea to widen and deepen the local peace movement, bring in more members for the Committee, and do something memorable: Do a joint action with Slidell. We met to plan it.

"Beer?"

"I believe I will have one."

"Are we celebrating?"

"Got into med school. First one. Might be others."

"Congratulations."

"I plan to continue in the Movement. The school I got into…half the faculty are old Bolshies."

"Of course you will. Let's get to it."

We decided on a simple script. The girls, carrying baby dolls and wearing peasant getup, would be "farming" out in front of the Chapel. We could liberate some gardening tools from the groundskeepers' shed, return them later. From the steps of the Memorial Building a figure in black leaps up and blows a bugle. A troop of guys with guns comes around the Memorial Building and starts shooting. The girls fall dead. We could do it just following a Convocation at the Chapel to guarantee an audience. We could repeat it in Saratoga later.

"It'll have to be in spring, for the weather."

"It'll take that long to bring the women on board."

"Also, bigger crowds at the later spring Convos." Convocations, lectures by invited speakers, had replaced compulsory chapel attendance only a few years before. Convocation attendance was required; you had to attend at least four per semester. By late spring laggards had to go to get the attendance cards; there was also a brisk trade in extra cards.

"Parker, I wanted to ask you something. Ali Acheson—is she OK?"

He grinned. "Far as I know she is. Acing the kinds of courses you take. Plus the French. Lives like a nun. For now. Why?"

"No special reason. Just asking."

I could have gone back with her, left from there No we were being followed She would have been cooked I could have had her drive me to some station on the Hudson No she had the exam We didn't think he would We thought we had all the time in the world When I sent back the letter she could have driven over here and

Allen Ginsberg came to read at a Convocation. All the little old ladies in Schenectady's poetry clubs showed up. Ginsberg opened, "Castro's balls are pink, Che Guevara has a big cock. America go fuck yourself with your atom bomb," and the little old ladies gasped so hard my back hairs stood up.

Dear Ali,
I told you how Allen Ginsberg was coming to read at a Convocation. He broke the place up with "Amerika", brought the house down with a few pieces from "Hydrogen Jukebox". Check it out if you haven't read him…I know you must have; he's Whitman's heir. OK, you prefer Emily Dickinson…

Perseverance furthers

My grandmother's health began to fail. Her breath came harder, her steps were smaller, the stairs higher. I was needed at home; I would go home. Home. *Nostos* I mailed my formal acceptance to the Bronx.

"You missed the fun," they said when I got back from a weekend visit home to tell them. "Ballasarian blew up the Organic lab. He was supposed to be sulfonating Toluene, and he picked up the Nitric instead of the Sulfuric off the Acids shelf. Made enough trinitrotoluene to set off the dinitrotoluene and take out two lab benches."

I won the intramural chess championship. Again.

Still no word from Dickie.

Dickie knew that story I told him

Professor Goldenberg showed up at lunch in the upperclass dining hall.

"I came to congratulate you, Mr. Seitz, on your medical school acceptance. It's a fine school, and quite interesting politically."

"I'm sorry, sir, I should have come to tell you."

"Yes you should have, but I came to talk about the historical and political aspect of the school. It is sometimes jocularly called the Little Red Medical School. Named for a man who was called a Fellow Traveler for his international peace activities."

"I know some of that, sir. I hope to remain active in the Peace Movement there."

"Do you? Ah, yes. Well, at risk of telling you what you already know, the school was able to assemble a world class faculty overnight in the early 50s by snapping up blacklisted scientists from all over the country, 'premature antifascists' as we ruefully referred to them. To ourselves. I doubt your political activities will do you harm there, perhaps quite the contrary if you keep up your studies."

"No fear there, sir."

He leaned forward suddenly, over the plate of salad, whispered, "But take care here. You have months left, enough time for a misstep."

"I will, sir."

"Visit me before you leave. I would offer a game of chess, but I don't want to be beaten that badly."

I made interesting things in the partially burned lab, only some intentionally. One was allyl chloride, the active ingredient in early tear gas. It was a byproduct of the reaction I was trying to perform; I must have overheated the reactants. It cleared the building, but did not bother me. This was how I discovered I was relatively immune to tear gas.

You masters of war

Nothing from Dickie.

Fantasies of how we could be together. Every one foundered on lack of money. Lack of power. Lack of nerve.

Parker called a meeting on Huron Street. Two girls—women—from Slidell were there. Emily was the tall one. She had long black hair and a long tan body. *How, in the middle of winter? Skiing?* We worked on the details of the script. She asked me what part I would play. She asked about med school, about how I had decided to become a doctor. She asked me where I was from, was as surprised as everyone else. The other one asked where we would get the guns.

"Not real guns," Parker said. "Toys. Cap guns."

"How about real explosions?"

"Too dangerous. We don't know how to handle explosives, and anyway that's all we need, possession of explosives."

"There's a rumor going around that someone here made tear gas in the chem. lab."

"Not a rumor. That was me. I did that. We definitely don't want that; it would disperse the crowd we're trying to gather. Same problem they had in the First World War."

Later Emily wanted to walk with me. "Nice historical perspective," she said.

"What's with your friend? This is a peace demonstration, a little agitprop drama, what's she want with guns, explosives, tear gas?"

"She's just excited, she's no problem. Zealous, maybe." *Irresponsible maybe*

"What we need is calm, sober. Nonviolence."

"We can rein her in. She'll be a real asset come the day. She'll fall down and play dead better than anyone."

Emily called me about the details. Then she called me again. I referred her to Parker. Parker called her back, but she kept calling me. She came down ostensibly to photograph the layout, figure out camera angles, and took some pictures of the dying elms. Parker called me.

"Come over."

Oh show me
The way
To the next whiskey bar
Oh don't ask why
Oh don't ask why

"Beer?" he asked.

"Why not?"

"So," he said. "What do you make of our female leads?"

"Emily is cool. The other one could be a provocateur."

He laughed. "You thought I was too."

"I thought you could be. Still do, sometimes, but your beer is better than the crap in the 'Skellar.

"I called you over for two reasons. Three. First, have you heard from Dickie?"

"No."

"Can I trust that? Where is he, Seitz?"

"Parker, let me ask you one. When you jack off, which hand do you use?"

"What the... Oh, I see, none of my business. You wouldn't tell anyone what you know about where he is."

I sipped my beer. "I gave my word."

"An Elephant's Faithful One Hundred Percent."

"Correct."

"Same with Alicia. Same answer. She still asks how you're doing, by the way. I told her you were accepted at med school. She had the same response as you."

"Meaning?"

"Whenever I mention her, especially if I say she asked after you, your eyes light up and your face tightens up like a screw got turned. Whenever I mention you to her, same look."

"Interesting."

"You're doing it right now. Stick to chess, Seitz. You'd never make a poker player. Neither would she. The two of you want each other. It couldn't be clearer. What's keeping you apart I don't know, but..."

"Why the sudden interest in my love life?"

"That's the third thing I called you over to talk about. We're out of order."

"I move we table this item and return to the planned agenda."

"Right. I want to ask you to write a reference for my CO application."

"Why do you need a CO? You're 4-F."

"Because that's still part of the System, and I want to work as a CO. I was thinking about it when I broke the leg."

"I'm not sure I'm a person who can attest to your lifelong commitment to nonviolence."

"You're better. You can attest to my turning from the ways of violence."

"As long as our friends from Slidell don't blow anything up."

"Which brings us to the third item on the agenda…Will you do it?"

"Write you a CO reference? I'd be honored, actually. Sure." *Who would have predicted this? Blos and Erickson? Maybe not even them.*

"Look, I'm trying to promote your thing with Ali Acheson for a reason. Three reasons. First off, I like you. Second, I like her, and she made it clear despite my best efforts that we were only going to be friends. Seitz, if you don't take this up, some other guy is going to come along who isn't your friend."

If I had a 4-F and a trust fund maybe I could do something about it. Would do something about it "What's the third reason?"

"Emily. She's coming on to you pretty strong, to me not so strong, and I'd like your permission to go after her."

"Like I could give her to you?"

"No, idiot. That the competition's OK. You don't move in on a friend's girl."

"She doesn't enter into it, then. It's just between us."

"Of course she… look, I have no idea if she'll go for me, but before I even try, I have to know it's OK with you."

She had the same look, the same quickness, the same interest. She just wasn't Ali.

Perseverance furthers

"It's OK with me. I'm leaving for New York in a few months. I'll be buried in work."

"You're such a tool. Have another beer."

"Why not."

515

"I think I have a lead on some toy guns. We need noisemakers, something that makes a noise. Caps aren't loud enough. I think I can get us Daisy Air Rifles."

"BB guns?"

"No, you cock it and it compresses air and makes a bang. Loud."

"Machinegun noises would be better. More dramatic."

"Nothing like that on the market."

"A Chinese String."

"A what?"

"Long string of firecrackers, one fuse. They go off in rapid sequence."

"My turn. Are you a provocateur?"

"Right. Nothing illegal."

"We just need some helmets, toys probably. Everyone has their own field jackets."

"The height of fashion. Gotta go." I stood up. And sat down.

"You alright Seitz?"

"I'm fine."

"Must be some new definition of fine. You want me to walk you home?"

"I'm OK." Huron Street was somewhat unsteady.

> *My beer is Rheingold, the dry beer*
> *Think of Rheingold,*
> *Whenever*
> *You buy beer*
>
> *It's not bitter, not sweet, extra dry flavored treat*
> *Won't you buy extra dry Rheingold Beer*

When I tried to walk up the stairs they wouldn't cooperate. I sat down at the foot of the stairs, next to the TV room.

"Oh, hey, guys, come see something new. Seitz is shitfaced."

"...To boldly go where no man has gone before..."

"Come on Spock, up we go. Where's your keys? Shoes off, that's it."

> *I belong to Glasga*
> *Dear Old Glasga tewn*
> *Bu' there's something the matter wi' Glasga*
> *'Cos it's goin' aroond an roond*

Bedspins. This was bedspins.

> *The waterfall of chestnut hair*
> *The eyes gray, or green, wide with surprise or joy*
> *The curve of her calf, the taper of her thigh*
> *The hair brushed thoughtfully back, just before speaking*
> *The thoughtful speech*
> *The concentration over a chessboard*
> *The lips, mobile or still, the times she kissed me*

Dear Ali,
Parker told me you asked after me. Here's how it is, Ali. I think about you all the time. I can't stop. I don't want to stop anymore. I don't know what to do. Another girl is coming on to me, a great girl, really great, and all I can do is think about you. All I can think about her is how she isn't you. She's pretty, even beautiful, witty, intelligent, and all she makes me feel is a longing for you

Next morning I had a headache bigger than my head. Breakfast was not possible. Balassarian was in the bathroom. He advised hydration.

"You need to drink water, lots of water."

517

"I need to make lots of water."

At lunch Goldenberg was there. "I missed you at breakfast, Mr. Seitz. You look terrible. Have you taken up drinking?"

You're not my father

"Not completely, sir, no. I think not."

"Good. It's the curse of this institution. This is an especially difficult period, just before graduation. Come with me to my office. I have something for you."

I was by now walking steadily. I saw amusement in his eyes.

In his office he moved some books aside and said, "Sit." He handed me a book, Isaiah Berlin, "The Crooked Timber of Humanity", a British edition. "You recognize the quote."

"Kant. 'Of the crooked timber of humanity, nothing straight is ever made'."

"I give you this now because I may not have the opportunity at Commencement. I will be taking my sabbatical. At All Souls, Oxford. Berlin is there. I may have to leave before the annual pageant where you go from Nott College to not college. *An old joke beloved of generations of commencement speakers.* I wanted to speak to you about something I think we have in common."

Holy shit, was he making a pass?

"I believe we have both been asked to write supporting essays for Mr. Parker's Conscientious Objector application."

"Oh. Yes. I agreed to do it."

"As did I. He is taking a very principled stance. One from which, despite his injury, he will later be able to claim he served. A principled and shrewd political move."

"A well-founded one nonetheless."

"Certainly. Of the crooked timber, Mr. Seitz. I thought also to tell you of my sabbatical activity. I plan to research and write a book on the commonalities of Capitalism, Socialism and Communism. For the popular market, possibly. Sound a tocsin, a la Rachel Carson and Michael Harrington."

"I look forward to seeing it, Professor."

"I will send you a copy, if it is published. You are very generous with your ideas, Mr. Seitz. You will be a great teacher."

"Doctor."

"Teacher. Doctors teach. At medical schools."

"I only plan as far as becoming a working physician, Professor. Not necessarily a researcher. I'll always be reading, of course. Can't stop."

"Mr. Seitz, are you familiar with Sartre's tetralogy, 'The Roads to Freedom'?"

"It's a trilogy. 'The Age of Reason'? 'The Reprieve'? Troubled Sleep'?"

"It's a tetralogy. Do you remember how it ends?"

"The fall of France, 1940. The captured French soldiers are herded into a prison train going to Germany."

"Yes. He didn't finish the last volume. He lived it. He and Camus edited 'Combat', the Resistance newspaper."

Avunculize *v. rare* [cf. *patronize*] To act like an uncle. —The Oxford English Dictionary

In my mailbox: a generic postcard of Wellsmith College, the single word: "Congratulations." In her aqua ink.

Dear Ali —

Thank you for the postcard. It has been such a long road. As you know, since you are also on it. I have so much I could tell you about the med school application process. So much

I put it in my desk drawer. With the others.

Two weeks later, an envelope postmarked Toronto, no return address, inside a single sheet of paper, refolded for the envelope; the single word CONGRATULATIONS, in letters cut out of newspapers and magazines, like a movie ransom note. *So he was in touch with her. And thought she was in touch with me*

What saved me was the Modern American Novel.

<u>20 Points.</u> In Thomas Pynchon's *The Crying of Lot 49* the author poses two visions of the world based in the same set of facts and experiences. Describe the two visions, and how Pynchon resolves them at the conclusion of the novel.

In *The Crying of Lot 49* Thomas Pynchon presents his protagonist, Oedipa Maas, with the legacy of her ex-lover Pierce Inverarity's stamp collection. The collection contains a number of stamps that may point to the existence of a centuries-long conspiracy determining the course of history in the Western world—or not. The evidence is ambiguous, and leads her into a web of human communication that is either a web in the sense of a conspiracy, i.e. a giant series of willed, manipulated connections, or a web in the sense of a creation spun by the perceiver, Oedipa herself (representing the reader), a phenomenon Pynchon calls "Paranoia". In the end, the question is not resolved within the novel. It cannot be. Oedipa enters an auction room, in which the outcome of the auction will reveal which vision is valid, and the author takes Oedipa, and the reader, no further. The reader must conclude for himself, as we all must, every minute of every day.

We met for the final run-through of the demonstration right after Spring Break.

"Coffee?" Parker asked.

"Thanks."

"Anything from Dickie?"

"You know, Parker, this time there is. From Alicia, a postcard congratulating me, I assume on getting into med school. Which I assume she knows about from you."

"Guilty as charged."

"But then this, I assume from Dickie. It's his sense of humor." I showed him the letter.

"Burn after reading."

"Hi Paul." Emily came in, carrying a bag of groceries, wearing one of Parker's work shirts.

The sweep of her hair
What it would be like to not feel lonely all the time
The awful daring of a moment's surrender
Which an age of prudence can never retract

"I'll make coffee," she said.

We inventoried the props, loaded them into Parker's car, and drove up to the Yaddo in convoy with the rest of the troupe. The girls met us there. We used a hill and tree as the Memorial Building steps. The girls, with baby dolls in slings, made as if to hoe and dig; the guys, in scraps of Army surplus, shouldered arms, marched around the tree, I bugled, the guys cocked the air rifles and fired, cocked and fired. The girls fell to the ground, spilling baby dolls randomly. Parker directed. It looked better on a second run-through, with a bugle call to announce the "troop's" entrance, and the guys marching more slowly and firing a ragged volley instead of a unified "bang". Good enough for agitprop.

521

Emily recorded it all for…what exactly? *Would this all some day be in the Smithsonian?*

Honors Biology Presentation: Paul Seitz: Excystment Triggers of D. nasutum

"…and so *Didinium nasutum* can survive for up to ten years dormant, in encysted form. Encystment is triggered by absence of Paramecium prey; excystment can be triggered by the presence of Paramecium. It follows that Paramecium might exude a chemical excystment trigger. My researches failed to reveal any such substance. As an alternative hypothesis, I propose that there could be a substance common in the creatures' environment that is brought to low concentration by the presence of Paramecium. High concentrations of this proposed substance, which we can call Substance X, occur in environments denuded of paramecium prey, trigger and maintain encystment; the return of paramecium to the environment of *D. nasutum* reduces the concentration of Substance X, triggering the release of *D. nasutum* from the encysted stage.

I propose that the next step in this research be a survey of the environment for a substance which decreases in concentration in an environment rich in paramecium, coincident with the excystment of *D. nasutum*."

Polite applause

Over a simmering fondue pot Professor Gundderson said, "Had you spent a little more time excysting didinia and a little less demonstrating against the War, Paul, you might just have found Substance X yourself."

"Professor Gundderson, I have to say…I'm not cut out to be a lab scientist."

522

"Your hypothesis is most probably correct, and could be an interesting step in protozoan ecology."

Now we know how many holes it takes to fill the Albert Hall "My problem as a scientist would always be that I'm good at generating hypotheses but lack the patience for the work necessary to growing the organisms, maintaining the cultures, all of it. I thank you for the trouble you took with me, but maybe the valuable discovery here is that I'm not going to be a research scientist. It will be a more valuable experience for another student to make that discovery."

"Paul, you are much too good at renouncing things."

Maybe something in the environment has to return and cause something else to reach a certain concentration

Parker's apartment was now part miniature darkroom. Emily's studies of Huron Street were hanging by their corners, still dripping fixer. She made coffee, padding around in jeans, barefoot.

"Tell me again who the speaker is."

"Some economist I never heard of. Talking about the cost of doing or not doing in Southeast Asia."

"Perfect."

"I don't know; I think it sounds sufficiently dull that the monitors will be selling a lot of fake cards."

"No, guys will be showing up fifteen minutes before the end and slipping in the back. Right after that it's Show Time. Em?"

"The girls will be here at 10:30. They'll come in two groups of four, one from North Terrrace, one from across the lots on South. They'll have the peasant outfits on under their coats. They can change back here after."

"So let's do this." We loaded the air rifles, coolie hats, rakes and hoes, and the boxes of flyers, in Parker's car and waited for midnight.

523

We parked behind the biology building and, using as much shadow as we could, carried the props to a rusty cellar door in the Memorial building, facing away from the Chapel. The flyers we left in the car; Parker would drive them over at 11:00 and the rest of the Committee would distribute them in the crowd. If there was a crowd. The door creaked open onto wet concrete steps, on which we hid the props. They dropped me at the dorm. Emily had her head on Parker's shoulder as he drove.

"Sure you don't want to come back for something?"

"Nah. Third wheel. See you tomorrow at noon."

In the end, it went off better than we'd hoped. I sat in on the Convocation to be certain it was going as scheduled, in the back where I could check action around the Memorial from a window. The girls showed up per plan. Then the guys. They lounged around casually. I left when the question session began. I could see Parker unloading the flyers just outside the south gate. With five minutes to go we distributed the props and the guys cocked the air rifles; when the first Convocation monitors in their blue blazers appeared on the steps to distribute attendance cards to the exiting audience I hit my mark on the Memorial steps and signaled the girls. The first thirty or so loiterers on the Chapel steps were treated to the sight of eight Slidell girls in what passed for Vietnamese peasant outfits raking and hoeing Library Field. Rumor rippled through the exiting crowd, and they gathered to see what was up. I blew the bugle and the little troop marched around the Memorial building, arms shouldered. By now the Chapel had emptied; there were students at the windows and at the windows of the dining hall and Phi Delt House. Some office workers were attracted from the admin buildings to the south.

I blew the bugle a second time, and the troop knelt and fired. The girls dropped to the ground, arms flung out, baby dolls flying in all directions. They had brought some stage blood along, a dramatic ad lib. The troop cocked and fired a second time; the girls on the ground jerked. Out of the corner of my eye I spotted Emily at the edge of the crowd, telephoto on her Nikon, clicking away. She was so intent she missed the Phi Delts charging out of their house, and was hit with the first egg. I blew the bugle a third time, and we retreated around the Memorial under a hail of eggs. Scuffles broke out between the Phi Delts and our guys distributing leaflets; some in the crowd, I was glad to see, came to their defense. The campus police showed up about then; it was definitely time to go. Carrying as much as we could, we abandoned the field, regrouped behind the biology building. I couldn't find Emily in the crowd. One of the girls was half laughing, half crying, raw egg in her long hair. "I needed an egg shampoo," she finally said. "Honorable wounds," said another girl.

"Everybody OK?" I asked.

"Sure. It's just eggs."

McCarthy came around the corner of the building. "Time to go," he said, and loaded four of the girls in his car. I threw the air rifles and bugle in his trunk; the coolie hats we left on the ground. The bloodied baby dolls, as planned, had been left on the field. Mortenson took the other four girls back to their car, and we dispersed. I was left facing Professor Gundderson in the window of his lab.

"A triumph, Paul," he said sarcastically. "I see you've successfully excysted several domestic chicken embryos. The War will surely be over by nightfall."

"There are a lot of people thinking right now, out in front of the Chapel, maybe reading informative leaflets."

"Feeling isn't thinking, Paul."

"They have to feel to want to think."

He sighed. "Perhaps. You might want to either come inside and look busy or head for your dorm."

525

"Thanks," I said. "I mean it. But I don't think I've done anything that violates a law or rule."

"You might have made some people feel and think, Paul. That's only barely legal."

I headed for Huron Street. The girls were there, cleaning egg off their costumes, faces, hair. The guys were in the mood for revenge, some of the girls too. Emily examined her camera for damage, pointed out where the UV filter had prevented goop from fouling her telephoto. She said she had some pictures of the Phi Delts involved; she could start developing the film as soon as the girls cleared out of the bathroom.

"No revenge," Parker said. "Not violent or destructive, anyway. Of course, there's no reason the newspapers, campus and local, won't be interested in those pictures. They'll want pictures of the demo, and oh look, a bunch of frat boys throwing eggs at defenseless girls."

"Defenseless my ass," one of them said.

"Leave it to me and Emily," he said.

When they'd all left Emily got to work. We examined the contact sheet with a magnifier; some of the pictures were first rate. "That was impressive, Parker," I said. "I happen to know you still have your keys to Phi Delt House. We could have done some damage."

"I wish you were still doing the radio thing. It would have been great to have live coverage. I never told you, how great that was, what you did for Dickie, and for Ali Acheson. The books. Slick. Her father never knew. He was drinking pretty heavily, by the way." *Really? That would explain a lot.*

"It didn't have such a brilliant outcome."

"Stick around. I'm going to start calling the newspapers."

"Got a chem lab."

Martin Luther King was assassinated.

<u>To:</u> Draft Board # 17, Wilton Connecticut
<u>From:</u> Paul Seitz, Nott College Class of 1968
<u>About:</u> William Parker

May 2, 1968

I am writing in support of the application of
William Parker for Conscientious Objector status.
I have known Mr. Parker since my admission to
Nott College in 1964. At that time Mr. Parker was
a typical Nott College sophomore, a fraternity
member, participating in freshman hazing, with no
affiliation that I know of with any peace groups
or religious organization.

I am aware of the requirement for grounding of
Conscientious Objector status in religious
conviction or extreme demands of conscience. I
believe Mr. Parker to have demonstrated the
latter, because he in fact does not require
Conscientious Objector status to avoid military
service; an injury has left him in the 4-F
classification. Such is his conviction regarding
military service and the obligation to fulfill
the Conscientious Objector alternative, and such
is his integrity, that he seeks Conscientious
Objector service in lieu of the military service
he cannot render.

I can attest to his level of this integrity in
other contexts. His convictions regarding
nonviolence grew as he progressed in his studies,
and he has taken pains to apologize to anyone he
believes he hurt prior to his commitment to
nonviolence. He has preached nonviolence and
nonviolent political protest, maintaining that
commitment even under extreme provocation.

I believe his application for Conscientious
Objector status to have great merit, and I
endorse it unconditionally. Thank you for your
attention.

Paul Seitz

Paul Seitz, Nott College '68

"Thanks Seitz. It says what you can say. It's very politic too, I must say. You steered around my current career quite neatly."

"What happens now?"

"We stick around here until Emily graduates, and we keep the protests going. We'll do the demo at Slidell in the Fall; by then we should have enough recruits for a real army."

"The peace movement is a great way to meet girls." Emily grinned. "Where are you going to get more air rifles?"

"That's the nice thing about being a trust-fund baby. You're a good friend, Seitz."

"Is that what I am?"

"I hope so. Who'd have thunk it? Something I've always wanted to know. Back your freshman year. Could you…would you…have been able to call in an army of crazed Brooklynites to lay waste to Phi Delt?"

"I can call spirits from the vasty deep."

"Why, so can I, or so can any man, But will they come when you do call for them?"

"You would have faced the rage of the Lincoln High School chess team."

"Those assholes still believe it."

"Good. Now that cities are burning it should give the future captains of industry pause."

"I sense your commitment to nonviolence is conditional."

"Legitimate response when no other legitimate avenue is open. I'm still working that out. I admire you, Parker. I do."

"Anything from Dickie?"

"Silence."

Robert Kennedy was assassinated.

One day I woke up and graduated. My mother came, my grandmother came and struggled to breathe. The bagpiper played, we straightened our mortarboards, putting the tassels on the correct side, marched in. Someone gave a speech. They announced the granting of diplomas. The guy next to me whispered, "Fait vos jeux, Mesdames et Messieurs." My name was called. The tassels were moved to the other side. I packed my trunk and duffle, handed them over to Railway Express, and accepted a ride from Parker and Emily to the station with my mother and grandmother. Parker shook my hand, said he'd be in touch. Emily kissed me on the cheek and whispered, "It could have been you."

The summer after the Summer of Love I worked in a lab at the med school, maintaining cell cultures, making micropipettes, sucrose gradients, precise solutions of many things, running the ultracentrifuge and the spectrophotometer. *We would like to thank Paul Seitz for his invaluable assistance* Not much different from being a waiter, really.

Dear Paul,

We've been in the Haight. Very crazy, not really political, more cultural. Drugs galore. Did a little acid, saw a lot of colors, Em was more turned on. I suppose dropping out is a political act, but not much of one. We may hang here for a while. Here are some of Em's pix; she sends love and regards. No word on the CO yet — P.

I wondered if Dickie was in the Haight. I wrote to ask, but the letter came back Addressee Unknown; they had moved on. I reposted it to Huron Street.

529

School started, harder than anything before. *Hollinshead: Textbook of Anatomy Strong and Elwyn's Human Neuroanatomy Balinski An Introduction to Embryology* Whenever I closed my eyes over a book she was there.

We were assigned four to a cadaver in Gross Anatomy Lab. Traditionally some are bothered by this. But this wasn't the first corpse I'd ever seen.

Johnson doubled the draft call, from 17,000 to 35,000 a month.

The Twelve Cranial Nerves: Olfactory, Optic, Oculomotor, Trochlear, Trigeminal, Abducens, Facial, Auditory, Glossopharyngeal, Vagus, Accessory, Hypoglossal. The mnemonic for remembering the Twelve Cranial Nerves: On Old Olympus' Towering Top, A Finn And German Viewed A Hop. The mnemonic for remembering the Twelve Cranial Nerves: Oh, Oh, Oh, To Touch And Feel A Girl's Vagina. And How!

She was in my dreams. Those dreams too. And my fantasies.

Perseverance furthers

My grandmother could just get the words out. "No girls since you brought her the car, Paul."

"She's still in college, Grandma. I can't talk to her until she graduates. And find out who she is now. If she's just a party girl…"

"There was more to her, Paul. She wanted to be a doctor too." She struggled to speak. "Real love is rare, Pavele. You never knew your grandfather. Ten years we had, and it left memories for a lifetime. There was only one. There was never another. Not like that. *Wait…you were*

only married three years I spent an hour with her. Maybe it's Bashert."
Fated. Destined.

You have the moment in the forest and the moment on the raft
What do these tell you

Six months into it I couldn't stand the dorm anymore. A few of us, having bonded over the corpse in Gross Anatomy, rented a house on a desolate back street in Pelham. Someone in the neighborhood kept chickens; a rooster crowed in the mornings. The Dyre Avenue subway rattled past. The kids played boxball, stoopball, stickball. And they played Ringelevio *Ollie Ollie Oxenfree The call to return to Home Base* Whispers of Home. It became a commune of sorts, everyone going in different directions, friends, cousins, cousins of friends, friends of cousins, dropping in, crashing sometimes for weeks.

We buried my grandmother next to my father and the grandfather I never knew.

I got deeper into the Movement, joining the big marches, the Fifth Avenue Peace Parade Committee, the Medical Committee for Human Rights (put a million people in the streets and someone's going to need an appendectomy, and then the tear gas…). We set up first aid posts, pulled people out of tear gas and bathed their eyes, stopped bleeding and called for ambulance evac, handled drunks and acid trips, you name it. I thought maybe she would be there, in the group *the peace movement is a great place to meet girls* every time I saw anything like a yellow ski jacket my heart leaped. It was never her. None of them was her.

531

Goodman & Gilman The Pharmacological Basis of Therapeutics Davis Dulbecco Eisen Ginsburg & Wood Microbiology We were still in classes. Sirens keened in the night.

I learned detailed anatomy from the formaldehyde-soaked corpse. Like a giant map, the arteries and veins like aqueducts, the nerves like highways and rail lines and power lines. *It wasn't the first corpse I'd ever seen*

I woke from sleep feeling her touch; she was never there. *Lilith, succubus.*

Ali Ali Oxenfree

Dear Eli,

Sorry to have given you such a hard time all those years ago. I thought I would tell you I had a kind of experience you called spiritual, when I was stalled on a mountain road at night. I felt this moment of intense quiet and ease in the face of a world totally empty of everything I knew. I have to say, I felt almost the same thing in the wake of a passionate kiss from an incredible girl. Soy, you said. So much else to tell, eventually. Writeme

—Paul (Seitz)

The protests grew, reaching a phase of campus strikes and takeovers. Brooklyn College had gone out in fall 1967; Columbia student activists had taken over the President's office and brought the campus to a halt in spring of '68. Parker and Emily were there, in an apartment on 108th Street. Thirty years later stock market analysts would fight for apartments in this block; in Spring 1969 it was a block falling from disrepair to abandonment, along with much of Upper Manhattan and the Bronx. The rats were fighting the roaches. Parker looked terrible and worse. Emily fired up a joint. He offered me acid.

"Pass."

"Turn on, Seitz. It's astounding. Maybe the way out. Huxley thought so." He put two pieces of blotter in my pocket.

"The Psychiatry Department where I am has been giving first year residents this stuff so they can experience psychosis."

"A little psychosis might be a good idea. Look where sanity has gotten us."

We learned to draw blood. We practiced on each other.

We saw Pontecorvo's *Battle of Algiers*. There was real blood in that, too.

I started on the wards. *Judge & Zuidema, eds. Physical Diagnosis: A Physiologic Approach to the Clinical Examination Walton Essentials of Neurology* The Van Etten building was un-air conditioned; it was hot among the strokes, comas, choreas, tremors, tumors. *People with strokes, comas, choreas, tremors, tumors.* Nixon! Tricky Dicky. *Dick Nixon before he dicks you.* Emily wanted to go to every big campus strike and the inevitable protests and police actions. Parker scorned it all; he now saw protest as futile, said, "All you can change is your own mind." On the hot rooftop and in the hotter apartment he and Emily argued. They argued on the beach when I took them there.

In June I was wakened from a nap after a night on call by Emily bursting in the door. There was no place to sit except the bed; still half asleep I pulled back and made room at the foot.

"I've left him, Paul." She had the camera. She always had the camera.

"I'm sorry to hear that, Em."

She pushed back against the wall, pulled her knees to her chin, and cried. "He's just gone, the Bill I knew. Since San Francisco he's been going further and further into his head, and there's no room for anything else. Certainly not for me." She pulled a joint out of her pocket and lit it, drew in a hit. She offered it to me; I shook my head. "Could you help me go back and get my stuff? I don't want to be alone with him anymore."

I looked at my watch. "I guess."

"There's no rush." She smoked the joint down, offered me the roach, stubbed it out. She'd stopped crying, had relaxed. "It could have been you, you know," she said. "I liked both of you, you actually more, but you never picked up on it."

"I knew, if that's what you mean, but Parker must have told you…"

"That you're saving yourself for someone, I know."

"I wouldn't put it that way. It's…I can't see her until she graduates. Or her father will pull the plug on her tuition."

"She told you that?"

"Her father told me that. He's pretty crazy."

"Or are you just not willing to take your friend's woman? Does the woman have any say in that?" She leaned over, unbuttoning a top button on the work shirt. Another button. Another. She had not worn a bra in years. "When does she graduate, Paul? Because I already graduated." She unbuttoned the last button, shrugged out of it. She unbuttoned a button on my shirt. Another. The door opened; *Music, loud*; Barry's voice said, "Oops, sorry." The door closed.

Perseverance furthers   The awful daring of a moment's surrender

I re-buttoned my shirt. "She graduates in a matter of days, Em. And I've come too far with this to complicate it now. I won't betray a friend."

"So I have nothing to do with it."

"I don't mean Parker. I mean her."

"She doesn't ever have to know."

For the length of time it took to imagine reaching out and touching her, just for one second one "But I would know."

She stopped then. "I guess that's what she finds attractive about you."

"What?"

"That."

"There's damned little else."

"You don't know what you're missing," she said as she buttoned up.

"I have a pretty good idea. I'm an idiot. Look, I'll help you get your stuff, but where are you going to go?"

"I was hoping I could crash here until I can hook up with someone or some group going to Woodstock."

"Sure." *Saw that coming.*

Parker yelled "Go away" when we knocked. She opened the door with her key. "You think you need protection?" he said when he saw me.

"Don't be ridiculous Parker," I said, "She just wants some help schlepping stuff."

"She going to stay with you?"

"She's going to crash at our place. Not with me."

"She really did a job on your head. Gonna carry that torch till it burns through you, right, man?"

"So close. When she graduates…"

"You don't know what the fuck will happen when she graduates. You haven't had any contact since I haven't, and that's a year. You don't know shit."

Emily stayed two weeks, took some pictures, and made a connection for Woodstock. "Paul," she said, "If this love of your life falls through, here's an address you can always reach me at. Call me. I'm not kidding."

"I know you're not. And I just might."

"Come with me to Woodstock."

"No can do, Em; I'm on the wards, I have patients, this isn't classes where you get a certain number of cuts."

"See what you can do for Parker."

"I'll try."

"You should have seen him in Chicago last year. This culture's gotta be brought *down*."

It's gonna take more than music, Em.

8/23/69

Dear Paul,

What you missed. So after two days of no sleep I wake up in the mud to Gracie Slick blasting out Don't you want somebody to love. Listen, this thing could have been a disaster but I watched a bunch of hippies set up and run a medical station and a food station, without "running" it. No hierarchies, just ad hoc action, gifted improvisation, doing whatever was needed.

It can be done, Paul. — Emily

The butterflies turned back into bombers.

Protest, Nott College 1968 Bill, Grant Park, 1968 Paul & Bill, Coney Island 1969 Night, Bronx Municipal, 1969 Paul After Night On Call (Portrait of the Doctor as a Young Man), 1969 Her pictures of Huron Street, of New York, of Woodstock and the street actions and riot at Kent State hang in galleries today, and a few on my walls.

I knew one thing: where she'd be one particular day. Perseverance furthers.

I daydreamed of crashing her graduation. On horseback.

June 1969. *Wilson Beecham and Carrington Obstetrics and Gynecology* July 1969. Men landed on the Moon *If they can do that maybe there would be someplace we could go* August 1969 *Nelson Pediatrics* I bought a used VW bug, yellow with one blue fender and a sunroof. *Give her a few weeks for a post-graduation trip.* Plus I had a week's vacation coming up between the minor and major rotations. *Friedman and Kaplan Psychiatry* Late August 1969.

I would say "Dr. Acheson I presume" No. I would slip into the seat next to her and say "Hi Froshie". No. I would take her hand, pull her to her feet, take her in my arms

I got a classmate to cover for me. I woke from a dream of her and went over to the campus for Freshman Orientation. Stood in the door of the Freshman lecture hall. Ran my eyes over the assembled class, finding the women; just ten. She wasn't there. She knew where I was, knew I was here, knew she should apply. Inconceivable she hadn't, inconceivable she hadn't gotten in. *Unless she had changed her mind. Or worse. Inconceivable.* Where was she? Where in hell was she?

537

If we could just have stayed on the raft

It was a sunny Saturday. I got some cash, gassed up the VW and headed up the parkway to North Greenwich. *There was a coolness to the air; leaves were beginning to turn in Connecticut.* I tried the radio; what luck, on WQXR the Rachmaninov Piano Concerto #2, possibly the most romantic music ever written. I bombed along, at least to the extent one can bomb along in a machine that could barely break the speed limit. My heart pounded. *With a wild surmise*

Off the Merritt I laid rubber to Vere Lake, careening around corners. *The little car hummed along, my heart swelling with the music. I burst through fresh leaf piles, yellows and reds, leaving vortices of downed leaves in my wake. The white houses stood out against the dark gray sky. I pulled into the drive, practically vaulted out of the door. The final chords of the Rachmaninov sounded and I rang the bell. No response; I knocked, and when it opened I pushed past the astonished maid.*

"Alicia" I shouted; she came to the head of the stairs.

"Paul," she cried, eyes wide. She flew down the stairs, hair flying.

Her parents appeared as I pulled her to me. "Mr. Acheson," I said, "Ali has graduated. I've come for her, you tyrannical sack of shit. Got any further threats to make? No priceless china anywhere nearby."

Ali laughed, wrapped herself around me. "Ready?" I asked.

"Any time, Paul. Just let me get my jacket."

"We'll be going out now, Mr. and Mrs. Acheson, with or without your approval."

"They can't be stopped," Mrs. Acheson said. "Leave them, Richard; they're in love and there's nothing we can do about it."

Ali appeared at the top of the stairs, hair flowing, radiant in the yellow ski jacket. It matched the VW perfectly. She laid her head on my shoulder; I spun gravel off the drive as we headed out to our lives.

None of that happened. None of it. The sky was blue, it was warm and humid, I came up the drive, and the house was cold, dark and shuttered. There was a realtor's lock on the door. It was clear no one had been there in a long time. I sat on the steps and thought. *Silent, upon a peak near Darien Ha Ha* I didn't know where to look for her, or for her mother. Thirty years later I could have found her with a few keystrokes.

Her father I could find. It wasn't even noon. I drove south, slowly now, to the boatyard. Behind a shack an elderly man was working on the guts of a small engine. I asked him if the Acheson boat had been taken out that summer.

"Who wants to know?"

"His nephew," I said, "I was supposed to meet him for sailing at the yacht club, and they say they haven't seen him."

"Neither have I. He had her overhauled completely, put in a backup motor, bigger fuel tank, extra sails, couldn't put her in the water till May, late for him. Then he showed up with a young woman, showed her all the new equipment."

"Blonde, dark hair, what?"

"Dark. Hey, what is this?"

"His daughter?"

"Young enough to be. Who the hell are you really?"

"Someone looking for the daughter." I pulled out my wallet. "Any idea where they went with all that new stuff?"

"No. And put away your money, kid. I really don't know. You could try the yacht club. He looked to be preparing her for a long trip."

The yacht club. "You can't park there," said a kid in a blazer.

"Can Abraham Lincoln park here?" I flashed a five.

"Five minutes," he said.

"All I need." The bar was just opening; the barman was just finishing wiping down the bar.

539

"What can I get you?"

"Some information. I'm looking for a guy, a member here, Richard Acheson. Actually I'm looking for his daughter. Word is they took their boat out for a really long trip, and anything you can tell me about where they might have gone—fact, rumor, anything…"

"Sorry kid, nothing I can tell you."

"Anything you could tell Abraham Lincoln?"

"Nope. I might have something for Andrew Jackson."

Romeo and Juliet, by Mickey Spillane

I gave him a twenty I couldn't afford.

"Story around the club is, after the big divorce he headed south, Florida, Caribbean, the Islands. No intention of coming back, word is. He thanked me for everything the last night I saw him here, so I think I believe it."

"Big divorce?"

"He and the wife split; it was the talk of the club for weeks, a year ago or so, maybe more."

I drove back to the city, to midtown, to Acheson's office, double-parked outside, ran in for long enough to see his name was no longer in the directory. I started to drive back to the Bronx, stopped at an East River overlook and gazed out for a while, just watched the gulls. I thought of riding the Ferry, but couldn't have stood it.

> *Frisch weht der Wind*
> *Der Heimat zu*
> *Mein Irisch Kind,*
> *Wo weilest du?*
>
> *Od' und leer das Meer.*

If we had just walked into the picture I felt like a prize fool. A schmuck, in Brooklynese.

> *The way she looked in jeans*
> *The waterfall of chestnut hair*
> *The eyes gray, or green, wide with surprise or joy*
> *The curve of her calf, the taper of her thigh*
> *The hair brushed thoughtfully back, just before speaking*
> *The thoughtful speech*
> *The concentration over a chessboard*

I took down the I Ching, threw the coins. This time I got Hexagram 5, Waiting, with a nine at the beginning.

> WAITING. If you are sincere,
> You have light and success,
> Perseverance brings good fortune.
> It furthers one to cross great water.

> Nine at the beginning means:
> Waiting in the meadow,
> It furthers one to abide in what endures.
> No blame.

("…There is a feeling of something impending. One must continue to lead a regular life as long as possible…")

I didn't think Ali was the woman on the boat, in spite of the line about crossing the great water. I thought about asking around at Wellsmith, but I didn't know who to ask. Dickie, Parker, her parents, the college, all the ties were gone, all the trails were cold. She knew where I was. She would have to find me. If she wanted to.

"So she vanished on you." Sam lit the joint, drew in a hit, passed it. "Your move."

I pushed a pawn. "I hurt her, Sam."

He took my knight, I took his bishop, he took another hit.

"Maybe she wasn't worth it in the first place."

"Maybe not." *But the longing seems to have no end*

He pushed a pawn; I saw his right flank attack two moves away, surprised him; castled Queen's side. He looked up, passed me the joint.

"How are Parker and Emily?"

I took a hit. "That's more a 'Where' question than a 'How' question." I could see it in his eyes: *Four years with these people and you're back where you started.* I passed him back the joint, reached over for the curved hemostat we used as a roach clip.

He brought out his other bishop *always one for the angles* took the hemostat and clamped the roach, took a last hit, passed it. "Let Cheryl and I set you up with someone, Paulie. Manufacturer's Hanover is full of bright girls."

I got a last hit off the roach. *The man with heavy eyes/Declines the gambit* "Not yet, Sam."

What a lousy way to have treated a guy who fought at Normandy, Anzio, Salerno

Wintrobe Thorn Adams Bennett Braunwald Isselbacher Petersdorf eds. Harrison's Principles of Internal Medicine and finally at last *Byrne & Levy Cardiovascular Physiology Goldman Principles of Electrocardiography* We learned that the heart is a pump, and it can fail. We learned that the brain is an organ like any other, and it can also fail. We learned that you can live without a brain but not without a liver. You can live without eyes and ears but not without kidneys.

The night is bitter, The stars have lost their glitter

A postcard from Jerusalem, the Wailing Wall:

Paul —

    They forwarded yours to me. You don't have to apologize or explain. I have had such a spiritual awakening as well. Her name is Margolit. I'll call you when I get back to the States. I'm sorry too. Same reasons.

        — Eli

Cross great water Europe She must be in Europe. Paris. Louvain. I could go
or Lyon, Rome, Milan, Geneva There isn't time or money

"Phone for you." Sam's voice: "Paulie? Bad lottery number. Know any docs from the Movement who'll write one of those letters to a draft board?"
"Gimme two days."

We learned that most of what we knew about sex was wrong. Most of what our instructors knew was also wrong.

I was passing Barry's room, headed for the kitchen. He was with Amazing Gracie.

> *Guinevere*
> *Had green eyes*
> *Like yours, lady, like yours*

543

And as I walked back from the kitchen

...She will be free...

Maybe that was it. Maybe she didn't want *anyone* now. A room of one's own...

Sam took another hit off the joint and handed it to me, dropping a tiny bit of ash on his tux front. "Best Man gets the pick of the bridesmaids, Paulie."

"Sure." He offered me the joint; I shook my head, reached over, brushed the ash off, adjusted his tie slightly. "You ready to do this?"

"Yeah. Oh yeah." *Silence* "Paulie?"

"What. Cold feet? She's a great girl, Sam."

"No. Nah." *Silence* "There's a secret. You're gonna know soon, and everybody's gonna know in about seven months..."

"Sammy. Mazel Tov."

"It was Plan B, Paulie. Good old Local Board Number 39 didn't buy the asthma diagnosis. Anyway, their second opinion guy didn't. Daddy's little parental deferment."

"Jesus fucking Christ Sam."

"It wasn't an accident, Paulie. We thought it through." He took another toke. "Paulie, you're almost a doctor. They'll fall at your feet."

Doctor Doctor Give me the news "Not what I'm looking for, Sam." I took a hit after all.

I once had a girl
Or should I say
She once had me

Was this love? Just stubbornness? Obsession? I had to ask myself

"No girls in your life, Paul?"

"No time, Ma."

"For the right girl there was time. For Alicia."

"I lost her, Ma. Vanished. I don't know how to find her."

"Try, Paul. Your grandmother thought it was Bashert."

Ali Ali Oxenfree

I was off on a Tuesday between rotations. I drove up to Northampton. The Interstate was finished now. I put on my Department of Health jacket, went to the alumni office, asked to see someone who could help me locate an alumna. They let me see the Deputy Head of Alumnae Relations. "Usually they wear a suit," she said.

"Usually?"

"Oh yes. We get one or two of you every fall. The girl they left behind. Or unwisely dumped. Or got dumped by. Usually they try to tell me the story. I'm sorry. I'm not a dating service. These records are private. Surely a doctor knows something about confidentiality." *You don't understand This is Bashert*

Sam passed the joint. Tipped over his king.

"Just in time for dinner," Cheryl said cheerily.

"You look beautiful," I said. "Radiant."

"I look like I swallowed a beach ball."

"Really," Sam said. "We're going to name it Brighton. Works for a boy or girl."

"Bound to be one of the two." *You have no idea the things it could be*

"I'll go check the roast." She went back into the kitchen. A moment later we heard a sort of splash. Looked at each other, like *pot roast doesn't make a sound like that* a second later we heard her: "Sam? Paul? I think...my water broke."

Sam took the last hit off the roach, sucked back hard. "How do you know?" he said, going in the door. "Oh. Surf's up."

Sam got the bag and grabbed a towel; I brought the car around. "Sit in front," I said. "Listen, one thing for sure: You're going to have this baby within 24 hours. That's how we do it. No long labor with no water." *Because your baby had been sailing happily on the warm waters of the sea in the middle of its world and now it isn't because the cervical plug went and now there's a danger of sepsis, that turns pregnancy into a Victorian horror*

She smiled weakly. "If we get stuck in traffic can you deliver me?"

I took her hand. "If I have to." *Shit I hope not* "Are you having contractions?"

"No. Not...I don't think so. Maybe small ones." *Braxton Hicks contractions*

I dropped them at the ER entrance, parked. In those days that was the end of the line until delivery; Sam waved to her as they wheeled her onto the labor deck and we found the Fathers' Waiting Room. "Can you stick around?" Sam said.

"You have to ask?"

"You just came off call. You're still in your whites."

"Go call your in-laws. Call your parents." It wasn't the dope; he was scared shitless. Or I was. We both were. He paced. I sat, too tired to pace.

Time passed. It must have.

"Funny the things you think about on no sleep," I said.

"Such as?"

546

"Odysseus comes home, here's his big-ass bow, that's so powerful only he can string it, plus he's a dead shot. How come he didn't take this thing to Troy?"

"So he took his second best bow. Cheryl would have said maybe it didn't go with his outfit." We laughed till our sides hurt.

"Not a single instance of him using a bow in the *Iliad*." I gasped. "Spears, short sword work only from our man of many wiles."

"Congratulations," he said. "You caught Homer nodding. Didn't you run some scam, taking an archery class to beat a phys ed requirement, up there?"

"It wasn't Troy, it was Schenectady. Check a map. We used to say 'Albany's the asshole of the world, and Troy is ten miles up," I said.

"Maybe Odysseus left it behind for Telemachus. Like, in case he didn't come back," he said. *Silence*

"So. Odysseus comes home, sees the Great Hall full of suitors, figures Penelope's twenty years older, so is he, he weighs up the odds, tells Eumaeus to rustle up a crew, Eumaeus is only too happy after twenty years of tending pigs, they sail back to Phaecia, Hey Nausicaa, I'm back."

"Definitely more plausible," Sam said. "Paulie. Any chance you could maybe, being costumed as you are, penetrate the inner sanctum and find out how she's doing?"

I stood up. "I could give it a shot." The labor deck was just like at Bronx Municipal, dimly lit for calm; better appointed, better painted, pictures on walls, nurses in scrubs all over the place, mostly splashed with fluids of, to me, known origin. *Life is wet* "Excuse me, could you tell me which room Mrs. Rabinowitz is in?"

"Who are you? Those aren't Downstate whites."

"No, I'm a friend, here with the husband, I'm a med student at…"

"I don't care who you are, you don't belong on this labor deck."

"Look, I was on call last night, and my best friend is out there worrying his ass off, so could you…"

She looked around. "Room six. Two minutes."

She was a sweat-soaked mess, breathing like a beached whale, eyes closed, exhausted, alone. The IV was running Pitocin to hasten labor but all it had done was intensify the fitful contractions. The hall was empty; I pulled the chart. Last check five minutes ago showed no progress from 4 centimeters despite the Pit drip. I backed up and bumped into the nurse. *Shit* "This doesn't look great," I said. "They thinking C-section?"

"If she doesn't start dilating soon. You know it has to come out in the next 12 hours, and better sooner than later. It's pretty likely."

"She could use some ice chips and some company."

"Two more minutes," she said.

I found the icemaker, found some paper towels, soaked them with cold water, went back in. Her eyes were open this time, but she didn't recognize me, or anything, at first. I wiped down her forehead; her head cleared, partly.

"That Dr. Paul?" she said, weakly. *How do they do it How*

"It's me, Cheryl; I snuck in. Here." I gave her the ice chips; she sucked on them greedily, mouth dry from hyperventilating.

She gripped my arm. "Can you stay? Please?"

"Not for long."

"I want Sam."

"I know. They won't let him in. Look, it makes some sense *Not much* I'll explain it all to you later, I only have a few minutes till they throw me out. Cheryl, the baby has to come out, and it may be the only way to do that is by C-section."

"A caesarian? Oh, no, Sammy loves to see me in a bathing suit…"

"They'll do what we call a bikini scar if they can, but this is for the baby, Cheryl."

"You know why we're having this baby?"

"Sam told me. It's a brave thing you're doing." *Stupid thing to say Stupid fucking war Stupid fucking country Stupid fucking everything*

A contraction hit; she hugged my arm until it eased off. I gave her the cup of ice chips. "Hold these," I said. "You can keep your mouth wet with these. I have to go before they throw me out. I have to go tell Sam." I found the nurse in the hall. "Thanks," I said. "I'll go prepare the father." But you can't prepare anyone for that. He was asleep for a time, a catnap really; I told him when he woke.

"How bad is this Paulie?"

"Not so bad," I lied. "We do C-sections all the time. *And lose babies And mothers* No big deal. Usually."

"Can I see her?"

"I'll ask." But she was already in the OR; the monitor had shown signs of fetal distress and they'd rushed her in. I came back out. "Almost over already," I said. "See? You both slept through it." His eyes said *Stop bullshitting me*

It was hours until they let us see the baby. All clean, pink, wrapped in a blanket, sleeping peacefully. "Well," Sam said. "A girl. And here I was worried I'd have to teach a kid stickball."

"You'll teach her chess," I said.

The law requires you to have this certificate in your possession at all times

My mother began volunteering with the Fifth Avenue Peace Parade Committee. "All us old Communists," she said, "We know how to get things done." That's where she met Herb. *We must march, my darlings*

We learned to suture by practicing on fruit. The skin of an orange has exactly the consistency of human skin.

The road gets rougher, It's lonelier and tougher

I flogged the VW up Route 7 to Rutland, to the intersection with 4 Waited until midnight Hey remember me Sure the guy who wanted to drive 103 in an ice storm How'd that work out for you Not so good I remembered what you said and came back It's about time I get off shift in a few Want to come back to my place

I came back Well you're too late I married the cook We own the place now

I came back Yeah that's great but I have this thing going with a prof from Dartmouth he's gonna leave his wife

Dear Emily…No. Too real.

"Phone for you." I woke up, too soon.

"Paulie? I have to talk to you. It's Cheryl. Something's really wrong. It's been days, she won't get out of bed, won't go near the baby. I thought she'd get over it, just nerves, tired, I don't know, but it's days now…"

"I'll be right there." On a few hours' sleep I flew to Brooklyn, slowed only when I thought I saw a cop. Parked a block away and ran. Sam answered the door, holding the baby asleep in his arms.

"She's in the bedroom. I told her you were coming." I knocked.

She was in bed, the covers drawn over her head, sobbing. I knelt by the bed, put a hand out to where I thought her shoulder might be. "Cheryl," I said as quietly as I could, "It's Paul. Tell me what's happening."

"You can't tell Sam."

"I won't."

"Promise."

"Unless it's something to keep you safe, and then I won't tell unless we discuss it." It was what I'd been taught to say on Psychiatry. It was supposed to instill confidence. It must have; she pushed the covers off her face. She was completely disheveled.

"I guess you're the family doctor."

"What's going on?" I said.

"I just don't want to do anything. I don't want to move."

"Why not?"

"I don't want to hurt the baby. If I go near her I might. I feel like I already did."

"What? How?"

"I should have had her naturally. I shouldn't have had the operation."

"You had to. If you hadn't…that would have hurt the baby."

"It was wrong. I'm all scarred up." And she started to cry. "I should be dead. There's something wrong with her and I did it and I should be dead."

"Cheryl, no, you…"

"I wanted to kill her. I had this thought I should kill her, it would be better, it's all my fault…" She trailed off into sobs of despair.

I know what this is. "Cheryl, listen. This happens to some women after pregnancy. The hormones go all wacky, and your thoughts and feelings do too, it makes them do that. This can be fixed."

"You can't fix this."

"Yes we can."

"Are you sure?"

"Of course." *Like hell I am* "There are psychiatrists at my place that know all about this. Experts. But I have to tell Sam…"

"Not about the killing part. Promise me, Paulie."

"Do you promise not to do anything like that? To not hurt yourself or the baby? To call me if you feel like you will? Can you promise that?"

"I think so. Yes."

I passed her a box of tissues. "Then I'll just tell Sam about the depression part. Tomorrow I'll get you guys a number to call. A psychiatrist at my school. *A ghost in a yellow ski jacket whispered A female psychiatrist* A woman in the Department. Deal?"

"A woman you said?"

"Yes."

"Deal."

I squeezed her shoulder one more time and went out to tell Sam. "She's having what's called a postpartum depression. The hormones go nuts after pregnancy, don't go back to pre-pregnancy levels…"

"Will she be OK?"

"Yes. But you'll have to get your mother and her mother to take care of the baby."

He called Cheryl's mother, then his; busy signals. He tapped his fingers on the end table. *Awkward silence.*

"So how are things at Manny Hanny?"

"Not so good. Small banks don't have much chance." He looked at the baby. "I think nothing small has a chance anymore." He tried the calls again, connected this time.

" I'll set you up with a woman in our psych department. Hang in there Sam. It'll be OK." *Shit I hope so*

In the surgical ER, the mounting casualties of the gang wars as the South Bronx came apart; stab wounds, bullet wounds. Abdomen. Chest. Head. Revolution was looking ever more unattractive. *The gains are speculative the suffering is here and now and certain Dickie I know that now*

Somebody calls you "We can conclude," Barry said, passing the joint, *You answer quite slowly...* "That at least one of the Beatles had a girlfriend with severe rotatory nystagmus."

The odor of pot roast had delighted me since childhood. Something else was in the air; Herb's things were in the bathroom. He wouldn't want to live in Brighton Beach. This could be my last trip home.

"Paulie, we want to..." my mother started.

I kissed her. "In a little, Ma. I just want to take a walk around the neighborhood." The El rattled and banged, crowds swarmed in and out of Mrs. Stahl's, over the boardwalk, the beach, the Pavillion. Missing tiles, bare concrete and reinforcing rods at the Moorish arches that carried the El over Ocean Parkway. On the Parkway the two-families and mutually antagonistic storefront synagogues. Century-old trees bordered the main roadway like the doomed elms at Nott. *Cheers to Lincoln Stinkin' Lincoln Raise your banners high* The school seemed smaller. Beyond, Coney Island Hospital, miniature of Bronx Municipal; I could walk in there and, as at any New York municipal hospital, feel instantly at home. Turned back, past the stairs from the El *Just a stumble Pavel Help me with the books* The building still smelled of a generation's cooking; somewhere in there was my mother's pot roast.

"Everything where it always was, Paulie?"

And always would be in my head "What did you want to tell me? Ask me?"

"Let me," Herb said.

"No," my mother said, "I have to do this. Paulie, Herb and I...I think you know we're together."

"Yes, of course."

"Herb's place is bigger. And it's in Manhattan. We wondered how you would feel if I moved in with him. To his place."

"How I would feel? That doesn't matter, this is your..."

"We're not asking your permission, Paul, it isn't like that," Herb said, "But you're entitled to have some feelings about this."

Dead is dead Pavel They need your blessing No Pavel, yours It's OK it's what doctors do we give people what they need What does a son do Pavel Or a lover "You kids today," I said. "You have my blessing." They laughed, relieved. *That's over*

The part I hated most was boxing up the books.

There was a moment I needed to get back to, and I couldn't. I was alone. There was the piece of blotter in the drawer. *Everything shone. Everything had its own light, its own ineffable light. And texture. She was there, and he was there, in everything, and the world felt back together. So terribly, terribly sad, when it faded. So empty, so completely empty. Emptier than it had ever been. Empty beyond bearing.* I cried. I slept. I cried again. *Now everything was dark, the forest was dark and now it was empty, empty. And then it…fragmented. Fell to pieces.* I didn't know how long this went on.

The Dean of Students looked me over. I tried to relax.

"Dr. Seitz. I asked you in today because I am told your performance on your surgery rotation is below your customary standard. You did very well in your preclinical studies, sailed through Part I of your Board exams, did well on all your rotations. Until Surgery. Is something going on you need help with?

"Nothing you can help with, no."

"Do you still want to be here?"

"More than anything in my life. Since I was a kid."

"So why have you failed to scrub in on three successive assignments, and maybe more important, why on a fourth do I have a report suggesting you were possibly intoxicated?"

"I was not intoxicated. I don't drink."

"There is more than one way to be intoxicated, as we both well know."

"Yes. I had been intoxicated. It isn't going to happen again. It was an experiment that went wrong."

"An experiment."

"I learned that Huxley was wrong."

"Huxley? Oh. I see. I appreciate the honesty."

"It's embarrassing, sir. I had a severe disappointment recently and I tried something…it got out of hand. Very temporarily. It hasn't happened again. And it won't."

"The report is two weeks old. Since then I understand you've been, how shall I put it, back to yourself."

"That is how I would put it."

"The student health plan includes psychotherapy, Dr. Seitz. I encourage you to…"

"Thank you, sir. I will definitely avail myself of it if I ever feel that way again. I promise you. Thank you, really. If you'll excuse me, I have work to do."

"You do, Dr. Seitz."

The awful daring of a moment's surrender Which an age of prudence can never retract

Shit. Close one.

Came out to the parking lot, could swear I saw a green MG pulling out. I blinked; another car was at the gate. Still tripping? *An MG is not exactly a rare sight at a school*

We learned what it felt like when a patient dies. Dies quietly, dies horribly, dies slowly, dies quickly, dies screaming or crying or raging or drowning in fluids or dies bleeding into lungs or gut or brain, or just dies. We tried to learn what to do to fix, to buy time, to palliate, to relieve, to turn the tales of suffering we listened to by the hour into clues to their cause and guides to their relief.

The wards became the world. The world vanished.

One out of three got better. One out of three got worse. One out of three maintained.

New York Times Book Review December 22, 1969

Capitalism, Fascism, Socialism, Communism
By Benjamin Goldenberg
250 pages
Little, Brown

The twentieth century has been one long contest between different systems for organizing plunder, at least in the vision of Benjamin Goldenberg, Phineas Hyatt Professor of History and Political Theory at Nott College, Schenectady, N.Y. Comes now Dr. Goldenberg to explain to us that all of these forms of politicoecomomic organization have not only common roots but a common end. He is, of course, in one of his own pet phrases, at least superficially correct. Marx himself saw Communism as an inevitable outgrowth of Capitalism, in fact requiring Capitalism from which to grow the necessary enlightened proletariat. Socialism, Communism's potentially democratic alternative, similarly depends upon Capitalism to provide the basis for wealth which must be organized for the public good, as does Fascism, its nationalist cousin. Here Dr. Goldenberg makes somewhat unclear he means the economic basis; there is a threshold of wealth and technology necessary to the organization, or "perhaps emergence," as he puts it, of the conditions necessary to sustain all four systems.

This invites the question: What is this threshold? Goldenberg passes lightly over this on his way to the fundamental source of those conditions, which all four systems have in common: the exploitation, he would say heedless exploitation, of the earth's resources, which leads inexorably to the exploitation of man by man, and beyond that, to the exploitation of man by himself, as if each of us is only what we have to sell.

Goldenberg locates this source in the Biblical injunction to have dominion over the earth, and a misinterpretation of the meaning of "dominion." He would substitute wise stewardship for heedless exploitation, demonstrating that he has been reading Rachel Carson as well as Adam Smith and Karl Marx.

Dr. Goldenberg raises troubling questions about the path we are taking in industrial development, of which his four governmental methods are, in his scheme, alternate versions. Each provides a quite different experience, on the way to the logical end—an earth emptied of resources necessary to sustain industrial civilization, possibly life itself. It decisively answers the question of whether the Free Market or the Command Economy are ends or merely means.

It is a disturbing vision, persuasively argued, clearly written, and urgently needed.

A package in the mail. On the back cover, the familiar face, in soft focus. On the dedication page, this: To my students, from whom I have learned so much, especially P.S, R.A, and W.P. (Signed, by hand, "To P.S."). And a note, with a second copy: "Give this to Mr. Acheson when you have the chance, with my regards."

When I thought about it, I thought—I still think—that Dickie saw deeper into this than any of us. Ali I think believed, with my mother, grandmother and Virginia Woolf, that equality for women would automatically solve the problems of perpetual warfare and bring social justice. I thought, and still think, action in the world as it is, is hopelessly compromised, that means corrupt ends and we must deal with the casualties. I know we were all hopelessly naïve, in the best possible ways.

The war went on and on. Every Fall and every Spring, the Marches on Washington. The Cambodia/Kent State protest. I was still there with the Peace Parade Committee's volunteer medical corps, the Medical Committee for Human Rights/Student Health Organization, running without running an aid team, taking care of minor lacerations, bad trips, tear gas inflammation, and giving out salt tablets, some to the aging men and women veterans of the Spanish war in their black berets.

"You know who we are?"

I sang "Viva La Quinte Brigada" with them. They refused the salt tablets. "What?" I said, "You didn't have heat stroke on the Guadarrama Front? At least give your wife one."

"I was there too. Drove an ambulance." *It is possible, Ali*

Suddenly another white coat was there. "This fine young doctor is right, people," he said. He took the elderly woman's hand. "I want you to be here to tell your stories to my children. And I want you to teach me how to drink from this." And he held up a bota. They laughed; I handed out the salt tablets and they came forward to show us how to drink from a wineskin.

I stuck out my hand. "Paul Seitz."

He took it. "Marv Kornbluth," he said.

My mother was there, with Herb. I thought I saw Parker at the Spring '71 Mobilization, but I lost him in the crowd—if it was him. Ali I thought I saw everywhere.

She must be angry at me. Or worse. But she knows it was necessary how could she be angry I'm not angry at her anymore, about anything That was so long ago

Perseverance furthers

I watched a mother of four whose history I had just taken die by inches as she bled into her brain from a ruptured aneurysm. I held a teenager's hand as, hideously burned, he slipped into death. I made house calls in semi-abandoned buildings to collect throat swabs from babies with strep, sputum from old men wasted by tuberculosis. The war went on and the Bronx was a casualty, burning and collapsing a building at a time. For every death in Vietnam, one in the Bronx. The veterans began coming home; some with undiagnosed malaria, some with alcohol and drug habits, some with nightmares that wouldn't let them sleep.

Outside my window a cardinal in a tree: CQ,CQ,CQ…Had I become a Golem?

The parties got more frequent. Barry said, "There's this girl, Third Year, Lish the Dish; if I could get her over here…"
"No way," Steve said, "She doesn't party. Total tool."

The last time I had the dream I got it. I didn't know why it had taken me this long to figure it out. WQXN. In the new chess notation, QxN meant "Queen takes Knight".

You loved her but you hadn't trusted her

I went everywhere: Bronx Municipal, Lincoln, the Mother House, the College Hospital, Bronx VA. I let my beard grow to just short of where one day there would be a tiny scar.

The parties got wilder. The friends, cousins, friends of cousins and cousins of friends continued to crash downstairs. Classmates showed up; we smoked more dope, dropped acid (some of us; not me, not again), got high, stayed just short of police involvement.

I learned how callow we had been and were. The things I thought I had learned in college, and all before it, were only half-understood quotations and juxtapositions of ideas. Fragments shored against our ruin, yes, at best. I learned that, as William Carlos Williams, poet and physician, said, "No ideas but in things". Blood. Bone. Brain. Flesh.

> *The way she looked in jeans.*
> *The waterfall of chestnut hair*
> *The eyes gray, or green, wide with surprise or joy*
> *The curve of her calf, the taper of her thigh*

In the end it was her eyes: quizzical, mischievous, alert, fiery. Intelligent. That's what was left. Those thousand-watt, gray-green eyes, seemingly lit from within. And sometimes her voice.

ESTRAGON: I can't go on like this. VLADIMIR: That's what you think.

Ali Ali Oxenfree I couldn't tell you exactly the day my heart finally broke entirely and I stopped hoping. So many were so much worse off than I was; I saw them every day in the wards and clinics, saw the coffins coming out of the bellies of the cargo planes on the TV news. But I had held happiness in my arms, warm and alive, and I had thrown it away. One night, both of us high, a friend of a cousin of a friend relieved me of my virginity in a procedure as neat and clinical as an appendectomy. And as anesthetized.

Well that's done and

Is that all there is?
Is that all there is?
If that's all there is, my friends, then let's keep dancing
Let's break out the booze and have a ball
If that's all there is

I discovered that Hemingway was wrong; we don't grow strong in the broken places. We grow numb.

April 7, 1973, 6:30 PM —
April 8, 1973, 7:30 PM

I love people who harness themselves, an ox to a heavy cart,
who pull like water buffalo, with massive patience,
who strain in the mud and the muck to move things forward,
who do what has to be done, again and again.

I want to be with people who submerge
in the task, who go into the fields to harvest
and work in a row and pass the bags along,
who are not parlor generals and field deserters
but move in a common rhythm
when the food must come in or the fire be put out...

The pitcher cries for water to carry
and a person for work that is real.

— Marge Piercy, 1973, *To Be of Use*

*M*ore infiltrated IVs, evening rounds to lock everything down.

"How ya doin, Mamie?"

"Better," she said. She was breathing better; the fluid we took off hadn't reaccumulated—so the Lasix had served its purpose—at least from what I could tell through a stethoscope. Still some rales, though. I called Ali over to listen. "That's what a successful pleural tap sounds like," I said. We checked the puncture sites; no appreciable blood or fluid. "We'll go look at your new X-ray," I told her. "Come with?" I asked Ali. She shrugged; we headed for the stairs.

"Gonzalez?" I said.

"Sleeping peacefully."

"I want to ask," I said, "Is there some way we could start over? As us now, I mean. No past history."

"You mean a lobotomy? Or a permanent conversational No Go zone? Hi, my name is Alicia Acheson, mine's Paul Seitz, I was just born yesterday. How could that work, exactly?"

565

"Yeah, pretty lame. I'm a coward, Ali. Was then, seem to be now."

"You're scared of me?"

"Of you now? Of the person you are now? No. About the person you were, the person I was, yeah, I guess I am."

"You trusted me today to stick a sharp instrument into your patient, into a little old lady that you like very much, and you're afraid to trust me to talk about the past."

Well, if you put it like that "I did trust you, yes, and I do, about things now...OK, so I'll be talking to 1973 Alicia."

"There is the third thing you've said that makes no sense to me. First about being scared of my father's influence, second about telling me something about an old chess game, now about..."

Silence

"OK, maybe that makes more sense than the other two. Paul, I'm still me, but grown. So are you. Grown. Adult. A lot of stuff resolved, or anyway over with."

"Ali, yes, true...look, here's something I know: We're great together, but apart we're not so hot, or anyway different from what we are together...does that make any sense?"

"It will take some explaining."

We were at X-ray. "What do the films show?"

"Looks to me like resolved pleural effusion."

"See here, tiny bit of blunting of the gutters. Should be sharp angles, here. Sharper."

"Oh. Yes, I see. Some little bit of fluid still there."

"See? Great together. Six years ago..."

"Paul. We were just nineteen. And you have no idea what was happening in my family."

"Dickie, you mean. I was a big part of that, remember?"

"That was only a small part of what was going on. You don't know what I was dealing with. And how...how could we part the way we did and then you just...stopped, not only stopped...I know something must have happened. What?"

How could she not know?

BEEEEEEEEP

"Every goddamned time." I was next up for an admission. It was Marvin; sure enough a ROMI. "Unit material. One more bed and we fill it and close the doors. Guy's got enzyme elevations but not major, ST elevations but not major—call it a feeling." I sighed; if I got this one, Ali would be up for the late night admit, and she still had to get Mr. Ukraine's history when that nurse showed up. And I wanted to be there for that, so maybe this wasn't so bad after all.

"What?"

"ROMI coming to the Unit. Go catch a nap; you'll be up for the late night, plus we have to interview our Vlassovite." She went, reluctantly, still eager for action she'd have enough of soon. Marvin and Katie were with the ROMI in the Unit; the nurses were just hooking up the monitor.

"Meet Mr. Molitor," Marvin said, "Mr. Molitor, Dr. Seitz. He'll be doing a thorough history and physical, and so will Dr. McCulloch."

Mr. Molitor smiled weakly, just a touch short of breath. "She'll be more fun," he slightly gasped. I wondered if he needed oxygen. It would be no fun getting arterial blood gases. This time I did my history and physical and left Katie to do hers on her own. She came over to review it as I wrote my note.

"Let's save some time on this one. Describe any outstanding history or physical findings."

"History—well, the striking thing, this is his third trip to the ER; no one could believe a 33-year-old man could be having an infarct."

567

"Happens all the time; black people, especially West Indians, have early onset hypertension. Guess they didn't want to believe someone so close to their own age could be having an MI. Until an enzyme went up. What about the physical?"

"I heard a murmur."

"Very good. What do you make it?" Meaning what kind, what grade.

"I heard a Grade III aortic murmur, so it must really be a Grade IV." Meaning the old med student joke about how to grade the volume of heart murmurs: A Grade I murmur, the cardiologist hears it. A Grade II murmur, the resident hears it. A Grade III murmur, the intern hears it. A Grade IV murmur, the med student hears it. A Grade V murmur, the patient in the next bed hears it. A Grade VI murmur, your deaf Aunt Sylvia in Dubuque hears it. It always gets a grin.

"No, you got it, I heard grade III too." Ali wandered in, looking slightly lost. "On call rooms are way over that side of the building."

"I can't sleep; I'm not tired yet. Anyway, I feel worse after an hour's sleep than on no sleep at all. Mr. Gonzalez is resting calmly, and no fever."

"Good news. Want to hear an aortic murmur? Katie, introduce her to Mr. Molitor."

Katie wrote her note. "What's your formulation?"

"Young black male, history of hypertension, shortness of breath without congestion, chest pain that could be cardiac, suspicious elevated SGOT; possible MI or anyway cardiovascular disease…"

"What about the murmur?"

"It doesn't fit," she said, and she was right.

"So what else could this be?"

"Coincidental. The enzyme could be coming from liver; the whole thing could be GI and the hypertension is a red herring, so is the aortic murmur, which could be functional."

568

"Could be subaortic stenosis," Ali said.

"Could be..." and we launched into a back-and-forth about the differential diagnosis of subaortic stenosis and aortic murmurs. "But none of the labs we have are any help. What should we be ordering?"

"Well, three days of EKGs, and SMA-12's *the standard '3 day Rule Out Myocardial Infarct workup', the ROMI Special* and maybe we should fractionate the enzymes *to rule out liver disease...*"

"Good."

"And I should get stool for occult blood."

"Ah."

"Anything else?"

"Cardiology consult Monday. The hypertension bothers me too...hypertension. Ulcer?"

"Renal functions are OK on ER bloods; crit and RBCs are OK too."

"Know how to get stool for occult blood?"

"Yes."

"Let's do it together. First day and all."

A rectal exam is never pleasant for either doctor or patient; one gets inured to it as a doctor. Not as a patient. "Mr Molitor. Comfortable?"

"Comfortable as anyone can be in a neon-lit room with a beeping machine attached to your heart, man."

"We go first-class all the way. And the food is four-star. Listen, one thing we still have to do—rectal exam."

"Why?"

"Your pain could be coming from heart, which is why the first-class accommodations, but it could also be coming from something like an ulcer. I know we went over this; you haven't had black stools or blood, but a tiny ulcer can leak without visible blood, and this way we can get a sample. It's no big deal; you just roll over on your side and we do the rest."

He sighed. "You make too much sense."

569

We gloved up, got the lubricant, laid out the sample card. I demonstrated, and got a surprise. I called Katie over; this was important.

"One more time, Mr. Molitor, and we're done." Katie slipped a gloved, lubricated forefinger into Mr. Molitor's rectum. Her eyes widened. She wiped the stool sample on the test card, and we settled Mr. Molitor back in bed. "Thank you Mr. Molitor," I said, "No more for now. Rest easy."

We went back to the end of the room with the chart. "So?" I said.

"That was like…he had no sphincter tone."

"It was like waving a stick in the Grand Canyon. Know why?"

"I'm about to learn something."

"He's gay. Homosexual. Something he would never in a million years tell us. This widens the differential. What do you think of now?"

"Sexually transmitted diseases. Aortic murmur, odd symptoms that don't add up…"

I knew she had the answer.

"…maybe syphilis."

"Bingo. The Great Mimic. Treponemes chewing on his aortic valve. Any additional orders?

"VDRL is already written."

"If that's positive, titers," Ali threw in, "It would be secondary syphilis."

Katie finished her note; she'd added the new information and orders. I countersigned them. "Go upstairs and tell Marvin about this," I said, "He's a great expert on syphilis."

"I bet."

"And. What did you learn?"

"A complete physical always includes a rectal exam?"

"Excellent. Go watch a ball game." She went to the roof.

"Is Marvin really an expert on syphilis?" Ali asked.

"Lewisburg. He knows more about it than Katie, that's for sure."

"You're really good at this, you know?"

"So you keep saying. What am I good at? Let's see. I just taught a good Catholic school girl how to stick her finger up a guy's ass for diagnostic purposes."

"Well, you did it without embarrassing her, the patient, or yourself."

"And then sent her up to the roof to let Marvin corrupt her further."

"Well, now that you mention, and since you bring it up, don't you find that a little creepy?"

"What, 'that'? It was a joke."

"He has to be at least five years older than her."

"Chronologically, yes. I've seen Marvin come on to nurses, pharmacists, ER clerks—not like this. My parents were about ten years apart. And I wouldn't think you would find this so creepy."

"Why not? Why not me? There's another cryptic remark, Paul. What do you mean, I wouldn't find this so creepy? Why the hell not? And what is she in your eyes? Maybe *was* a Catholic school girl, ten years ago. Now she's a med student. You think she can't do this?"

"Of course I think she can do this; she's great."

"So why do you call her a Catholic school girl? How do you see her? Child or adult?"

Boats against the current

"You're the one saying she can't handle a relationship with a guy five years older. Is this about Katie?"

"No, it isn't about Katie, it's about how women are seen around here. How do you see me? You teach me, you respect my opinions and back me to superiors; you also make completely baffling references to my—to our—past, so..."

571

"So this is about us, so yeah. Ali…Alicia, I owe you an apology. A big apology. I know I hurt you. I hurt myself. I owe you an explanation. You also owe me one."

"How do I owe you one?"

" 'You don't know what I was dealing with'."

Silence.

"OK, we owe each other explanations."

"And this is not a terrific place…"

BEEEEEP

This time it was her beeper, and it was a good thing she hadn't gone for that nap, because it was the admit of the day.

"Marvin says call out all troops, we have a Doriden OD."

"Oh shit, I hate those." We ran into Marvin and Katie coming down from the roof.

"Why those, especially?" She turned to Katie. "Paul hates Doriden overdoses."

We pounded down the stairs. "Who gets to explain?" I asked Marvin.

"What do you know about Doriden?" he asked the air.

"It's an obsolete minor tranquilizer," Ali said. "I didn't know it was still available."

"It never should have been. It was supposed to be safer than Miltown. Equanil. Before Valium replaced them. But it has one unique and interesting feature. Anyone? No? Dr. Seitz, enlighten our students."

"Enterohepatic circulation."

"Entero…" Katie said.

"Means it goes into the gut, gets absorbed, rides up the portal vein into the liver and gets metabolized, but some gets sent to the gall bladder. From which it is promptly secreted into the gut again, is reabsorbed, returns to the liver for another trip, etcetera. Which means levels rise, putting the patient to sleep or into delirium, then fall, putting him into irritable, delirious withdrawal, then rise again… and this goes on all night. So we get them all hooked up to IVs and tubes, they wake up and pull everything out and demand to leave, maybe get as far as the elevator bank, and keel over, we reinsert tubes, over and over."

"Sometimes they get combative. Nasty overdose," Marvin added. "Dr. Acheson has drawn the deuce of clubs. But we will be there to help, will we not Dr. Seitz?"

"All for one and one for all."

"What's the treatment for this?" Ali asked.

"Supportive. Hydrate, keep electrolytes up, nourish, wait, try to encourage detox when awake and alert. Rate of success: close to nil. But we try. To avoid injury, mostly."

"Where would he get this stuff?" Katie asked. "If it's off the market."

"Ah, but it isn't. Just very uncommon. A few of our less scrupulous colleagues along the Concourse will write a script for the right price."

"Jesus."

"Not involved in the trade as far as I know." *All we get to do is treat the casualties*

We were at the ER. Ali led the way to the bedside; her patient after all. He was unconscious, IV taped to one wrist, wrist taped to a board. The ER crew were only too glad to sign him over to us. Marvin had a brief conversation with the ER resident.

"I just closed the house—ICU is full; one bed left for in-house transfers and we've got some fragile ones: Mamie. Anything else tonight goes to the Mother House. That's the only good news in this situation. Let's get him upstairs before he wakes up for the first time."

A lot of the next few hours are a blur, partly because of how it ended. I remember he woke up in the elevator, started shouting to be let up, let go, but he was restrained on the gurney. We'd have to wait until he conked out again to transfer him to a bed, which wouldn't improve his mood. When we rolled him into the Unit, Ali pushed a pillow under his head. She tried to get a history, but only got threats of mayhem if he wasn't allowed up and out.

"Mr. Donnelly. Do you know where you are right now?"

"The infirmary."

"What infirmary?"

"Attica." Great. The state prison.

"Admission papers say he just got out. Scored some pills his first day," Marvin said.

She asked him the date and his name and age, got only curses and threats for answers. After about five minutes he fell back into a stupor. We moved him to a bed, hooked up a monitor, did a physical, each of us positioning him for the others. A 23-year- old man with no notable physical findings beyond some interesting tattoos.

"What do you see?" Marvin asked Katie.

"Nothing contributory," Katie answered.

"What do you NOT see?" Marvin asked her.

She shrugged, puzzled. Ali was also stumped.

"No tracks," Marvin said, meaning no needle marks of intravenous drug abuse. "This one's a pillhead. No opiates, at least not yet. Maybe some hope here. We'll see when he wakes up clear."

And then he was up again, pulling wildly at the restraints, ranting at us and the world. This went on for 2 solid hours, with the periods of stupor shortening, the periods of angry delirium lengthening.

"Can we knock him out with something? He's disturbing the other patients."

"Can't—he's already got rising and falling levels of a tranquilizer in him."

We apologized and explained as best we could to Mr. Molitor, waited for 11:00 when the Ukrainian nurse would, please God, come on shift.

At length she did. Her face lit up when we told her the story. "We will be able to help him," she said. "The Tolstoya Funt, the Tolstoy Foundation, it's a Ukrainian nursing home. He'll have a place there."

"Right now we need to get a history," Ali said. "Can you help?"

"I will try. My Ukrainian is pretty good, but rusty. It will be a pleasure to use it again."

His name was Ivan Vovchok, he was 62, and he had lived alone in the apartment, in a neighborhood gradually turning Puerto Rican, then being abandoned, for three years after his wife died. He'd worked as a machinist until all the local factories closed. Yes, he smoked, two packs a day, and drank, wine and vodka, but only rarely got drunk. He had been increasingly short of breath for a year, with short periods of dizziness, but no chest pain. A string of Slavic sounds was translated by Nurse Schevchenko as, "I'm healthy as a horse." But when he fell, a few days ago (vodka may have been involved) he could not get up, "Couldn't keep my breath." Ali's review of systems turned up nothing new. I came over from Mr. Donnelly's bed and pointed to the missing fingers.

"Vlassov's Army?" I asked. This time we were treated to the full story, courtesy of Nurse Schevchenko's translation. He had indeed been in Vlassov's Army, a lieutenant. He'd been a sergeant in the Red Army in 1941, when the Germans had overrun the western Soviet Union and taken hundreds of thousands of prisoners. He'd survived labor camps; new arrivals informed the POWs that they were considered traitors by their government, that retreating troops were being shot by commissars; when Vlassov began recruiting for the Germans he saw a possible way out, even though he hated the Germans as much as he now feared his own government. He might at least return to home ground. When Vlassov marched them on Prague he knew he'd made the right choice; if they were heroes to the Czech people he could have a new homeland.

"Could he have done that?"

"He could have passed for Ruthenian."

"What's Ruthenian?" Marvin asked.

"Ukrainians who lived on the Austro-Hungarian side of the Carpathians. Catholics, but spoke Ukrainian, had other aspects of Ukrainian culture."

"How do you know all this shit?"

"If it's in a book, Paul knows it," Ali said. *Ah, sarcasm*

But the Red Army was right behind; after fighting the Germans for Prague, he saw the Czechs welcome the Soviets as liberators. As I suspected (as I'd learned happened from my father's stories) he'd taken the uniform of a dead German private; the paybook papers were intact, and he was able to surrender to American troops as a Sudeten German deserter. One Wehrmacht private looked pretty much like another, one European language sounded just like another to them, and he'd picked up jackleg German in the camps. A cousin in a Pennsylvania mine was his connection to America, but he hated the mines and came to New York after a few years. He was amazed that a young American knew anything about Vlassov's Army. "Tell him my father was a Czech," I told Mrs. Schevchenko. This brought a smile and a nod, as did her news of the existence of the Tolstoya Funt.

He'd never encountered a Captain Seitz.

"This will be a story," Ali said.

"It will."

We huddled over the EKG again. "These elevated ST segments and flipped T could be signs of an old inferior wall MI," Marvin said.

"Maybe a year ago, could account for the increasing weakness and shortness of breath."

"And ongoing atherosclerosis knocking out the conduction system, giving him the trigeminal beats. Or alcoholic cardiomyopathy. But his liver seems OK. No hypertrophy, no enzymes or protein."

"Could cut out at any minute. The heart is as we know a most unreliable organ. He's still having runs of trigeminy. Is he on any meds?"

She'd never asked; we were at the beginning of the exhaustion curve, the time after midnight when you start forgetting simple things, making errors. We went over with Mrs. Schevchenko and hit pay dirt.

"He says after his wife died he was depressed; a year ago they gave him something for that."

"Gave him what?"

"He says he doesn't know. Something with a T."

"Tofranil?"

"He says could be."

"When was the last time he took it?"

"He says he doesn't remember. Today? Yesterday?"

"Katie, what do you know about Tofranil?" Marvin asked.

"Tricyclic antidepressant, noradrenergic, serotonergic, very anticholinergic."

"What happens with overdoses?"

None of us knew that one precisely. "Cardiac arrythmias. Usually escape rhythms, tachyarrythmias." He added, for Katie's benefit: "Slows the sinoatrial node, heartbeat gets uncoordinated; lower centers take over."

"I know escape rhythms."

"If he's been drinking, or missing some O's to the brain, he could have accidentally overdosed himself."

"Or he's been throwing extra beats for a year?"

Ali pulled the chart to rewrite her note to include the new information, add Tofranil OD to the differential diagnosis. She was writing up her admission note on Donnelly, feet propped up against the door. Which was when I noticed that Donnelly had been awake and had worked out of his restraints. He was only restrained at the wrists, and was out of the bed, IV pulled out and dripping blood and fluid, faster than we could get out of his way; he pulled Ali out of her chair and left her blocking the door. But she rolled to her knees and stood, chased him out to the elevators, shouting for him to stop.

"Call Security," I yelled, and followed. As I feared, he'd quickly given up on the elevators and turned to the stairs, which Ali was blocking, talking soothingly. He'd kept the restraint belt, and now he swung it at her head. She ducked, skidded on the perpetually wet linoleum, went down, still blocking the door. He hauled off to swing the belt at her again, but I caught it, and his attention. He whipped it back out of my hand, swung it at me, and connected, despite my block, not too heavily, with the side of my jaw. My head rang for a second; things started to happen in slow motion:

1. Marvin, Katie and the nurses appeared.
2. Two New York Health and Hospitals Corporation police came rushing out of the stairwell.
3. Donnelly began swaying on his feet and slumped as another round of Doriden absorption raised his serum level. Marvin, Katie, nurses and police got him on a gurney and back to bed.

For some reason I was leaning against the wall. Ali had her arm around me, and I briefly considered just staying there, like this, and then my head cleared completely. "The correct procedure, Dr. Acheson," I said, "Is to call Security."

"Paul, I'm so sorry. Thank you. Are you OK?"

"Pretty much. You?" She nodded.

"Maybe could use a stitch," Marvin said. I walked into the Unit bathroom, with the rest of the Musketeers; everyone had an opinion. I cleaned the small cheek laceration with a 4X4, applied pressure, winced at the betadine. "Butterfly should do it," I said, and Mrs. Schevchenko brought one. I started to open it, but Ali insisted on applying it. Sitting down seemed like a good idea.

"Go get some Z's," Marvin said. "I'll sleep here, if I sleep; call you if there's a floor admission or anything." Which was SOP when the Unit was full; resident took first call for the Unit. There was an old bed on the disused sun porch we kept for these occasions.

"You sure?"

"Yeah, I'll call if I need you. Donnelly isn't going anywhere for a while, I just need to be here if a monitor goes tilt."

"I'll stay," Katie said. "I couldn't sleep anyway."

"You'd be surprised."

"I have notes to finish," Ali said.

"Paulie. Go," Marvin said.

He was right, I should go. A brain with a little sleep might be a handy thing later in the night. I went down the stairs, stopped at 4, walked around just to make sure. Gonzalez was snoring peacefully. So was Goldstein. Gordon was awake, planning his return home. Mamie was asleep on her side; I whipped out my stethoscope and took a listen; a few crackles, nothing worse. Miss Fascelli snored like a bear. And twelve others in the midst of diagnosis or treatment or dying. I was surprised to see Callie on her way out. "Shouldn't you be gone by now?" We walked down the stairs together.

"Donna called in late; husband not home in time."

"What is it with nurses and cops?"

"We both do shift work, and anyway, what should I marry, a doctor? No thanks. I get enough of you at work. What happened to your face?"

579

"Attempted rearrangement by a Doriden OD."

She grimaced. "Can't wait to meet him."

"Doubt you will—he'll sign out AMA. More like AMF."

"But you tried to stop him, right?"

"Not exactly. But close." We had reached the first floor; she was going out the main doors, I was headed for the courtyard.

"Dr. Seitz? Can I tell you something?"

"Anything."

"The reason I—we—put up with all your and Kornbluth's crap is: you never ever leave for your on-call room without checking the floor first. And you teach your students that too; that Dr. Acheson came through before too."

"Thank you, Callie. That means a lot to me. And I'll tell Marvin. But Dr. Acheson—we didn't teach her that; she did it on her own."

"Then there's another one."

"Get some sleep."

"You too."

The ER was quiet; a few late night asthma cases, night shift injuries for the surgeons, but ambulances were going further north tonight, we had all we could handle. The chill in the air surprised me; I hadn't been out of the building for hours, and I didn't have my jacket. The on-call rooms were in the old nurses' residence building, from the days when nurses were virginal, nun-like creatures who lived on the hospital grounds. Most of the rooms on the lower floors had been converted to administrative offices or storage rooms. The building loomed gray and shadowed in the floodlights. More stairs, a door, a closet-sized room with a bed, a nightstand and a lamp. Half the window was floodlit. I took off my shoes and lay down in my clothes. With the Unit full it didn't do to have to get dressed if there was a call. I called the Unit. "This is Dr. Seitz. I'm in on-call 7."

"OK doctor."

But I couldn't sleep. Partly it was flashback to the belt buckle coming at me, and more important, coming at Ali. If he'd hit her with that thing I would have killed him. I imagined grabbing the belt, wrapping it around his neck and pulling. I imagined her head bloodied, carrying her down to the ER for sutures, X-ray...I didn't let it go further than that. The things that didn't happen. Thinking about killing him was better than thinking about her with a skull fracture, but not by much. Four years marching against the War, doing first aid at the Fall and Spring Mobilizations, going down with gangs of med studs, sleeping on dorm room floors. Not to mention Dickie and the bodhidharma. I did not have my father's or Dickie's visceral commitment to non-violence. Maybe neither did they.

And I loved her. Face it. I had to face it. I loved Dr. Alicia Acheson. But maybe not Alicia Acheson. She was on to it, too; I could not think of her now without thinking of the girl I knew she had been. Was that fair, or right? People didn't change that much. Or did they? I had; I could barely remember my pre-doctor personality. Doctor isn't something you do, it's something you are. It's something that does you. If doctoring had taken her out of herself, made a new self... *The truth is, I didn't deserve her. I had loved her and this is how I'd screwed it up.* I turned out the light.

Or if I could just say to myself, that old self doesn't matter. What if we had just met? If I'd never known her before, if all I would ever know about the teenaged Ali was what she chose to tell me. *I loved her competence I loved the way she thought How her skin felt Her hands How her breath tasted*

I heard footsteps on the stairs. They came down the hall toward my door. I watched the knob, just visible in the gray light from the window. The steps moved on down the hall.

I would have killed the man who hurt her. I didn't even think when he attacked her; I just acted. I would have let him hit me if that was

581

what it had taken. Hell, I had. I couldn't fight a feeling like that. And could it be wrong? Of course it could, but it didn't feel wrong. It felt damned familiar. Remember that supposed old Arabic saying: What you can't have, shit on. Had I done that?

How, out of all Earth's teaming millions, was it this one girl? How, after all the girls I'd ever seen in school, at chess matches, in libraries, on trains and buses, at rallyes, at peace marches? How, after mooning over her for years, was it not Naomi Ackerman? How, after partly undressing me and herself, was it not Emily? How, when I could sometimes still hear her little moan of pleasure, was it not Maxine?

It would be stupid to trust her, trust her family. It had been stupid all along. *The awful daring of a moment's surrender Which an age of prudence can never retract* But she said her family was broken up. And she was a med student, and a good one, definitely not part of the family plan. And that there were facts still unknown to me. *I wasn't finished being stupid. Think this through scientifically. All the facts aren't in.* None of this fit the woman I'd worked with today. There was the pattern: When I was with her, all doubt melted away; when I thought about things alone was when the canker of doubt bloomed. As with Eli and his religion, were prudence and rational intellect the wrong tools for this job? *You are making a forest of words. Remember the real forest* What did she feel toward me? She obviously had feelings for me. Love?

I drifted into a half-sleep. In the empty chair by the bed she sat, I could see her, legs crossed, one shoe dangling off her toe. The French say: Un coup de Foudre. *I loved the way her mind worked, how she casually but thoughtfully examined an X-ray or a cardiogram, how she wouldn't leave before checking the floor, how she staked out her ground and fought. Her competence* How had that girl become this woman? *He was the boy* How had that boy become me? *The feeling of her hands on my face as she applied the butterfly.*

582

A long-banked fire was flaring. I heard footsteps on the stairs. They came down the hall toward my door. I watched the knob, just visible in the gray light from the window. The knob turned. The door opened. She stood silhouetted in the weak hall light. The light caught stray wisps of hair escaping from the clips and pins. "Paul?" she whispered, "You awake?"

"You're eight years late," I said.

"Eight years late?"

"August 1965. I waited up for you, waited for you...in case you decided to come visit."

She laughed softly. "I waited up for you."

I sat up, swung my feet over the side of the bed, turned the lamp on. "You did?"

"I did."

I didn't know what to say to this.

"Well, I'm here now." She took the clips out, shook out her hair. The ice around my heart melted. "Are you really OK?" she asked.

"Mostly. I'm very tired and maybe mildly concussed. Not the first time I've been hit."

"Well, it was for me. I'm just starting to shake."

I resisted the urge to hug her to me. It seemed the wrong response. *Not the first time she'd dragged me into*

"I mean, he's just a kid, no older than us, there has to be some hope for him."

"Maybe, but you can't risk stuff like that. He needs your skills, not your sacrifice. You have to promise yourself never to do that again."

"You sound like my father. Promise you'll never..."

"Is there something wrong with your hearing? I said promise *yourself*."

"...Yes. You did. Sorry. Nothing wrong with my hearing, or anyway not with my ears. My father..."

"How is the good Richard Acheson Esquire?"

"Only a vague idea. Living with a succession of women in a Manhattan apartment, after cruising the Caribbean for a few years, maybe he took up piracy. Or in hell. No contact since I went to med school. Longer than that. God, I'm tired."

Silence.

"Why, Paulie? No calls, no letters, and, and this really, really hurt, why return my letter unopened?"

"I wrote a thousand letters to you in my head. My whole life was a letter to you."

"Pity you never wrote them on paper and sent them."

"Ali, I'm so, so sorry. It was one of the worst things I've ever done, and I did it because I couldn't think of a safe way for us to communicate and I had to send you a signal to stop you writing, maybe get him off our backs, make him think he broke us up, you know that, and I'm a coward. *The truth is, I don't deserve you.* I was afraid for you. For both of us. I thought, my God, doesn't she know the risk she's running? Myself, I thought I could protect, but I couldn't have protected you. I thought, what guts you have, and I'm a miserable coward, I wasn't worth it. And I was angry, too. Didn't you know the risk you were exposing me to? My family? Maybe we should have just gone in and told him to shove it up his ass…I was afraid of him, of what he could do to your life. To all of our lives."

"Him…him who? What are you talking about?"

Silence

"What? Your father."

"You are certainly no coward. Why would you suddenly be afraid of my father?"

"I was then. *I was then. That was me then, not now.* After the run-in with him at his office…"

"What run-in at his office? What the hell are you talking about?"

"You don't know about that? How could you not know? He said he was going to tell you by close of business that day, his exact words. I figured he must have told you, he was trying to scare you and me both. He never told you? Oh my God, he never told you. Ali, you think I just…"

"What I thought is, I thought I knew you enough to know that you wouldn't just do that, ditch me like that, and anyway you only sent it back after a month. Which meant to me you must have thought it over, long and hard, and you must have had a reason. Plus Parker told me your eyes lit up every time he told you I'd asked about you. And you kept asking him if I was OK, which meant you still cared, and something worried you, something had happened. And Alice thought…"

"Oh, I had a reason. Son of a bitch, I had a reason."

"You had a meeting of some kind with my father. At his office."

"Yes, what we expected. Mike, Michael, the guy who had been following Dickie and me around, practically kidnapped me at Grand Central."

"The day I drove you to the bus?"

"Next day. I crashed at Yale, a faculty friend of my father's; took the train to New York the next day. Michael. One of the firm's investigators."

"The one you and Dickie thought was keeping an eye on him."

"Yeah, well, we were right. It wasn't Mike watching you and me; remember the blue Chevy? That guy followed me to New Haven, and I shook him off in the Yale library. But I didn't want them staking out my mother's place, scaring her. I let them find me at Grand Central. Mike watched the trains…you never knew?" She shook her head. I told her about the scene at her father's office. All of it, every word I could remember.

" 'If you like the type'?"

"Come on. A masterpiece of indirection. It wasn't a moment for emotional honesty. I had to keep the eyes off you. And I was scared he..."

"You were really scared he could do all that? Or would?"

"Jesus, Ali, I was nineteen. They knew about Dickie and Bina, had this dossier on me and my family, I figured from informants, and he would know the same way if we were in contact. I had Sammy check him out, do a little investigating through acquaintances... Didn't you say you thought he interfered with your med school applications? Yeah, I thought he could. Sammy did. He himself said he sat in the middle of a huge web. The point for me was to not disturb the web, he said. I was scared for you. I didn't know if he knew you were in on Dickie's run before I brought you the car. Seemed like not. The whole point was to keep suspicion off you. Bring you the car—Surprise!—without implicating you with the old man. To let you keep free to find your own way."

"You were part of my way. Didn't you get that? How much clearer could I have made it? What do you need, an act of Congress?"

All I had to do was raise one eyebrow, and she heard what she'd said and exploded. I pulled her to me to stifle the laughter; we shook, gasped with it. When I'd caught my breath I said, "Shh, you'll wake up the surgeons."

She sat back again, collected herself, struggled to resume a serious look, but something had loosened, something important.

"Shit, Ali, I'd love to have stood up in his office and told him we were deeply in love so go fuck yourself, but that isn't something I could do without deciding it with you first. I didn't really know if you were that in love with me that you would jeopardize your whole future..."

"You didn't, huh?"

"And I knew you don't like to have other people make plans for you. I thought I didn't have the right."

That silenced her. We stared at each other. *Her move Oh God, her move*

"I think…you're right. You were right, Pavel. But you didn't even try to discuss it with me…"

"I figured I had a matter of hours. I had 30 cents—enough to risk a dime in a pay phone, and carfare home. So I placed a Person-to-Person call I couldn't pay for and yelled into the phone to tell you I had called. The Chock Full O'Nuts on 40th and 6th thought it had one nut too many."

"That was you? The yelling, my roommate told me…I thought it was my father. I didn't go near a phone for days. But…you could have visited. You could have come later. With Parker. We could have talked this over."

"Sure, travel with a known off-campus agitator. I didn't know who, if anyone, could be watching us, watching Parker, watching you, and who your father might be connected with. If only by rumor. I never spotted anyone, but…this professor, he's a historian and ex-OSS, knew about your father investigating where Dickie went, kept warning me to be careful, and frankly scared the hell out of me. And he was right. COINTELPRO; the FBI and CIA were watching us activists. Still are, probably. We would have had to be perfect. He would only have to catch us once."

"You could have communicated through Parker."

"We did communicate, sort of, through Parker. Look in the top pocket of the lab jacket."

She unfolded the worn, faded Wellsmith postcard. "You carry this around?"

"For luck. Close to my heart, yes? Crazy. Dumb."

"You are a romantic."

"When it's time. An amulet. I thought it would bring you to me eventually. Magically. There was no other way. Seems to have worked.

I thought you knew. I thought you understood the signal, what I was doing. I would come for you when we wouldn't have to worry about your father anymore, or you would come for me. I had a fantasy of crashing your commencement."

"That's a picture."

"On horseback."

She laughed. "What stopped you?"

"I was on Pediatrics. Plus I don't know how to drive a horse. Plus I thought your family would be there. Your mother wasn't any too happy with me when she came to pick up Dickie's stuff. I expected to see you at Freshman orientation…When you didn't show up it damn near killed me. I went up to the house to find you. I thought you'd have contacted me by then, you'd graduated. I was prepared to beat it out of them. The house was empty, the boat was gone, even the bartender at the yacht club didn't know where you all went, and your father's name was gone from his office's directory. End of trail. I tried the alumnae office at Wellsmith. They threw me out. You would have to come for me. And you didn't… But about Parker, to tell the truth I didn't completely trust him at the start, in '67. And anyway he would tell someone who would tell someone. I didn't know you people well enough to know who I could trust. In Brooklyn I know; at Nott, not."

" 'You people'. Sometimes I think you don't know anything but books and chess and Brooklyn."

"I know the Bronx. That's Brooklyn with hills." *And I know that I love you* "I didn't know what he'd really do about you and me if we ever really…"

"Really what?"

"Started going together. He was vicious, Ali. Not just angry; cold, calculating, intimidating, vicious. And bat-shit crazy. He accused me of turning an Acheson over to the Soviets."

"He was pretty deep into right-wing politics about then."

"Yeah, no shit. Parker told me he was drinking pretty heavily, did you know that?"

"Of course I know that. I told Parker."

"So I figured, the best thing for the moment was to cut contact with the Achesons. All of you. Icarus, me, flying too close to the sun. Better for you, too, at least until you graduated. I told you, he threatened to stop paying your tuition and take you out of school on the spot if I ever went near you. I had no doubt—I have no doubt—that he could have pulled you out of school. Dickie told me he threatened him the same way. You told me yourself, he didn't care about you. And the boat, the phone, the library card, the car. For God's sake, Riley. I couldn't be the reason for you losing your shot at living in the library. How long would you care for me then? And, this was scary. He talked about getting my scholarship revoked; that would have tossed me out of Nott and made me draft bait. He threatened my mother's job, Ali. He talked about moving a stolen car across state lines. Across an international border. I didn't know what lengths he'd go to, to keep his daughter from...going with a Jew. This Jew, anyway."

" 'Going with'?"

"Give me a break; I'm a little concussed. I wondered what it would be like waking up with you every day, having conversations like that...it was 1967, Ali. People didn't just move in together then, remember? Jesus, I had fantasies of marrying you, moving in with my mother and grandmother, we could go to Brooklyn College, but I couldn't transfer all my credits and finish in four years; again, draft bait."

"There's another picture."

"Yeah, isn't it? I was nineteen, I said, couldn't protect you. That's how I thought of it."

"You wanted to help, but you didn't know how."

"What? Oh." I smiled, looked away. "Yeah. But also, I wanted you desperately. I sent back the letter. Figured he'd find out. Maybe back him off. Figured you'd understand the signal. Then the heartache started."

She laid a hand on my arm. "I remember the kiss. Whenever I was lonely I thought of that day. You said, *no matter what.* I should have flunked that exam. Couldn't concentrate."

Silence. A kiss is just a kiss

"...Did...Did you ever think I had turned you in? Or said something that..."

"It crossed my mind. But no, I couldn't think that."

"Why?"

"Why? *Because I couldn't see you ever doing that. No good reason. Not a matter of Reason. Because I thought you loved me.* I thought later, a thousand times, of calling you, catching a ride over, telling you about it. But I thought there was a chance you wouldn't believe it. Believe me. He said he was going to tell you to stay the hell away from me, but I knew he wouldn't tell you all the rest. As it is, that shrewd, treacherous bastard never told you anything. Let you think I'd just dumped you. Very effective, so much better than telling you to keep away from me. Why dirty his hands? Then if I had come over later you'd never have believed me. Maybe thought he'd given me money..."

"There was no money. And I know you. Alice figured..."

"I had no evidence. He's your father. Prize bastard but famous lawyer."

"Of Oldwasp, Irish, Jew, Jew And Jew."

"Yeah. Yes. OK. Yes. Ali, again, we were eighteen, nineteen. We were in college. What were we going to do? Confront him? Go to his office and tell him to fuck himself? Run away? Join Dickie? He vanished. He's underground. Or he's in an ashram someplace. Where does that leave my mother? Or us? And that's if you did believe me, which I thought maybe you wouldn't. I said, I had no evidence."

"So why should I believe you now?"

"Do you?"

"Sure I do. It explains why he brought the Dresden piece home. After the separation I went to see my mother, saw it there. She never knew why; never explained that. You just did. But I would have believed you anyway. Why would I not? How could I not, for all the reasons you just went over. It all sounds just like him. I trust you, Paulie. Far more than I would ever trust him. There has to be some other reason."

"There is. Was. I was afraid of him, sure. But I was also afraid of you. And of myself. You would have wanted to defy him…"

"That's for sure."

"…and so would I. So did I, and a word from you and I would have. It was too big a risk, bigger than an ice storm. Not just to you, or us, but to everybody. Make no mistake, we would have tried, we would have been that stupid, that immature, and we would have lost, and I was scared. My mother and grandmother had been through enough. I was all they had."

"He thought you were after my money. Some joke. 'You aren't the first'. Hell no. He was. There isn't any money. Wasn't any. My trust fund? He was the trustee, and he drained it. Dickie's too. Our trust funds are that damned boat. That's why Dickie needed the rallye money. And money from me. When he asked Mother for the keys to the safe deposit box to get his passport, and incidentally mine, what he was really after was the MG title papers. She told him there were two boxes and she didn't know which one it was in and gave him both keys. The first box he opened had the MG papers but he was curious—why two boxes?—so he checked the other one. He found the trust fund documents. The funds stood at about zero."

"Jesus."

"Yes, Jesus. Dickie didn't tell me until November of '66. He didn't want to discourage me from going to Paris."

591

"I wish he had."

"Yes, well, he had to tell me then because I wrote him that I was going to surprise you with a ticket, for Christmas."

"You never told me. That's why the gap in the letters from Paris. I thought you didn't write because you were mad at me…"

"I know what you thought. He didn't want you to know because he was afraid of our getting serious and about me tapping the fund for med school because it would have been discovered that there was no fund. He knew I'd blow up. Father would have been criminally liable. And Dickie didn't want for things to blow up right then. But I didn't want another penny from them. It would have been years of litigation, my aunt said, and in the end there was no money. I just wanted to be free of him, and anyway it was all unnecessary…"

Dickie you bastard That's why that crap about only a friend "So we run away. And we support your extravagant spending, how?"

"My…"

"After Dickie left. Your reputation was all over the Little Ivy League, and for all I know the Ivy League too. You were famous, Ali. You had this secret life. You were never at school on weekends, or almost never. And I think it saved my ass at school, and maybe Dickie's."

"How's that?"

"Michael said to your father he could investigate Dickie's disappearance without my information. Evidently he did, and in the process of this supposedly secret inquiry managed to raise the question of whether Dickie and I and a favorite professor—the one who kept warning me to be careful—were gay. I think Dickie is cleared of that one by his old prep school buddies and a couple of Slidell and Miss Porter's girls. Only one thing saved me: a legendary Wellsmith beauty who people saw me drive off with for a day, and kept asking after me. Parker told me."

"I'm glad for you. But did you ever wonder how I lived that fabulously extravagant life and still aced Organic Chem and Physics and got into med school?"

"Can't say I did. I was trying not to think about you at all. And failing completely."

"So Parker told me."

"A day didn't pass that I didn't think of you. You're bright enough to do well and still…But Jesus, ski trips, parties in Boston, New Haven, I mean, you were known to vanish for whole weekends. There was this story of you passing out at a piano at a Yale frat party and sounding a chord when your head hit the keys … then I didn't know if I loved you or hated you. Loved what you had been, hated what you'd become, and I thought you knew about his threats, and you kept writing, I thought doesn't she care what danger she's putting us all in? I was so angry at you, keeping on sending those letters he would have to know about, how could she know and care so little, keep exposing us all to the risk of this crazy man; it fit the picture."

"So that's how you thought of me. Think of me. It makes a kind of sense, if you thought all along that I knew, that he had told me to stay away from you."

"Not today, Ali. It doesn't fit the person I've gotten to know today."

"Maybe it does." She touched the bandage on my cheek. "I'm starting to see you may have been sort of right. I mean about me. And to do what you did. You're right, I would have wanted to take him on, no matter what. And I could have dragged you into it, Ivanhoe, you wouldn't have said no. The boy that drove a stupid car over mountain roads in an ice storm wouldn't have shrunk from that."

"No. I wouldn't have, because…"

"You really were thinking with your dick."

"It functioned more or less as a compass that night."

She grinned. "But you took a hell of a risk, sending back the letter."

593

"It was like on the boat. I thought he'd told you, I didn't know I was running any risk. I would never have done it if I'd known there was that risk."

"If Alice hadn't been there we might have lost each other. She said never, ever just throw away what you felt at that bus station. It never occurred to you that he didn't tell me? Wouldn't tell me? Would leave me to think you'd dumped me?"

"It didn't; I counted on how much he loved to humiliate you, order you around. I figured he couldn't resist the chance to tell you, bully you again, the son of a bitch. As for risk, I figured him telling you to stay away from me was as good as an engagement."

"Funny."

"And who exactly is Alice?"

"Dickie never told you?"

"No. You never did either."

"Alice is part of what you didn't know and don't know yet. Look. I didn't know what was going on with you. But I had a deal with Dickie, and here's how it worked. I did one spending spree with my mother at Bergdorf's, one time. Stocked up. I pretended to wreck the car. More than once. Those scratches you put in it helped. Had the garage fake bills. I told her I was in therapy, got her to send money for that too. I wrung my mother for money. Then I wore the stuff practically out, all the time begging more money. Let the word spread that I was a real fashion plate, a social butterfly. Going for my MRS. What they wanted me to be. My father probably bought it because he thought he'd broken us up. Huh. Anyway…go to one frat party at Yale, one at Amherst, one at Williams. Get invited again, tell the Amherst guy I was at Yale, the Yale guy I was at Williams, the Willimas guy I was at Amherst. So sorry. What I was really doing? Studying my ass off and sending the money to Dickie. Post Restante, American Express offices, wherever. He warned me my mail would be watched, so you were right

594

about that; he sent contact addresses through an old girlfriend, I think Bina. All of which you would have known, been in on, if you'd stayed in touch. *And I don't know what I'm going to have to do to help...And what I'm going to have to do now* And you would have known where I was all those weekends. I was at my aunt Alice's. I didn't have time for anything else. My advisors kept telling me I'd have to be twice as good as the guys to get into med school. And oh yeah, that's a true story about the piano—only, one, it was at the lounge at my House at Wellsmith, and two, I didn't pass out, I fell asleep when I was trying to pull an all-nighter before an Organic exam. Oh, and the trip to Hartford helped me too. The whole campus knew I ditched school weeks after I got back from Paris, the day before a big exam to go off with this Frenchman who gave me his car."

"What Frenchman..."

"The beret, idiot."

I didn't know what to say. "I said I was a coward."

"What did you think, Paul, that in my despair I had turned to drink?

"Your brother did, for a while..."

"I'm not him."

"I had a pretty good view of you people up close, for four years..."

" 'You people'. There's your problem. How is that different from how my father thought of Jews? Stop it. I'd like to know why you would think so little of me."

"I didn't...I didn't think it was happening. When I asked Parker he said you were OK. Yeah, I didn't entirely trust his definition of OK. I just...thought...I was afraid it could happen. Or would. *There was the cowardice* There was this girl at Slidell, Bina's roommate..."

"Bitsy Reade. Bina told me that story, Albert. I'm not Bitsy Reade. Never knew her. I was determined to be a doctor, as determined as you were. You knew that. Nothing was going to stop me, not my father, not even any crap with you. And here I am."

The girl was pretty special but she didn't hold a candle to this woman "You have every right to be angry at me, Ali."

"You're damned right I do. But," she said more softly, "I set it all up, the wild kid I was pretending to be. Dickie never told you the car was going to be a way to funnel money to him?"

"No. Told me you should have it because your father refused you a car when you refused a deb party, same thing you told me. Straightens out the karma. If I'd known, I'd have offered him my share of the rallye money."

"Exactly. That's what he thought you'd do. What did you use it for?"

"Med school expenses. App fees, interviews, microscope, books, lab fees, with what was left plus some summer job money, I bought the VW."

She looked away. "That's why he didn't tell you." Then she said softly, "I would have wanted to take him on. I didn't understand then, about not having money. So. Another Goddamned secret."

"I think maybe Dickie had it all, what my father would have called, compartmentalized."

"Compartmentalized."

"Yeah. Two parts to the operation. My part, getting him to Montreal and getting the car to you. Your part, using the car as one way to rack up plausible reasons for your parents to send extra money. Once you had the car, my necessary role was over, no matter how things turned out between you and me. And what I didn't know I couldn't tell anyone, most particularly your father. It was logical, brilliant, pure Dickie."

"Pure Dickie in not taking into account the cost to the people around him. He used us, Paul. He counted on our loyalty to him, our gratitude. But he didn't entirely trust us. Typical Acheson. Always a plan. Watch out for me, I'm an Acheson too. Why didn't he just apply for a Year Abroad program?"

"He did. He didn't get it. Grades. We were Plan B. And Plan B worked, Ali, it worked great."

"Yes, for Dickie. He's a let-the-chips-fall-where-they-may man. And we were the chips. He's my brother, I love him. But."

"He asked me once if I was serious about you."

"What did you tell him?"

"That if I was, I wanted whatever it was to grow by itself, without any fertilizer from him. I was afraid you'd see that as more family pressure…"

"I wouldn't have seen it that way. Not about you."

"I was afraid to risk it. I wanted it to be between us. I thought that's what you would want. Then we had that day driving together, and I thought, what a schmuck I'd been. Then the meeting with your father, and I thought I was crazy to want to have anything to do with any of you."

"The Achesons have that effect on people. Look, Dickie did know there were some feelings on my side. Serious feelings. He knew I wanted to bring you to Paris."

"Funny, then. We were working on the car, and I'd shown him the letter about that embassy guy. Dickie the Buddhist regarded himself as an expert on women, and he said you were being so open and honest with me you couldn't want to be more than a friend. That's why I got so crazy about the embassy guy. But I reasoned my way out of that one, and he realized at the very end that I loved you, but he thought, I mean he worried, he asked me, and these were among his last words to me, in Montreal, if what I was really in love with was rescuing damsels in distress, I guess because of all the things with your father, and how I drove Bina's drunk roommate home that time… He asked me to think about it, and I did."

"That's pretty astute, for Dickie. Was he right?"

"Honestly? I don't know, if at any point that was part of the attraction. I told him I enjoyed the times with you when there was nothing to do with your father even more. I thought about it, it was separate from how I thought about you, your brains, your wit, your forthrightness… I loved everything about you. Don't tell me it wasn't part of the attraction for you too."

"Sure, at first, but…it was the same for me, Paul."

"It wasn't any part of it after Paris, that I know, that day at Motor Vehicle. I was in love with that girl. It sure isn't part of it now. You aren't in any distress, I mean not fighting with your father, which is what Dickie meant. You're magnificent, Ali. Dickie thought he'd failed you. It was one of the things that set him looking for the Buddha. He told me to do what I could for you. He told me to protect you. And him. He called me Snow Lion. That's the protector of the Buddha."

She reached out and punched my bicep.

"Ow."

"So this was all for my own good? My big brother and my nobly self-sacrificing admirer-from-afar taking care of me? That's what it was, more men knowing what's good for me." But she was thinking. "Dickie couldn't take my father on for himself and me both. So he passed the job on to you. And God bless you, Paul, you seemed to relish it, and not just for me. A hundred years of WASP anti-Semitism, avenged."

"I took on Bob today too. That isn't why I did it."

"I know. But I think that's why you enjoyed it."

"Huh. Maybe. I don't know. I just know it broke my heart to see him treat you that way, see you bullied. Bullying I understand. I couldn't just stand by…"

"That's why it's called the Unconscious. Listen to the psychiatrist. What Dickie never understood, that you did: What I needed was to stand up to the old man *myself.* Unresolved Oedipal issues. Huh, that's more insight than I would credit Dickie with."

"You never saw him in full Buddha mode. I think he would have put it that he wanted to be sure I was in love with a woman, not a Cause. But, your father wasn't symbolic; he was a real bully. He knew how crazy your father could be. He was there, remember, when you took the wheel on the boat...Goldenberg once called Dickie a Conscientious Objector in the Hobbesian struggle."

"A deserter, more like. He says there's talk of starting a school for Tibetan Buddhist studies in Colorado, but I don't know how he'll ever come home."

"So was it all a calculated conspiracy? A brilliant piece of opportunism? Or neither. Think we'll ever get to ask him?"

"He's a draft dodger, Paul. You know that. He can't come back. Think we'll ever be able to go to Dharamsala? After our loans are paid off maybe. Did you ever try to do any of that stuff to my father? Sabotage his office, make trouble for him?"

"No. I really don't know if I could have. I had this instinct, there in his office, that I could probably keep him from hurting me too much, but not from hurting you. And I couldn't live with that, and the best thing to do was pretend there was nothing between us. If he had fucked with your schooling, or mine, I sure would have tried. Sam said I probably could have done a very little. It wasn't important; it was just important for him to believe I could. He seemed to believe his own myths." I started to tell her about the scene in the freshman dorm.

"I know what you meant. Dickie told me that story. The Internationale. So did Parker, when he asked if I thought you'd work with him, and if I thought he could count on you for more than just a few revolutionary songs. I told him about the car and the ice storm. You are no coward, Paulie. When it's a matter of consequences only to yourself, you stand up. When the consequences fall on others you take that into account, you stop and think. That isn't cowardice, Paulie. That's what makes you different from Dickie. And maybe me."

"I'm no saint."

"You're good enough for me. If it hadn't hurt so much I should be thanking you. It worked. He never, not once in those last two years at Wellsmith, threatened to stop my tuition. Not even my allowance. Not even the car. Not once. You thought it was necessary. You thought I knew why you were doing it. But did it ever occur to you that maybe taking me out of school was an empty threat? After I refused a coming out party and ditched the diplomatic corps, Wellsmith was the only place I could meet those wealthy suitors. Did you ever think of that?"

"I didn't credit him with that much sense where you were concerned. He seemed more interested in subjugating you. Or maybe I just didn't want to think about you meeting wealthy suitors."

She grinned.

"Don't make fun. It terrified me. Any suitors. Parker would have told me, and believe me, that would have changed the equation."

"Huh. I should have faked one. Brought you out of your lair."

"It would have, like a shot. You really think he messed with your med school applications?"

"The last lash of the dragon's tail. You stymied him. And we made it, didn't we? You graduated, I'm weeks away. And we're having this conversation. In spite of everything." *In spite of everything*

"Dickie would have said using people is inevitable as long as there is Desire."

"Do you still feel desire, Paul?"

"Oh yes. God yes."

"Me too, Paul."

"Ali, I was so scared the spark had died. That I'd killed it. This morning…"

"Never, Paulie. But we have a lot to work out…"

Silence. *God, we were tired. Were we even still making sense?*

"Shit. This isn't the time or place…"

"It doesn't ever seem to be. Tell me the rest of it."

"I admit it felt great facing down your father, Ali…"

"I wish I'd been there for that."

"…but the best part of it was seeing you again. Falling in love again. But I gave you up, Ali. I'm a coward."

She touched the bandage, touched around my cheek. "You're no coward, Paulie."

"Not that kind. Afraid to trust, maybe."

"You trusted me today. Know where I live, Paulie? A fabulous dorm room. Latest of a long line. I got that room of my own but it's not even a basement apartment."

"Why didn't you sell the car?"

"I need a car. I need *that* car. You practically killed yourself bringing it to me. It's the last thing I had from you. And from Dickie, damn him. And it's the last thing I had from home, after Riley died. I'm squeaking by on a tiny inheritance from my aunt that's not nearly Ginny Woolf's £ 500 a year. It's going to be exhausted soon. I'll need that salary. But I'm free. It was just enough for that. I never took a penny of their money and never will. Uh, did you never think you'd succeeded? That maybe I didn't need protecting? There's something you don't know, that made it all unnecessary…"

What did she mean? "Poor little rich girl, my mother used to call you. 'What ever happened to that poor little rich girl?' she'd say. Meaning why was I not in contact with you. My grandmother told her there was more to you than that. She was a big fan of yours. Told me, too."

"Rich no more, Paulie. House is gone, in the divorce. My father it turns out couldn't cover the settlement without selling the family manse. Title was joint, even though it was my mother's family's place. If he'd kept the Dresden at the office he could maybe have kept that, so I guess you did zing him after all." *Musing upon the king my brother's wreck*

"That's why he wanted you to be a deb? Make a rich marriage? So he could afford to divorce your mother without paying child support? And hide that he'd looted the trust fund?"

"Something like that."

"Ali, I'm sorry."

"He kept the boat."

Silence.

"Where are you interning?"

"I'm not. Straight to a Psych residency."

"So we'll be caught up, both residents. I know you want to study female adolescent development…"

"You *did* read my letters."

"Read them? I still have them. Except the one. Residency where?"

"At Bronx Municipal. I did Peds at Lincoln. One abused girl after another. I did OB at Jacobi. I delivered a fourteen-year-old girl of her second child. I can't turn away from that. I'm not going anywhere, Paulie."

" 'Bad things happening in my family'. I thought that was finding out about us, pulling you out of school."

"No; it was the divorce. The separation, anyway."

"How come Parker never told me about the divorce?"

"The separation. Because I never told him. I never talked about it with anyone. That isn't something you talked about in that world, at that time." She looked away. "It wasn't something I wanted to talk about anyway. Then she moved in with a guy, summer of '68; that blew it wide open. Huge scandal in North Greenwich."

"Talk of the yacht club."

"Exactly. But Parker and I weren't in contact anymore. He wasn't even in contact with his family. I don't know where he went…"

"I do. Chicago. The Haight. Upper West Side. From there I don't know…Ali, I'm not going to lose you again. I have shed blood for you. And your father's out of the picture. *We* are free, Ali."

"Yes, you have shed blood for me. All my fault. It wasn't just myself I was endangering, was it. Or ever was. I'm just beginning to realize that. Tell me, did it ever occur to you that sleeping with me would have been great payback for him too?"

"No. What? No, of course not. You think I would…?"

"No, Paulie, I think you never would."

"Sleep with you?"

She did one of her 'Huh' chuckles. "Not for that reason. Look, this is the longest we've been able to talk. The phone could ring any minute, or I'm going to fall asleep any minute." She reached up and began gathering her hair into a twist, clipping and pinning, so she wouldn't lose time if her beeper went off. We had been leaning forward on the bed; she yoga-style, me with my head hanging. I snapped off the light.

"One last thing," she said. "Did it occur to you, you could have made a bargain with him; tell him where Dickie was going in return for seeing me?"

"Yeah. Sam asked me that one too. How would you have lived with the guy that did that? How would I?"

"Right answer."

"If you had known…?"

"Never. But, the 'compartmentalization'. He didn't trust us, Paul. In case my father tried that."

"I think…he did. He just didn't trust Desire."

603

"Do you?"

I reached over and pulled her to my side. We leaned back, fell against the pillow, my arm around her shoulders. She leaned into me. And we drifted off.

RRRIIINNNGGG

BEEEEEEEEEEEEEP

We were awakened by all hell breaking loose. Every phone in the place was ringing, both our beepers going off. I pulled shoes on, reached for the phone.

"Paulie? It's Vovchok. Run."

We ran, tucking stuff in clumsily as we went. Down to the courtyard, across it, our breath steaming, in the ER entrance, up the stairs. She started gasping as we passed the fifth floor; I pulled her up the last three flights. Very effective arrival: out of breath and barely awake. Marvin was reading the EKG, nurses were charging up the defibrillator cart, Katie was pushing 50 cc amps of Bicarb into the IV.

"Get me an airway," Marvin said, but he didn't need to; I had already flipped the laryngoscope open, Ali had pulled his head back, and I was reaching around for the Ambu bag and tube. Ali whipped out her stethoscope; I squeezed the bag as she listened to his lungs, shook her head.

"Shit." I moved the tube back a touch, squeezed again. This time Ali gave a thumbs up—we had air going to lungs.

"Hit him." I hauled off and pounded his chest once, in the approved motion, hard enough to break ribs.

"Start pumping," I told Ali, and she did. "Katie, bag." She started squeezing the Ambu bag. Nurse Schevchenko began lining up amps of Bicarb; *prevent acidosis.* "What have we got?"

"Damnedest V-tach I ever saw. Anyone ever seen this?" He flashed it in front of me, then Ali and Katie.

"Paul," Ali said, "Take over. Please." I took her place, pumping Mr. Vovchok's chest. *Live, damn it.* "I've seen that. On psychiatry at Louvain. It's called Torsade de Pointes, it's a kind of V-tach. You see it in antidepressant ODs."

"Oh, yeah, right, I read about this. Only thing we can do is keep pumping him, if he goes into V-fib, shock him."

"Can we give propranolol?"

"No," I said, "If we slow the SA node we lose hope of recapture."

"Exactly. Keep pumping. And don't lose track of the Bicarb. How many amps so far?"

"Four, doctor."

"OK, an amp every three minutes. Spell each other pumping every three minutes."

We rotated pumping, bagging, pushing Bicarb.

"This is ridiculous, we're waiting for him to go into V-fib. How long?"

"Ten minutes, doctor."

"OK, we're going to shock him." Marvin took the paddles, checked the lights. "Clear."

We all jumped away from the metal bed. Marvin positioned the electrodes, hit the trigger. Mr. Vovchok's body jumped. We pumped him, bagged him, pushed another amp of Bicarb.

"Still in V-tach. Again. Ready? Clear."

Shock, jump, pump and bag. "No good." We pumped, bagged, pushed Bicarb, waiting for the machine to recharge. "Three's the charm."

It was. Mr. Vovchok's heart settled back into regular sinus rhythm. He started to stir, breathe; I pulled the airway, but I had a bad feeling. We all did, because of the same thought. The Tofranil was still in him, would be for days, it was so slow to metabolize. This could easily happen again. We might need the airway. "Leave the EKG hooked up," Marvin said, "And draw up a few more amps of Bicarb. And two amps of epi on long needles. Might as well be ready. Dr. Acheson, tell me about Torasade de Pointes."

"It means row of bayonets. See what the waves look like? Bayonet blades, in a rank. French Lit minor, two years at Louvain…it can go to V-tach any time."

"Very impressive. On psychiatry. What did they do?"

"Called a cardiology consult."

"Terrific."

There was light in the east. I looked at my watch. "Just going six," I said.

Marvin nodded wearily. "We could call cardio at eight."

"Could we send him up to the Mother House?" Ali asked.

"There isn't much more they could do for him there. He could die in the ambulance. And the Ukrainian translator is here. Natalia, can you stay beyond your shift?"

"I could, Dr. Kornbluth, if I have to. How long?"

"Long enough to translate for the cardiology consult. I'll call at seven, not eight."

"Thank you, doctor."

"No; thank you. Dr. A, you have another patient to check on. See how Mr. Gonzalez is doing and call me." Off she went. "She's hanging in."

"She'll be fine," I said.

"How about you?"

"I'm OK. Better than OK, actually. We've been getting reacquainted."

"You dog, you."

"Well, I shed blood for her."

606

"So you did, and she bandaged you, you dog."

"I'm a dog? What's with you and Katie?"

"Baseball will bring us together. We have seats upstairs for the next month in the extremely far bleachers." He leaned forward, into the aisle. "Katie—watch the EKG."

"If it's alright by you assholes I'd like to sign out of here." Mr. Donnelly made his presence known.

"He's been conscious for an hour," Katie said.

"Been watching you, Red," he said, "Wanna bust out of this dump with me?"

"Mr. Donnelly," I said, "What do you remember of the last 12 hours?"

"I remember I got some business I gotta take care of. I gotta meet a man. Today. This morning."

"Mr. Donnelly, you were admitted to this hospital with a toxic overdose of a very dangerous substance. If you leave this hospital you could become very dead."

"Listen, asshole, if I don't leave this hospital I'll be very dead. Did I hear you say it's 6 o'clock?"

"About. Closer to 6:30 now."

"AM or PM?"

"AM."

"I'm outta here. Get me out of this rig."

"Sorry, no can do; you were a very bad boy last night."

"I'm gonna be a lot worse if you don't let me outta here. I know where to find you."

"Mr. Donnelly, you're threatening me. That gives me two choices. I can call the police, who after last night don't like you very much, or I can have you held for psychiatric observation. Which of those would you prefer?"

Marvin said, "Let me do this. Mr. Donnelly, this fine young doctor just gave you the two choices he faces if you continue to threaten him and anyone else in this hospital. There is a procedure for signing out Against Medical Advice. I suspect you know that. Your move."

"Threaten? Me? I'm sorry, my head must still be spinning a little. Get me what I have to sign."

RRRIIINNNGGG.

"Get that, will you Dr. S?"

"Gonzalez is sitting up ordering breakfast. You'll be happy to know Mrs. Tolliver is still breathing easily."

"Great. Does Gonzalez have orders for today's Librium?"

"Ahhhhh, no; I'll write them and bring the chart for one of you to countersign."

"Right. Donnelly is signing out AMA."

"What? No. I'll be right up."

She blew into the Unit as Donnelly was handed the pen. "Mr. Donnelly, I'm your doctor, and I'd like to speak to you before you do this."

"Listen, doll, I've done all the talking I'm going to do about this."

"You could die if you leave here now."

"And for sure I'll die if I don't. Now get the fuck out of my…please get out of my way and let me go."

"Would you consider coming back and talking to one of our psychiatrists about getting clean?"

"Jesus Christ on a fucking crutch." And he pushed out the Unit door.

We just looked at her.

"What? He's my patient. What are you doing letting him sign out?"

"Letting him?" Marvin said. "He was threatening violence if he didn't. Was afraid of some if he didn't. What do you think he meant by being dead if he didn't leave?"

"I don't know. Needed another fix?"

"No, Doriden doesn't work like that. He's involved in something criminal he had to do, probably drug-related. Probably used some Doriden to get relaxed, and didn't take into account his time in prison lowered his tolerance. He has to meet a man, he said, and is desperate to do it. Whatever consequences there are of signing out are dwarfed for him by the consequences of not making that meeting. What does that tell you?"

"That he's still impaired in his judgment."

"He's oriented, alert, able to inhibit irritation when he has to, is neither weak nor ataxic, and is not obviously incompetent to refuse treatment. He is free to sign out AMA. And may I remind you—he's my patient too."

She thought about this a minute. "Sorry," she said, "I'd just like to have had a chance to talk him around. I don't say it would have come out any different."

"It does you credit. Listen: You aren't going to know everything, love them all, or cure them all. You especially won't cure folly. We don't have a treatment for that. He never really was a patient, just an emergency patch job. He lives to fight another day. Maybe he'll remember some day that somebody cared." Marvin headed for the desk to phone the on-call Cardiology Fellow. "Write a note: patient demanded to leave, was oriented, alert, appropriate, neither weak nor ataxic, signed out AMA."

"More like AMF," I muttererd.

"AMF?" Katie asked.

"Adios Motherfucker."

She laughed. Ali heard, and gave me a hard look. Which was when Mr. Vovchok's monitor went

BEEEEEEEEEEEEEEEEEEEP.

Katie and I were standing on the right side of Mr. Vovchok's bed; Ali was on the left, next to the EKG. She looked at it and dropped it like it was on fire, and faster than I could get the airway in she grabbed the syringe full of epinephrine on an intracardiac needle, found the sweet spot under the fifth rib and rammed it home. She drew back, saw the drop of bright red left ventricular blood, and pushed.

The monitor stopped beeping, came to life, showed slow, steady beats.

Silence. Long silence.

Marvin came around to the EKG, ran the strip through his hands. "Right you were," he said. "He was flatlined. Nice work. Very very nice work, Dr. Acheson. Write a note, nice and neat for the Fellow."

She half staggered over to the desk, as if walking on a cloud. She had revived a dead man, restarted a stopped heart in one quick, unthinking motion. When you do that, it shocks you. You realize how little, how small a gesture, separates life from death. It exhilarates you, and it shakes you, and it shook her. It shook us all.

And it could happen again.

I stopped myself from intruding, tried to look busy. Marvin called the Mother House for the Cardiology Fellow, called the ER to tell them Donnelly had signed out, we had a Unit bed again. Sat by the phone. Ali tried to write her note. She stared blankly. It was time to bring her back from the dead zone, I knew from my own tours there.

"You cheated the Reaper," I said. "You started a stopped heart. It was brilliant, Ali. But the job isn't over till the paperwork is done. Katie, cut that EKG strip, bring over the batch showing the Torsade de Pointes and the flat line segment. Now. Clip the parts just before the run of Torsades, and the segment just after we shocked him back. Write that up, and tape it to the chart, folded up. Then do the same with the segment just before he went flatline, and write that up: 'Administered 2 cc of epinephrine; reverted to RSR'."

She stared at me for just a second, the awe beginning to fade, to be replaced by the bureaucratized routine of Medicine.

"The Cardiac Fellow will find that very useful."

"Right. Should we run a full EKG?"

"Could do. Couldn't hurt. The Fellow will probably run his own."

RRRRRRRRRRIIIIIIIIIIIIINNNNNNNNNGGGGG

"Dr. Seidenberg for you, Dr. Kornbluth."

Marvin took the phone. "Sy? Top of the morning to you. Rise and shine, we have a fascinoma....Yes, I know what time it is, stop whining...OK. 62-year-old white male, speaks only Ukrainian, but we have a translator if you pull some pants on and get your ass here fast enough, maybe an old inferior infarct, but on Tofranil and maybe accidentally OD'd. Keeps having runs of trigeminy, went into the damnedest V-tach on us..."

"Torsade de Pointes," Ali said.

"Torsade de Pointes," Marvin said, nodding at her. "Shocked him out of that, an hour later he goes flatline on us, the world's best subintern shoves epinephrine into his pump and he's in RSR but I don't know for how long...Yes he's lucky, but I think his parents were married...Sure, we'll be here." He put down the phone. "Good man, Sy. He's interested. What time is it? Where's our replacements?"

611

A good question. We were pretty much done.

"Only a little after seven," I said. "How about we go check the floor, you holler if we have to run another arrest."

Mr. Gonzalez was now awake, no longer tremulous, no longer delirious. I had my own listen to Mamie, let Katie listen; Mamie was still breathing. What her electrolytes would show, we'd see. Mr. Gordon was ready to go. Mrs. Goldstein wanted to talk. She was feeling well enough to go home, she said; I told her to sit tight, let us monitor the numbers and her blood pressure. At mention of blood pressure she settled back on the bed; this was the only thing more sacred than bowel movements. That left Miss Fascelli.

"Good morning Miss Fascelli," I said, "How are we this fine morning?"

"I'm pretty good; you look like you haven't slept."

"I haven't, not much, but I get the rest of the day off. You got the new insulin dose this morning; some doctors that are awake will use the needle in your foot to test your sugar like we did yesterday. If it's OK they get to take it out and you get to go home."

"Where's Dr. Fast-talker?"

"Up watching the ICU. He had a busy night. I'll tell him hello from you."

"Ah, he's too young for me anyway."

"You take care," I said, "I'd rather run into you on the Concourse than here."

"Dr. Seitz," she said, "Go get something to eat. Some coffee. You look like hell."

"I'll do that, Miss Fascelli, as soon as my relief shows up."

"She a human being now?" Ali asked.

"Yeah." I said. *She had restarted more than one heart*

When we went back upstairs our relief had shown up, and so had Seidenberg. He was getting a history from Mr. Vovchok, with Natalia's help. I signed out to Mickey Solowitz, Ali signed out to a classmate of hers I didn't know, stressing the Librium withdrawal. The Third Year was late. I made sure Mickey would get Mrs. Goldstein's Dig level and Miss Fascelli's Glucose Tolerance Test. "She'll kill you and eat you if you don't," I said. "Also watch Mr. Molitor. He hasn't told us everything he should have; no sphincter tone, we sent a VDRL—might not hurt to have Cardio have a look at him too, as long as he's here." I planted this idea on Marvin as he signed out to Charlie Gilbert.

"Can wait till Monday, we'll have more labs, but yeah, his option."

"You guys had some night," Charlie said. And, quietly, but not quietly enough, "Is that the legendary Lish the Dish you spent it with?" *Incoming Hit the deck*

"Alicia Acheson," she said.

Charlie flushed, said, "Sorry, Dr. Acheson."

"Make it up to me," she said. "Take care of my patients."

"Will do," Charlie said.

She smiled, pushed the glasses up her nose. "Call me Ali," she said. *Nicely played*

"It's all yours," Marvin said, "And remember, and this is key, Bodaceous Bob will be here covering Gendleman."

"Shit. That's his car under the portico, isn't it."

"Affirmative. We might have offered to help move the crap off it, except that he's such a complete and total douche bag. Good luck. Time to go, children. Restoratives, coffee, and we owe Katie breakfast." This meant the cafeteria again; we were blood-spattered, noisome, and none too steady on our feet. Local coffee shops wouldn't seat us. "When was the last time anyone took a leak?" Marvin asked. "Thought so. Kidney rounds." We hit the head.

"Paul, I was thinking of asking a favor. Not sure how this is going to work out. I wondered if, if things do work out...I owe Katie dinner, you could get a ride with Ali and if I could maybe borrow Hitler's Revenge?"

"Sure. If things go that way."

The eggs swam in something that looked like it came out of a tugboat's bilges. Orange juice looked OK, coffee passable—simply a caffeine delivery system. It looked wonderful. Toast can't be ruined. I pulled in a stack, slathered on butter. Ali was still slightly dazed. Nobody spoke; adrenalin was running down, hadn't yet been replaced by caffeine's effects. We ate. Started to revive. Around us silverware clanked, plates and trays banged and crashed. Suddenly Seidenberg was standing there.

"You people look like homemade shit."

"Feel like it too," Marvin said, "Pull up a chair."

"You saved a life tonight, young lady."

"Thank you," they both said.

"Sy, this is Dr. Acheson, this is Dr. McCulloch, and they both earned kudos."

"There's enough credit to go around. First off, I think you're right, he's getting a cardiotoxic effect from the Tofranil." He pulled out a length of EKG. "See this? Look how long the ST and T segments are. He isn't repolarizing fast enough to be ready for the next beat, throws him into V-tach, or he flatlines. I pulled my pharm book; there's a vague reference. But if you slow the beat, you get escape rhythms. Damned if you do, damned if you don't. I think we'd better get him up to the Mount of Flowers; we can watch him better."

"What about the language problem?" Ali asked.

"We can get a translator from this Tolstoya Funt, the nurse says. She says he'll be special to them."

"He will," I said. "Fought Hitler, fought Stalin, fought Hitler again—he's a hero of Ukrainian liberation. A one-man tribute to the fucked up politics of the twentieth century."

"Who isn't? I'll take your word for it. Sounds crazy, but I assume this has something to do with the missing fingers."

"It does." I was too tired to explain.

"Good. Dr. Acheson, we'll take good care of your patient."

"Give us some follow-up, will you Sy?"

"Will do, Marv."

"Sorry to call so early."

"No, that's OK. Go clean yourselves up. I'll see Molitor tomorrow—we'll have more numbers."

Marvin broke the next silence. "He's right, you know. There's more than enough credit to go around. Katie, you spotted the trigeminy. We wouldn't have seen it if you hadn't bird-dogged the EKG. Paul, we'd never have gotten a history if you hadn't figured out the language from his amputations. And Ali, well, where do we start? That was some move, getting that adrenalin into him."

"I don't know how I did that. Dumb luck, it felt like."

"And you recognized the weird arrythmia pattern."

"More dumb luck."

"No, Edison said chance favors the prepared mind."

"My mind wasn't prepared. Paul prepared it. He showed me how to do a pleural tap, so I knew how to put a needle into a chest. And he showed me how to make information out of physical findings."

"Paul also knew better than to push propranolol."

"You saved his life," I said. "You listened to all of it, and you made the right decisions, Marvin. He would never have lived to get the epi if he hadn't survived the V-tach, and he wouldn't have been in the Unit to survive it if you hadn't paid attention to the seriousness of the arrythmia."

"Mr. Donnelly saved his life." Katie said. "He pulled you all away so that Ali was in just the right position to hit him with the intracardiac epi."

615

"Bodaceous Bob saved his life," Ali said, "He admitted him as a social admission."

"Natalia Shevchenko and Wanda Kaslowska saved his life," I said. "They…"

"We all saved his life, " Marvin said. "Everything that led up to that moment saved his life. Everything we did, everything we know. You know what the Talmud says? 'He who saves a life, saves the world entire.' We have saved the world entire. *She had restarted more than one heart* Not a bad night's work. And you know what? We get to do it all over again in 24 hours. Katie? You awake?"

"Sort of. Is it always like this?"

"No. Sometimes it's even worse. Seriously? Stuff like this happens all the time, but usually not all in the same day. Usually we get to see some of a ball game. I promised you dinner. Will you take me up on it?"

"You mean Monday?"

"No. Today. Tonight."

She considered this.

"It was a bet. You won. You can say no, but I'll only keep asking. It's a debt of honor."

"Sure. What the hell. Yes, actually. I need to get home and get cleaned up, though."

"Dr. Acheson. Can you give your old friend a ride so he can lend me his car?"

"I suppose. If he would like a ride."

"I would like a ride, Ali."

"Sure."

She had hung the jacket over the back of the chair; I fumbled the keys out, threw them to Marvin. And we were alone, without obligation to beepers or phones. I got us more coffee.

"I feel like we cheated God," she said, "And I don't think I even believe in a God. Cheated the Universe, maybe."

"The Universe doesn't care."

"But I do."

"Exactly. Seems like that's an obligation of consciousness. To recognize the suffering the Universe ignores. Do something about it."

"What if I hadn't been there?"

"But you were."

"What if I had missed?"

"But you didn't."

"What if I had?"

"Scary, isn't it. One day you will. I have."

"What did that feel like?"

I looked away. "It felt like shit. One time I nailed one as perfectly as you did today. It was at the Mother House, it was 7 AM, I was just coming in, took a shortcut through Surgery, and they called a Code twenty feet from where I was. I run in, one intern is pumping, nurse is bagging, that's it. Nobody else there. The EKG shows flat line, I did what you did, Boom, heart starts beating. Felt top of the world. Patient arrested again six hours later and died."

"We play this game with death. Like in the Bergman flick."

" 'The Seventh Seal'. No. We're playing for other people's lives. Always."

She caught the note in my voice. "Meaning what?" she said. "Tell me."

"You sure? This is about the worst thing I ever did. Worse even than sending back the letter to you. What gave me the damned strength, if that was what it was, to do that."

"Tell me."

"It was in late February of '64. I was coming home from school, down Brighton Beach Avenue, from a block away I saw my father

617

coming down the el stairs. He started to fall, caught himself. I ran to him, a full block, I thought he'd slipped on an icy patch, but when I got there he couldn't breathe. I got an arm under his shoulders, I was almost as tall as I am now, I had to lean over, I told him to leave the books, we'd come back for them, but I ended up hoisting the briefcase too. If I hadn't done that…I don't know. I got him to the house, he took a Nitro, thought he could get up the three flights. Insisted on it, after a rest. I helped him up the stairs. He said he felt better, went into the University room. I started to boil some water for tea for him. I heard a crash…"

"Oh, Paul, no."

"He was dead when I reached him. I could see he wasn't breathing, his eyes were staring open, like he'd just seen something great…that he would never tell anyone." I started to cry. "If it happened now I could save him. If I knew then what I know now, I could have saved him. Tried to, anyway."

"That's why you want to be a cardiologist."

"I know. It's completely neurotic."

"No it isn't. Secondary autonomy. It means something you start doing for neurotic reasons becomes gratifying for itself, for good reasons, and you'll be a good cardiologist, Paulie. Freud was wrong, or incomplete. He should have said, to love, to work, and to tolerate loss."

"Every time I save a life, it's like I've saved him, but I haven't, so it doesn't last and I have to do it again…"

"And pretty soon you've saved a lot of lives. A lot of worlds. I know…"

"I called my grandmother. I should have done that first thing. Told her I'd found him like that. My grandmother came right over, took charge. Called an ambulance, called police, all the things you do. We had to meet my mother at the front door. That was maybe the worst. We had to tell her. She let out a scream, dropped her pocketbook and

618

book bag, God, always the books…My grandmother took charge of her too. She'd lost a husband too, but that husband was my mother's father, you see? It was a repeat for both of them. They cried together."

"Did you?"

"Somebody had to make tea. Call my mother's school, tell them to get a substitute teacher. Call the funeral home…"

"It wasn't me you didn't trust all those years ago, it was the Universe. Paul. Something I learned in psychotherapy. Something bad happens, and you think it's your fault. It isn't, but you have a choice. You can believe everything is under your control, so if anything goes wrong it's your fault, and you cling to that idea because you think if you caused it you can fix it. Or you can give up that relatively comforting idea and realize that things aren't under your control."

"We need the fantasy of control so we can do this job."

"But not when we're off the clock."

"I thought you said you were never really in therapy, that about prep school, nothing was wrong."

"With that. There was plenty else wrong."

"You haven't told me everything."

"Not yet."

Neither had I "That wasn't the worst thing. None of that was the worst thing."

"What was?"

"The worst thing I did was I went to Nott College. I took the scholarship, instead of going to BC and staying home with my mother."

"She had your grandmother."

"That she did. My grandmother moved in with her. And they took me to the train and I got on the train and left. His life insurance paid what the scholarship didn't, at first. That's it. That's the worst thing I did as a child. The worst thing I did as an adult, you know. I did it to you."

"You're a good man, Paulie. A mensch. He taught you well. To do what's necessary. It's what he wanted for you. It's what they wanted for you."

"The look on your face says maybe he taught me too well."

She just shook her head.

"When they put me on the train my grandmother said '*Gay gesunt*'."

"Go in health. You lived with this all four years at Nott?"

"Plus… I was angry. At him. For not taking care of himself. For being older. For being sick. For scaring my mother. For scaring me. At myself, for feeling those things. At the world, for scaring him…I looked into transferring to BC. You know about that."

"I want to help but I don't know how."

"You are helping. This was help. There's no one else I can ever tell." I blew my nose on a napkin. "It felt like he had been holding my hand, and he let go. Like a piece fell out of the world. The world was whole, and then it wasn't."

"So we play with death."

"We don't beat death. We stall the fucker. We play with him. Smooth his rough edges. Sometimes that's enough. Sometimes not."

"Some day it will be us."

"Yup. There we'll be in the nursing home, in wheelchairs, IV in one arm, catheter bag hanging off the other end, over the PA system comes the Stones. *I can't get no…Satisfaction…*"

"It could happen tomorrow. Or today."

"Could be. You just finding this out?"

"No." She looked away now. "I'm just feeling it. Just letting it in. The possibility of it. There's…No. Not now. When I was on Peds I decided I didn't ever want to have kids. To take the risk, I mean."

"Then you did OB and changed your mind."

She laughed. "I did."

"Then you did Psych and thought you were crazy."

"I did. I had reason. Didn't you ever think I was crazy?"

"It occurred to me, that possibility."

"Not funny Paulie. I was a teen runaway, did you ever think about that? If I hadn't had a rich family, I could have been one of those girls at Lincoln, on the streets. But I had a rich aunt. Then three years of acting. Talk about games. It was all an act. The party girl. Go to Killington to ski once, spend the other times talking to Parker—about you, mostly. Refuse other invitations or beg off at the last minute, saying I had another engagement, go to one frat party at Yale, do the same thing, let everyone think I was at another party somewhere else, make sure word got back to my parents I was working that hard on my MRS. You know what? My mother wanted me taken care of as much as he did. She never took the med school ambition seriously. All the time I was at my aunt's in Danbury. All so easy; people are ready to believe anything about you if you're a stereotype."

"I also thought…your mother came to get Dickie's stuff, and she was pretty broken up. I also thought, maybe you were, I don't know, remorseful, and you were going along with the family program out of remorse, or sacrifice, or pity…"

"She forfeited that consideration, Paulie; more of what you don't know. Paul: Here I am. It's a long story…"

"I have time. All day, if you want."

She shook out her hair. "I have to go home. You're giving me that 'You're so beautiful' look again, but look closely, Paul; I have blood and urine all over me and I smell like a corpse."

"So do I. It's in a noble cause. You've never been more beautiful to me than you are now. Come to my place. Come home with me." I think it suddenly hit both of us, how many we had lost, *and I didn't know the whole story yet.* "I think I understand you better," I said. *I had not thought death had undone so many* "We've both had so many losses, let's not lose each other again. Keep talking. Come home with me."

621

"Whoa, why would I…" She smiled. "Because you shed blood for me, I'll just come home with you?"

"No. Better reason. I have a bathtub."

"At the Commune? No thanks."

"No longer at that address."

"Really? Where do you live now?"

"At the Mother House's apartment building. The Mountain of Flowers' very own real estate empire."

"The one you can take call from?"

"The very one. I can exchange our soiled whites, we can whip up a little lunch. We can keep talking."

"A bathtub," she said. The dorm didn't have anything but showers. And an empty room. She looked away. "There's this story about de Beauvoir. She was visiting Nelson Algren in New York. They were lovers. He didn't have a bathtub, so he took her over to a friend's place, who had a bathtub…" We picked up her soiled lab coat; she offered me my jacket back.

"Keep it for now," I said.

She flipped me the keys. "This time you drive. You know where we're going."

The MG coughed, sleek and unreliable as ever. But it started up and purred. "Like a kitten," I said. *Old friend from another Sunday*

"I tune it myself. It sticks in second."

"Yeah? Sweet. Sticks in second?"

"Yes. And the wipers are still worthless."

"Synchros are worn. We gave the gearbox quite a workout." I reached down and turned off my beeper. Reached over and turned off hers. "Free at last."

Bob's car was still buried. The gate went up, and we were off the hospital grounds, back in the land of the living. Up Gerard, to Jerome Avenue, and north under the elevated. Little traffic on a Sunday morning. At Fordham Road I pulled over so she could lean out the window to pick up a Sunday Times.

PRESIDENT PLANS NEW IMPORT FEES ON 'GAS' AND OIL...BOYCOTT OF MEAT ENDS WITH A CALL FOR NEW PROTESTS... NIXON SENDS HAIG ON INDOCHINA TRIP AS OUTLOOK DIMS; *Won't Speculate on Trip... COLSON REPORTED PASSING LIE TEST Takes Credit For 'Leak' A 'Grubby Business'* ... 1969 CAHILL FUNDS ARE INVESTIGATED... *Peace Agency Helicopter Believed Down in Vietnam; Report Disputed Heavy Shelling in Delta...3 KILLED IN CORONA AS PARAPET FALLS; Roof Structure on 8 Stores Collapses Onto Street... Wagner and Others Cited in $30-Million Fraud...*Men Report Seeing Edge of the Universe; *A Wall to Vision... Black P. O. W. Is an Echo of 1966*

The shadows of the el flickered over the grimy windshield; trains thundered overhead. Right on Gun Hill Road, along the north side of the Mother House, down Wayne, into the garage. She pulled her pocketbook out from its hiding place under the seat.

"It's just a studio," I said, unlocking the door.

"Jesus, Paulie, you have all the books." She found the Kafka immediately.

"Welcome to the University of Brighton Beach, Gun Hill Campus. Turns out it's portable."

"I wonder what color the walls are."

"Don't remember. Saves on paint. Christ, I'm tired."

"You have things in the fridge."

"I do, yes."

"Nice stereo. KLH 6's?"

"Graduation present to myself."

"Your father's chess set?" She picked up a knight, put it back down.

623

"For me, said my mother."

"And there is a bathtub…it could use a scrub."

"My bathtub is your bathtub. Look, here's an idea. I can shower, which will clean out the tub—I'll scrub it. Then you take a bath while I run over and exchange the whites."

"Any bath salts?"

"No. Sorry."

"No other women here, then."

"None that needed bath salts. Actually, none Ali. I've lived like a damned monk…"

"I know. From Parker. That you didn't dump me for some Slidee. It was another way I knew something had happened. How about a robe?"

"That, I should have." I went to find it. "Old and comfy."

"Mmmm. Go shower. And I can help scrub the tub. Men can't keep clean."

I closed the bathroom door, emptied the pockets, stripped off the tunic and pants, socks and underwear. I pulled out a scrub brush, a shampoo bottle, took a leak, started the shower, let it warm up. Tried not to think, just to shower off, wash my hair. *I can tune it myself who taught you, the rude mechanicals stop that shit that is at an end you just met this beautiful woman she's a very competent physician there was this girl you once knew she was spectacular but she doesn't hold a candle to this woman you just met the truth is you don't deserve her the reason you aren't good separately is you think too much Remember the forest* I dried off with the second best towel, rubbed my hair, wrapped the towel around my waist. Shaved while the hair dried, carefully avoiding the butterfly. Took a deep breath. Opened the door. Steam everywhere. She had put on the robe; the soiled whites lay in a heap. We took turns scrubbing the tub, me hoping the robe would part, if only for a moment. She looked at me, too.

"Looking good, Paulie. Lean and mean."

"Have a soak." I said.

"The main challenge will be not falling asleep in the tub."

"Want some music?"

She had looked over the records. "Something not classical or Kurt Weill."

"I have Dylan, Beatles, Stones, Joni Mitchell, Judy Collins, Crosby Stills…"

"Crosby Stills."

I put it on the turntable, and she started running her bath. I pulled out a sweatshirt and jeans, a pair of work boots. Pinned on my name tag. Pulled the towel across my hair one more time. My mother believed colds and pneumonia came from going out with wet hair.

"Hey," I said, "I'm going."

"What?"

Susanna and the Elders

I opened the door enough and repeated it.

"Leave it open a little," she said, "So I can hear the music better."

> *Will you come see me*
> *Sunday in the afternoon…*
> *What've you got to loo…ooo…oose*

I gathered up the whites and headed across the street, into the oldest part of the complex, the early-century red brick with classic portico and cupola. Skyways led at crazy angles to the huge later additions in M.C. Escher-like connections of upper to lower floors; tunnels led across streets and service alleys, gated and fenced. On a Sunday at 9:30 it was just waking up, although its minions in white had been toiling away since 7:00. Past the auditorium and cafeteria, stairway to ER and ICU/CCU, and side corridor to Pulmonary. *You blew this twice before*

625

Just before the corridor jogged right to the new main entrance an unmarked staircase led down to the laundry.

> *Dear Playboy Advisor,*
> *The goddess of my dreams is currently naked in my bathtub. I have fantasized this moment for most of my adult life. What should be my next move?*
> Anxious To Get This Right
> *Bronx, NY*

> *Dear Anxious,*
> *If you don't know the next move, the Advisor cannot help you. Hint: Do you have Protection?*

Corridor full of wheeled canvas hoppers.

> *Dear Abby,*
> *I recently re-contacted a woman who has been the Girl of My Dreams for seven years. She gives every indication of being still interested. I cannot ignore the doubts and hesitations that caused me to lose her, but feel sure these factors are now irrelevant. How can I banish my doubts and reassure her of my unconditional affection?*
> Ardent but Anxious
> *Bronx, NY*

> *Dear Ardent,*
> *Are you more anxious than ardent, or the other way around? Prudence is important, but some doubts are neurotic. You might want to seek professional advice.*

626

One of Hades' underlings took the two soiled sets of whites, to the tune of high-pressure steam and spinning dryers, passed over new ones.

New England Journal of Medicine
To the Editor

It is well known that heart issues frequently require careful physical examination. Auscultation is of course crucial. Palpation of peripheral areas yields information on pulse strength, but when all this information is in, and there is still no diagnosis, how may one proceed?
Paul Seitz, M.D.
Bronx, NY

Dr. Seitz,

The physical examination is important, of course, but if this does not lead to a correct diagnosis, perhaps the history is incomplete.

A toothbrush. She'd need a toothbrush. Hospital gift shop wasn't open yet. I popped in to Admissions, looked for a friendly face.

"Can I help you, doctor?"

"I hope so. A friend just arrived unexpectedly, needs to crash for a day or two. He could use a toothbrush. I wondered if maybe you could let me have one of those patient welcome kits…" *Ever the resourceful prevaricator But: All's Fair…*

"I don't see why not—here you go."

Who knew; maybe the comb, kidney dish and nail scissors would come in handy too. I passed the bronze bust *The model farm at Kinnereth on the lakeshore of Tiberias Can become ideal winter sanatorium* of the hospital's namesake, a turn-of-the-century British philanthropist who, according to legend, never gave the hospital a penny. The tip of the nose gleamed from being rubbed by generations of house officers for luck on their Board exams, licensing exams, presentations at Grand Rounds, or anything else. I paused to rub the nose. Out the door on to Gun Hill Road.

Protection. I made a sprint for the drug store at the corner of Jerome. A train sped overhead, festooned with graffiti. In those days you had to ask. "Three-pack of lubricated Trojans." The bored pharmacist handed it over without a glance. OK. Ready for anything.

Be prepared
That's the Boy Scout marching song,
Be prepared

Another sprint up Gun Hill.

Helplessly hoping her harlequin hovers
Nearby
Awaiting a word

She'd flipped the record. She came out of the bathroom, hair wrapped in the third best towel, the best towel wrapped around her and tucked. The long legs pink from the hot bath.

"Toothbrush," I said, holding out the admission kit.

"That was thoughtful. There's a comb, too. You know, we didn't think this thing through. There are so many things I need from…"

"Not more than you needed a bath. There is such a thing as too much thinking."

"You're right. I'm too relaxed to think."

"Want a nap?"

"Maybe after I dry my hair. You wouldn't happen to have a hair dryer?"

"Sorry."

"No problem. It'll air dry. Probably good for it." She stepped back into the bathroom, exchanged the towel for the robe, and shook out her hair. It hung long and straight. She began toweling it. *Degas: Woman at Bath. Renoir: Bather Gathering her Hair* "I have to comb it out. Otherwise it'll look like crap."

"Not from where I'm standing."

"Trust me." She held out her hand. "Comb."

I slapped it into her hand in the approved OR manner.

"I could use a chair. And some phone books to sit on, if this is your only mirror."

I brought them. She started combing out her hair. When she sat, she crossed her legs and the robe parted. She said softly, "So tell me how you almost came visiting me in my bedroom."

"Oh, well. Like you said, we were what, seventeen, right? I lay there thinking about you..."

"Yeesss."

"Don't make fun. I was scared."

"Of getting caught?"

"Sort of. Although I also thought that would have suited your purposes at the time."

She laughed. "I can see where you would think that."

"At first I thought you might come to me. I stared at that doorknob, at the light under the door, for it felt like hours. I gave up. I tried to go to sleep. But I couldn't get you out of my head. I was going home next day, or maybe the day after, right? So I'd only have this chance. I was this kid from Brooklyn, and if I muffed it, I'd never ever have another. So I thought and thought about how to go about it, and it was difficult because not all the blood was in my brain..."

"Hah!"

"...and I realized I was scared more of you. Of what we might do, what you might want. That I didn't think I'd be very good at."

629

"Paulie, if you had come, the most we would have gotten to was second base. Maybe. I think you thought...still think...I was more experienced than I was."

"All those townie boys. The rude mechanicals. Looked a lot older. Looked at you like they knew you very well."

"And I flirted with them and tried to make everyone think they did. Fooled you, didn't I? Paulie, they were boys. Yeah, I went riding with a few of them to get a rise out of my father, and mostly *nothing happened*. But I could count on them bragging, right? And it was your grandmother who made me realize all I was doing was trying to hurt my father, and these boys were just using me to do the same thing, to one of the town's rich men. Humiliating me to humiliate him. None of them cared any more for me than he did."

"Ali, none of this matters. None of it. None of it. I don't care. For seven years, whenever I close my eyes, I see you. It's like you're painted on the inside of my eyelids. It's like I knew who you were going to be."

"Who I was going to be? What am I to you Paul? A fictional character, in a story? This is you we're talking about, so it has to be a classic. Who am I? Daisy? With the green light at the end of the dock? She wasn't too terrific a person. Julie from 'Brideshead'? Sorry, Paulie, this is Brideshead Revised. Natasha from 'War and Peace'? No, wait; I know, this is beautiful, this is great: from 'Zhivago'. I'm Lara. I'm soiled goods turned to gold, is that it? By the magic of modern medicine. Cue the balalaikas."

I couldn't move. I didn't move.

"Wake up Paulie. Real Person here. Actual person. Troubled obnoxious teen, messed up young woman, tired med student. See? Flesh. Hair, not chestnut waterfall. Nose is too big. Breasts are too small. Legs are too skinny. Rotten taste in boys, but better taste in men, or I thought maybe."

"You..."

"Shut up. Listen to me. Listen to ME. Are we clear? Channels open? No fictional character static? OK. Here is something about you, Paulie. I absolutely trust you. I have for years. In spite of everything. For one reason. I know, like I know nothing else, that you will never, ever humiliate me. You know how I know?"

"I don't seem to be earning any trust here…"

"Olaf the Walrus."

"Olaf the…"

"Olaf. That day in Brooklyn I was beastly. I treated you and Dickie like crap. I treated everyone like crap. I treated myself like crap. I wish I could take all that back, all of it, but I can't, because I'm not a character in a story. You could have let me walk around for the rest of that day reeking of fish, but you didn't. Even Dickie, the sainted Dickie, would have. But you didn't."

"I didn't because when I was eleven…"

"I know why you didn't. Dickie told me that story when I was mad at you for leaving without saying goodbye."

He did? "He did?"

"You told it to him, and he told it to me. So I know who you *were*. You weren't always a saint either. You had to learn by doing something stupid too. You're no innocent. And I know who you *are*. Those parties at the Commune are famous."

"Those stories are highly exaggerated."

"Exactly. Like the stories about me."

She was right. "Point taken." *But wait.* "Hold on a moment. You know about the Commune. How long did you know I was there?"

"From about six months after I got here."

"You could have called me. You could have come over any time. You could have come to a party. They were open parties."

"And what would you have thought of me then?"

"Thought? I would have thrown my arms around you and dragged you into my room. I would have…"

She smiled. "We maybe would have had some version of this conversation first."

"Yeah, probably. So why didn't you call, or just drive over?"

"You had returned my letter. I was hurt. It was your move. And it hurt more when you didn't try to contact me."

"I had no idea you were here. I never heard your name. I heard there was this girl they called Lish the Dish. Clocked in at 800, 900 millihelens. I figured it was a girl named, I don't know, Lishinsky. I was buried on the wards. You know how that is."

"Now I do. I didn't then. I also figured you were still scared of me. Or something. I thought, maybe I'd been so, I don't know a good word, needy, always looking for reassurance, that you'd gotten tired of it…"

"No, Ali, look, even when you were, they were needs I enjoyed meeting. And the girl I found in '67 wasn't at all needy, certainly not the doctor I met yesterday. Even back when you were, when you weren't looking for reassurance you were saying and doing things that made me glad to be alive…"

"Or you had maybe lost interest, and you were too embarrassed or something to confront me."

"Ali, every day for four solid years I've woken up thinking 'today could be the day she'll call'. I couldn't understand it. I thought all along you knew about your father and why I had made such a show of sending back the letter."

"I woke up every day thinking the same thing. It was your move. I thought, what would be your response if I just show up? But I knew I would run into you on a rotation, and then I could see how you felt…"

"Look, I wasn't still scared. Once I was out of college your father couldn't hurt me, and once you graduated he couldn't hurt you. I went looking for you. I told you last night. A few weeks after you graduated I went up to the house. It was empty. The guy at the boatyard told me your father had had the boat refitted for long distance sailing and left with a woman young enough to be his daughter, and I was 99% certain it wasn't you. I checked the directory at his office and his name was gone."

She had returned to combing out her hair. "I'm getting hungry for lunch. Listen, when I'm done with my hair I have to put on a little makeup, and I have to pee. Were you planning to watch that too?"

"Sorry." I left, looked out the window. El trains were shunting in and out of the Woodlawn station. End of the line. It was close to noon. *There was plenty else wrong. Can I do this? I can do this. I want her that much. And why not? Why the hell not?*

She came out, the firm but delicate face made more perfect by a few deft shadings.

"We didn't think this through. I can't spend the day in a bathrobe. Can I borrow a shirt? Where are those clean whites?"

She picked a plaid lumberjack shirt worn soft by years of use. "Is there a washer in the building? If you have some laundry to do I could add my stuff to it."

We put together a laundry and I took it down to the basement laundry room. When I came back she was wearing the shirt and the clean whites. *No bra. No...* She was padding around the kitchen, rummaging around for cookware. *What was she thinking*

"Can I help?"

"I was thinking a salad at first, but you don't have lettuce. Salade de tamates?"

"I was going to do some grocery shopping today." I started to take her in my arms, but she took evasive action. "We still have some work

633

to do. You have garlic, oil, and a little spaghetti. You know spaghetti agli'olio?"

"Sure." I sliced garlic and she started sautéing it. The little apartment soon filled with a delightful odor. I broke a few handfuls of pasta in half, started a pot boiling.

"Music?"

"Judy Collins?"

> *On the firefly platform on sunny Goodge Street*
> *Violent hash smokers shook a chocolate machine*
> *Involved in an eating scene*

We divvied up the pasta, poured over the oil, added cheese. I was hungrier than I thought. And I wanted her so badly I could taste it. And she wanted me. Nothing else mattered. Nothing. *Why were we eating instead of…*

> *Crashing in the neon*
> *Lights in the stoneness*
> *Smearing their eyes*
> *On the crazy cult goddess*

"Mmmm. Explain Millihelens."

"Helen of Troy was the face that launched a thousand ships. A millihelen is enough beauty to launch one ship."

"And Lish the Dish scores in the 800 to 900 range."

"I didn't know, Ali. I didn't put it together until yesterday morning, when I saw the MG parked. Marvin had set it all up. He's one of the residents who said he was comfortable working with women trainees, asked Sarah for them in fact. You aren't supposed to know that."

"Sharing secrets is good for a relationship, remember? Marvin is maybe willing for the wrong reasons."

"Not entirely. Marvin genuinely likes Katie. Nobody asked me. If they had, I would have been willing for the right reasons. You know that. You met my mother and my grandmother. Both worked, both radicals in their time. Those are my models, Ali."

She touched my cheek. "I know that, Paul."

"I'm saying this because I know it's important to you. I have some idea how much shit you've had to take. How hard you had to work to get here. Even before you told me."

"You have no idea."

"Some."

"You don't."

"OK. Will you tell me?"

"Sure. A sample. How do you remember the Twelve Cranial Nerves? Don't bother; I know, and I have a sense of humor, but still. Twice yesterday I was mistaken for a nurse. There are no female changing rooms in any surgical suite at any hospital at this school, did you ever notice? And they razz the girls that change with the nurses. I told the guys if they peeked they'd be struck blind. And Bob, one among so many. And by the way, what exactly does 'castana' mean? I heard that a lot today. Yesterday."

"Slang for a chestnut-haired woman. Appreciative, not derogatory."

"Still. I'd rather be appreciated for other things when I'm working. I've been groped, Paul, been grabbed by patients while examining them. And not just patients."

"Who…?"

"Professors, Paul. I've been propositioned. Grades were mentioned."

"How did you…?"

She smiled grimly. "Variation on an old theme. Experience helped. I got clever. Told each one I was already taken by a more powerful colleague. 'Oh, pardon, mon Professeur, je suis engagé'. Like a taxi."

"Is there anyone I need to kill?" *That's what's…*

"Pas necessaire. There's some *I* need to kill."

"Right, sorry."

"And back here, of course—and this affected both of us, didn't it?—I've never been Dr. Acheson, I'm Lish the Dish."

"For what it's worth, I think you handled Charlie beautifully his morning."

"Thanks, but I'm really tired of having to handle anything."

"How did you get through it?"

"Friends. I had three pre-med friends at Wellsmith, but we all went to different schools. At Louvain…that's a long story. My class here was like yours; ten women, ninety men. Two were married."

"None of the guys interested?"

"Not a one. Lish the Dish is all business. Probably scared them off."

"Probably would have scared me off."

"Maybe. I'd like to think not. We went for meals, coffee, studied together, one by one the women got engaged, got married, we all went our separate ways on clinical rotations…talked about what we were going through. I read a lot." She looked around at the shelves. "That hasn't changed. Same as you. Get the laundry? I'll wash the dishes."

I ran down *I want to kill Chaskis* transferred the laundry from the washer to the dryer, ran back up. "What are you reading?"

"Marguerite Duras. Trying to keep up my French. Tried to read Proust. Couldn't do it. Love lives of useless petty aristocrats. I'd like to read about the loves of the worker bees. Oh, and we talked about guys."

"Oh."

"I wasn't going to wait forever, Paulie. I'm not a nun. I had a few blind dates. One classmate's cousin. If anything developed, I was going to come to you and tell you. We have history. Deep history. In Hartford…I would have gotten on that bus with you. I'd have gone anywhere with you." *Where would we have gone…*

"What about…interns, residents…?"

"I told you once. I don't date older men."

This is the time. The unavoidable time. Look her in the eyes.

"Ali…I was telling you what happened that night. At the house."

"So tell me." She leaned back, prepared to be amused.

"OK. That night. I was scared. But then I wasn't. Or I was more desperate than scared."

She laughed. "You were thinking with your dick."

"You bet I was. I started out. I figured the best way, the least risk of running into anybody, waking anybody, was to go outside, down the magnolia, onto the terrace, and back in the servants' entrance…"

"That's insane. That way you'd be *more* likely to run into someone."

"A servant, the cook, yes, so what? I wanted a snack, so I'm on my way to the kitchen, or I got lost…"

"You think servants are that stupid? Or discreet? Where were you getting your ideas, P. G. Wodehouse? Agatha Christie?"

"Well, that's what I thought, I guess I figured that's why you and Dickie showed me the service corridor, remember? Like you were showing me the way." *Northanger Abbey*

"We were just giving you a tour of a Gilded Age home, like the Hampton Court Palace tour."

"I'm telling you what I thought then, not now. Anyway, that wasn't the only reason. Riley slept at your door. I figured he'd woof the house down."

She was still holding a fork, still amused, smiling. "He probably would have."

637

"So I climbed out the window onto the tree and down to the terrace, came around to the servants' entrance. That's when I saw the pool guy going in."

"The pool guy? Mr. Chaskis? You saw Mr. Chaskis going in the…"

"Couldn't miss him. Full moonlight."

"*That's* what stopped you? What time would this have been?"

"One, maybe 1:30."

"And he was going in the servants' door."

"He was. He did. I waited for maybe a half hour, an hour—he didn't come out. Ali, this does not matter. I said I don't care and I don't. It will never come up again."

Her eyes widened. "So that's why you thought I should be understanding of Katie and Marvin, the age difference."

"Well, yes. And it will never come up again. I love you, Ali. I've loved you for years. Even when I tried not to. I've loved you all day, since yesterday. I don't ever want to lose you again."

"So who was I, Paul? Who am I?" she said quietly, "Lady Chatterley? Strindberg's Miss Julie?"

"I really saw…"

"You idiot, Paulie. You stupid, stupid idiot." She threw the fork she was drying across the room, leaving a gouge in the little table. "You thought he was coming to see me? You idiot."

"I saw your light go on. And I figured you told him it was over, you were leaving for school, the end. What is this?"

"I was crazy, but I wasn't *that* crazy. He was there for my mother, you idiot. He was my mother's lover. Had been for years. That's why they divorced, my parents. Why my mother went along with all my father's shit. The man you call 'the pool guy' is the owner of the biggest pool company in Westchester and Fairfield counties. You idiot. I put the light on because I heard him on the stairs. I thought it was you. I never thought he'd come over while we were all there."

"He was probably avoiding Riley too."

"He's one of the wealthiest men in that part of the world. He's who she's with now. My mother, not me. He was coming to work on the pool, she said, and sent us to New York, sent me with you. Remember? You idiot, Paulie."

What could I say? "I thought she was getting you away from him."

"Idiot, idiot. She was getting us out of the way. Paul, I was seventeen. Seventeen! Even if you didn't have any faith in me, at least figure to yourself, why would a grown man risk all that for a crazy girl, the daughter of a powerful man who could ruin him, put him in jail?"

"I was on my way to risk that same thing, for that same girl, wasn't I?"

"It's why I was so messed up, Paulie. He and my mother had been sleeping together for years. Didn't you ever wonder why we had a pool when we had a lake? Why the pool was always broken? Why my mother was always out? Why I was so crazy when she sent me to New York with you? Why when we were up in the magnolia the morning after the trip to Brooklyn there were no marks in the lawn of any heavy equipment, or any work on the pool? Is this all falling into place?"

It was.

"I was maybe eleven, twelve when I found out, the exact same way you did—I was using the service corridor to get to the kitchen for a midnight snack, and ran into Mr. Chaskis. Whenever my father wasn't home, and that was plenty except in sailing season, he was there. And I was supposed to keep this a secret. My mother called me in, explained that this was grownup stuff, and that mommies and daddies sometimes had complicated lives, but it was all OK as long as nobody talked about it, and if I shot my mouth off—she didn't put it that way—a divorce would be all my fault. I couldn't even tell Dickie."

"Did you?"

"Of course I did. We were allies. He told me she was full of shit about it being my fault, but right that if Daddy found out it would mean a divorce. The double standard, after all. But it terrified me. Divorce. What was that? So we—I—had to keep him happy. Which wasn't easy, because what he wanted from me—for me—was so…not me. You could have asked me, Paulie. Or asked Dickie."

"Oh, sure. 'Miss Acheson, I know we've only been acquainted a short time, but I was just wondering, are you sleeping with the pool guy'? Or, 'Hey, Dickie, old man, I am just curious, is your sister sleeping with the pool guy'? Or I could have asked the pool guy."

"OK, I guess not. But you could have asked me eventually—if you hadn't been afraid to disturb the web. Or was what you were really afraid of was this? Was this why you wouldn't talk me out of going to Paris? To get me away from Chaskis?"

"I never…maybe. Mostly to get you away from your father, since Dickie was going to set him off again, but maybe…it would explain why I was so angry about the embassy guy. I couldn't even explain that to myself. I know, that's why it's called the Unconscious."

"Was this the real reason you didn't keep contact with me? The first time? What I might answer if you asked me?"

After a few seconds I said, "Yes…maybe the second time too. Then, like I said, it stopped mattering. I wanted you so much I stopped caring. I don't care."

"You know what the real problem is? We did the infatuation part, now we're doing the relationship part. We never did the Getting to Know Each Other part."

"Why didn't you tell me your mother was having the affair with Chaskis?"

"How? 'By the way, Paul, my mother has been having an affair for years with the owner of the pool service'. When would I have slipped that into the conversation? And why? I didn't know until today that you

640

had seen him that night. And I did tell you—when it made sense for you to know what was happening to me." *When was that?* She got up and went to the window. "That's Woodlawn Cemetery out there, isn't it."

"It is. Beautiful place to go for a walk, if you haven't had your fill of death."

"I have relatives buried there. My mother's side."

"I heard, I don't know if it's true, Jenny Jerome is buried there. Winston Churchill's mother."

"She's one of the relatives."

"Great. We can name our first son after streets that run in the family. Jerome Seitz Third." I put my arms around her, under her breasts, pushed my head against her back, nuzzled some hair out of the way, kissed her neck. "You know, Ali, if we're ever going to have family we'll have to create our own."

She stiffened, loosened my hold. "Not yet, Paul," she said.

"Ali, I wanted you when I thought it was you with him, and I want you now. It doesn't matter."

"It matters plenty to me. We're going to have this all out. All of it. And you owe me a listen."

"You don't have to..."

"Yes I do, and yes you do. Nothing between us is ever going to be 'not talked about'." Not no privacy, that isn't what I mean; I mean no secrets, nothing unexamined. I've lived my whole life with secrets and things not talked about and things buried, and I will not live like that anymore. I can't. I love you and I trust you and I want like hell to be with you but if you can't do that, I won't. You stopped calling, you ignored my calls, you returned my letter. And I say that's because you weren't ready to do that. To have that kind of relationship. Maybe I wasn't either."

"I was nineteen. I'm twenty-five. I'm ready now." I sat down on the couch.

"Good. Then shut up until I'm finished. We're going to wind the clock back. I'm going to show you the letter you sent back unopened." She got her pocketbook, rummaged around, pulled out an envelope. There was her undergraduate dorm address, faded some, the November 1967 cancellation.

"Open it."

I opened it. Inside was her envelope addressed to me, cancelled Northampton, Mass, October 1967. Still sealed.

"Open it," she said. "Read it. Who says there are no second chances?"

"Out loud?"

"Yes."

"You've been carrying this around for five years, at the bottom of your pocketbook..."

"No. I kept it for when I knew I'd run into you. On a rotation at Morrisania...I mean, yes, I kept it, because I thought you had a reason for acting as you did, and one day we'd meet. I thought, I couldn't afford to think otherwise, it was devastating when I got it back unopened..."

"Ali..."

"...and I thought, he had a reason, the postmark is a month later than mine, he thought about this for a month, I'll see how he feels about me, and how I feel about him, and if it's right I'll give him the letter. And tell him the whole story. The second chance. Read it."

I read, out loud: "Dear Paul, My aunt Alice. I'm named for her. She was my aunt and my godmother. My mother's older sister. I've told her about you, and she says I should tell you the whole story of what has been going on in our family for the past bunch of years. She was a WASP... Ali, all your relatives are WASPS."

642

"Funny. No. Read."

"...which stands for Women Airforce Service Pilots. There were three sisters. She was the oldest. She was a trained pilopt, and a good one. Amelia Earhart made that alright for rich girls when she married George Palmer Putnam."

"Him you know."

"G.P. Putnam's Sons. Translations of the *Quixote*, *Rabelais*..."

"But the WASPs you don't know. There aren't any books, and they didn't make a movie...she met Amelia Earhart on the circuit, once, before the War. Anyway, read."

"The War came, they needed every hand. Women went to work in arms plants… My mother was a Rosie the Riveter at the Brooklyn Navy Yard, Ali. Do I really need a history lesson just now?"

"Paulie, shut up. This is about who I am. You need to know who I am. Because I'm not who you think I am. This is a letter. You don't get to answer until the end."

"My aunt Alice flew everything. She flew target-towing missions, and it was dangerous because some of the men deliberately shot at her tow plane instead of the target. She got to fly B-17s over to Atlantic coastal bases, shuttle back, fly some more. She shook them down, handed them opver to the boys who flew them over Germany, and some of them she saw again and some she didn't."

"After the War the army fired the lot of them, just dumped them. The family figured, or hoped, she'd settle down, marry, crank out little aristos, but she didn't. She loved to fly. She started an air charter service. Had all kinds of wealthy clients. She ran it out of Danbury Airport. She toopk a house in Danbury, and she hung out with aviation types. Pilots, mechanics. The family was scandalized, but she refused to be rejected. She came to all family functions, and they figured out she'd be there anyway, so it would cause less of a scene to invite her. She cleaned up real nice, as they say, didn't show up in greasy coveralls. As a businesswoman, she was a modest success. She told me once: 'Know how to make a small fortune in aviation? Start with a large fortune'.

"She was quite good loopking...Loopking?"

"The O and P keys used to stick on my typewriter. And I was pretty upset. Read."

"She traveled all over. Europe mostly. Sometimes she chartered planes over there. A few times she flew wealthy clients around Europe. Sometimes she went alone, sometimes not... That's who got you the de Beauvoir. 'The Second Sex'."

"Yes. Of course."

"I never thought to ask where you got it."

"Or where I was weekends. You never asked a lot of things. You just thought you knew all about it."

I thought this over. "True. Guilty as charged. I plead insanity. Oh God, you must have been alone in that house for days at a time, weeks…"

"Read."

"She was my Auntie Mame. When things got hot around home, I'd catch a ride to Danbury. Sometimes she flew down and picked me up in her plane. Not Dickie. Just me. Dickie gets airsick, too. I've pretty much lived between her place and my other aunt and cousins in Boston since I broke with my father. One of the great things about having the MG is I can visit her every weekend I want to. She taught me a lot of things. All kinds of things. About all kinds of things. Things I would never hear at home... Like what?"

"Read."

"Like that everyone always gasses on about French cuisine, but Italian is better. Do you know spaghetti agli'olio? Lucky for Brooklyn, huh? Every wine snob says Rose wine is garbage but they have their heads up their ass—her words. That's just an example. She only has strong opinions.

"She said since the War, women were treated like domestic animals. She told me my mother had a promising career in teaching literature, and had been Summa at Wellsmith, and had dropped her graduate work at my father's insistence after Dickie was born. Which she had never told me herself. She taught me chess. She taught me how to turn a wrench. I can tune the MG myself. *I imagined her in a courtyard at Wellsmith telling some girl to rev it, turning the idle screw Imagined us in the garage four floors below doing the same* Some things she didn't have to tell me. Some things she just *was*.

"I got older. And I found out by accident that my mother was having an affair with Mr. Chaskis, the man who built and serviced all the swimming pools, and my mother said I shouldn't tell anyone because that could lead to a divorce, and it would be my fault. It would just make Dad's drinking worse. I was stunned when Alice was delighted. Said my mother had finally found a man who made her happy. But she was appalled by what my mother said about keeping my father happy. She reassured me nothing would be my fault, and that a divorce would probably be the best thing to happen for my mother, and it didn't have to be hard on me—I'd have her, I mean Alice, no matter what. And she'd keep me out of the way if it got rough. And that my father started drinking after the War, when he couldn't sleep, dreamed about being torpedoed. That wasn't my fault either.

"I got older. She told me the debutante thing was a deathtrap for a girl with a brain, and I had a brain. She told me sex was a great pleasure but true love was rare, and that a woman had to navigate between those two. She told me sex was like a dance, not like a game or a sport. I said that worried me because I wasn't a very good dancer, or athlete, and she said she meant it's a shared, cooperative experience, not a gymnastic event. Guys always look at me like a wolf looks at a lamb chop, Paul, but I told her you always look at me like you want to share something.

"She was on and off with a guy, one of the mechanics at the field. I say mechanic, but he was more a mechanical engineer, he loved airplane engines. He was also a published poet. I saw some of the poems he wrote her. They've been published by City Lights: 'Odes to an

Aviatrix'. You're such a bookworm, maybe you know the book... I do, actually. I think I have a copy."

"Quel surprise. Read."

"She could have gotten me the Borges books, but I preferred getting them from you. In case that wasn't clear.

"When Dickie went underground she was surprised. She didn't think he had it in him. She always underestimated him.

"She told me this: She told me that most men were interested in what was between a woman's ears or what was between her legs and she told me to find a man who was interested in both. But she said the same went for women, although it might look different; we were interested either in what was between a man's ears or what was between his legs, or in his wallet. And too many women settled. And she said I should never be satisfied until I found a man about whom I could say I was interested in both. It had to work both ways. I told her about you. ...I'm interested in both, Ali. You know I want a partner, not a pet."

"I know that. So am I. And you know that. That's why I'm still here, Paul. Whatever else, we've always respected each other's ideas and abilities, and you have never called me 'baby', and you've been trying to get me into bed since this morning."

"Since August 1965, actually..."

"It doesn't stop there. Keep reading."

"...and she said I'd never be happy living like my parents, with the secrets, the lies, the accommodations. She said my parents used money to insulate themselves from the world and she used hers to jump into it. She said a life that would make me happy would also bring me pain, but it was pain I would prefer to my parents' kind of pain. She saw what I was doing to myself, to sabotage their wishes for me, and urged me to be straight with them. I heard you say almost the same thing. So did your mother and grandmother. It took me months to figure out how to do it. You know that story. By that time I was living at her place when I wasn't at school. The next thing that happened, a few months after you brought me the car, my father walked in on my mother and Mr. Chaskis. It was quite a scene...Why did your father never have your mother watched? Have Michael do a little surveillance?"

"Hmm. Who says he didn't? But I don't think he'd have used anyone close to him, to the firm. Too embarrassing. Read."

"The separation was final a few weeks ago; the divorce will be I don't know when. It was horrendous. Like my father had a right to complain. Dickie told me once he slept with anything that wasn't moving faster than he was. But he's fighting her for every penny, because he couldn't cover her demands without selling the house. And she's even worse—Mr. Chaskis' pool service company is one of the biggest businesses in Connecticut. She doesn't need a penny from him.

"Here I am at school, and my home is gone, and I don't know that I have a home to go to. My father is still pressuring me to be a good WASP stereotype (not the aviatrix kind). Dickie is God knows where—I don't contact him, he contacts me, when he needs money. My mother I think wishes I'd graduated and been out on my own. I think she was waiting for that; then she was going to leave my father. She wasn't anticipating him coming home to install a new compass in the boat.

"Alice took me on an extended trip to Europe again this summer. I want you to know my plans. I'm going to apply to med school. Definitely. You know how I've thought about being a doctor for years and years. Meeting you kind of solidified that. Made it seem possible. I can't really explain, except to say I think after spending time with you, and your note (did you think I forgot that?), and your reassurance, I think I can do this. Be some use in the world. I told my aunt, and she said even if my parents were still battling, the money would be there. That was important, because you remember my trust fund? Doesn't exist. My father was the trustee, and he emptied it. Or maybe never filled it. I found that out from Dickie when I thought to surprise you with a ticket to Paris. Family business—he would never tell. I don't know if there is anything we can do about that, but Aunt Alice said it wouldn't matter; I wouldn't need that money, she would always have the money to keep me in school and she wouldn't need it…. That's what I didn't know?"

"It's only the start. Read."

"She said I had a lot of work to do, but she said I should keep you in sight. Not lose track of you. Never lose track of a boy who makes a gift of 'A Room of One's Own'. And kisses you and tells you to never forget, no matter what happens.

"I've been following the second part of the Plan, pretending to be the social butterfly and sending the proceeds to Dickie. You know I have my ways of foiling unwanted relationships, so don't worry about me, or about <u>us</u>. It's all a show. I'm spending my weekends with Alice.

"You won't be able to find me through Dickie, and I won't be able to find you. Nobody knows where he is. So it's up to us to stay in touch with each other. You can always find me through her at P.O. Box 247, Danbury. I don't know why you didn't answer my letters. How could we part that way and then nothing? You said remember, no matter what happens. I know something must have happened. What? *Love, Ali*"

I hung my head, waited until I could speak, past the lump in my throat. "I need to take the girl who wrote that letter in my arms, Ali."

"You'll have to settle for a later version. There was one problem. My aunt smoked like the proverbial chimney. It's a wonder she didn't blow herself up on the tarmac. As it is, when I was about sixteen she found the lump. She caught it early, but I don't have to tell you about breast cancer. They did the mutilotomy, she got a prosthesis, but she knew there wasn't forever. It's how she knew she wouldn't be needing money forever. Actually, though, she did pretty well for years. When she was dying, she hated how little doctors could do, but she said just think how much more you're going to know. She gave me her Fifinella shoulder patch, from her uniform. She took me to Europe. London, Paris, Rome, Venice. Venice was her longtime favorite. She always spent a month in Venice, every two years. She took me away, Paulie, because it got so ugly. The point is, no one got to ask me anything. My father never got to actually ask me if I had known, and if so why I didn't tell him and on and on. She kept me out of it."

"Did you try to contact Dickie?"

"Tried. Didn't succeed. All we had was his last Post Restante number. We left a message, never heard back. Tried classified ads too. Nothing. He'd already left Europe. Just heard from him months ago, first time since '68.

"Is that it?"

"She died in the middle of my second year. The inheritance comes from her."

"I'm so sorry for your loss, Ali."

"She was a big fan of yours."

"She never met me."

"She might as well have. You say you couldn't stop thinking about me—I couldn't stop talking about you. One thing she loved: You weren't afraid of my father."

"Yeah, well…is that it?"

"No. There's plenty more. She was the final reason I went to Louvain. At first…women physicians are no novelty in Europe, Paul. I was accepted here, but she was hospitalized in Paris, she liked the approach they offered her there, she was among friends. She told me to come here, she'd be fine. I loved her so much, Paul. I owed her so much. I had to try, I had to be there with her. I burned up the rails with my student card, until she came to see a surgeon in Louvain. She was dying then for real; she died in Louvain. I sat with her, I talked to her, I played chess with her, I read to her."

What I didn't get the chance to…"There was a guy."

"There was a guy, a classmate. I was lonely, Paul, Alice was dying, and he was a nice guy. Jean-Jacques. Tall, of course, skinny, funny, well-read, from a Socialist family from Charleroi. I probably would have gone for him even if Alice wasn't dying. He was you in French, Paul. Except that he wasn't. My French is so good, I thought, I could always stay in Europe, if things develop…"

I took her hands. "Did they?"

She looked away. "Should have. Did, up to a point, then didn't. He wasn't you. He kept doing things that reminded me he wasn't you. I don't know. He never showed me a New York sunset, never gave me a Virginia Woolf book, never defended me from hostile marine life, never defied my father, never practically killed himself bringing me a stupid car…" She looked at her hands in mine, looked away. "When you touch me, when you kiss me, it's electric. It's fireworks. With him…I might as well have been shaking hands. I remembered my Eliot; there was no history. Actually there were, could have been, plenty of guys, but…we have such history. I talked to Alice. She said, why was I wasting my time with a copy when the original was still out there."

"Thank you, Alice."

"Don't joke, Paulie. Not about this." She looked at me straight on, piercing me the way she had once done on the raft. "So. Jealous?"

I searched myself. "There's an eighteen-year-old boy somewhere in here who would gladly kill this Jean-Jacques. But that boy's an idiot, a long time gone. No, not jealous in the way I felt when you were in Paris, I think you mean. Only of the time that should have been ours. I'm glad you had someone when you needed to. But why didn't you write to me? To tell me you were in Louvain? I'd have hopped the next flight. I was…I did acid once. Parker gave it to me, and I had it around…"

"Did you really? And you were worried about *me*."

Whoa. Right. "Yeah. Some right I had. I haven't done it again, and I haven't smoked dope in years now. Anyway…it was a bad trip. At first it felt like you were there, but then…I almost got tossed out of school, I think, I was on Surgery, missed two days, had to explain it to the Dean… my head went to this really dark place. I felt *abandoned*, Ali."

"Then you know how I felt. I was hurt, I told you. But I did write to you at the school. When I knew that she was dying. Late '69, early '70. It came back Addressee Unknown."

"I'd moved to the Commune by then. Phone wasn't in my name…"

"Then she died. She was the last, Paul. What did you say this morning? Like a piece fell out of the world. "

"Why didn't you come to me? Why, Ali?"

"I tried to find you. I knew you were here somewhere; I'd been accepted here, and they were willing to take me as a transfer if I passed my Part One Boards, which I did, but I got the same response you got at Wellsmith. I tried to call your mother; she isn't listed in Brooklyn anymore…"

"She's with a guy named Herb, on the Upper West Side…"

"So that's who that was. *What?* But I told you, I didn't want to find you like that, just drop on in. If I did, and…but I knew where you would be on one particular day."

"What day?"

"Your graduation, in the quad. I watched from my dorm window, Paul. I saw you, you were wearing those work boots and jeans under the gown. Your mother was there with, it must have been, Herb."

"Why didn't you just come down? It would have been the greatest reunion ever. Or when you knew where I was, why didn't you just come over? You were what, embarrassed?"

"No, something more. I couldn't do it. There isn't going to be anyone at my graduation. Paul, I've lost everyone who ever loved me, that I ever loved, except one. You were the last. I was afraid you'd dumped me, and if I went to see you and you…if you were…if you sent me away I would know, I would lose any hope that you'd ever…"

"Oh, no Ali, no…"

"I'm the coward, Paul."

Silence

651

"No. It makes perfect sense after what I did. I wish I could have met Alice. That we'd found a way while we were still in college."

"She said a room of one's own always has room in it for the right people."

"Oh God, we could have met at her place. We could have…"

"If you'd read the letter. She was the one though, who agreed, you must have had a powerful reason. You know how she knew, she said? Because of the very first time we met. When my father dragged me to Nott with Dickie. And you told my father you were giving me the book. I should know who you were from that moment, she said. The books later—icing on the cake. But the real reason she knew, she said, she noticed you didn't just mark the letter 'Return to Sender'. You could have, but you didn't. You put it in an envelope with no return address, like you were trying to keep anyone from knowing I'd even sent it. And you typed the address, disguised it like some official letter, no handwriting to recognize. She said, you were a chess player, and you must be desperate, something really bad must have happened, she even guessed it was, could be, my father, she said 'Paul has castled, he's hunkered down, setting up for the long game'. He isn't as free as you are, she said, I didn't know what it was like to have to watch every penny; well, I know now…Those local boys…I told you, I wanted something male to care about me other than Riley. I didn't want them all over me. De Beauvoir, talked a good game, said we had to free ourselves from our bodies. But you. You I wanted. So much I didn't know what to do, what to say. The others, all they wanted was to get something off the rich girl. But you. You scared the hell out of me. Because you I *needed*. You terrified me. I knew you'd never humiliate me, but I learned from your grandmother that I could humiliate myself. And I would never again do that."

"That's why you didn't call me?" I could see fire in her eyes. "That isn't why."

"You're damned right that isn't why. It's only part of why. I told you, Alice told me my body was trying to tell me something. Only she didn't say 'body' exactly."

I started to laugh, but she said, "And she said I would have to deal with my anger at you if that was what was keeping me from going home because it would just leave me lonely."

I took her hands again. "It's OK," I said.

She pulled her hands away. "It's OK? Really? You think it matters if it's OK with you…"

"No, no…it's OK to tell me. To say it. I won't run away. I swear."

"It's why I couldn't go to see you at the Commune and your Graduation. Why I was afraid you'd send me away. I think sometimes I have my father's temper. I didn't think I could see you without wanting to kill you."

"So, why? All of it."

"Because of how angry I was at you. Damn you, Paulie. Bastard. Even at my father…I didn't know it was possible to be so angry. Enraged, more like. When you sent the letter back I took a train into Manhattan, tried to find Sammy in Washington Square, maybe he could tell me, he was gone, nobody knew where…"

"NYU for economics and accountancy. He graduated to horseplaying and the stock market. Bankrolled by our rallye bets, which he partially financed…"

"Shut up. I fantasized calling your mother. I thought that would be a bad idea. I was ashamed. I'd be at Alice's and I had the car, and I'd think, it's maybe two hours or so to Schenectady, I could be there in two hours and tell you the hell off. I fantasized it a thousand times."

"I would have told you about your father…"

"I know that now. But it didn't matter. Wouldn't have mattered. The fantasy always ended the same way. I'd go up there and kick your door in, slap you across the face, take you by your scrawny neck, and it always ended the same way—with us in bed. You had me twisted into a pretzel, Paulie. God, I hated you, I loved you, I needed you, and I didn't want to need any man like that. My aunt had to settle me down, tell me to be patient. Good Yankee girls don't do things like this, don't feel things like this, isn't that the stereotype? Work. Go to med school. His. Show up in his face. You're what he wants, and if he can't see that, well, you'll be a doctor, won't you."

"I…"

"Shut *up*, Paulie. I need to get this out now. You said, all of it. I'd go back to school, I'd get hung up on some Organic Chem problem, want to call you, and the rage would take over, I'd think, screw him, I can do this on my own."

"And you did. Partner."

"Yeah, I did. Didn't I."

"That'll teach me."

She grinned. "Bastard. You bastard. It was what I needed. Be my own champion, you said. Bastard. Of all the screwed up ways to do it…That's how I found out I didn't need you anymore. I wanted you. Which, I found out, is a different kind of needing. A much less scary kind."

"Where does that leave us?"

"I could have killed you. Wrung your neck. A thousand times. Too chicken. Every time I picked up the phone, every time I thought of driving over to the commune, every time I thought, oh, I'll just run on over to the Ed office and ask Sarah where he is…Then, I told you, first time since '68, I got the letter from Dickie in Dharamsala. He asked me how you were, how *we* were, and I wrote back, told him what happened, told him I thought you weren't interested, and he wrote back and told me I must be nuts, you were crazy about me, told me how crazy, Govinda." She grinned. *Oh* "So finally I did it and asked for this rotation…"

"You…wait, you…?"

"Yes, you idiot, I couldn't stand it anymore. I had to find out how you felt. How I felt. And to minimize the risk, it had to be this way, meet up even, completely even, in a place where we would have to behave professionally. Where I would have to behave professionally. You see?"

I saw. *Dickie, Dickie you bastard Thank you Love and friendship are the last to go If they go Desire…* "It's the first Acheson plan that ever really worked."

"Didn't it just. I found out you were still the same guy. The boy I loved had turned into a man I could love." She turned away. Murmured, "Did love. Do love." Then louder, "You are exactly what I wanted. What all of me wants. You are also smug, overconfident in your own often premature judgments, and just a touch paranoid. Your misinterpretations of me and my life are all about your prejudices, do you see that? This isn't a chess game. You don't always know the next move. You need to ask me stuff. Not assume. You need to *listen*. And you could use a haircut."

True. She's right "I could use your help with all of that. You're what *I* need. And want. With all my heart."

"Well, you have possibilities."

"Thanks."

"Idiot. I don't care about any of that anymore. Almost every minute since yesterday you've been exactly what I needed. What I wanted. Including leaving me alone when I needed that."

"Infuriating, isn't it?"

"Wiseass. It is, yes, damn it. You didn't give me a single chance to tell you off. Even after dinner, when you were irritating the hell out of me. Then Donnelly showed up."

"And did it for you."

"No. That's just it. When he knocked me down I saw you behind him. There was murder in your eyes, Paulie. I knew you would do anything to keep him from hurting me and if he hurt me you were going to kill him."

"Depend on it."

"And then you took the blow meant for me. I saw him hit you and if the cops hadn't shown up *I* would have killed him. I love you, Paul. I was the first one to you, I was so scared he'd really hurt you…" and she touched my cheek, where under a butterfly dressing, a small scar was beginning to form. She nestled down next to me, spent. *God, the fire in this woman* "I lied before. To myself. If you had come to my room that night I don't know what would have happened. I might have just…given myself to you. Not that I was so sure how to do that. And it scared me."

"I don't know if I would have been up to the gift. Or up to refusing it. I wasn't, ah, prepared. Emotionally or contraceptionally."

"Either way, what would we have done then?"

"Good question. At seventeen?"

"And then you pulled back. Still there, but at a distance. Now I know why."

"I was just as scared as you."

"I can see why. Oh God, Paul, I set it all up. I set myself up. For you to believe it was me Chaskis was there to see. It was a performance for my jerk father, you believed it—but partly because of the stereotypes in your head."

"But I came back. I tried to give you up, but I couldn't, so I thought—I was 17, Ali—I thought, well, what you wanted was to get away from him, that you'd sent him away, you said you'd made a vow not to date older men…"

"I meant my brother's prep school friends."

"…and you would need a guy with…more experience. So I spent a year trying to get some."

"Idiot. How much did you get?"

Jacob lay with Leah before he lay with Rachel I smiled. "Not much. As your brother must have said. *Calypso* Except once…it was…"

"Nothing, Pavel. We're both human. Good. I don't know that I'd measure up…"

"Stop it. What I learned was that I didn't want to have sex, I wanted to have sex with *you*."

"Paul, you know…we're docs, so we know this…this doesn't always go so well the first time."

"I think it only has to go well enough to want to do it a second time. Are you still scared?"

"Honestly? Just a little. I'm still a lousy dancer. I don't want to disappoint."

"Honestly? It isn't tennis. You can't possibly disappoint. Ever. I love you."

"Well, a boy I loved once told my father chess players don't bluff." She looked away. "With Jean-Jacques, the tip-off should have been, one night at a coffeehouse we played chess. When I started beating him he found an excuse to have to leave. In a million years, I thought, Paul wouldn't do that. But we're scientists, right? So I did an experiment. The next time we…I pretended, fantasized it was you. Boom. Fireworks. Alice laughed. She said see, I'd have to find you. Jean-Jacques was pretty surprised when I dumped him. Huh. He probably spread it around that all you have to do to get rid of me is excite me. Didn't matter. I was going home."

There seemed nothing else to say. Except…I pushed the pieces off the board, picked out the white king, a white bishop and a white rook, the black king and black knights. I set them up. "That reminds me."

"What in hell are you doing?"

"I have a chess problem to show you," I said. "This is my response to your letters. Even though I wanted to steer clear of the Achesons, until you graduated, I wanted desperately for you to know this chess problem. I mailed it from Bedford Hills, no return address, took a train up there to mail it. Signed it Albert Myles. You never got it?"

"No."

"I couldn't have sent it from Brooklyn or Schenectady without...disturbing the web." I set the pieces up exactly as they had been eight years ago.

"A chess problem. That you thought was so important for me to have."

"Look." She examined the position. "The problem is: is it mate in three for white?"

"This is the end of the game we played that night."

"It is. Look carefully. I looked at it for months. I didn't feel right about it. What I tried to do was see what your father saw, because I still didn't know what a bullshit artist he was. I was a kid; I thought nobody ever lied about chess. I tried to play it from white's point of view, to get mate in three. I couldn't. That's what took me months. It's black's move. After that scene in his office I had a revelation. What if he was wrong. Or bullshitting. I set it up again and played for black. And I saw it. The important thing. So. Your move."

She examined the board as if it were a minefield. She saw it almost immediately. Moved the knight to create the fork. "Check."

I moved my king to protect the rook; without hesitation she took the rook, and I took the knight.

Stalemate. Tie game.

She tipped over the white king. She tipped over the black king. Then she placed the two horizontal kings side by side.

"Now?"

"Now, Paul."

I pulled her gently to me, cradled her head, kissed her long and deeply. We kissed where we had left off in a bus station six years ago, in a Manhattan bookstore, on a raft at a lost lakeside house. She ran her hands under my shirt, started to lift it as I unbuttoned the old flannel shirt she was still wrapped in, kissed her neck in the sensitive spot where the nerves and carotid artery run just underneath the sternocleidomastoid muscle. And on down, to her breasts, kissed each one. We stood. I unbuttoned her whites; she helped me push them over her hips, stepped out of them, pushed them away with one bare foot. She unbuckled my belt; I helped push the jeans down, kicked them away. Kissed her, ran a hand down from her breasts to where her thighs met. She reached for me. She closed her eyes. Her breath caught. Her heart was racing. Mine too.

"Still a little nervous?"

"A little. You have…"

"This time I do. Dance with me." We opened the couch *her lips her mouth her hands her arms her breasts the nipples so soft then hard* and began the exploration of each other's bodies and their pleasures that continues to this day. *Oh God, when she took me into her Ali Ali Ali   Oh Paul   The Joy   The world felt whole again*

Her eyes opened. "You've been watching me sleep."

"I have."

"What time is it?"

"About 5:00."

"AM or PM?"

"PM."

"Mmmmmm. Stop. There's stuff we have to do."

"I wanted to show you another procedure. See one, do two."

"Mmmmmmmm."

"Now what time is it?"

"About 5:30."

"Shower. Laundry." She threw off the blanket and headed for the bathroom, naked, a vision surpassing eight years' imaginings. She ran back and pulled up the blanket, gave a little shiver and folded herself into me.

"Paul, do you think…I think…I suppose…I wonder if…we really were too anxious, too scared I mean …to do this before."

"You mean when you kissed me so passionately and then swam away?"

"Yes."

"Or the time I fought with myself on the phone to not tell you I loved you so you'd go to Paris?"

"All the pauses. Yes. Among other times. Paul, we weren't ready yet."

"We were kids." I put my arm around her shoulders. "Sex was scary back then. You could get PREGNANT. You could get A DISEASE." She was laughing now, laughing with her whole body. "Worse, you could DO IT WRONG."

"Well, we were children."

"What are we now?"

"Wiser children?"

"I was ready when you got back from Paris."

"Me too. But where would we have gone? Plus, we had work to do. But you know what? I think all those years we were both scared. And we found ways of being apart."

"We had a lot of help."

"Didn't we just."

I turned, traced, with one finger, the outline of one perfect breast. "Rumor has it that this gets even better with practice."

She stretched, buried her face in my chest. "I can't imagine feeling any better than I do right now, this minute."

We lay for a while, listening to street noises. I watched the play of light on strands of her hair where it fell across my face, the red highlights shining in the brown.

"What a pleasure," she murmured, "After eight years in dormitories, to have a day with a private bathroom, a tub, a refrigerator, a stove."

Her face Her body Her hands Her heart. Her mind. "All yours from now on, if you want."

"…What are you saying?"

"Move in with me. Tonight. Now." *One should not marry such a maiden*

"You mean live together? I wasn't…"

"Yes. You'd have all that stuff, and we could talk all night. Play chess. Do this whenever we want." *Defy a three-thousand-year-old oracle*

"I don't know, Paul. We still have to get to know each other. In more than the biblical sense." *Still scared?*

"What better way than to live together?"

"It's…"

"Ali, I can't come home to this, knowing you're a mile away…it would kill me. I'd end up sleeping outside your door like Riley. Look, you'll have to move out of the dorm when you graduate in two months. You're paid up there until then. Move in with me. If for some reason it doesn't work out, you can move back to the dorm." *I'll kiss you awake every morning*

She was still tucked into my shoulder, playing her fingers over my chest. "You make it sound pretty reasonable. Just give me some time to think it over. To digest it."

What was there to think about? "Sure. But look, there's plenty of room…"

"I don't have much stuff. Books, clothes. Most of my stuff is at my mother's place. The good Mrs. Chaskis…about the time she realized I was seriously going to med school she decided to realize I'd been funding Dickie the whole time. That I was in on it. I didn't deny it. Cold cordiality since then. When she finds out I'm with you…"

"We could, like, not tell her if you…"

"No more secrets. No more intrigue. No more lies, Paul. Look where it got us. She'll hear it. From me."

"Right answer."

"We'd need a bigger bed."

"We'll get a bigger bed."

"Let me think about it."

"Think about what?"

"Nothing really. I just want to be sure my brain is involved in this decision."

I laughed. "Right. Hey. You know what? We've never been on a date."

"We've been on life. OK, ask me out."

"Dr. Acheson, will you do me the honor of accompanying me to dinner?"

"It would be my pleasure, Dr. Seitz. But my shirt's all creased. I bet you don't even have an iron."

"Cover it with a lab jacket."

We crossed the street and checked the CCU for Vovchok. He was there; we had a brief exchange of attempted conversation, mostly exchanged smiles. We left a note for the CCU social worker to contact the Tolstoya Funt.

She stopped suddenly in the corridor, leaned into my arms. "That was all…really something," she said.

I hugged her to me, pushed some hair back off her forehead, kissed her. "I'm going to have to be someplace else when they discuss your grade. But you should have seen yourself. I don't just love you. I admire you, Ali. You're a hell of a person and a hell of a doc."

"You ain't bad yourself." She smiled. "But that wasn't all I meant."
Well now

We dined at the Mother House's famous free-to-students cafeteria, on her student card. It could have been Maxim's. She caught me looking at her again.

"What? Something stuck in my teeth?"

"No. I was just admiring you some more. I think there's a roomful of people wondering what this seriously gorgeous woman is doing with the scruffy beanpole."

"Paul. Seriously. I didn't want to make this decision in afterglow. What I'm doing is I'm thinking about moving in with you."

"And?"

She looked away. "Dickie was wrong to worry. You didn't take the big chance to stick it to my father. You wouldn't do that without talking it over with me. Then you waited for me all that time. Even when you thought I was making it with the pool guy. Even when you thought I had …might have…become a drunken party girl."

"Yes. You were worth waiting for. In case you were wondering." I took her hands. "Parker said you were OK. I'd have come for you, and damn your father, if..."

She looked down at my hands holding hers. "I'm not that easy to live with, Paul. Alone a long time now."

"Me either. I'm sure there will be Moments. I'll risk it."

"I was right about you years ago. You grew up, Pavel. You're a mensch."

"I'm an idiot."

"That too."
Silence

"You know my attitude toward marriage and why…I would only do this if it's voluntary. I mean, we're both there because we want to be, not because a piece of paper says we have to be."

"I know marriage isn't the only kind of relationship. I think my grandmother was with my grandfather long before they were married. There's my mother and this guy named Herb…" And then it hit me. "Ali, I just thought…the reason your father let me go that day in his office…never bothered you at school…it had nothing to do with the stupid heroics with the vase, or my idiot threats of vengeance, it was that he realized if I raised any fuss and you raised a stink it would all come out about the trust funds…he never tried offering me money."

"I told you. Because there wasn't any to offer."

"He could have sold the boat."

"Never. That was his life. That was him. It was his skill. It was a piece of the only good thing he ever did in his life. That I know of."

"I suppose so. He did save his crew."

"Paul. Ever notice, the boat had no name?"

"What's the significance of that?"

"LSTs don't have names, only numbers. I think he never really ever got off that burning LST. Not in one piece, anyway. Some part of him died with that boat."

"You've made a study of your father."

"At some point, Pavel, you stop studying books and start studying people. I made quite a study of you."

"I guess you had to."

"I did."

"Any conclusions?"

"Working on it."

She seemed distracted again, the look I'd noticed before, last night. "What is it, Ali? You're miles away."

"There's this...Paul, you said the worst thing you ever did was to leave your mother and grandmother and go to Nott. That's where I met you. At the other end of that train ride was me. That worst thing you think you ever did probably changed my life. I don't know what my life would have been without your encouragement...without you."

"I know what mine would have been, because I know what it's been like without you."

"But the thing you feel the most guilty about...is the thing that brought you and me together. Is that...could it be that's maybe why you misread everything, why you got me so wrong, why you couldn't find a way to..."

And there it was. I sat back, rocked by this. It made sense. How everything had been misperceived. No. How I had misperceived it. I had taken psych too. When you make a correct interpretation you get a memory or a fantasy. "You know what?" I said. "When I found my father's Kafka translation, just before coming up to the lake...I also found a book of love poems he wrote for my mother. I think...like I'd found a missing piece for her..."

"Probably. I think you did."

"So it was OK to...Ali," I said. "After the summer at your place I had a recurring dream. I mean it was a little different each time, but the common thing was, there was a train, and you or we would be on it and it always ended with you saying 'Paul, do you know what you're doing'? One time it crashed but we were OK, and then you said it."

"That's...what do you think it meant?"

"At the time I thought it meant would I know what I was doing with you. I mean, sexually. Now I think, it meant, did I know what I wanted to do. With you. Once when I visited my father's grave I imagined a conversation with him and he told me to ask myself that."

"What did you answer?"

"I answered that I wanted…everything. Life. Everything. Which I think we couldn't have had then. You were right before. It was too scary. I wanted you so very much…"

She took my hand. "As I wanted you."

"Damn it. Damn the time we lost. *Silence* So…what if I'd started out for your room a few minutes earlier, never saw Chaskis."

She smiled. "Assuming we hadn't been caught, it would have been somewhere between awkward and incandescent."

"Earthquake Rocks Western Connecticut."

She laughed. "But what then? Burn up the phone lines, burn up the roads, drop out of school? Or find some way to screw it up? We'd never have got here. To this. Paul. Pavel. What was scary was how much we both wanted love. Needed to be loved. If we…it would have been like a drug…"

"…that we needed to find the right dose of." We both sat back. *Solved that one*

"Paul. It doesn't matter anymore. None of it."

And suddenly it didn't "My mother…she'll be awfully glad to see you again. She's been asking me about you for years. She'll make a pot roast the size of a bus. And I don't care about any piece of paper either. I want to be with you. You decide how to do that. If you want."

"I think I'll risk it."

"Think so?"

"Well, nobody ever *admired* me before."

"Something you'll have to live with. There doesn't have to be any risk. We can't haul much in the MG. Take enough for a week, and we can get the rest later. If you still want."

She grinned. "You used to know how to sweep me off my feet. As little as hours ago."

666

"We aren't kids anymore. I did the sweeping last time around. Now I'm thinking long-term. I'm thinking about your attitude to marriage. And to rooms of your own."

"Paul, let's go get my things. I think we understand each other."

"As long as you're certain."

"Yes. Everything we decide, we decide together."

"Wouldn't have it any other way." We walked out into the oldest part of the hospital, mustard yellow walls, walnut wainscoting, clean but worn linoleum. She stopped at the bust in its niche and rubbed its nose.

"No risk, huh? You're confident enough to offer a money back guarantee?"

It's bashert I took her hand. "Twice you dropped into my life like a miracle, and I will never forget that's what it is. Never."

"That's what you are for me, too, Paul," she said.

"Dr. Acheson—I'll be at your graduation. No matter what." And for the second time that day I, too, rubbed the aloof philanthropist's bronze nose.

April 8, 1973
7:30 – 10:30 PM

$\mathcal{I}$ remember.

There once was an ugly duckling
With feathers all fuzzy and brown

Danny Kaye, the great Jewish comic actor (as my father called him) sang that song to me over and over until I wore the record out. You know the end; the duckling turns out to be a cygnet, and becomes a beautiful swan. I was too young to wonder what a swan raised as an inferior duck might feel like. That was for later.

The other ducklings and swans I knew were in the Boston Public Garden: Jack, Kack, Lack, Mack, Nack, Ouack, Pack and Quack. When we visited my Boston cousins (mother's side) Father took me on the Swan Boats in the lake, where Michael the kind policeman stopped traffic so Mrs. Mallard could lead her eight ducklings from the Charles River to the Lake. I loved my father then. He read me "Make Way for Ducklings" and I thought he would always be there to stop traffic for me.

My parents' arguments got worse and worse, until one day when I was four I was in the dining room and I heard their voices in the kitchen become really, really loud. I was standing in the kitchen door when I saw my father hit my mother. That's what I remembered in psychotherapy on the worst day of my life. There were a lot of bad days I remember very clearly, *and you figured in a lot of them in different ways* but the day I recovered that memory was the very worst. I called my brother, and he confirmed it; he was the one who had taken me upstairs and read to me until things calmed down.

I thought I went into medicine because I wanted to help people, and into psychiatry because I wanted to bring female developmental concerns into focus—Freud's formulations were invariably anthropocentric. A gynocentric psychology, I thought, would look entirely different. But the things you do for neurotic reasons that work, you keep doing because they work.

Mother said to Father, "That is the last time you will ever touch me," and she walked out onto the porch. And went to Boston. Where her sister lived. And the ducklings, now all grown into swan boats.

She came back, of course, but the chill in the house was Arctic. Father was gone more and longer, "at work in The City", and when he was home I wouldn't let him near me. I cried when he approached. Finally, when I was maybe six he bought me a puppy. I mean us; me and Dickie, but Riley attached himself to me; he was my dog. Mother wouldn't let him sleep in my bed, or even in my room, so he slept at my door until I went to college. Dickie read to me until I caught on to reading; Riley sat with me when I read. I read Winnie the Pooh and Black Beauty (over and over) and Nancy Drew (all of them; the North Greenwich Town Library had all of them) and one day I got the measles and was in bed for two weeks with no lights because in those days people believed measles could make you blind if you used your eyes (and there is a measles keratoconjunctivitis, so it isn't completely ridiculous that people believed this) and this terrified me, so when the doctor came I asked about it and he reassured me, told me light didn't cause the problem, germs did. So when I recovered, the first time I went back to the library I asked about germs and they showed me Paul deKruif's "Microbe Hunters" and I read that over and over until the library asked me to give someone else a chance and my aunt Alice bought me a copy. That was my first really grown-up book.

I'm named for my aunt Alice; she was my godmother, wanted to eventually teach me to fly, but honestly I couldn't imagine it. I had zero athletic ability. I was this tall, skinny kid, all legs and no coordination. She said great, my legs would be long enough to reach the rudder pedals, but I could trip over myself playing Fetch with Riley. Dickie tried to teach me sports but it was hopeless. Alice taught me to play chess. Pretty soon I could beat her. And Dickie. And I found that books and chess and excessive height were pretty good ways to alienate peers, especially when added to a house on a lake and effortless A's in school.

> *The other birds*
> *In so many words*
> *Said hmmph*
> *Get out of town*

The first time my father saw me playing doctor, using Riley as a patient, he laughed so hard he almost fell. I was pretending to draw bloods, using an alcohol pad I had filched from Mother's makeup vanity, and Riley was doing a pretty good imitation of a reluctant patient. Father recovered himself and came over to hug me. "Some day you can marry a doctor," he said. What I remember is, he smelled the same as the alcohol pad.

It seemed to me they argued about money, especially after he got the boat. I knew his LST was sunk by a U-boat off Anzio. I was about ten when I understood what that meant; I must have been reading something about the War. "The Diary of Anne Frank"? Maybe. A

Landmark series history book? Could have been. He was at the D-Day landings too, and there was a Landmark Book about D-Day. He started to be around more in sailing season. He took Dickie out on the boat all the time; never me. I don't remember being bothered by that; I could always go flying with Aunt Alice. Besides, we lived on a lake, and the one thing I could do, athletically, was swim. It seemed I was built for that. Riley could swim too; it turns out Golden Retrievers are aquatic mammals. We had cousins down from Boston, summers. Eleanor was more than a year older than me, almost as old as Dickie. She more or less took me under her wing, and treated Dickie with the disdain a girl who develops early feels for a boy who is old enough to respond but too young to respond in ways that don't make him look like an idiot. I didn't completely understand, but it was exciting to be around Eleanor. She promised subversion and adventure. She could also be capricious and cruel. Dickie sniffed around her the way Riley sniffed around the occasional stray bitch, and it was fine when she was cruel to him. But if there was another girl around who had, you know, "got her growth", it was me on the receiving end. I could not comprehend this. I had got my growth—I was taller than either of them. This made them laugh harder. One night Eleanor came down to dinner in pearls and heels. We were having guests in addition to the cousins, guests with teenaged sons. She swept into the room in a cloud of Canoe. We all walked over to Swede's for ice cream later; Dickie and I might as well have been a pair of toddlers.

Eleanor hung back with the older boy (he must have been all of fifteen; she was about to be thirteen); I heard them on the darkened porch, in the glider, when I went up to read. Whisperings and rustlings. I imagined scenes from "Nancy Drew". Next day she said he was a "good kisser". Dickie looked somewhere between disgusted and forlorn.

That was also the summer Mother decided we needed a pool. We had a lake, but she said it was dirty, and too cold to swim in a lot of the time. Mr. Chaskis owned the local pool service company; you saw his trucks everywhere. He showed up one day with his men and machines and dug out a huge chunk of lawn. Riley woofed himself hoarse. Next day he was back with the cement trucks, and there was plumbing, and so on, and Mother was always there to supervise, and bring out cold drinks. I hated the pool. Because I loved the lake and its cool water, under which was a whole subaqueous world of plants and insects and frogs and turtles and fish. In the pool was nothing. In fact, it was mostly broken. Leaks, plumbing problems; when we started back to school they were still fiddling with it, Mr. Chaskis was there once a week at least, usually more often. Sometimes he was just leaving as the school bus pulled up the drive. Mother started to go out at night; we were old enough to take care of ourselves, and there was a cook for dinners. We played and pulled all kinds of pranks in the service corridors, which was a whole world within the walls, dimly lit, with their own outside doors. There hadn't been live-in servants for years; those rooms were unused, but the service corridors were both handy shortcuts and equally handy secret routes for water balloon attacks and the like. Then one late night when I was almost twelve I was hungry and used the service corridor and stairs from my room to the kitchen, and ran into Mr. Chaskis doing the same thing.

It is not clear to me who was more scared. We both recoiled. He said, "You're Alicia, aren't you. I was, ah, just getting a bite to eat." I drew myself up and in my best Nancy Drew voice I attempted to say, "What are you doing here?" but it came out with a quaver, and by that time my mother had opened the service door to the master bedroom.

"Alicia, come up here, dear, we need to talk. Robert, why don't you have your snack in the kitchen. I'll be right down."

Mother was in a dressing gown, and her hair was down, and I knew I had done something awful. She sat me down, was very gentle, said adult relationships could be very complicated, things happened that it was best not to talk about, because then everyone had to *deal with them* and that would be the fault of whoever talked. So it was best to never mention this to Dickie, or to Father, because they might not *Understand*. I could hear the italics and the upper case U. I had graduated to the Jeeves stories.

She did not say I shouldn't mention it to Aunt Alice, and that was how I got the Sex Talk. A good thing, too, because without it I would have been utterly unprepared for menarche except for some claptrap from Eleanor that I had dismissed as ridiculous. But which had been somewhat accurate after all. Anyway, Alice was glad for my mother, said it was nice her sister had found a man who could make her happy, even if she had to buy a pool to do it. But she was appalled by Mother making it sound like anything that could happen from this would be my fault if I talked about it. She was in fact disgusted. She lit a cigarette, walked around the room a little. "Your mother gave up a promising professional life to marry that...your father," she said. "She graduated Summa from Wellsmith, and she started toward a doctorate in French literature. Your father showed up between wars, on his way from the Atlantic to the Pacific, and got her pregnant. That's your brother Dickie. She went back to finish her degree part time, and he got her pregnant with you. I'm sorry, dear, I put that badly; I made it sound like your fault. And after all, if it hadn't happened that way, your precious self wouldn't be gracing my life the way it is. God, this really is complicated. Look, here is the simple way to put it: It's all about what you want to do with your life, until a child is born; then it is all about the child." She looked at the cigarette in her hand, stubbed it out. "Children have to be raised. It's work, and you have to sacrifice things

676

in your own life because the child needs you. You're responsible. Do you see?" I didn't then; I didn't want to. "Remember when Riley was a puppy? How you took care of him until he could take care of himself?"

Then I saw, to the point I became a child psychiatrist.

She took my head in her hands, turned it into a hug. "I want you to know," she said, "That no matter what happens, you always have a home here. With me."

I asked her what could happen.

"I don't know," she said, "Divorce, maybe."

That was a terrifying word in 1959. In that world.

"No matter what she does," my aunt said, "Your father will find out, and it will not ever, ever be your fault." *But it always felt like it was*

I know now what she meant, that Mother and her lover were being careless, as if they didn't care at all, and it was just a matter of time. At age eleven, I understood this dimly at best. Of course I told Dickie. He was, beside aunt Alice, my best friend. My only friend. Only non-canine friend. *Until you showed up*

But I only told you all that later.

***

I drove us across the Bronx to my dorm at the school, to my room of my own. One floor down from where you had lived. There wasn't much. Books, (textbooks, the Duras, the abandoned Pleiade Proust) desk stuff, clothes, shoes. The iron. We threw things into suitcases; some better things I left on hangars, folded.

"I don't think you've ever seen me in a dress," I said.

"Something to look forward to," you said.

"You bet it is. I'm very good loopking."

677

When you stopped laughing you said, "There aren't many books."

"Not by your standards. Some are stored in my mother's basement, but really my books are all at the Strand; I just haven't bought them yet. Oh. I do have these." I pulled open a drawer. Under a worn Nott sweatshirt were the Borges books, Cyrano and the Woolf. "I got them from a boy who loved me. And was smart enough not to say so too soon."

You picked up "Labyrinths", turned some pages. *Seeing there ghosts of your father's notes?* "It was more lucky and neurotic than smart. I was just reading my own anxieties," you said.

"Which worked fine, they were mostly the same anxieties as mine. A pair of power tools." I kissed him. "You always take me on my own terms, Paul," I told you. "Even Dickie, with all his sympathy, never did." *That's more important than anything*

"I always liked the terms. I'm not that good a person, Ali. I'm very selfish. I want the feeling I get when I'm with you."

"Lucky for you: I'm selfish the same way. You're a *good enough* person. This isn't about good. This is about love. You always seem to have what I need. Right down to a bathtub. A room of my own isn't enough for me. It has to have you in it, Leonard."

"Mine, too, Virginia."

Suddenly at the door: "Hey Ali. Hey, whoever you are. What gives?"

"Marsha, this is Paul. I'm…we're…" I was suddenly overwhelmed with trying to explain.

"Paul Seitz," you said, extending a hand.

She shook it. "I know you. You were on the next floor of the Klau Pavillion when I was on Medicine last year. You better work fast, there's this guy in her past who has rights of first refusal."

"Marsha, this is the guy. I'm moving in with him."

She stepped back. "This is the guy? He's been here all along? And you're…?"

678

"Long story. Marsha, he has a bathtub."

"Oh, well, that makes all the difference." She turned to you. "So can friends use this tub?"

"Ask Ali. It's her tub now too."

"Ali?"

"Sure. Why not? We'll tell you the story. With full orchestration. It's got everything: romance, politics, hair-raising escapes, a really great villain…"

"And deep idiocy," you said.

"Truly. Come for dinner when we're settled." *Not If. When.*
Marsha left.

"Paulie, you know I'm not moving in with you for the bathtub. That's just a joke."

You gave this big grin. "You have an MG. We're even."

"Seriously, I meant it before when I said meeting you maybe changed my life. I was wrong last night. I might never have tried to get to med school without the jump start from you. Maybe I could have turned into Bitsy Reade."

"No. Never. We know that now. Alice would never have let that happen. You would never have settled for anything less. Here you are. This is your room, Ali. You got yourself here. And we'd have met here. We did meet here. I was just thinking, I've loved you in three different versions. I like this one the best."

"You'd better," I said. "It's the one you're stuck with. I can say the same." *God, you needed a haircut*

You pulled me to you, you hopeless romantic. "But when we make love I kiss all three versions," you said.

God, I love you "Moi aussi. Il y'a longtemps que je t'aime."

"That's what gives it depth," you said.

"When I thank you it's for the jump start. And for being a friend, even before what else you are to me."

"Stop already. You've thanked me enough." Your eyes said *A thousand times over*

"Not yet." Here was the boy who had defied my father without even thinking. And who had known when not to. Who couldn't take his eyes off me. Who laughed at my jokes and made me laugh. Who taught and learned. And *listened*. Who I'd wanted to walk into a painting with, who I would have followed onto a bus going wherever it was going. Now a man. And a more than competent doc. Who thought I was beautiful, even admirable, and valued and respected my work. Who wanted me exactly as I was. Who made me feel loved. And suddenly I knew what had happened in the time we'd been apart. "Paul. It's OK. It's all OK. The room of my own—it's portable. It's in my head. Not this." I swept my hand around the room. "It's in here, in me."

I watched your face become thoughtful. "You have yourself to thank for that," you said finally. "I guess we both had a lot to figure out. Does more free psychoanalysis come with this relationship?"

"It does. Upon request. Mostly. *I've kept that promise haven't I* Nothing not talked about."

It took so little time to empty the room. I thought of all the time we could have had together, all the lonely hours we could have filled with each other. There would be more; our residency and fellowship rotations would pull us apart on separate schedules for years to come.

"Take us home, Paul."

"Saddle up."

"Move 'em out." You laughed, like music.

> *Let us be lovers*
> *We'll marry our fortunes together.*
> *I have some real estate here in my hand*

The Dan's Supreme market on the Post Road was open until nine. We stocked up on breakfast things, salad things, pasta, some chicken, burger meat. And (laughing like kids) bubble bath, which was as close to bath salts as Dan's could provide. Drove back to Gun Hill. The fatigue was beginning to catch up with us both. We put away the food, hung out anything that would suffer from being packed, made room and threw the rest into drawers. And settled into bed.

But I couldn't just sleep; I was up on my knees, leaning over you, my hair in your face, like the first time, on the raft. "We're really here."

You sat up; we kissed. Deeply. The bed rocked, like the motion of a raft on a long-ago lake. "We're really here."

RRRRRRRRRIIIIIIIINNNNGGGGGGG

"What the fuck?... Hello."
I heard Marvin's voice.
"Marvin wants to know if I'm going to need a ride tomorrow morning."
I put my arms around you. "I don't think so," I said.

The next day the alarm woke us. There was work to do. There would always be work to do. We would always have that.

Alumni Notes

Marriages

Dr. Paul Seitz, '72, Assistant Professor of Cardiology, Medical Director of the South Bronx Medical Clinic, and Dr. Alicia Acheson-Seitz, '73, Assistant Professor of Child Psychiatry, Director of the South Bronx Teen Mental Health Program. The couple wrote their own vows. Pictured with them beside the couple's vintage MG, officiating at the nondenominational ceremony, are the bride's brother Richard Acheson III, Professor of Advanced Studies in Tibetan Buddhism at Naropa Insititute, and William Parker, Mayor of Eldorado, Colorado. Also in attendance were Drs. Marvin Kornbluth, '69, and Kathleen McCulloch-Kornbluth, '74. The two couples met on a rotation at the now-closed Morrisania affiliate. June 14, 1980, Boulder, Colorado (The picture is part of a collection of photographs of the wedding and much more by Emily Bohlen-Parker: "Paul and Ali's Wedding: An American Odyssey", on view at the New Photography Gallery, 110 Spring Street, New York, from September 12 through October 18, 1980).

Births

To Dr. Paul Seitz, '72, and Dr. Alicia Acheson-Seitz, '73, Martin Jerome Seitz and Alice Sarah Seitz, September 23, 1980.

Faculty and Alumni Publications (a partial listing):

Acheson, R (ed). The Prayer Wheel, A Tibetan Buddhist Anthology. 1998, Boulder, Colorado, Naropa Institute Press.

Acheson-Seitz, A. Disturbances in normal female adolescent development: Familial and extra-familial influences. *Psychoanalytic Study of the Child*, 40, 204-237, 1985.

Canfield, M, Posen R, Acheson, A. Alcohol-related suppression of REM sleep and dreams in post-traumatic stress disorder. *International Journal of Alcohol Studies*, 16, 127-134, 1980.

Goodwomyn, N. & Martin Seitz (trs). Kafka's Zurau Aphorisms. 1977, New York, City University Press.

Kornbluth, M & McCulloch-Kornbluth, K. The Ends of Treatment and The End of Treatment: End-of-Life Decisions in Modern Medicine. 1997, Baltimore, Johns Hopkins University Press.

Parker, W & Bohlen-Parker, E. The Huron Street Statement: An Illustrated Memoir of the '60s. 2000, New York, Archive Press.

Rabinowitz, S. The Little Man Gets In: Investing for the Rest of Us. New York, Adam Smith Press (1986); 2nd edition (1998), 3rd edition (2004).

Seidenberg, B, Kornbluth, M, Seitz, P. Cardiotoxicity of cardiac drugs. *American Journal of Cardiology,* 86, 578-585, 1977.

Seitz, P. Toxic Arrythmias. In: Seidenberg, B, et al, (Eds). Textbook of Cardiology. 2005, New Haven, Yale University Press.

Seitz, P, Acheson-Seitz, A. Toxic arrythmias in pediatric psychopharmacology: A review. *Journal of the American Academy of Child and Adolescent Psychiatry,* 45, 923-933, 2006.

Shantih Shantih Shantih

Acknowledgments

The real-world inspirations for Nott, Slidell and Wellsmith Colleges, the Medical School, and the Mother House are all readily identifiable. I stress "inspirations". The characters are, of course, fictitious.

All of the books, poems, essays and stories mentioned are available in numerous editions, and were in the years mentioned. The textbooks (and their chapter headings) are all real and exact. So are the New York *Times* front page headlines for Sunday, April 8, 1973. Professor Goldenberg's book is, alas, a fiction.

The Strand bookstore and the Café Reggio are very real. So, in their time, were S&G Catering and Mrs. Stahl's Knishes. So, in his, was Olaf the Walrus (as described).

Philip K. Dick's *The Man in the High Castle* is available in numerous editions, including a recent Library of America edition of Dick's novels; the edition mentioned, with its cover map of a United States under Axis occupation, is the Popular Library paperback; this cover also graced the G.P Putnam hard cover (both 1962). Dick used and acknowledged the Bollingen Foundation/Pantheon (Bollingen Series XIX) edition of the Wilhelm/Baynes *I Ching* of 1950 (in two volumes) found in the Nott College library; it was reissued as a single volume, with additional material, in 1967 by Princeton University Press. Both editions have the Jung introduction.

T. S. Eliot's *The Wasteland* is available in numerous editions, and on line. The version of the Fire Sermon used here is my own condensation of several English versions.

The Zurau Aphorisms of Franz Kafka, wonderfully translated by Michael Hoffman (New York, Schocken Books, 2006) is the inspiration and basis for my attempted renderings of first drafts of a 1950s/60s free version of the Aphorisms.

The description of a draft card is from my own, issued in 1966. I still have it in my wallet; it must, after all, be carried at all times.

Sartre's "Roads to Freedom" has a recent American translation (Sartre, J-P: *The Age of Reason, The Reprieve*, tr. Eric Sutton; *Troubled Sleep*, tr. Gerard Hopkins, 1992, Vintage International); as this book was written Continuum International (2009) issued a translation of the uncompleted fourth book, *The Last Chance*, tr. Craig Vesey.

The Hotel de la Harpe exists, or did when my wife and I stayed there on a shoestring in 1971. The Rat Man also is real; he was immortalized in Paul West's *The Rat Man of Paris* (Doubleday, 1986). One afternoon in 1971 he complimented my wife, as described.

"She wouldn't be the first". In 1951 eight teachers at Erasmus Hall High School were suspended after refusing to deny membership in the American Communist Party.

As this book reached completion, the Womens' Airforce Service Pilots (WASPs) were at long last awarded a group Presidential citation.

All medical procedures and slang are from 1973. Much is now obsolete.

Formed originally to provide medical support to the Civil Rights movement, the Medical Committee for Human Rights soon began to provide the same services to the Peace Movement later in the 1960s, along with its student arm, the Student Health Organization. The story is told in *The Good Doctors: The Medical Committee for Human Rights and the Struggle for Social Justice in Health Care* by John Dittmer (New York, Bloomsbury Press, 2009). Some of us still have our armbands.

Closed and derelict from 1976 to 1997, despite a doctors' sit-in protest, the Morrisania Hospital complex still stands in the Bronx at 167th to 168th streets between Walton and Gerard Avenues. The main building was renovated as housing for the poor and homeless, with job training centers, by the Women's Housing and Economic Development Corporation. Within sight of its rooftop, the City of New York spent millions to subsidize the building of a new Yankee Stadium on the last municipal park land in that part of the Bronx.

Music: All the songs heard in the background were available at the times indicated.

Roberta Flack/Fox & Gimbel: Killing Me Softly

Carly Simon: You're So Vain

Crosby, Stills & Nash: Guinnevere, Suite Judy Blue Eyes, Helplessly Hoping

Danny Kaye: There Once Was An Ugly Duckling, I Belong to Glasgow (Will Fyffe)

Neil Sedaka & The Tokens/Solomon Linda: The Lion Sleeps Tonight

Frank & Nancy Sinatra: Something Stupid

Richard Rodgers/Lorenz Hart: I Could Write a Book

Steely Dan: My Old School

Scott McKenzie/John Phillips: If You're Going to San Francisco

Bertolt Brecht/Kurt Weill: Alabama Song

Harold Arlen/Ira Gerswhin: The Man That Got Away

The Beatles: Norwegian Wood, Lucy in the Sky With Diamonds

Jerry Leiber/Mike Stoller: Is That All There Is

Tom Lehrer: Be Prepared

Judy Collins/Donovan: Sunny Goodge Street

Simon & Garfunkel: America

About the Author

Andrew Levitas, M.D. is Associate Professor of Psychiatry and Medical Director of the Center of Excellence for Mental Health Treatment of Persons with Intellectual Disabilities of the Department of Psychiatry, UMDNJ/SOM. He is a graduate of Union College, Schenectady, New York and the Albert Einstein College of Medicine, Bronx, New York. He did his medical internship at Montefiore Hospital, Bronx, New York, residency in Psychiatry at Downstate/Kings County Hospital Center, Brooklyn, New York, and his Fellowship in Child Psychiatry at the University of Colorado Health Sciences Center, Denver, Colorado, where he later taught the "Literature and the Unconscious" course. He is Board Certified in both Psychiatry and Child Psychiatry. He is the 1999 recipient of the Robert D. Sovner Award for psychiatric services to persons with intellectual disabilities.

Dr. Levitas is a member of the Scientific and Clinical Advisory Committee of the National Fragile-X Foundation, the Advisory Board of the Fragile-X Advocate, and was Associate Editor of Mental Health Aspects of Developmental Disabilities from 1997 through 2009. He is a member of the Advisory Board and scholastic contributor to the *Diagnostic Manual on Intellectual Disabilities: A Clinical Guide for the Diagnosis of Mental Disorders in Persons with Intellectual Disability*, and the author and co-author of numerous scientific papers and book chapters on psychiatric aspects of intellectual disability.